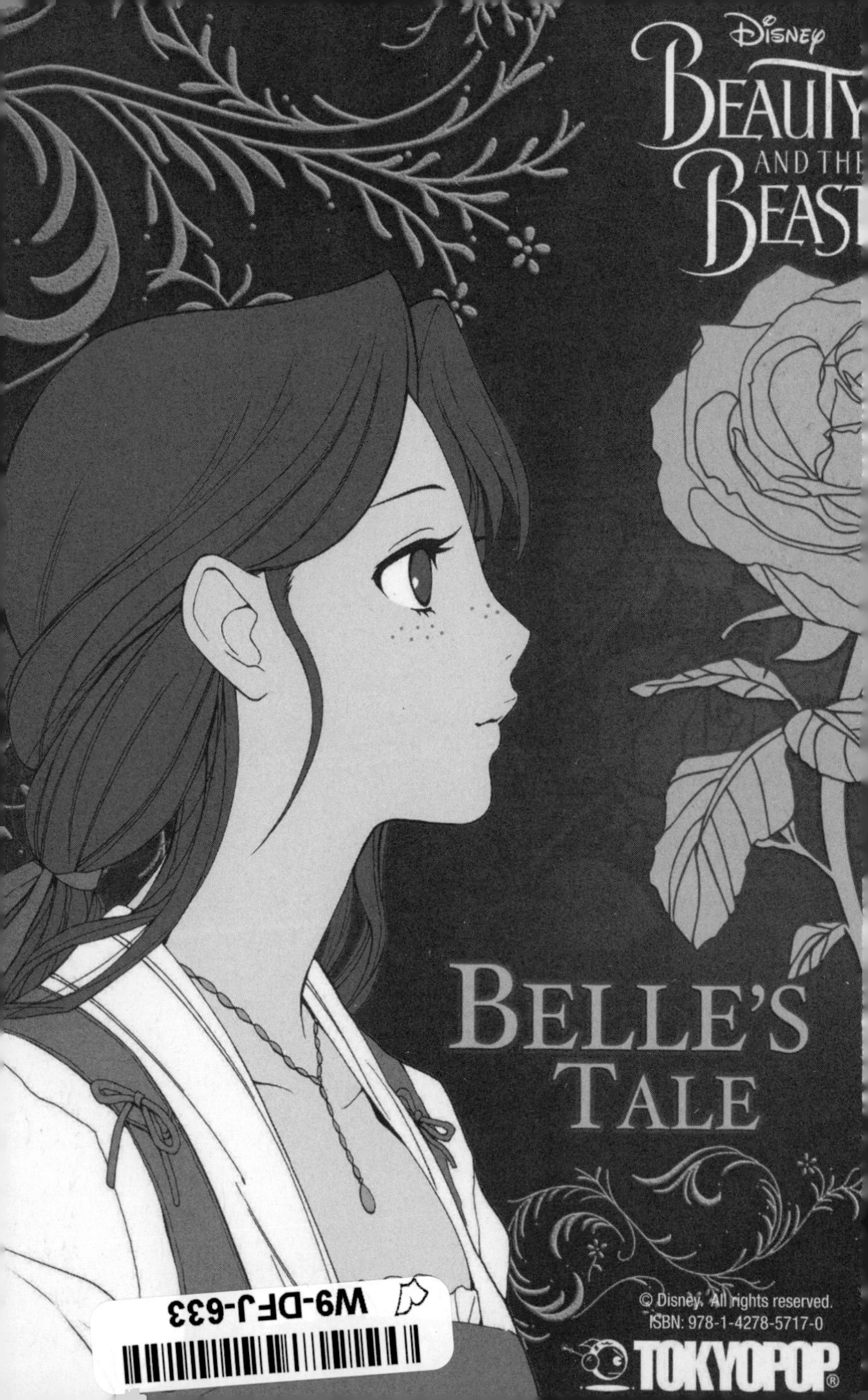

Disney

Beauty and the Beast

Belle's Tale

ISBN: 978-1-4278-5717-0

TOKYOPOP®

Contents

Dear Readers:

Welcome to a very special project: the twin companion *BEAUTY AND THE BEAST* manga set! This particular manga is *BELLE'S TALE*, where we relive the story from Belle's perspective.

While our talented Japanese artists iterated and iterated to embody the Beast's ferocious yet sensitive nature, our artists focused on intricate details and nuances when illustrating Belle. Working closely with the Disney team, the artists evolved the perfect balance of shojo manga and classic Belle. Be sure to study the Concept Art section found in the back of the book to experience this artistic evolution.

Certainly, the locations and set pieces from the film are reflected in this manga through careful recreations. Notice the detail you'll find in the Villeneuve prison scene, or Belle's bed in the Beast's castle. Every angle needed to be anticipated by the artists since there are no cameras to record such images. In some cases where the film references were not always available, the artists had to rely on their imaginations and highly disciplined fingers.

And with no songs emanating from each page of the book, Belle's inner thoughts are expressed by traditional shojo manga monologue. We recommend playing the movie soundtrack – or even humming it quietly! – while reading Belle's diary-like comments.

So, join Belle on her journey finding her inner strength and embracing the possibilities of a life pursuing one's dreams.

TOKYOPOP is proud to bring you *BELLE'S TALE*!!

--- Team TOKYOPOP

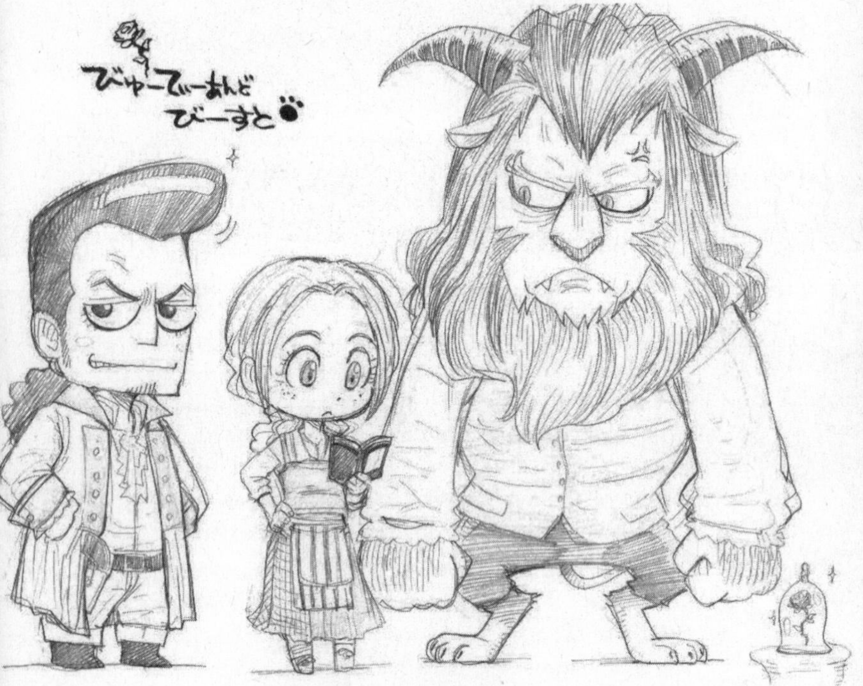

びゅーてぃーあんど
びーすと

DISNEY

BEAUTY AND THE BEAST

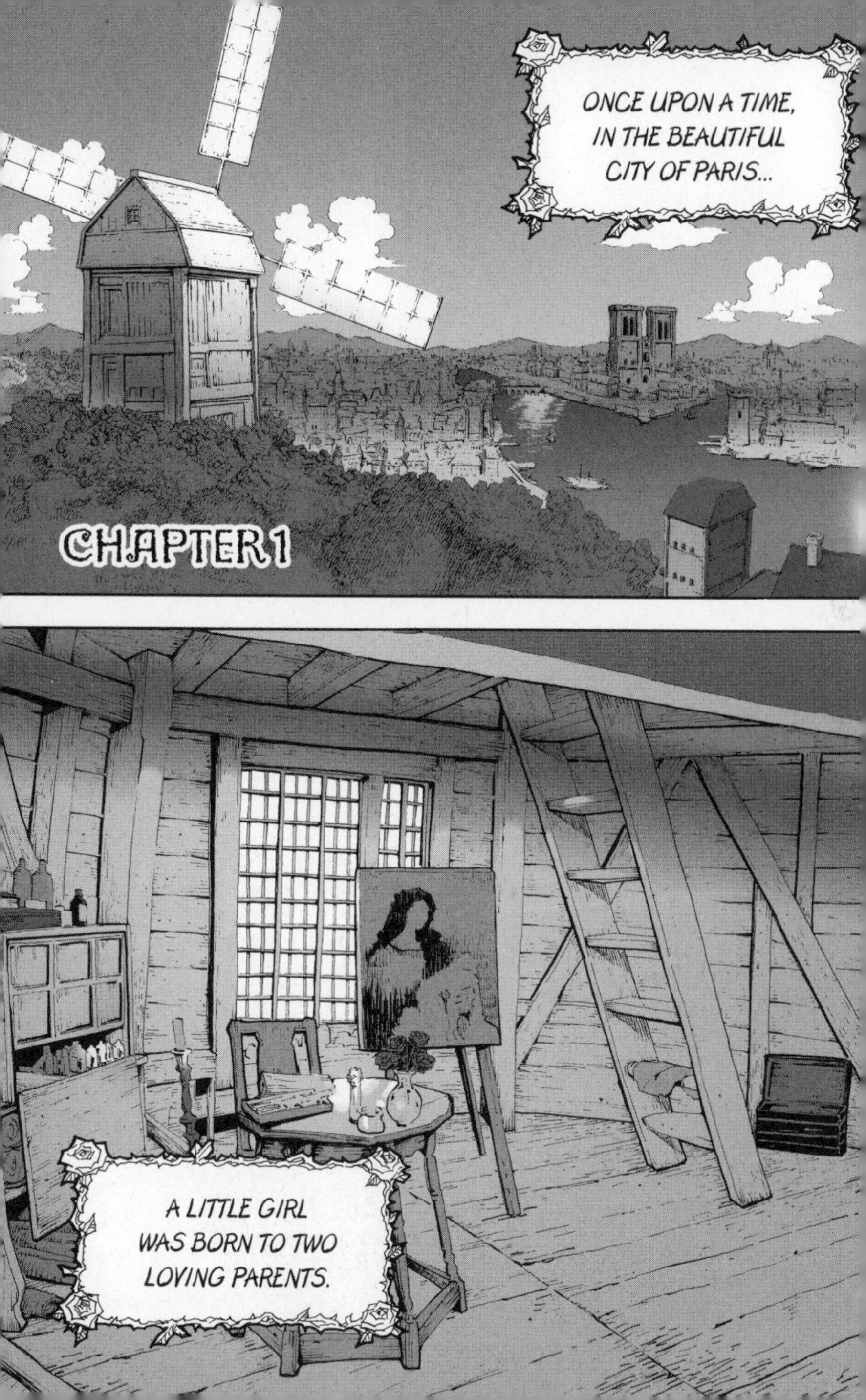
ONCE UPON A TIME, IN THE BEAUTIFUL CITY OF PARIS...
CHAPTER 1
A LITTLE GIRL WAS BORN TO TWO LOVING PARENTS.

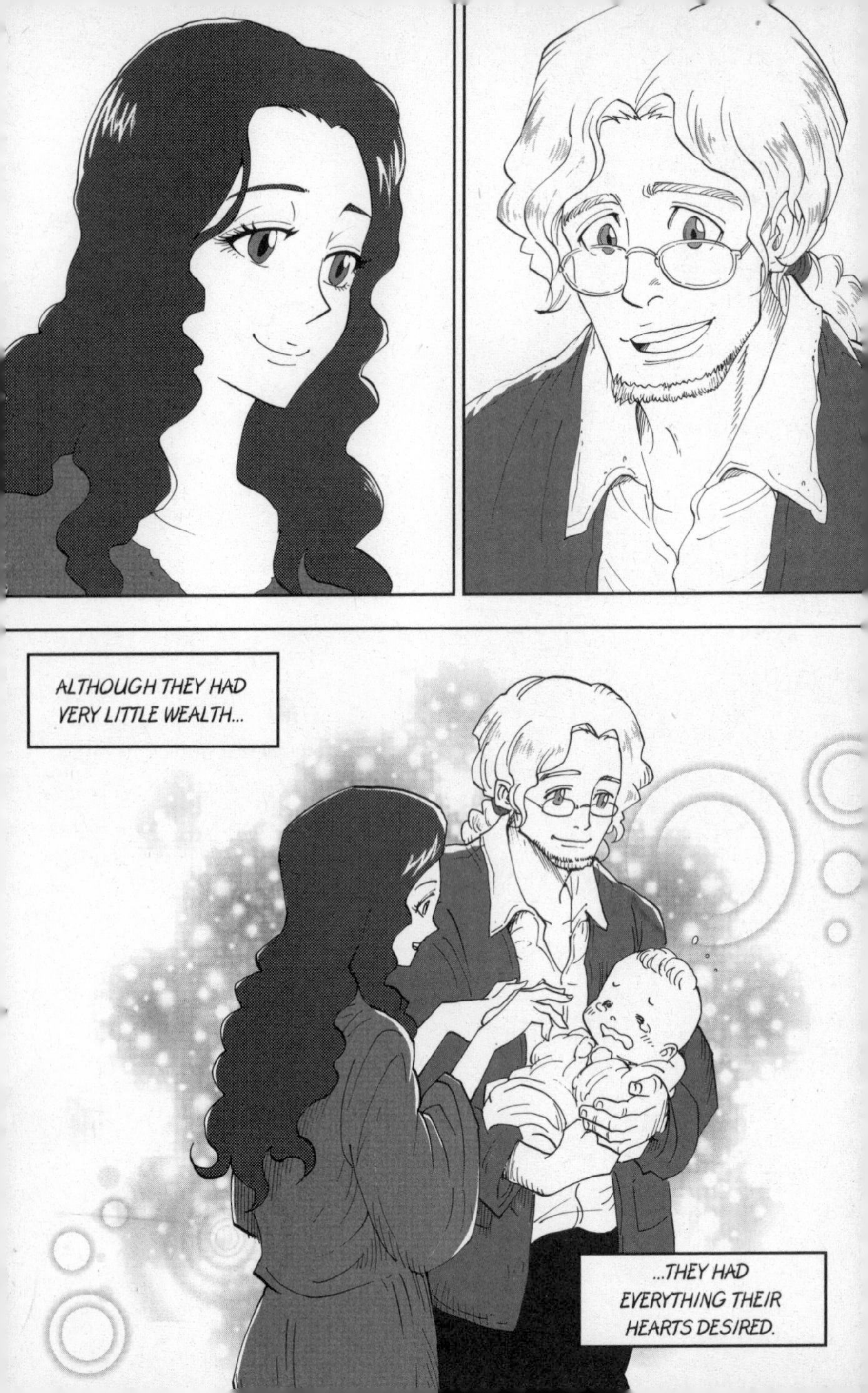
ALTHOUGH THEY HAD VERY LITTLE WEALTH...
...THEY HAD EVERYTHING THEIR HEARTS DESIRED.

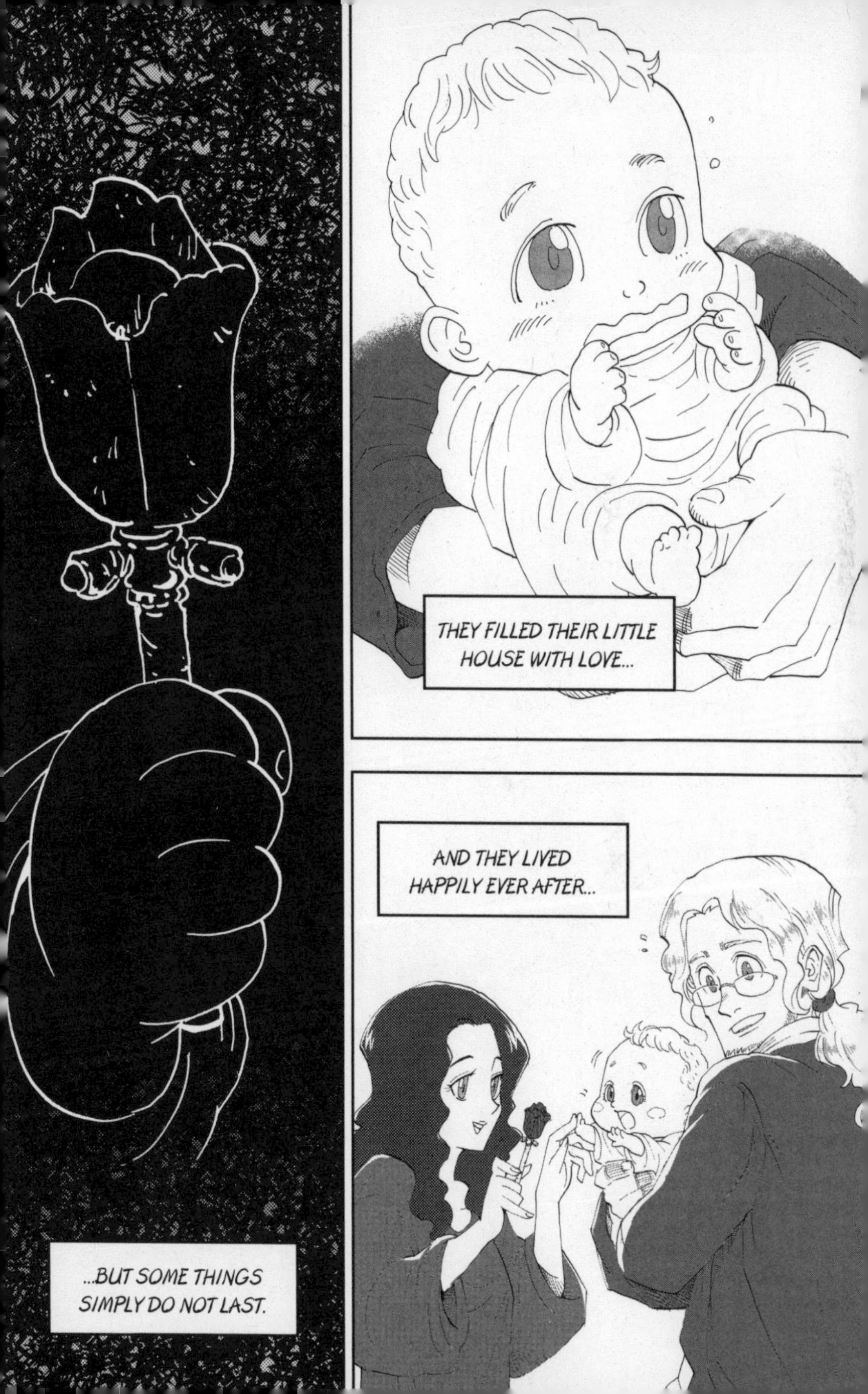
THEY FILLED THEIR LITTLE HOUSE WITH LOVE...
AND THEY LIVED HAPPILY EVER AFTER...
...BUT SOME THINGS SIMPLY DO NOT LAST.

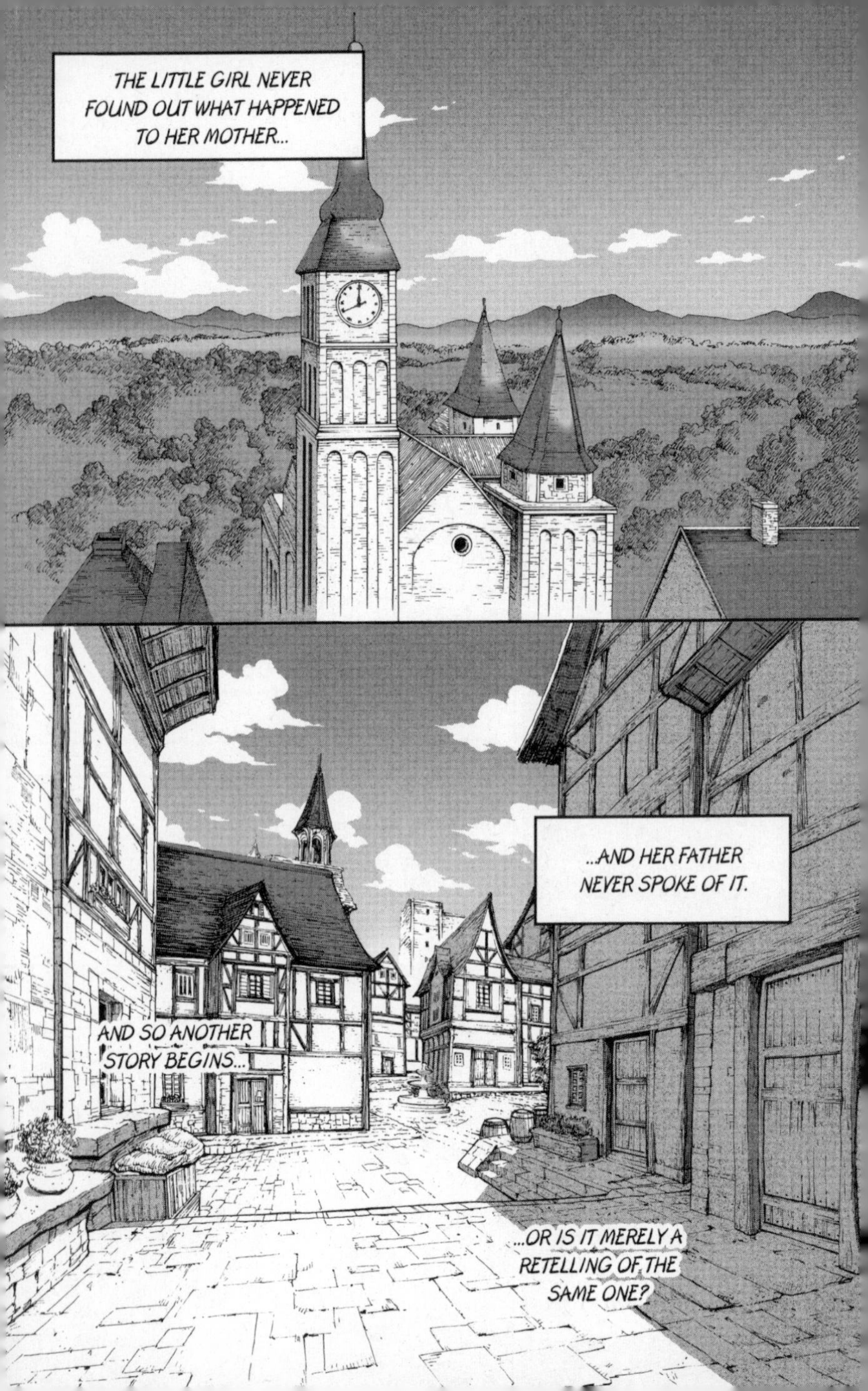
THE LITTLE GIRL NEVER FOUND OUT WHAT HAPPENED TO HER MOTHER...
...AND HER FATHER NEVER SPOKE OF IT.
AND SO ANOTHER STORY BEGINS...
...OR IS IT MERELY A RETELLING OF THE SAME ONE?

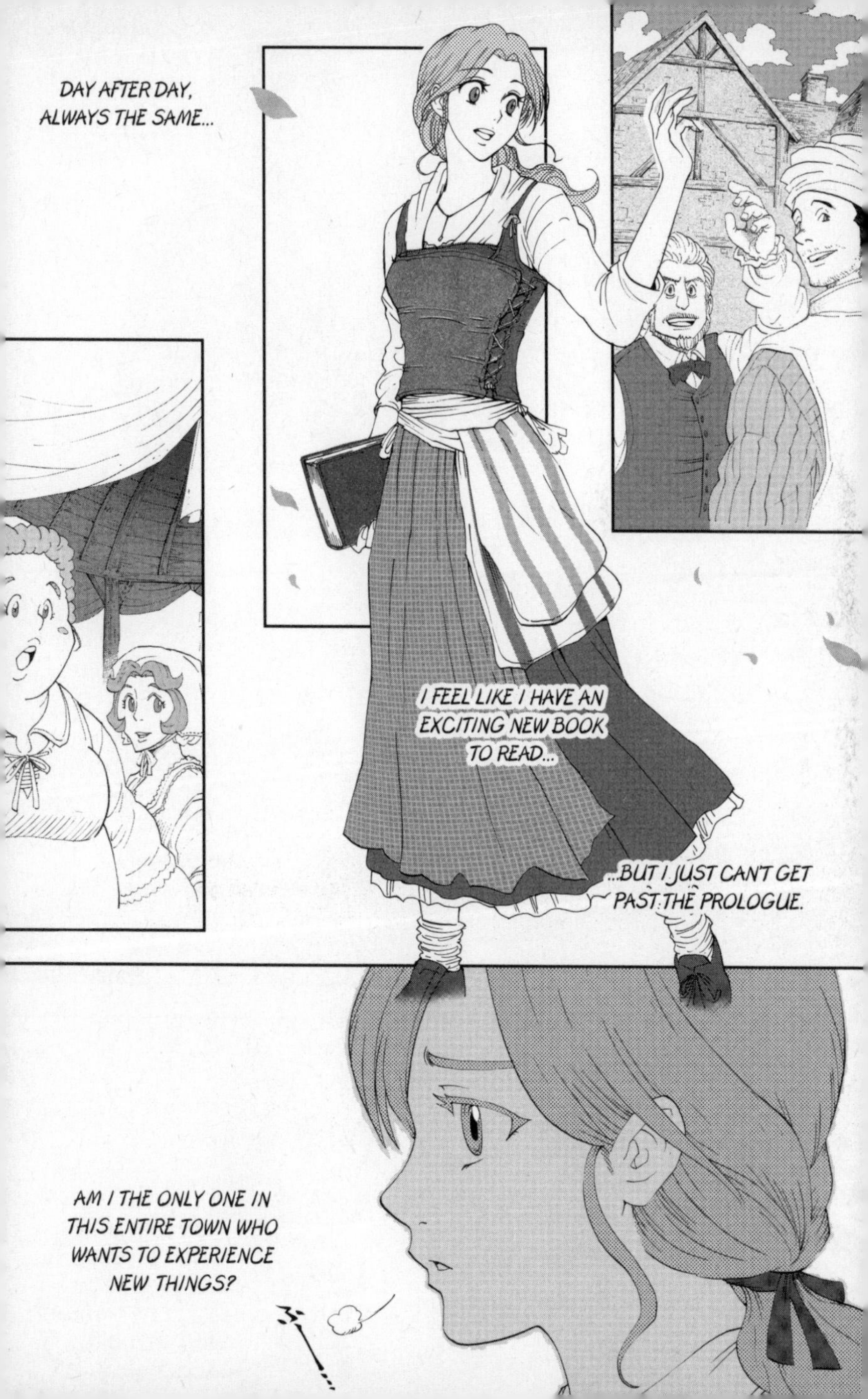
DAY AFTER DAY, ALWAYS THE SAME...
I FEEL LIKE I HAVE AN EXCITING NEW BOOK TO READ...
...BUT I JUST CAN'T GET PAST THE PROLOGUE.
AM I THE ONLY ONE IN THIS ENTIRE TOWN WHO WANTS TO EXPERIENCE NEW THINGS?

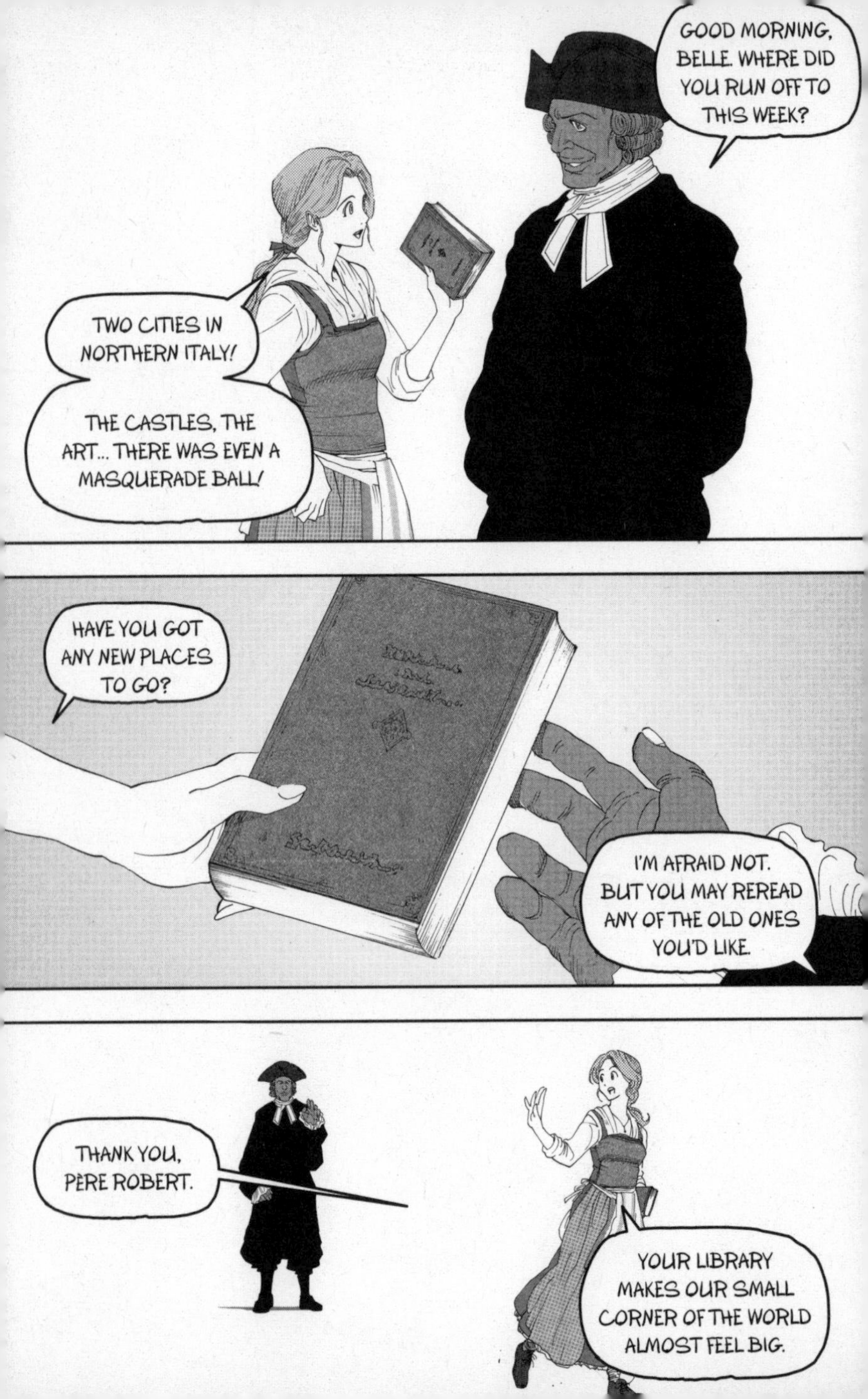
GOOD MORNING, BELLE. WHERE DID YOU RUN OFF TO THIS WEEK?
TWO CITIES IN NORTHERN ITALY!
THE CASTLES, THE ART... THERE WAS EVEN A MASQUERADE BALL!
HAVE YOU GOT ANY NEW PLACES TO GO?
I'M AFRAID NOT. BUT YOU MAY REREAD ANY OF THE OLD ONES YOU'D LIKE.
THANK YOU, PÈRE ROBERT.
YOUR LIBRARY MAKES OUR SMALL CORNER OF THE WORLD ALMOST FEEL BIG.

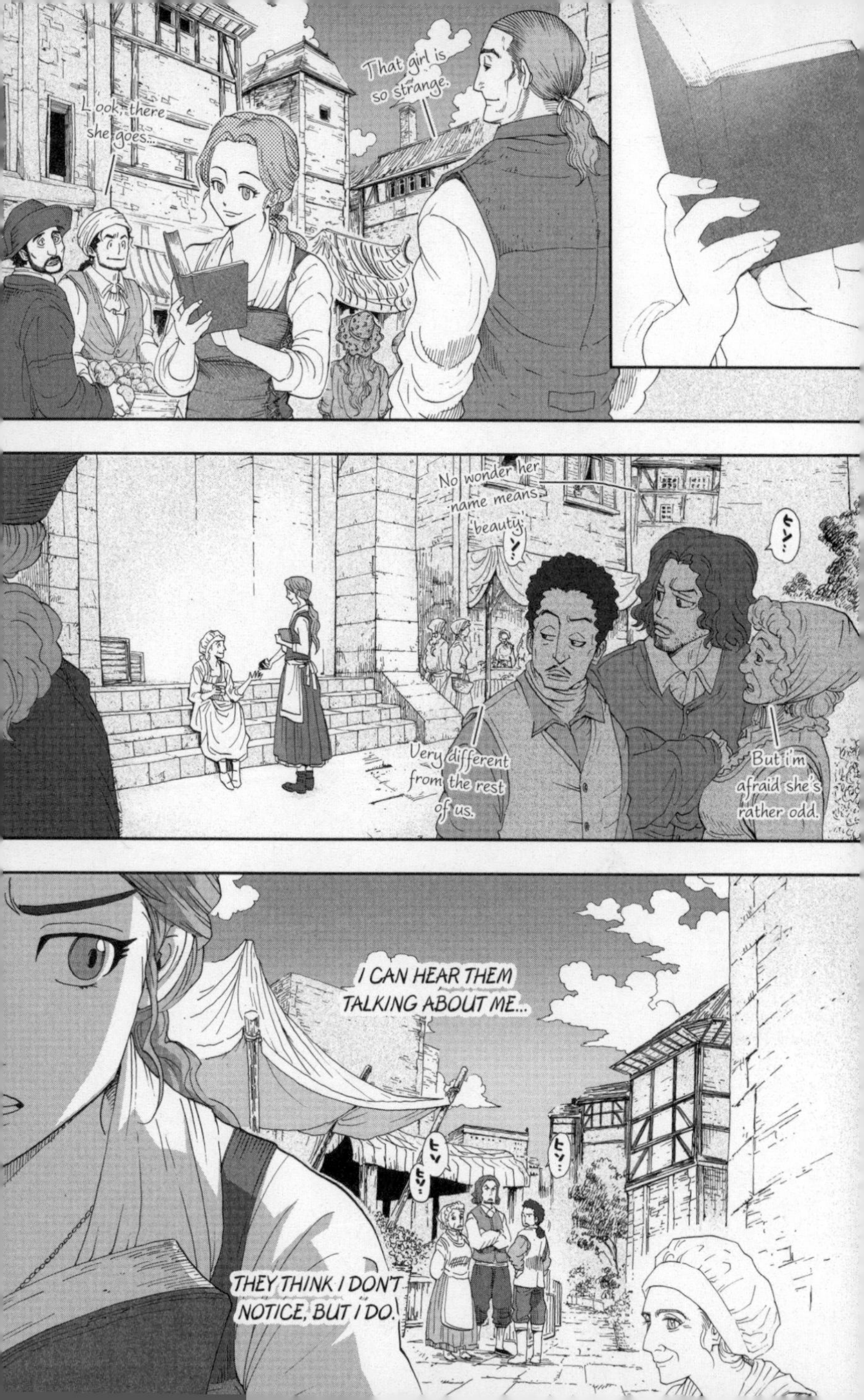
That girl is so strange.
Look, there she goes...
ヒソ...
No wonder her name means beauty.
ソ...
But I'm afraid she's rather odd.
Very different from the rest of us.
I CAN HEAR THEM TALKING ABOUT ME...
ヒソ...
ヒソ ヒソ...
THEY THINK I DON'T NOTICE, BUT I DO.

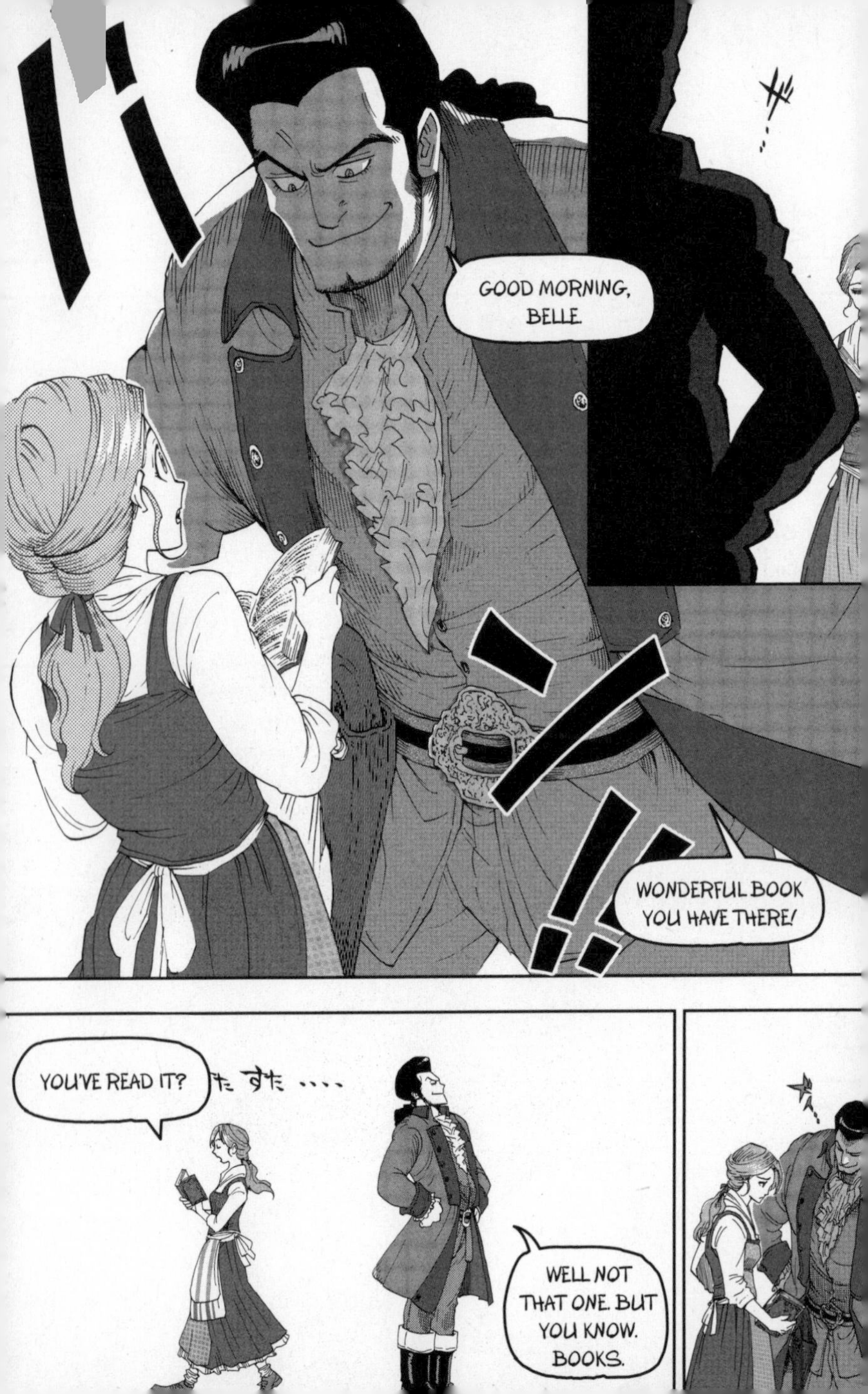
GOOD MORNING, BELLE.
WONDERFUL BOOK YOU HAVE THERE!
YOU'VE READ IT?
た すた ・・・・
WELL NOT THAT ONE. BUT YOU KNOW. BOOKS.

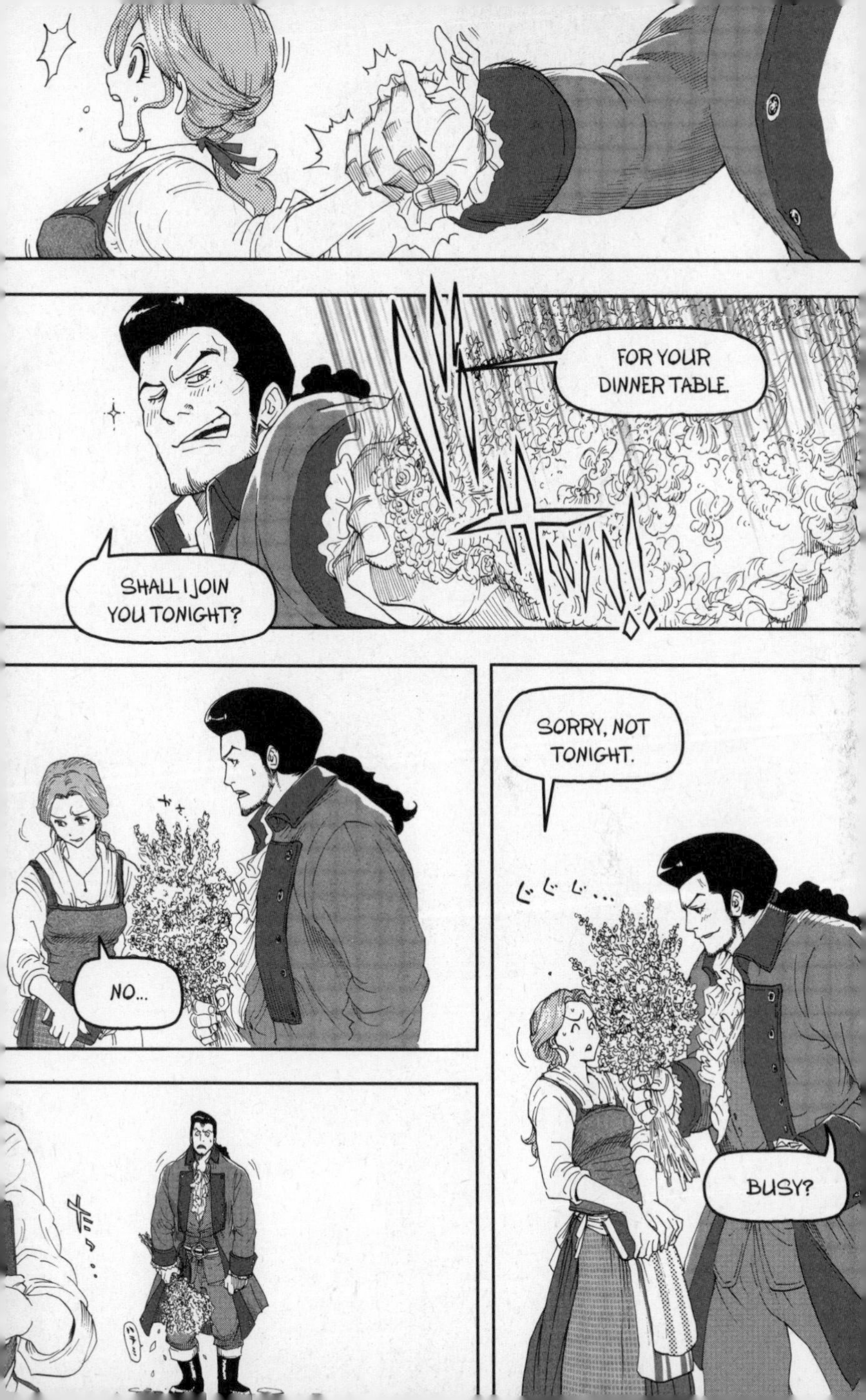
FOR YOUR DINNER TABLE.
SHALL I JOIN YOU TONIGHT?
SORRY, NOT TONIGHT.
じじじ...
BUSY?
NO...

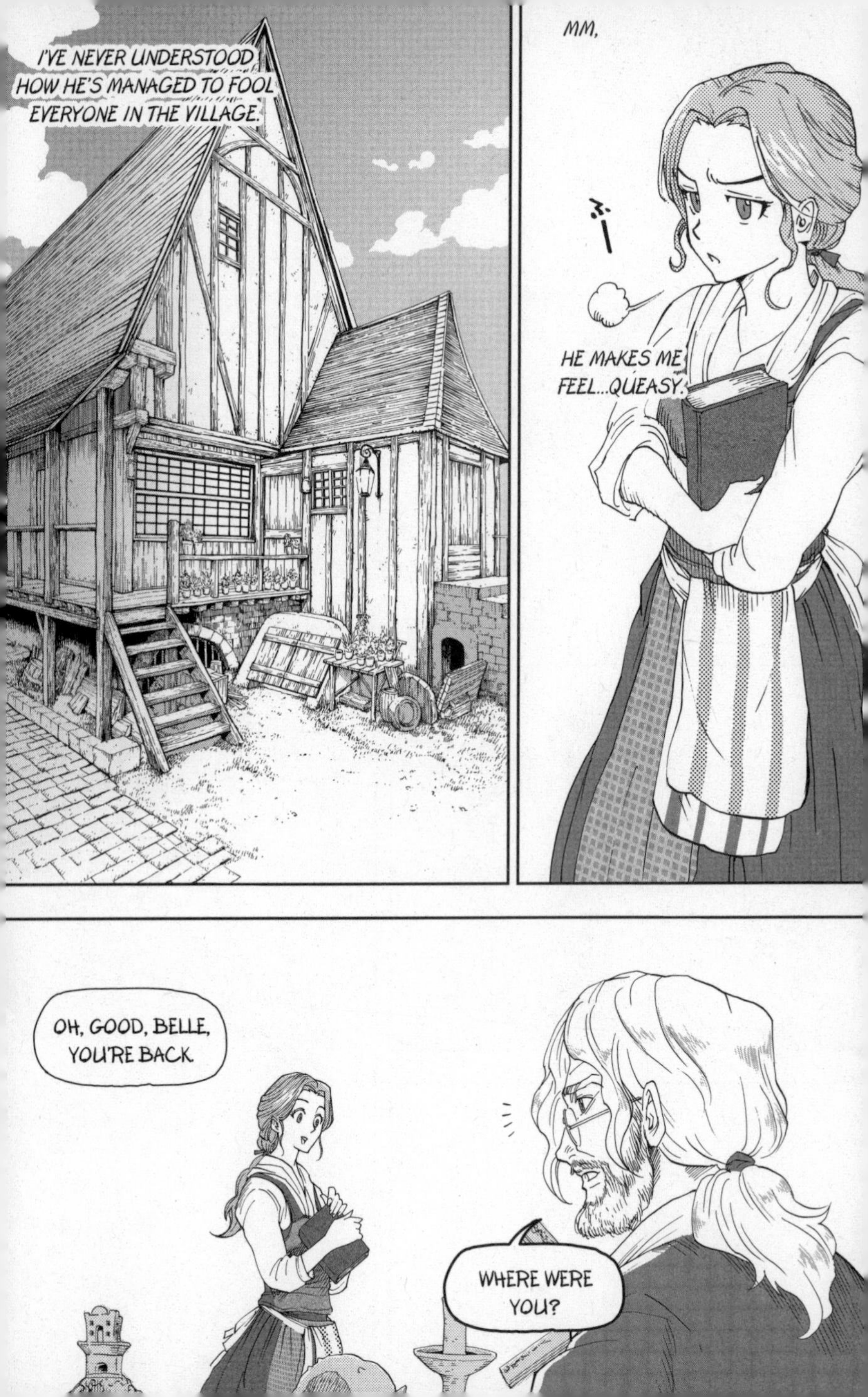
MM,
HE MAKES ME FEEL...QUEASY.
I'VE NEVER UNDERSTOOD HOW HE'S MANAGED TO FOOL EVERYONE IN THE VILLAGE.
OH, GOOD, BELLE, YOU'RE BACK.
WHERE WERE YOU?

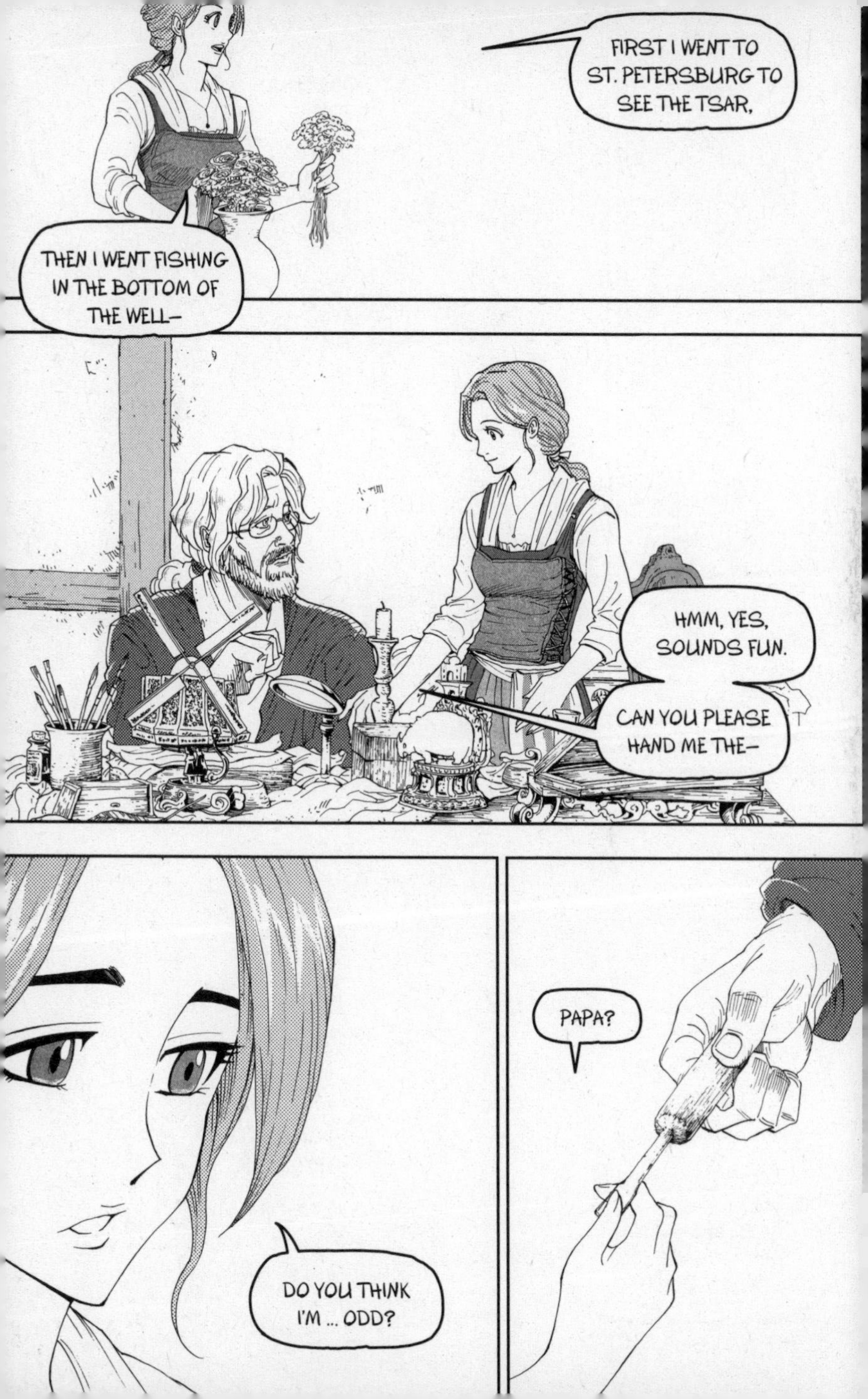
FIRST I WENT TO ST. PETERSBURG TO SEE THE TSAR,
THEN I WENT FISHING IN THE BOTTOM OF THE WELL–
HMM, YES, SOUNDS FUN.
CAN YOU PLEASE HAND ME THE–
PAPA?
DO YOU THINK I'M ... ODD?

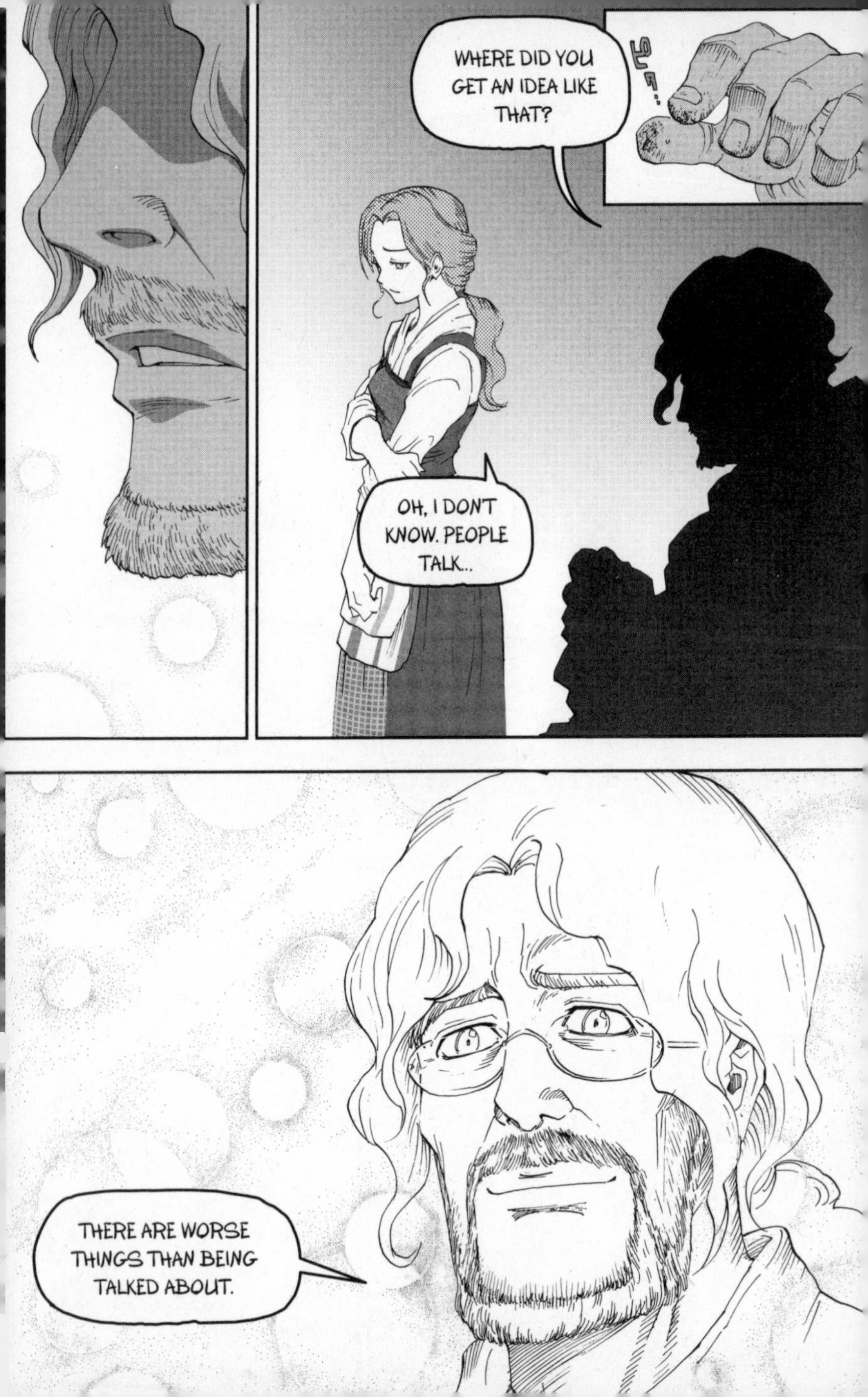
WHERE DID YOU GET AN IDEA LIKE THAT?
OH, I DON'T KNOW. PEOPLE TALK...
THERE ARE WORSE THINGS THAN BEING TALKED ABOUT.

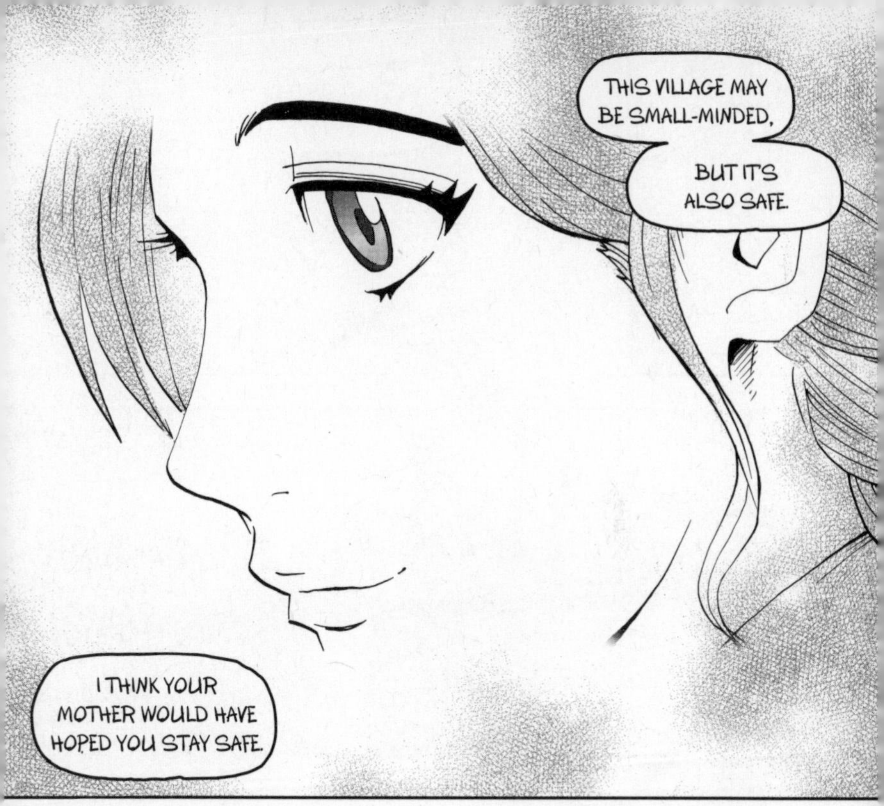
THIS VILLAGE MAY BE SMALL-MINDED,
BUT IT'S ALSO SAFE.
I THINK YOUR MOTHER WOULD HAVE HOPED YOU STAY SAFE.

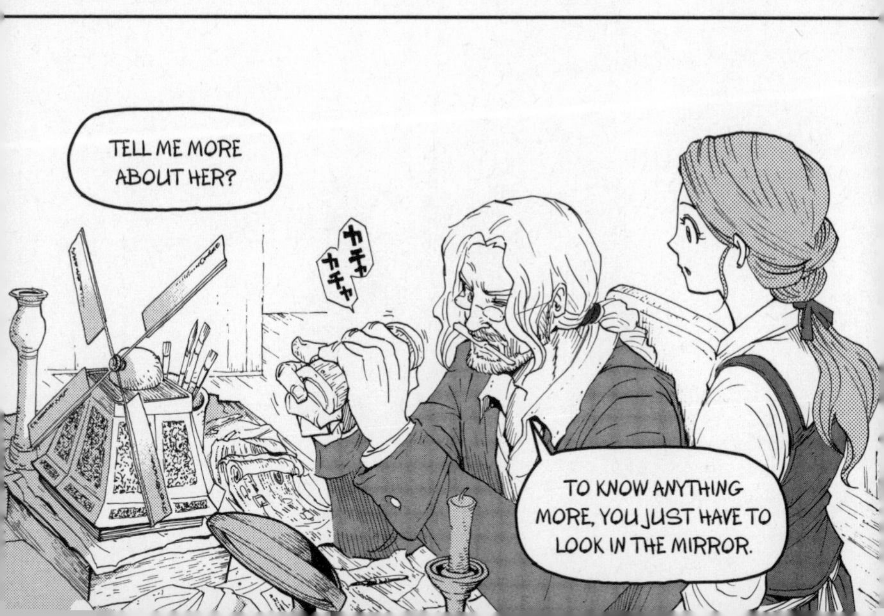
TELL ME MORE ABOUT HER?
カチャ カチャ
TO KNOW ANYTHING MORE, YOU JUST HAVE TO LOOK IN THE MIRROR.

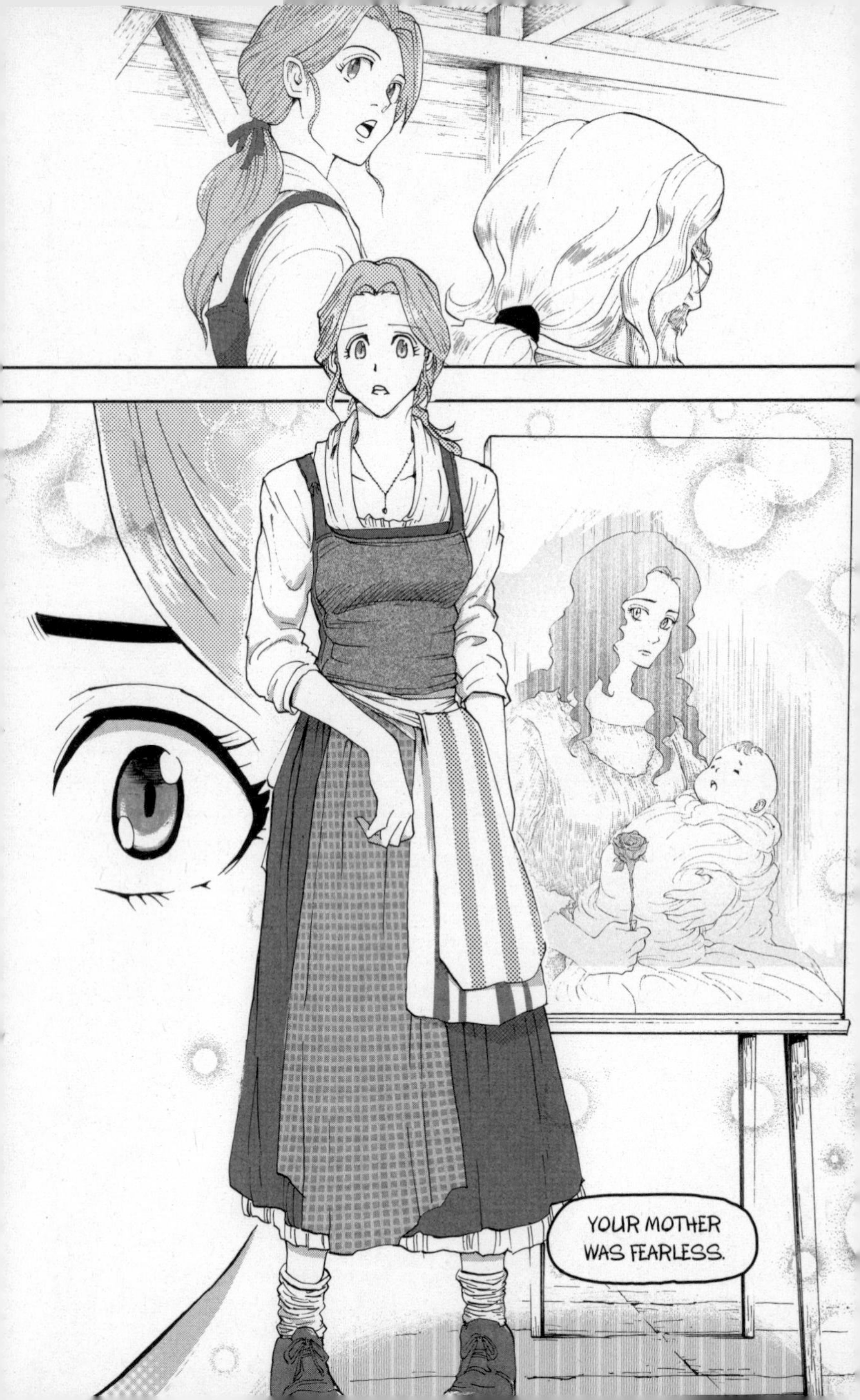
YOUR MOTHER WAS FEARLESS.

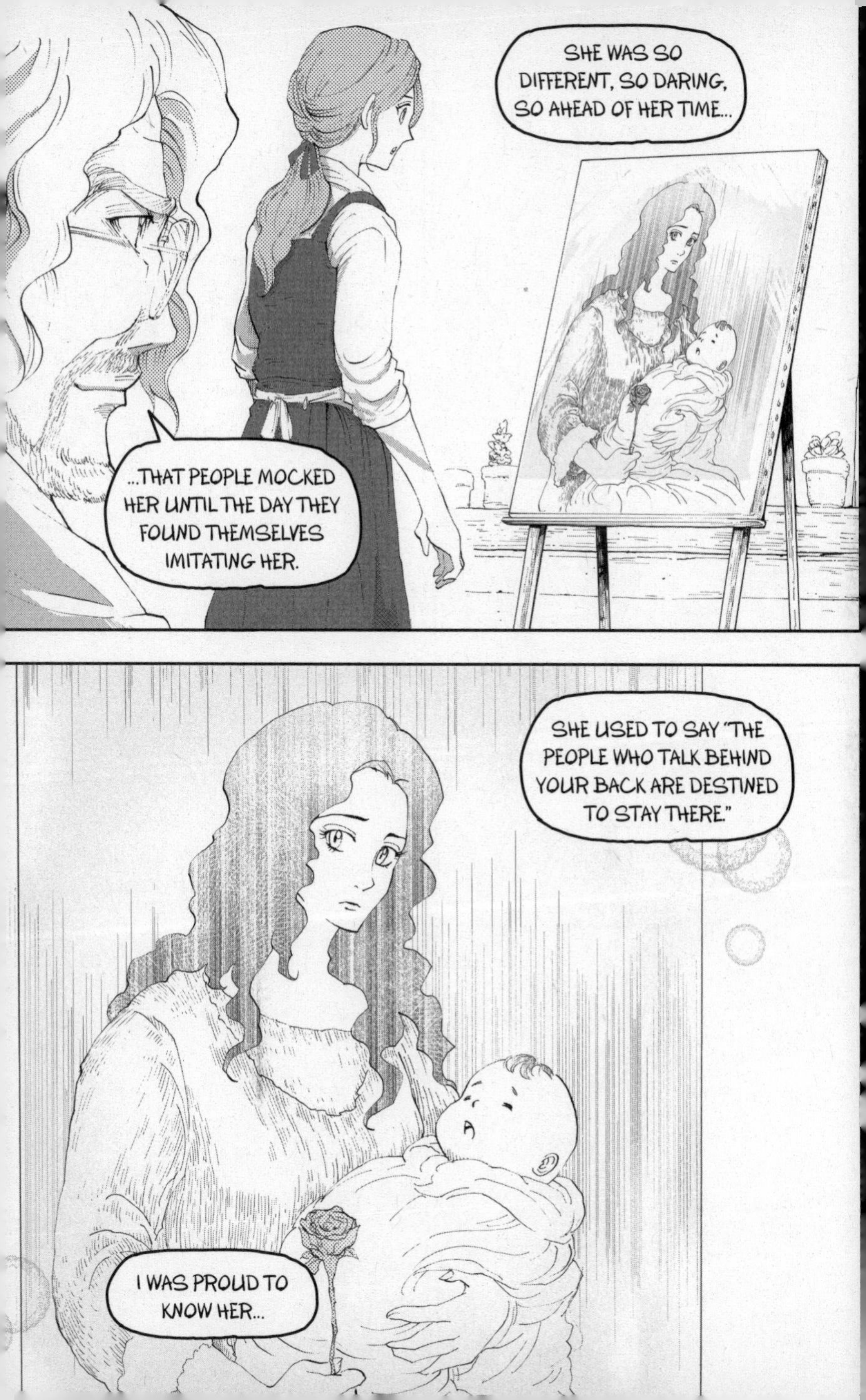
SHE WAS SO DIFFERENT, SO DARING, SO AHEAD OF HER TIME...
...THAT PEOPLE MOCKED HER UNTIL THE DAY THEY FOUND THEMSELVES IMITATING HER.
SHE USED TO SAY "THE PEOPLE WHO TALK BEHIND YOUR BACK ARE DESTINED TO STAY THERE."
I WAS PROUD TO KNOW HER...

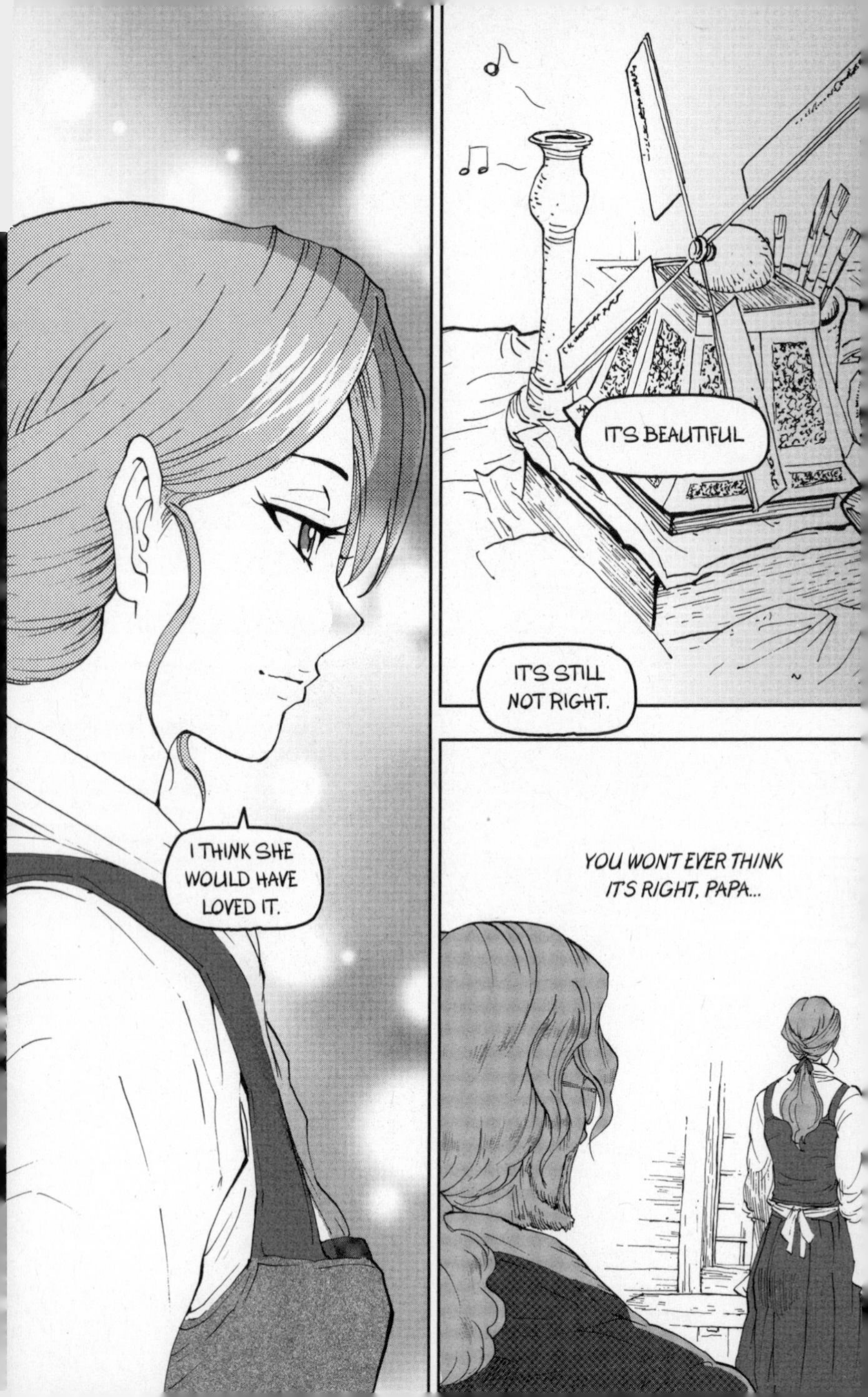
IT'S BEAUTIFUL
IT'S STILL NOT RIGHT.
YOU WON'T EVER THINK IT'S RIGHT, PAPA...
I THINK SHE WOULD HAVE LOVED IT.

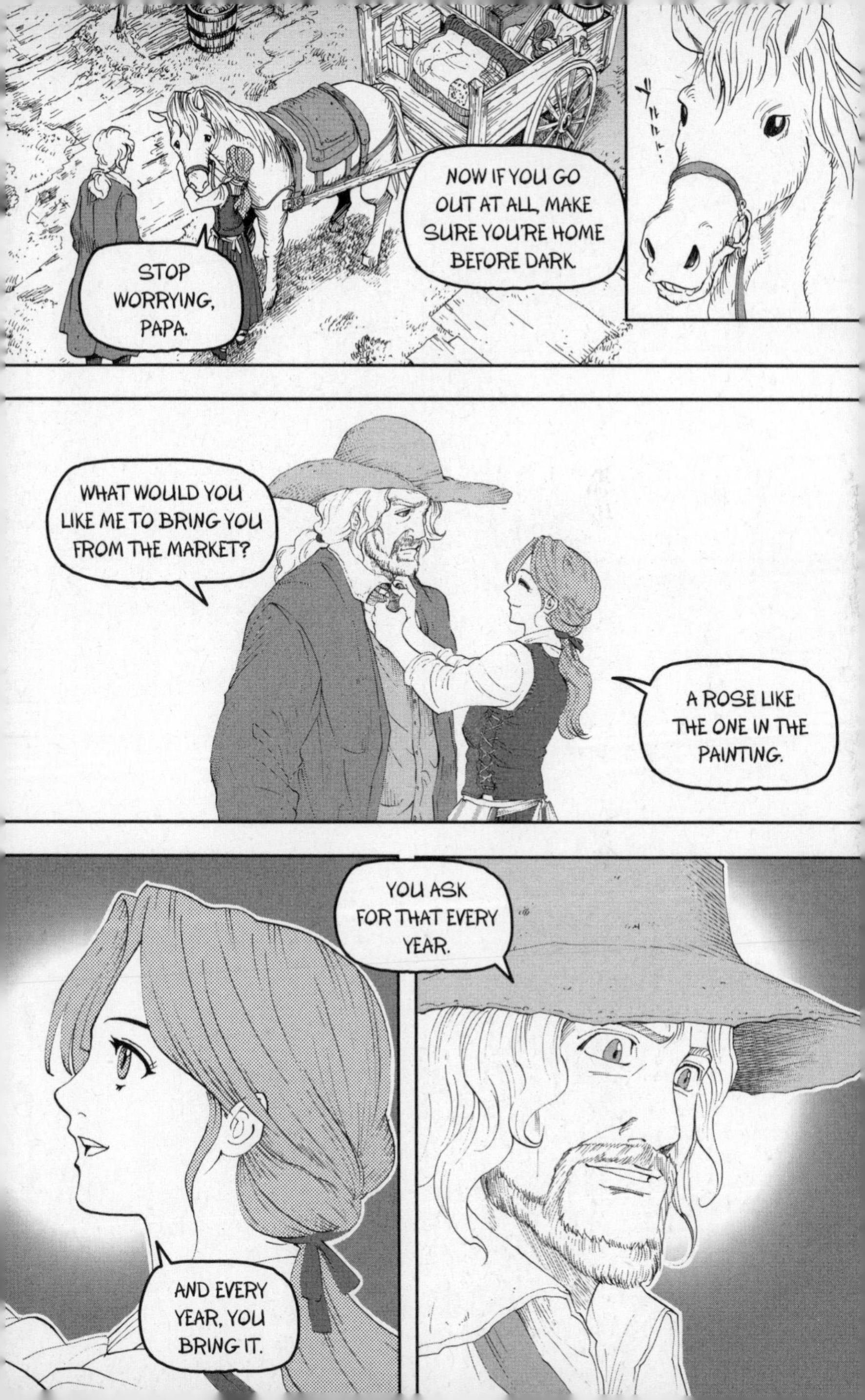
NOW IF YOU GO OUT AT ALL, MAKE SURE YOU'RE HOME BEFORE DARK.
STOP WORRYING, PAPA.
WHAT WOULD YOU LIKE ME TO BRING YOU FROM THE MARKET?
A ROSE LIKE THE ONE IN THE PAINTING.
YOU ASK FOR THAT EVERY YEAR.
AND EVERY YEAR, YOU BRING IT.

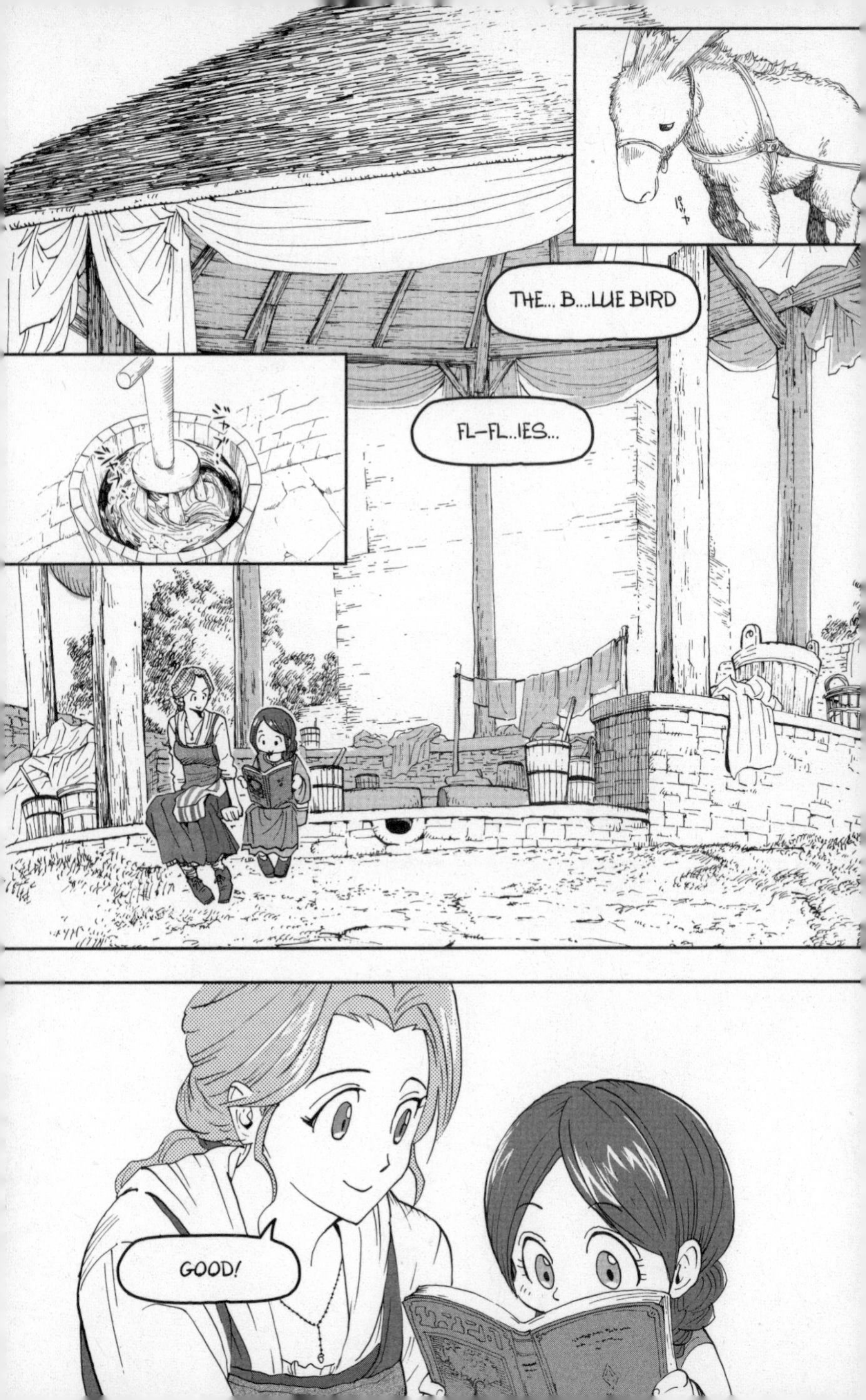
THE... B...LUE BIRD
FL–FL..IES...
GOOD!

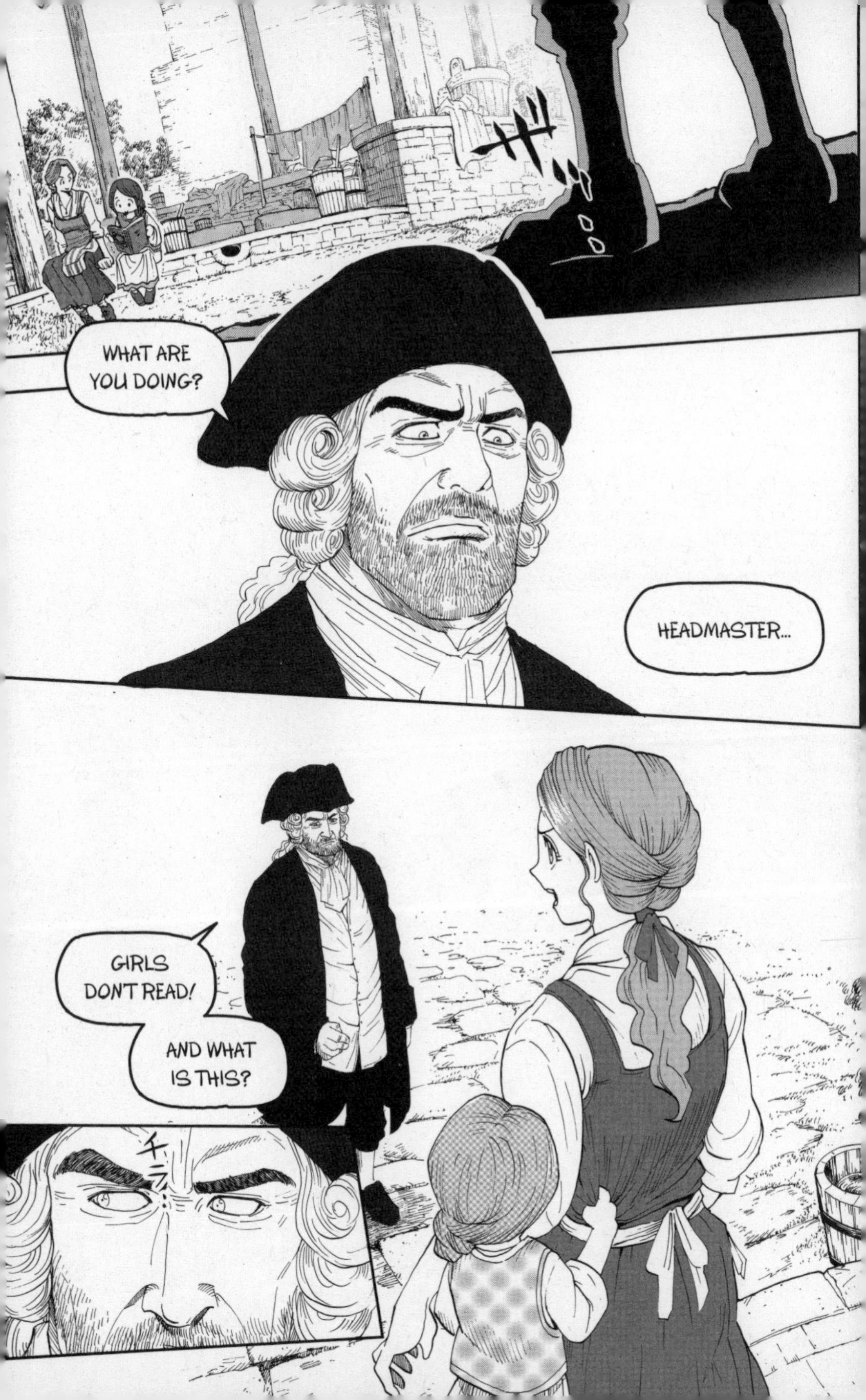
ザッ
WHAT ARE YOU DOING?
HEADMASTER...
GIRLS DON'T READ!
AND WHAT IS THIS?
チラ

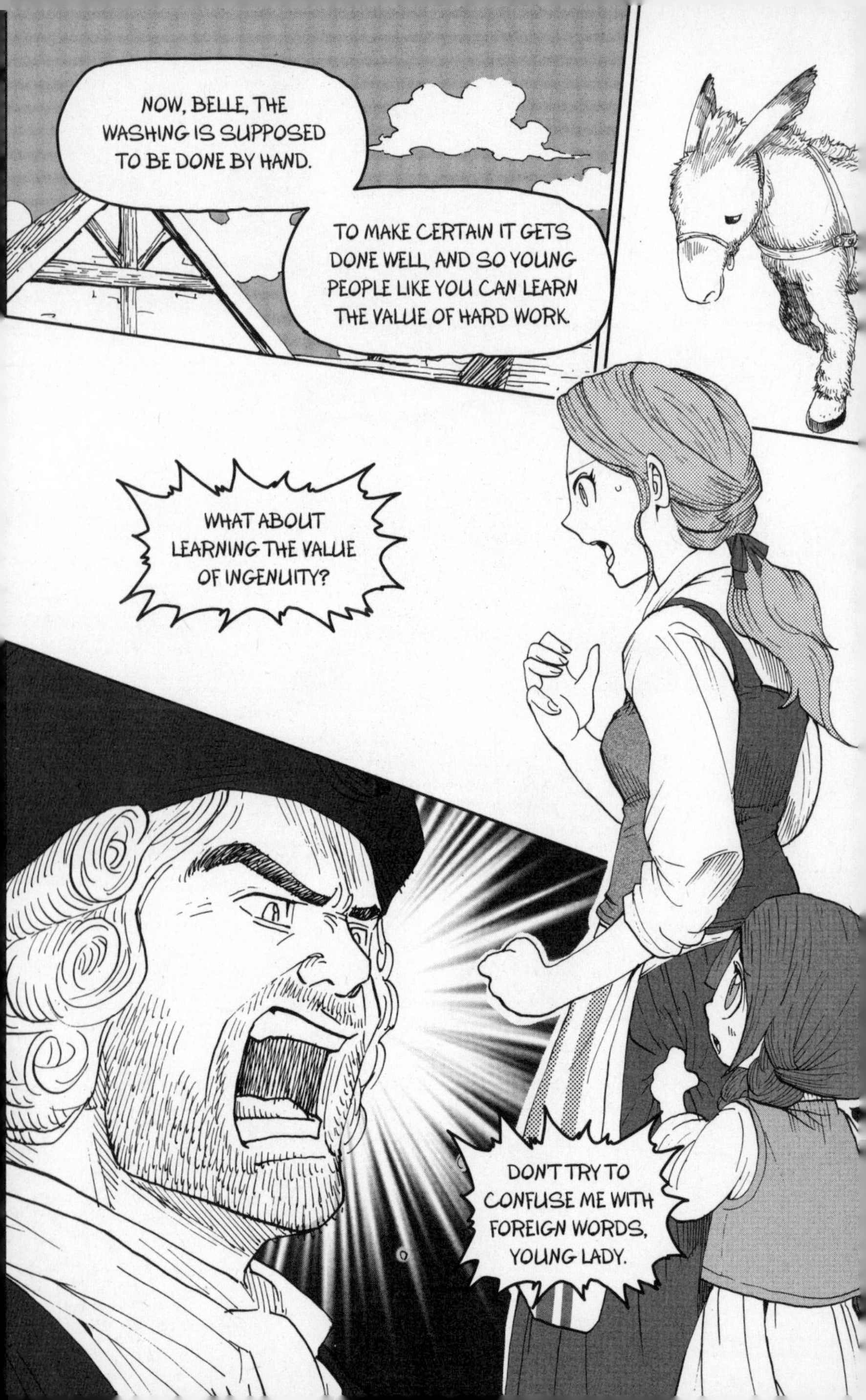
NOW, BELLE, THE WASHING IS SUPPOSED TO BE DONE BY HAND.
TO MAKE CERTAIN IT GETS DONE WELL, AND SO YOUNG PEOPLE LIKE YOU CAN LEARN THE VALUE OF HARD WORK.
WHAT ABOUT LEARNING THE VALUE OF INGENUITY?
DON'T TRY TO CONFUSE ME WITH FOREIGN WORDS, YOUNG LADY.

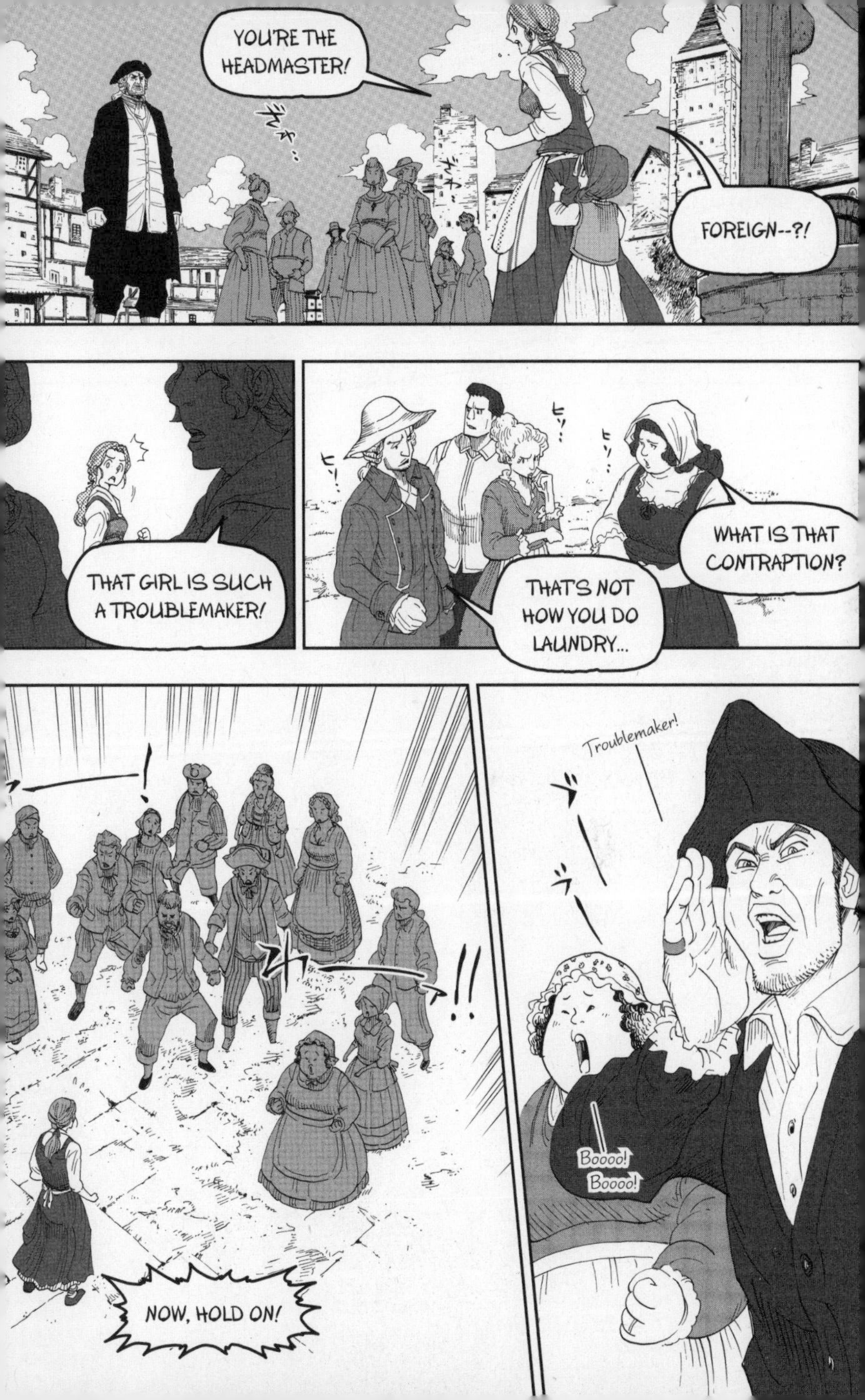
YOU'RE THE HEADMASTER!
FOREIGN--?!
WHAT IS THAT CONTRAPTION?
THAT'S NOT HOW YOU DO LAUNDRY...
THAT GIRL IS SUCH A TROUBLEMAKER!
Troublemaker!
Boooo!
Boooo!
NOW, HOLD ON!

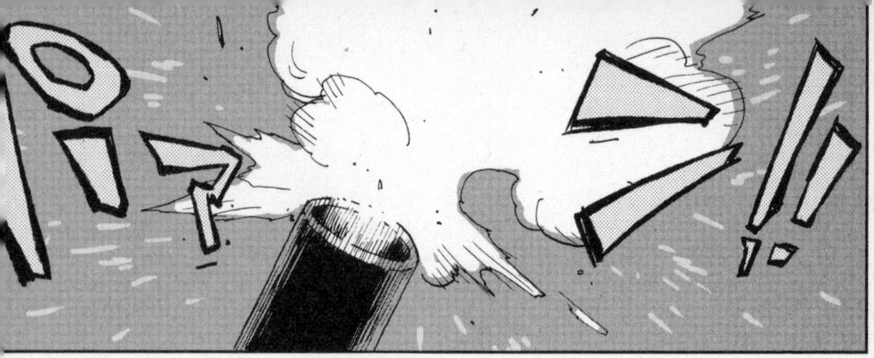

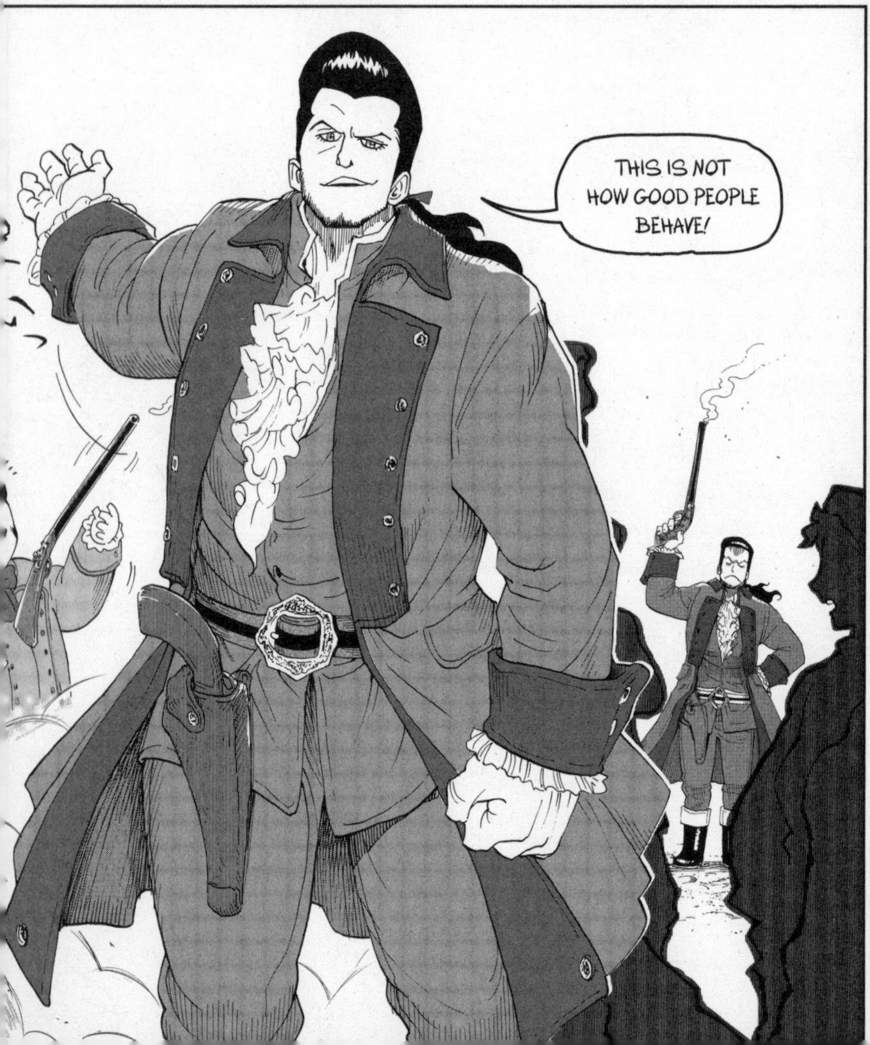
THIS IS NOT HOW GOOD PEOPLE BEHAVE!

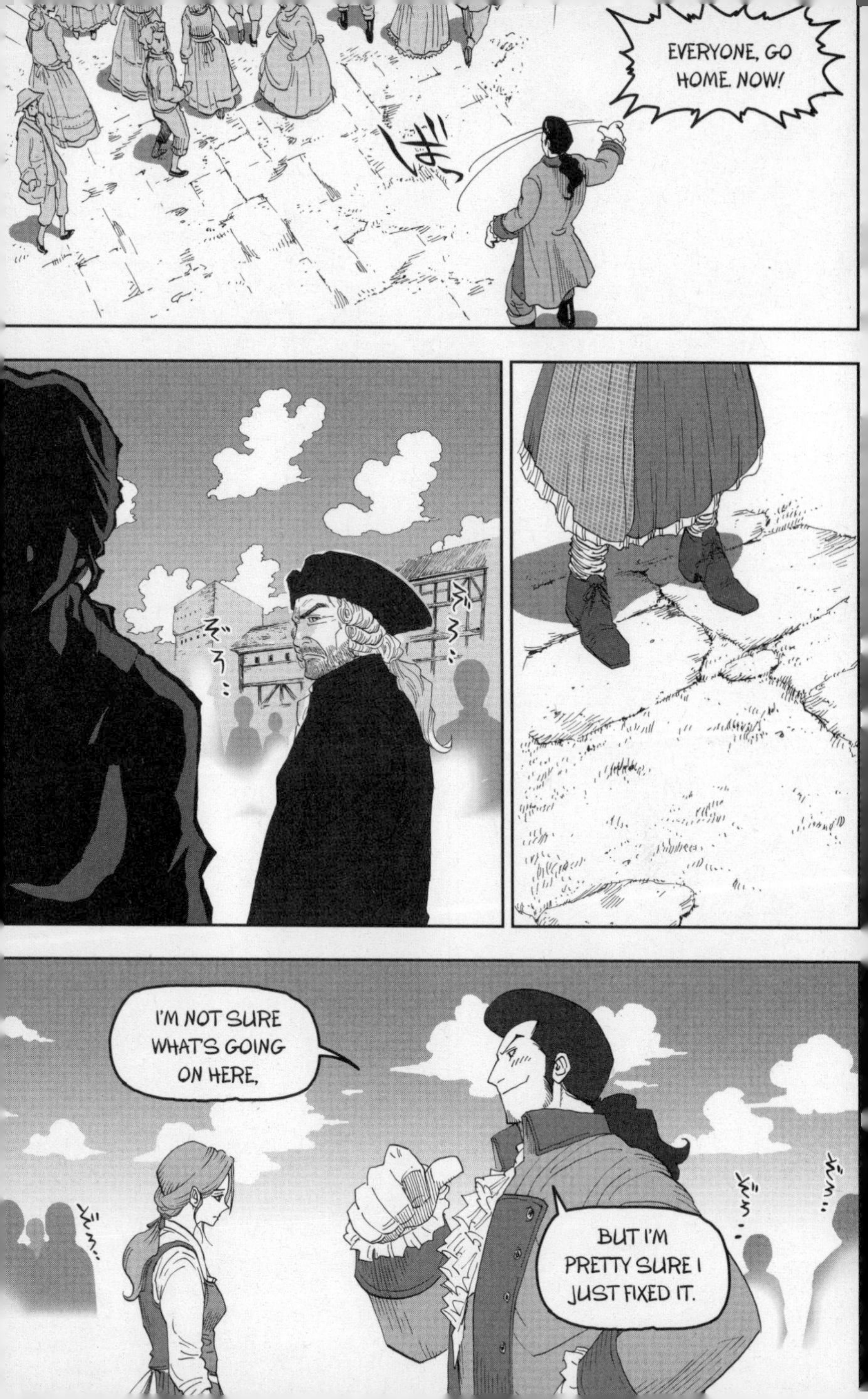
EVERYONE, GO HOME. NOW!
I'M NOT SURE WHAT'S GOING ON HERE,
BUT I'M PRETTY SURE I JUST FIXED IT.

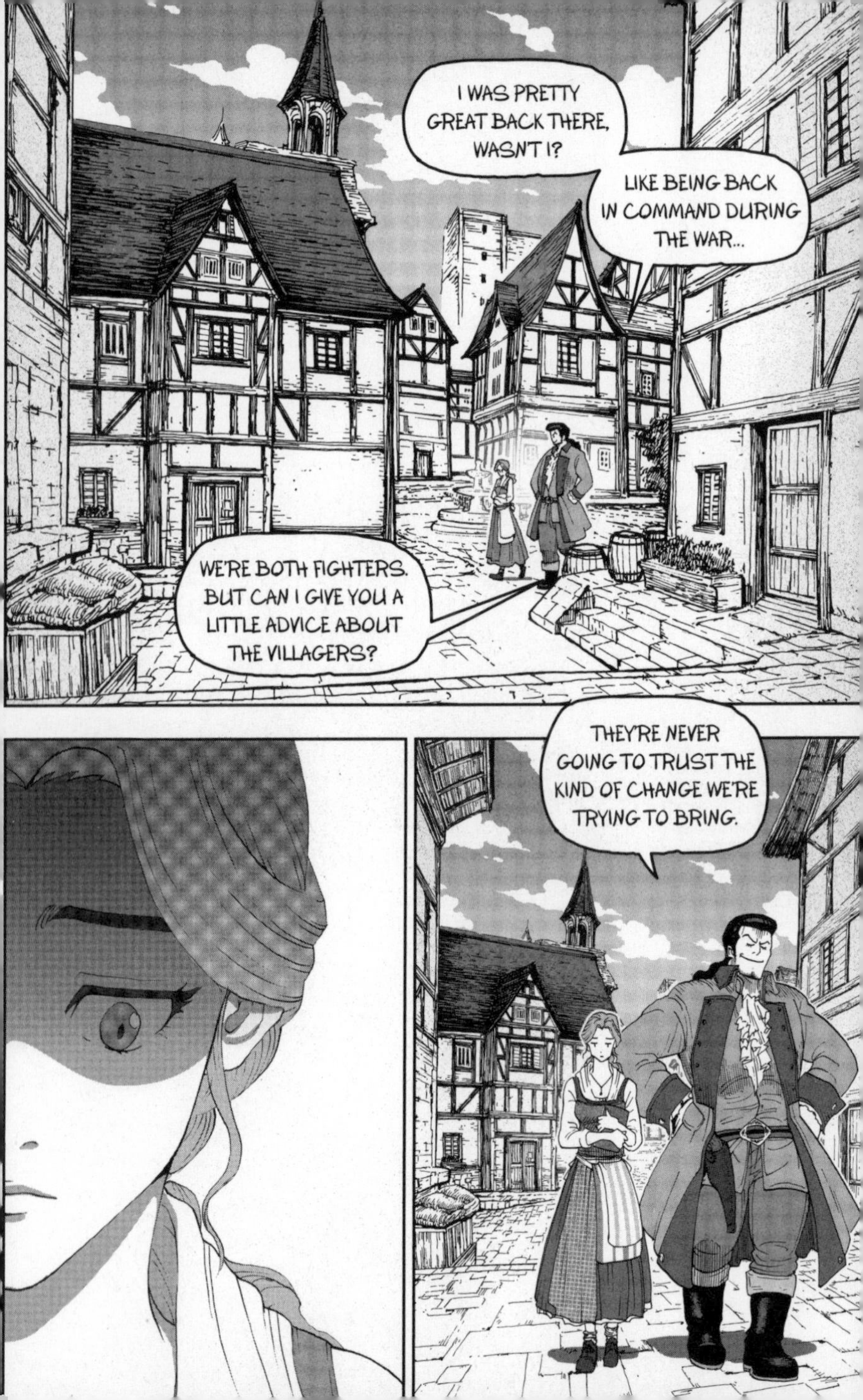
I WAS PRETTY GREAT BACK THERE, WASN'T I?
LIKE BEING BACK IN COMMAND DURING THE WAR...
WE'RE BOTH FIGHTERS. BUT CAN I GIVE YOU A LITTLE ADVICE ABOUT THE VILLAGERS?
THEY'RE NEVER GOING TO TRUST THE KIND OF CHANGE WE'RE TRYING TO BRING.

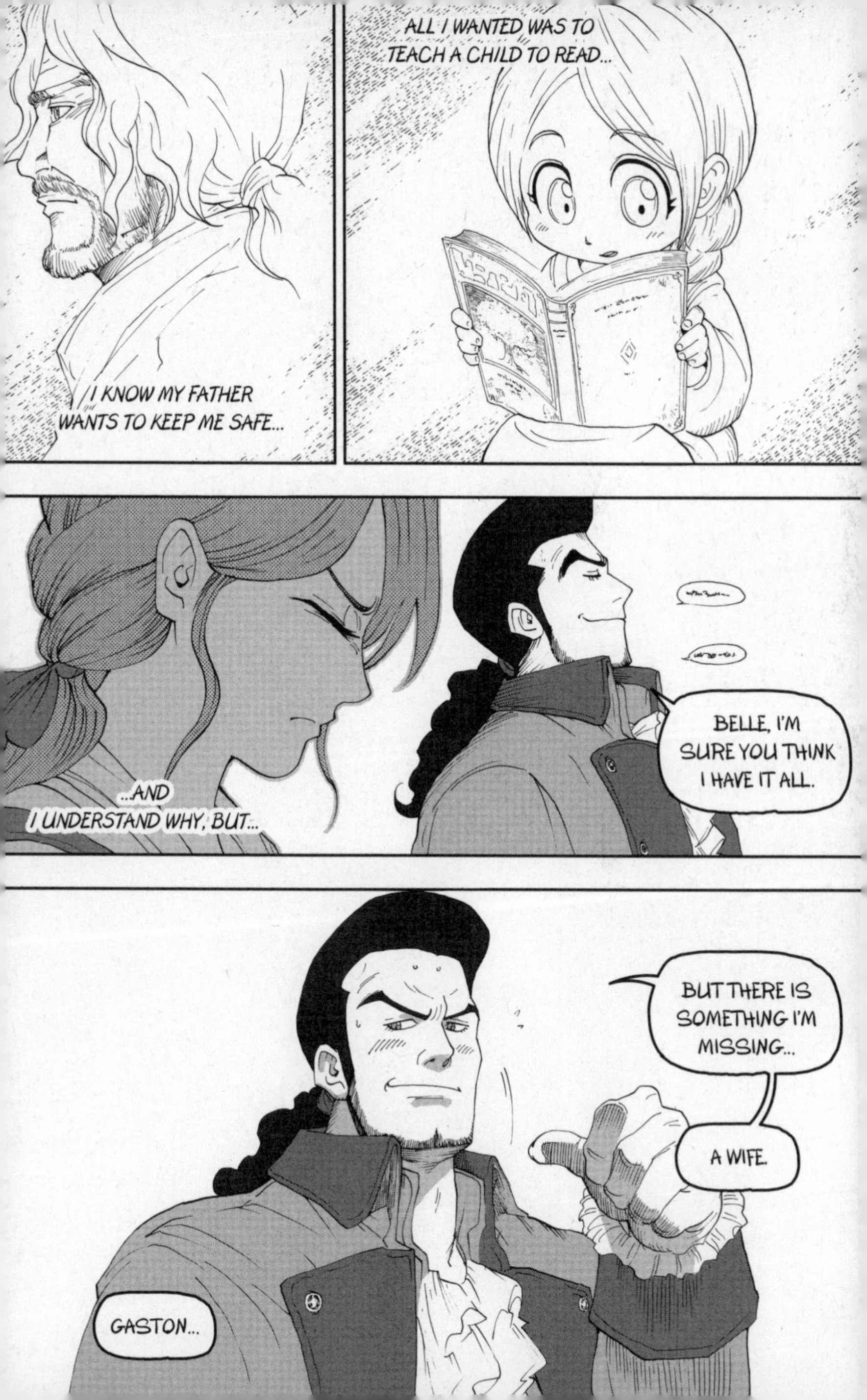
ALL I WANTED WAS TO TEACH A CHILD TO READ...
I KNOW MY FATHER WANTS TO KEEP ME SAFE...
BELLE, I'M SURE YOU THINK I HAVE IT ALL.
...AND I UNDERSTAND WHY, BUT...
BUT THERE IS SOMETHING I'M MISSING...
A WIFE.
GASTON...

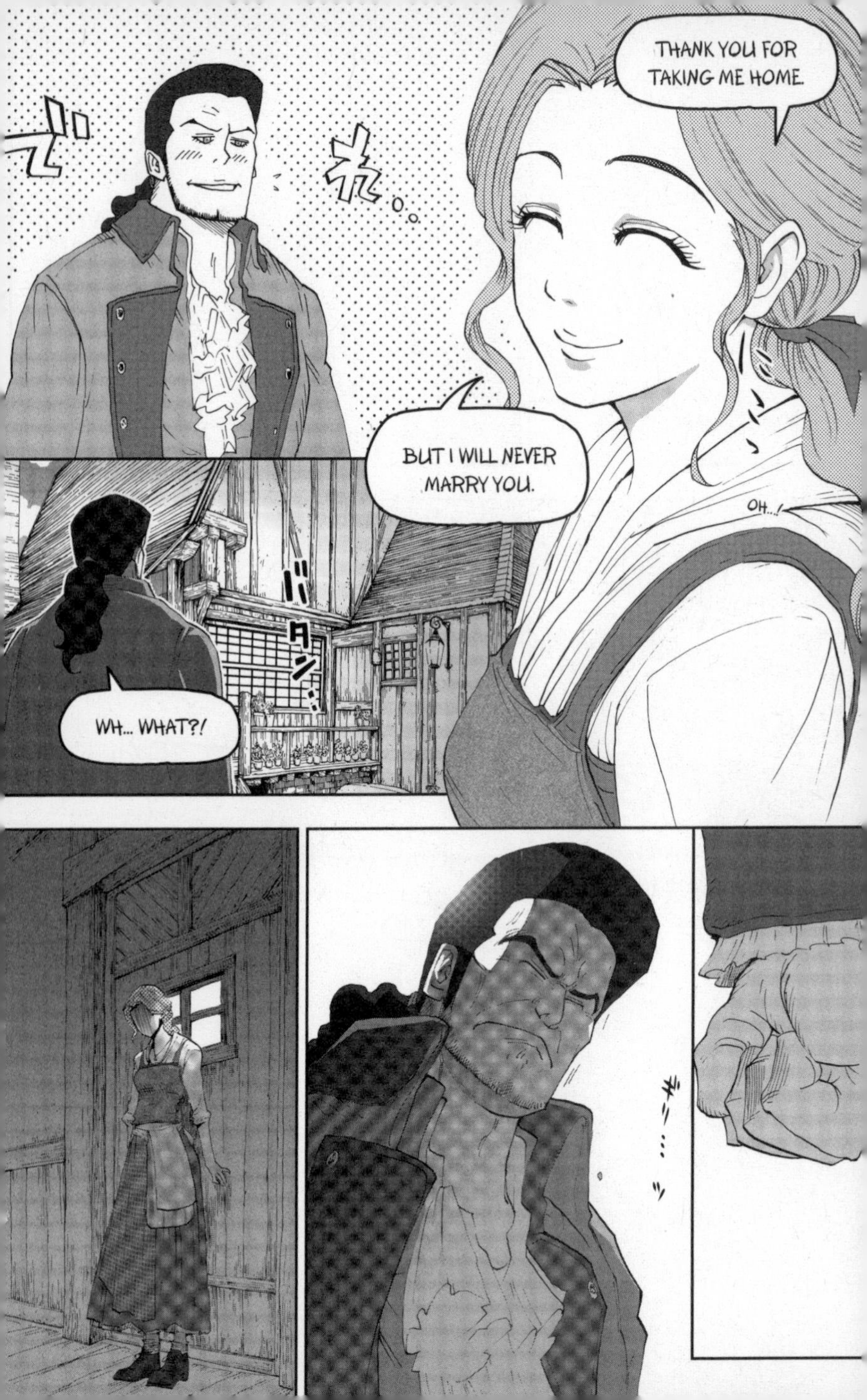
THANK YOU FOR TAKING ME HOME.
BUT I WILL NEVER MARRY YOU.
OH...!
WH... WHAT?!
バタン…

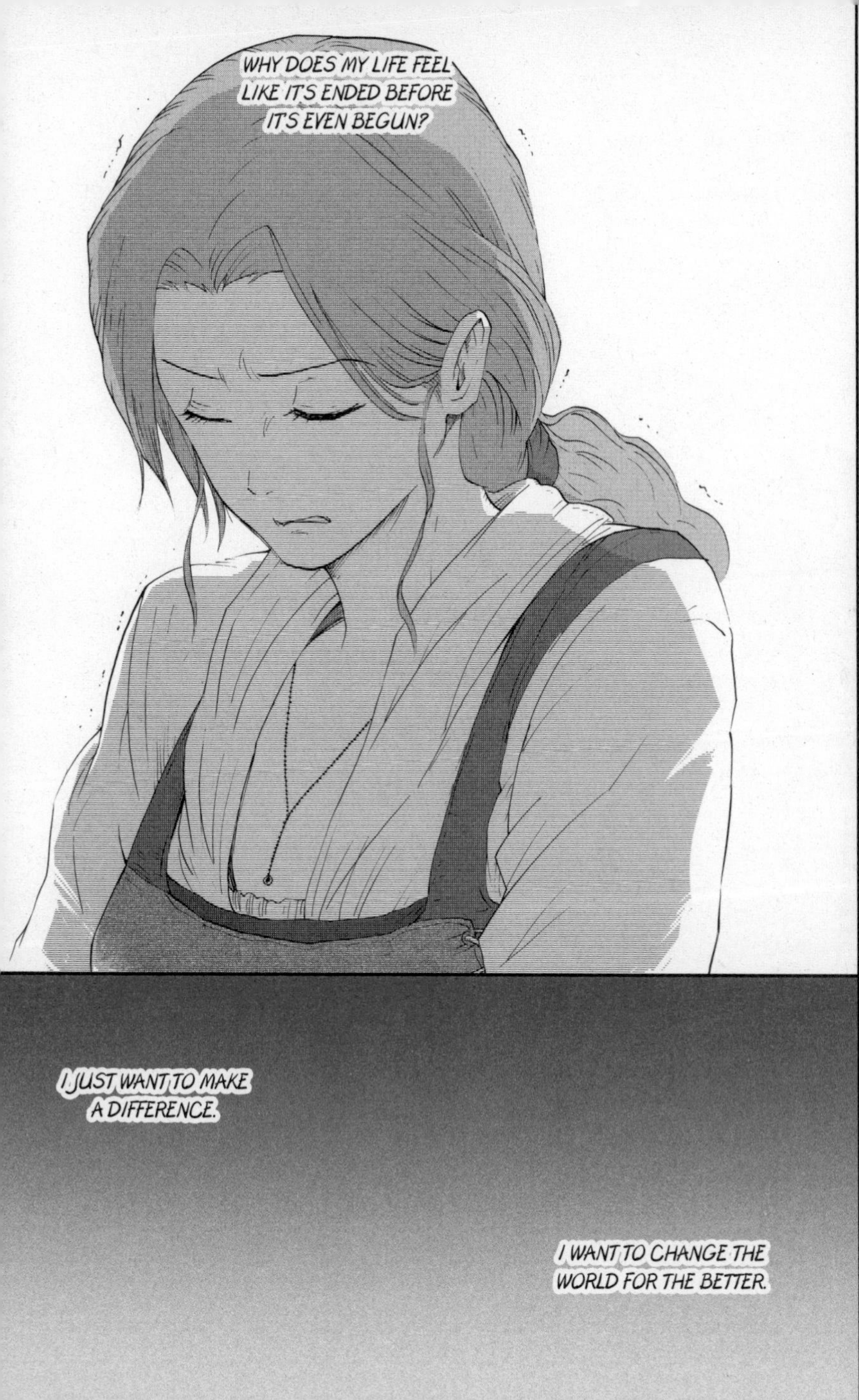
WHY DOES MY LIFE FEEL LIKE IT'S ENDED BEFORE IT'S EVEN BEGUN?
I JUST WANT TO MAKE A DIFFERENCE.
I WANT TO CHANGE THE WORLD FOR THE BETTER.

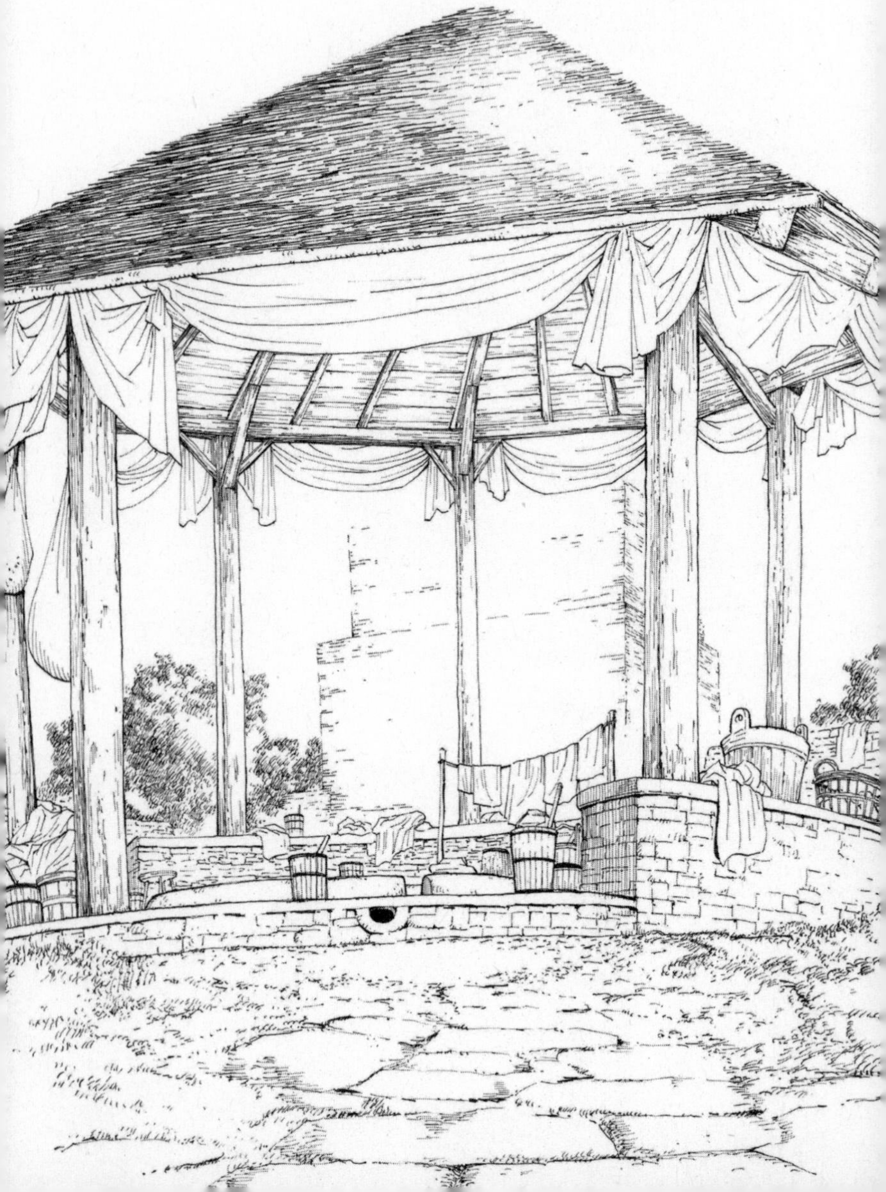

CHAPTER 2

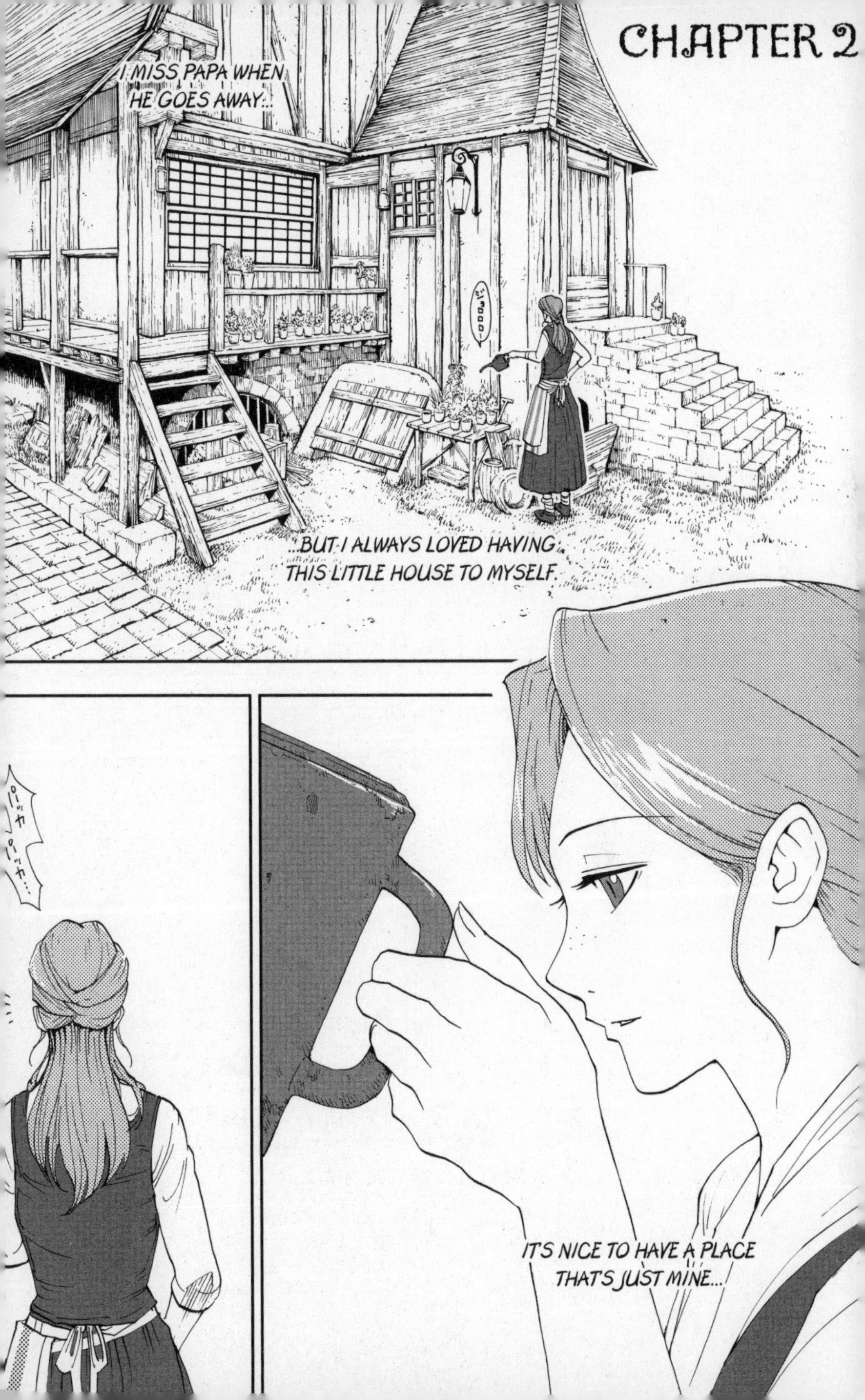
I MISS PAPA WHEN HE GOES AWAY...
...BUT I ALWAYS LOVED HAVING THIS LITTLE HOUSE TO MYSELF.
IT'S NICE TO HAVE A PLACE THAT'S JUST MINE...

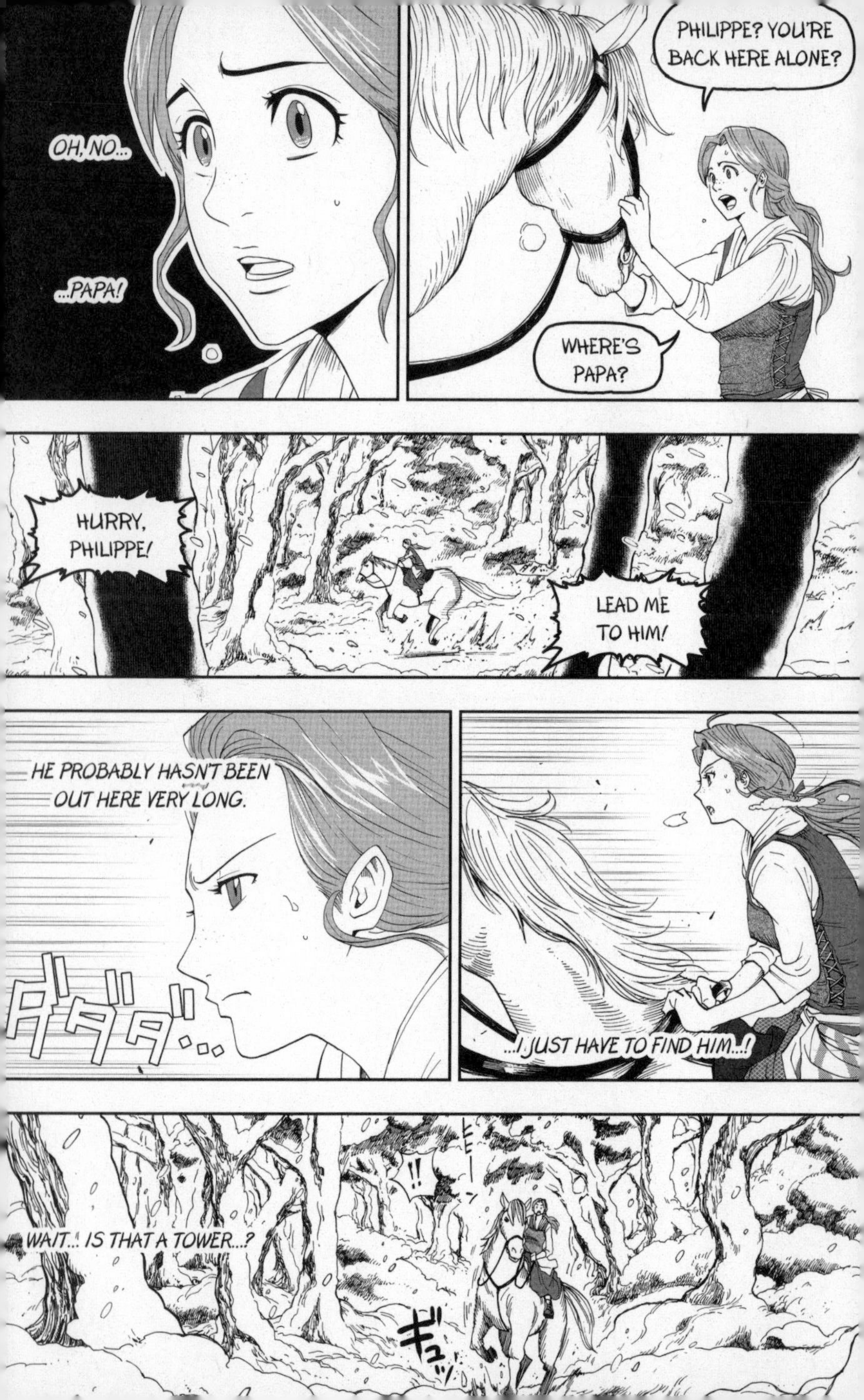
PHILIPPE? YOU'RE BACK HERE ALONE?
WHERE'S PAPA?
OH, NO...
...PAPA!
HURRY, PHILIPPE!
LEAD ME TO HIM!
...I JUST HAVE TO FIND HIM...!
HE PROBABLY HASN'T BEEN OUT HERE VERY LONG.
ダダダ...
!!
WAIT... IS THAT A TOWER...?
ギュッ

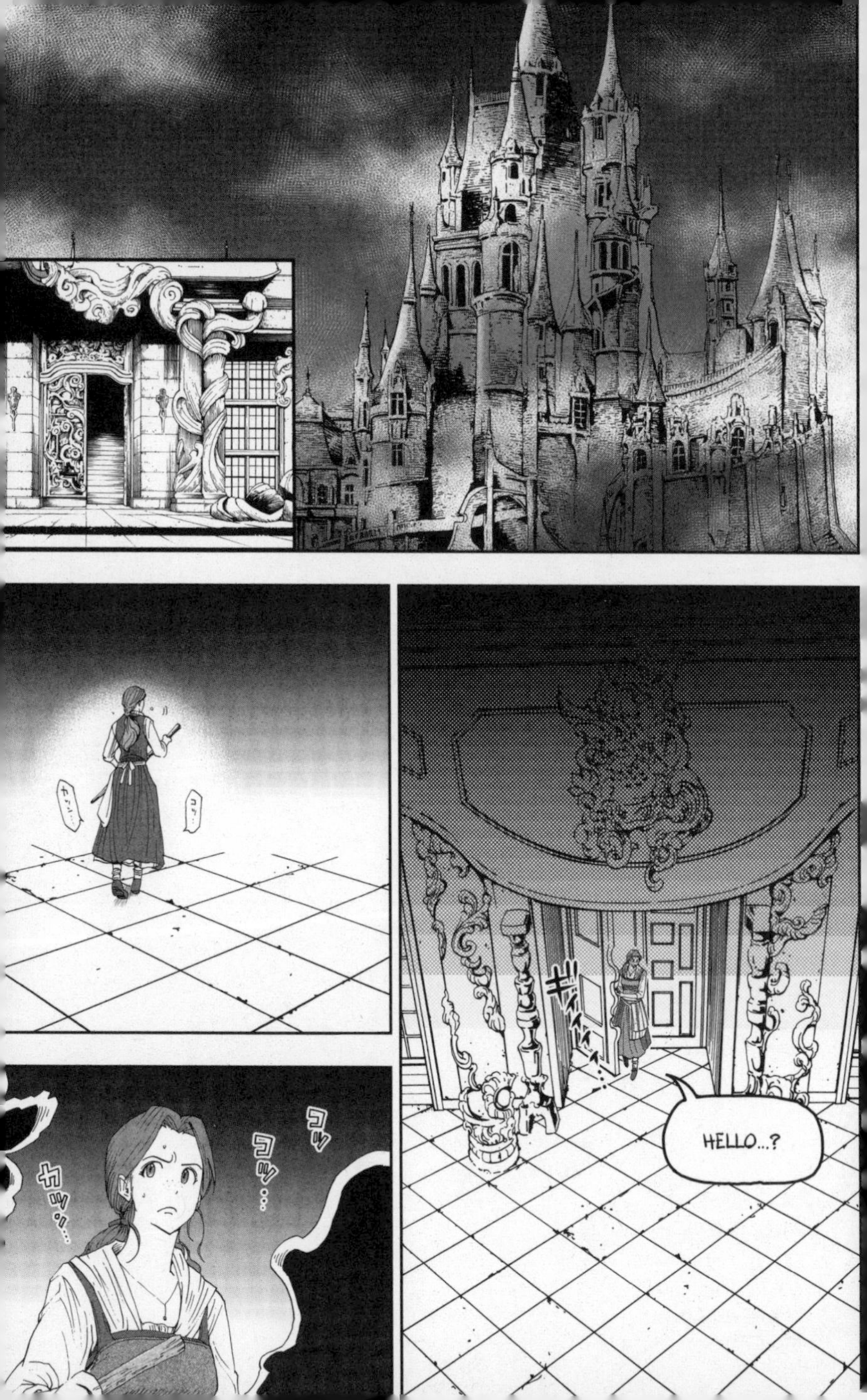
HELLO...?

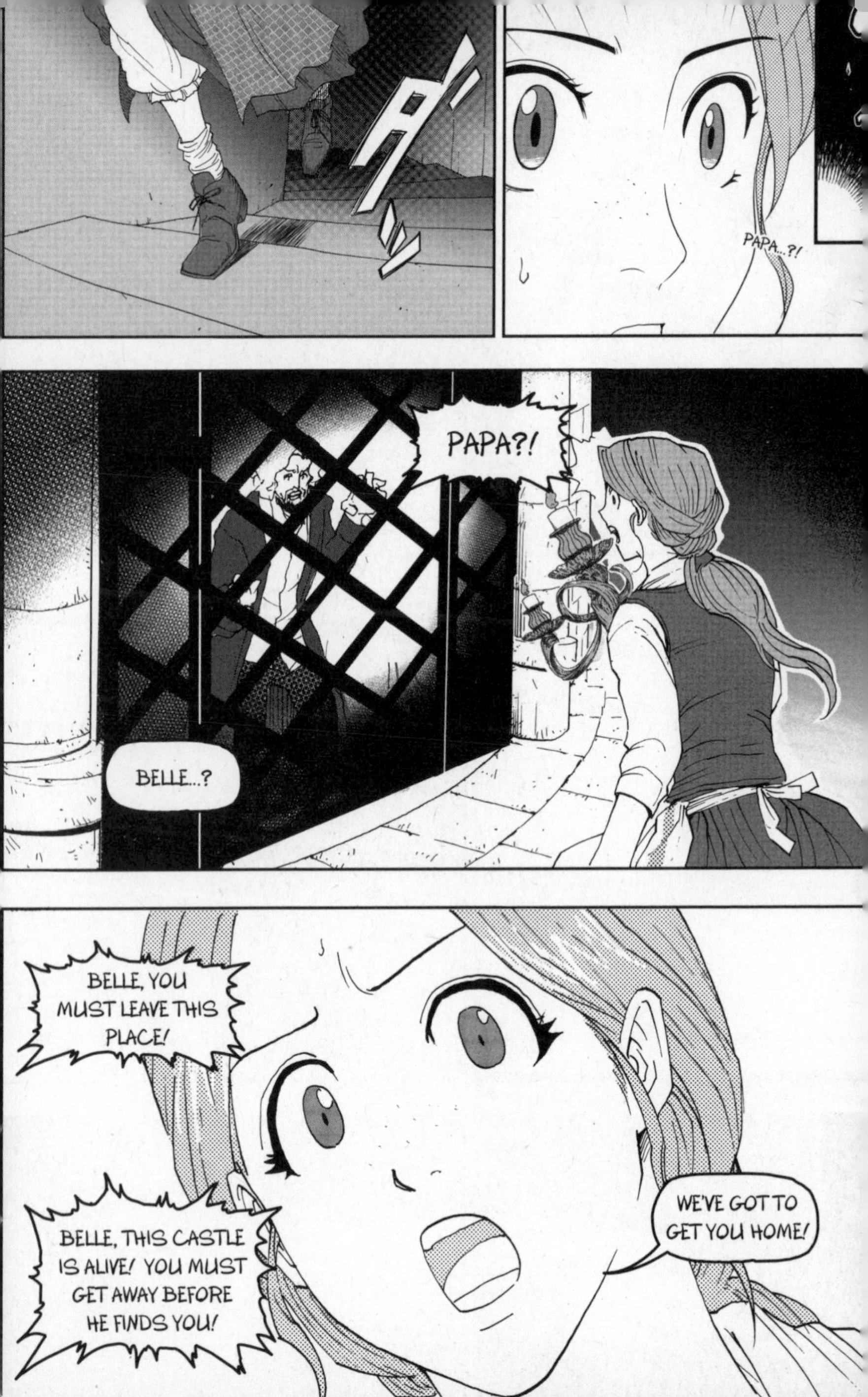
PAPA...?!
PAPA?!
BELLE...?
BELLE, YOU MUST LEAVE THIS PLACE!
WE'VE GOT TO GET YOU HOME!
BELLE, THIS CASTLE IS ALIVE! YOU MUST GET AWAY BEFORE HE FINDS YOU!

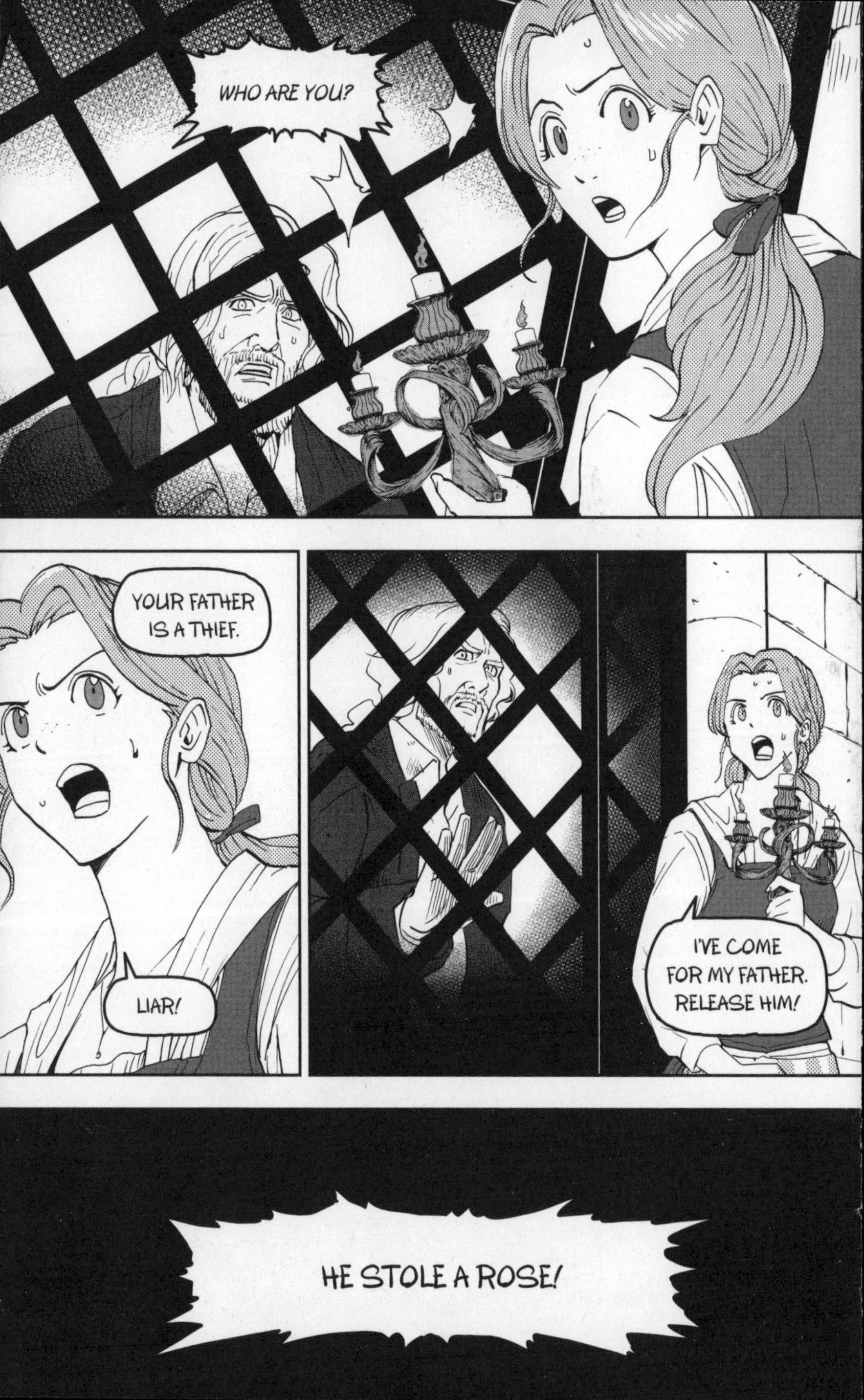
WHO ARE YOU?
I'VE COME FOR MY FATHER. RELEASE HIM!
YOUR FATHER IS A THIEF.
LIAR!
HE STOLE A ROSE!

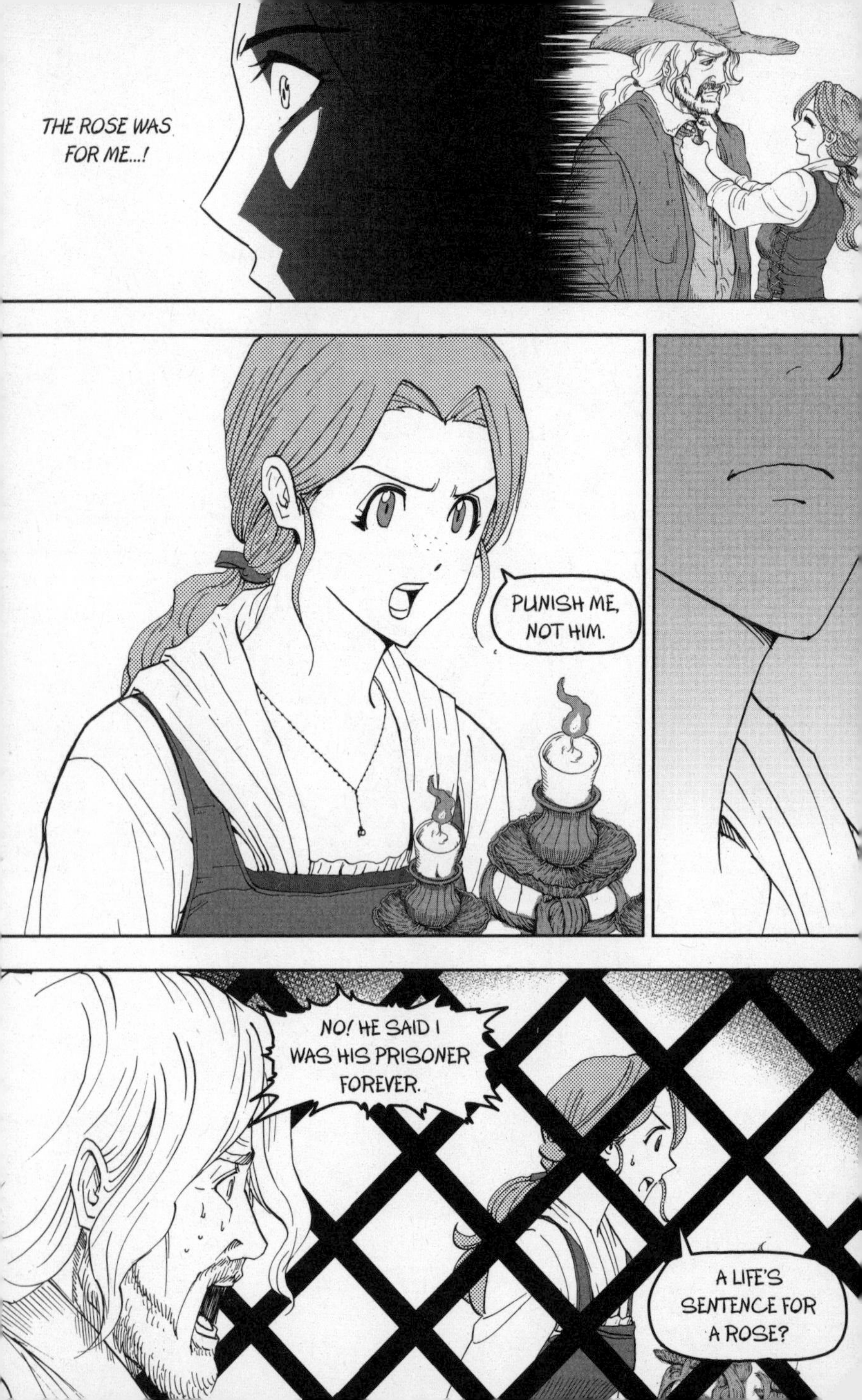
THE ROSE WAS FOR ME...!
PUNISH ME, NOT HIM.
NO! HE SAID I WAS HIS PRISONER FOREVER.
A LIFE'S SENTENCE FOR A ROSE?

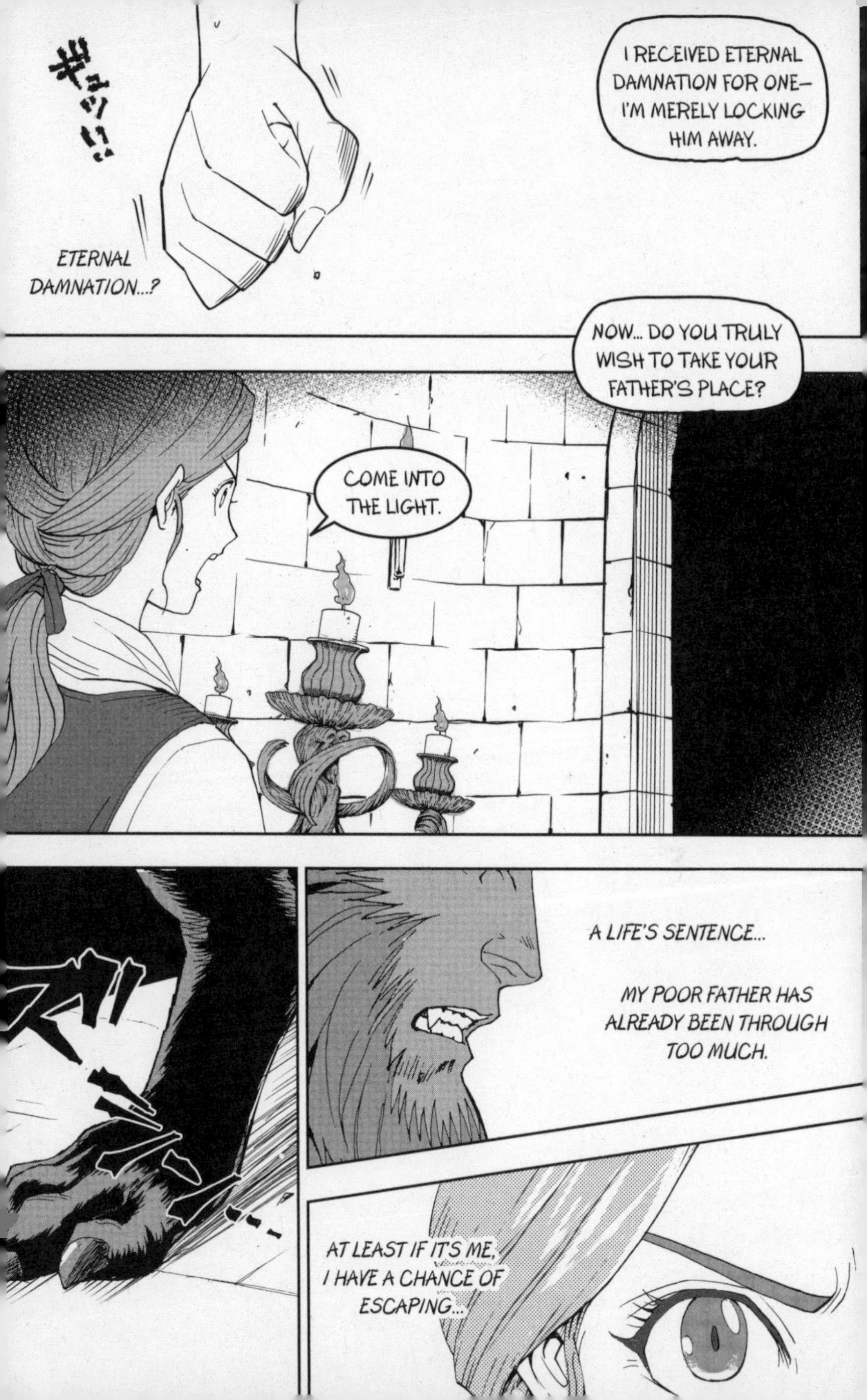
I RECEIVED ETERNAL DAMNATION FOR ONE— I'M MERELY LOCKING HIM AWAY.
ギュッ!!
ETERNAL DAMNATION...?
NOW... DO YOU TRULY WISH TO TAKE YOUR FATHER'S PLACE?
COME INTO THE LIGHT.
A LIFE'S SENTENCE...
MY POOR FATHER HAS ALREADY BEEN THROUGH TOO MUCH.
AT LEAST IF IT'S ME, I HAVE A CHANCE OF ESCAPING...

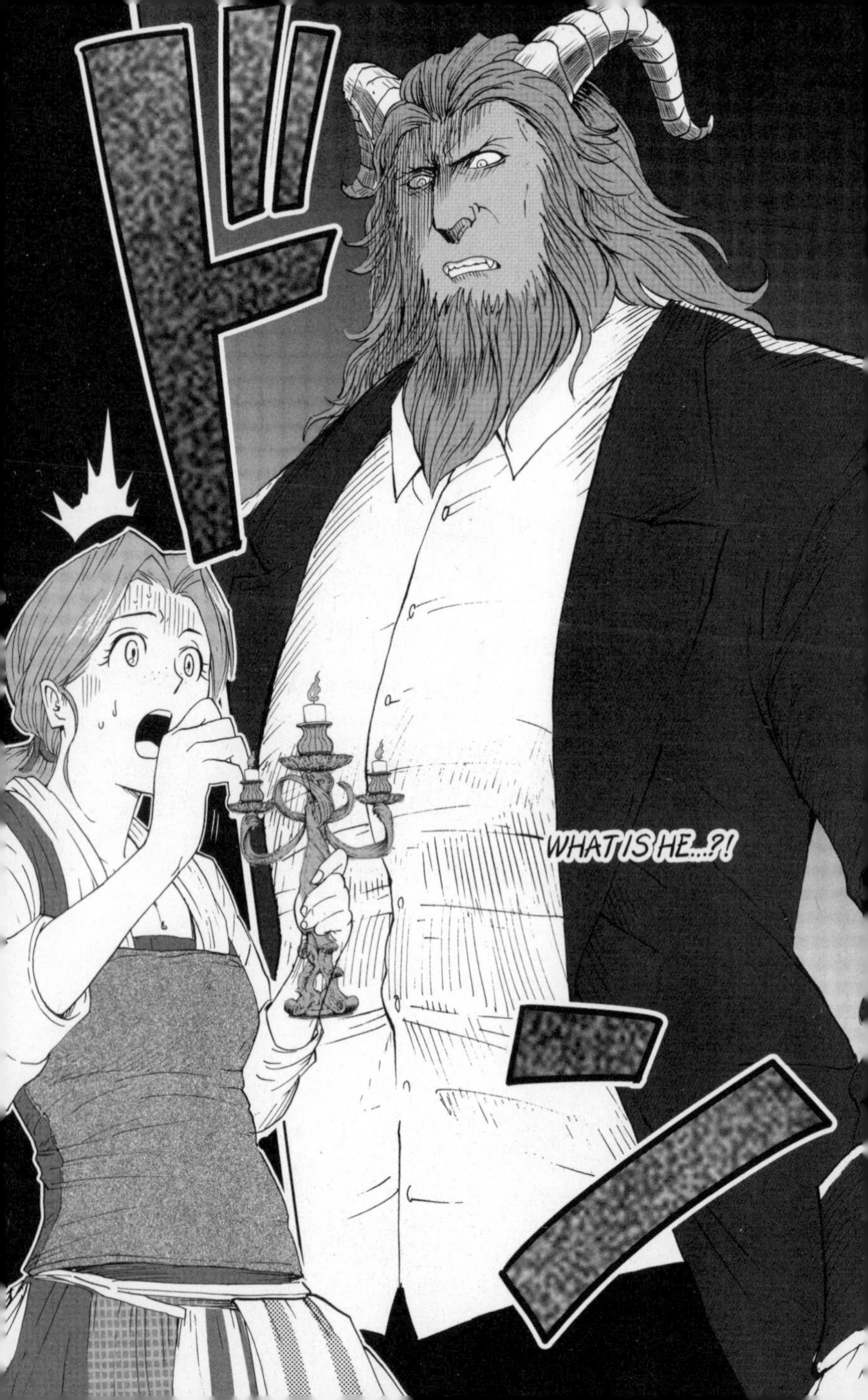
WHAT IS HE...?!

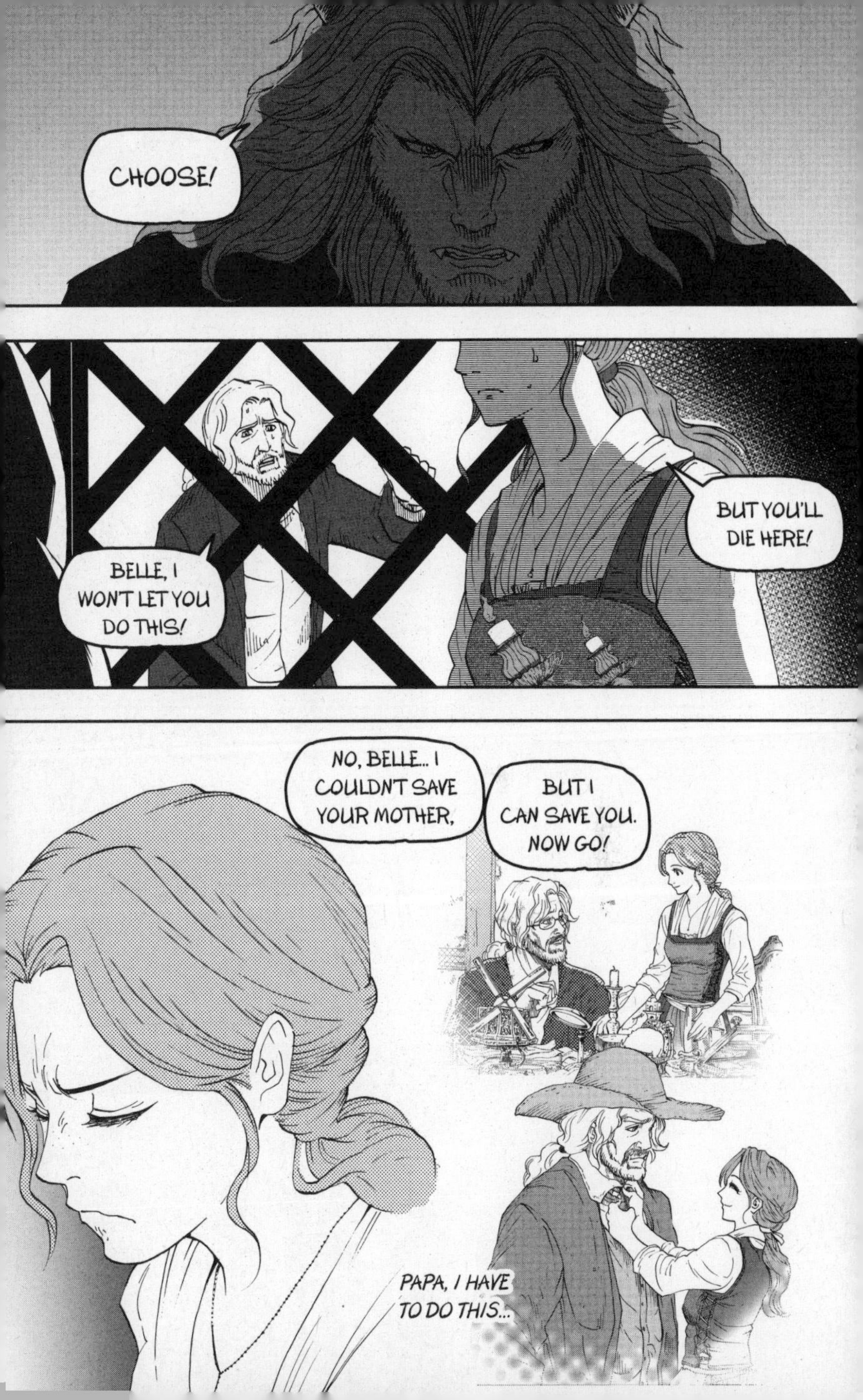
CHOOSE!
BELLE, I WON'T LET YOU DO THIS!
BUT YOU'LL DIE HERE!
NO, BELLE... I COULDN'T SAVE YOUR MOTHER,
BUT I CAN SAVE YOU. NOW GO!
PAPA, I HAVE TO DO THIS...

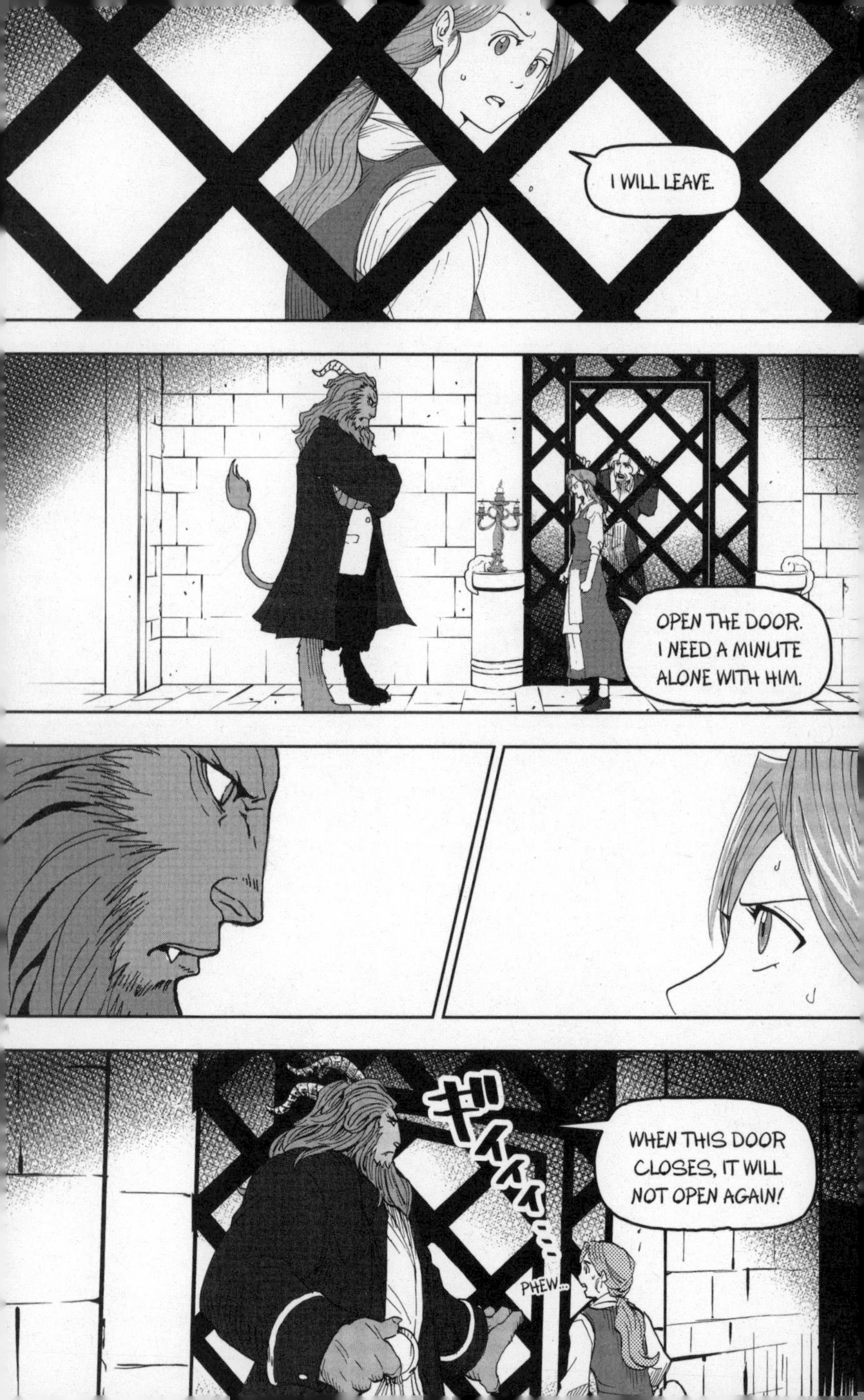
I WILL LEAVE.
OPEN THE DOOR. I NEED A MINUTE ALONE WITH HIM.
WHEN THIS DOOR CLOSES, IT WILL NOT OPEN AGAIN!
ギィィィ…
PHEW...

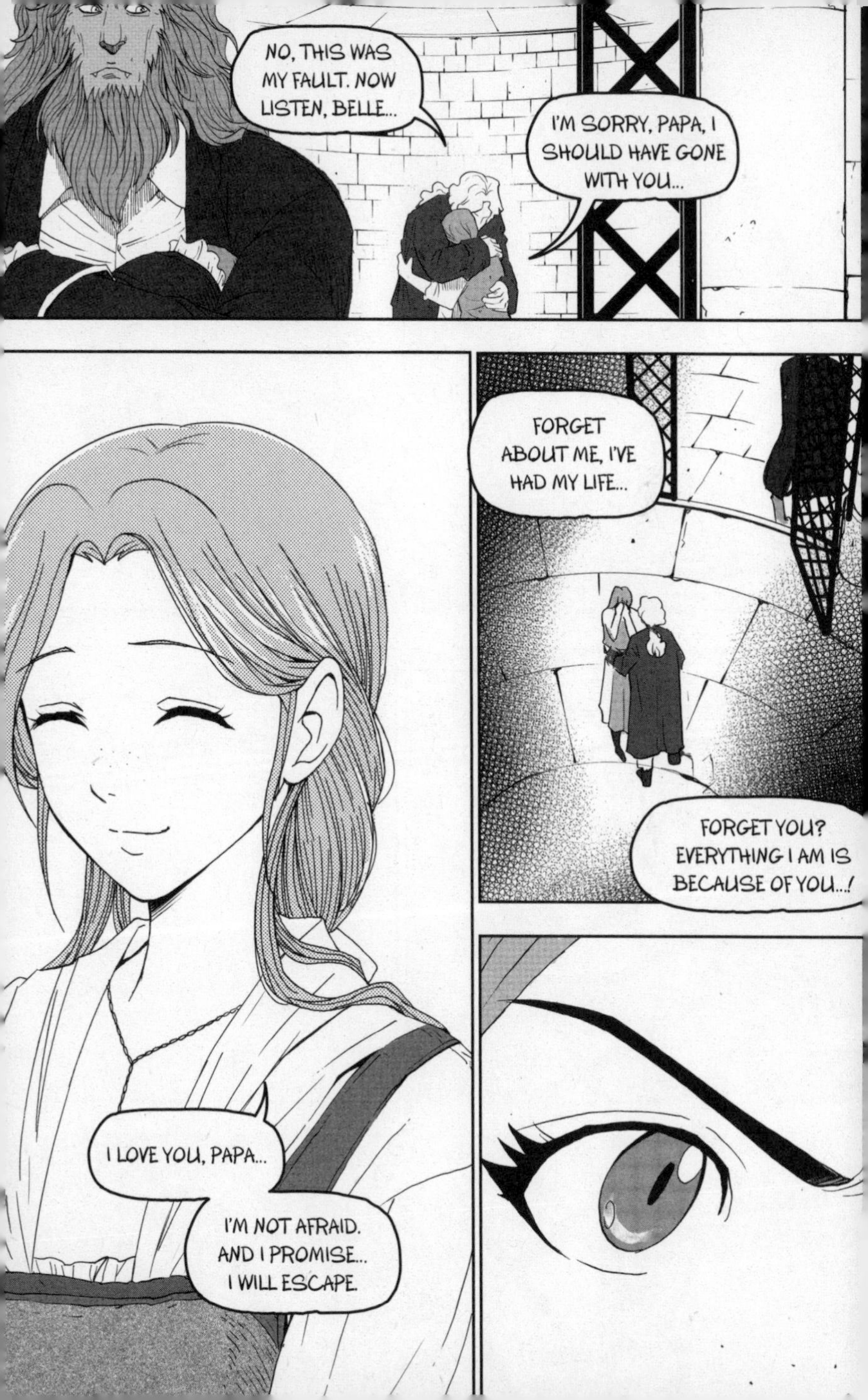
I'M SORRY, PAPA, I SHOULD HAVE GONE WITH YOU...
NO, THIS WAS MY FAULT. NOW LISTEN, BELLE...
FORGET ABOUT ME, I'VE HAD MY LIFE...
FORGET YOU? EVERYTHING I AM IS BECAUSE OF YOU...!
I LOVE YOU, PAPA...
I'M NOT AFRAID. AND I PROMISE... I WILL ESCAPE.

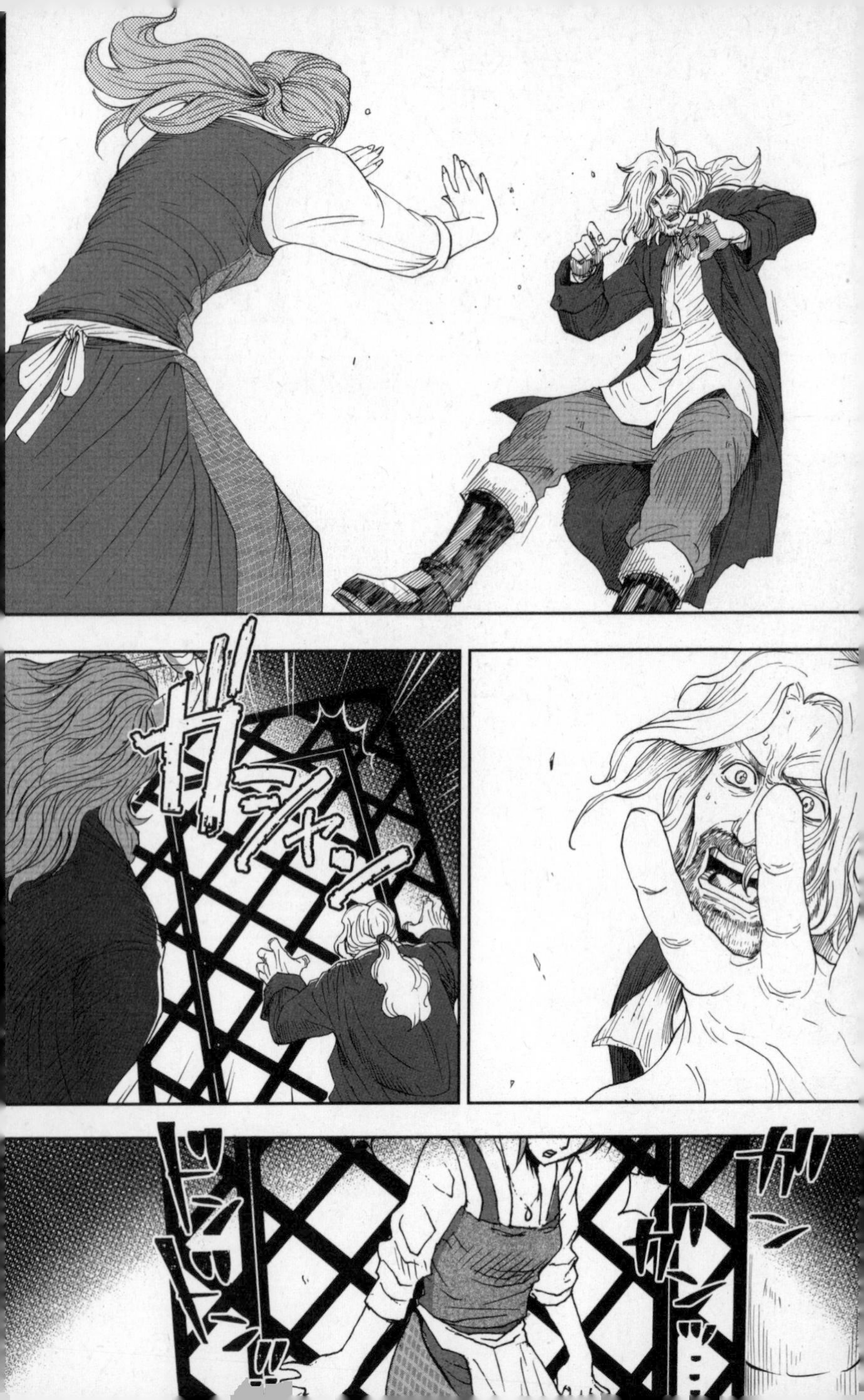
ガシャン
ガン
ガン…

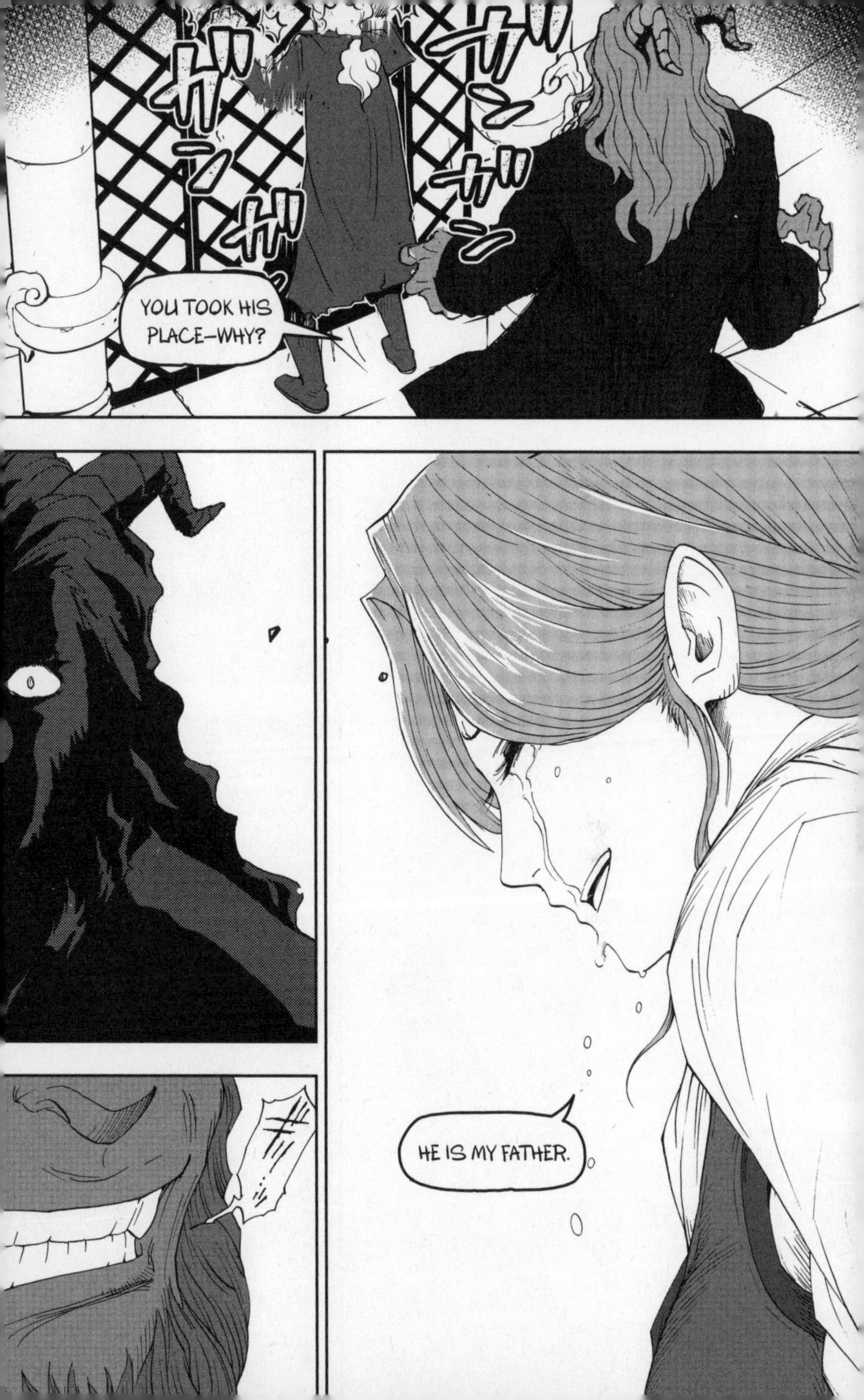

YOU TOOK HIS PLACE—WHY?
HE IS MY FATHER.

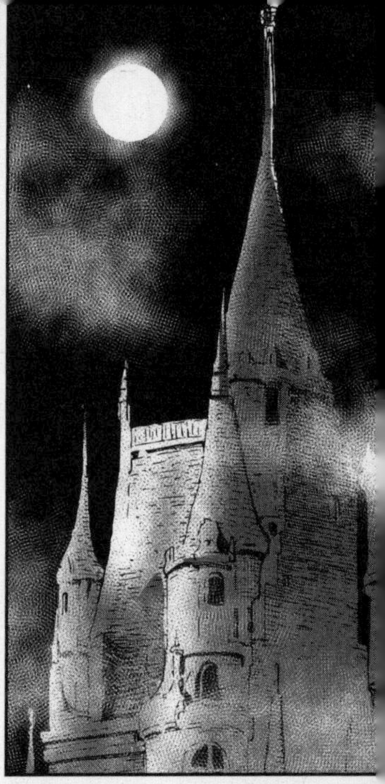

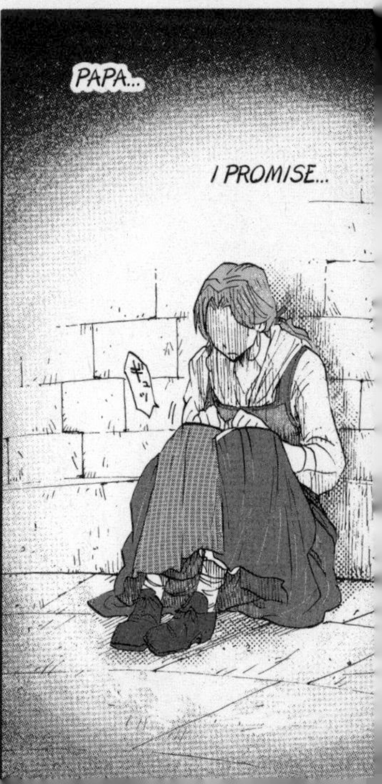
PAPA...
I PROMISE...

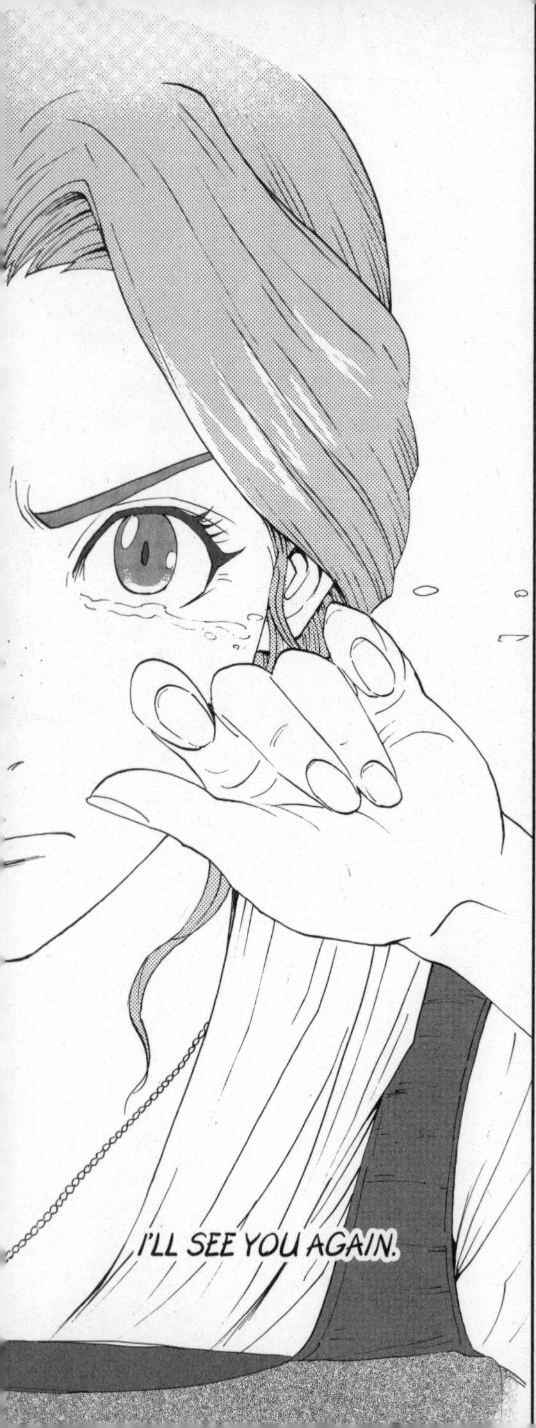
I'LL SEE YOU AGAIN.

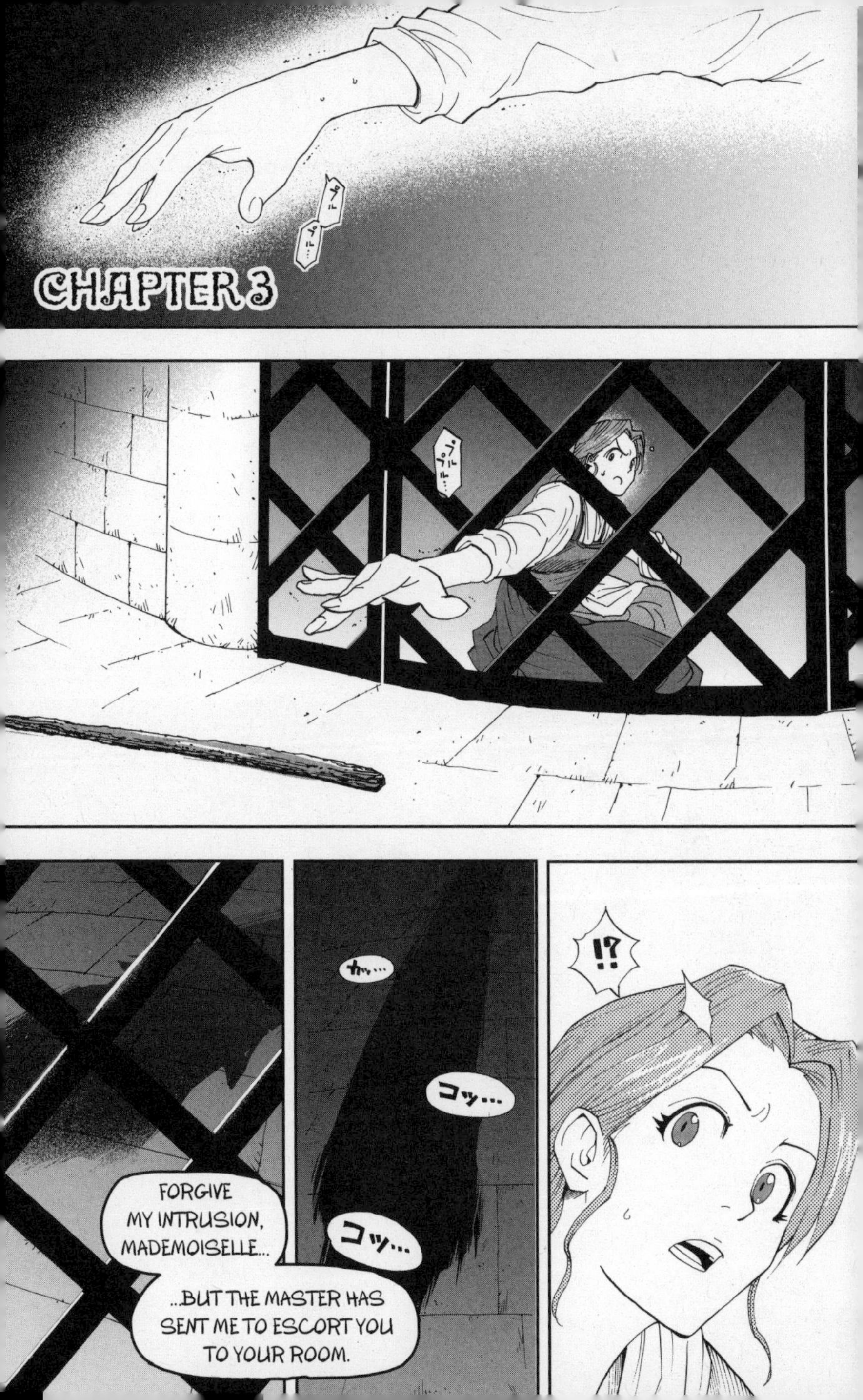
CHAPTER 3
ドプ
...ドプ
!?
カッ...
コッ...
コッ...
FORGIVE MY INTRUSION, MADEMOISELLE...
...BUT THE MASTER HAS SENT ME TO ESCORT YOU TO YOUR ROOM.

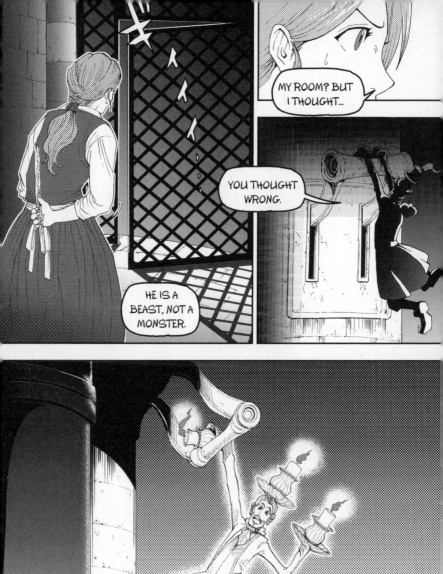

MY ROOM? BUT I THOUGHT...

YOU THOUGHT WRONG.

HE IS A BEAST, NOT A MONSTER.

'ALLO.

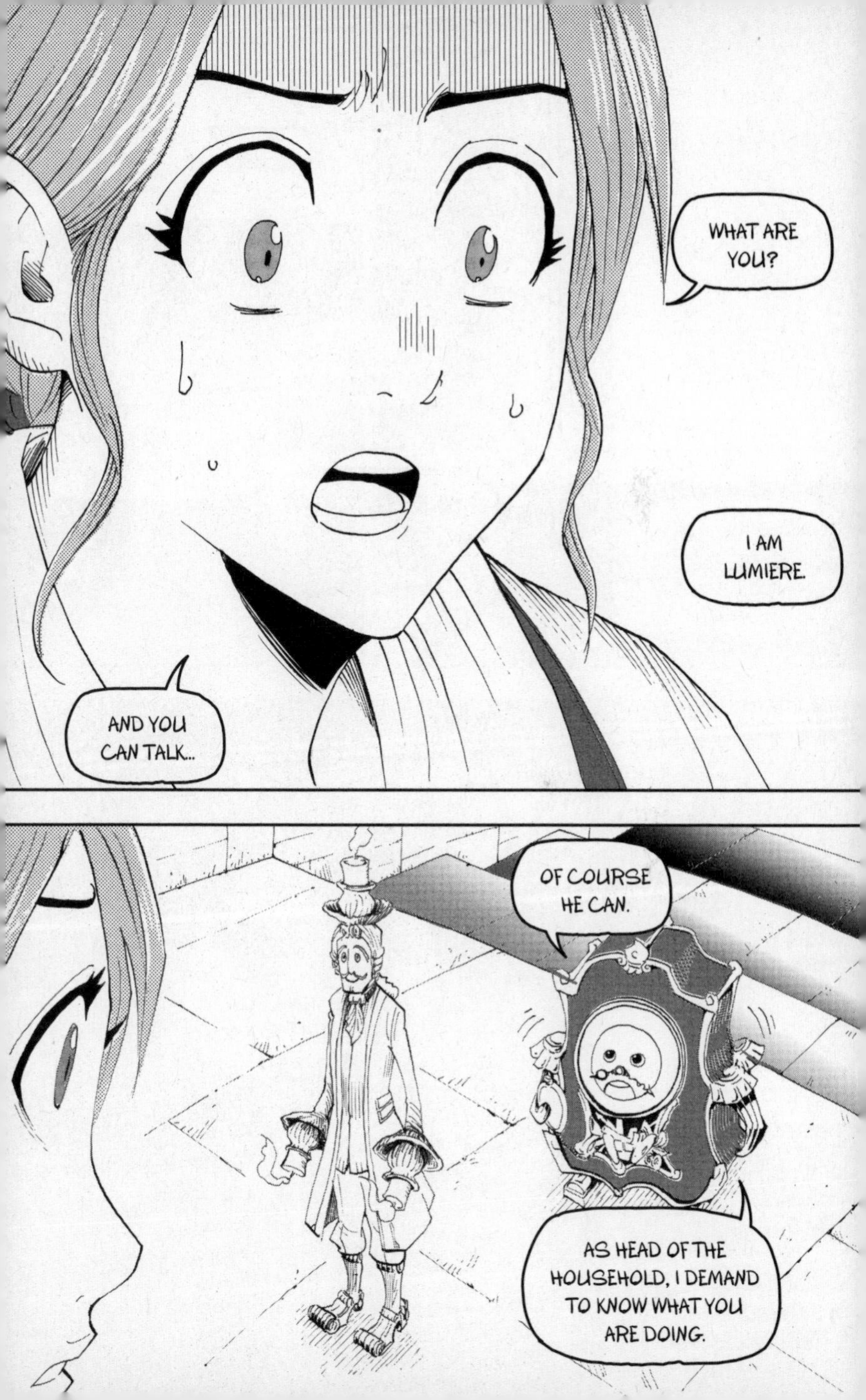
WHAT ARE YOU?
I AM LUMIERE.
AND YOU CAN TALK...
OF COURSE HE CAN.
AS HEAD OF THE HOUSEHOLD, I DEMAND TO KNOW WHAT YOU ARE DOING.

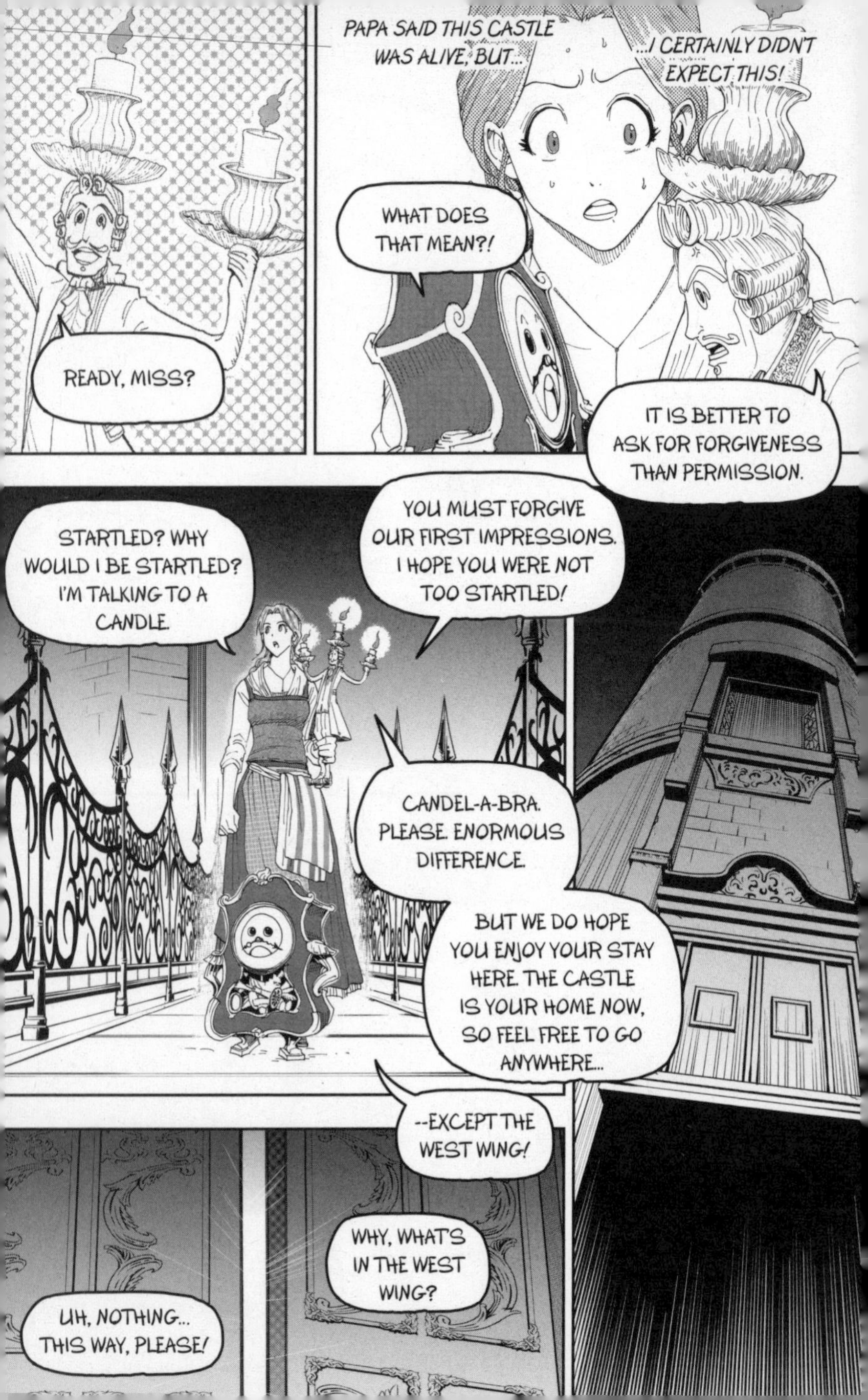
PAPA SAID THIS CASTLE WAS ALIVE, BUT...
...I CERTAINLY DIDN'T EXPECT THIS!
WHAT DOES THAT MEAN?!
IT IS BETTER TO ASK FOR FORGIVENESS THAN PERMISSION.
READY, MISS?
BUT WE DO HOPE YOU ENJOY YOUR STAY HERE. THE CASTLE IS YOUR HOME NOW, SO FEEL FREE TO GO ANYWHERE...
--EXCEPT THE WEST WING!
YOU MUST FORGIVE OUR FIRST IMPRESSIONS. I HOPE YOU WERE NOT TOO STARTLED!
STARTLED? WHY WOULD I BE STARTLED? I'M TALKING TO A CANDLE.
CANDEL-A-BRA. PLEASE. ENORMOUS DIFFERENCE.
WHY, WHAT'S IN THE WEST WING?
UH, NOTHING... THIS WAY, PLEASE!

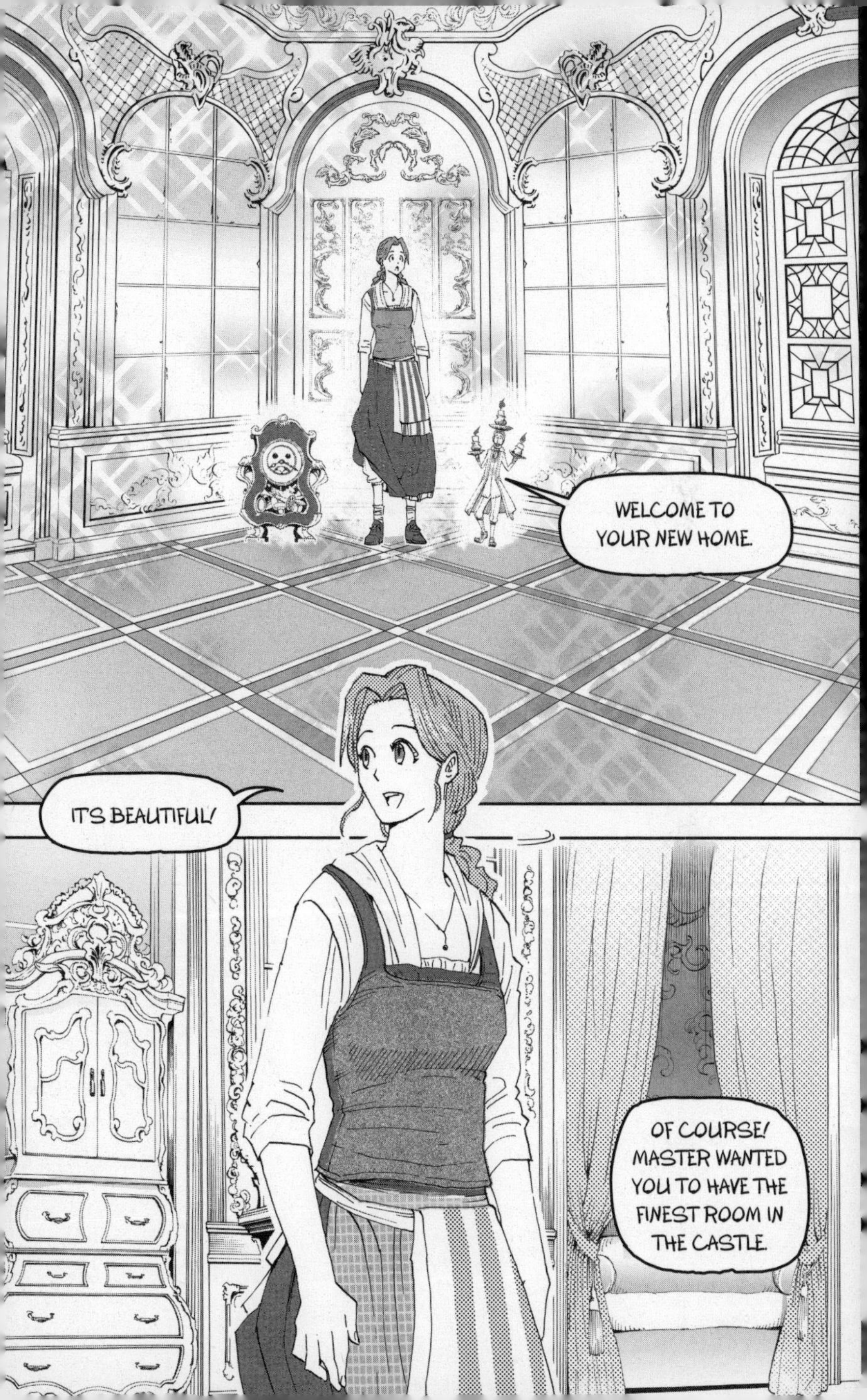
WELCOME TO YOUR NEW HOME.
IT'S BEAUTIFUL!
OF COURSE! MASTER WANTED YOU TO HAVE THE FINEST ROOM IN THE CASTLE.

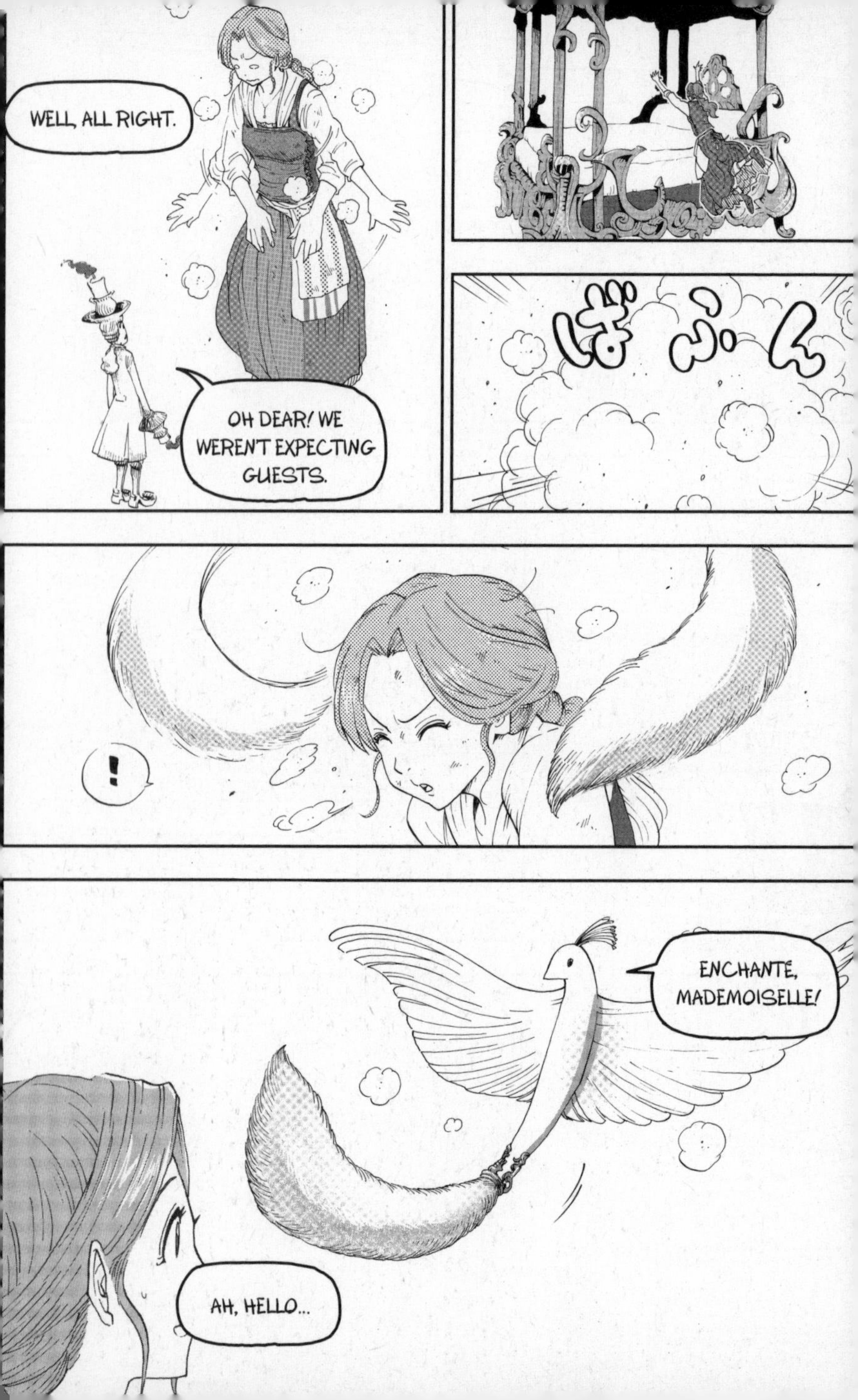
ぼふん
WELL, ALL RIGHT.
OH DEAR! WE WEREN'T EXPECTING GUESTS.
!
ENCHANTE, MADEMOISELLE!
AH, HELLO...

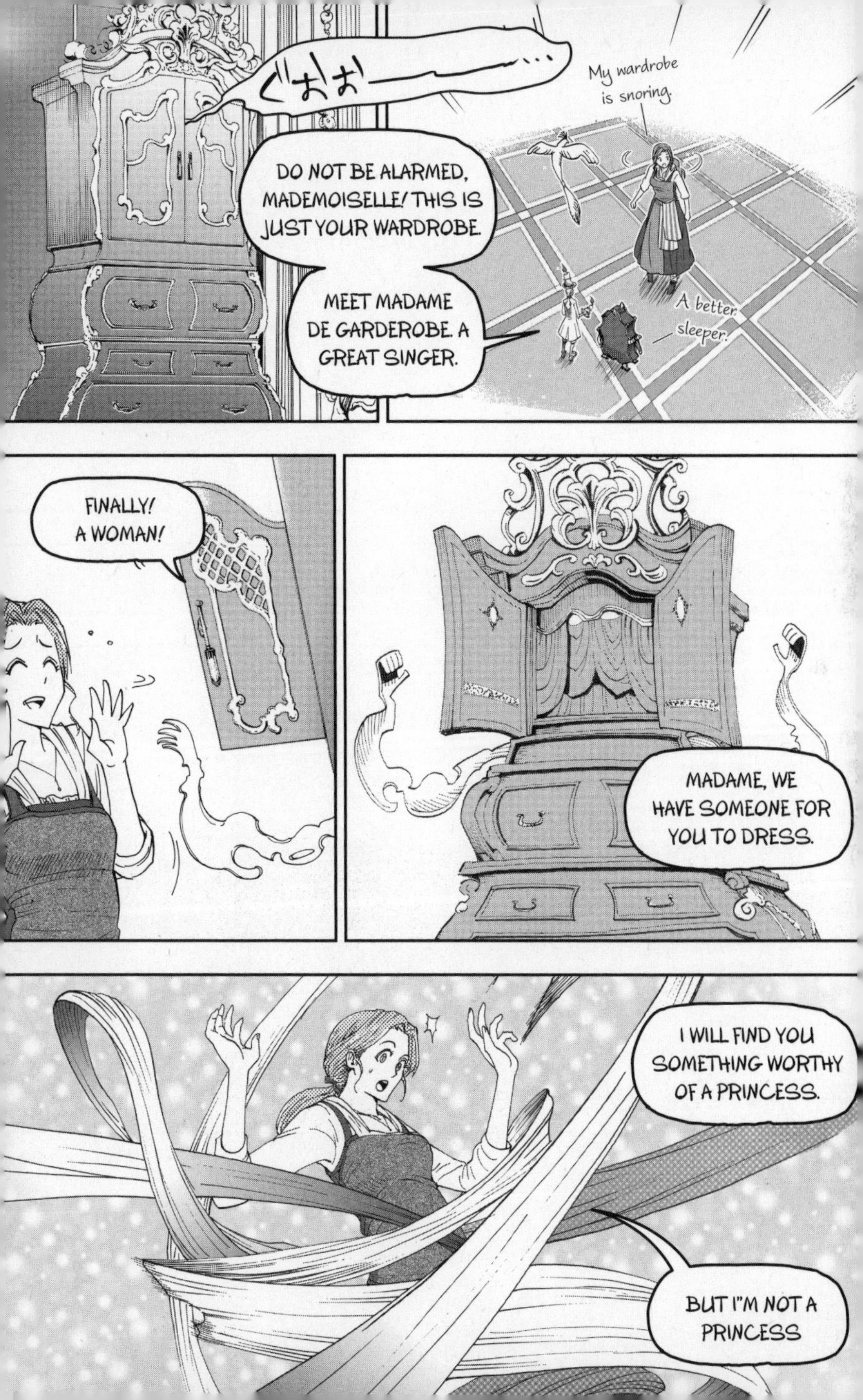

My wardrobe is snoring.
A better sleeper.
ぐおお———…
DO NOT BE ALARMED, MADEMOISELLE! THIS IS JUST YOUR WARDROBE.
MEET MADAME DE GARDEROBE. A GREAT SINGER.
MADAME, WE HAVE SOMEONE FOR YOU TO DRESS.
FINALLY! A WOMAN!
I WILL FIND YOU SOMETHING WORTHY OF A PRINCESS.
BUT I'M NOT A PRINCESS

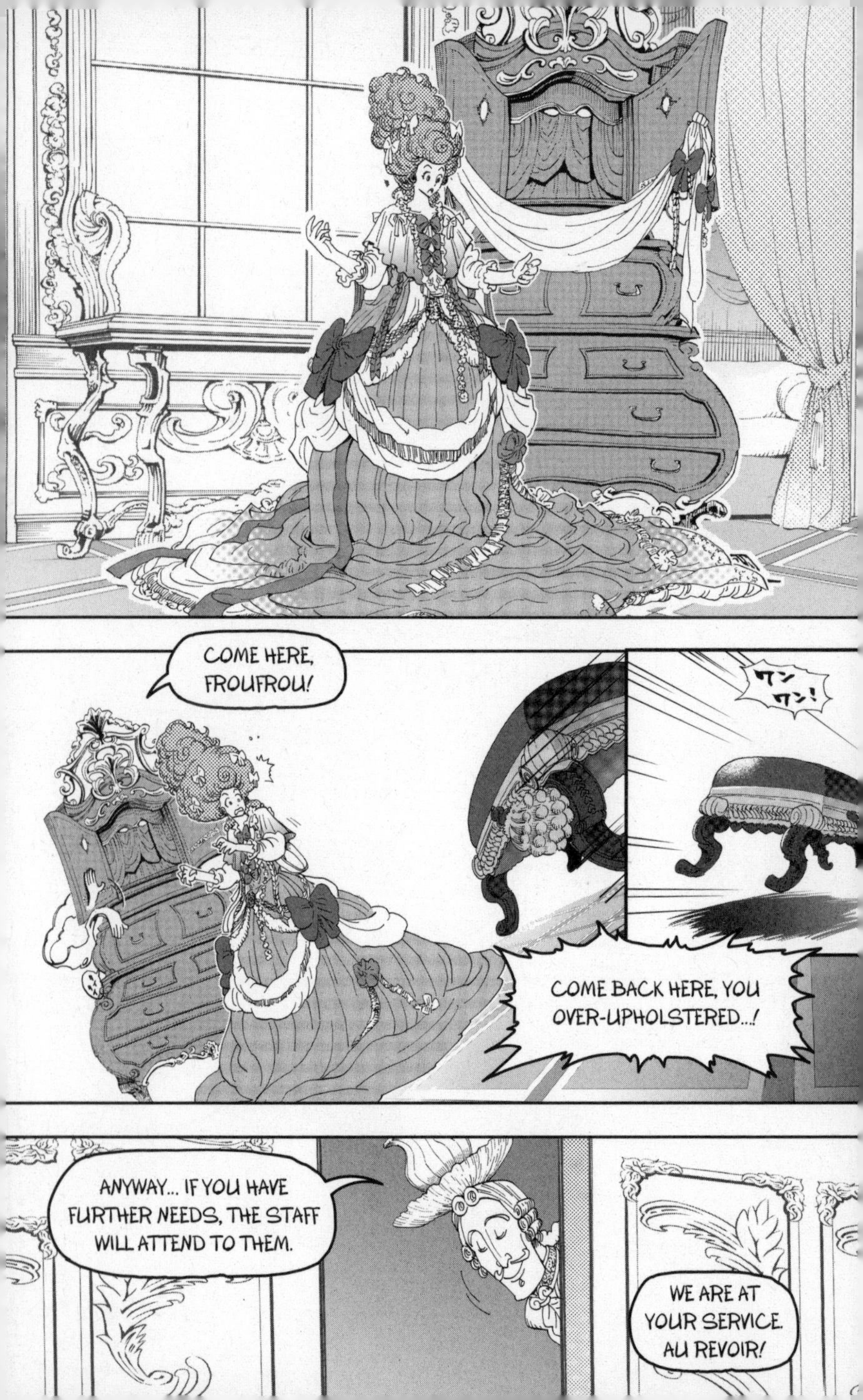
ワン
ワン!
COME HERE, FROUFROU!
COME BACK HERE, YOU OVER-UPHOLSTERED...!
WE ARE AT YOUR SERVICE. AU REVOIR!
ANYWAY... IF YOU HAVE FURTHER NEEDS, THE STAFF WILL ATTEND TO THEM.

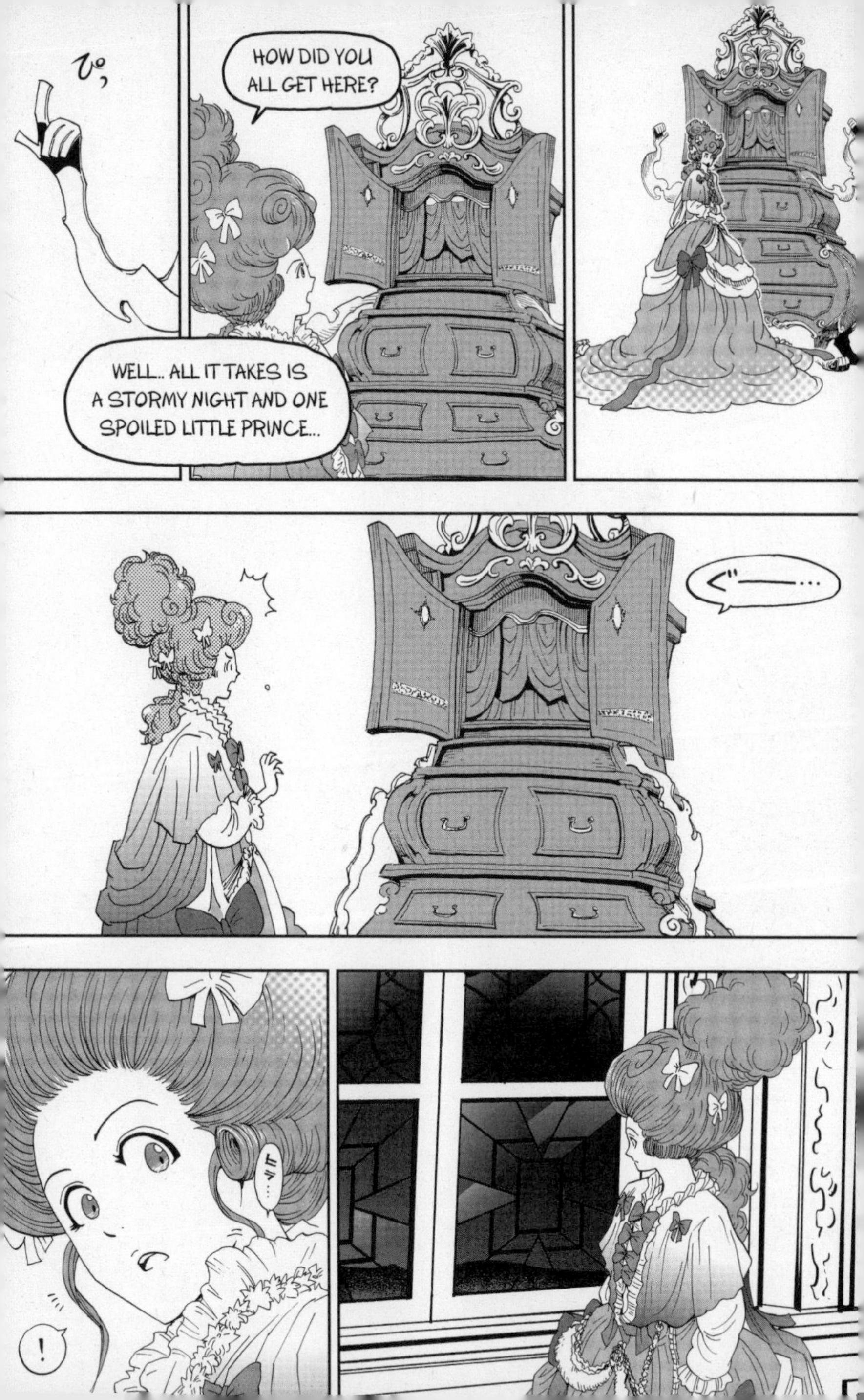
HOW DID YOU ALL GET HERE?
WELL... ALL IT TAKES IS A STORMY NIGHT AND ONE SPOILED LITTLE PRINCE...
ぴ,
ぐ———…
ヒラ…
!

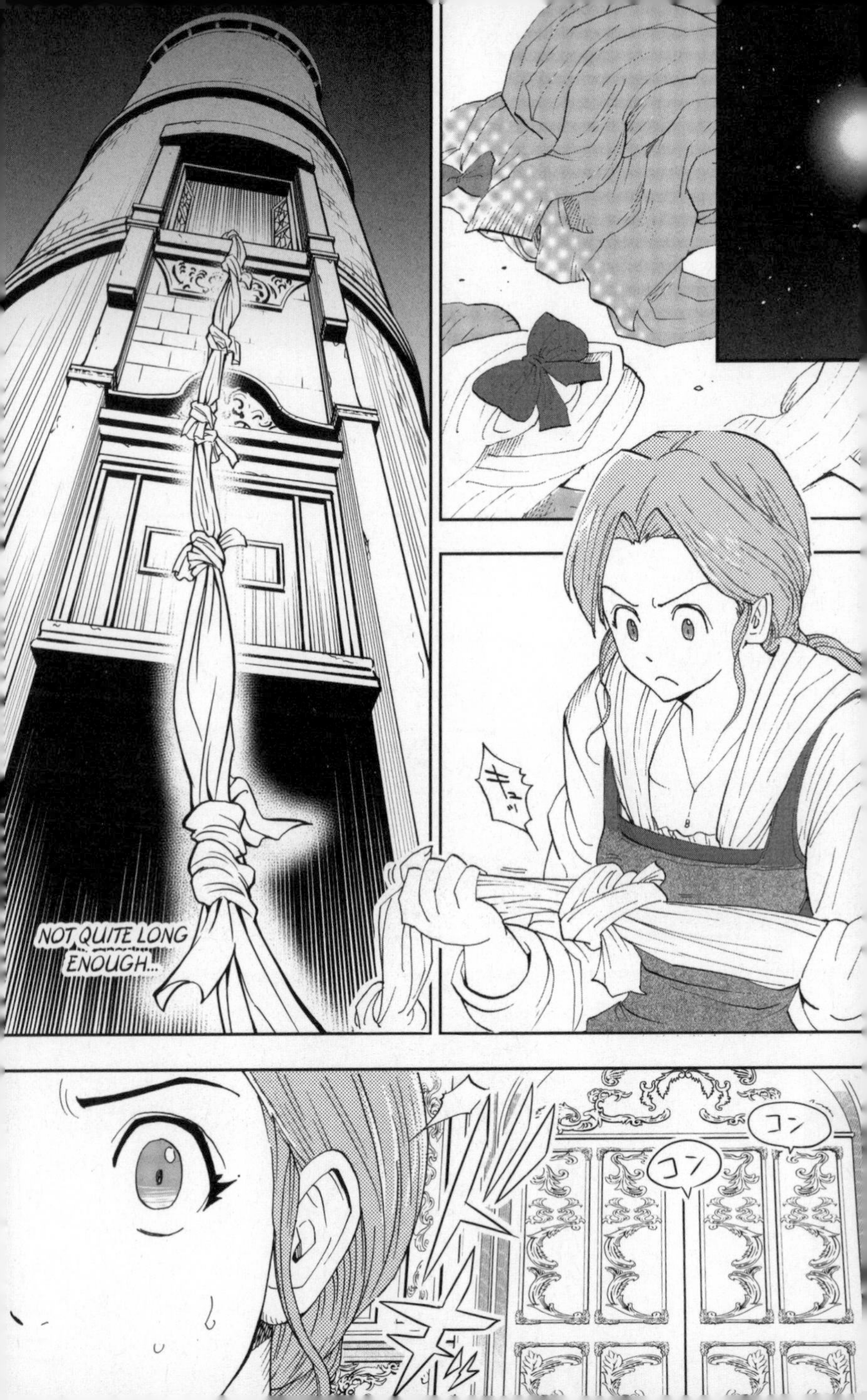
NOT QUITE LONG ENOUGH...
キュッ
コン
コン

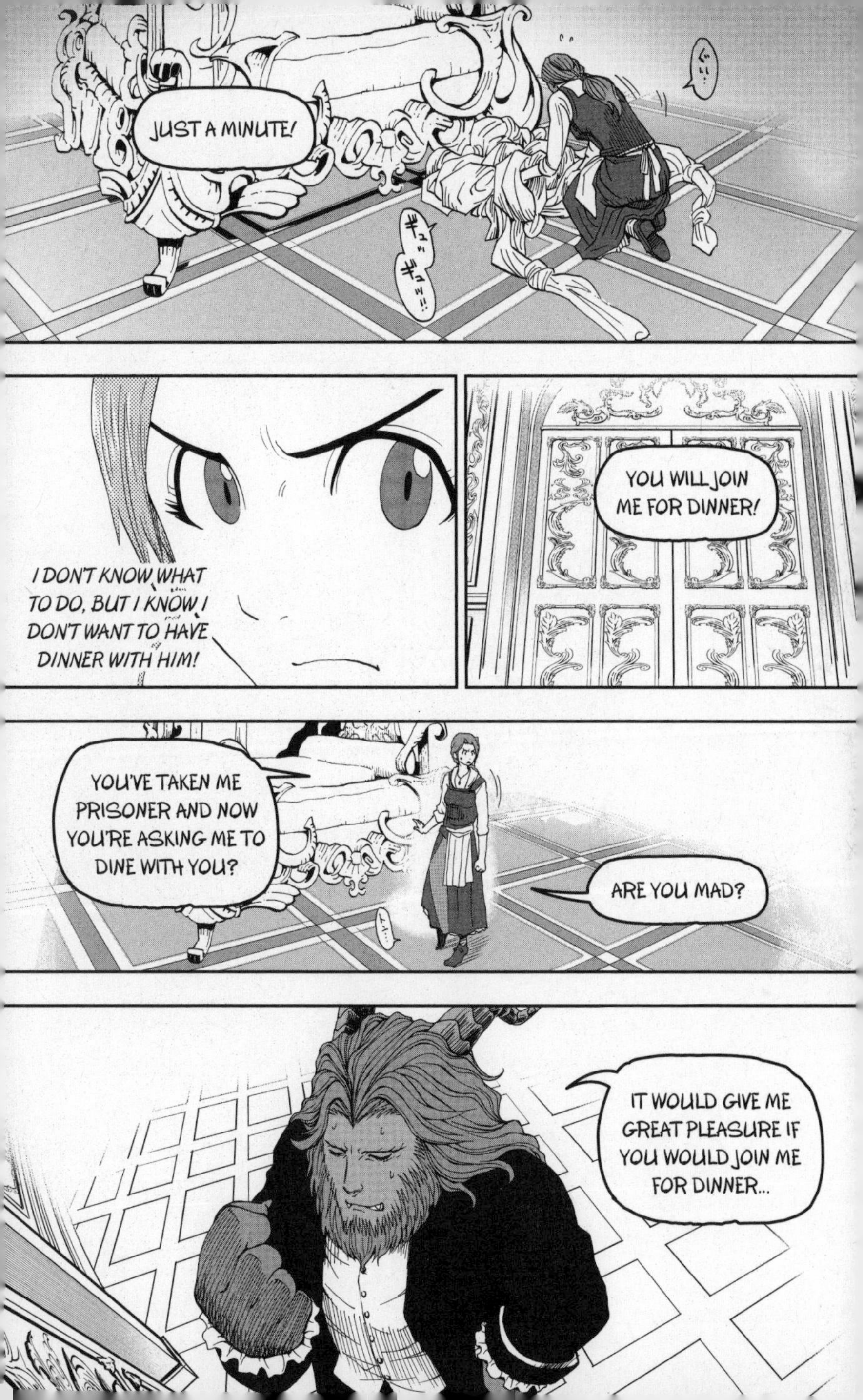
JUST A MINUTE!
YOU WILL JOIN ME FOR DINNER!
I DON'T KNOW WHAT TO DO, BUT I KNOW I DON'T WANT TO HAVE DINNER WITH HIM!
YOU'VE TAKEN ME PRISONER AND NOW YOU'RE ASKING ME TO DINE WITH YOU?
ARE YOU MAD?
IT WOULD GIVE ME GREAT PLEASURE IF YOU WOULD JOIN ME FOR DINNER...

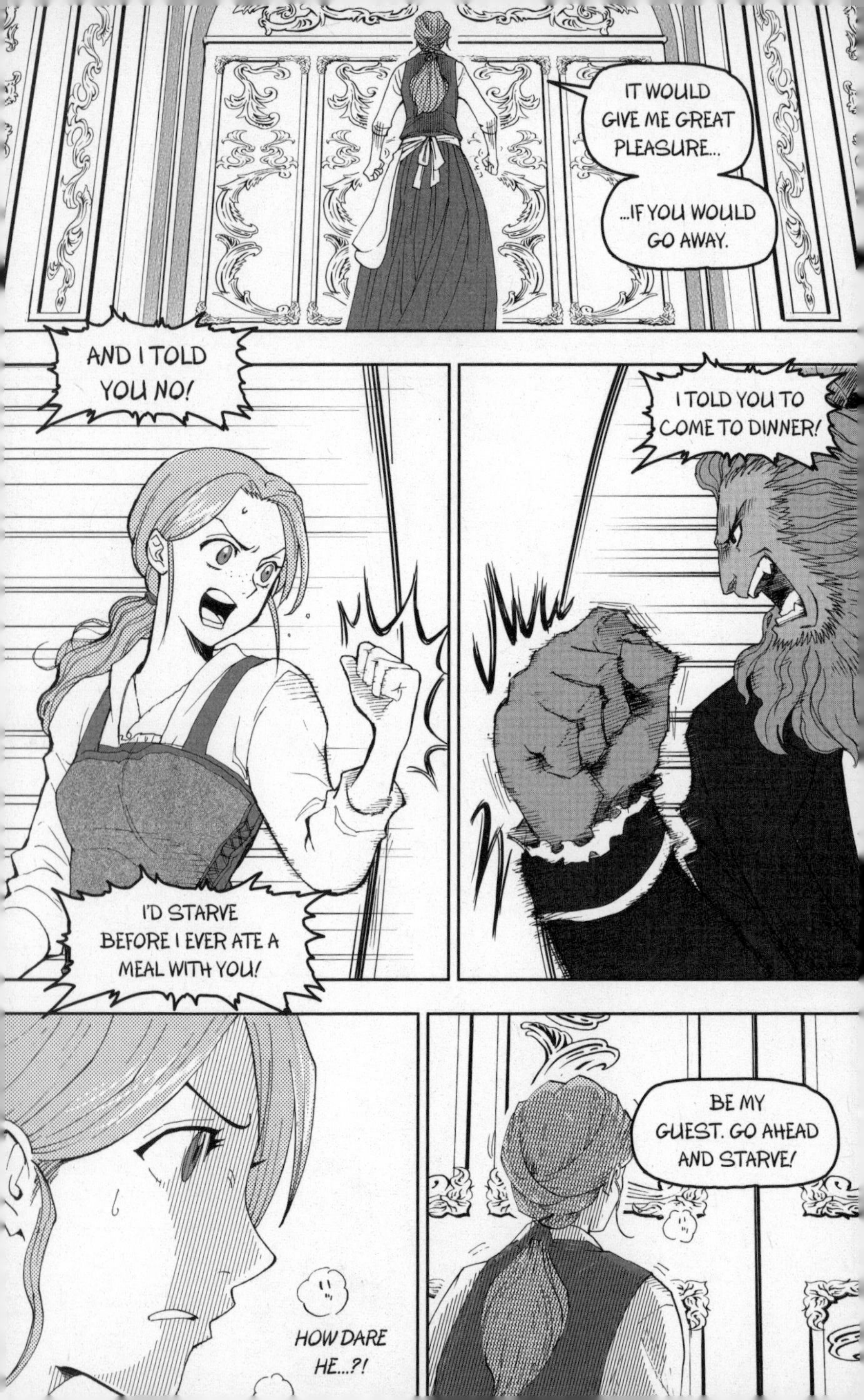
IT WOULD GIVE ME GREAT PLEASURE...
...IF YOU WOULD GO AWAY.
I TOLD YOU TO COME TO DINNER!
AND I TOLD YOU NO!
I'D STARVE BEFORE I EVER ATE A MEAL WITH YOU!
BE MY GUEST. GO AHEAD AND STARVE!
HOW DARE HE...?!

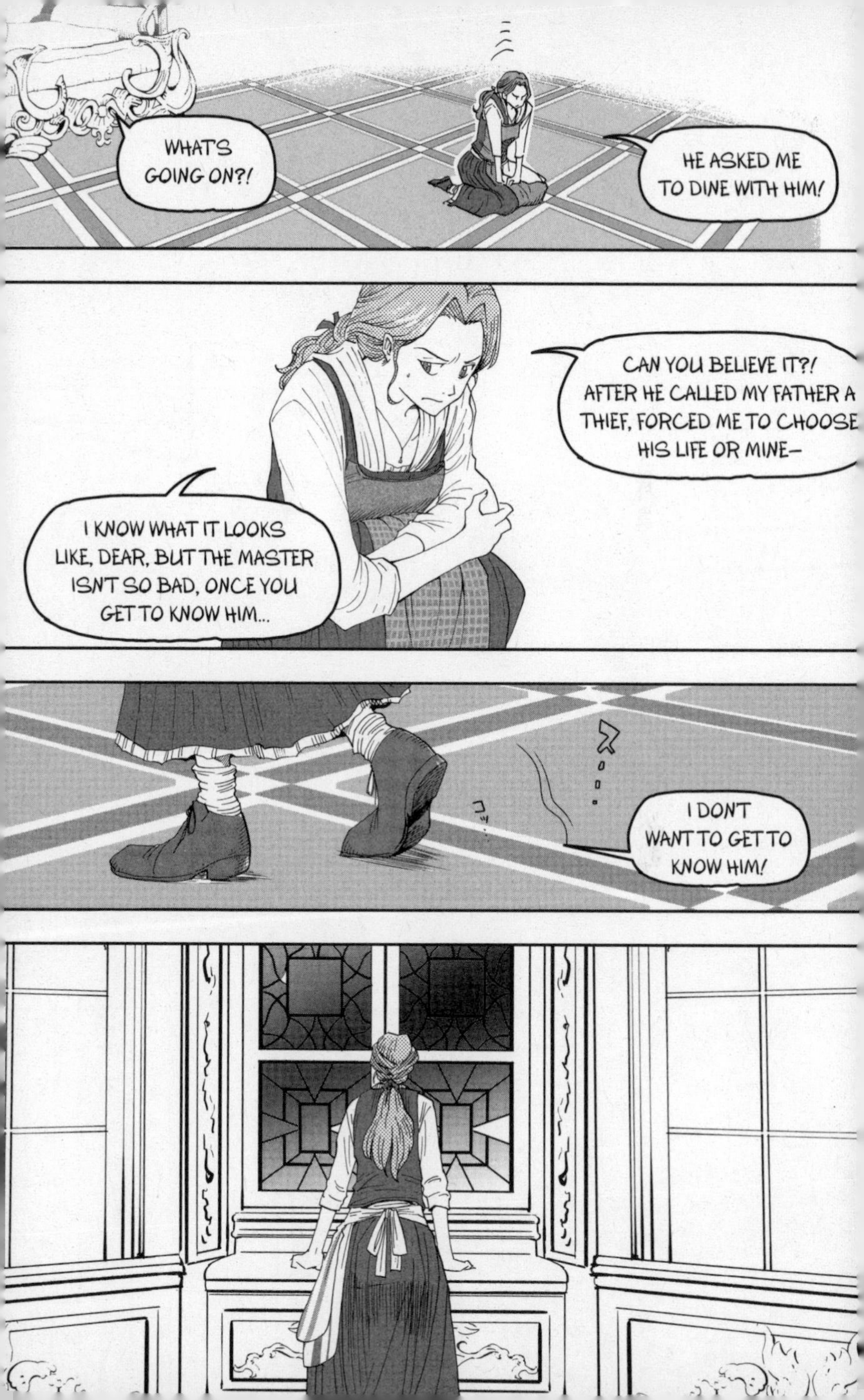
HE ASKED ME TO DINE WITH HIM!
WHAT'S GOING ON?!
CAN YOU BELIEVE IT?! AFTER HE CALLED MY FATHER A THIEF, FORCED ME TO CHOOSE HIS LIFE OR MINE—
I KNOW WHAT IT LOOKS LIKE, DEAR, BUT THE MASTER ISN'T SO BAD, ONCE YOU GET TO KNOW HIM...
I DON'T WANT TO GET TO KNOW HIM!

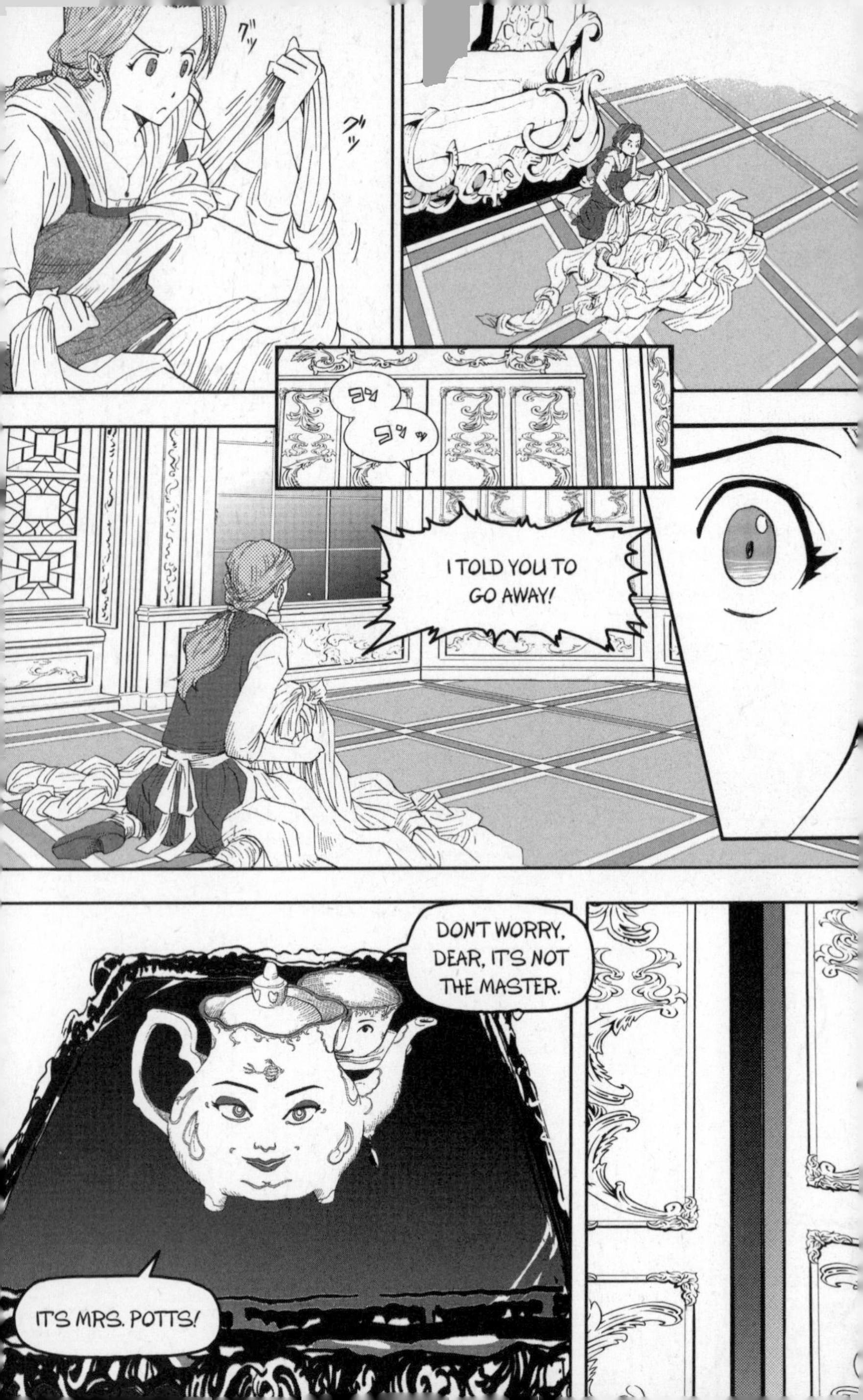
グッ
グッ
コン
コンッ
I TOLD YOU TO GO AWAY!
DON'T WORRY, DEAR, IT'S NOT THE MASTER.
IT'S MRS. POTTS!

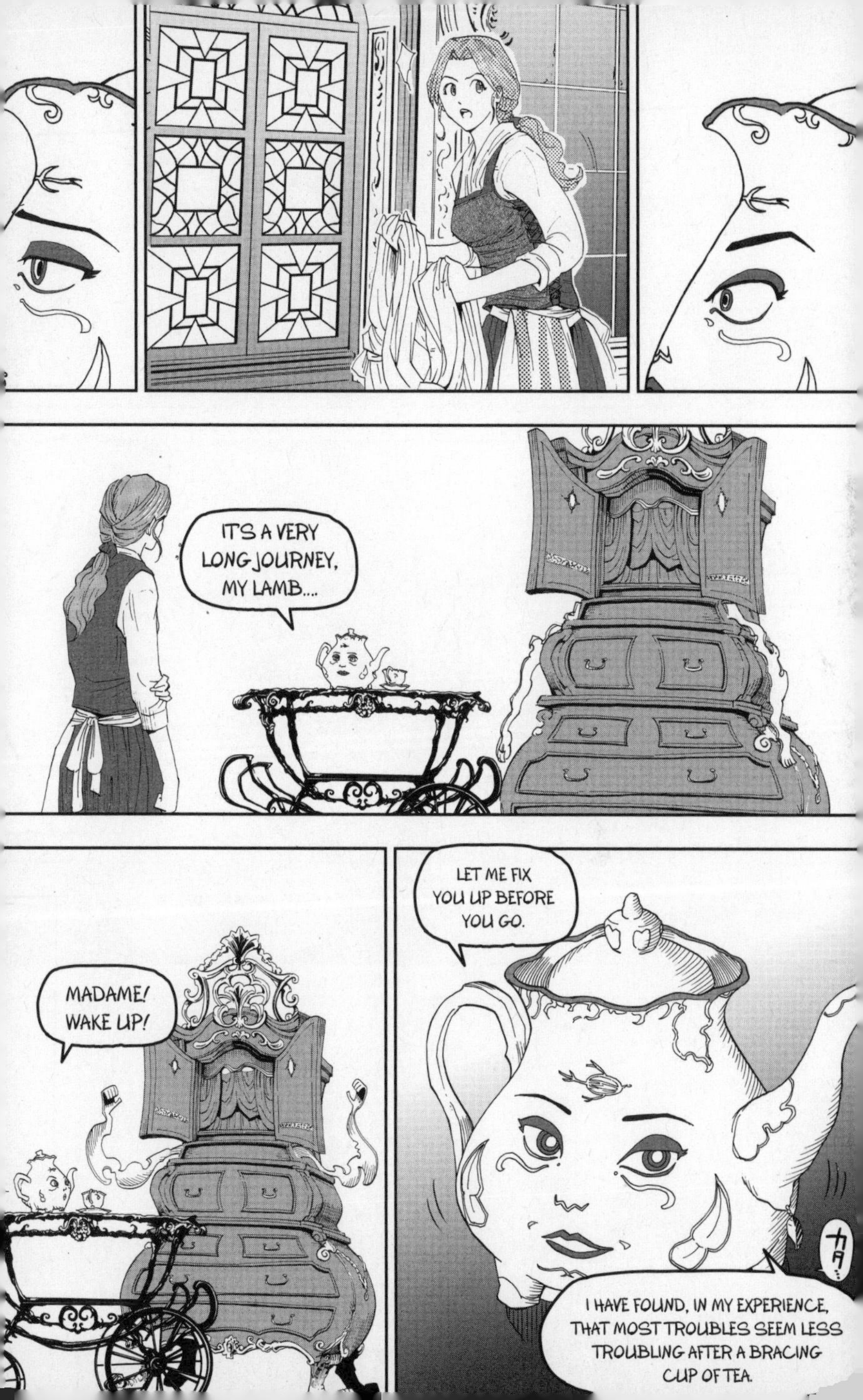
IT'S A VERY LONG JOURNEY, MY LAMB....
LET ME FIX YOU UP BEFORE YOU GO.
カタ…
I HAVE FOUND, IN MY EXPERIENCE, THAT MOST TROUBLES SEEM LESS TROUBLING AFTER A BRACING CUP OF TEA.
MADAME! WAKE UP!

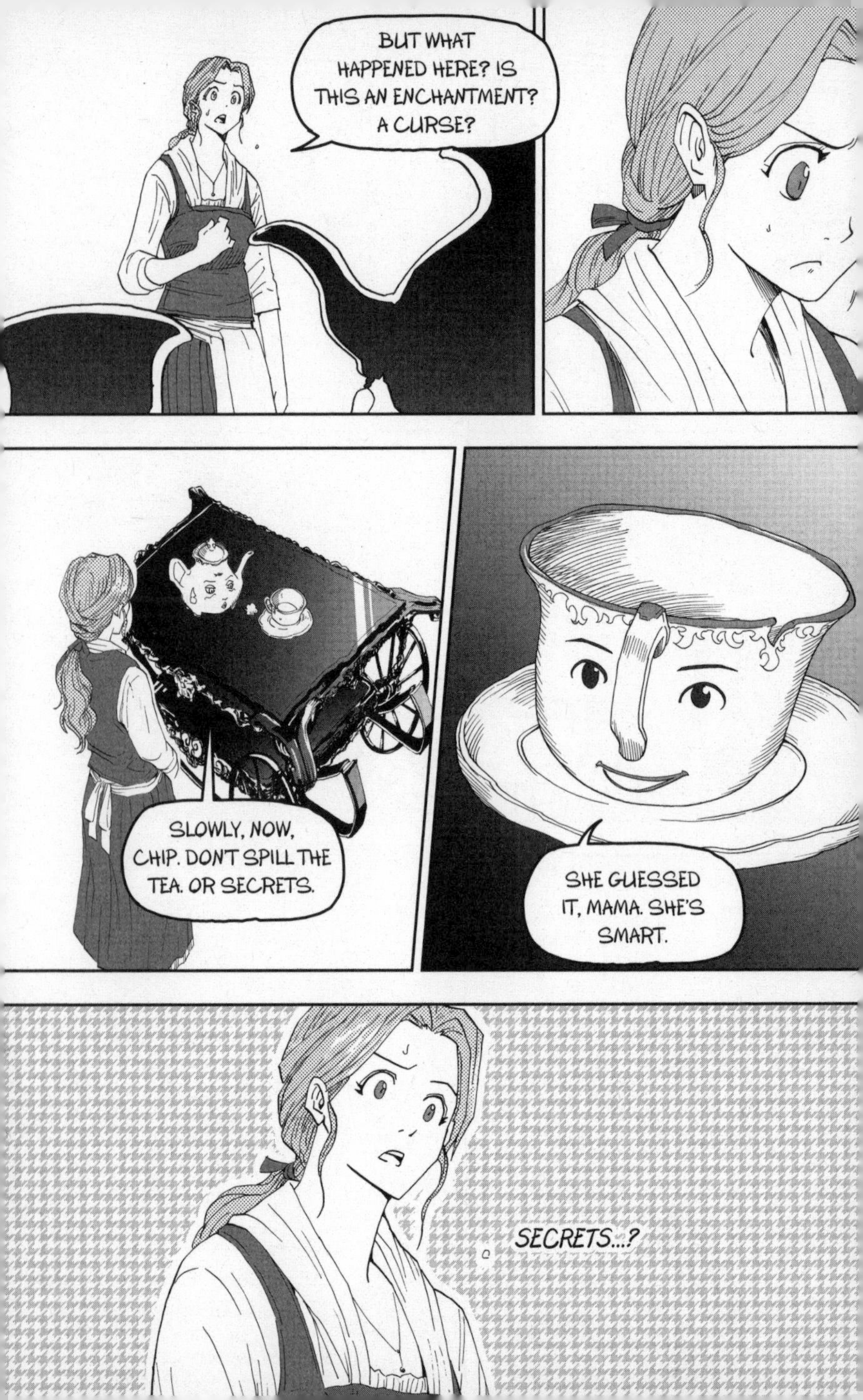
BUT WHAT HAPPENED HERE? IS THIS AN ENCHANTMENT? A CURSE?
SHE GUESSED IT, MAMA. SHE'S SMART.
SLOWLY, NOW, CHIP. DON'T SPILL THE TEA. OR SECRETS.
SECRETS...?

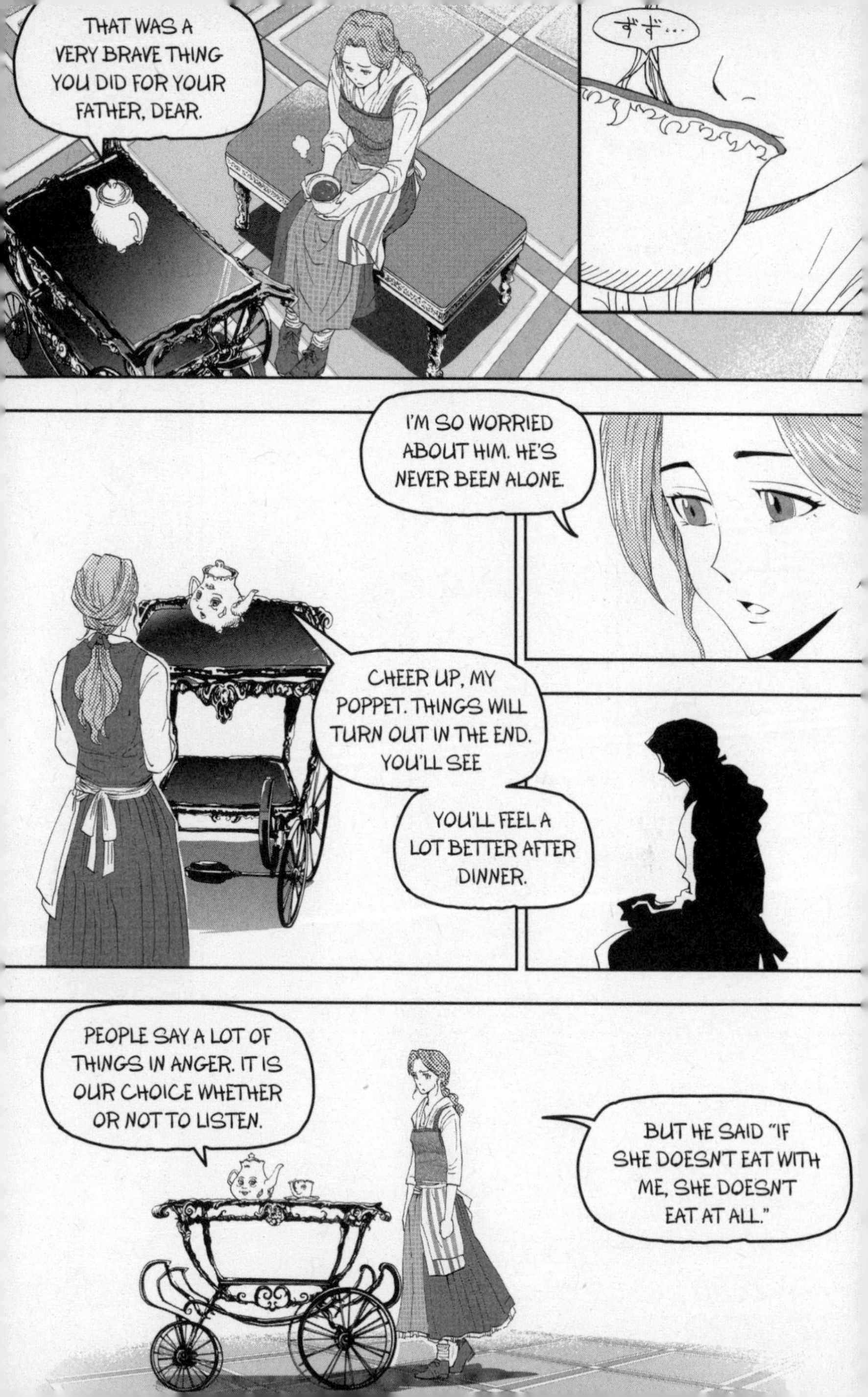
ずず…
THAT WAS A VERY BRAVE THING YOU DID FOR YOUR FATHER, DEAR.
I'M SO WORRIED ABOUT HIM. HE'S NEVER BEEN ALONE.
CHEER UP, MY POPPET. THINGS WILL TURN OUT IN THE END. YOU'LL SEE
YOU'LL FEEL A LOT BETTER AFTER DINNER.
BUT HE SAID "IF SHE DOESN'T EAT WITH ME, SHE DOESN'T EAT AT ALL."
PEOPLE SAY A LOT OF THINGS IN ANGER. IT IS OUR CHOICE WHETHER OR NOT TO LISTEN.

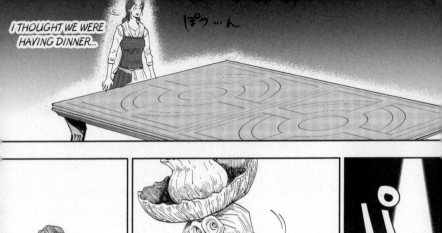

I THOUGHT WE WERE HAVING DINNER...

ぽつ゛ーん

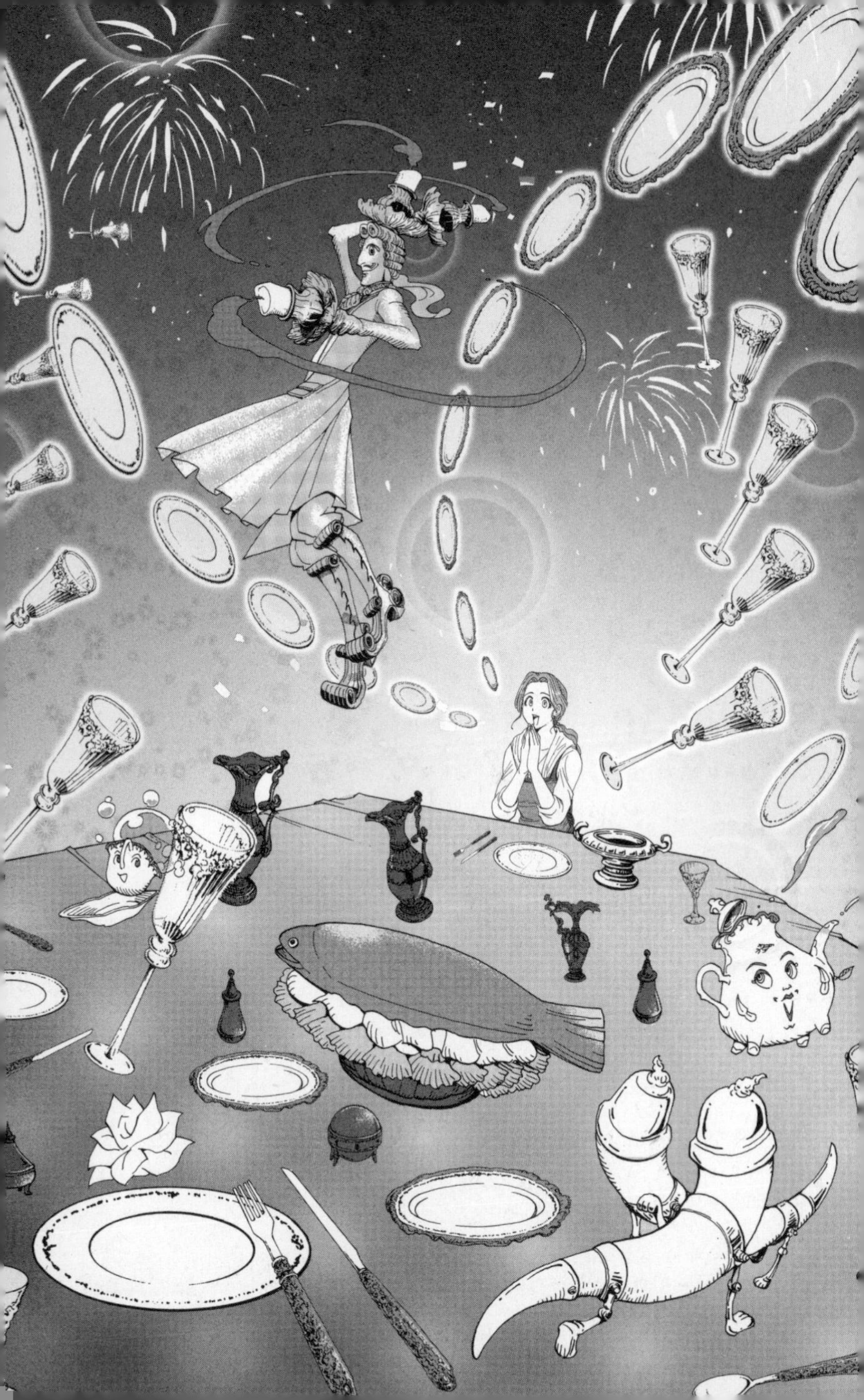

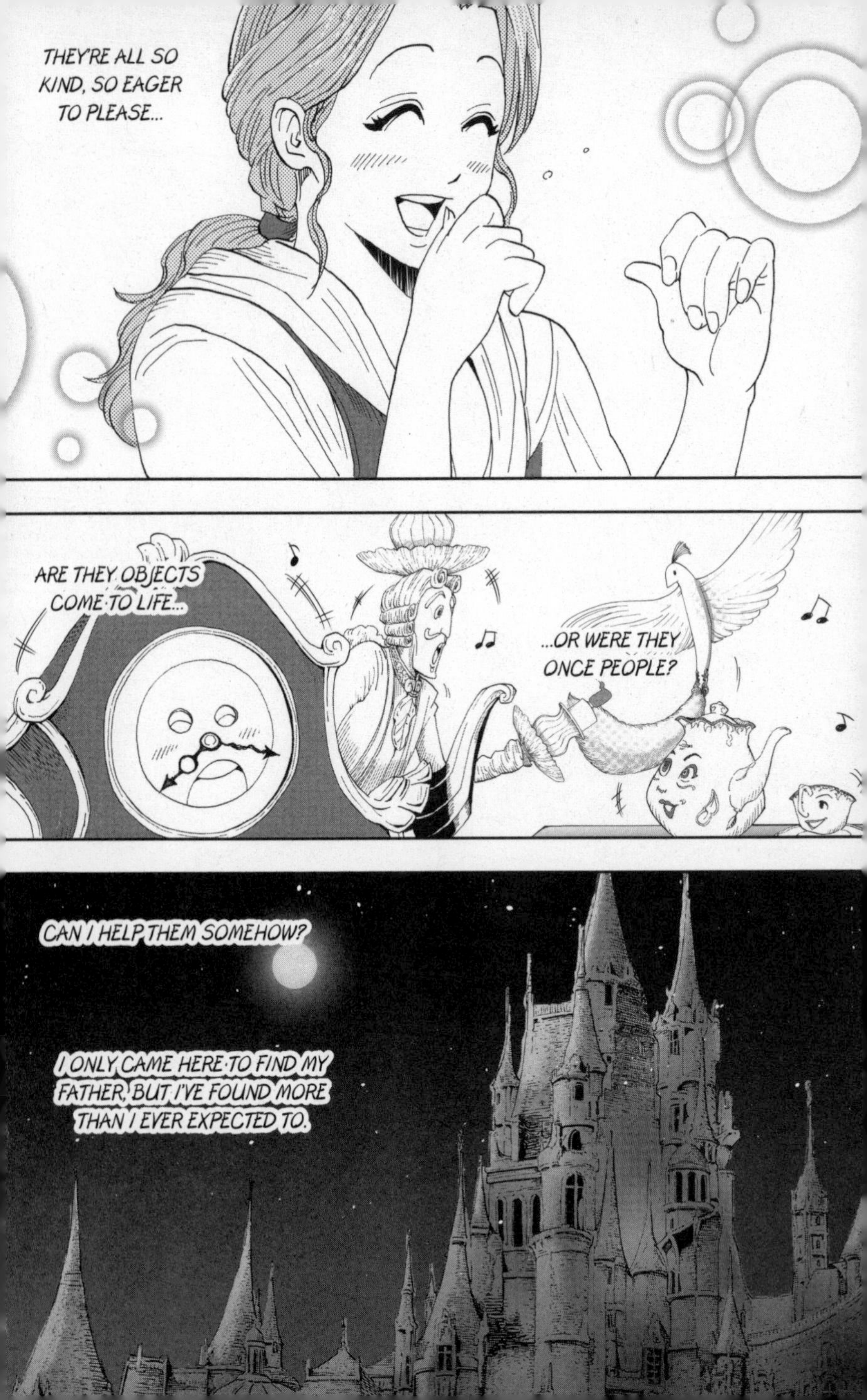
THEY'RE ALL SO KIND, SO EAGER TO PLEASE...
ARE THEY OBJECTS COME TO LIFE...
...OR WERE THEY ONCE PEOPLE?
CAN I HELP THEM SOMEHOW?
I ONLY CAME HERE TO FIND MY FATHER, BUT I'VE FOUND MORE THAN I EVER EXPECTED TO.

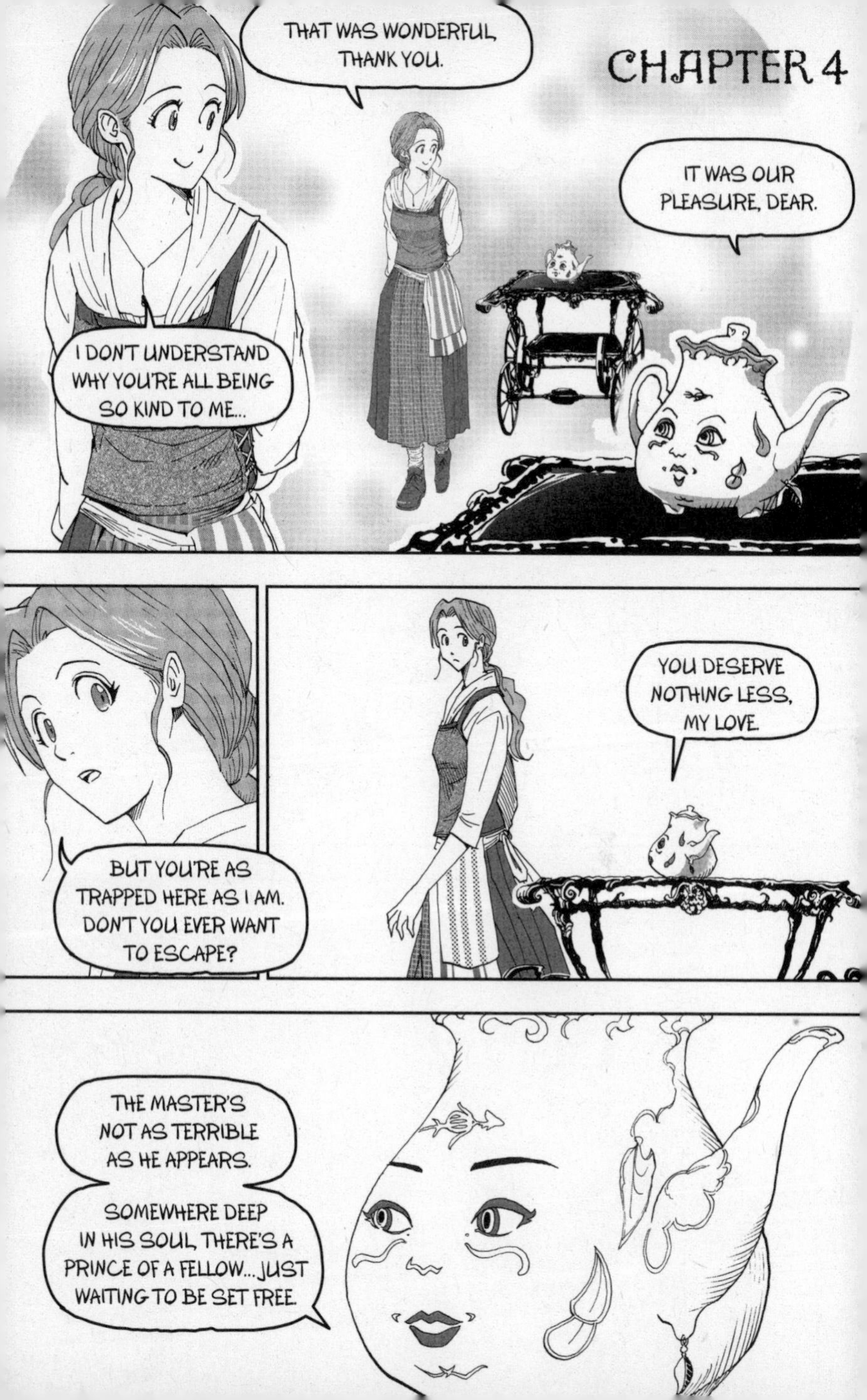
CHAPTER 4
THAT WAS WONDERFUL, THANK YOU.
IT WAS OUR PLEASURE, DEAR.
I DON'T UNDERSTAND WHY YOU'RE ALL BEING SO KIND TO ME...
YOU DESERVE NOTHING LESS, MY LOVE.
BUT YOU'RE AS TRAPPED HERE AS I AM. DON'T YOU EVER WANT TO ESCAPE?
THE MASTER'S NOT AS TERRIBLE AS HE APPEARS.
SOMEWHERE DEEP IN HIS SOUL, THERE'S A PRINCE OF A FELLOW... JUST WAITING TO BE SET FREE.

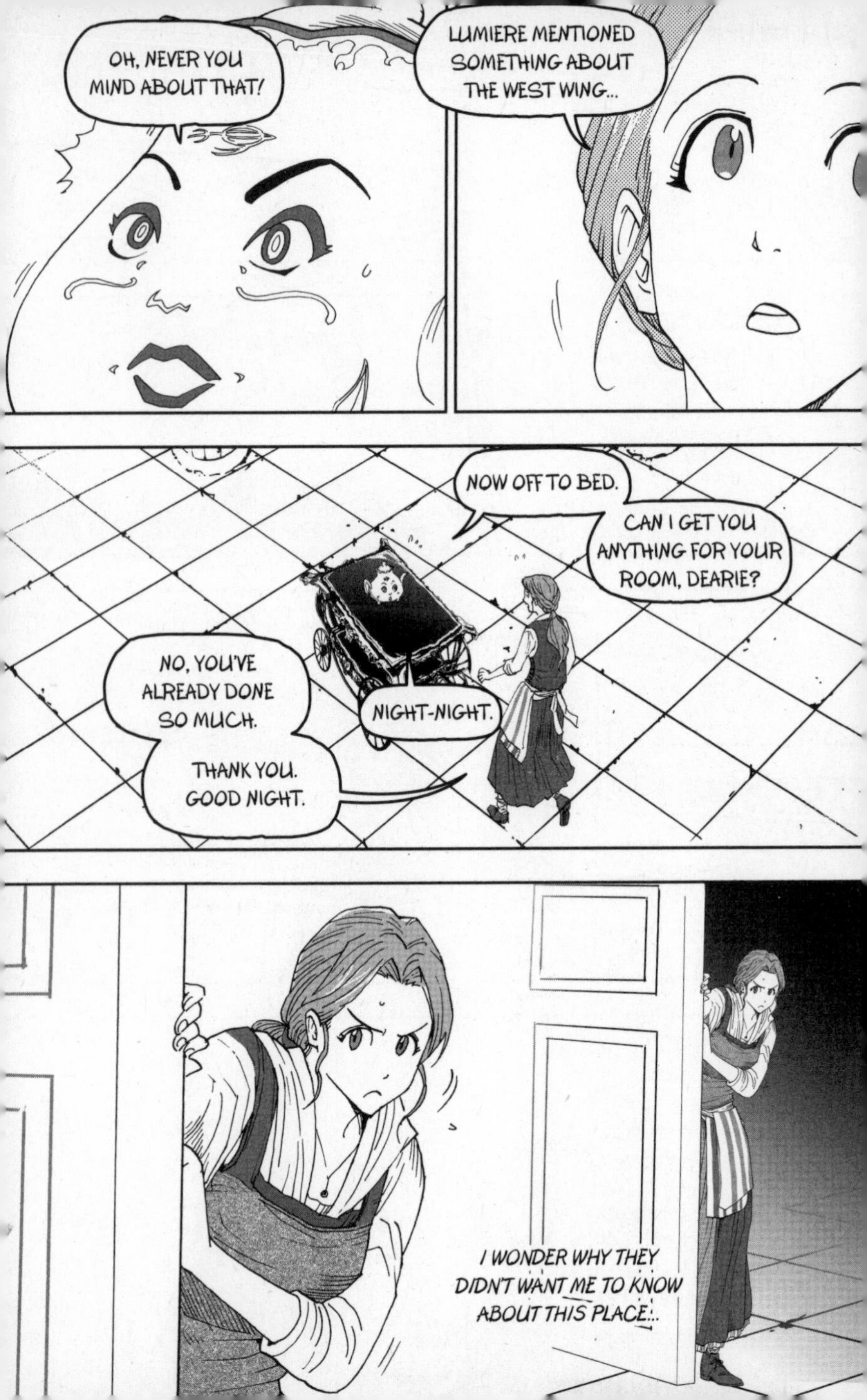
LUMIERE MENTIONED SOMETHING ABOUT THE WEST WING...
OH, NEVER YOU MIND ABOUT THAT!
NOW OFF TO BED.
CAN I GET YOU ANYTHING FOR YOUR ROOM, DEARIE?
NO, YOU'VE ALREADY DONE SO MUCH.
THANK YOU. GOOD NIGHT.
NIGHT-NIGHT.
I WONDER WHY THEY DIDN'T WANT ME TO KNOW ABOUT THIS PLACE...

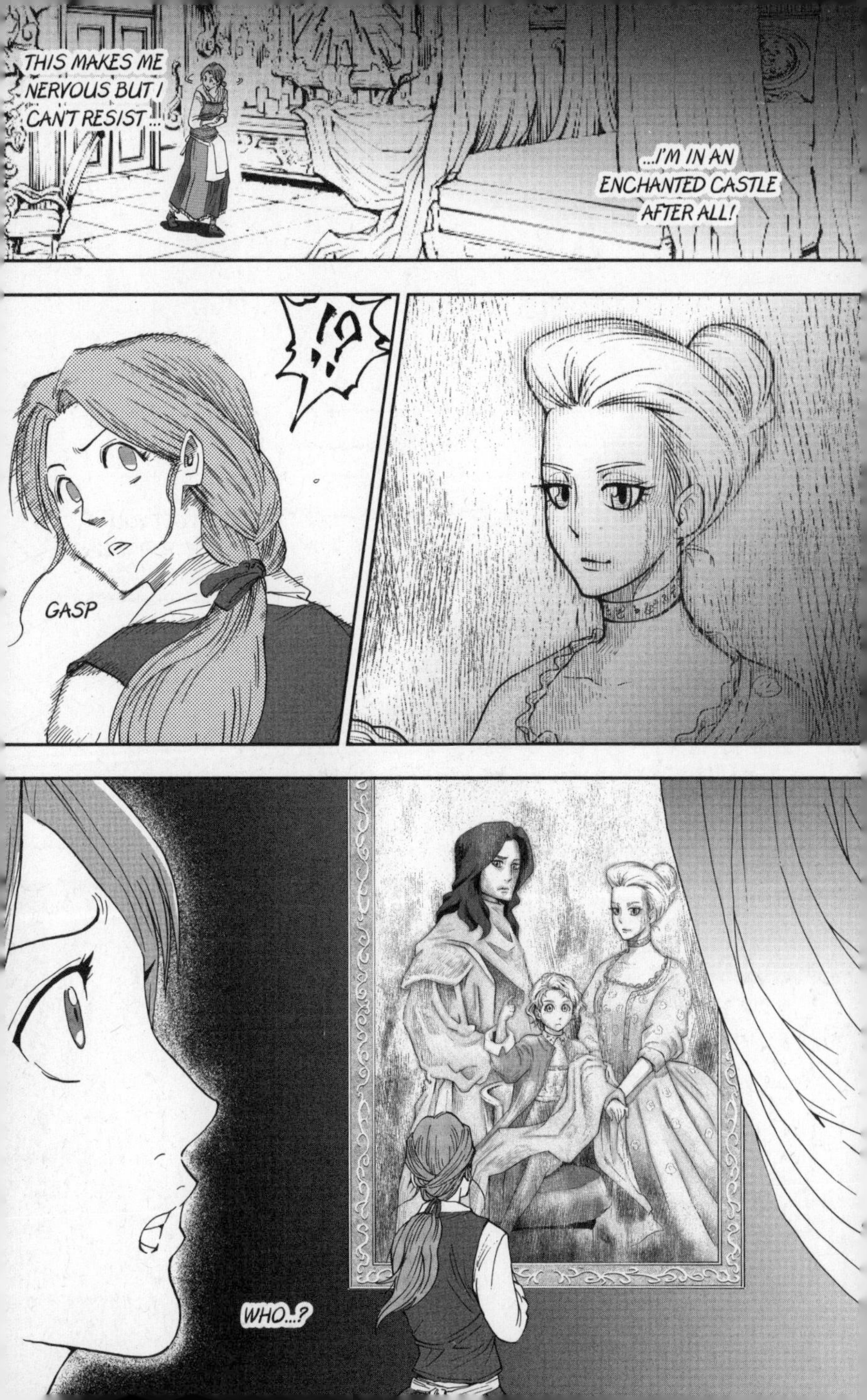
THIS MAKES ME NERVOUS BUT I CAN'T RESIST...
...I'M IN AN ENCHANTED CASTLE AFTER ALL!
!?
GASP
WHO...?

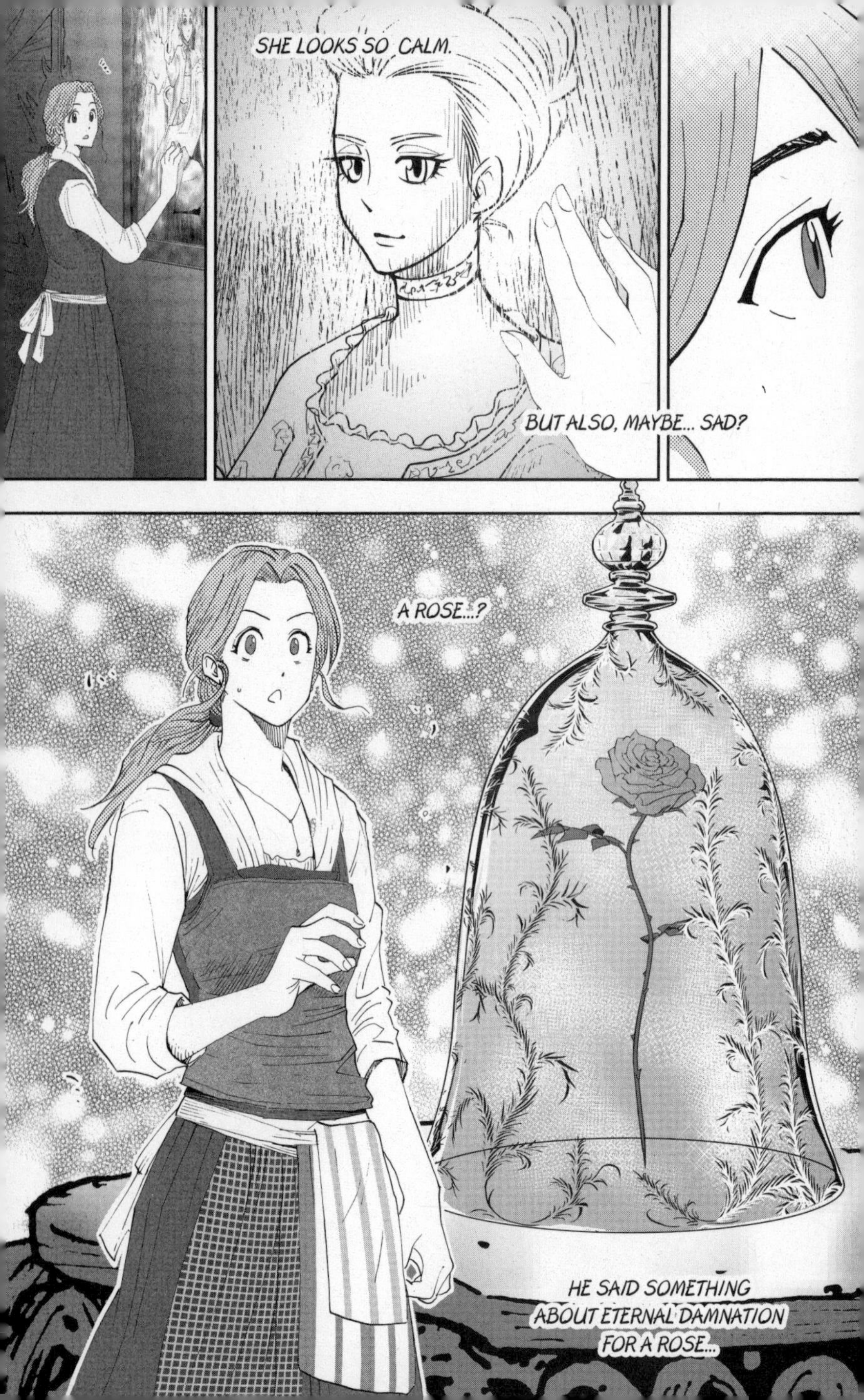
SHE LOOKS SO CALM.
BUT ALSO, MAYBE... SAD?
A ROSE...?
HE SAID SOMETHING ABOUT ETERNAL DAMNATION FOR A ROSE...

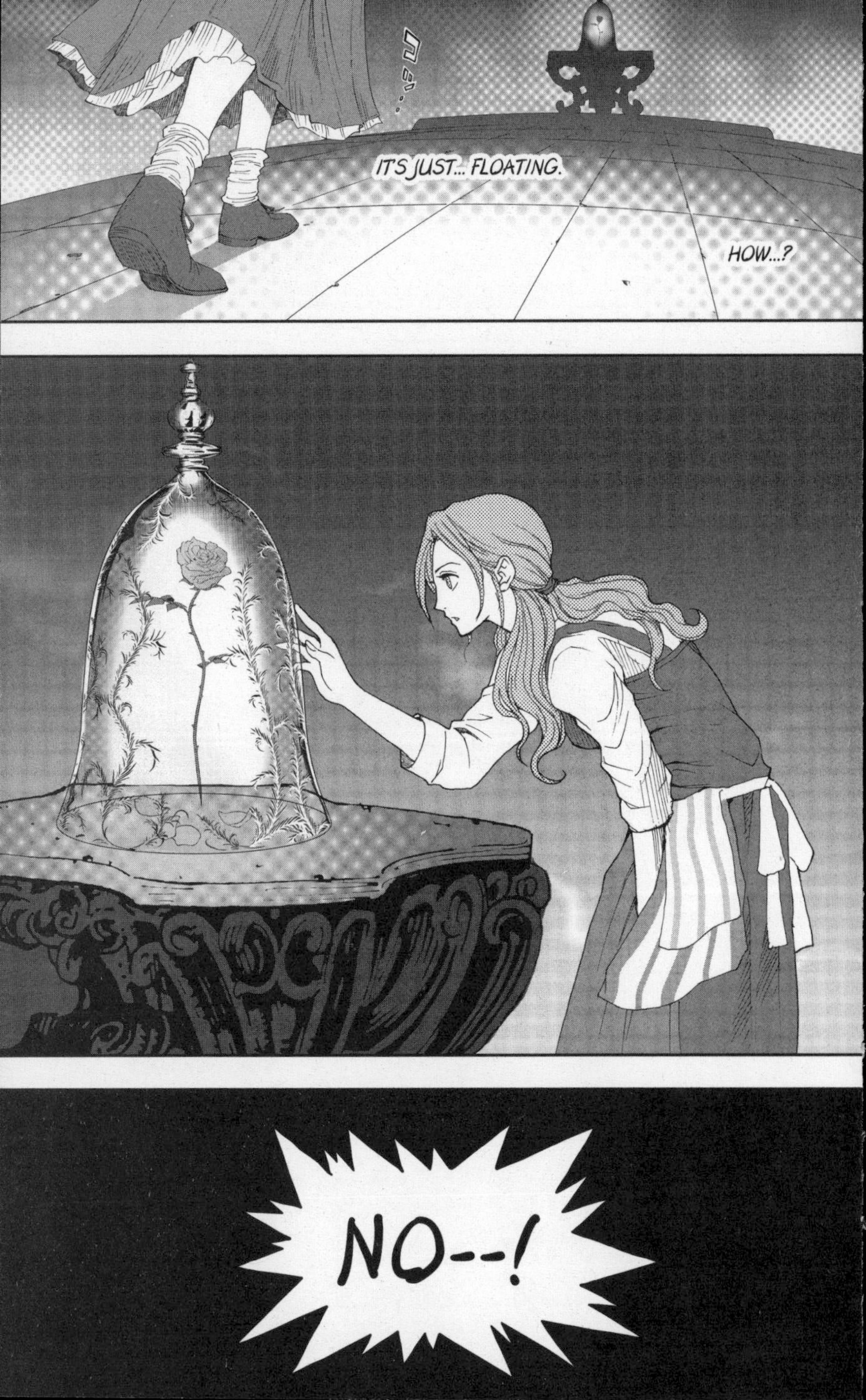
IT'S JUST... FLOATING.
HOW...?
NO--!

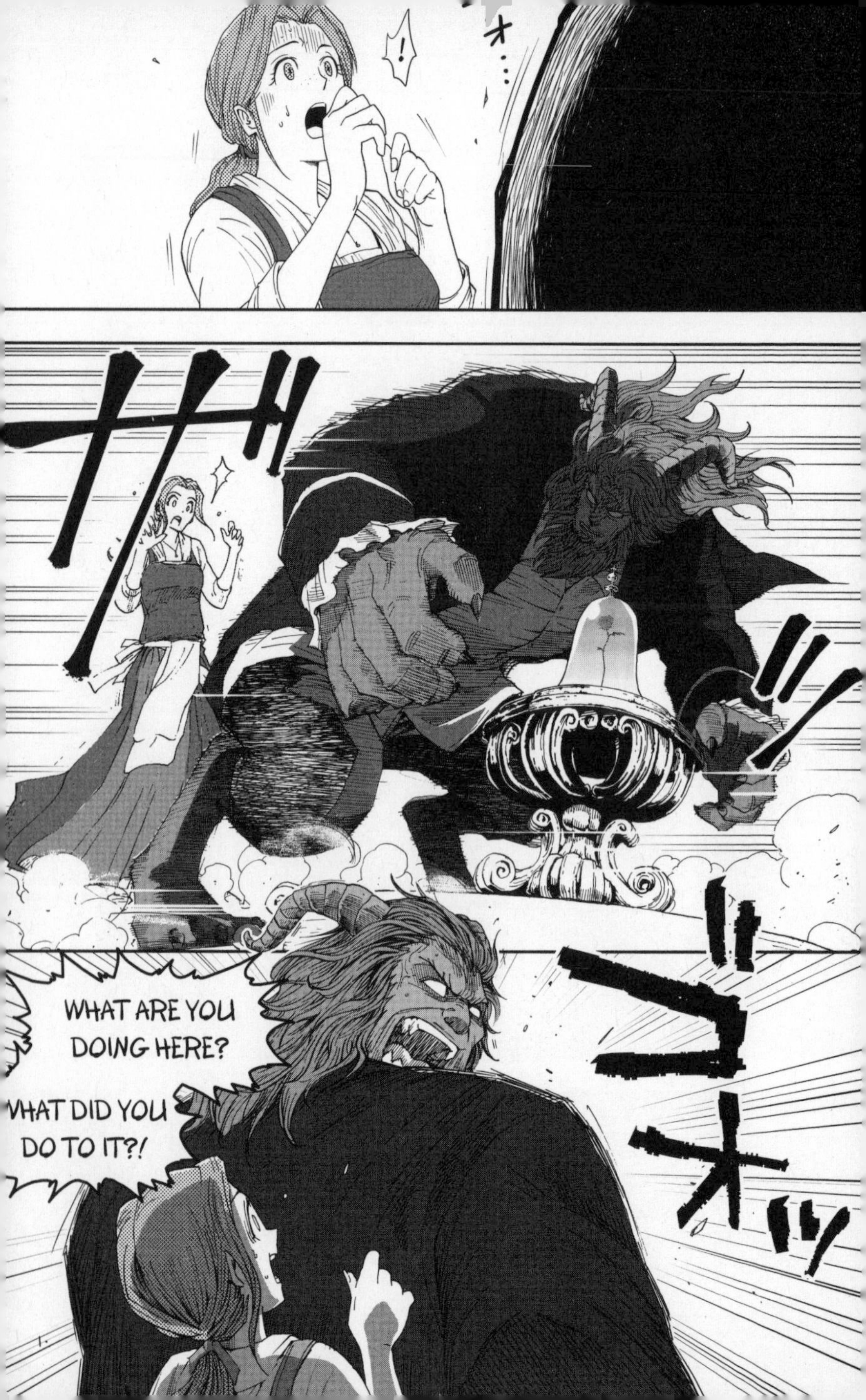
ゴオッ
WHAT ARE YOU DOING HERE?
WHAT DID YOU DO TO IT?!

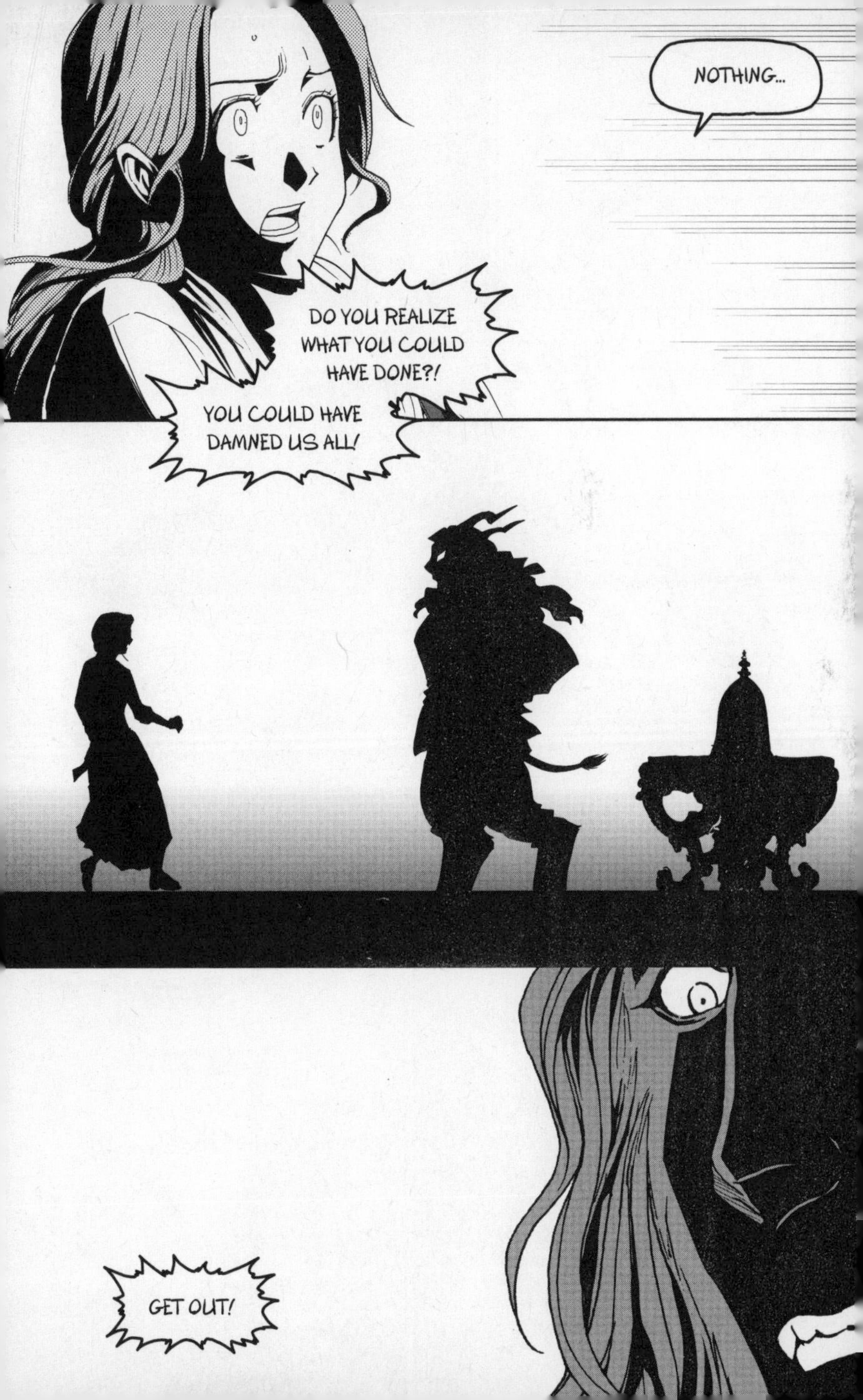
NOTHING...
DO YOU REALIZE WHAT YOU COULD HAVE DONE?!
YOU COULD HAVE DAMNED US ALL!
GET OUT!

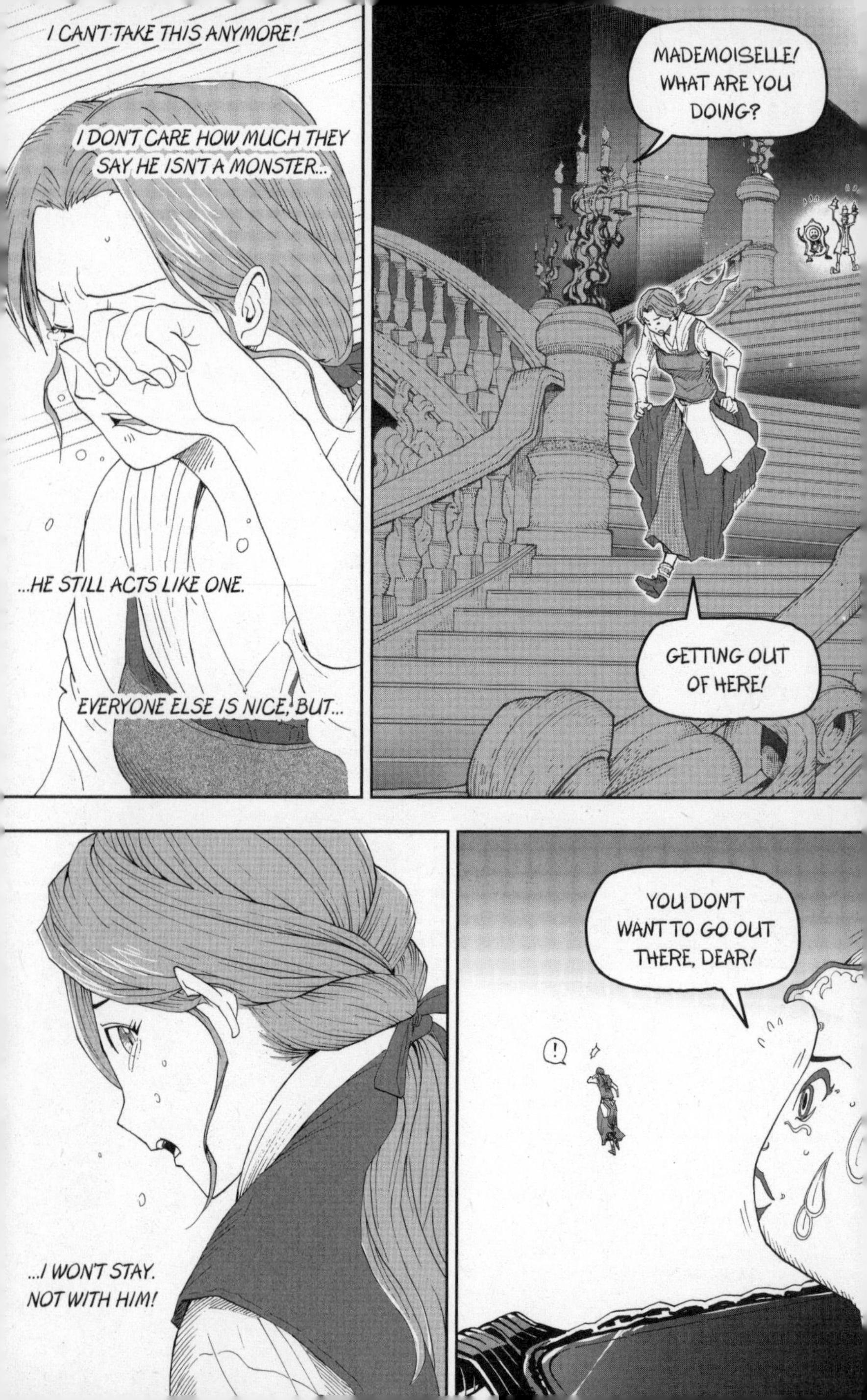
MADEMOISELLE! WHAT ARE YOU DOING?
GETTING OUT OF HERE!
I CAN'T TAKE THIS ANYMORE!
I DON'T CARE HOW MUCH THEY SAY HE ISN'T A MONSTER...
...HE STILL ACTS LIKE ONE.
EVERYONE ELSE IS NICE, BUT...
YOU DON'T WANT TO GO OUT THERE, DEAR!
!
...I WON'T STAY. NOT WITH HIM!

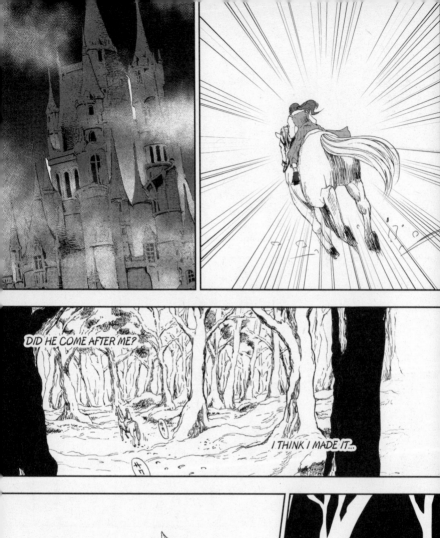

DID HE COME AFTER ME?

I THINK I MADE IT...

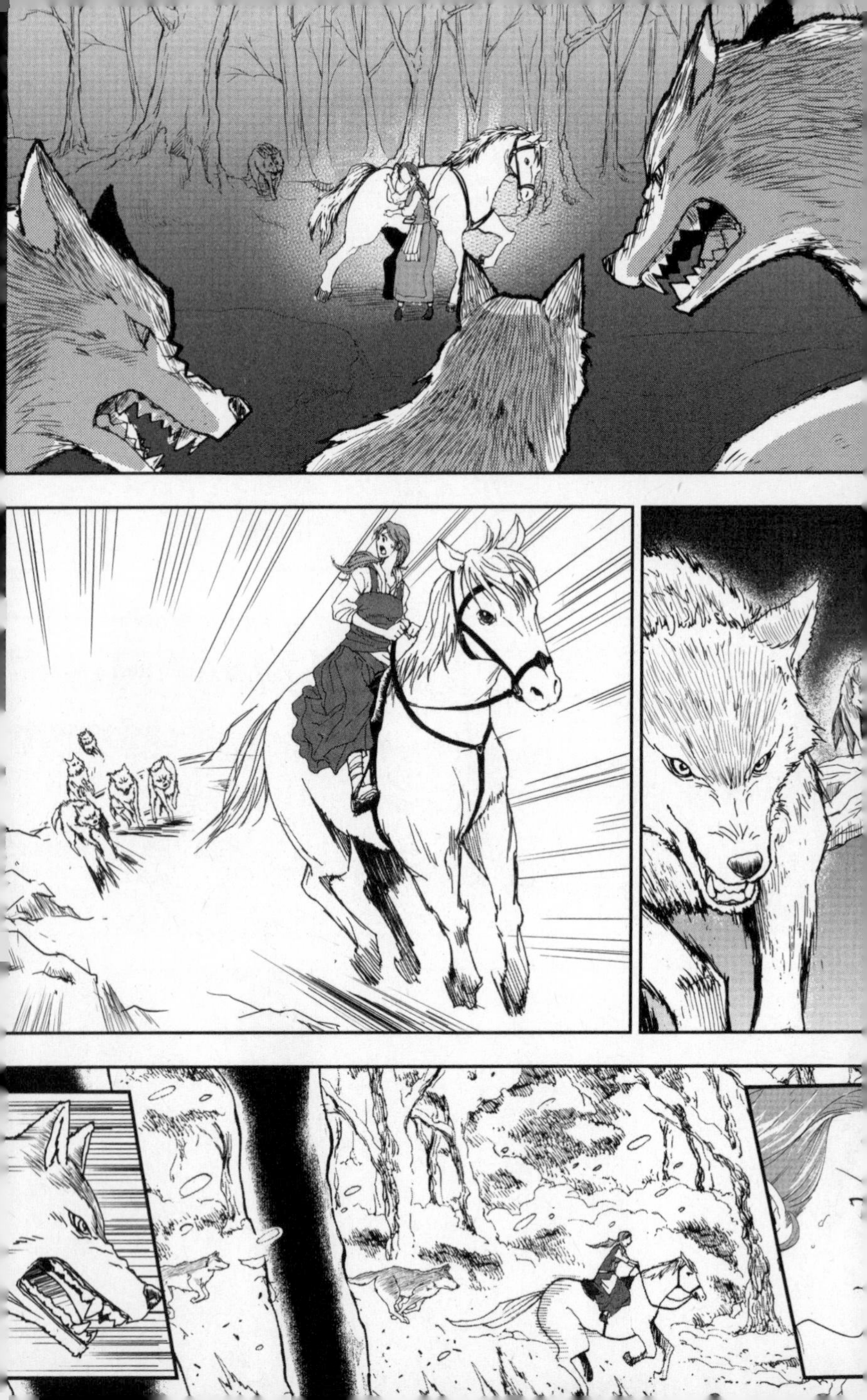

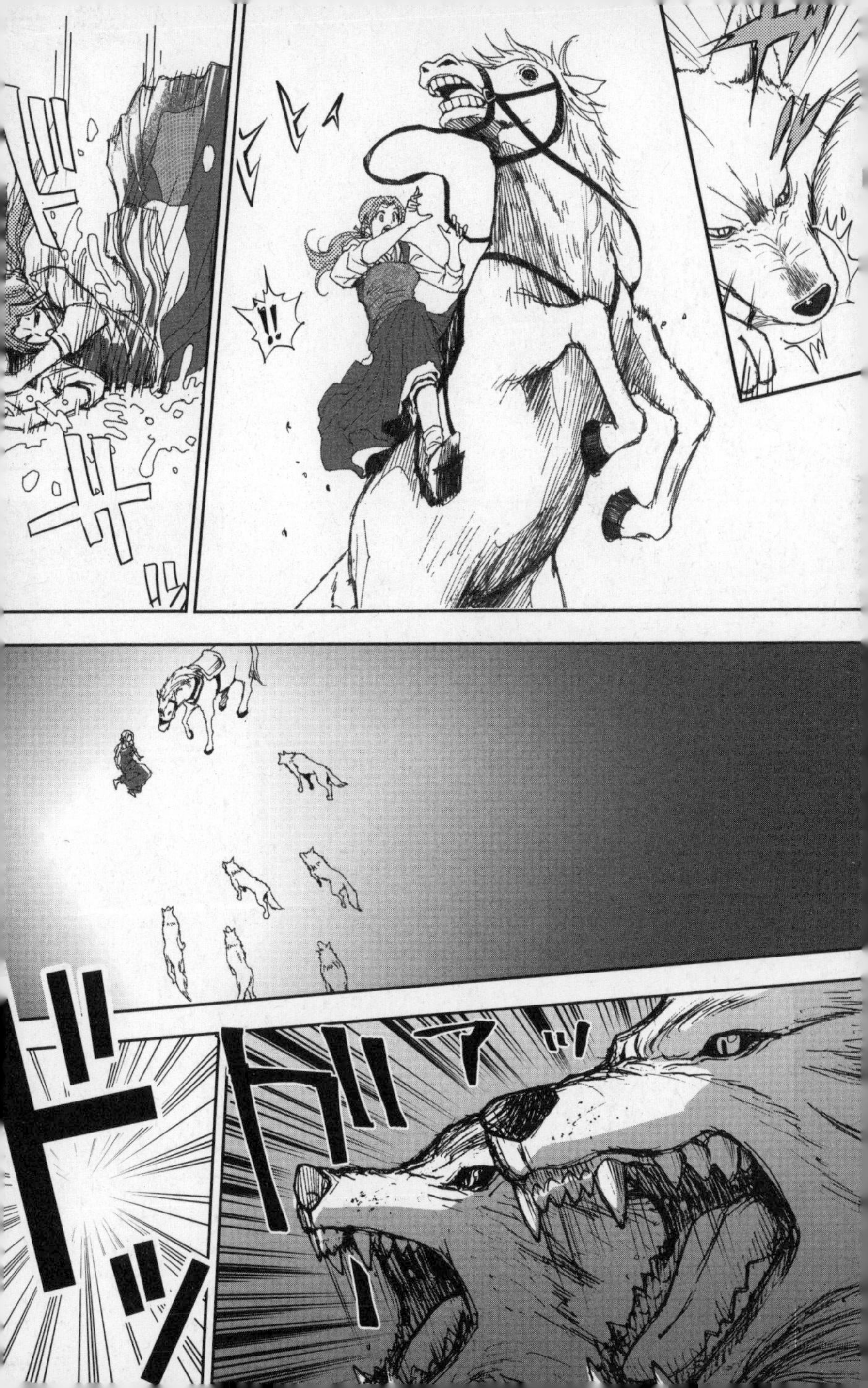
ヒヒィ
!!

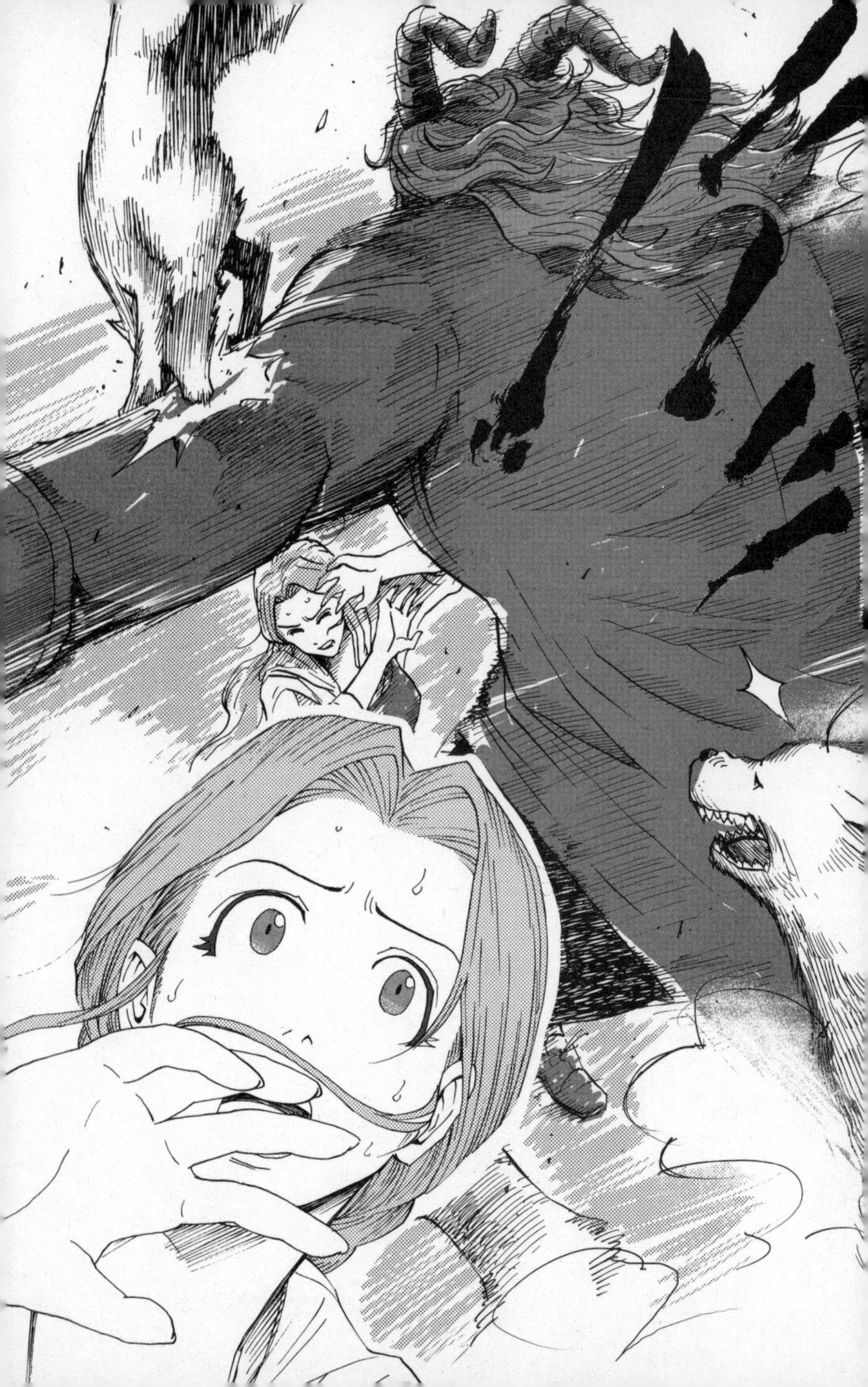

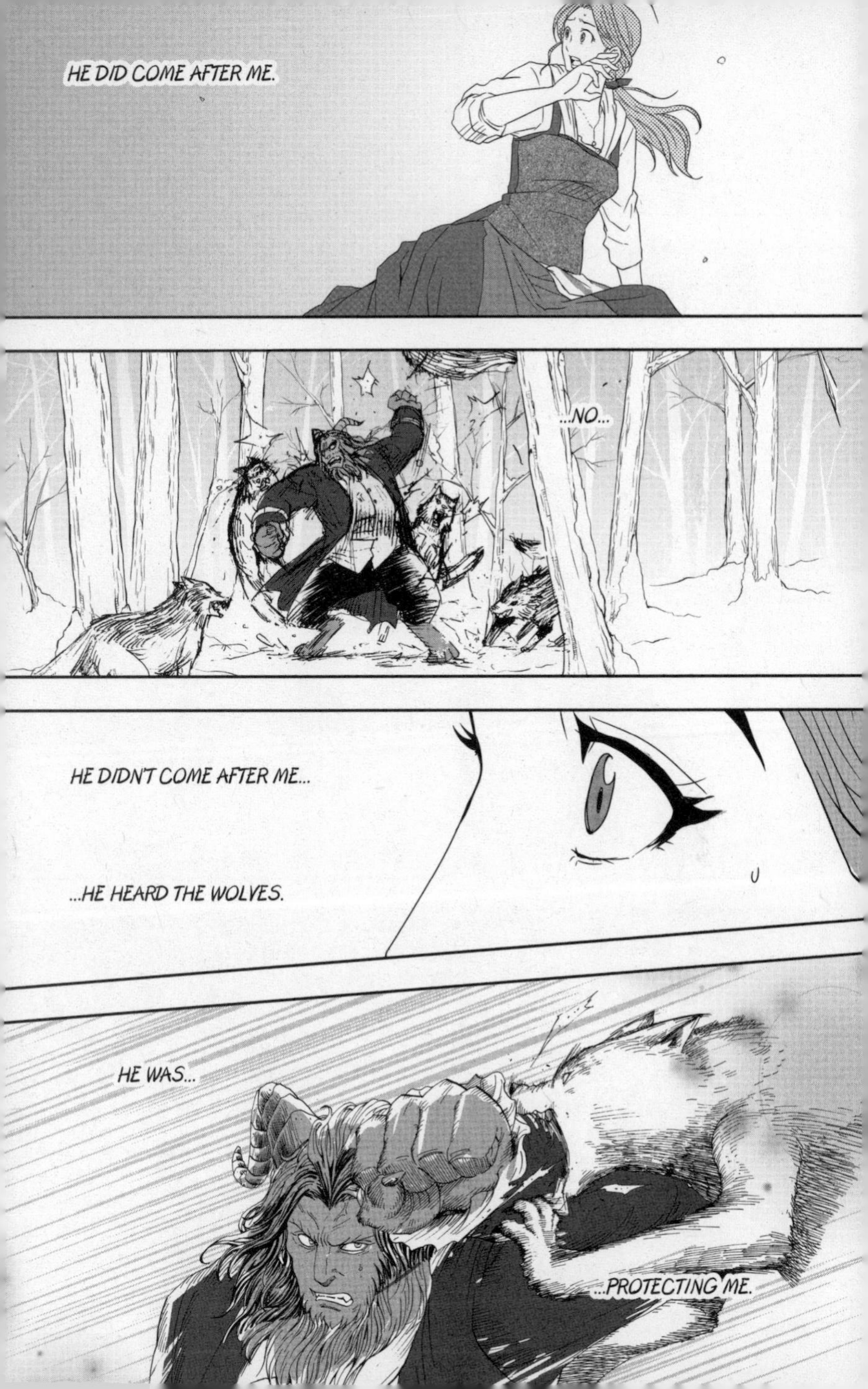
HE DID COME AFTER ME.
...NO...
HE DIDN'T COME AFTER ME...
...HE HEARD THE WOLVES.
HE WAS...
...PROTECTING ME.

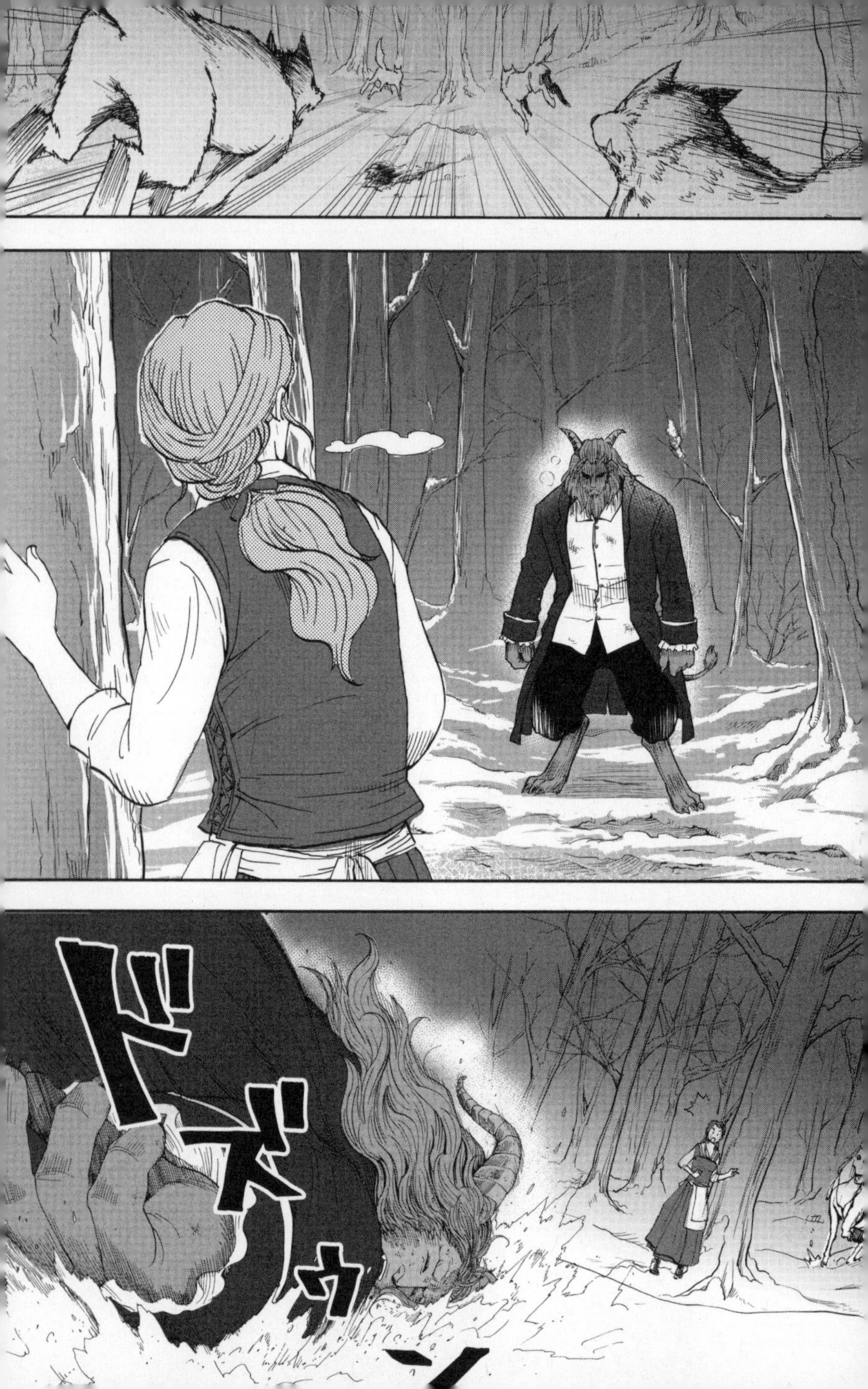
ドズゥーン

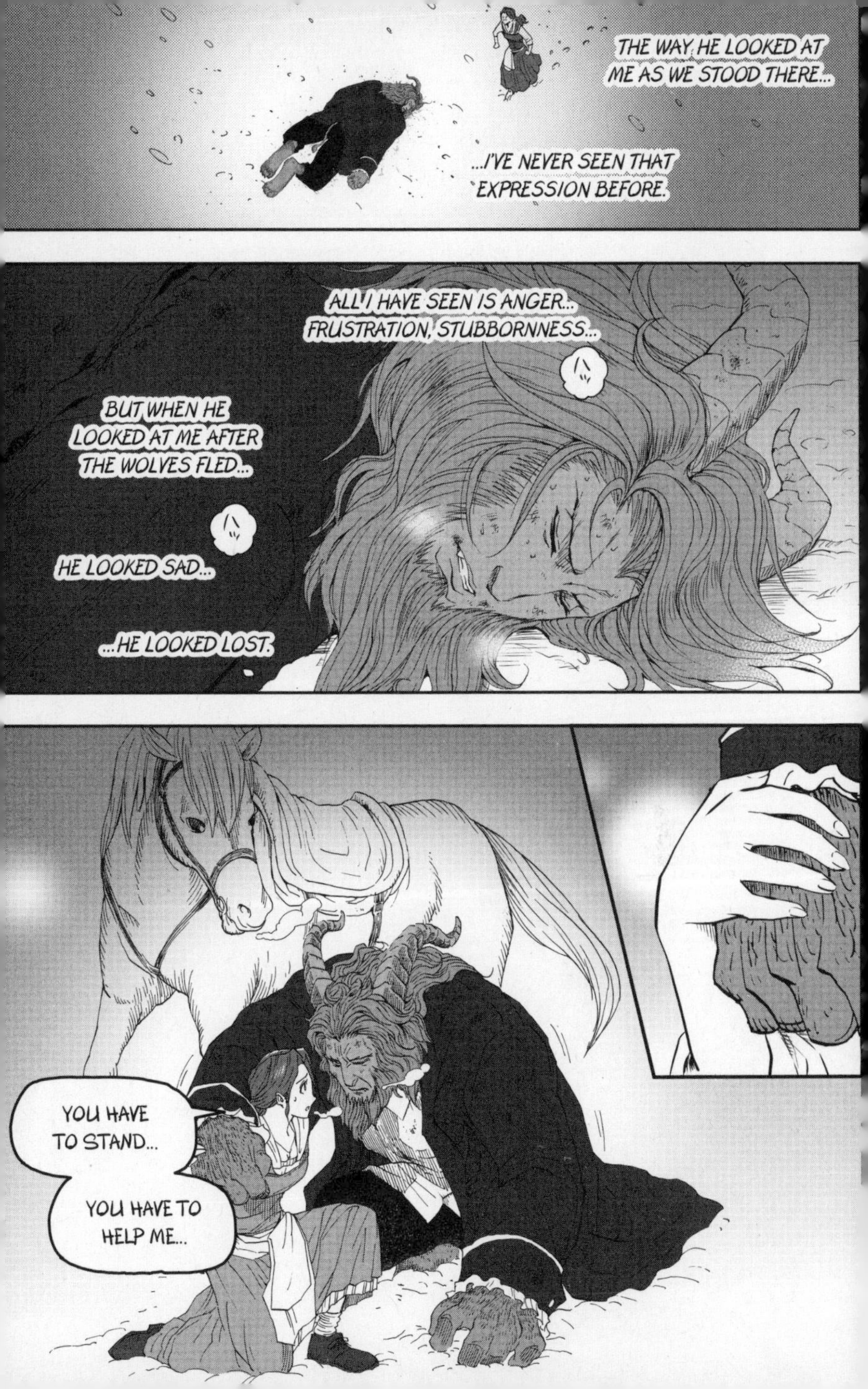
THE WAY HE LOOKED AT ME AS WE STOOD THERE...
...I'VE NEVER SEEN THAT EXPRESSION BEFORE.
ALL I HAVE SEEN IS ANGER... FRUSTRATION, STUBBORNNESS...
BUT WHEN HE LOOKED AT ME AFTER THE WOLVES FLED...
HE LOOKED SAD...
...HE LOOKED LOST.
YOU HAVE TO STAND...
YOU HAVE TO HELP ME...

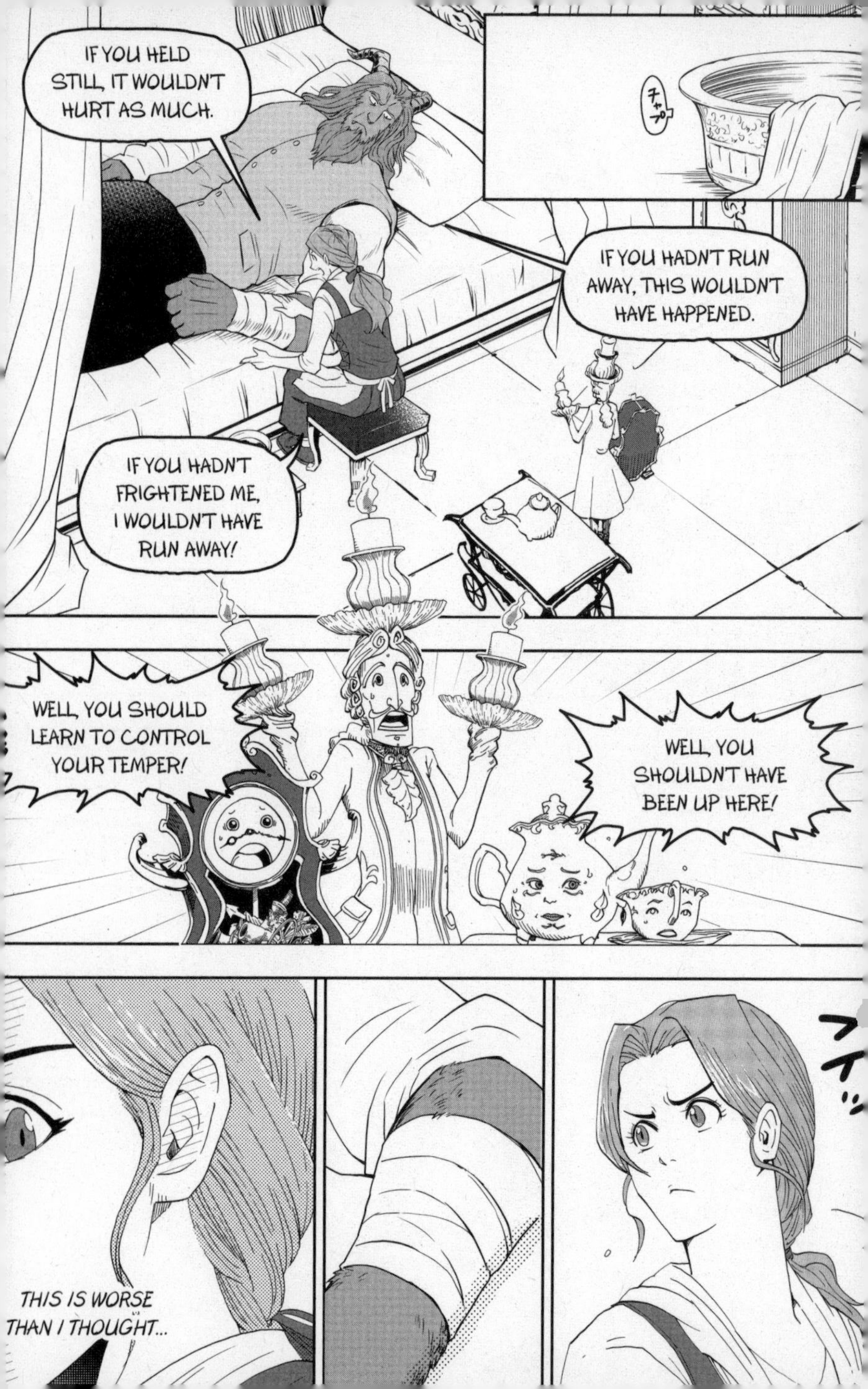
IF YOU HELD STILL, IT WOULDN'T HURT AS MUCH.
IF YOU HADN'T RUN AWAY, THIS WOULDN'T HAVE HAPPENED.
IF YOU HADN'T FRIGHTENED ME, I WOULDN'T HAVE RUN AWAY!
チャプ
WELL, YOU SHOULD LEARN TO CONTROL YOUR TEMPER!
WELL, YOU SHOULDN'T HAVE BEEN UP HERE!
THIS IS WORSE THAN I THOUGHT...

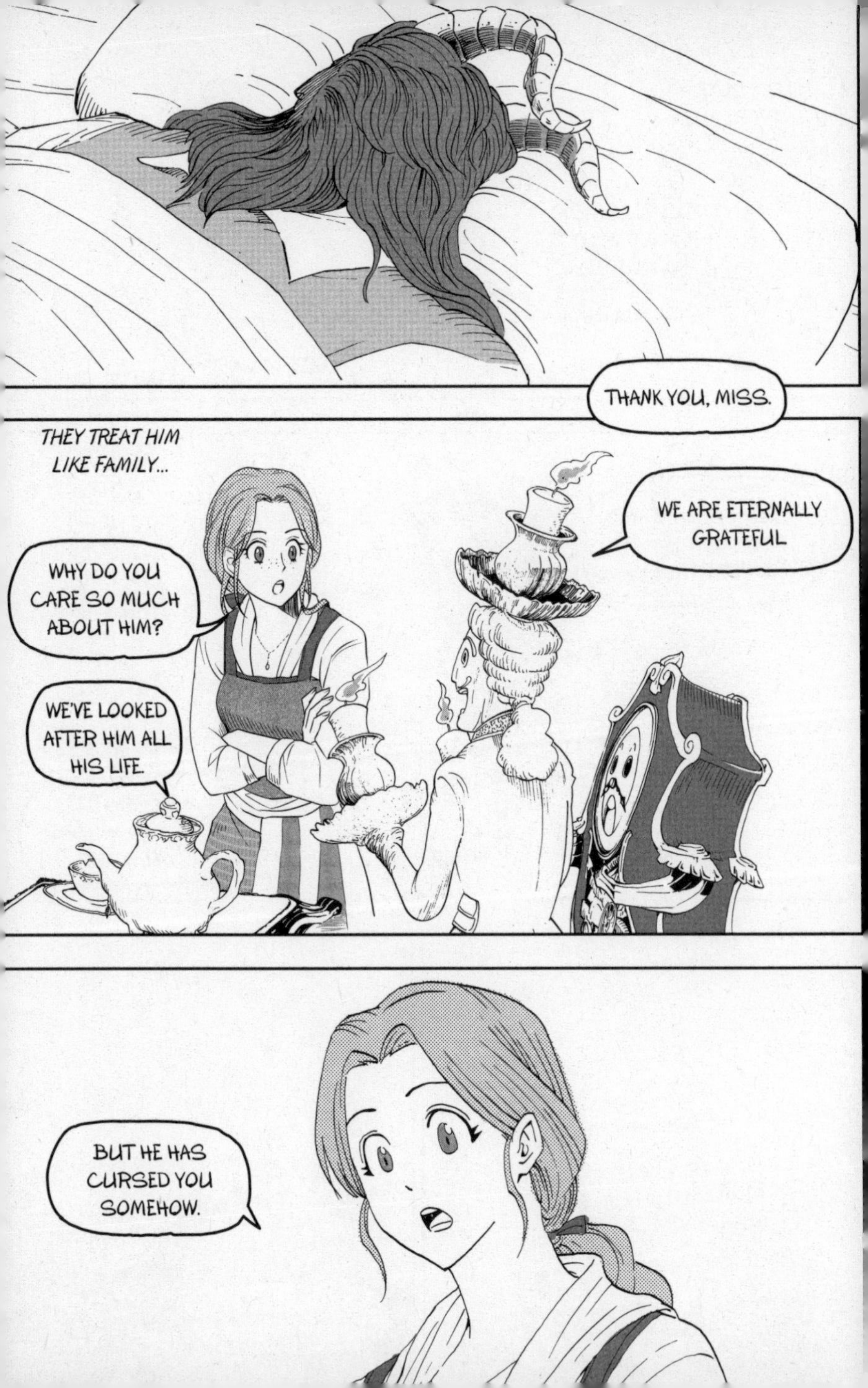
THANK YOU, MISS.
WE ARE ETERNALLY GRATEFUL
THEY TREAT HIM LIKE FAMILY...
WHY DO YOU CARE SO MUCH ABOUT HIM?
WE'VE LOOKED AFTER HIM ALL HIS LIFE.
BUT HE HAS CURSED YOU SOMEHOW.

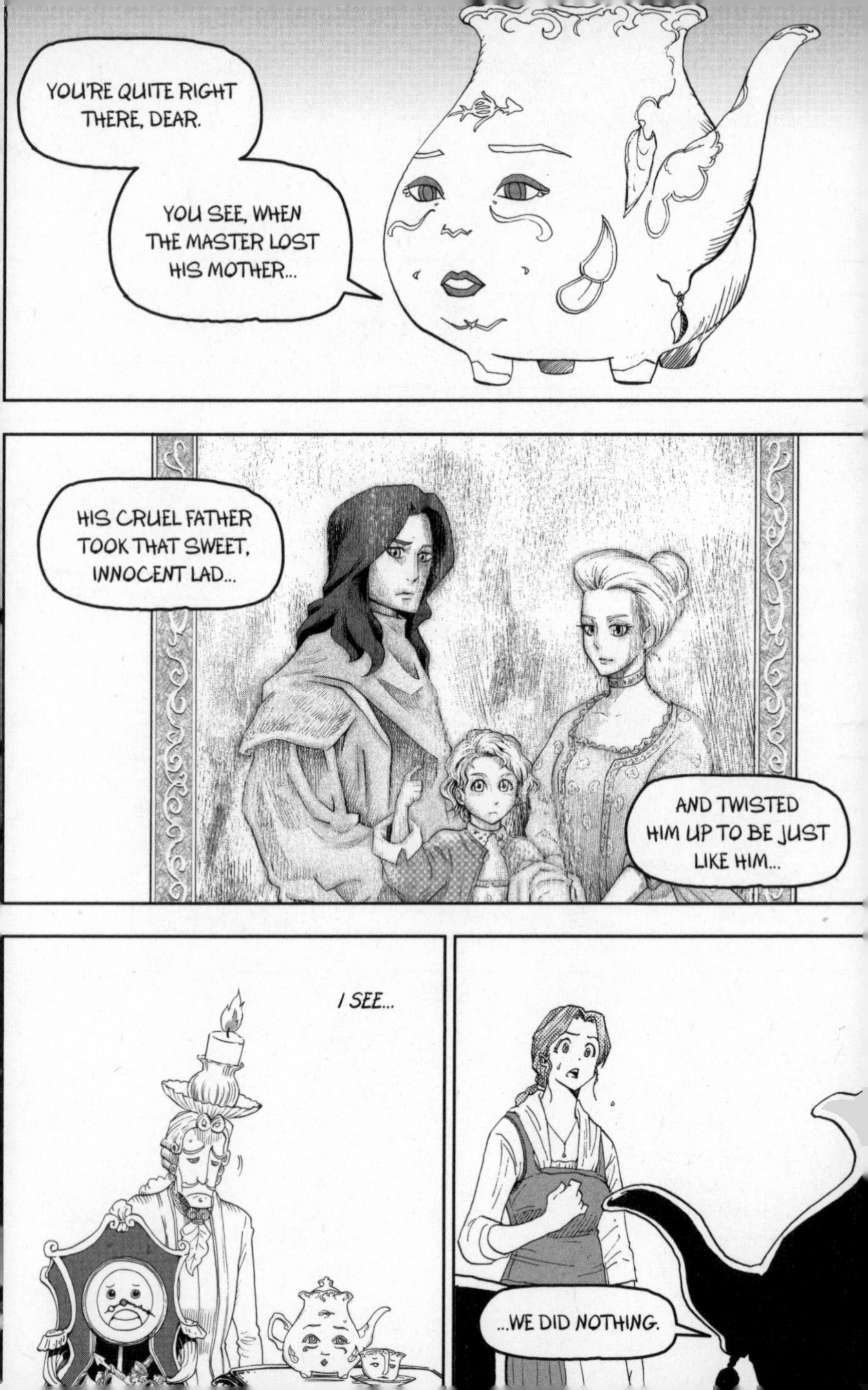
YOU'RE QUITE RIGHT THERE, DEAR.
YOU SEE, WHEN THE MASTER LOST HIS MOTHER...
HIS CRUEL FATHER TOOK THAT SWEET, INNOCENT LAD...
AND TWISTED HIM UP TO BE JUST LIKE HIM...
...WE DID NOTHING.
I SEE...

IT DOESN'T EXCUSE HIS BEHAVIOR... BUT...

...IF THAT WERE ME...

...I THINK I WOULD BE PRETTY ANGRY, TOO.

I THINK, IF I HADN'T BEEN RAISED WITH LOVE...

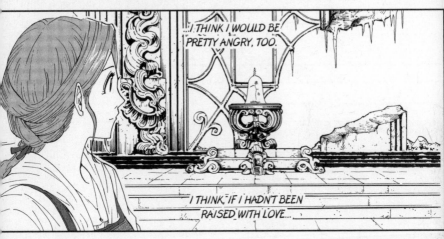

...IT MIGHT BE HARDER FOR ME TO RECOGNIZE IT.

THIS ROOM DOESN'T LOOK SO SCARY IN THE SUNLIGHT...

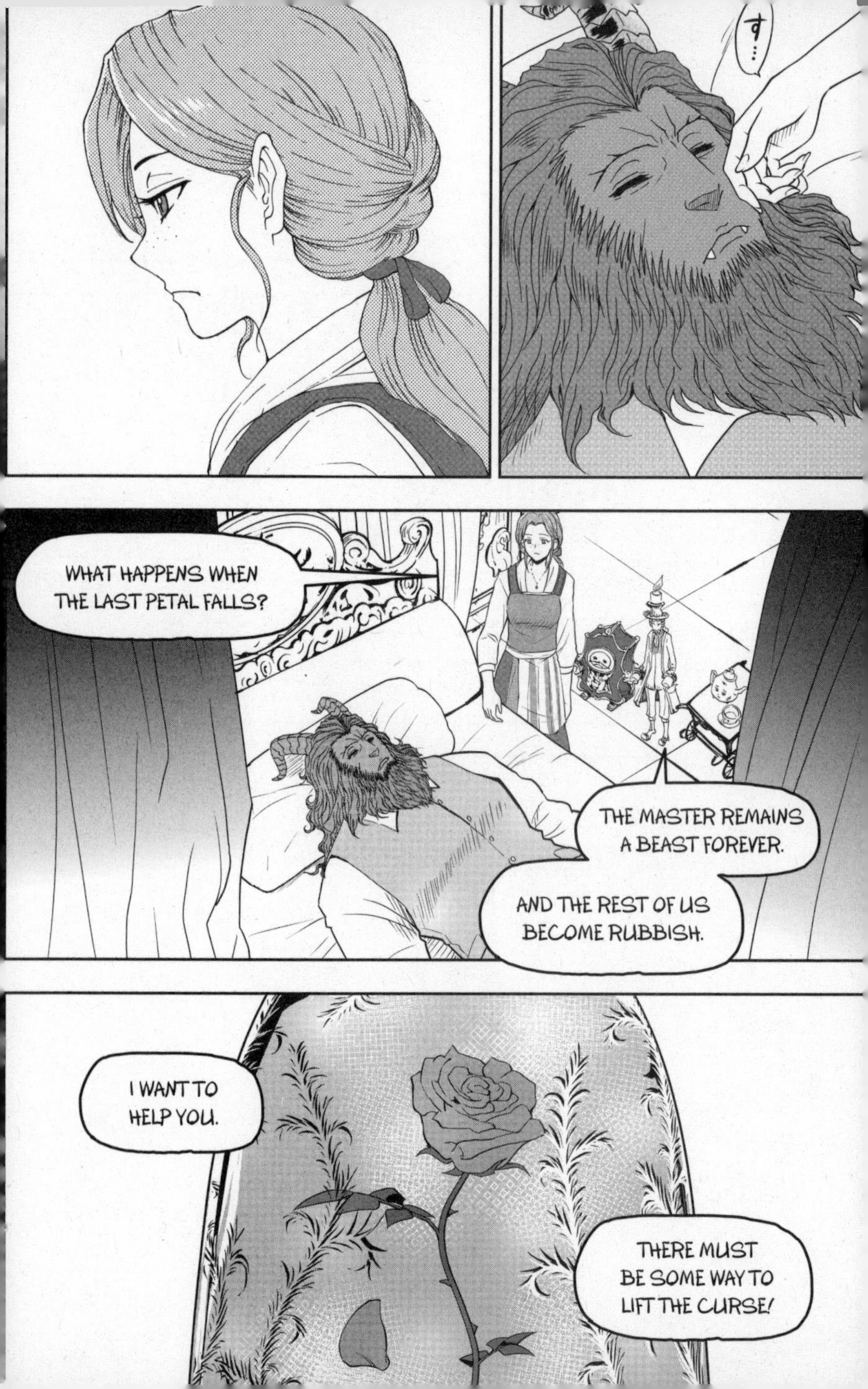
す…
WHAT HAPPENS WHEN THE LAST PETAL FALLS?
THE MASTER REMAINS A BEAST FOREVER.
AND THE REST OF US BECOME RUBBISH.
I WANT TO HELP YOU.
THERE MUST BE SOME WAY TO LIFT THE CURSE!

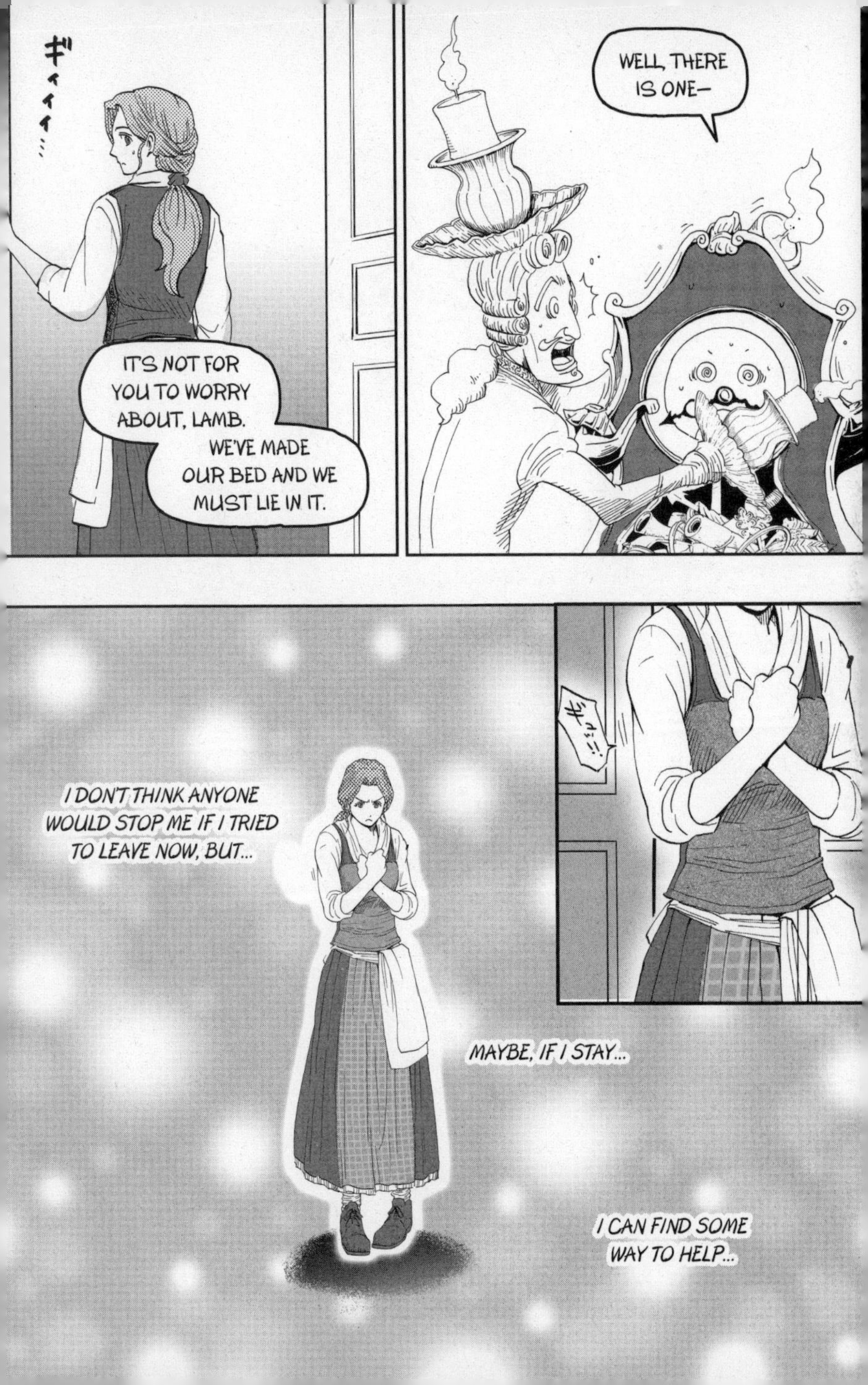
WELL, THERE IS ONE—
ギィィィ…
IT'S NOT FOR YOU TO WORRY ABOUT, LAMB.
WE'VE MADE OUR BED AND WE MUST LIE IN IT.
I DON'T THINK ANYONE WOULD STOP ME IF I TRIED TO LEAVE NOW, BUT...
MAYBE, IF I STAY...
I CAN FIND SOME WAY TO HELP...

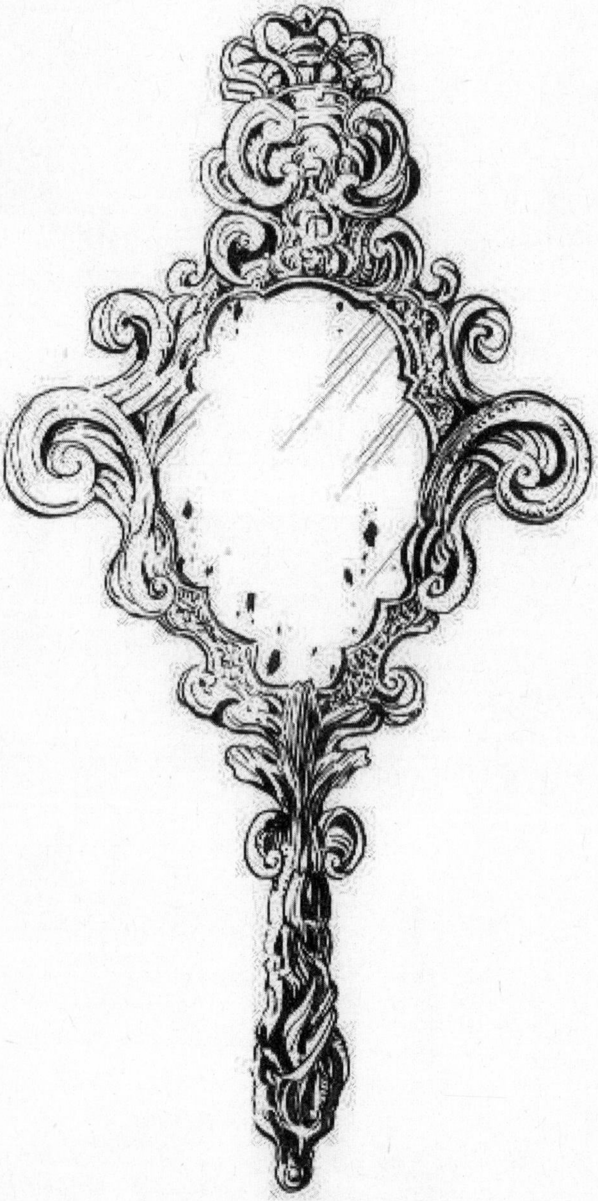

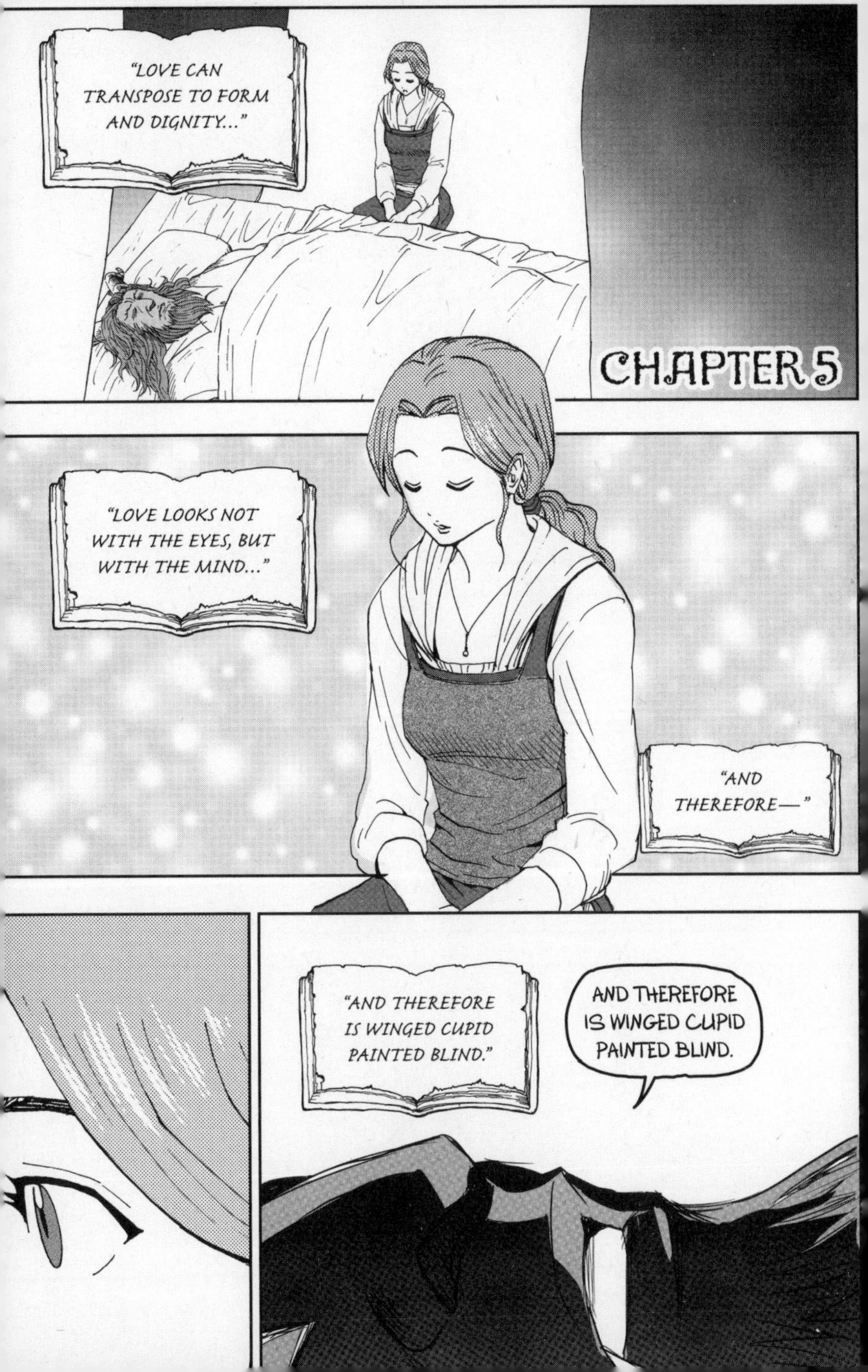
"LOVE CAN TRANSPOSE TO FORM AND DIGNITY..."
CHAPTER 5
"LOVE LOOKS NOT WITH THE EYES, BUT WITH THE MIND..."
"AND THEREFORE—"
"AND THEREFORE IS WINGED CUPID PAINTED BLIND."
AND THEREFORE IS WINGED CUPID PAINTED BLIND.

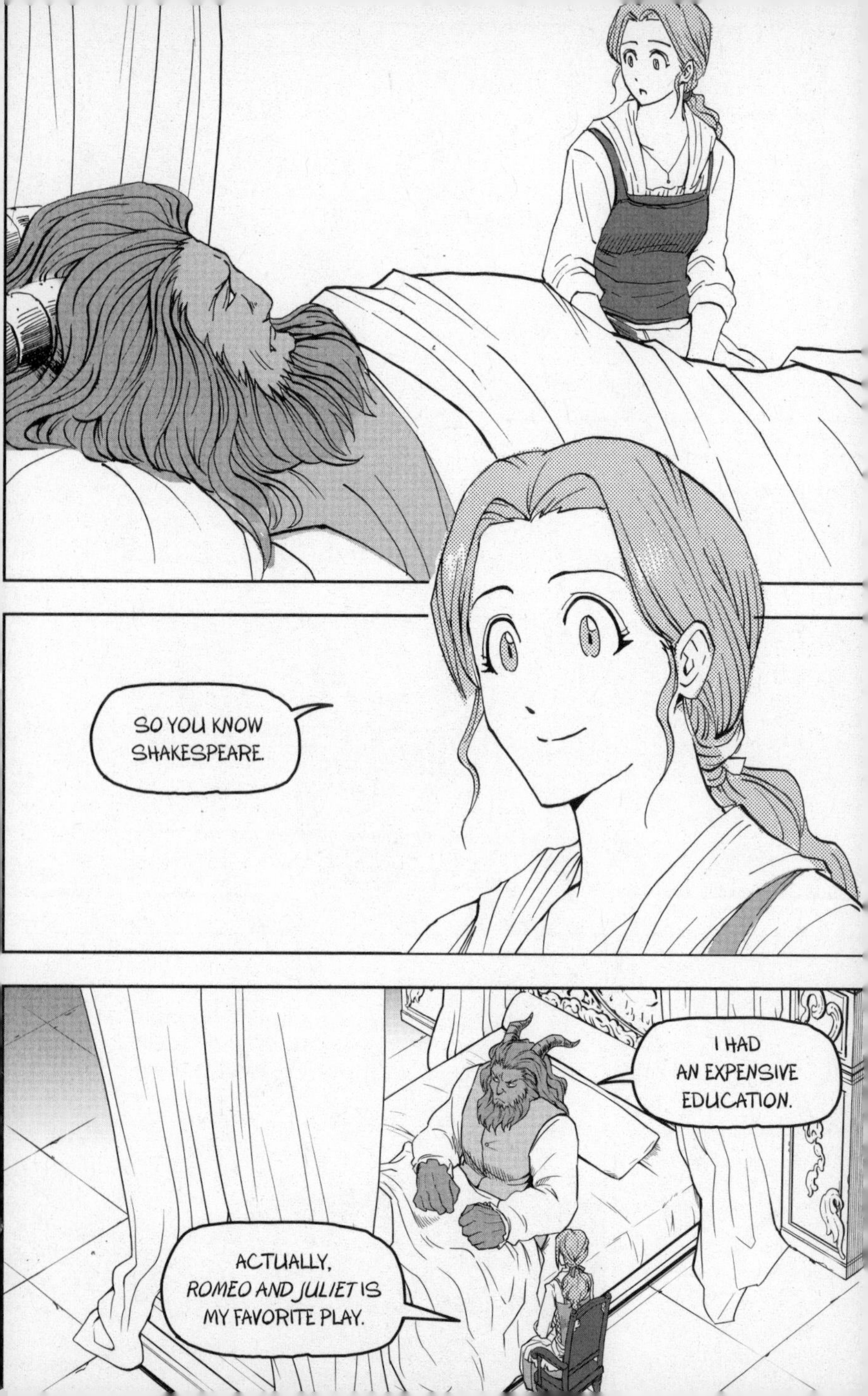
SO YOU KNOW SHAKESPEARE.
I HAD AN EXPENSIVE EDUCATION.
ACTUALLY, *ROMEO AND JULIET* IS MY FAVORITE PLAY.

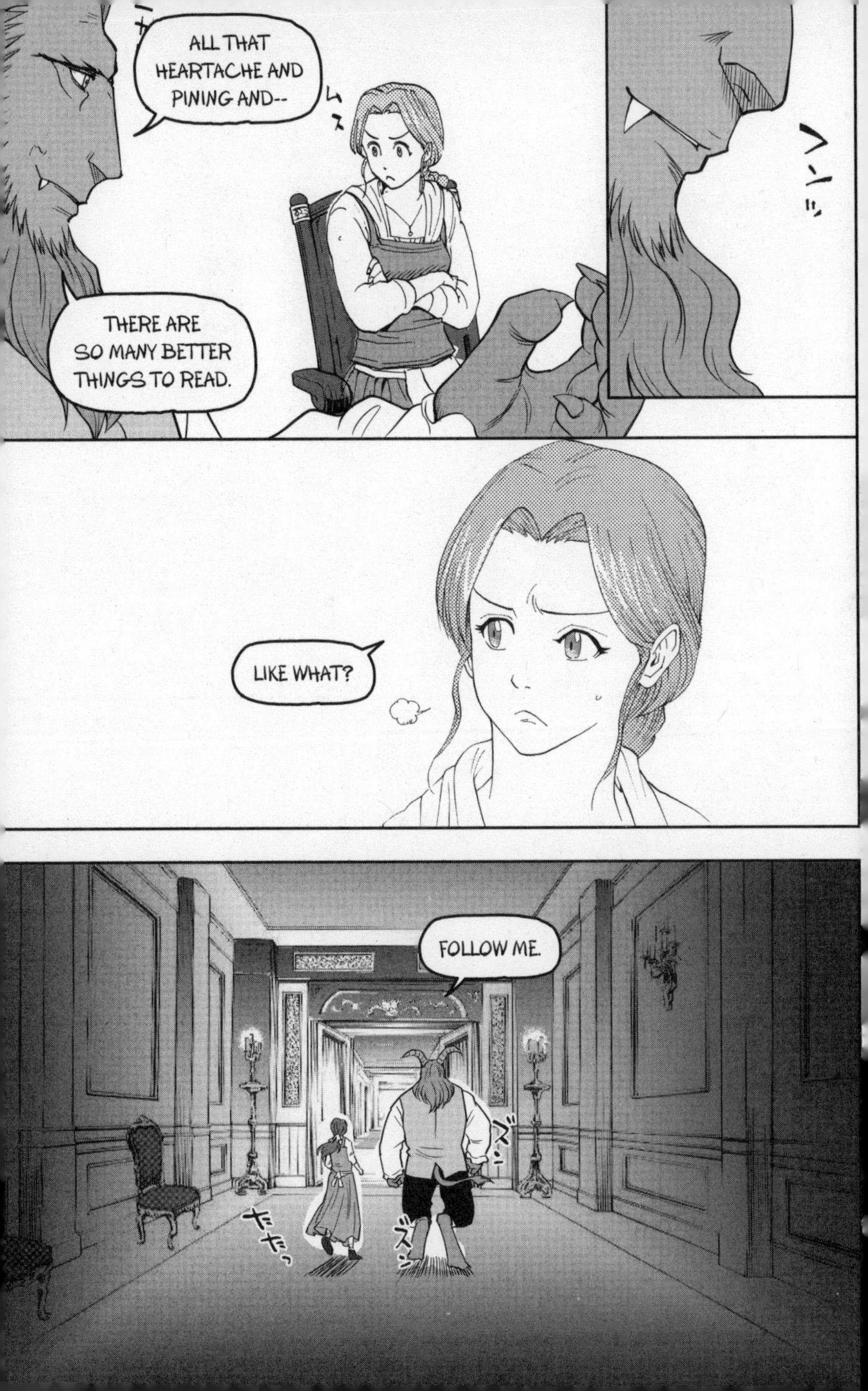
ALL THAT HEARTACHE AND PINING AND--
THERE ARE SO MANY BETTER THINGS TO READ.
LIKE WHAT?
FOLLOW ME.

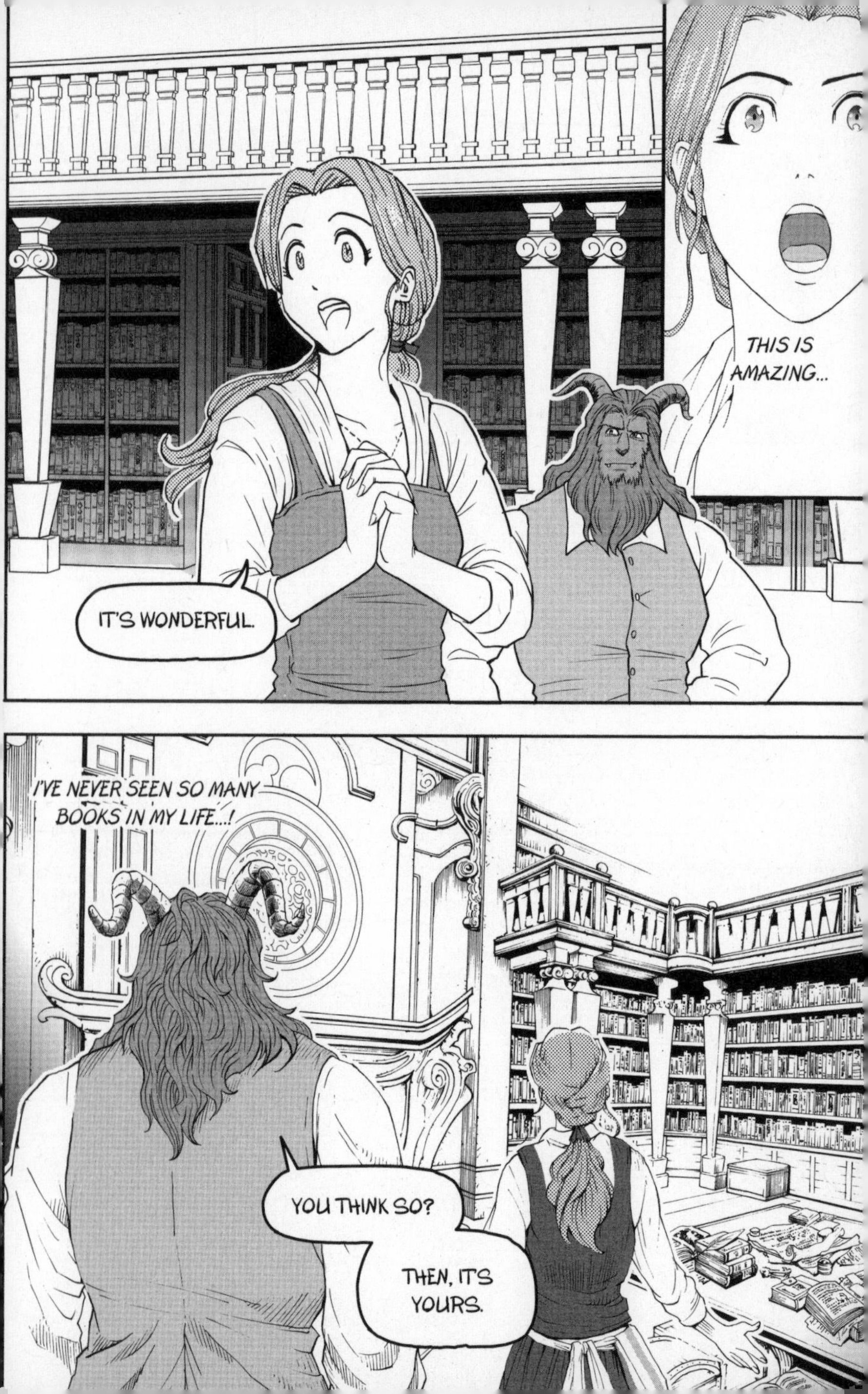
THIS IS AMAZING...
IT'S WONDERFUL.
I'VE NEVER SEEN SO MANY BOOKS IN MY LIFE...!
YOU THINK SO?
THEN, IT'S YOURS.

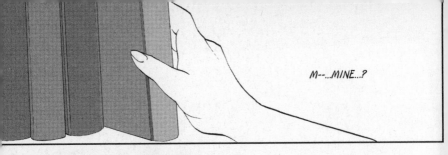

M--...MINE...?

YOU CAN BE MASTER HERE.

THAT WAS...

SO KIND OF HIM!

ドキ...

ドキ...

I FEEL A LITTLE DIZZY.

MY HEART IS POUNDING.

I WONDER IF SOMETHING CHANGED...

...OR IF THIS SIDE OF HIM WAS ALWAYS THERE.

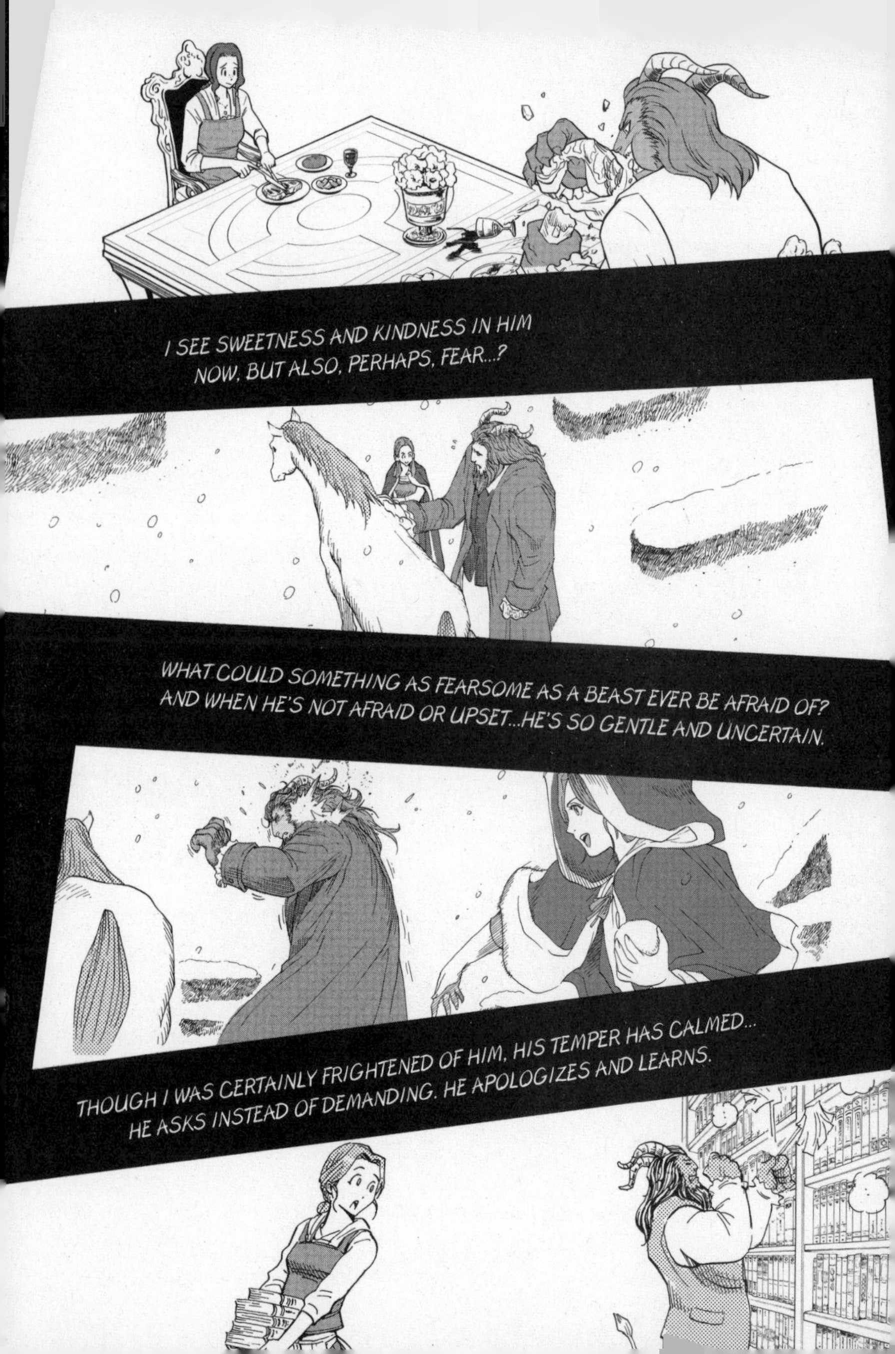
I SEE SWEETNESS AND KINDNESS IN HIM NOW, BUT ALSO, PERHAPS, FEAR...?
WHAT COULD SOMETHING AS FEARSOME AS A BEAST EVER BE AFRAID OF? AND WHEN HE'S NOT AFRAID OR UPSET...HE'S SO GENTLE AND UNCERTAIN.
THOUGH I WAS CERTAINLY FRIGHTENED OF HIM, HIS TEMPER HAS CALMED... HE ASKS INSTEAD OF DEMANDING. HE APOLOGIZES AND LEARNS.

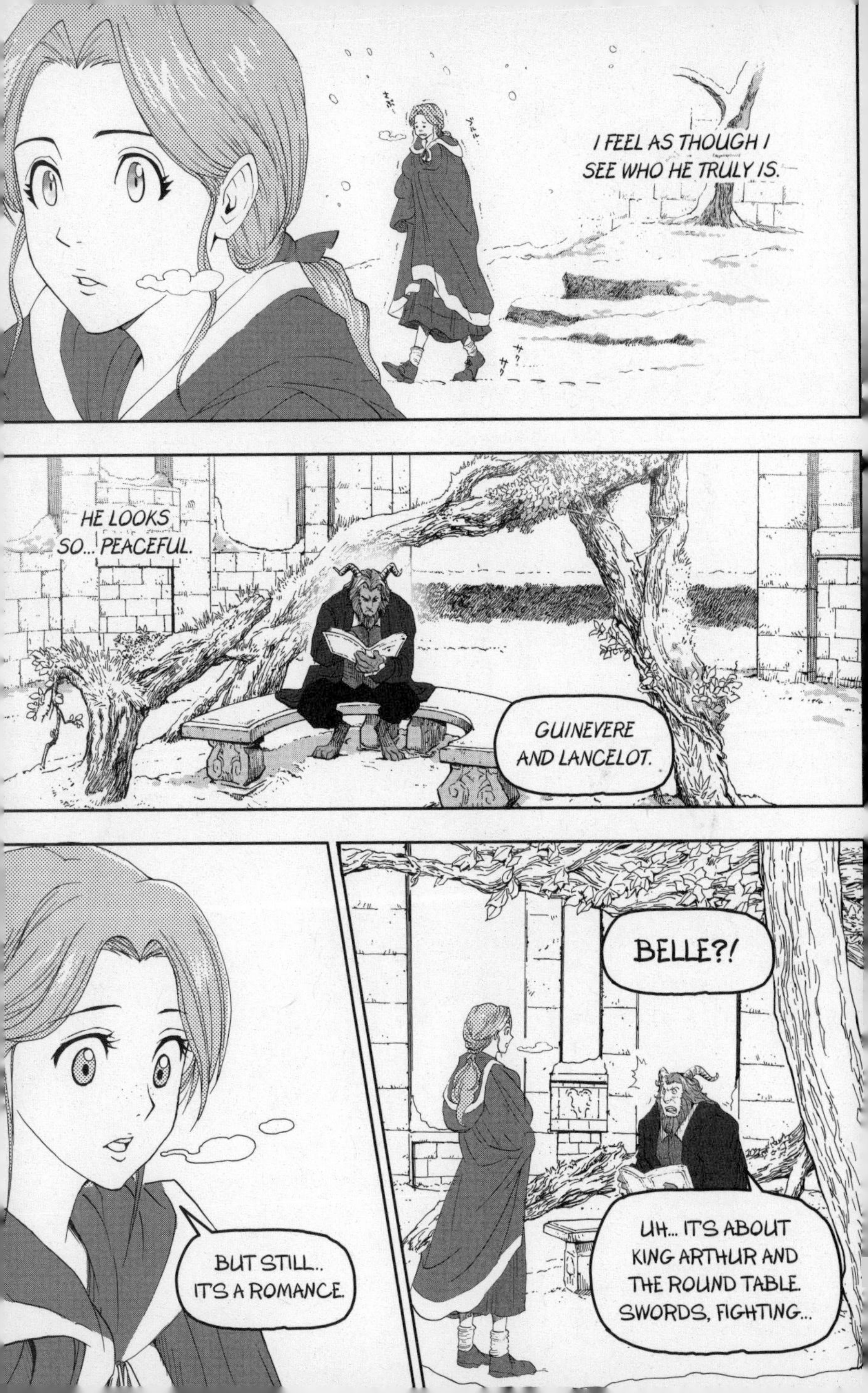
I FEEL AS THOUGH I SEE WHO HE TRULY IS.
HE LOOKS SO... PEACEFUL.
GUINEVERE AND LANCELOT.
BELLE?!
UH... IT'S ABOUT KING ARTHUR AND THE ROUND TABLE. SWORDS, FIGHTING...
BUT STILL.. IT'S A ROMANCE.

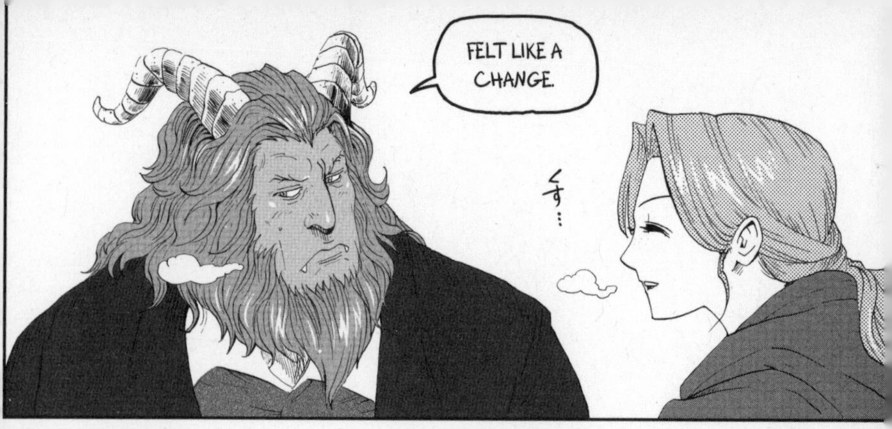
FELT LIKE A CHANGE.
くす…

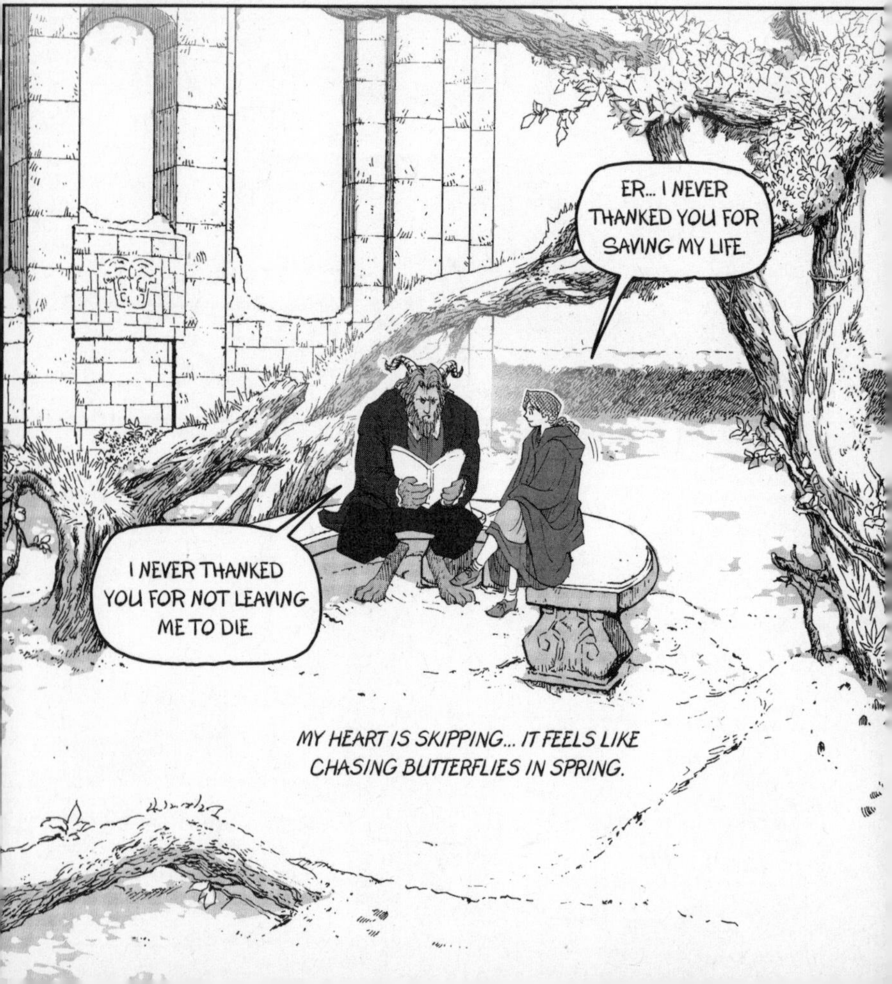
ER... I NEVER THANKED YOU FOR SAVING MY LIFE.
I NEVER THANKED YOU FOR NOT LEAVING ME TO DIE.
MY HEART IS SKIPPING... IT FEELS LIKE CHASING BUTTERFLIES IN SPRING.

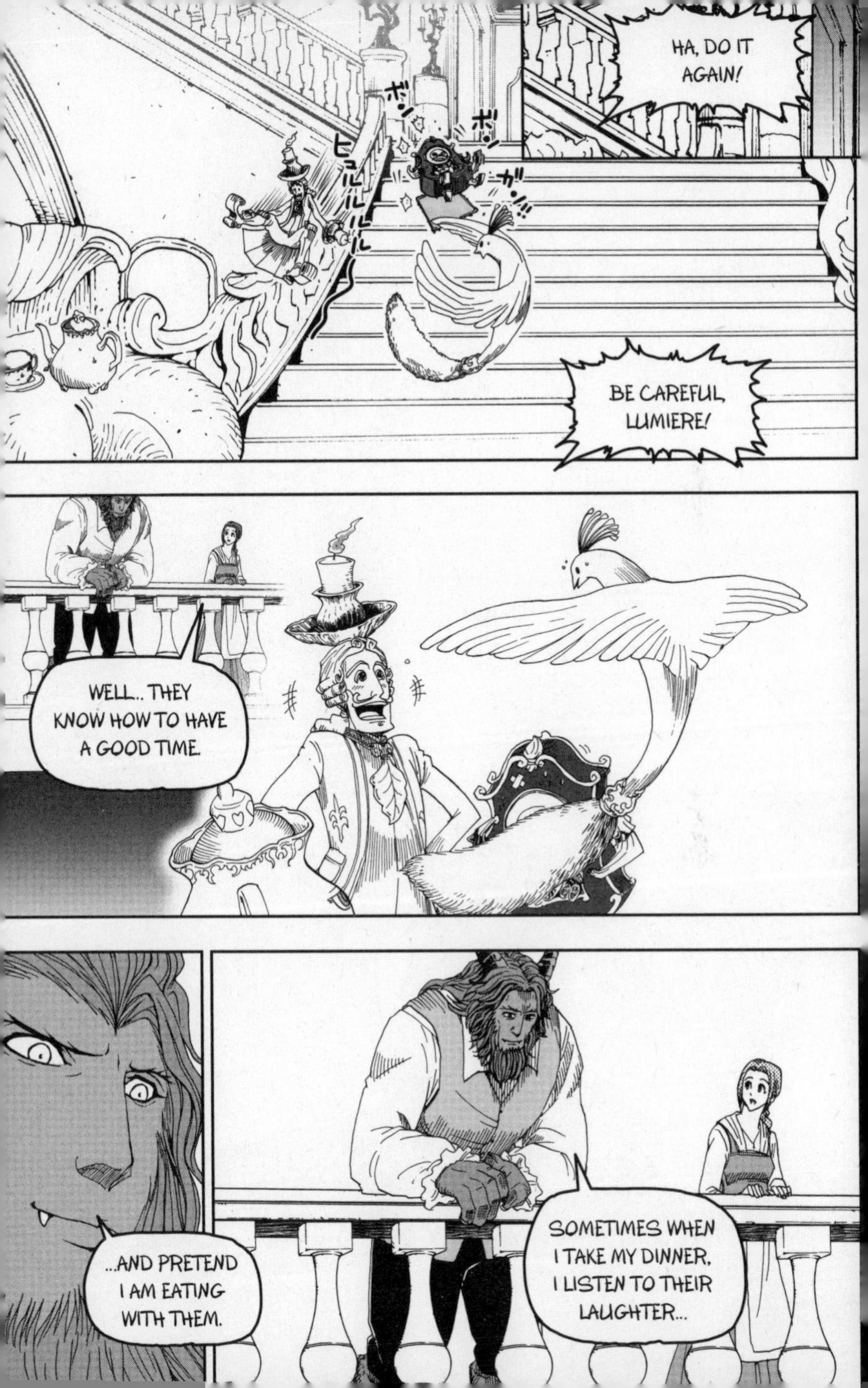
HA, DO IT AGAIN!
ボン
ボン
ガン!!
ヒュルルルル
BE CAREFUL, LUMIERE!
WELL... THEY KNOW HOW TO HAVE A GOOD TIME.
SOMETIMES WHEN I TAKE MY DINNER, I LISTEN TO THEIR LAUGHTER...
...AND PRETEND I AM EATING WITH THEM.

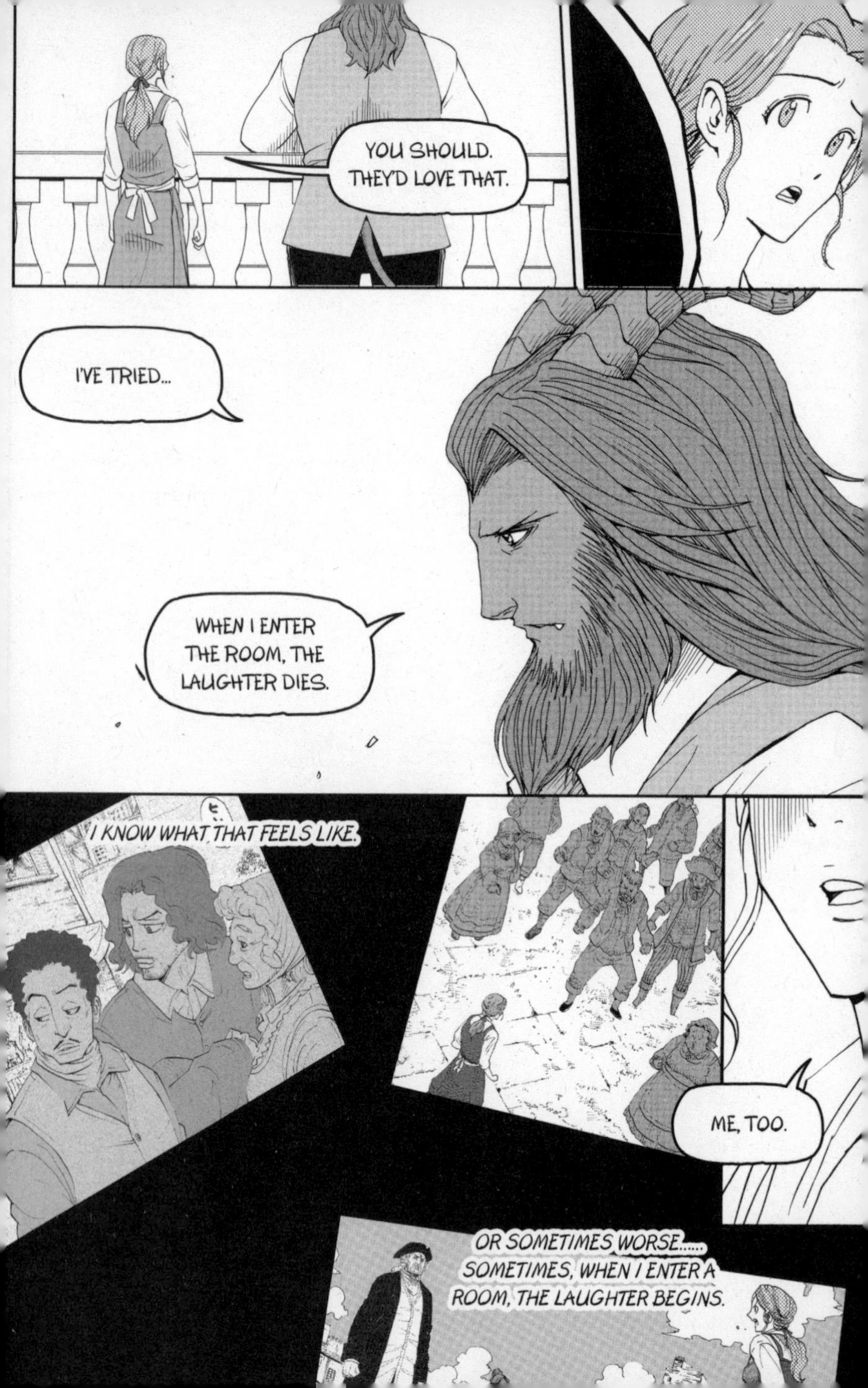
YOU SHOULD. THEY'D LOVE THAT.
I'VE TRIED...
WHEN I ENTER THE ROOM, THE LAUGHTER DIES.
ME, TOO.
I KNOW WHAT THAT FEELS LIKE.
OR SOMETIMES WORSE..... SOMETIMES, WHEN I ENTER A ROOM, THE LAUGHTER BEGINS.

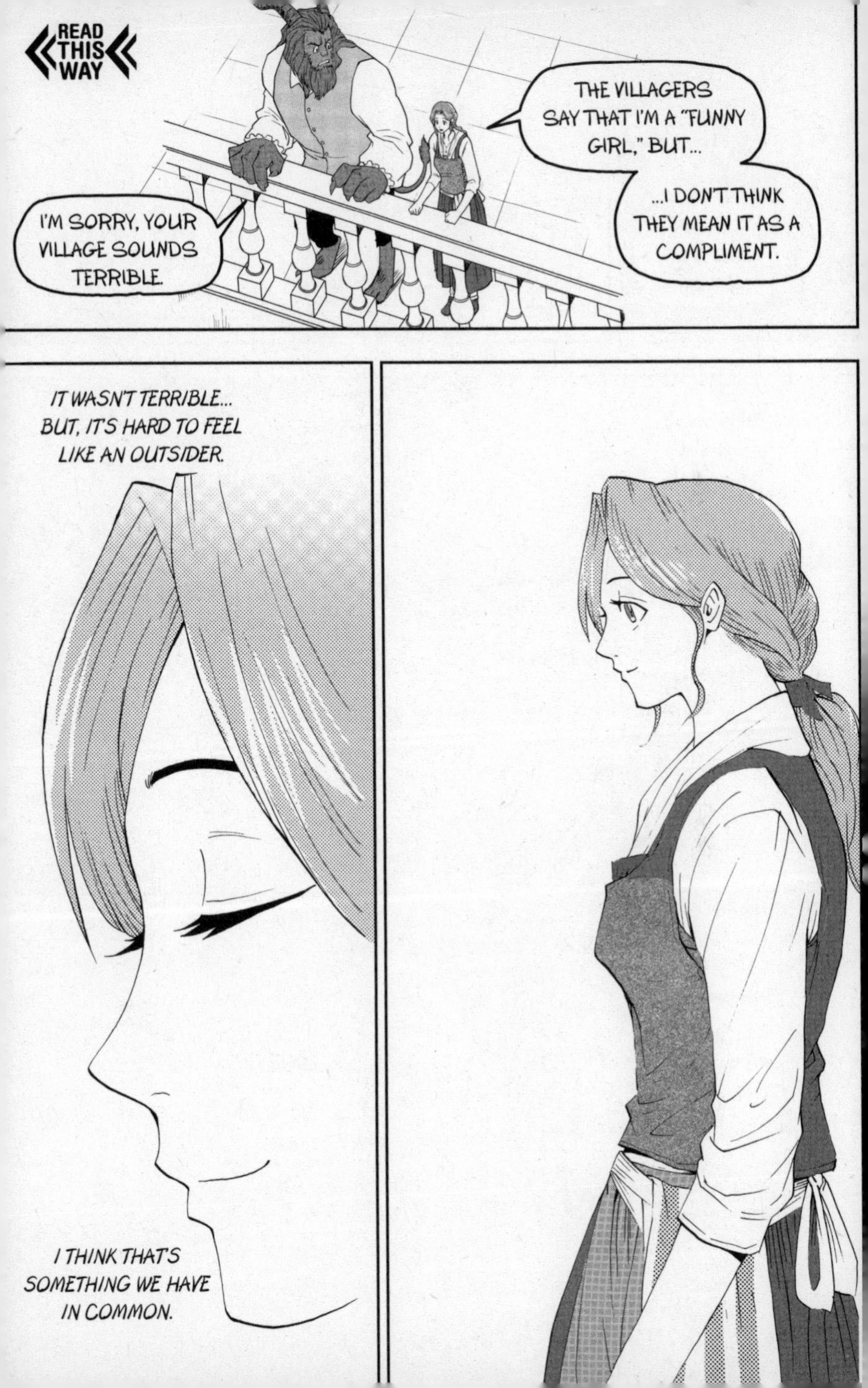
READ THIS WAY
THE VILLAGERS SAY THAT I'M A "FUNNY GIRL," BUT...
...I DON'T THINK THEY MEAN IT AS A COMPLIMENT.
I'M SORRY, YOUR VILLAGE SOUNDS TERRIBLE.
IT WASN'T TERRIBLE... BUT, IT'S HARD TO FEEL LIKE AN OUTSIDER.
I THINK THAT'S SOMETHING WE HAVE IN COMMON.

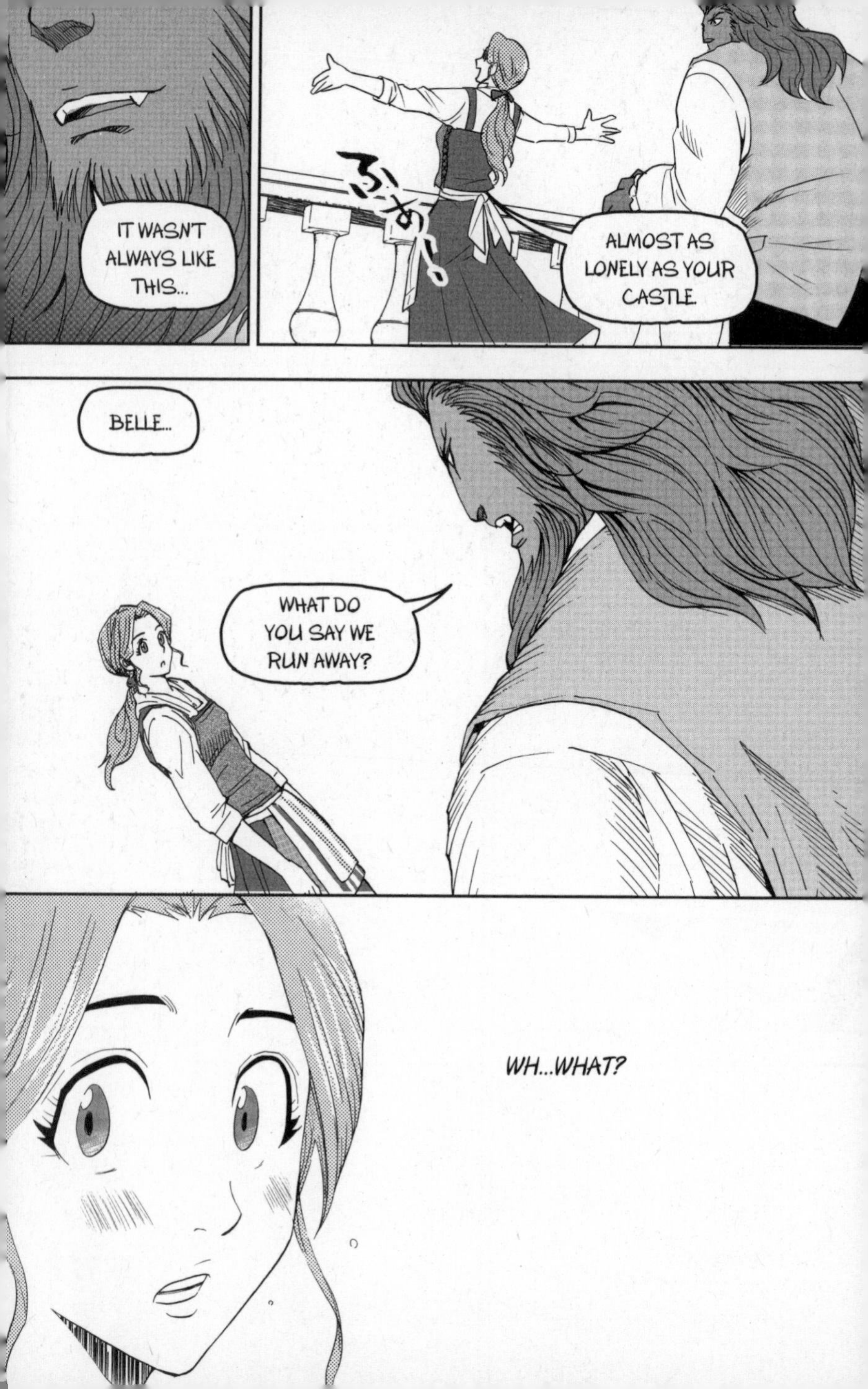
ALMOST AS LONELY AS YOUR CASTLE.
IT WASN'T ALWAYS LIKE THIS...
BELLE...
WHAT DO YOU SAY WE RUN AWAY?
WH...WHAT?

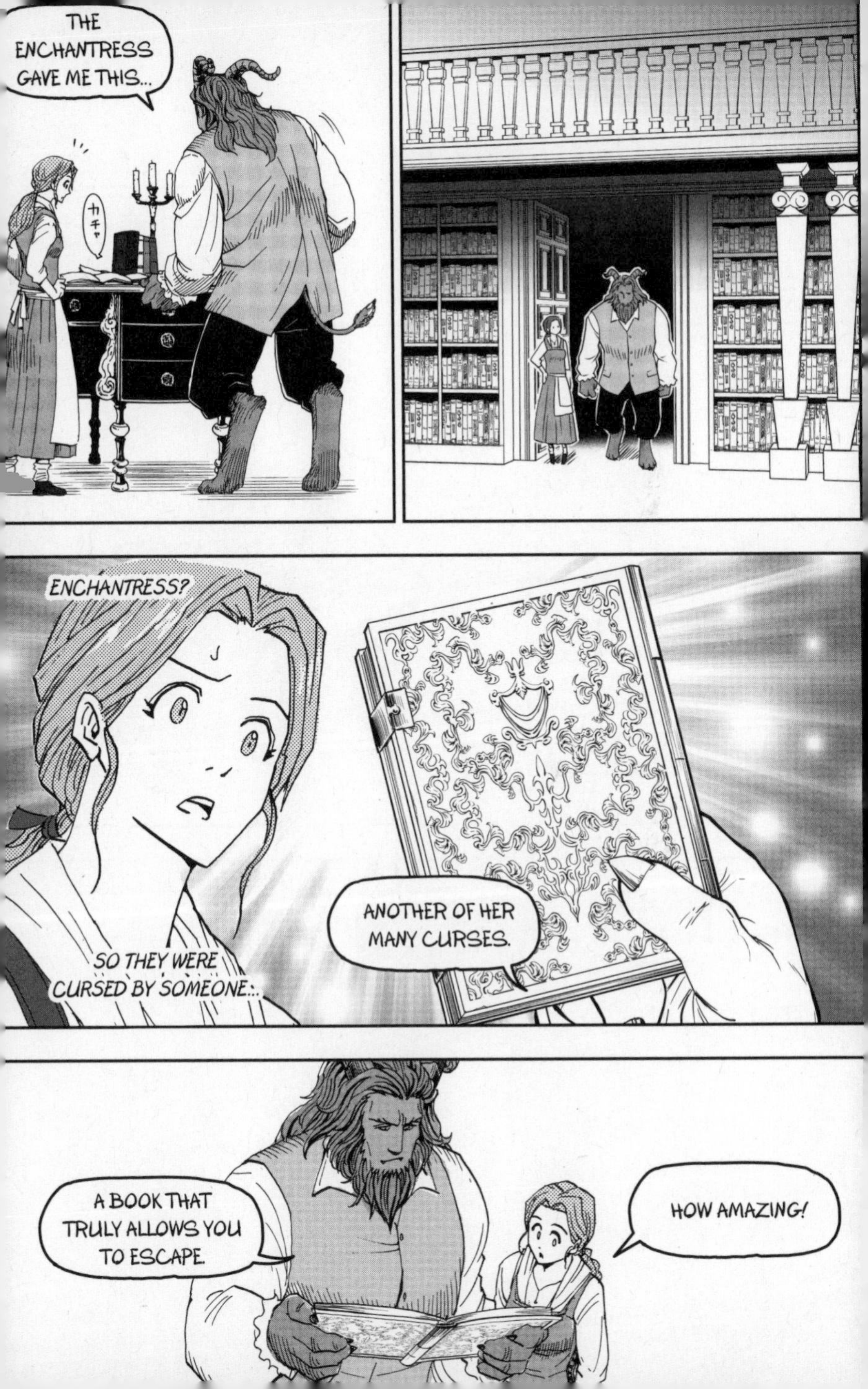
THE ENCHANTRESS GAVE ME THIS...
カチャ
ENCHANTRESS?
ANOTHER OF HER MANY CURSES.
SO THEY WERE CURSED BY SOMEONE...
HOW AMAZING!
A BOOK THAT TRULY ALLOWS YOU TO ESCAPE.

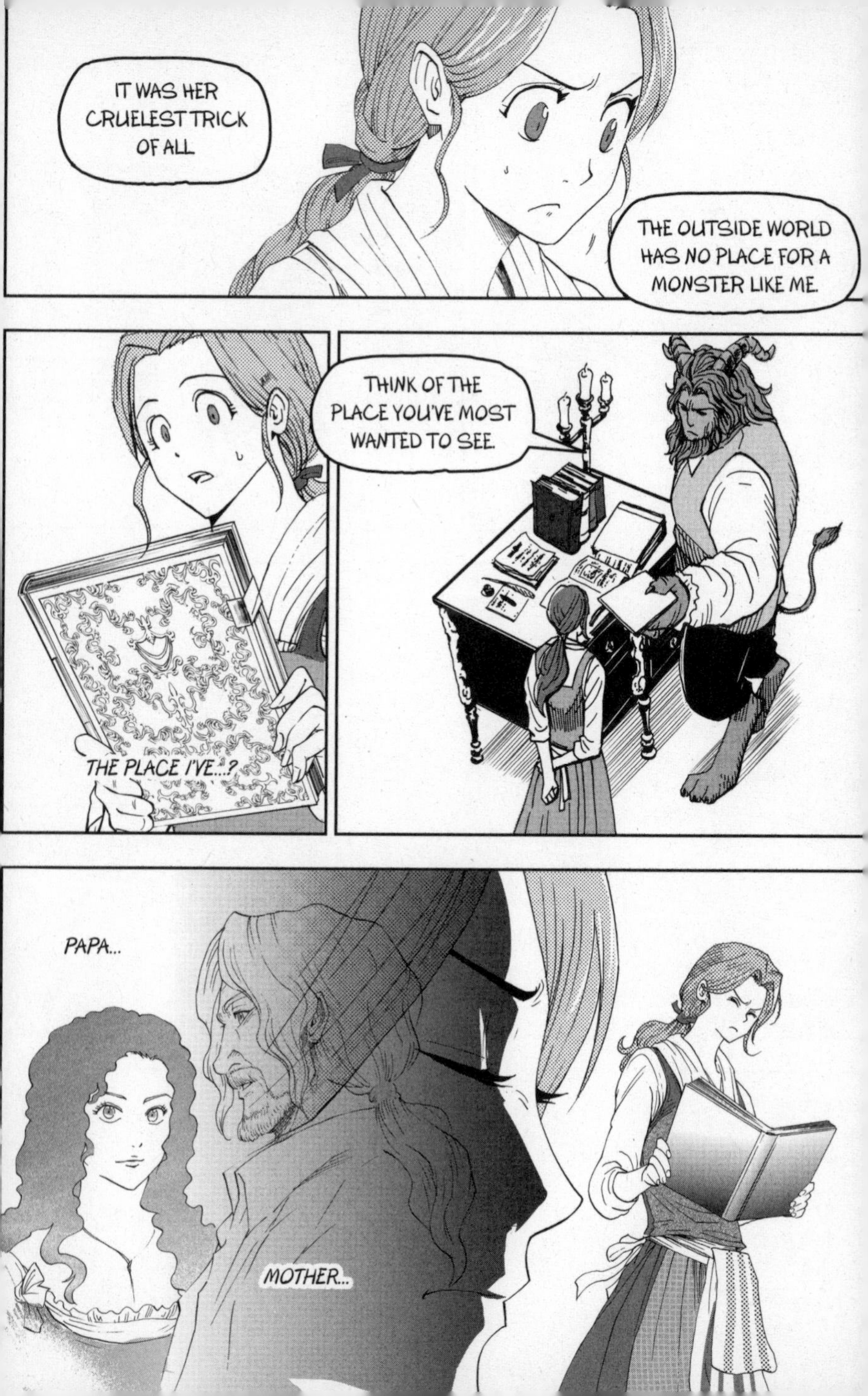
IT WAS HER CRUELEST TRICK OF ALL
THE OUTSIDE WORLD HAS NO PLACE FOR A MONSTER LIKE ME.
THINK OF THE PLACE YOU'VE MOST WANTED TO SEE.
THE PLACE I'VE...?
PAPA...
MOTHER...

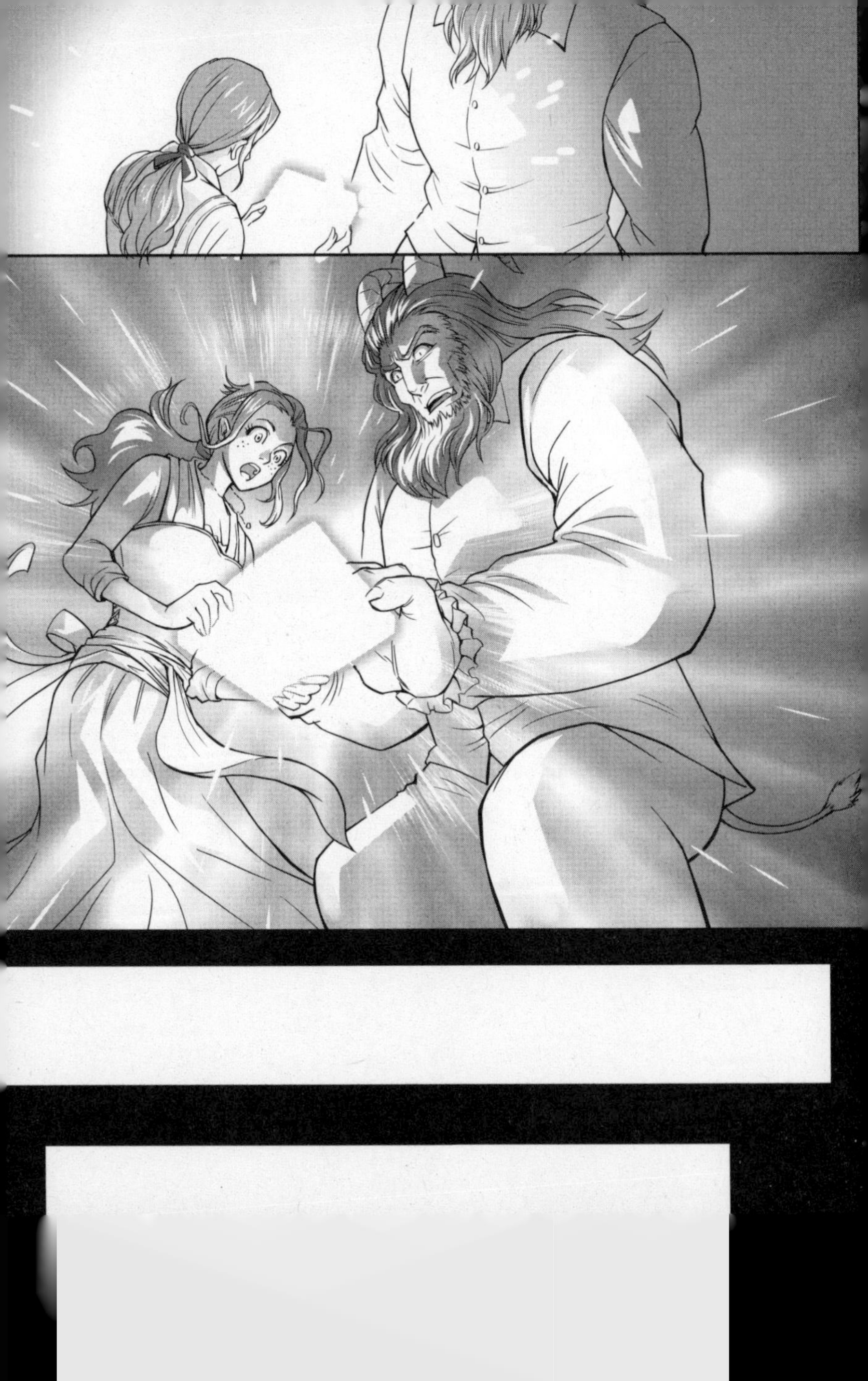

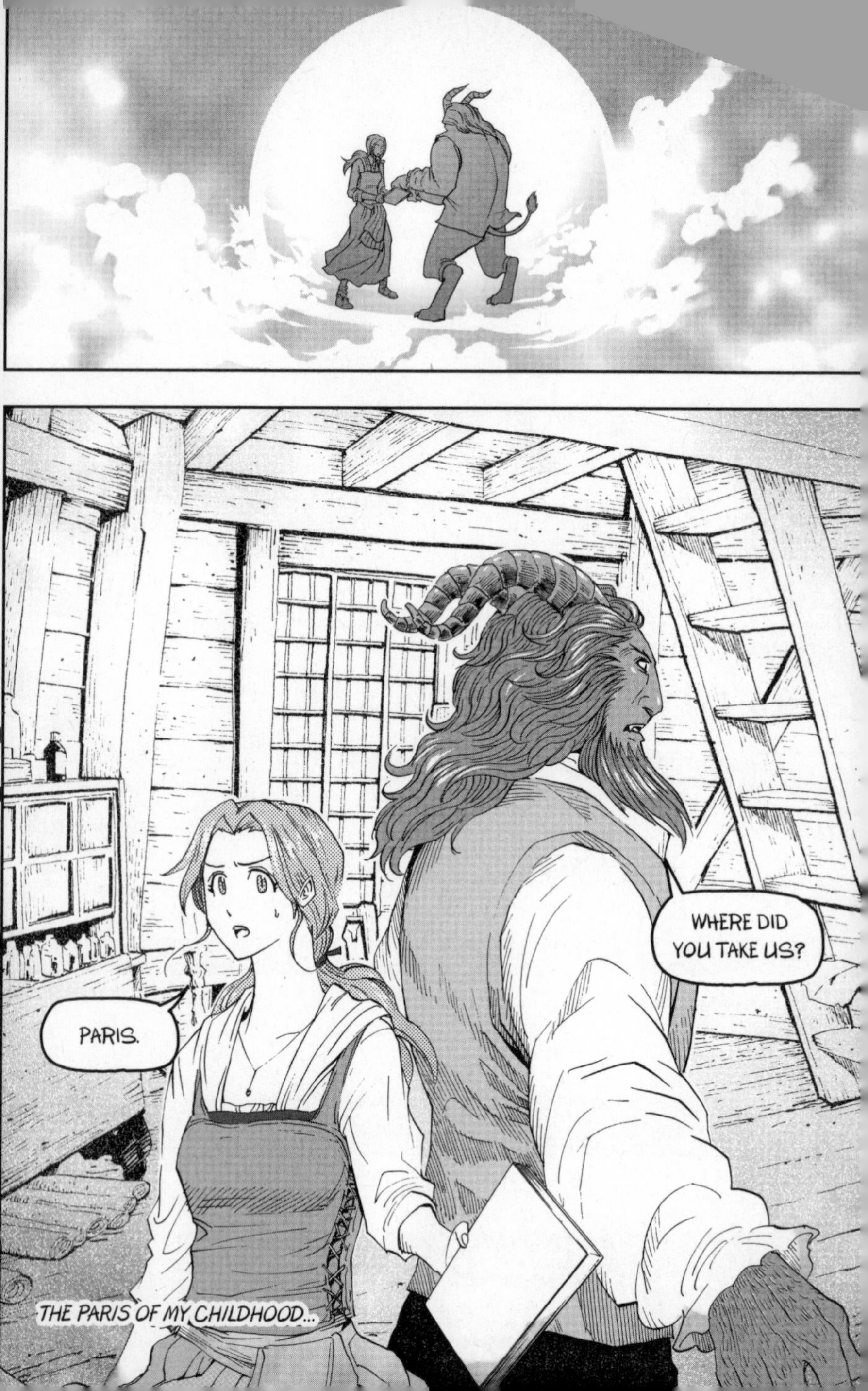
WHERE DID YOU TAKE US?
PARIS.
THE PARIS OF MY CHILDHOOD...

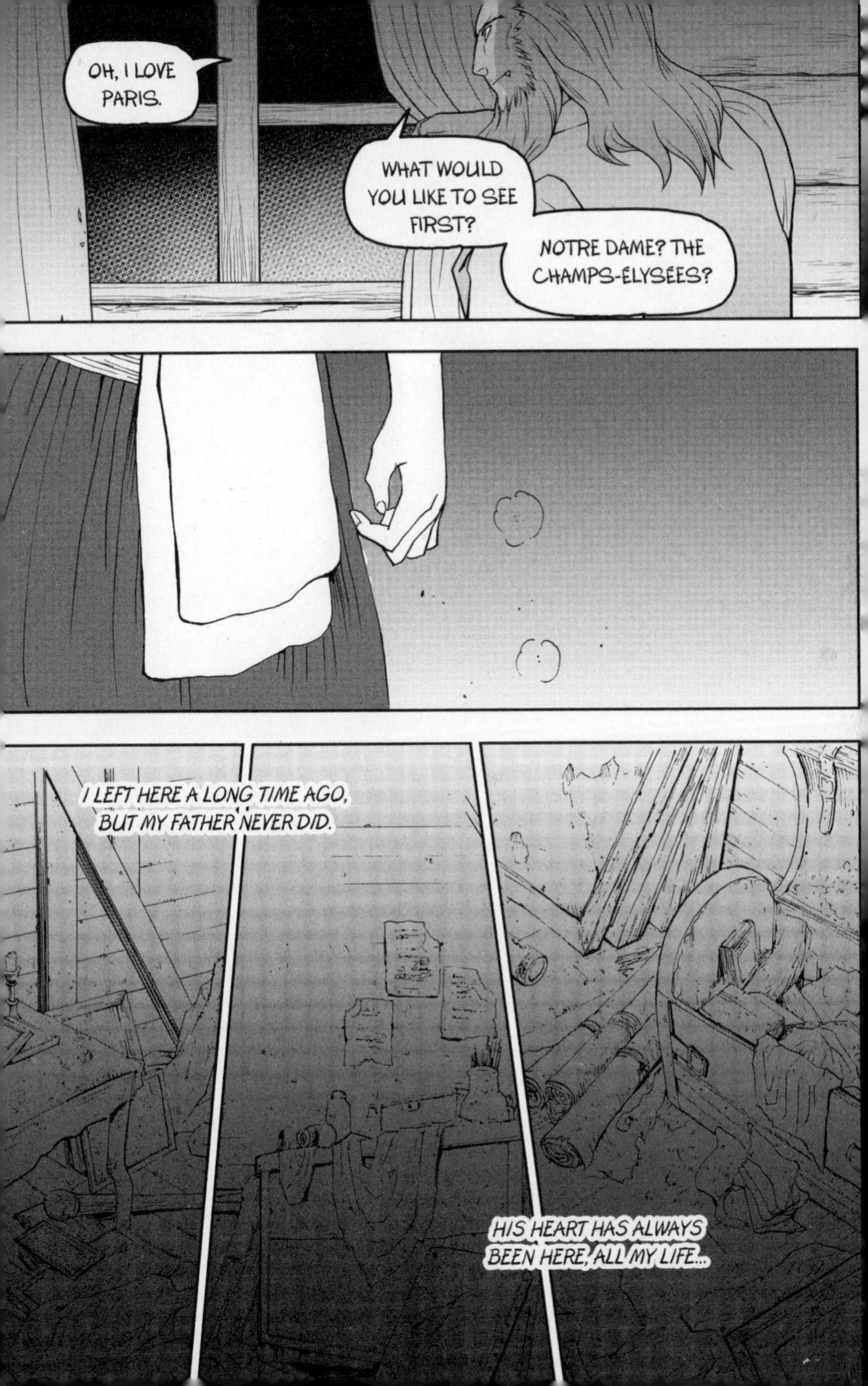
OH, I LOVE PARIS.
WHAT WOULD YOU LIKE TO SEE FIRST?
NOTRE DAME? THE CHAMPS-ELYSEES?
I LEFT HERE A LONG TIME AGO, BUT MY FATHER NEVER DID.
HIS HEART HAS ALWAYS BEEN HERE, ALL MY LIFE...

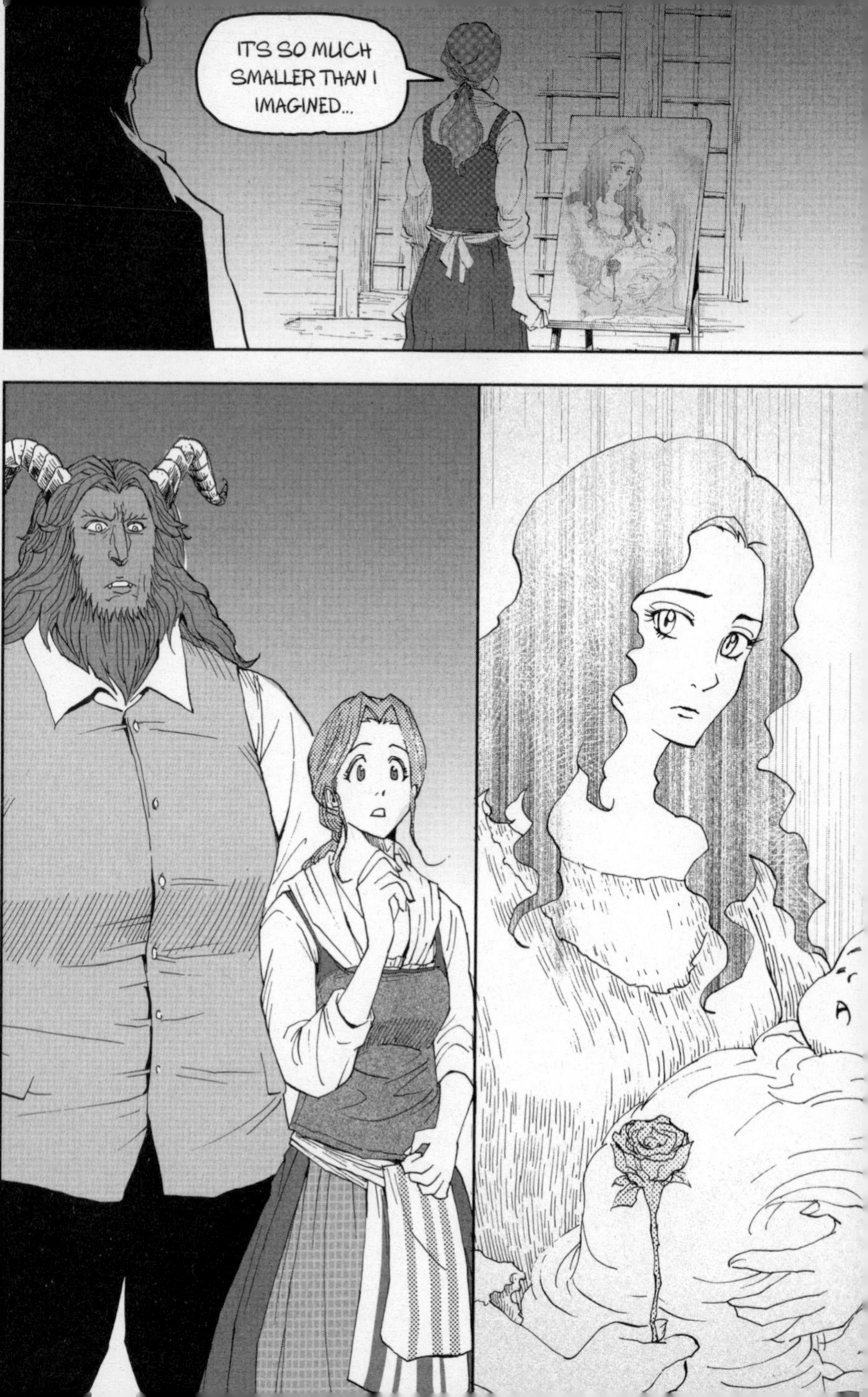
ITS SO MUCH SMALLER THAN I IMAGINED...

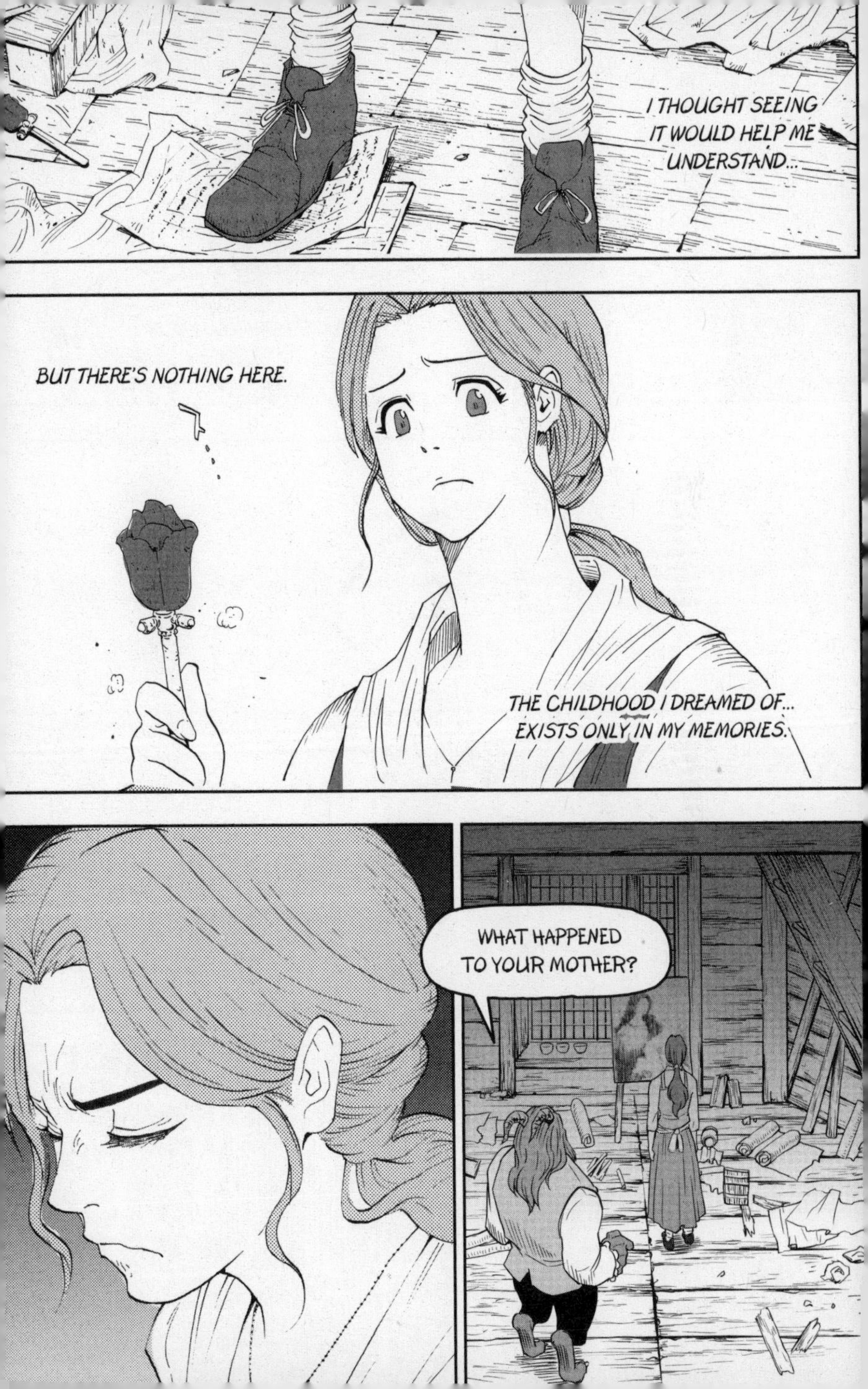
I THOUGHT SEEING IT WOULD HELP ME UNDERSTAND...
BUT THERE'S NOTHING HERE.
THE CHILDHOOD I DREAMED OF... EXISTS ONLY IN MY MEMORIES.
WHAT HAPPENED TO YOUR MOTHER?

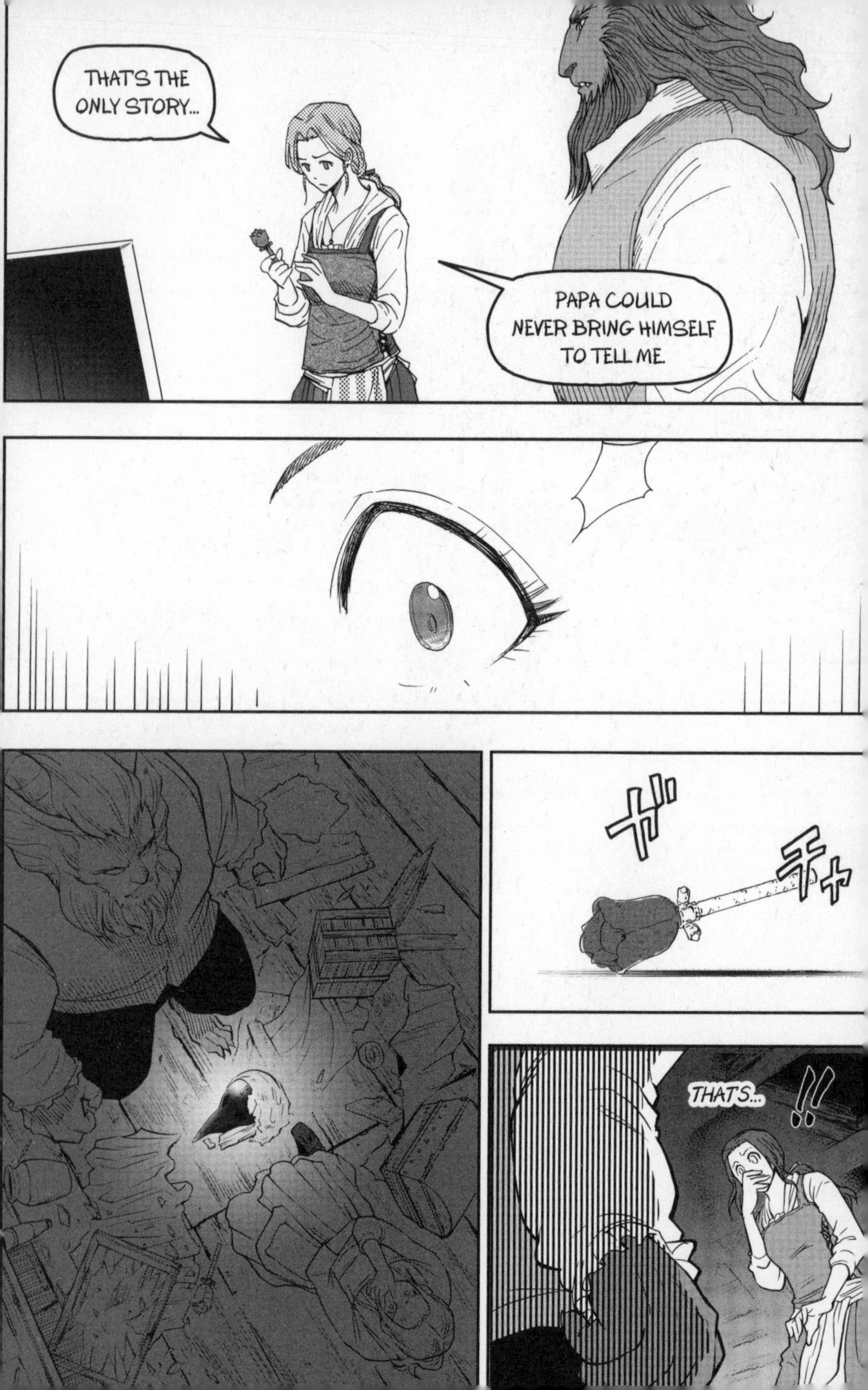
PAPA COULD NEVER BRING HIMSELF TO TELL ME.
THAT'S THE ONLY STORY...
ガ
チャ
THAT'S... !!

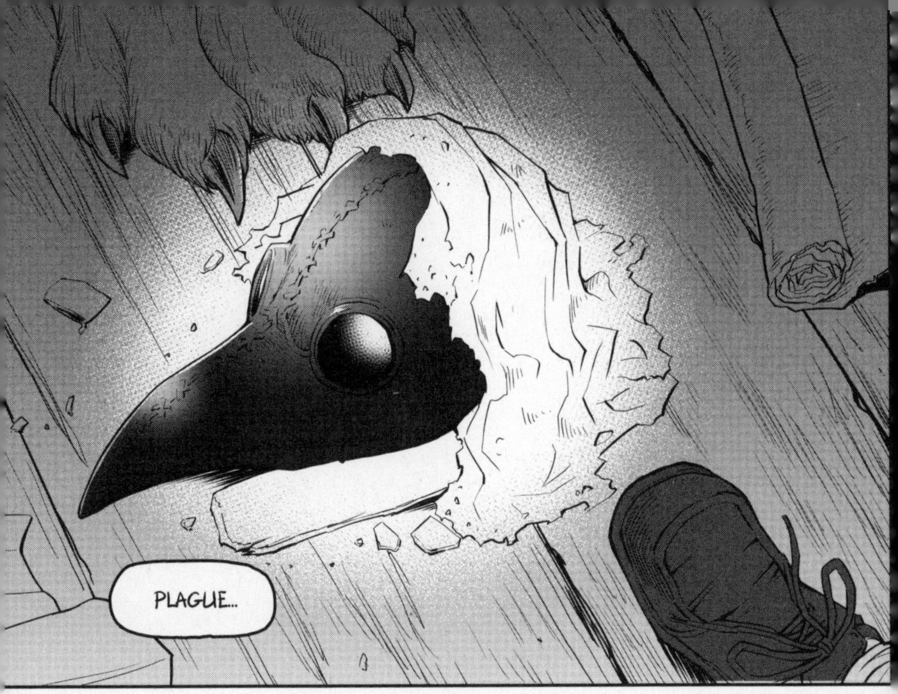
PLAGUE...

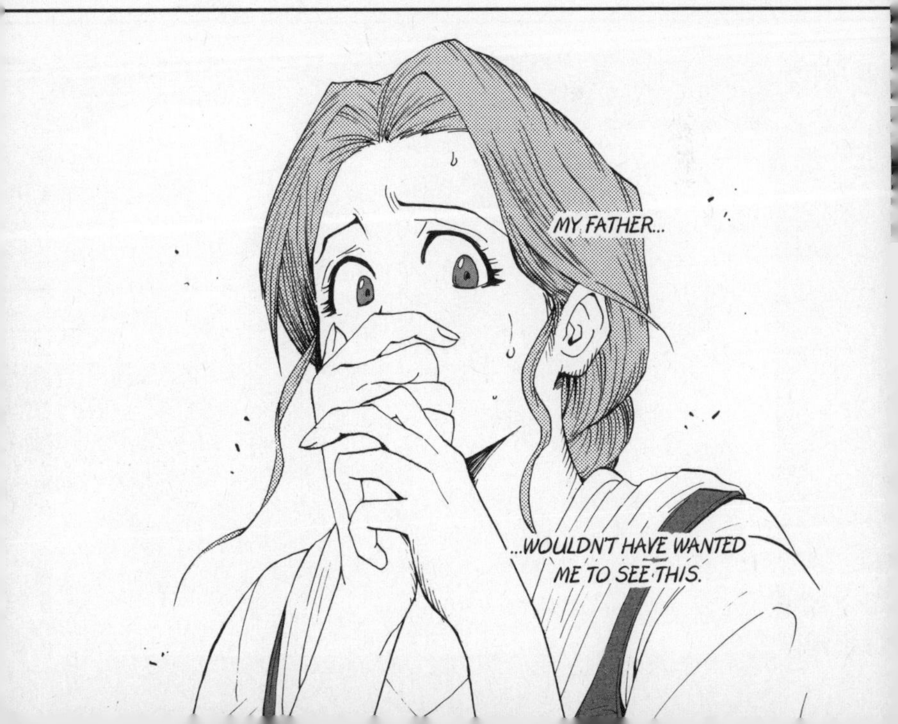
MY FATHER...
...WOULDN'T HAVE WANTED ME TO SEE THIS.

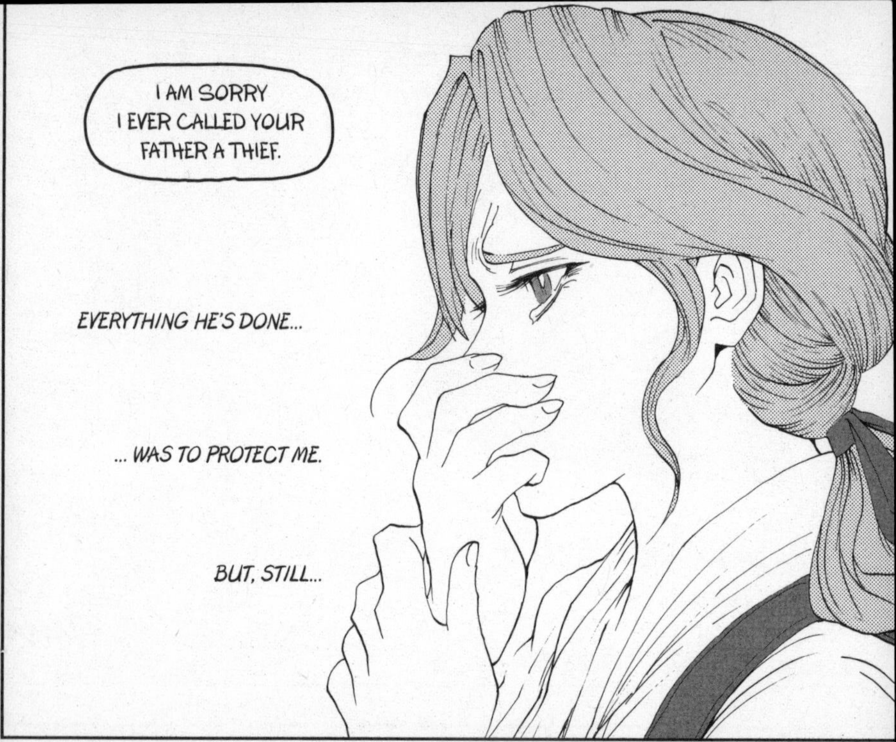
I AM SORRY I EVER CALLED YOUR FATHER A THIEF.
EVERYTHING HE'S DONE...
... WAS TO PROTECT ME.
BUT, STILL...

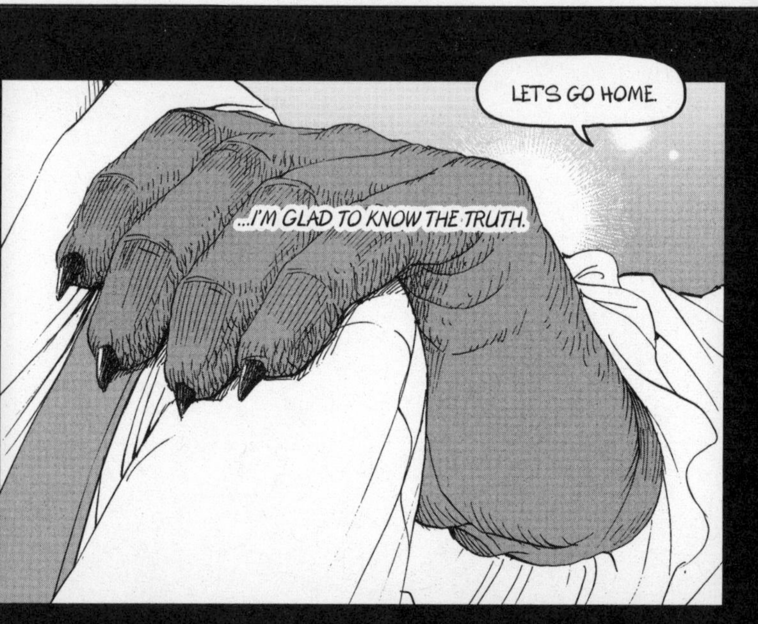
LET'S GO HOME.
...I'M GLAD TO KNOW THE TRUTH.

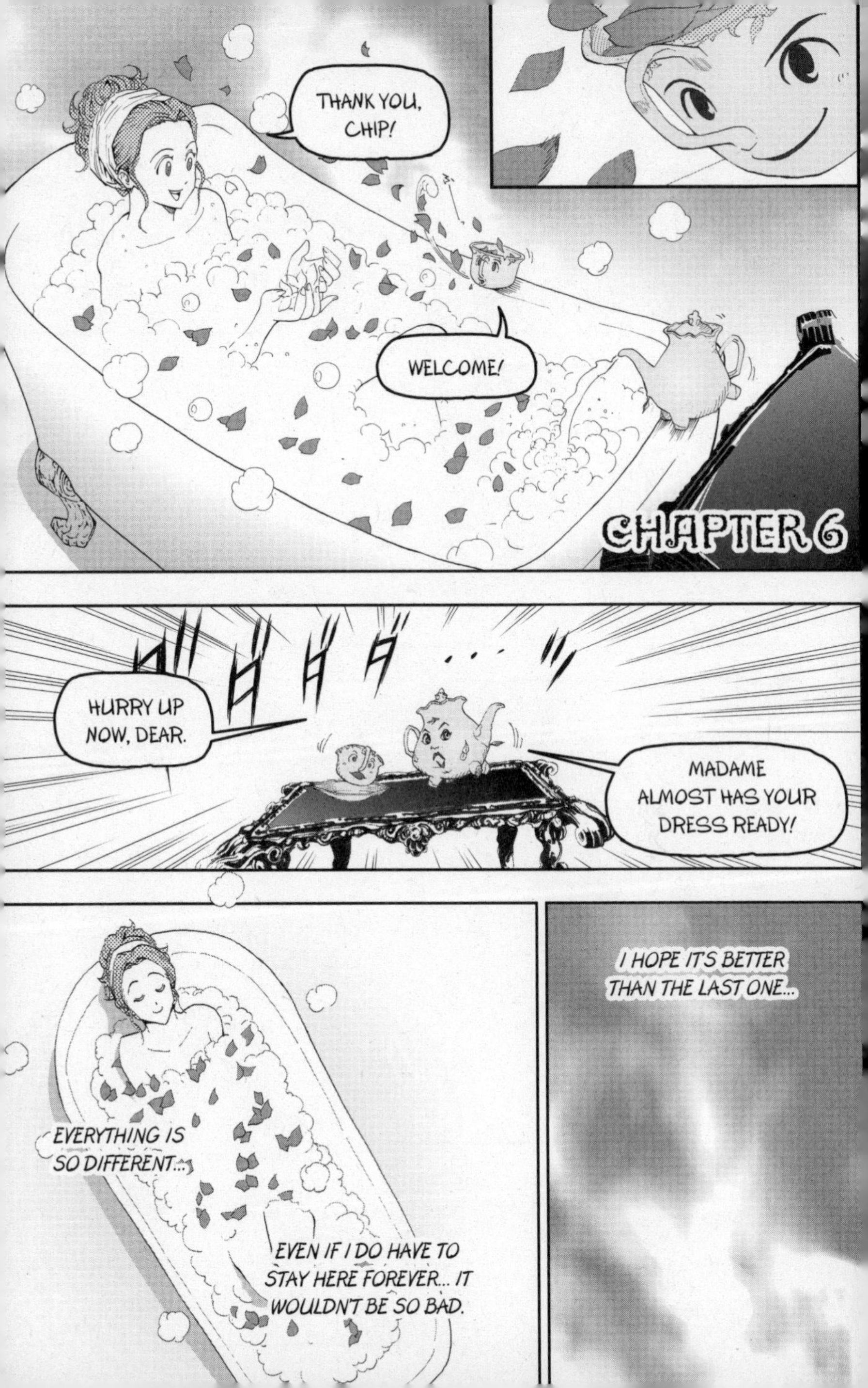
THANK YOU, CHIP!
WELCOME!
CHAPTER 6
HURRY UP NOW, DEAR.
MADAME ALMOST HAS YOUR DRESS READY!
I HOPE IT'S BETTER THAN THE LAST ONE...
EVERYTHING IS SO DIFFERENT...
EVEN IF I DO HAVE TO STAY HERE FOREVER... IT WOULDN'T BE SO BAD.

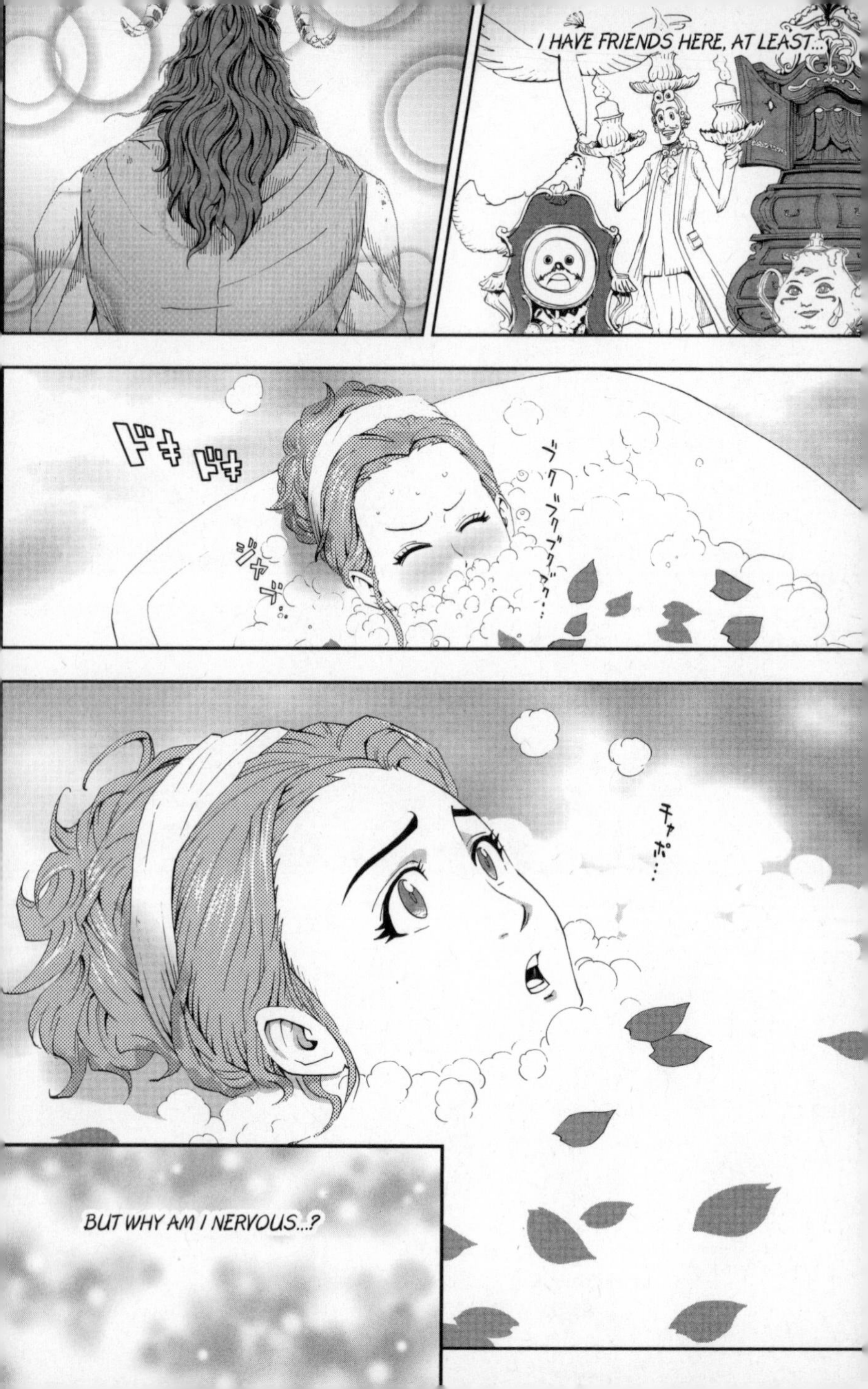
I HAVE FRIENDS HERE, AT LEAST...
ブクブクブクブク…
ドキドキ
ジャブ…
チャポ…
BUT WHY AM I NERVOUS...?

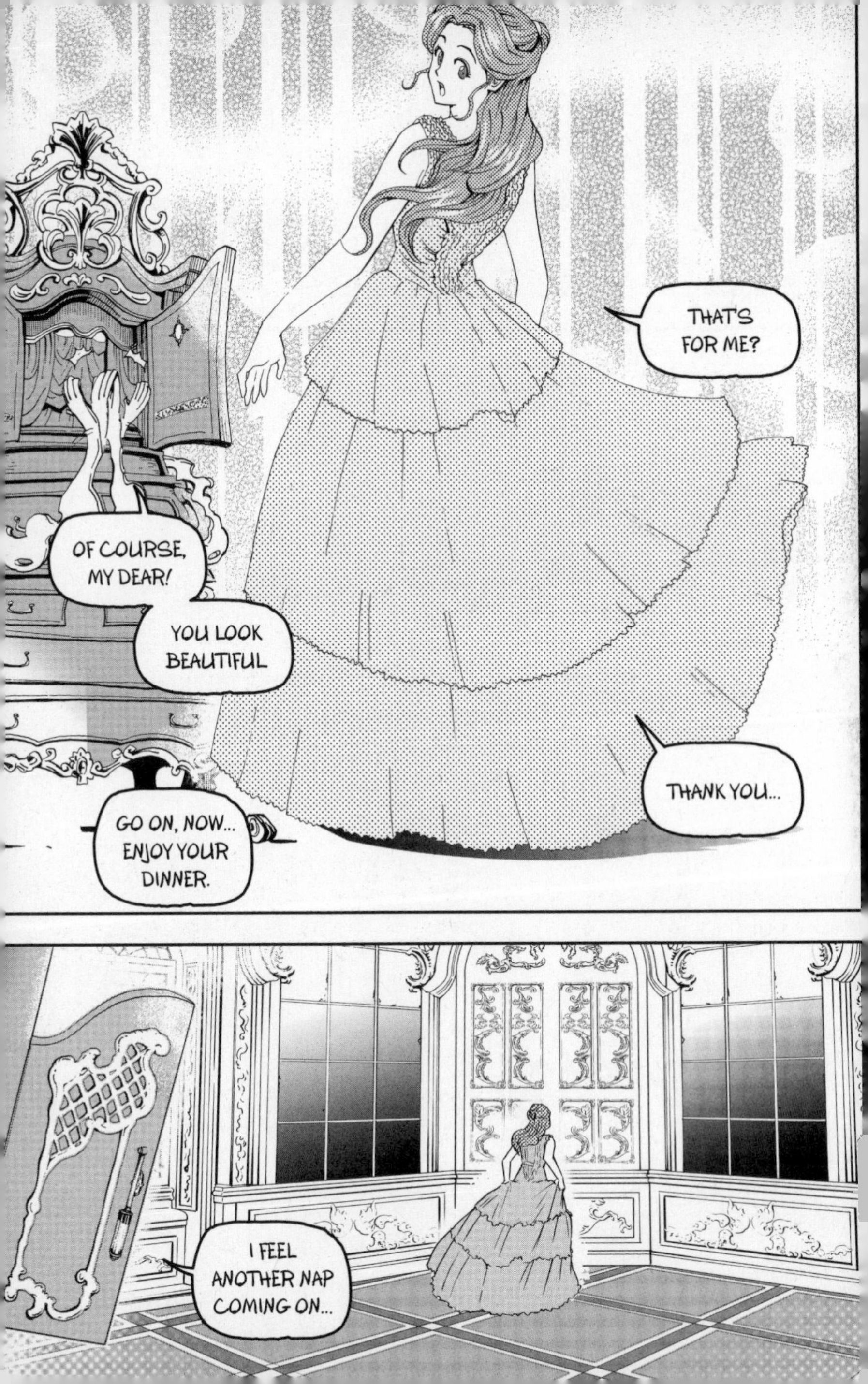
THAT'S FOR ME?
OF COURSE, MY DEAR!
YOU LOOK BEAUTIFUL
THANK YOU...
GO ON, NOW... ENJOY YOUR DINNER.
I FEEL ANOTHER NAP COMING ON...

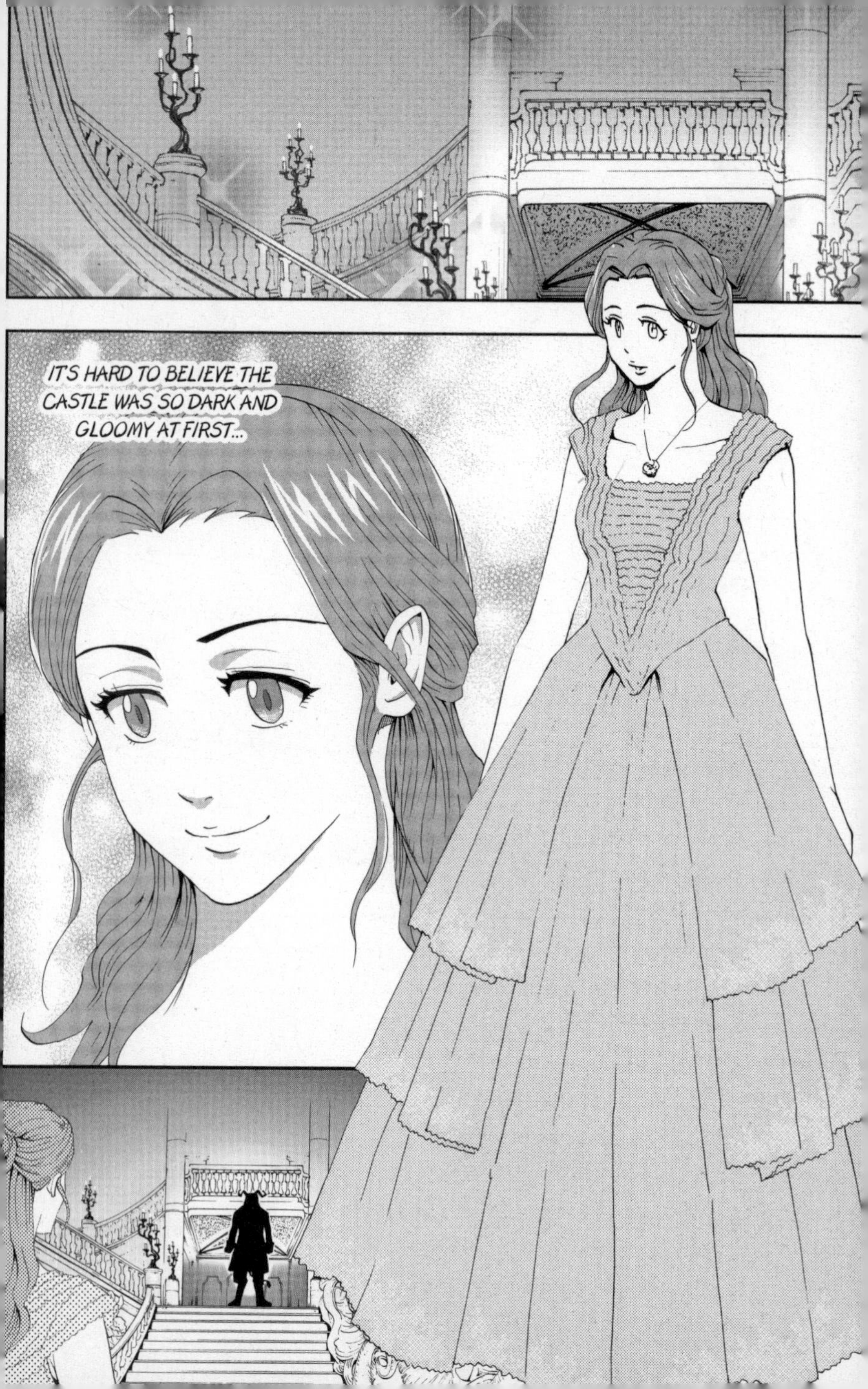
IT'S HARD TO BELIEVE THE CASTLE WAS SO DARK AND GLOOMY AT FIRST...

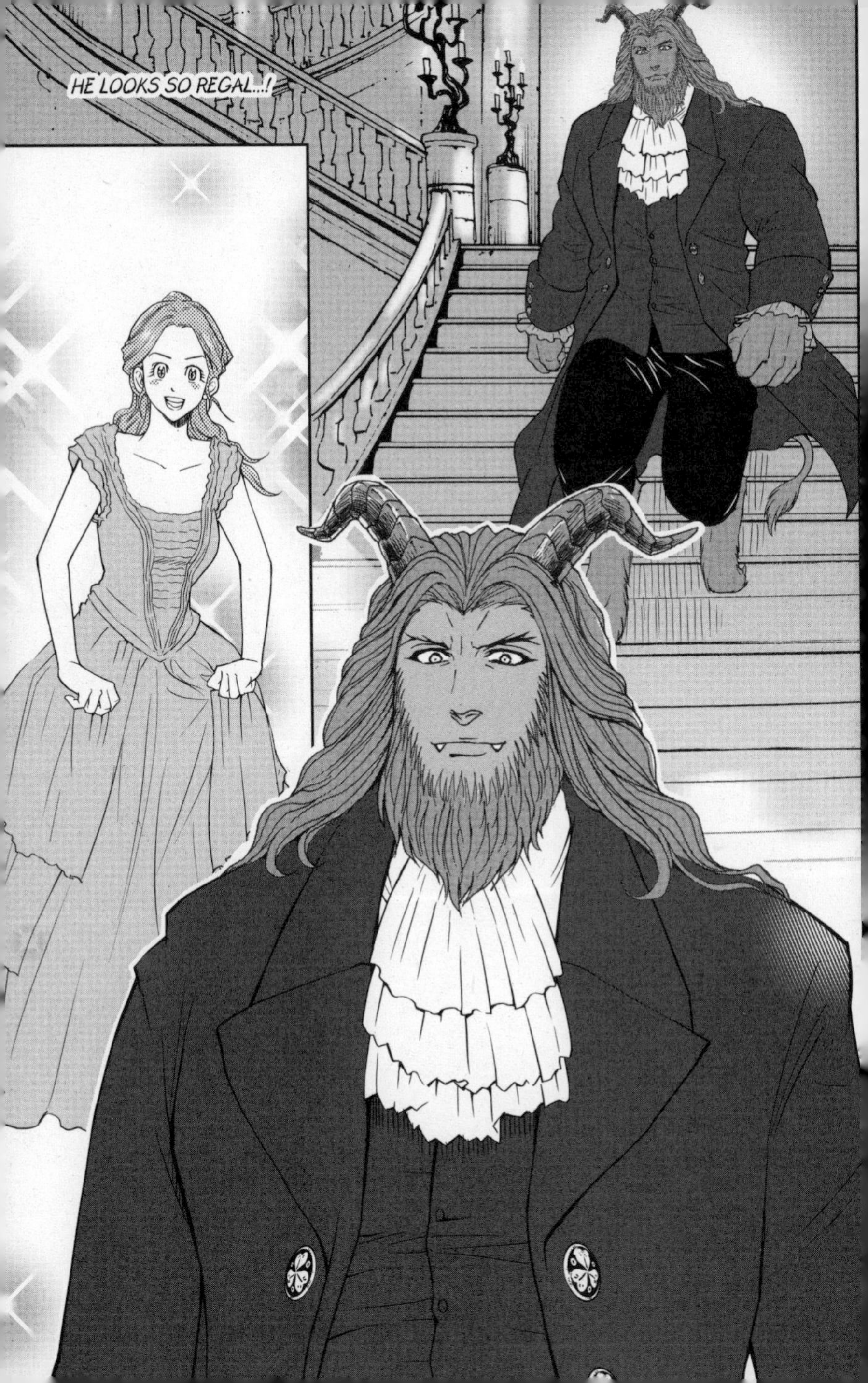
HE LOOKS SO REGAL...!

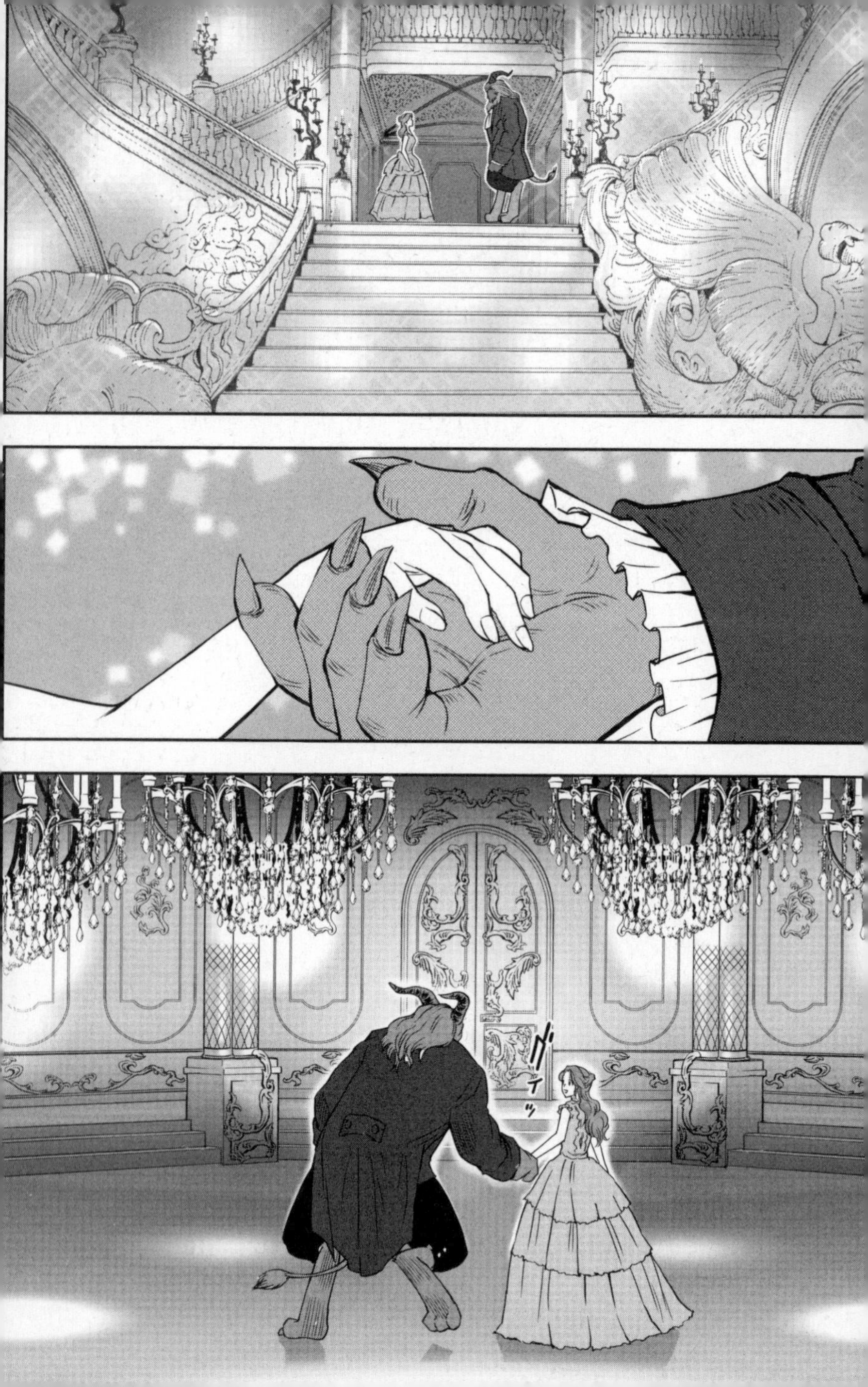
ギィッ

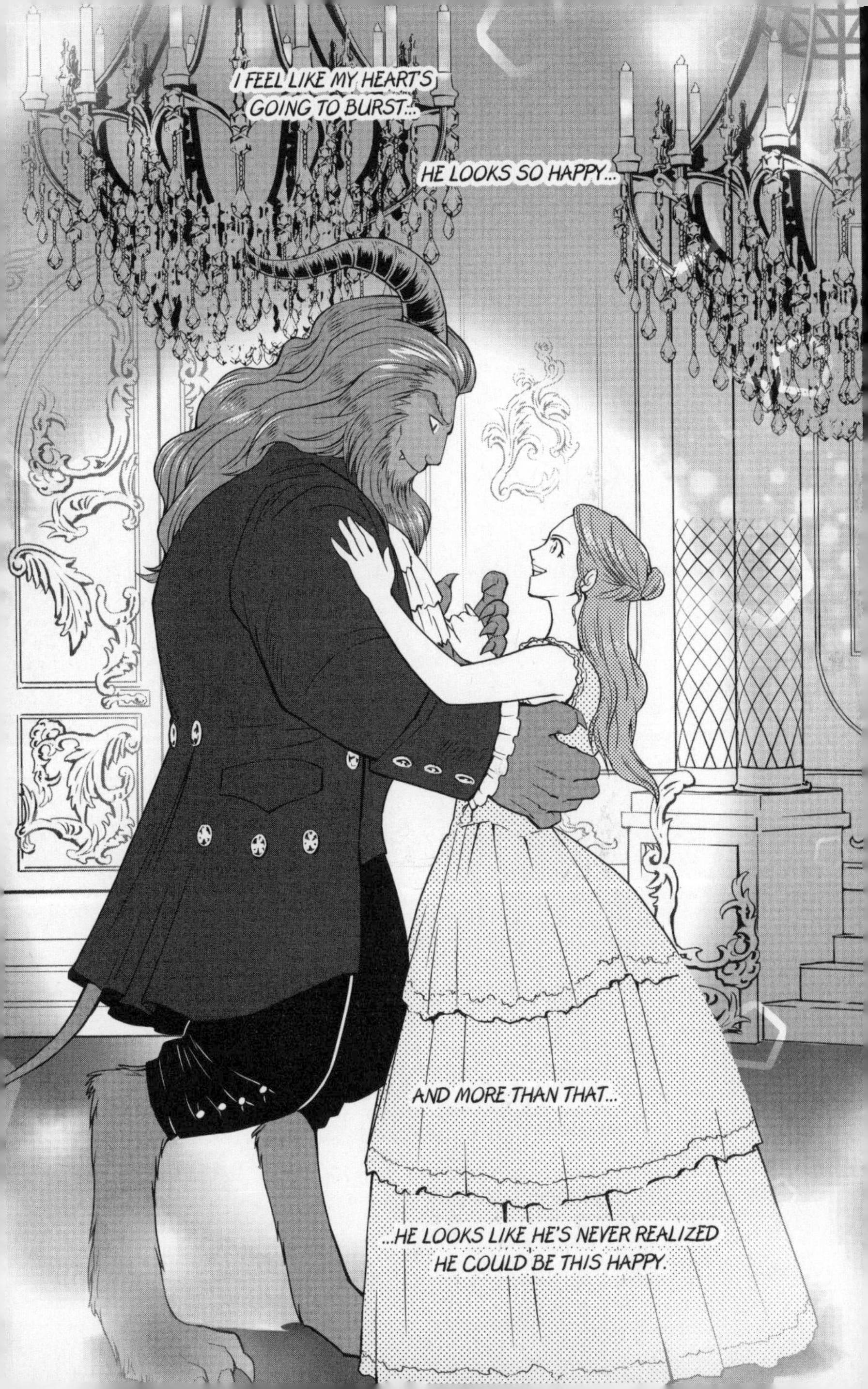
I FEEL LIKE MY HEART'S GOING TO BURST...
HE LOOKS SO HAPPY...
AND MORE THAN THAT...
...HE LOOKS LIKE HE'S NEVER REALIZED HE COULD BE THIS HAPPY.

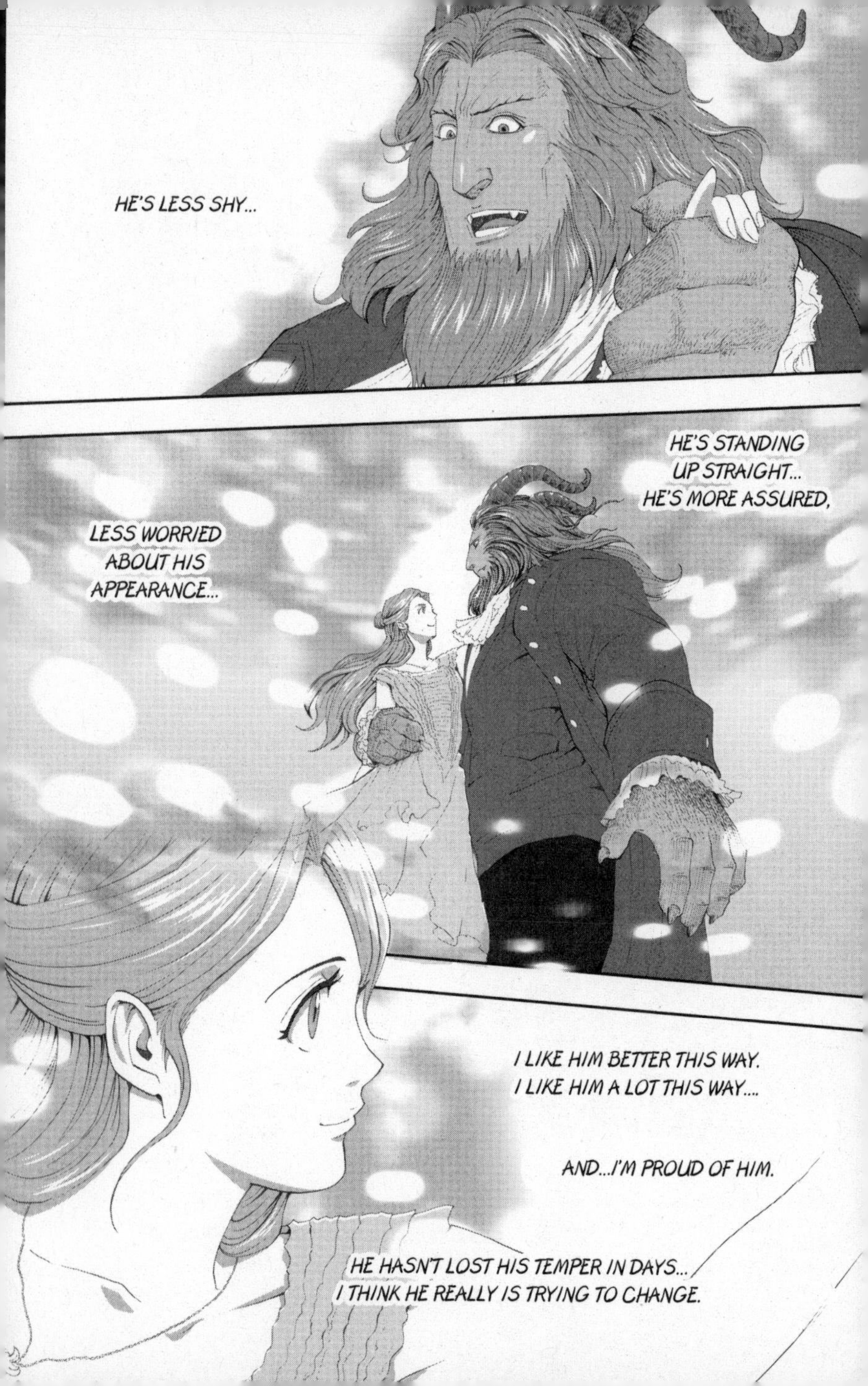
HE'S LESS SHY...
HE'S STANDING UP STRAIGHT... HE'S MORE ASSURED,
LESS WORRIED ABOUT HIS APPEARANCE...
I LIKE HIM BETTER THIS WAY. I LIKE HIM A LOT THIS WAY....
AND...I'M PROUD OF HIM.
HE HASN'T LOST HIS TEMPER IN DAYS... I THINK HE REALLY IS TRYING TO CHANGE.

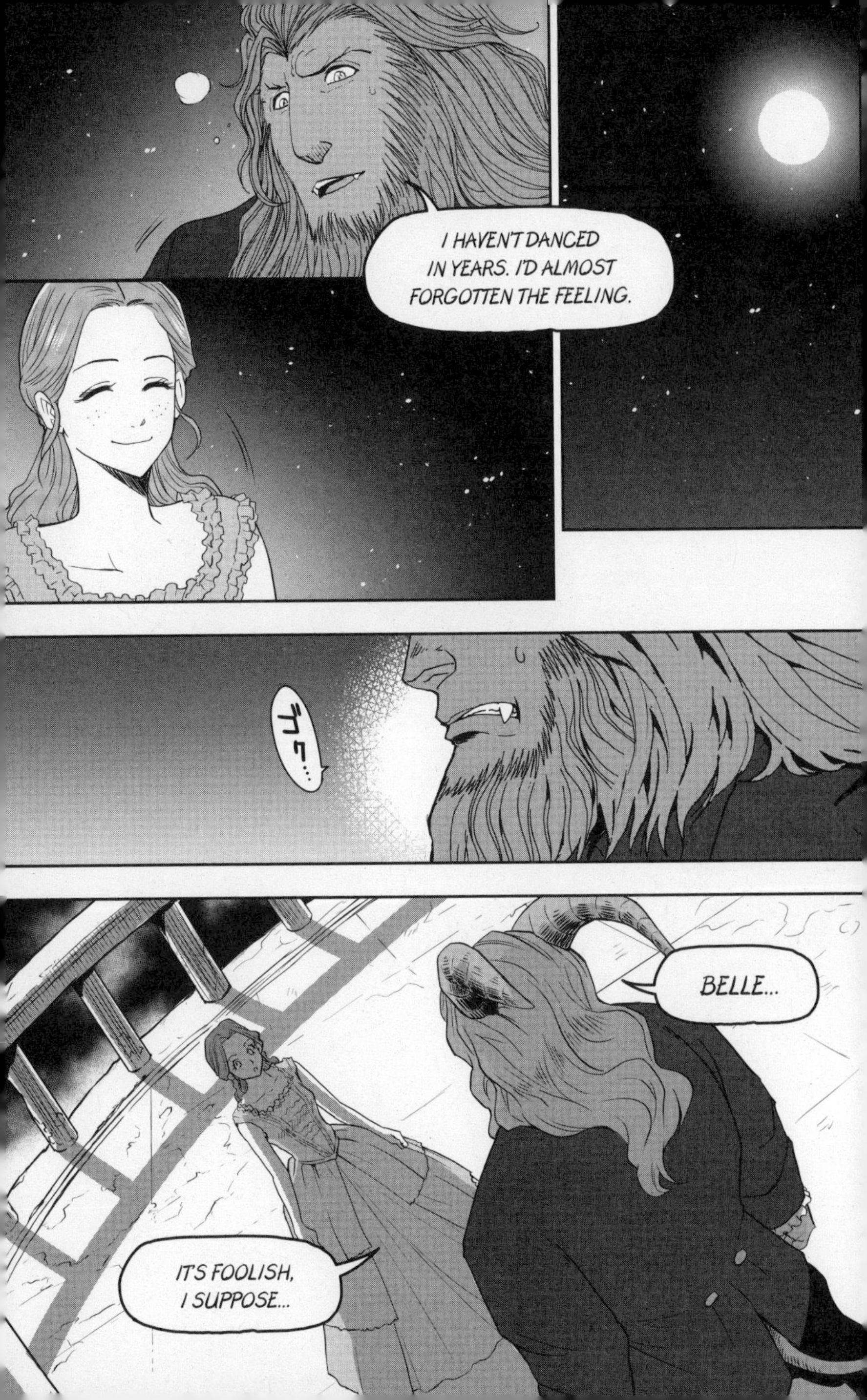
I HAVEN'T DANCED IN YEARS. I'D ALMOST FORGOTTEN THE FEELING.
ゴク…
BELLE...
IT'S FOOLISH, I SUPPOSE...

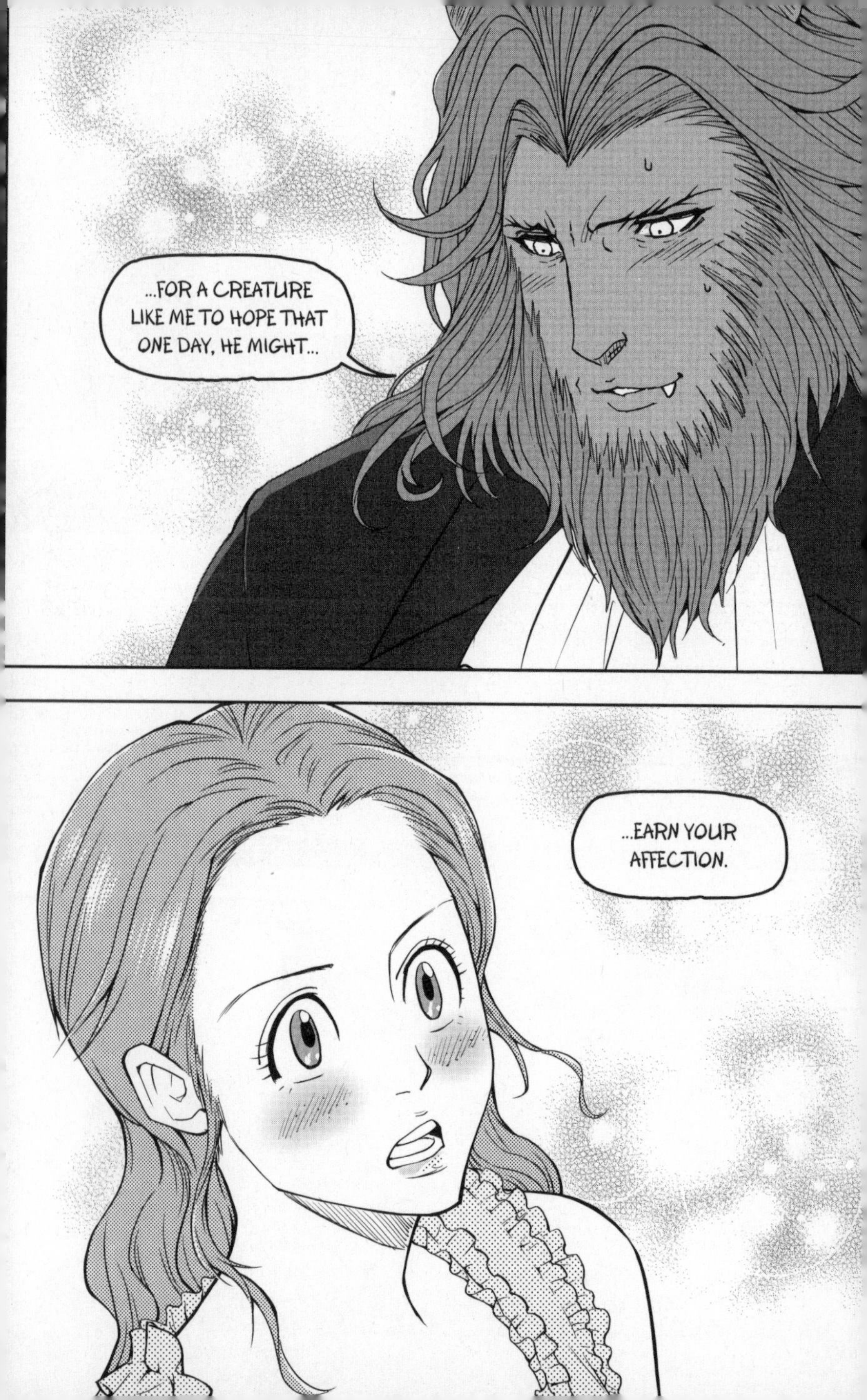
...FOR A CREATURE LIKE ME TO HOPE THAT ONE DAY, HE MIGHT...
...EARN YOUR AFFECTION.

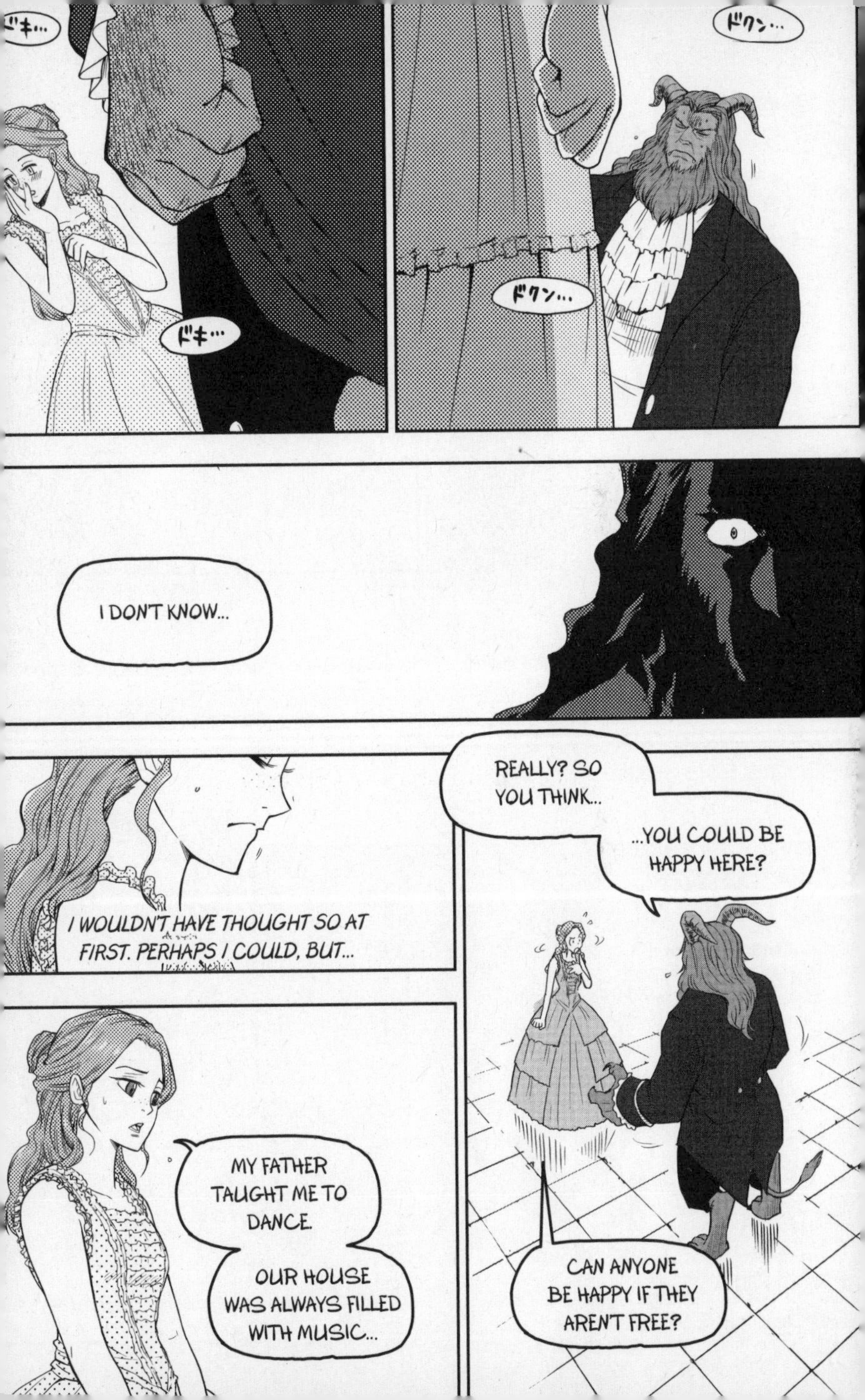
ドクン…
ドクン…
ドキ…
ドキ…
I DON'T KNOW...
REALLY? SO YOU THINK...
...YOU COULD BE HAPPY HERE?
CAN ANYONE BE HAPPY IF THEY AREN'T FREE?
I WOULDN'T HAVE THOUGHT SO AT FIRST. PERHAPS I COULD, BUT...
MY FATHER TAUGHT ME TO DANCE.
OUR HOUSE WAS ALWAYS FILLED WITH MUSIC...

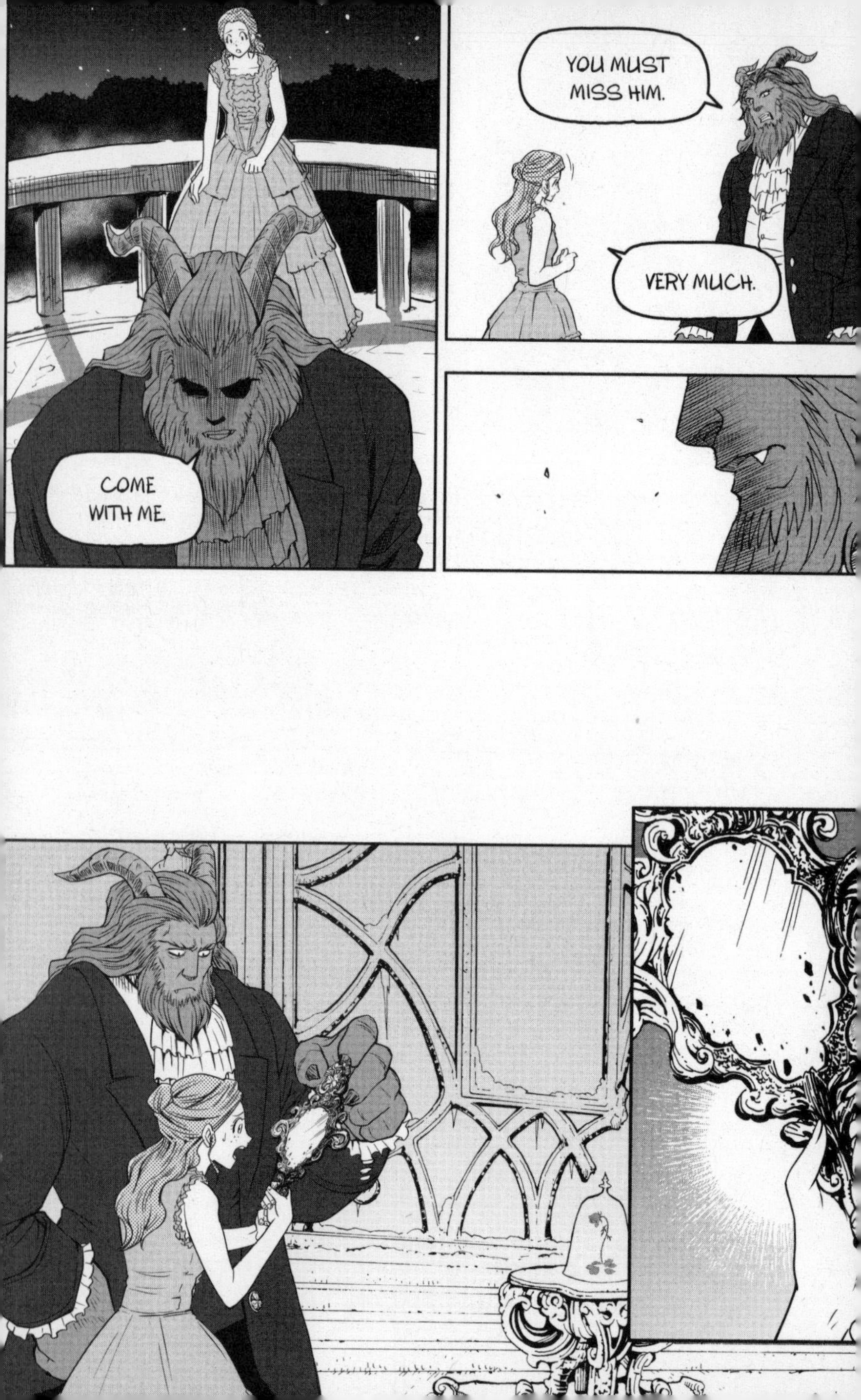
YOU MUST MISS HIM.
VERY MUCH.
COME WITH ME.

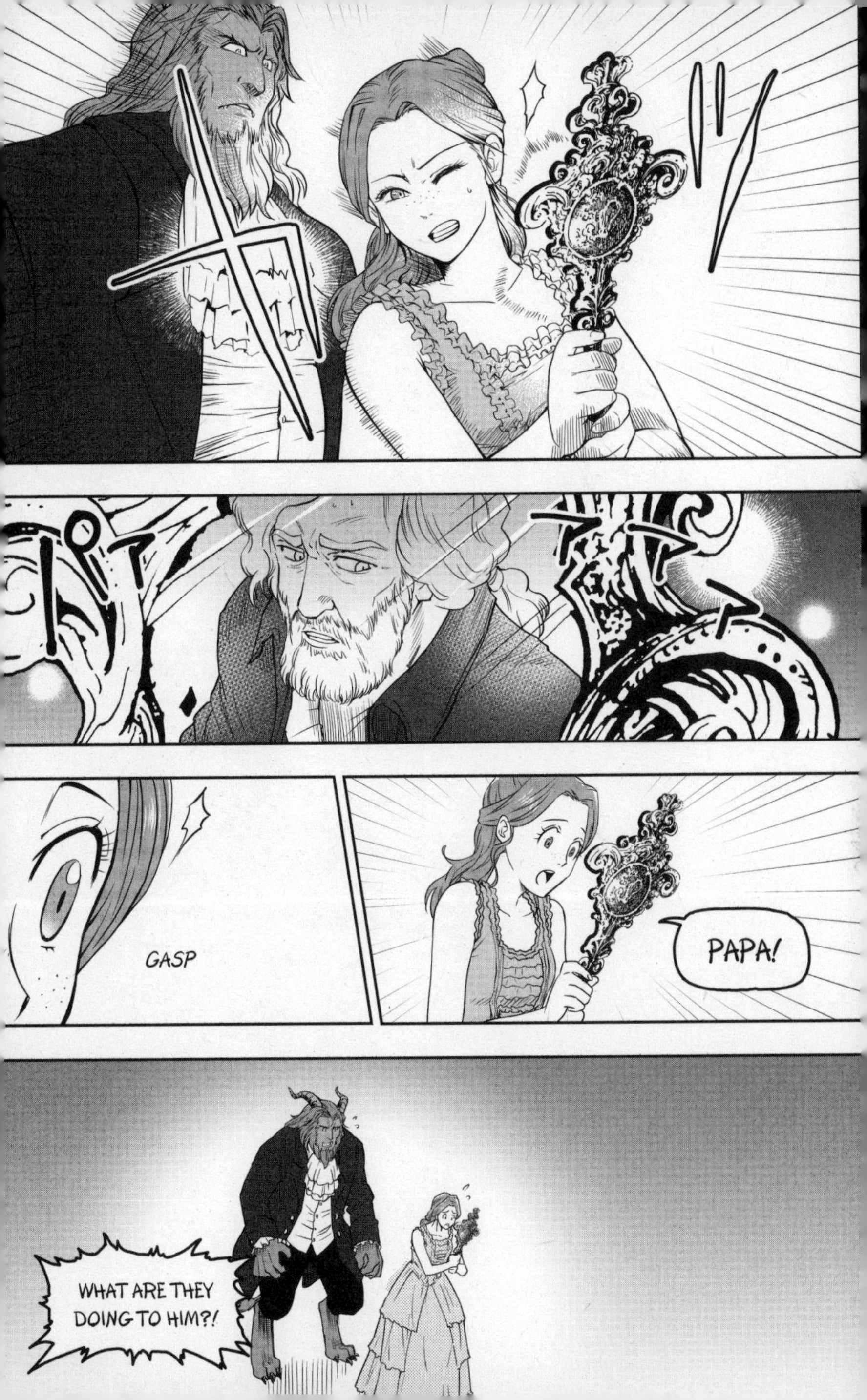
PAPA!
GASP
WHAT ARE THEY DOING TO HIM?!

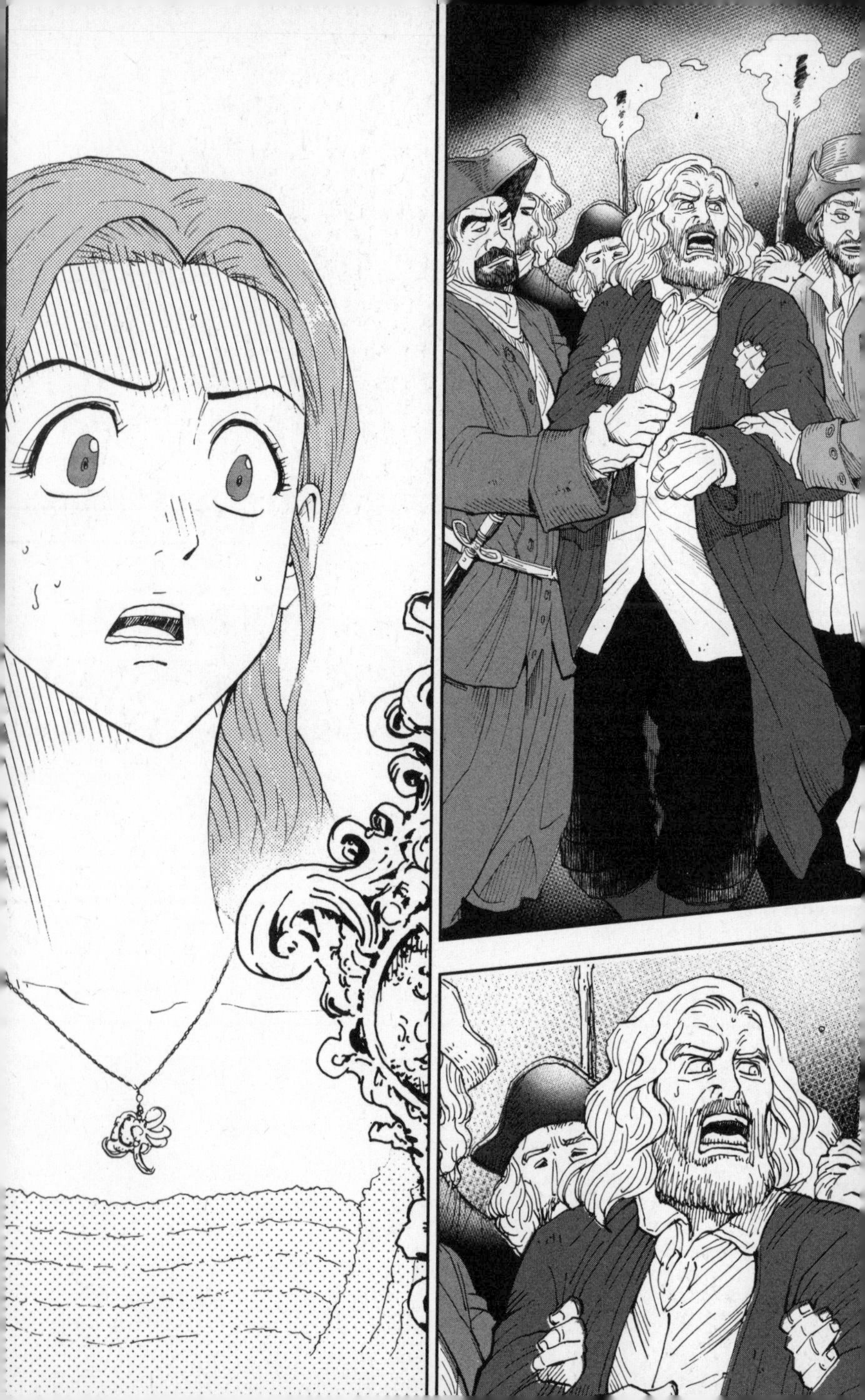

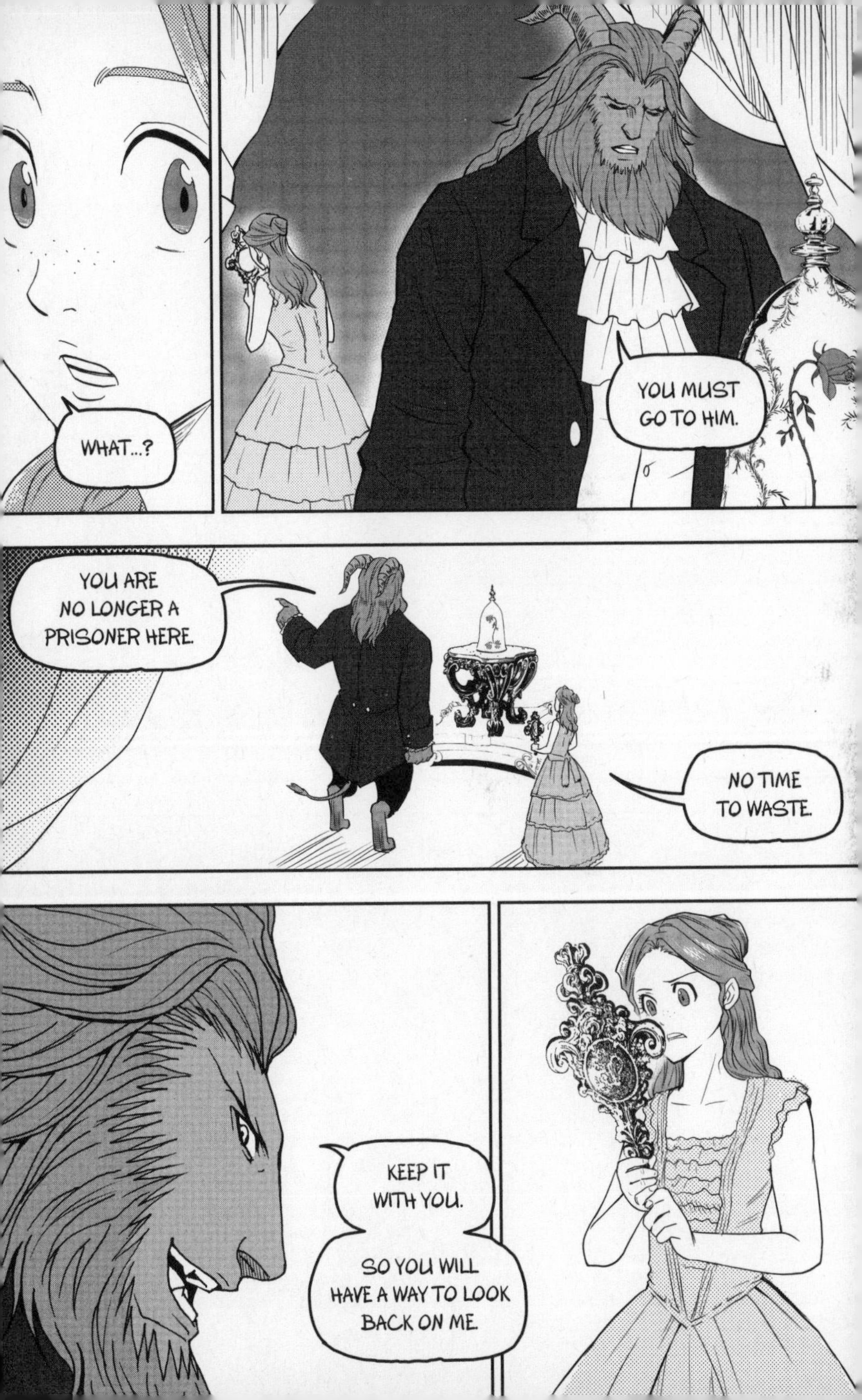
YOU MUST GO TO HIM.
WHAT...?
YOU ARE NO LONGER A PRISONER HERE.
NO TIME TO WASTE.
KEEP IT WITH YOU.
SO YOU WILL HAVE A WAY TO LOOK BACK ON ME.

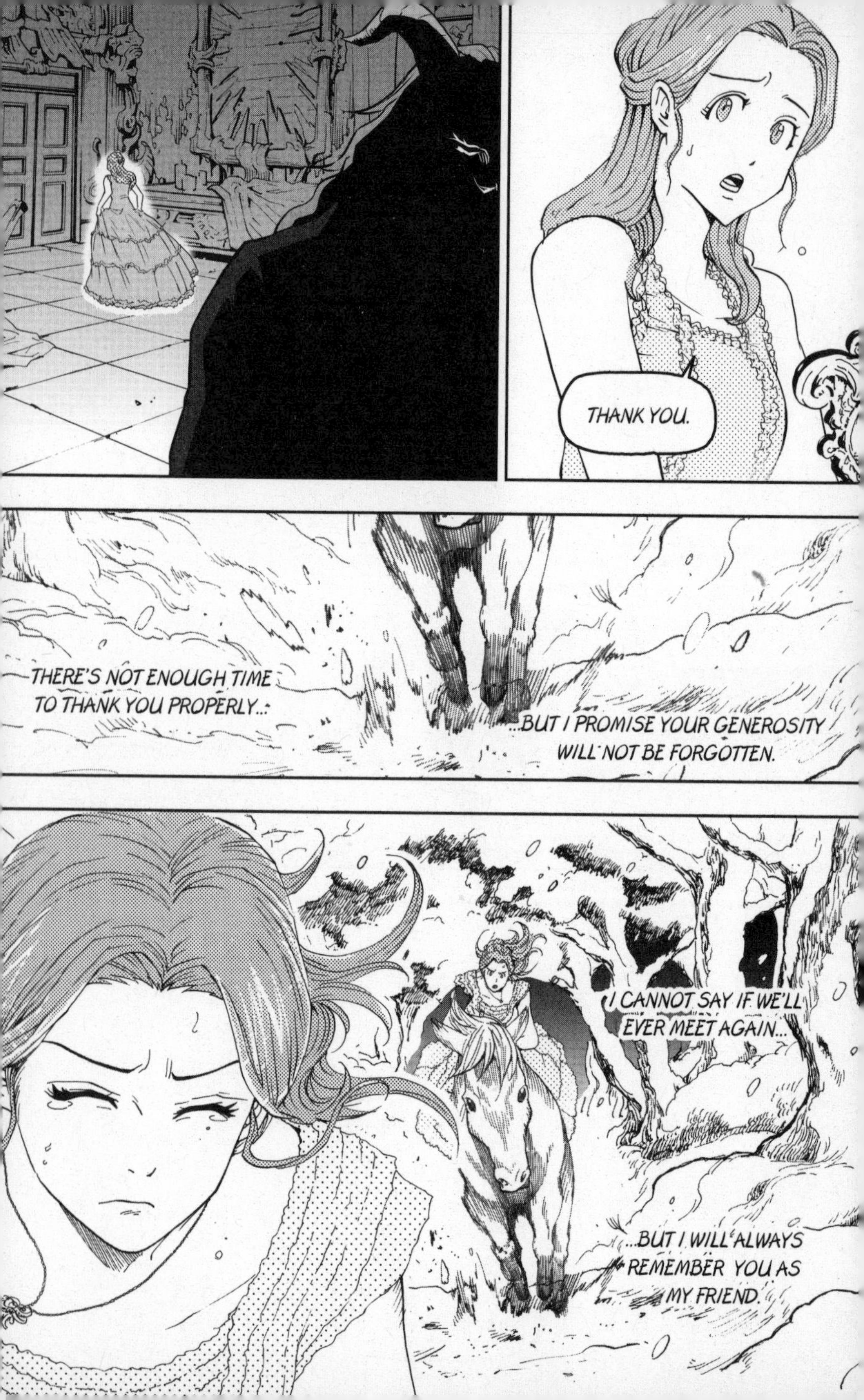
THANK YOU.
THERE'S NOT ENOUGH TIME TO THANK YOU PROPERLY...
...BUT I PROMISE YOUR GENEROSITY WILL NOT BE FORGOTTEN.
I CANNOT SAY IF WE'LL EVER MEET AGAIN...
...BUT I WILL ALWAYS REMEMBER YOU AS MY FRIEND.

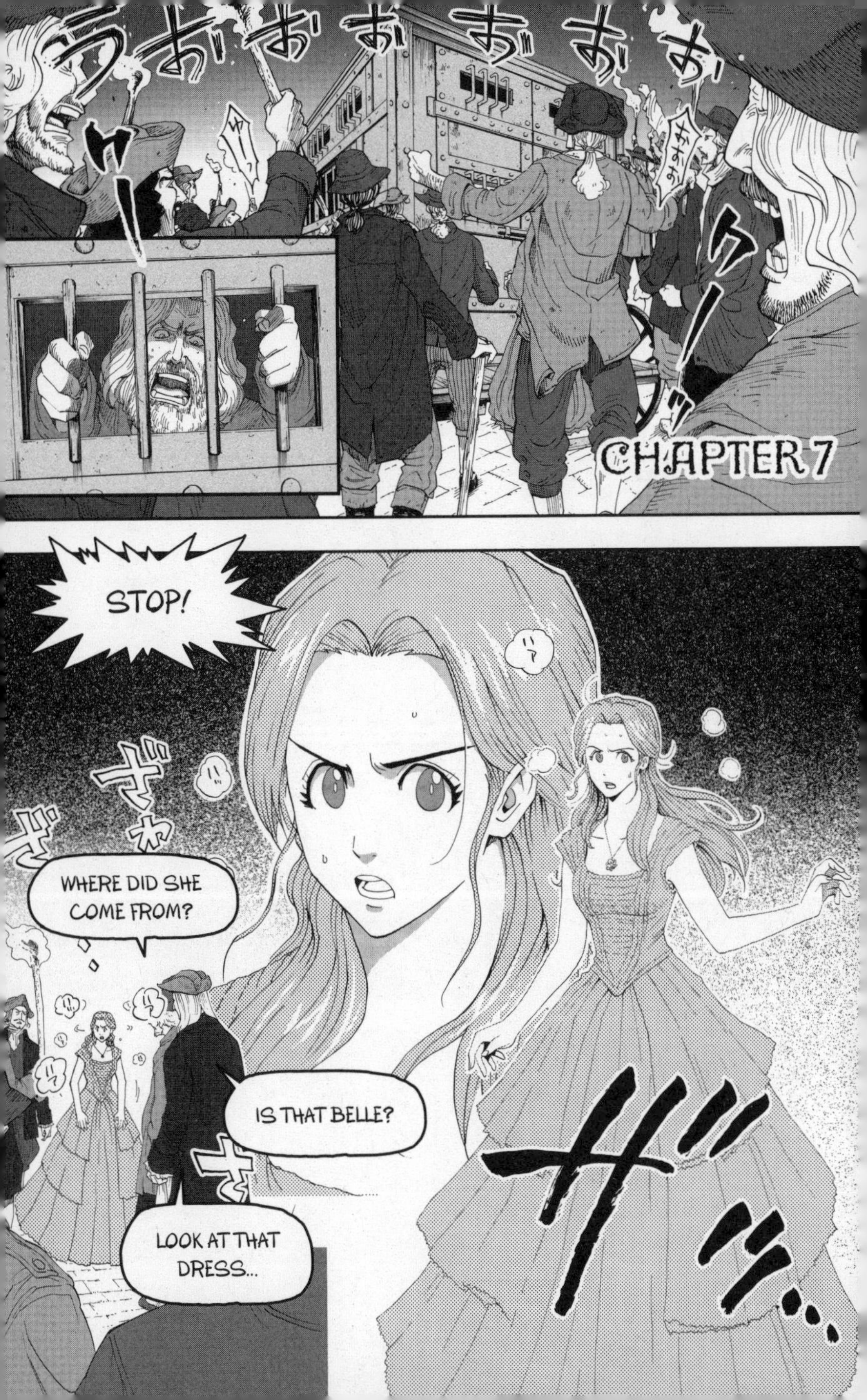
CHAPTER 7
STOP!
WHERE DID SHE COME FROM?
IS THAT BELLE?
LOOK AT THAT DRESS...

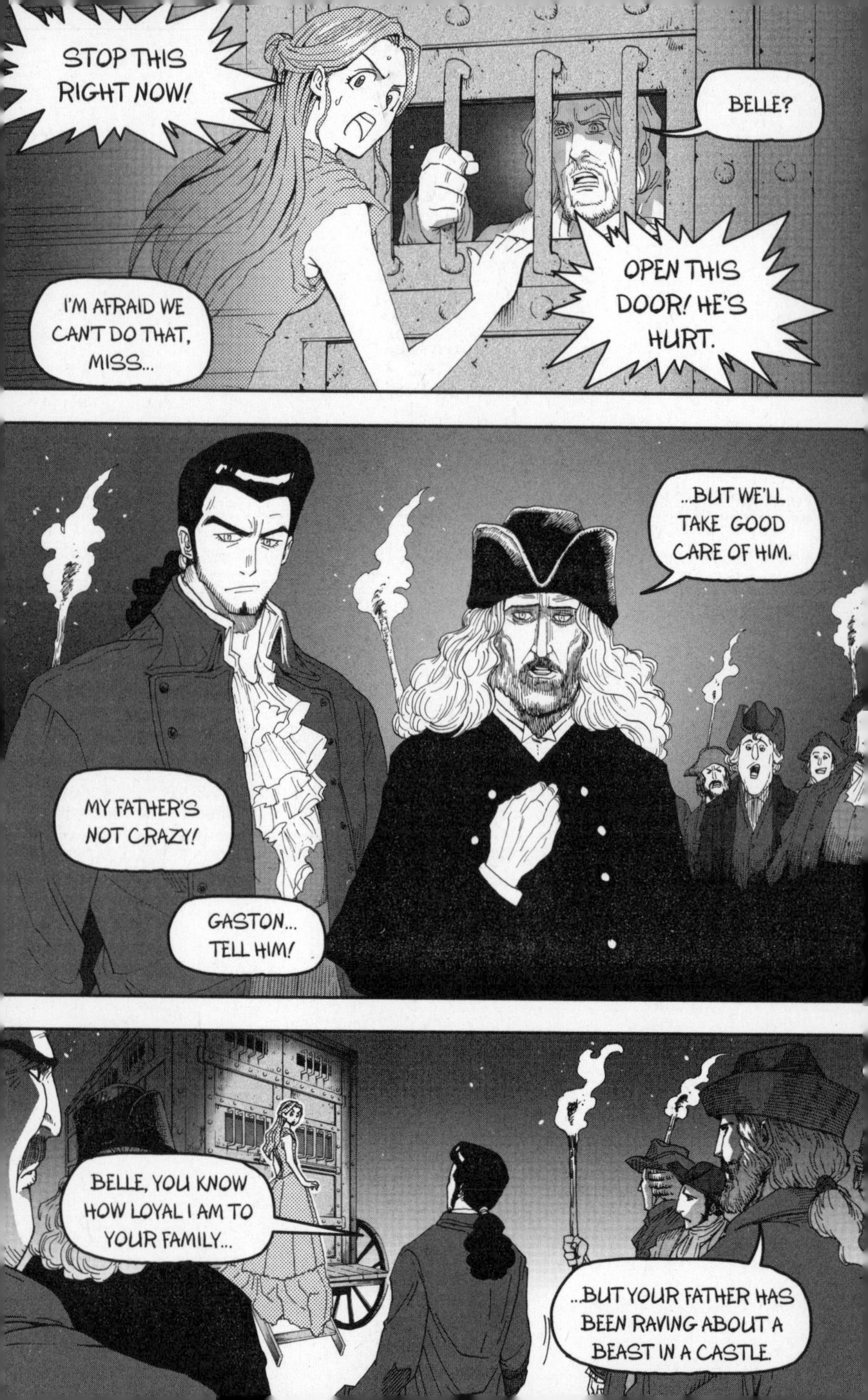
BELLE?
STOP THIS RIGHT NOW!
OPEN THIS DOOR! HE'S HURT.
I'M AFRAID WE CAN'T DO THAT, MISS...
...BUT WE'LL TAKE GOOD CARE OF HIM.
MY FATHER'S NOT CRAZY!
GASTON... TELL HIM!
BELLE, YOU KNOW HOW LOYAL I AM TO YOUR FAMILY...
...BUT YOUR FATHER HAS BEEN RAVING ABOUT A BEAST IN A CASTLE.

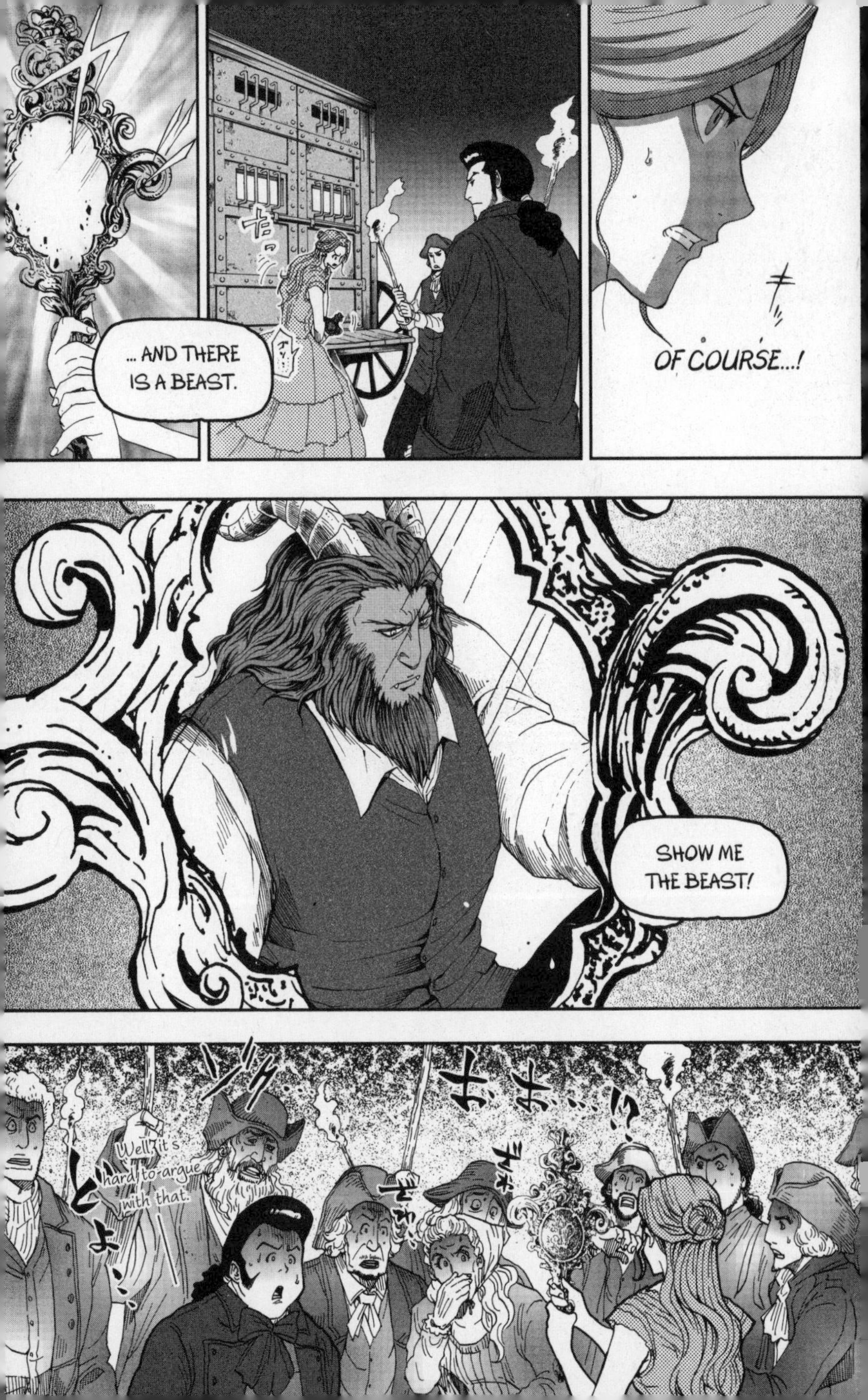
OF COURSE...!
... AND THERE IS A BEAST.
SHOW ME THE BEAST!
Well, it's hard to argue with that.

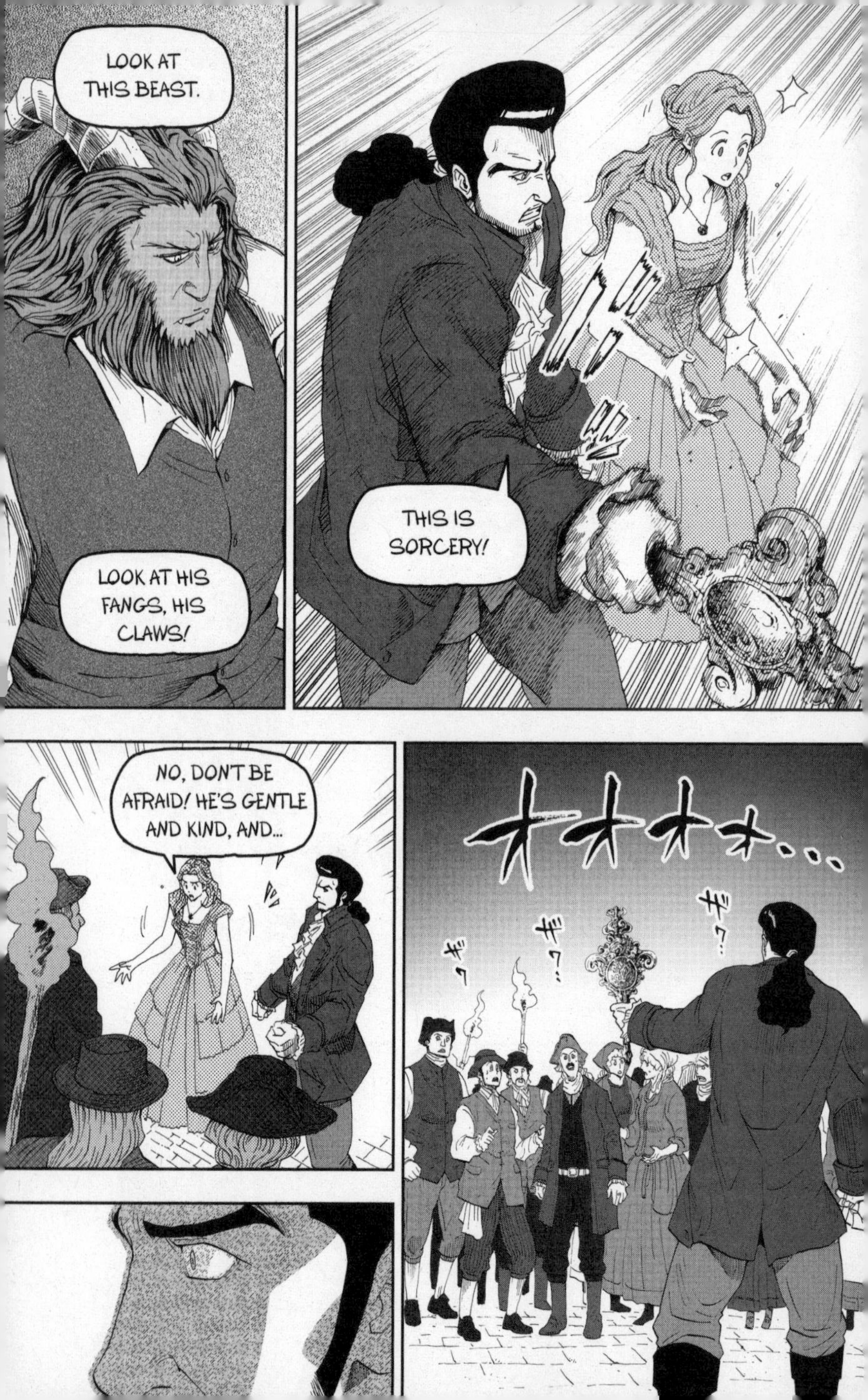

THIS IS SORCERY!
LOOK AT THIS BEAST.
LOOK AT HIS FANGS, HIS CLAWS!
オオオオ...
ザワ
ザワ
ザワ
NO, DON'T BE AFRAID! HE'S GENTLE AND KIND, AND...

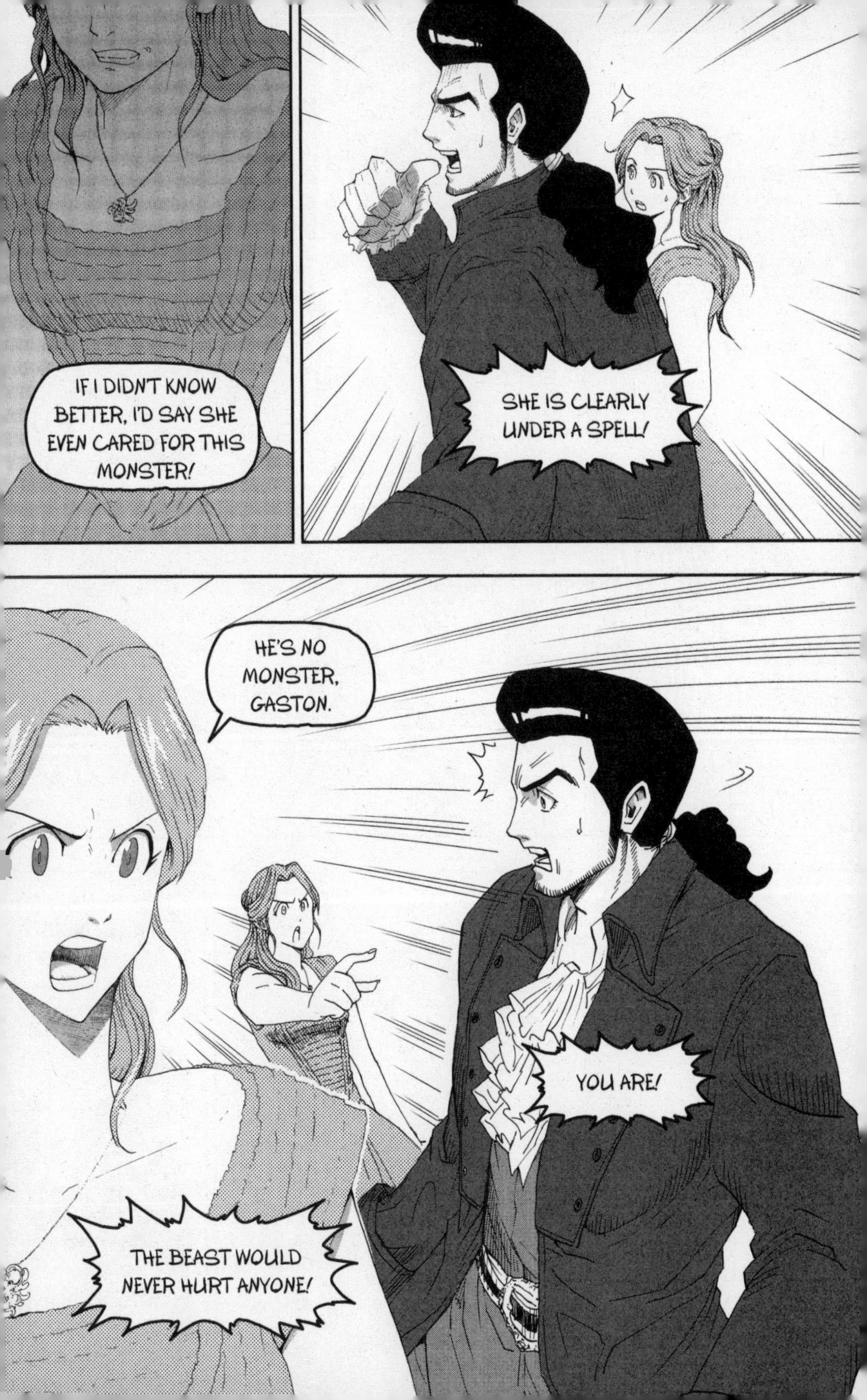
SHE IS CLEARLY UNDER A SPELL!
IF I DIDN'T KNOW BETTER, I'D SAY SHE EVEN CARED FOR THIS MONSTER!
HE'S NO MONSTER, GASTON.
YOU ARE!
THE BEAST WOULD NEVER HURT ANYONE!

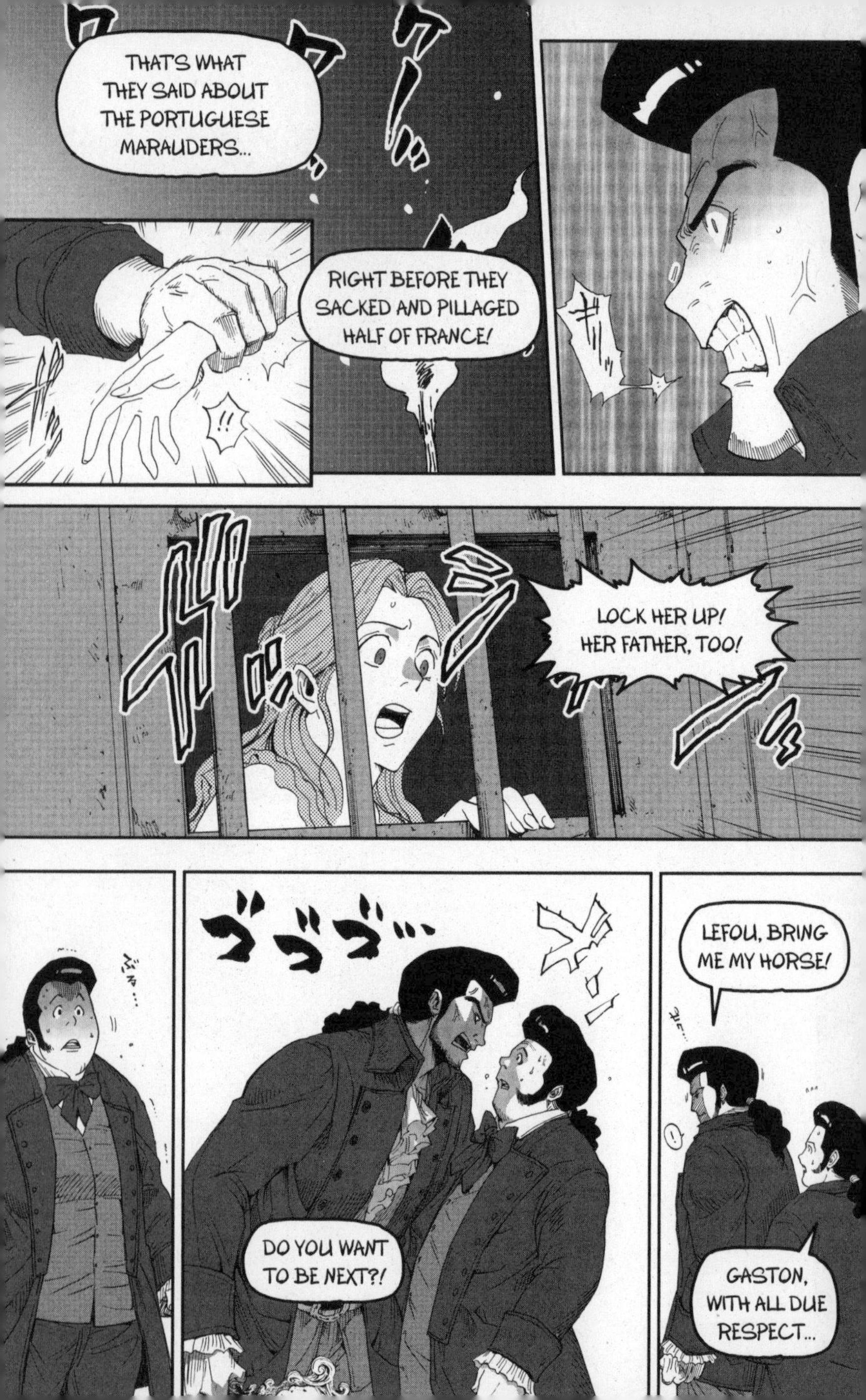
THAT'S WHAT THEY SAID ABOUT THE PORTUGUESE MARAUDERS...
RIGHT BEFORE THEY SACKED AND PILLAGED HALF OF FRANCE!
LOCK HER UP! HER FATHER, TOO!
LEFOU, BRING ME MY HORSE!
GASTON, WITH ALL DUE RESPECT...
ゴゴゴ…
DO YOU WANT TO BE NEXT?!

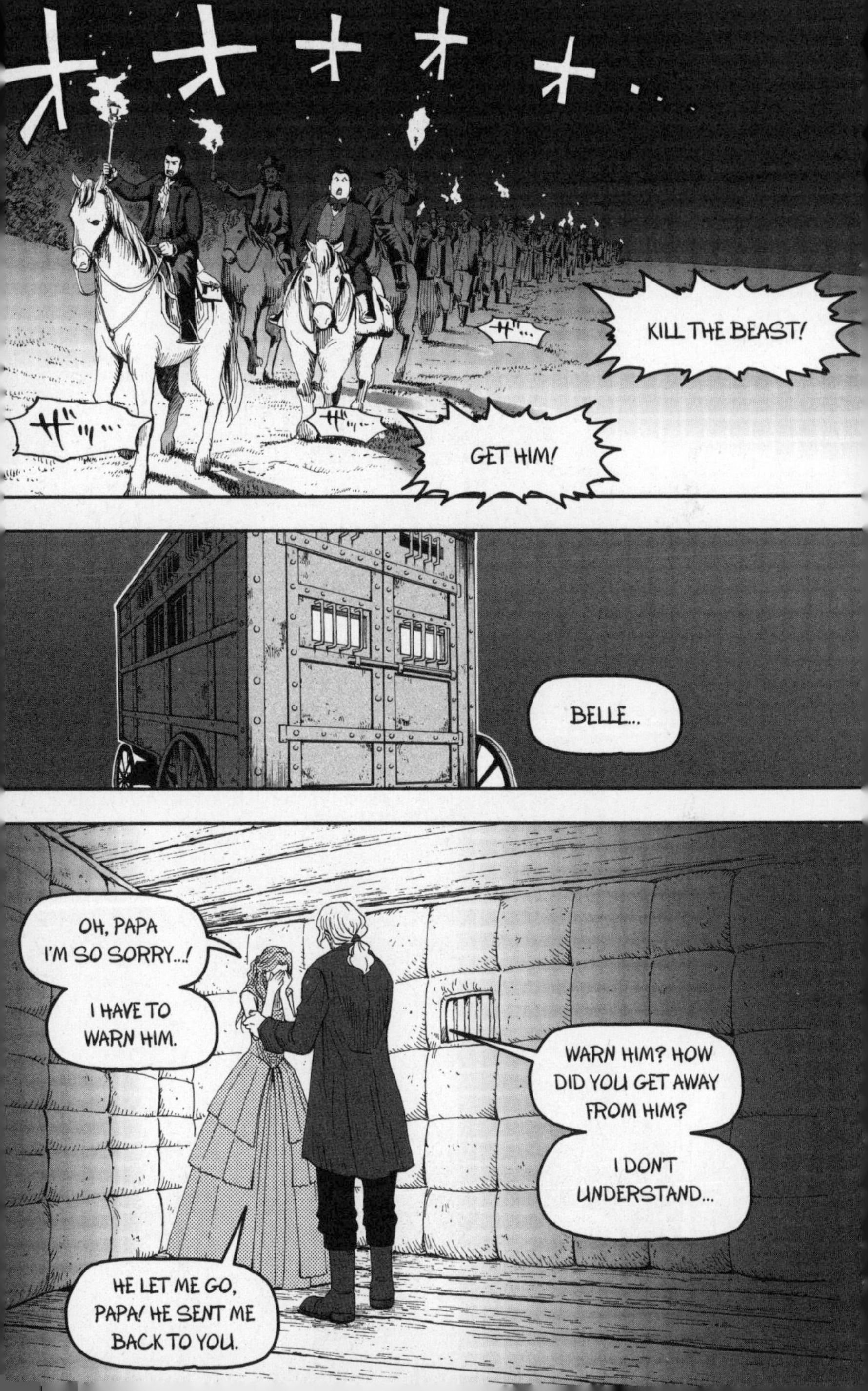
オオオオオ…
KILL THE BEAST!
ザ"…
GET HIM!
ザ"ッ…
ザ"ッ…
BELLE…
OH, PAPA I'M SO SORRY…!
I HAVE TO WARN HIM.
WARN HIM? HOW DID YOU GET AWAY FROM HIM?
I DON'T UNDERSTAND…
HE LET ME GO, PAPA! HE SENT ME BACK TO YOU.

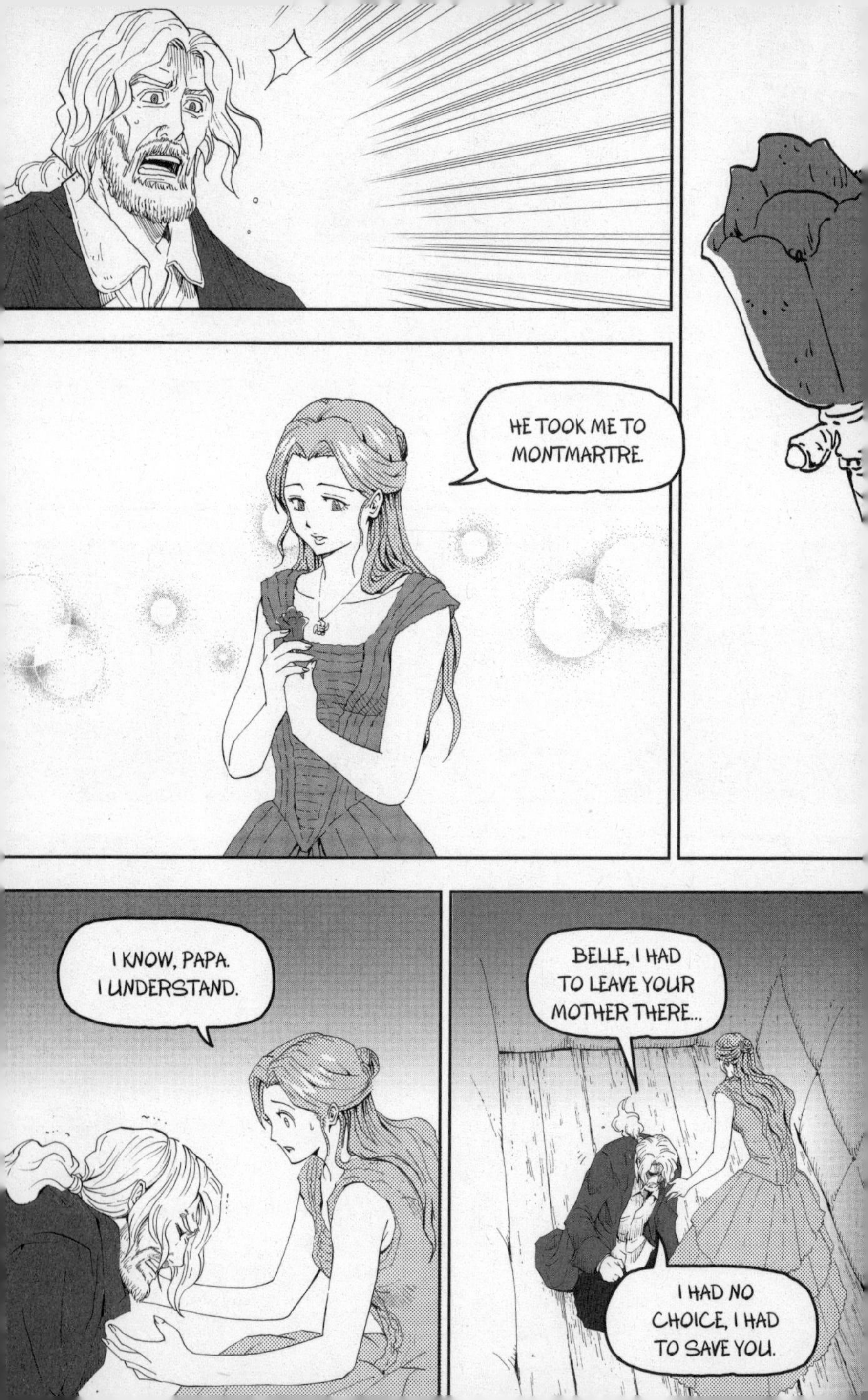
HE TOOK ME TO MONTMARTRE.
BELLE, I HAD TO LEAVE YOUR MOTHER THERE...
I HAD NO CHOICE, I HAD TO SAVE YOU.
I KNOW, PAPA. I UNDERSTAND.

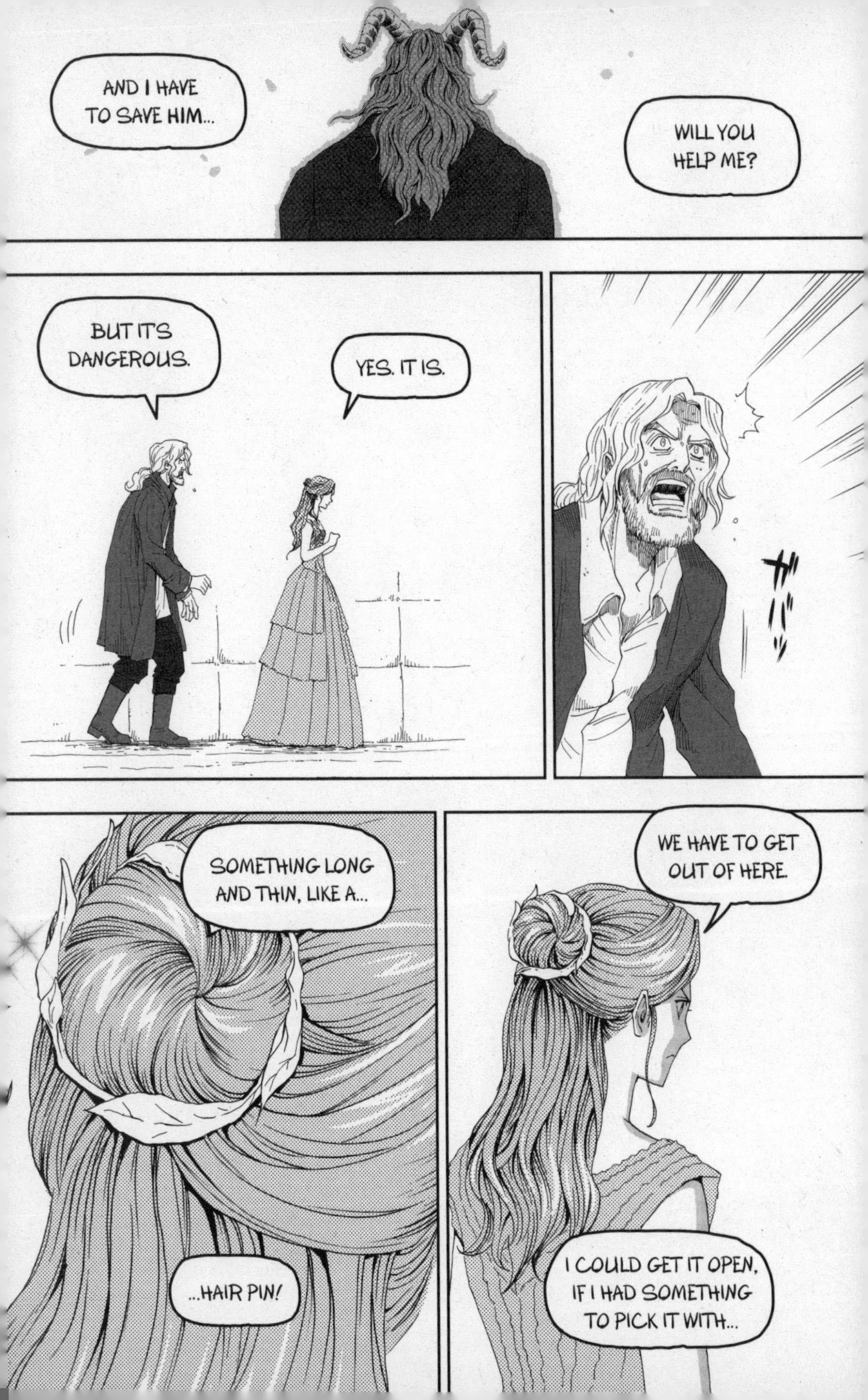
WILL YOU HELP ME?
AND I HAVE TO SAVE HIM...
ガバッ
YES. IT IS.
BUT IT'S DANGEROUS.
WE HAVE TO GET OUT OF HERE.
I COULD GET IT OPEN, IF I HAD SOMETHING TO PICK IT WITH...
SOMETHING LONG AND THIN, LIKE A...
...HAIR PIN!

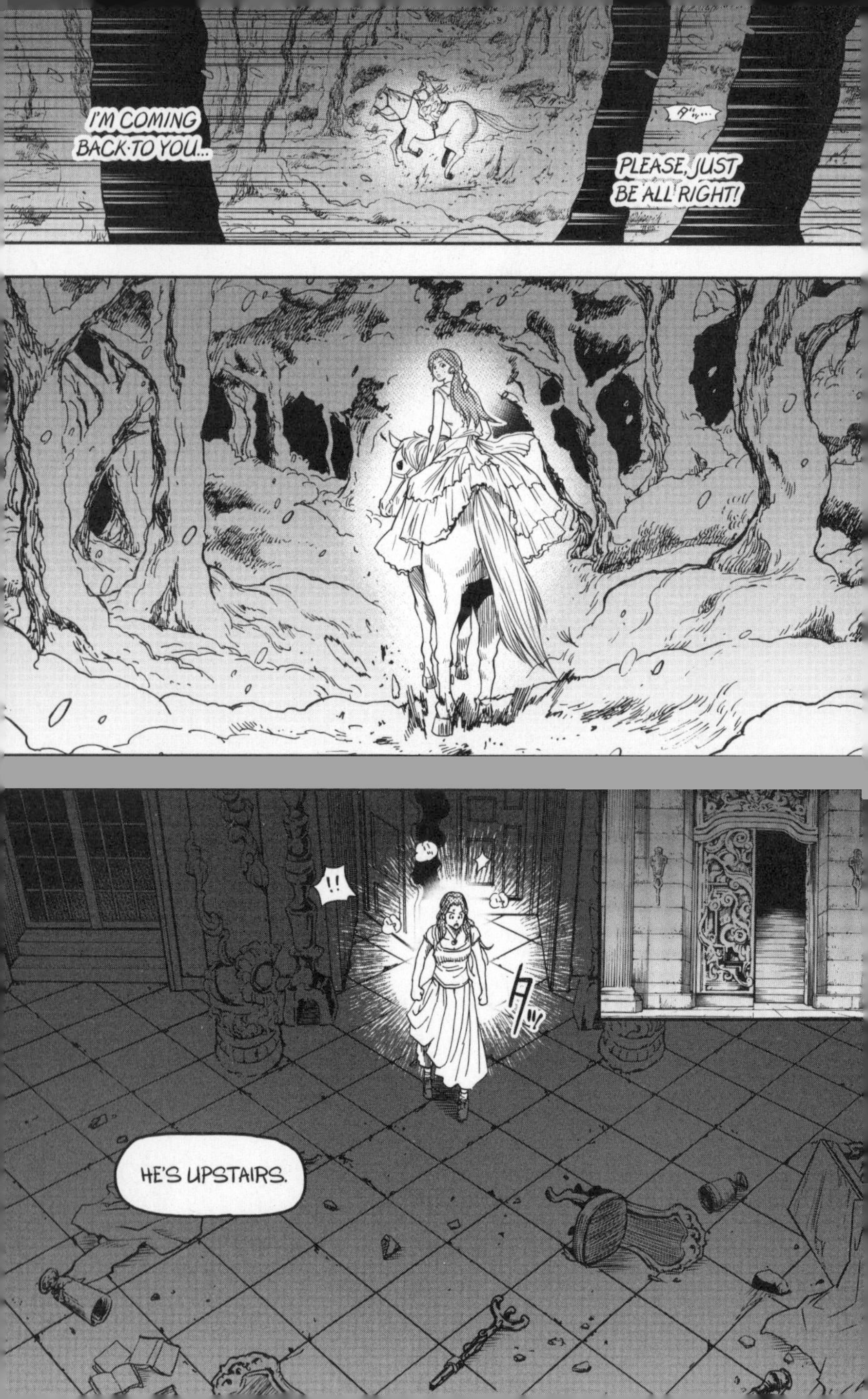
ダッ…
PLEASE, JUST BE ALL RIGHT!
I'M COMING BACK TO YOU...
!!
ダッ
HE'S UPSTAIRS.

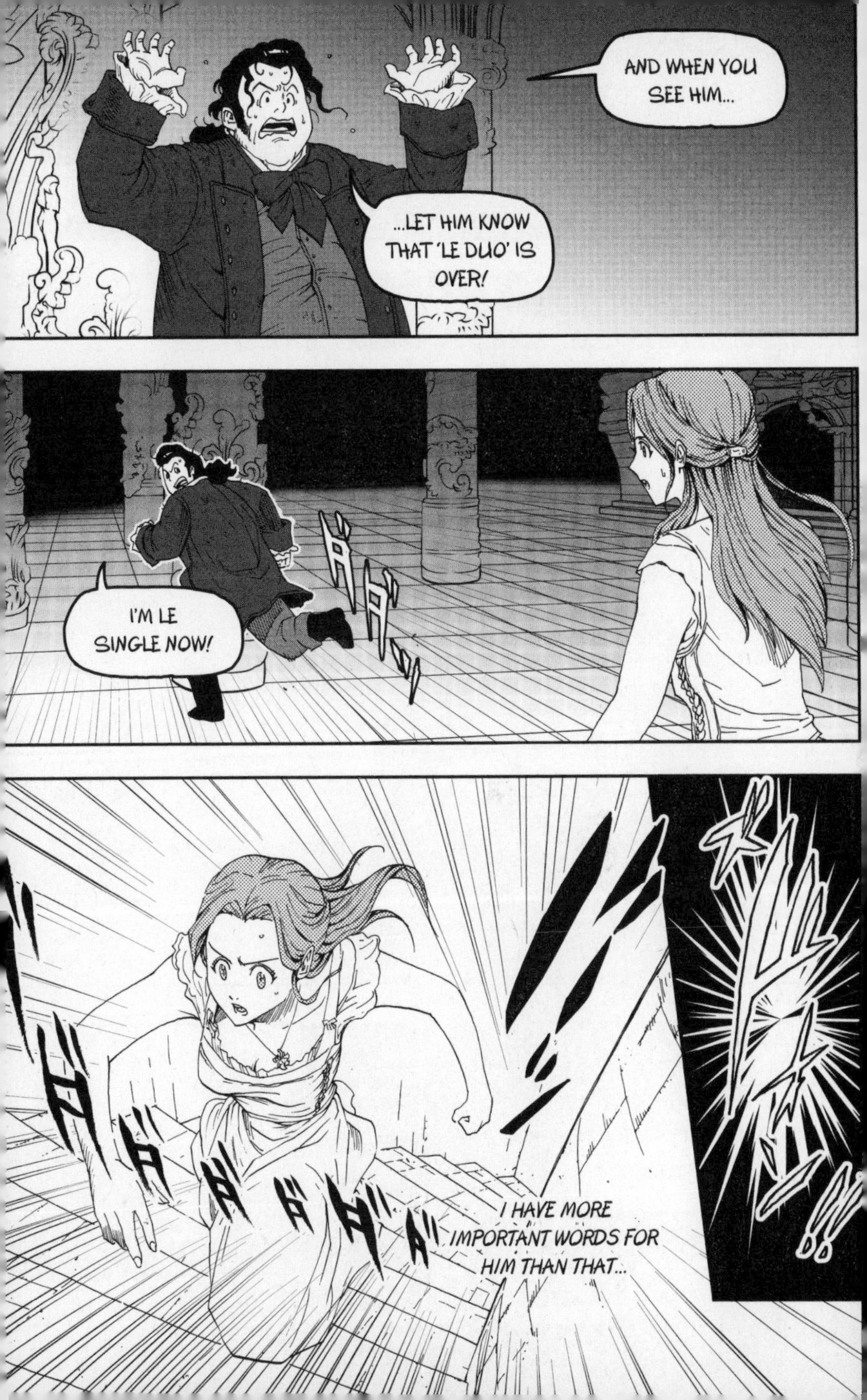
AND WHEN YOU SEE HIM...
...LET HIM KNOW THAT 'LE DUO' IS OVER!
I'M LE SINGLE NOW!
I HAVE MORE IMPORTANT WORDS FOR HIM THAN THAT...

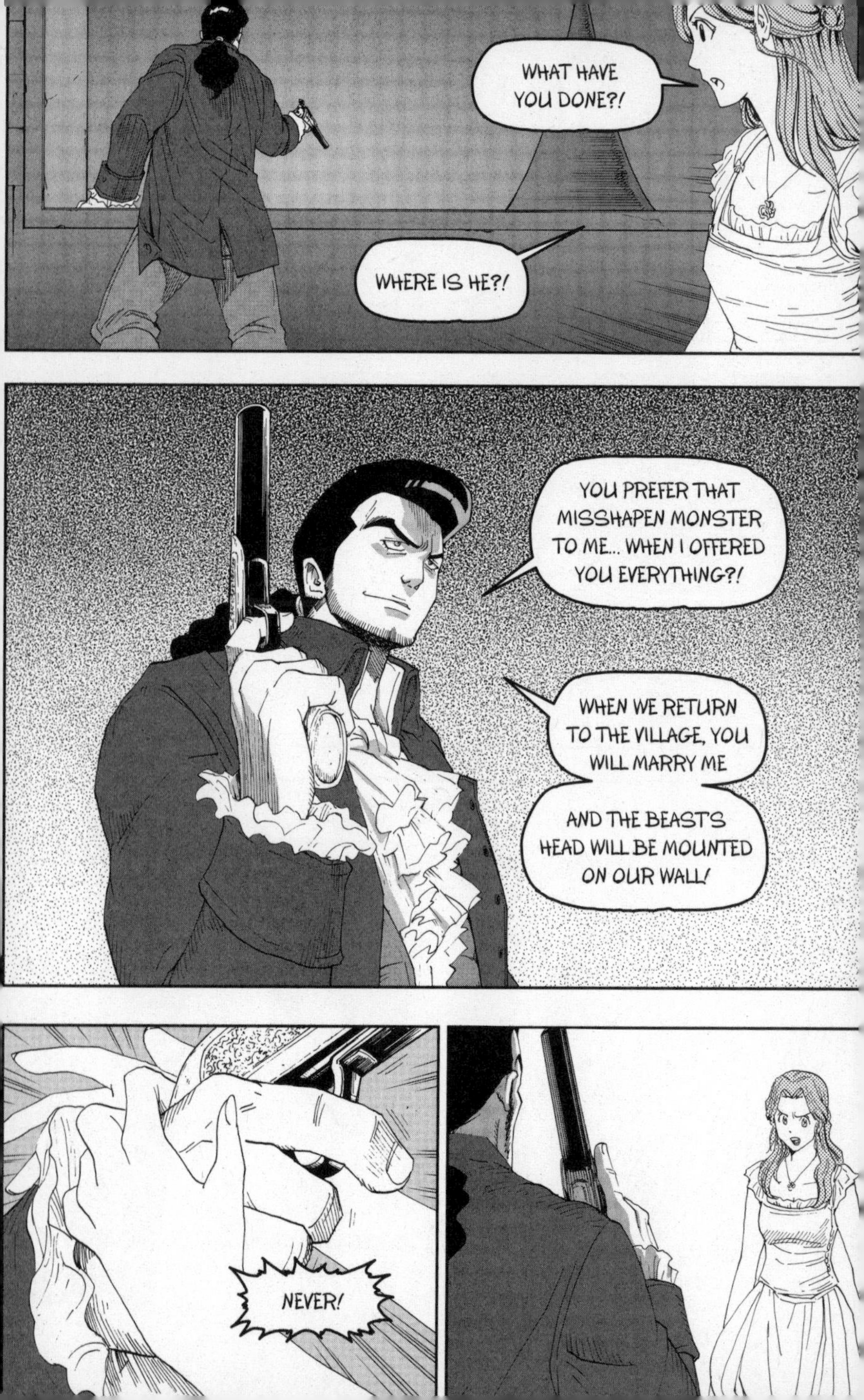
WHAT HAVE YOU DONE?!
WHERE IS HE?!
YOU PREFER THAT MISSHAPEN MONSTER TO ME... WHEN I OFFERED YOU EVERYTHING?!
WHEN WE RETURN TO THE VILLAGE, YOU WILL MARRY ME
AND THE BEAST'S HEAD WILL BE MOUNTED ON OUR WALL!
NEVER!

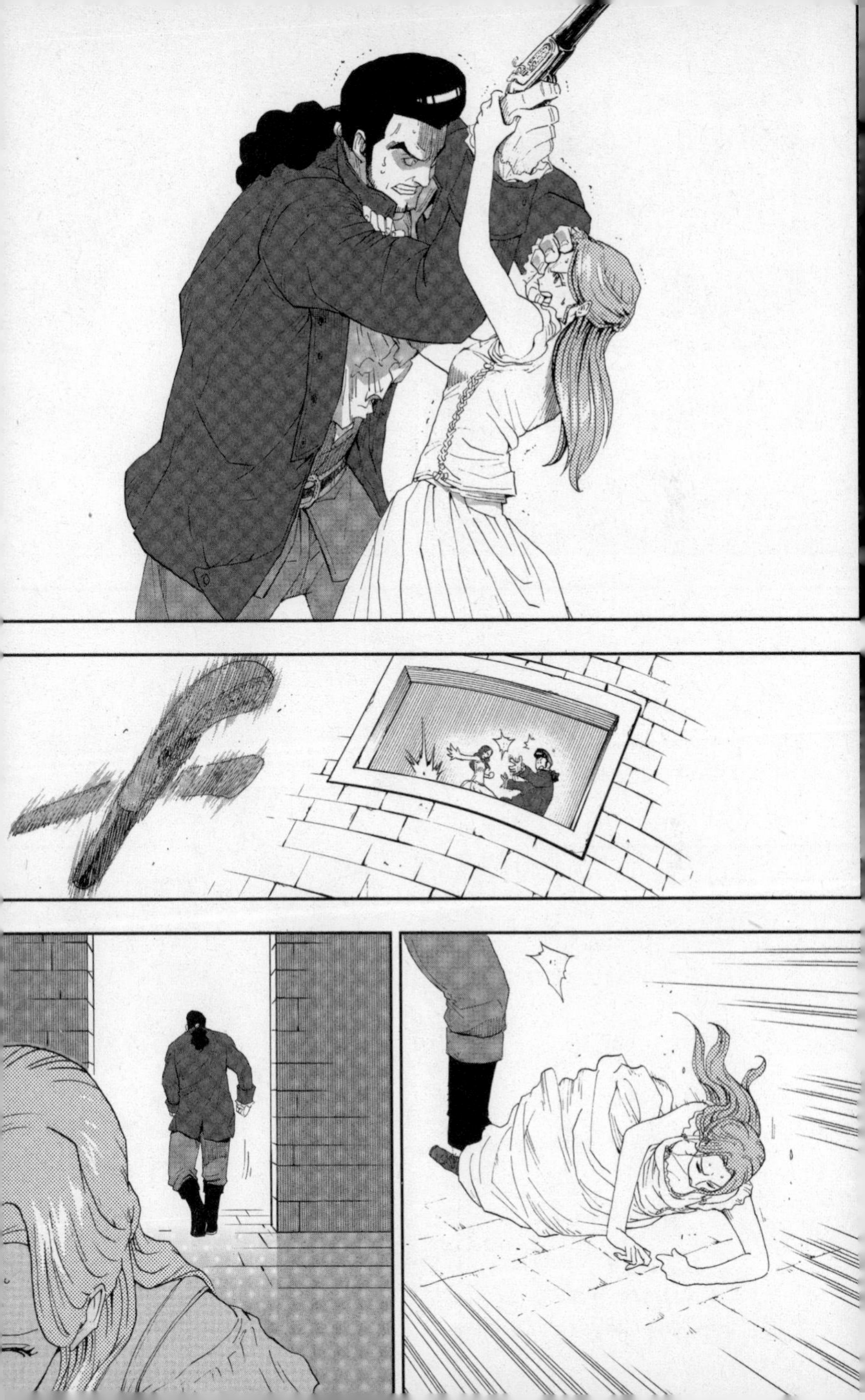

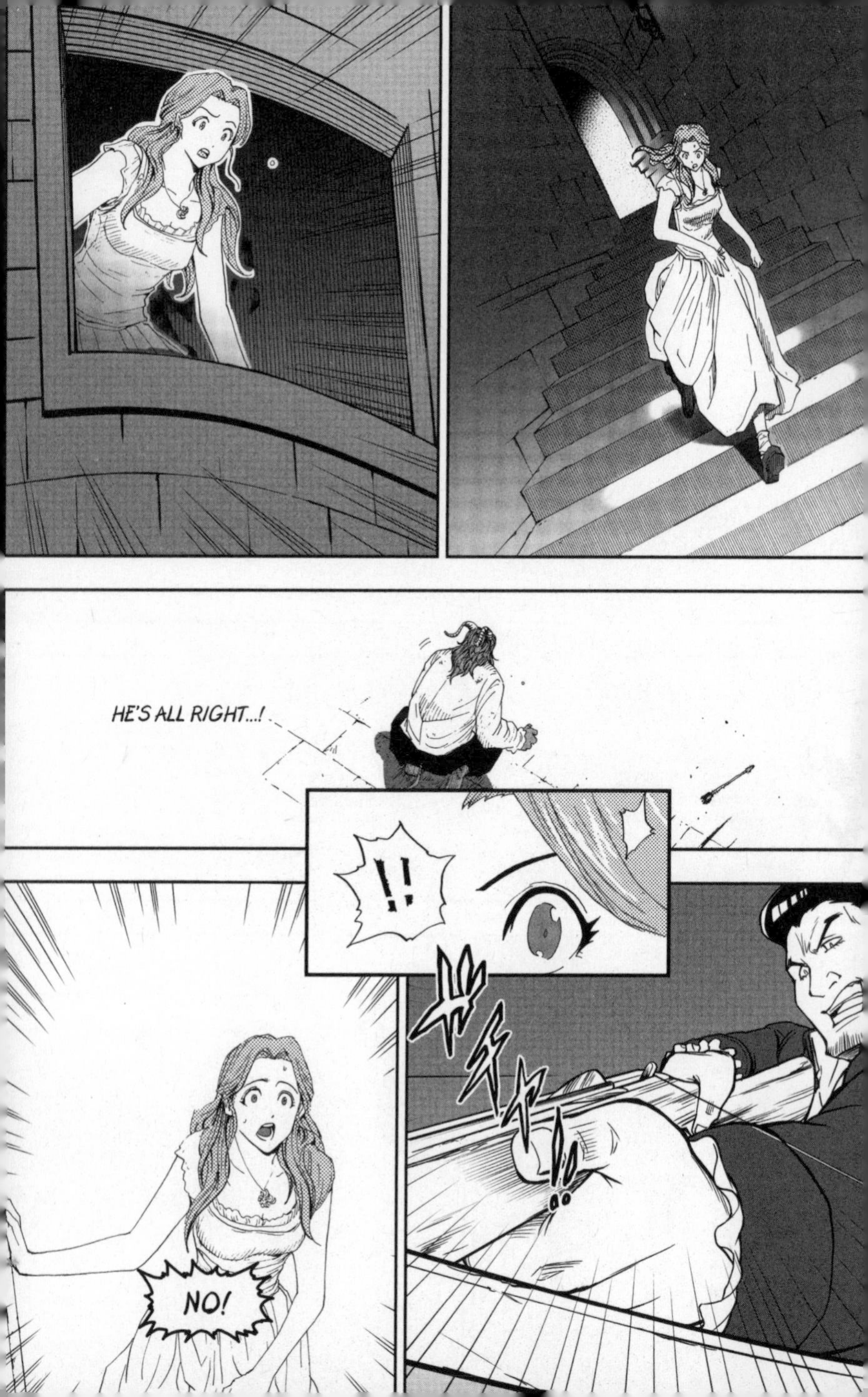
HE'S ALL RIGHT...!
!!
NO!

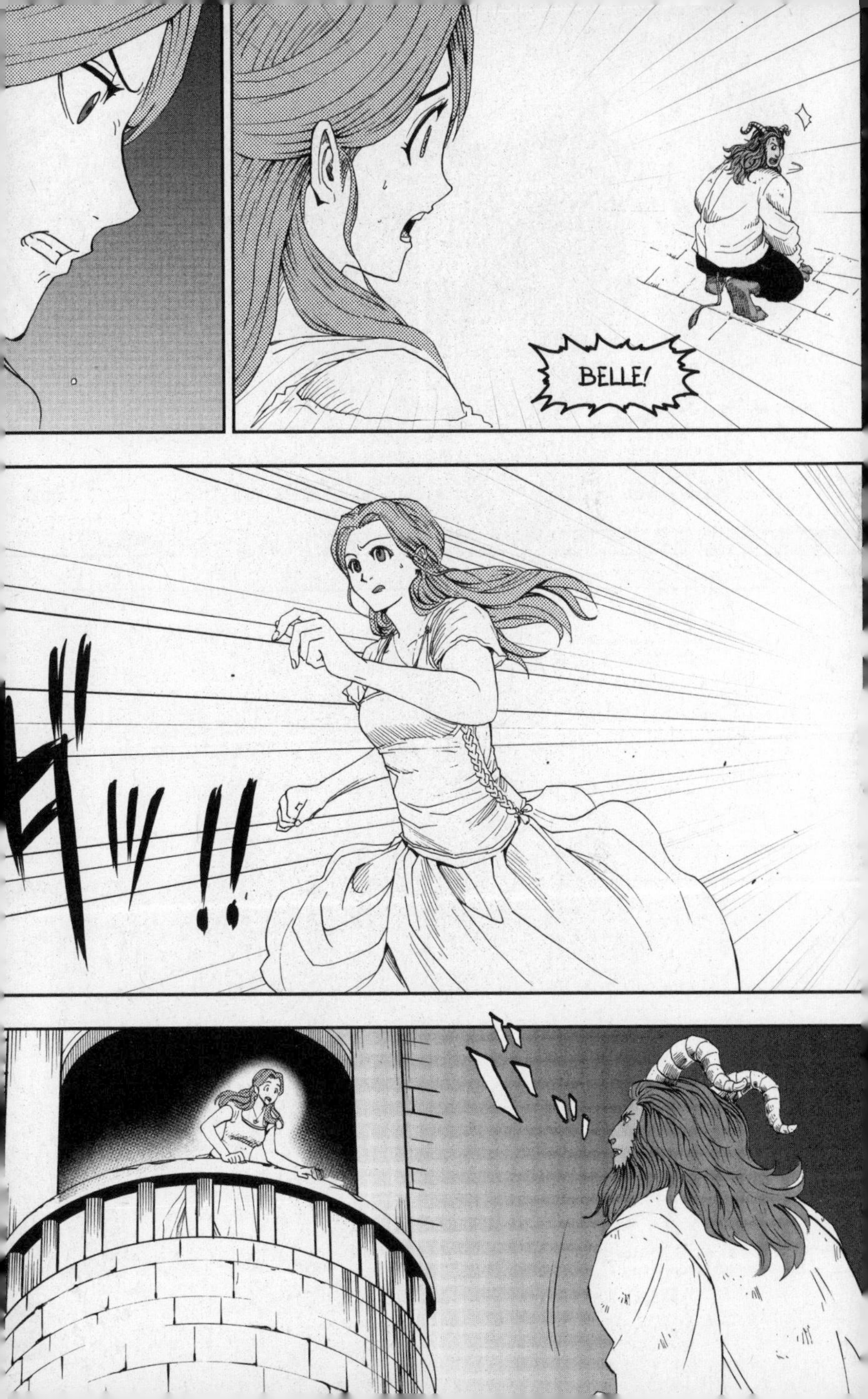
BELLE!
ガッ!!

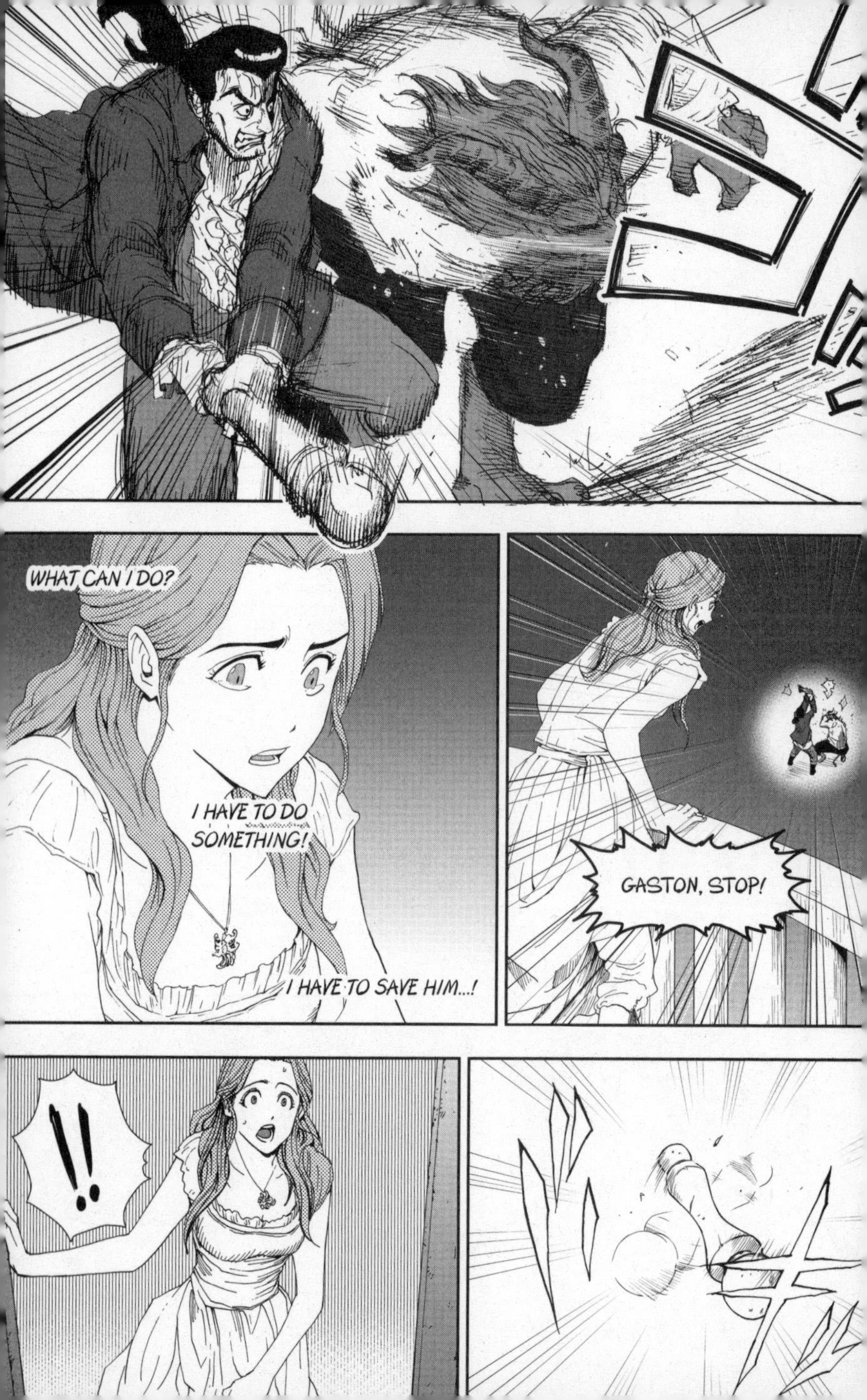
GASTON, STOP!
WHAT CAN I DO?
I HAVE TO DO SOMETHING!
I HAVE TO SAVE HIM...!
!!

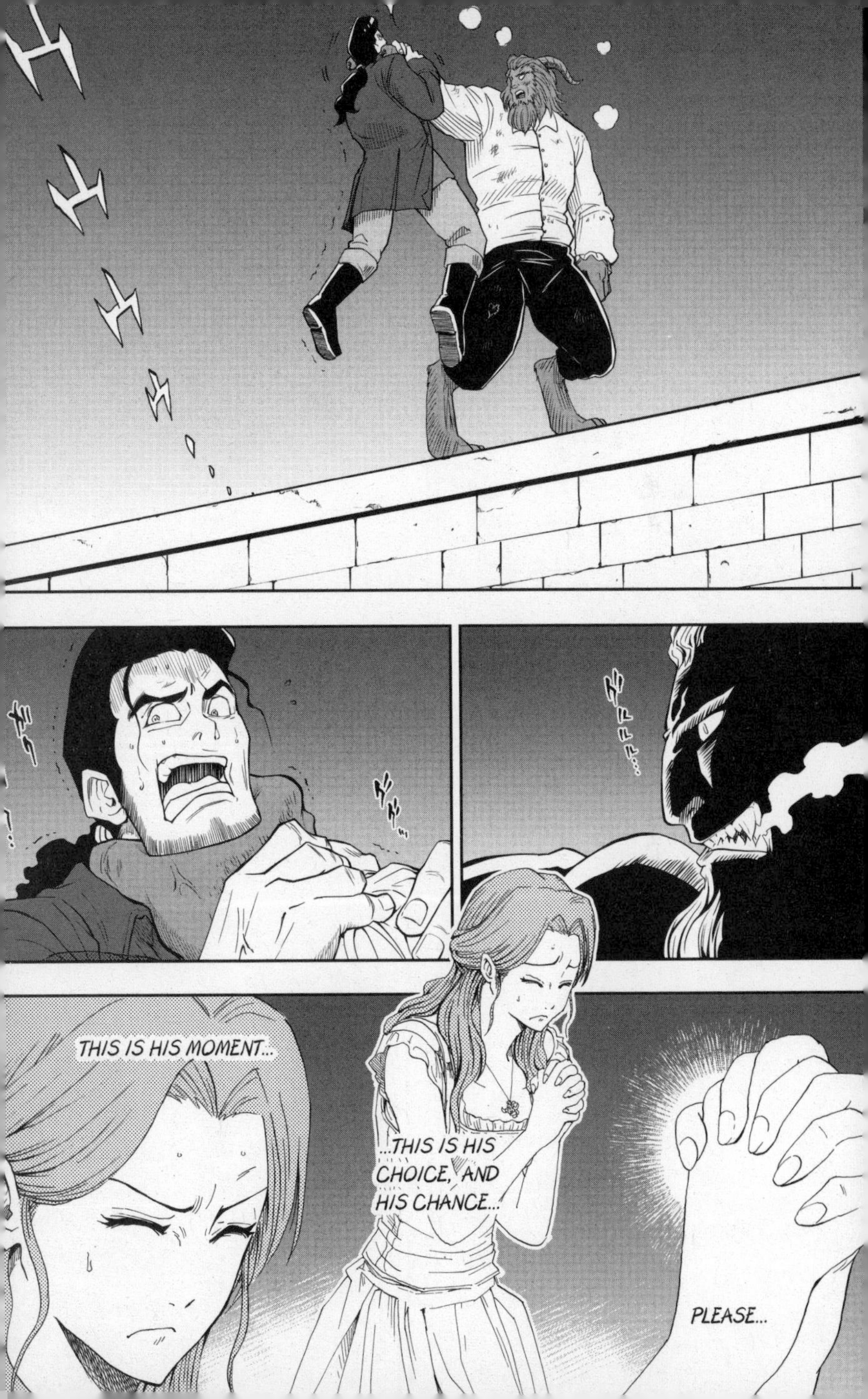
THIS IS HIS MOMENT...
...THIS IS HIS CHOICE, AND HIS CHANCE...
PLEASE...

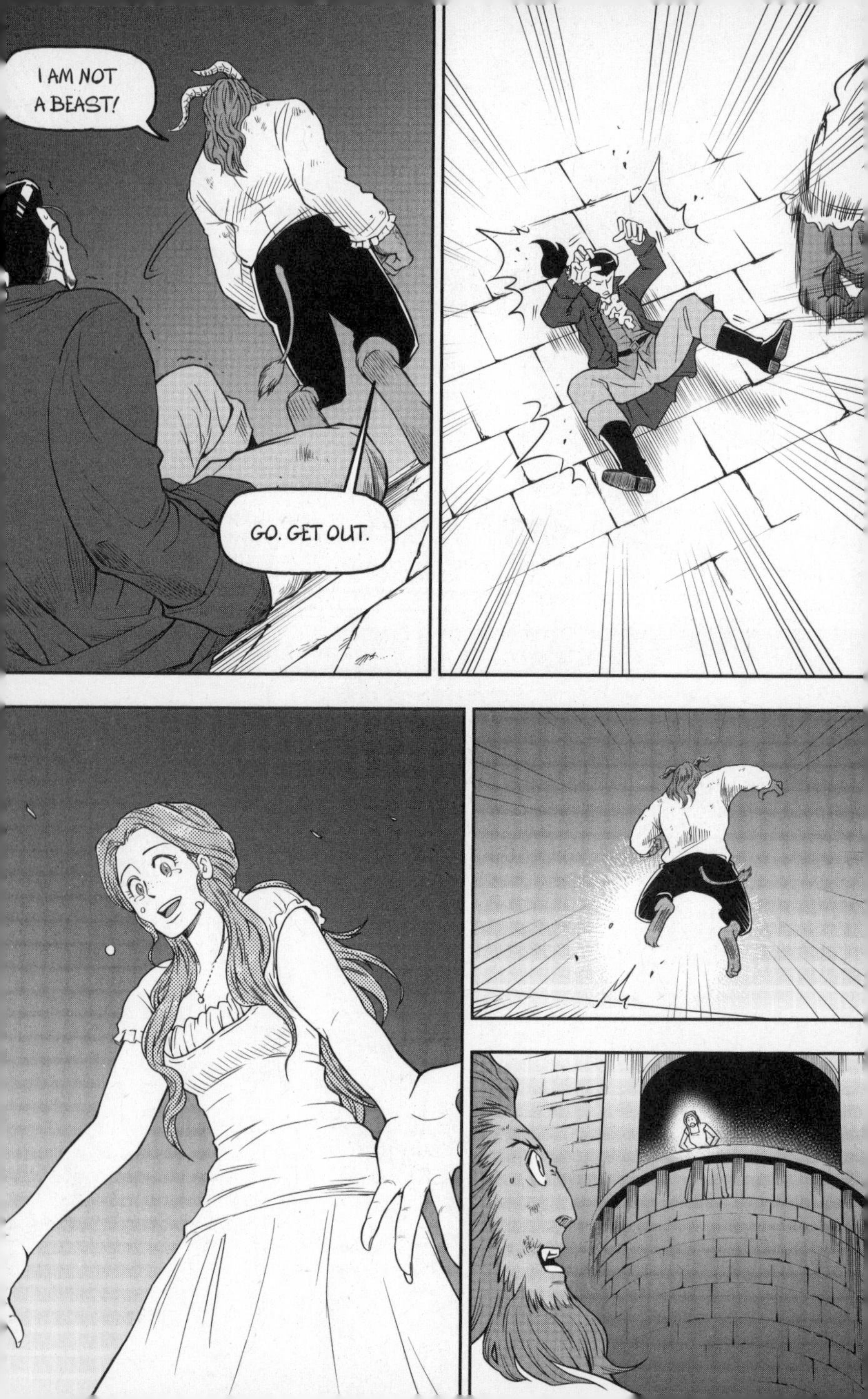
I AM NOT A BEAST!
GO. GET OUT.

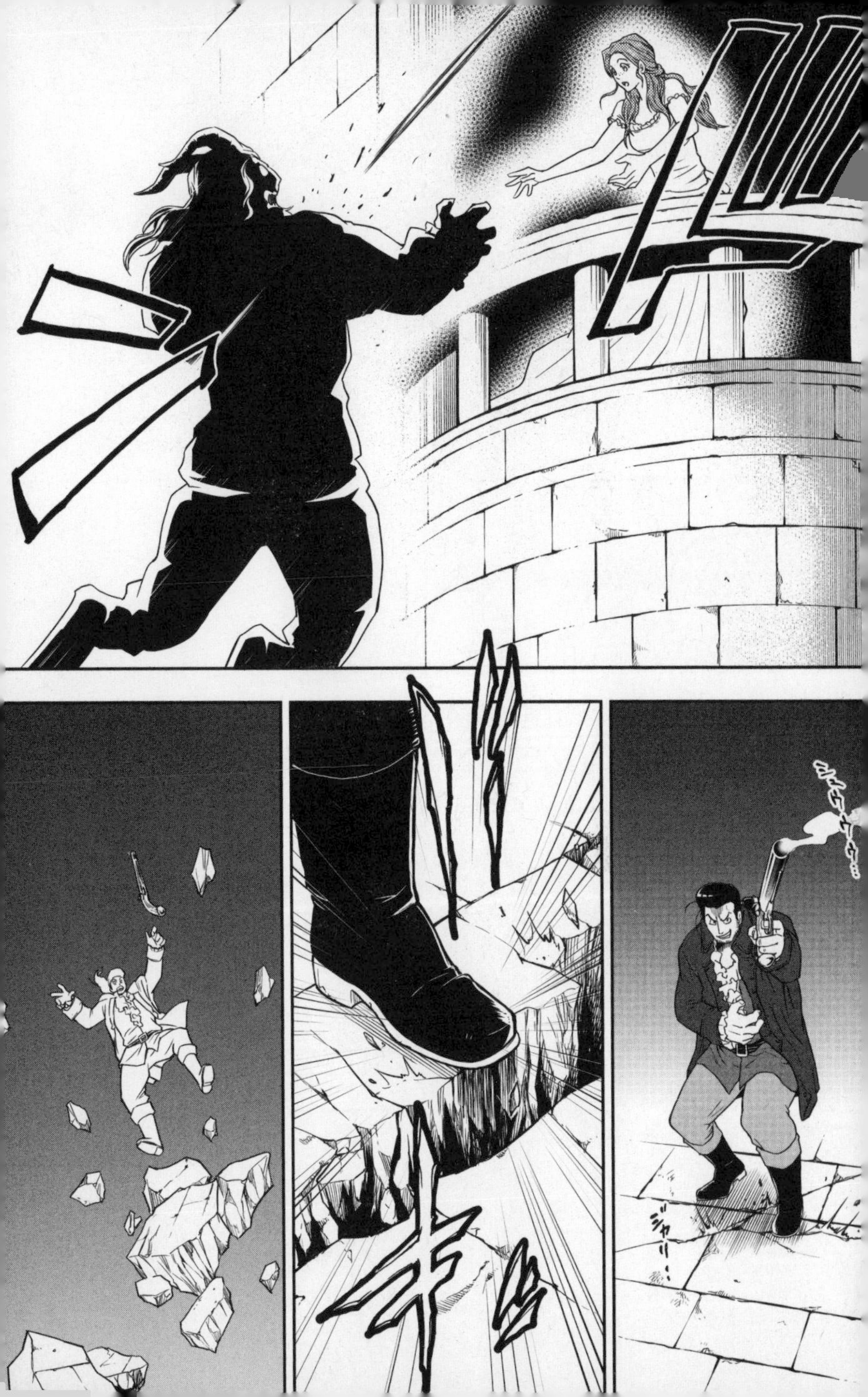
シュウウウ…
ジャリ…

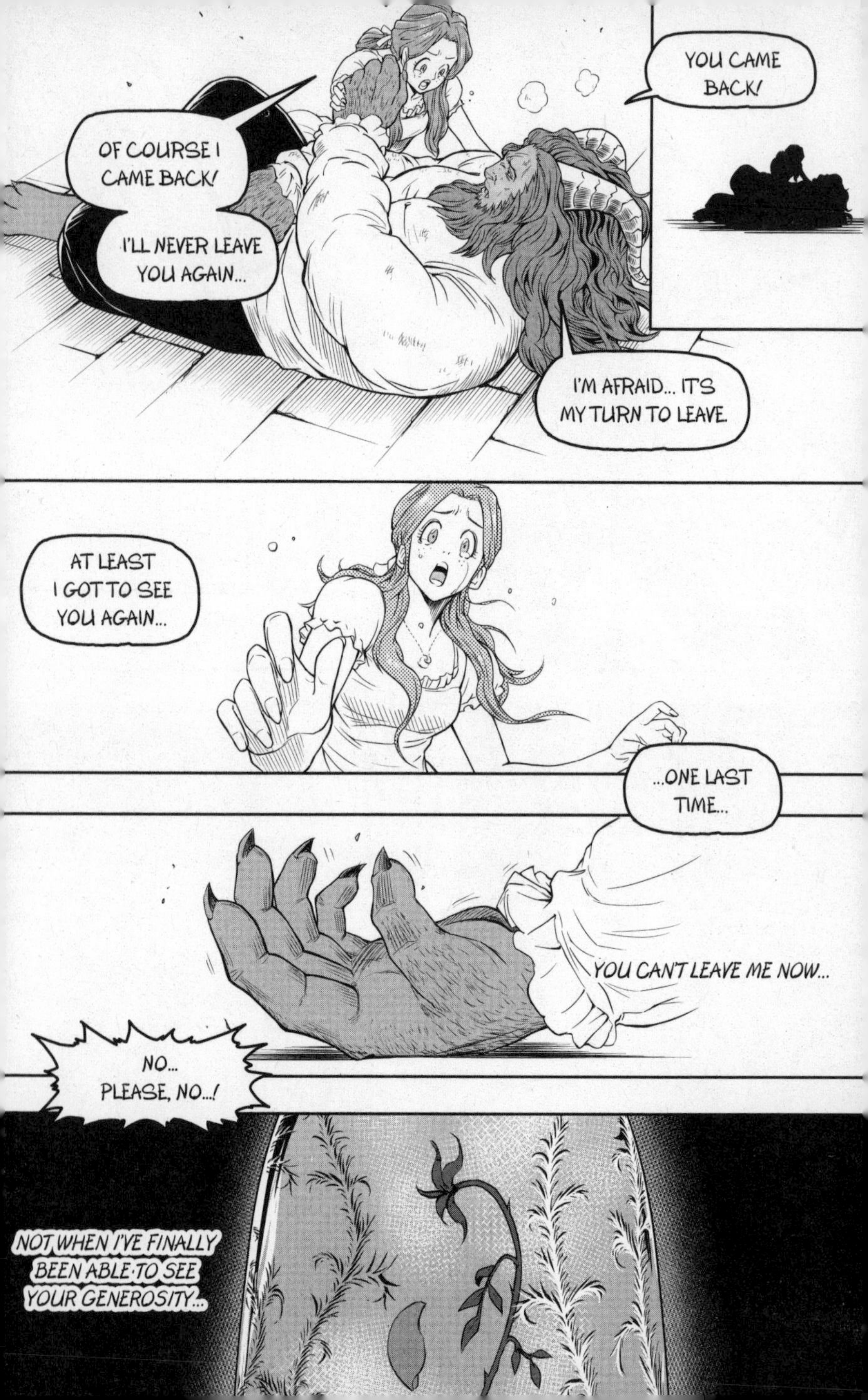
YOU CAME BACK!
OF COURSE I CAME BACK!
I'LL NEVER LEAVE YOU AGAIN...
I'M AFRAID... IT'S MY TURN TO LEAVE.
AT LEAST I GOT TO SEE YOU AGAIN...
...ONE LAST TIME...
YOU CAN'T LEAVE ME NOW...
NO... PLEASE, NO...!
NOT WHEN I'VE FINALLY BEEN ABLE TO SEE YOUR GENEROSITY...

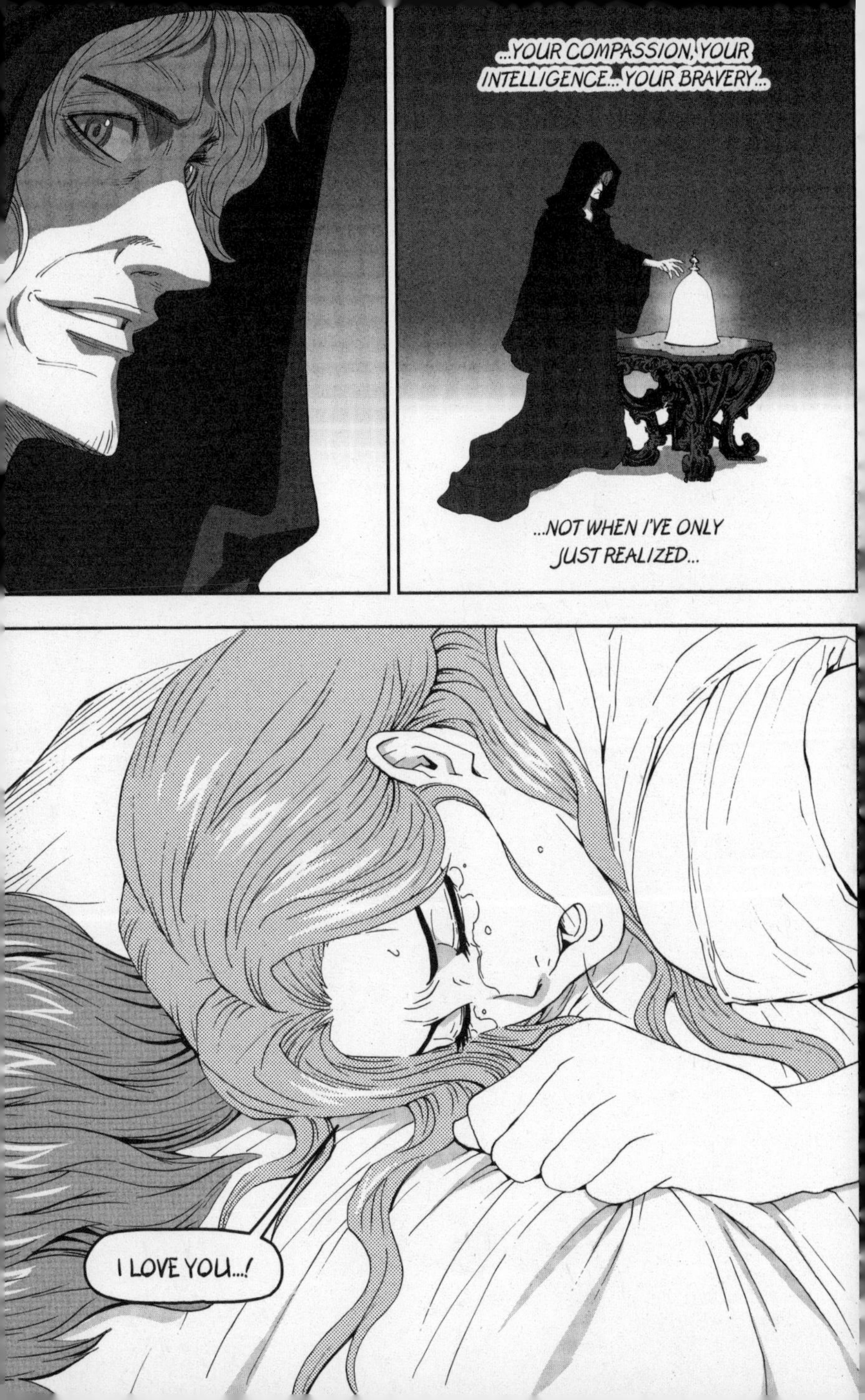
...YOUR COMPASSION, YOUR INTELLIGENCE... YOUR BRAVERY...
...NOT WHEN I'VE ONLY JUST REALIZED...
I LOVE YOU...!

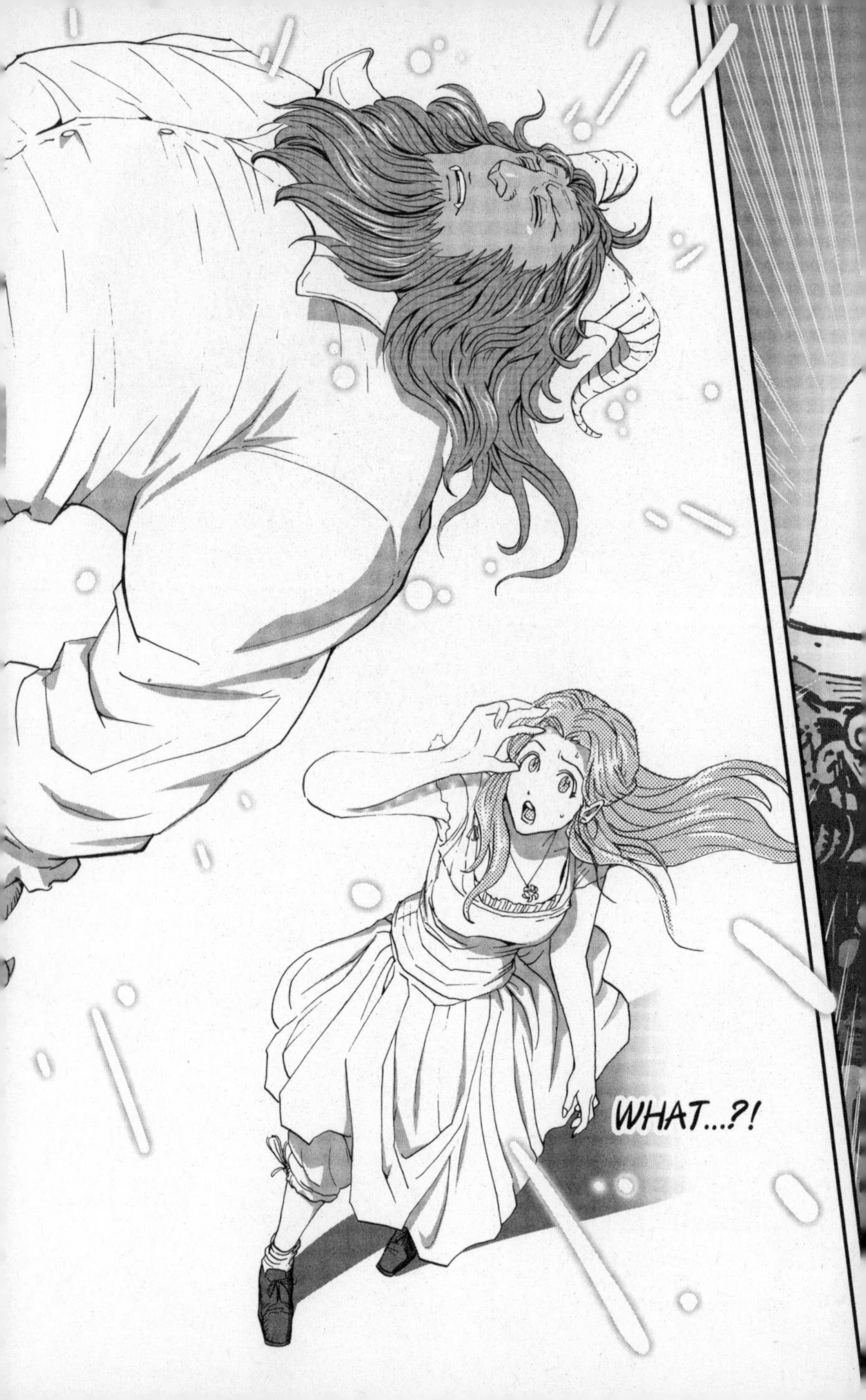
WHAT...?!

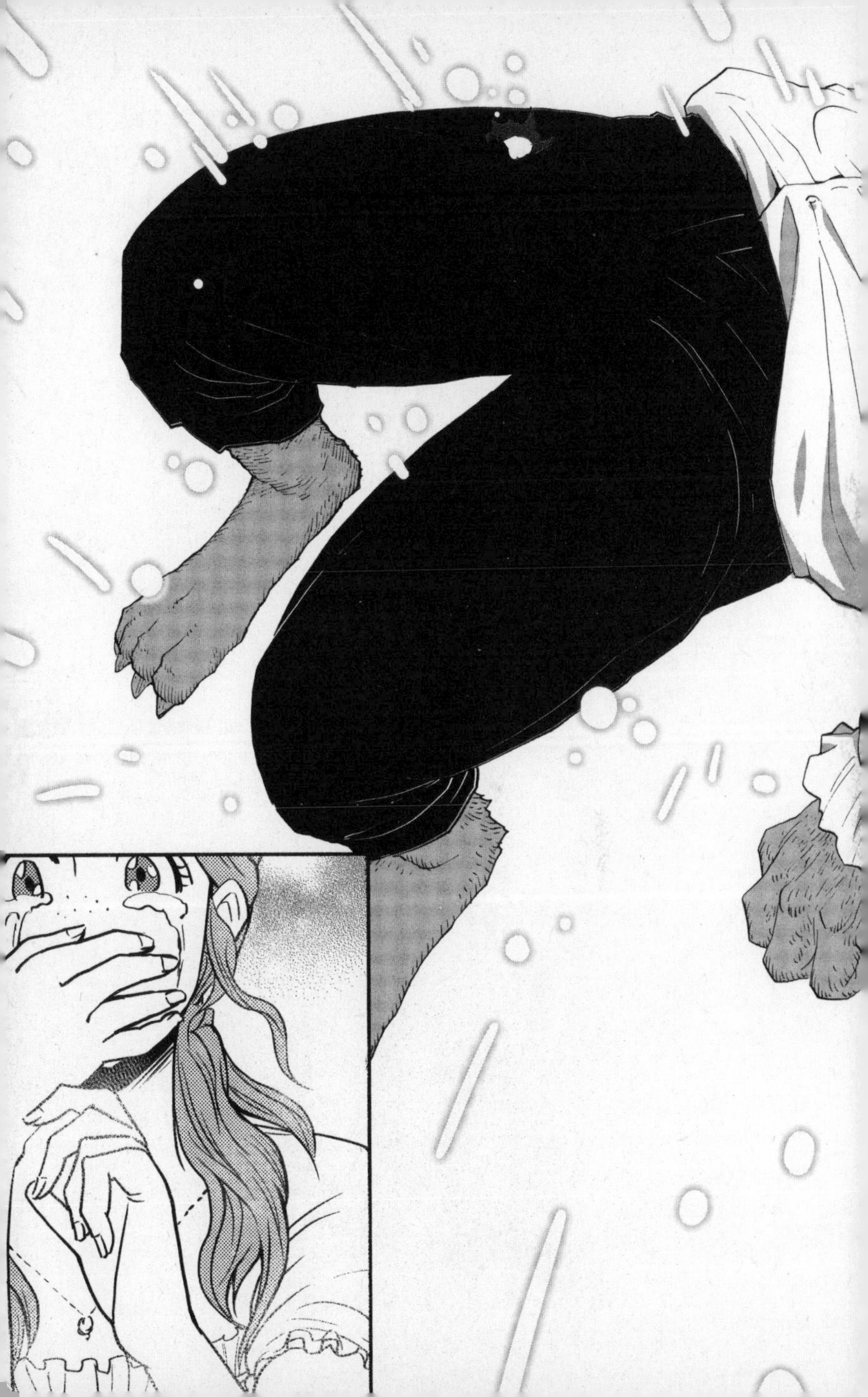

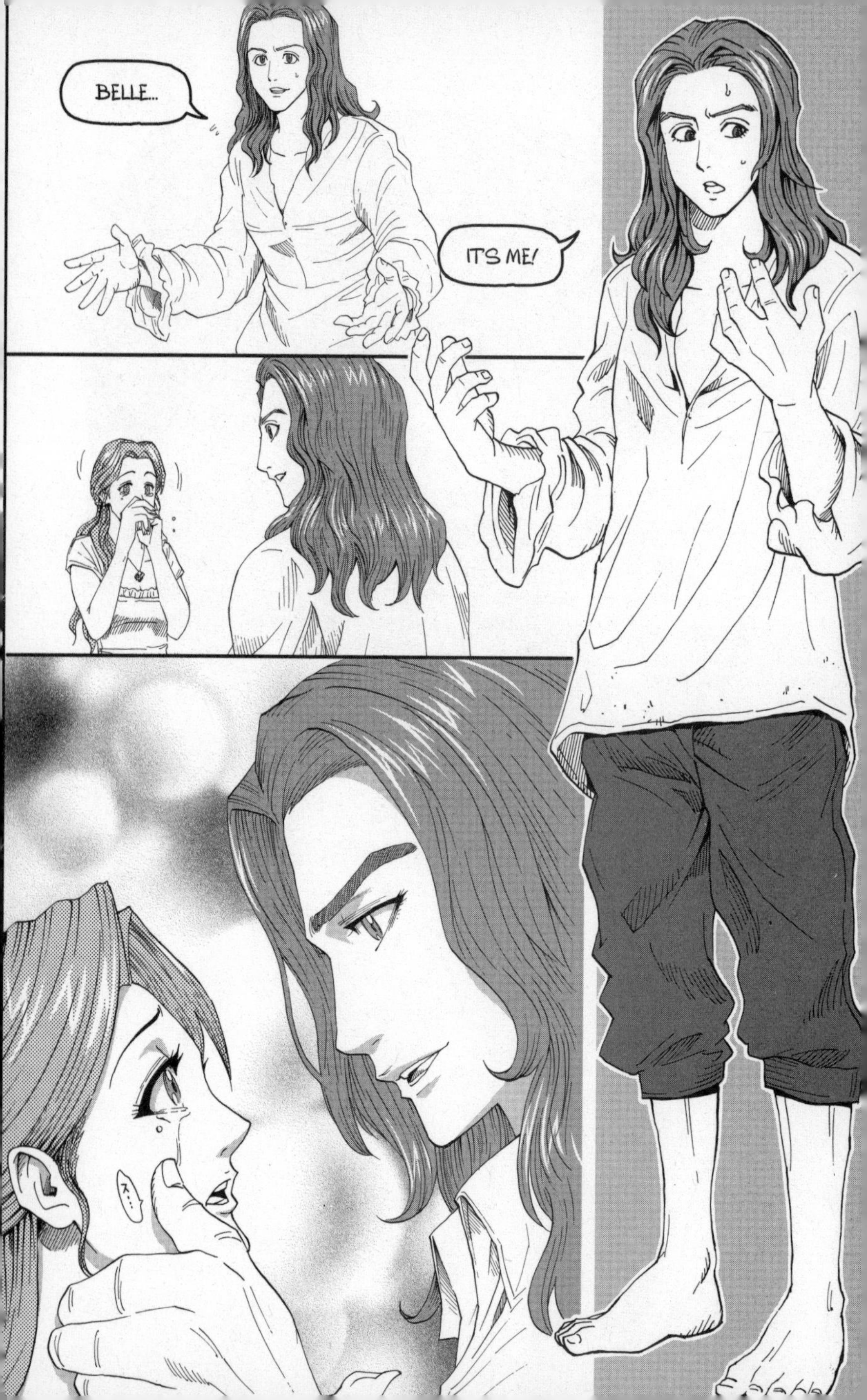
BELLE...
IT'S ME!
ス…

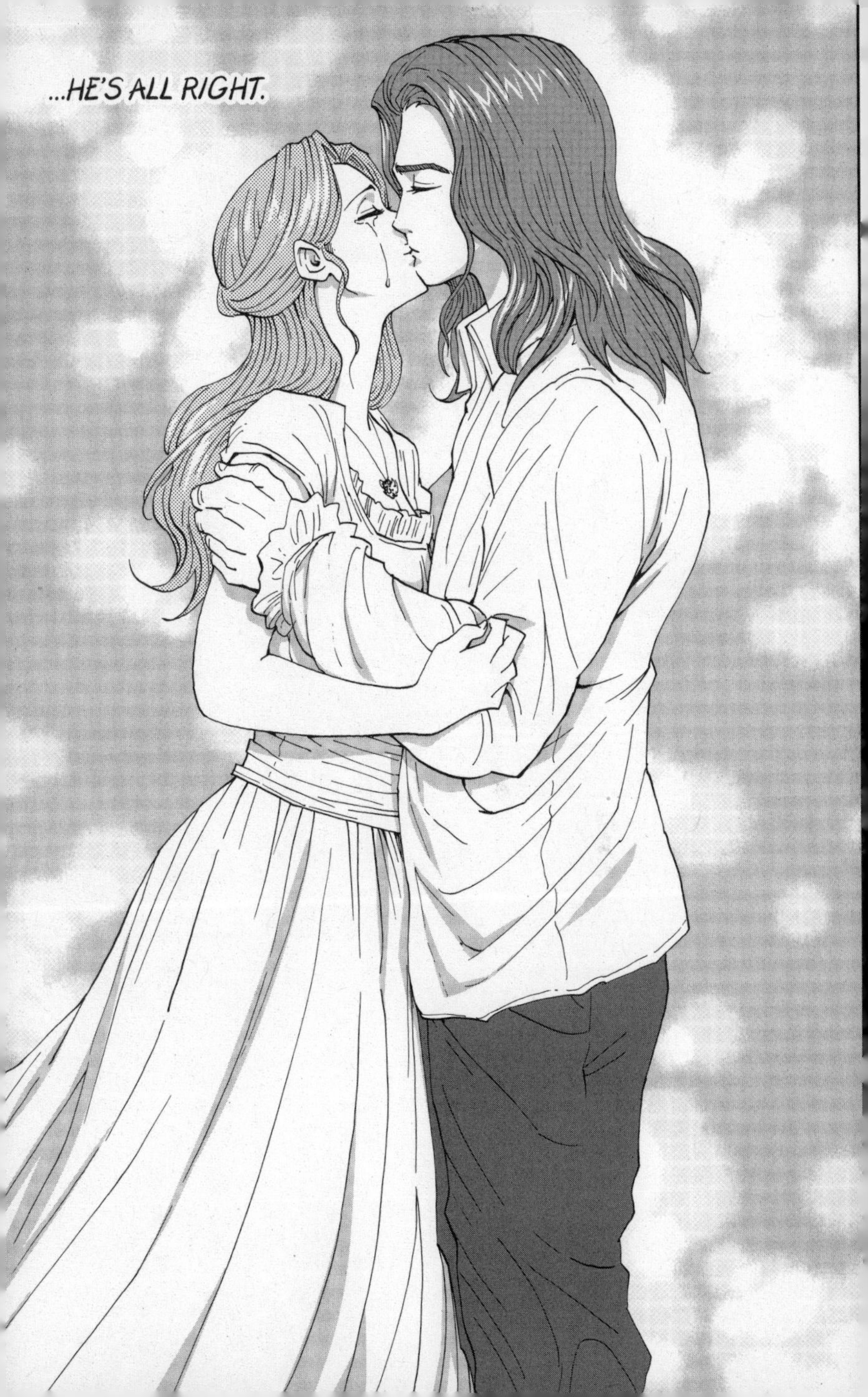
...HE'S ALL RIGHT.

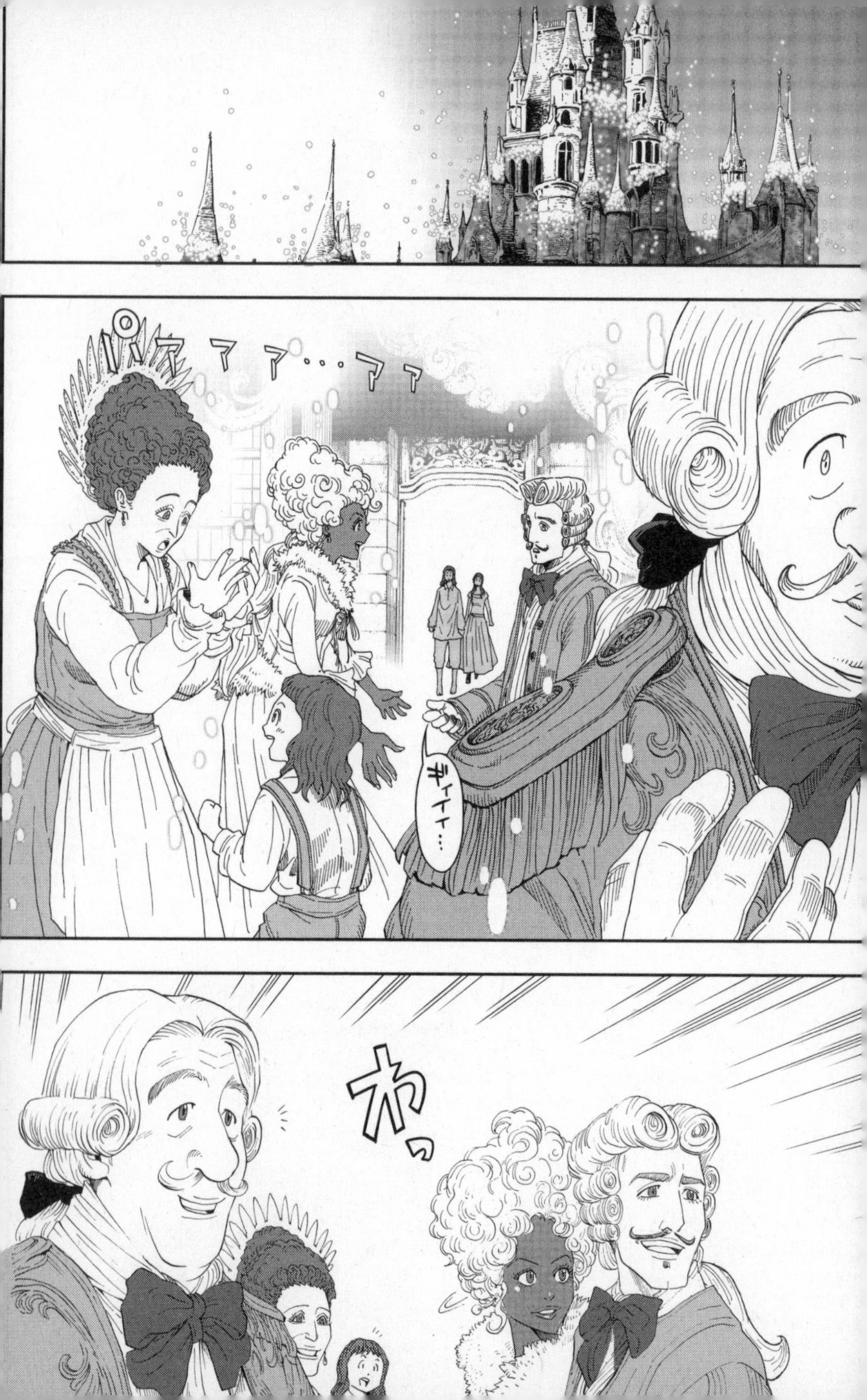
パアアア…アァ
ギイイイ…
わっ

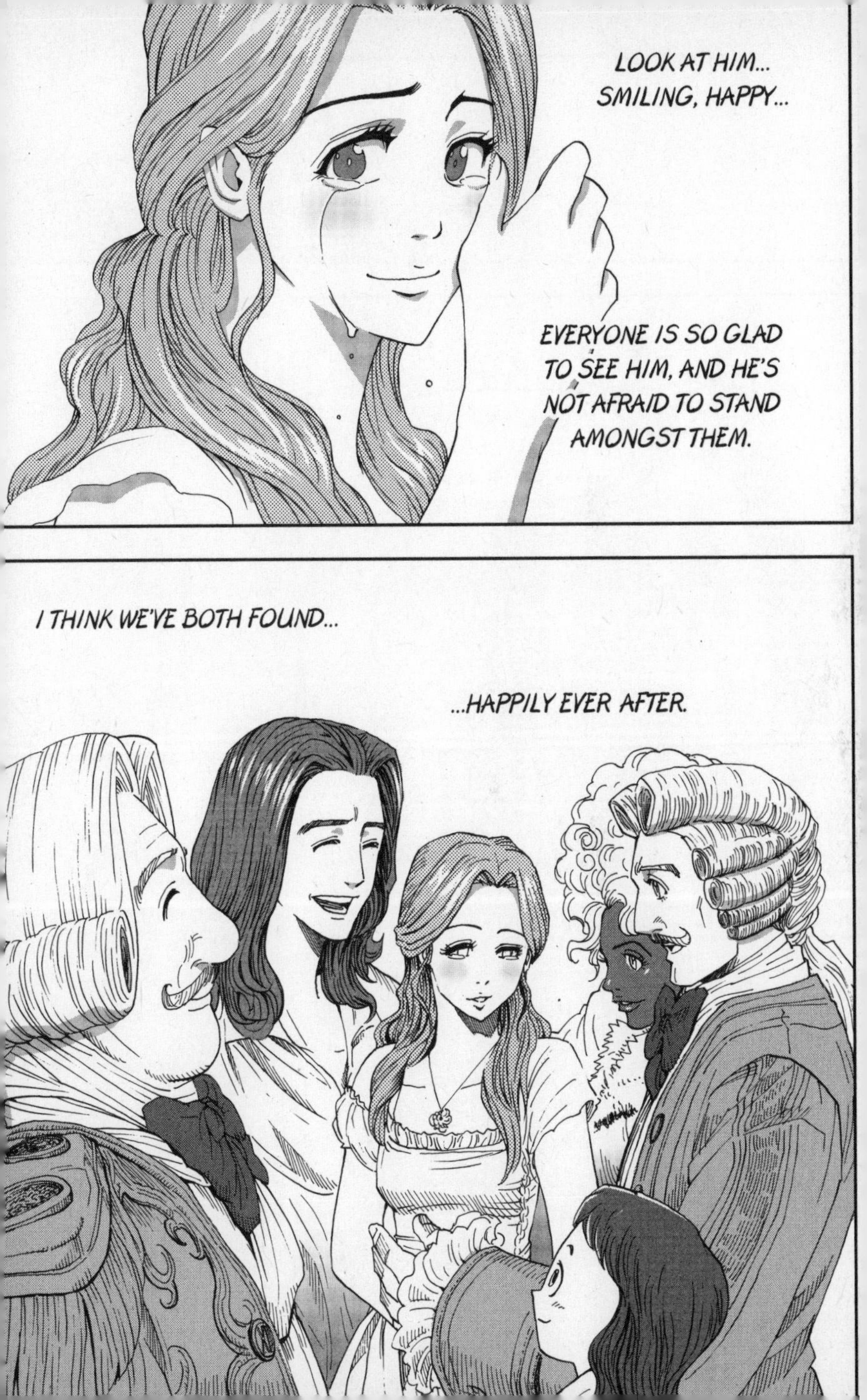
LOOK AT HIM... SMILING, HAPPY...
EVERYONE IS SO GLAD TO SEE HIM, AND HE'S NOT AFRAID TO STAND AMONGST THEM.
I THINK WE'VE BOTH FOUND...
...HAPPILY EVER AFTER.

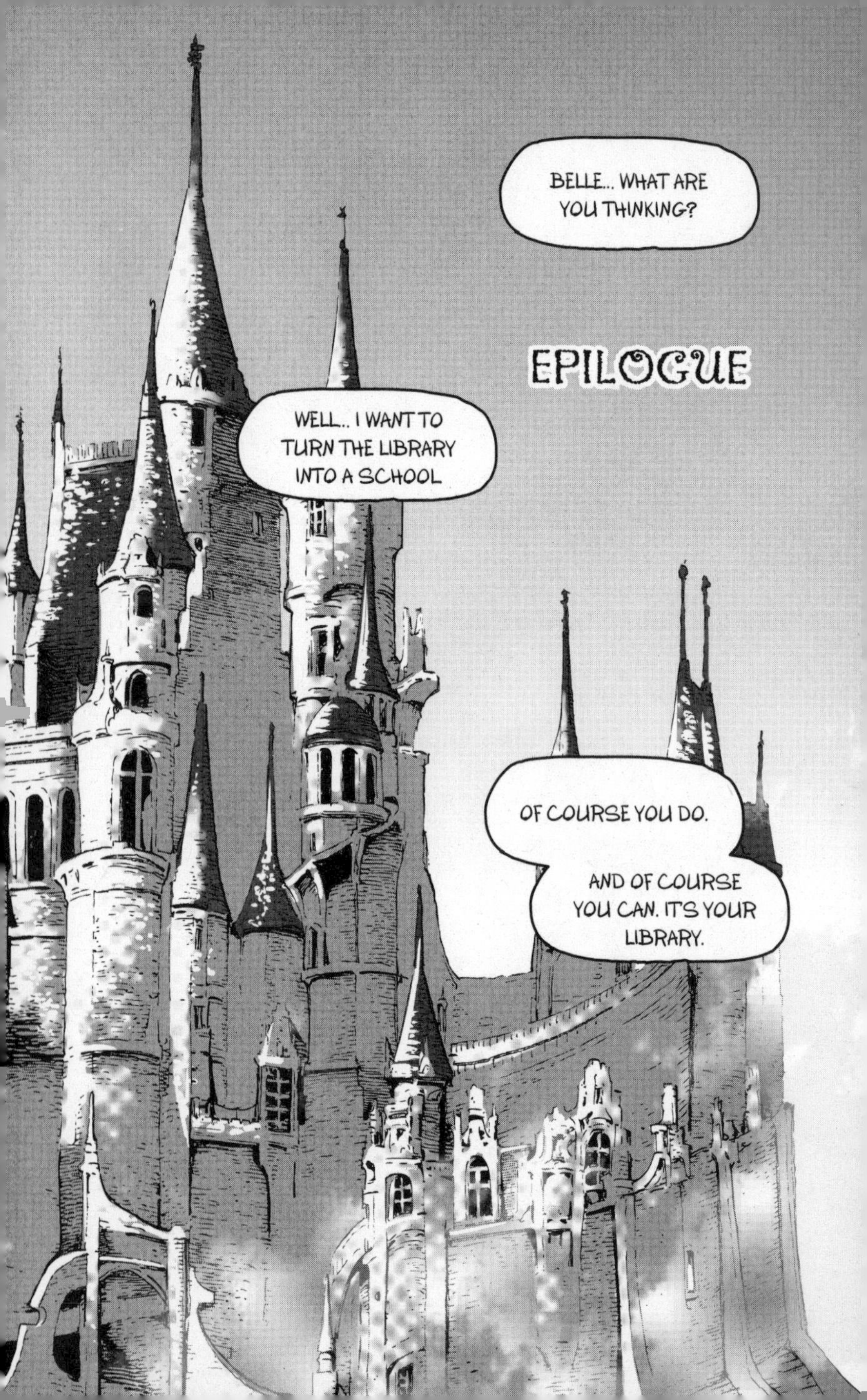
BELLE... WHAT ARE YOU THINKING?
EPILOGUE
WELL... I WANT TO TURN THE LIBRARY INTO A SCHOOL
OF COURSE YOU DO.
AND OF COURSE YOU CAN. IT'S YOUR LIBRARY.

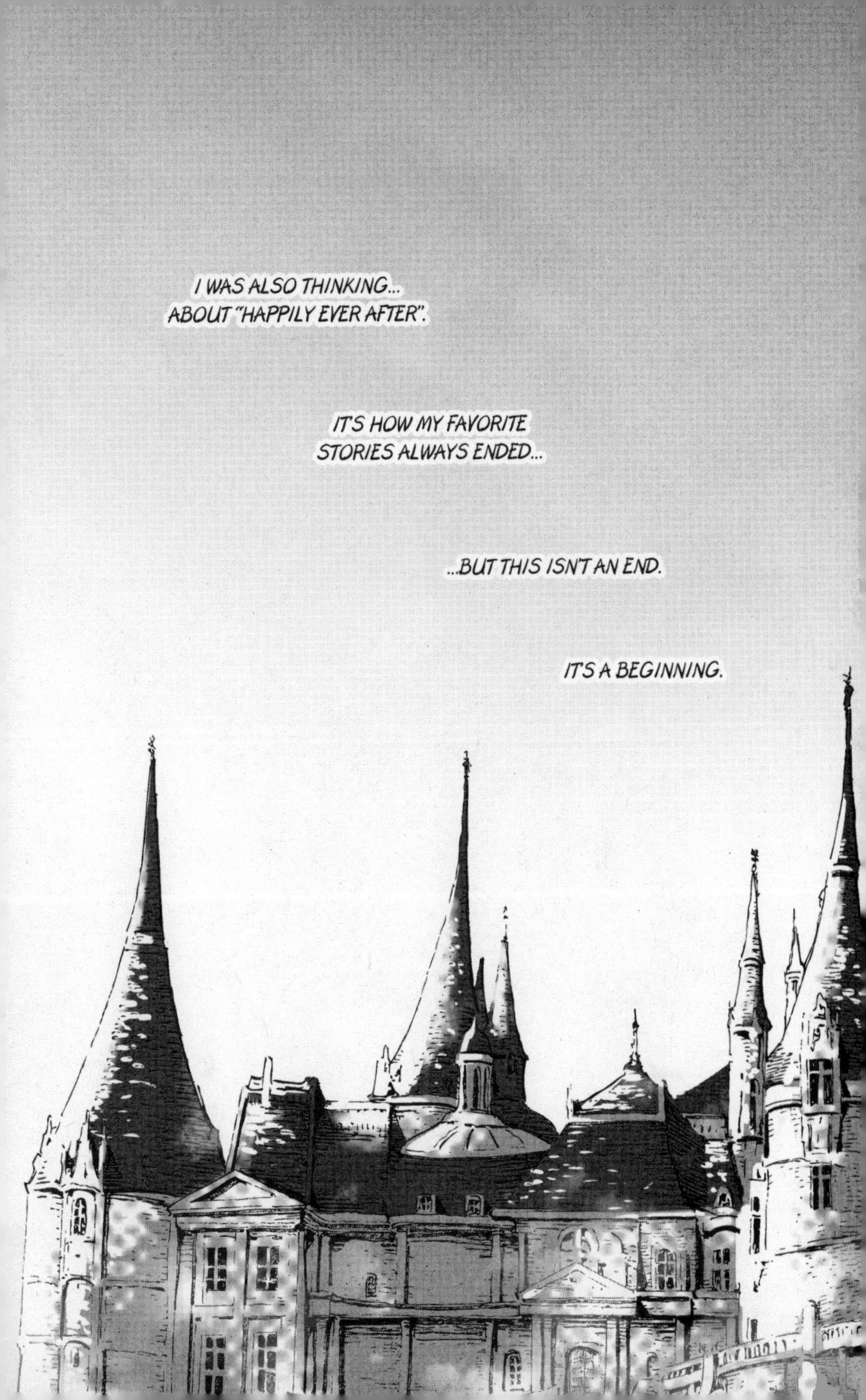
I WAS ALSO THINKING... ABOUT "HAPPILY EVER AFTER".
IT'S HOW MY FAVORITE STORIES ALWAYS ENDED...
...BUT THIS ISN'T AN END.
IT'S A BEGINNING.

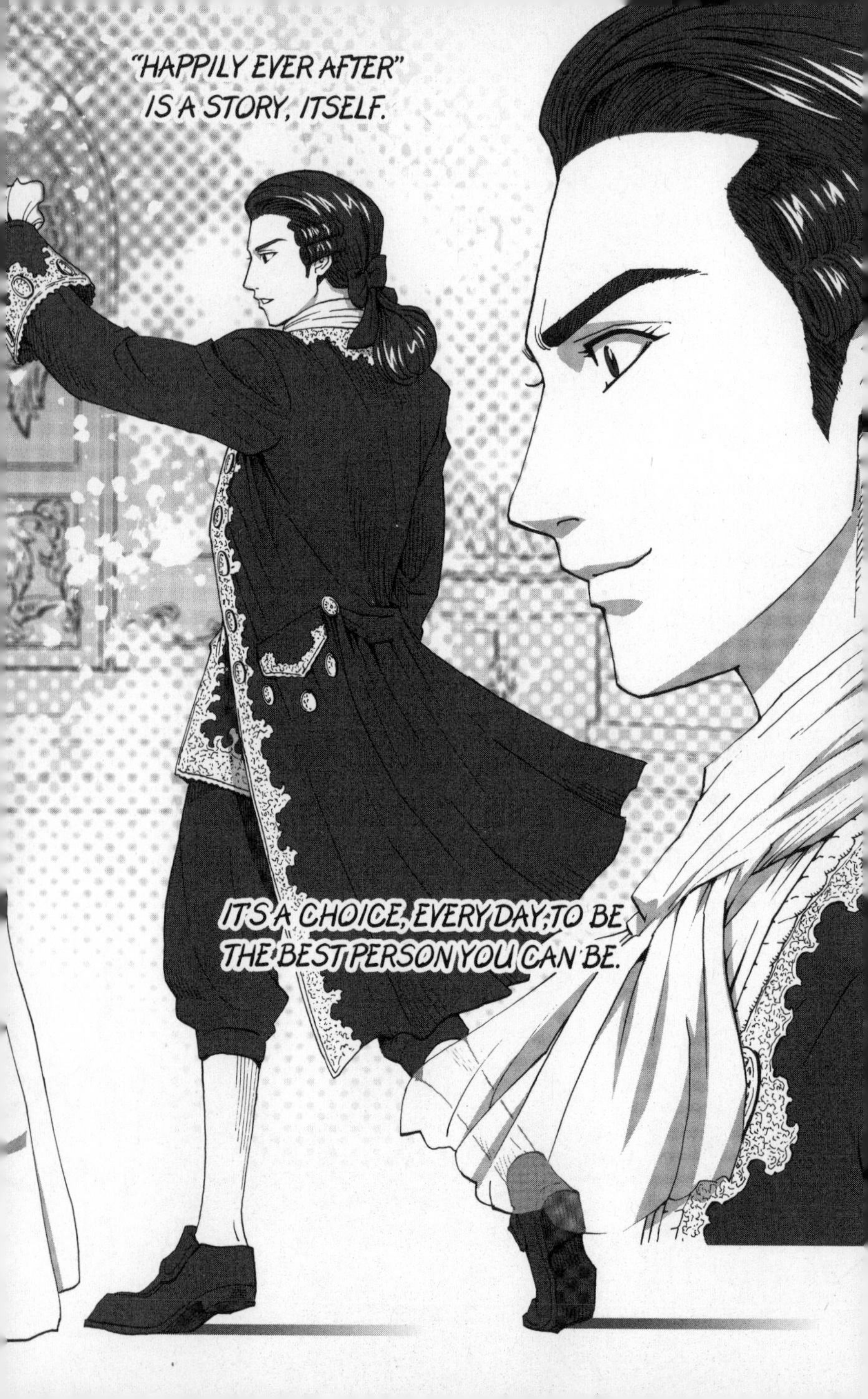
"HAPPILY EVER AFTER" IS A STORY, ITSELF.
IT'S A CHOICE, EVERY DAY, TO BE THE BEST PERSON YOU CAN BE.

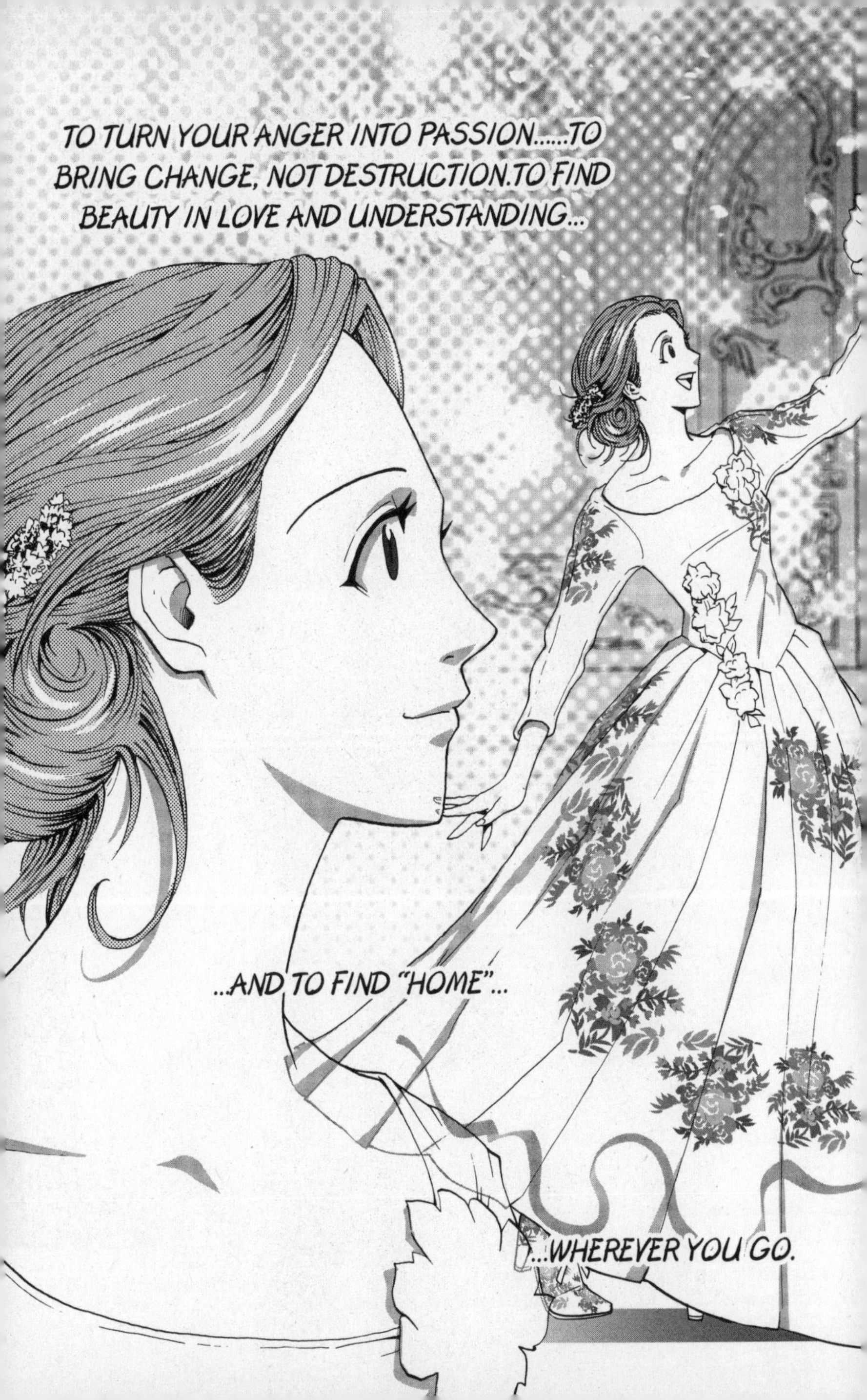
TO TURN YOUR ANGER INTO PASSION......TO BRING CHANGE, NOT DESTRUCTION. TO FIND BEAUTY IN LOVE AND UNDERSTANDING...
...AND TO FIND "HOME"...
...WHEREVER YOU GO.

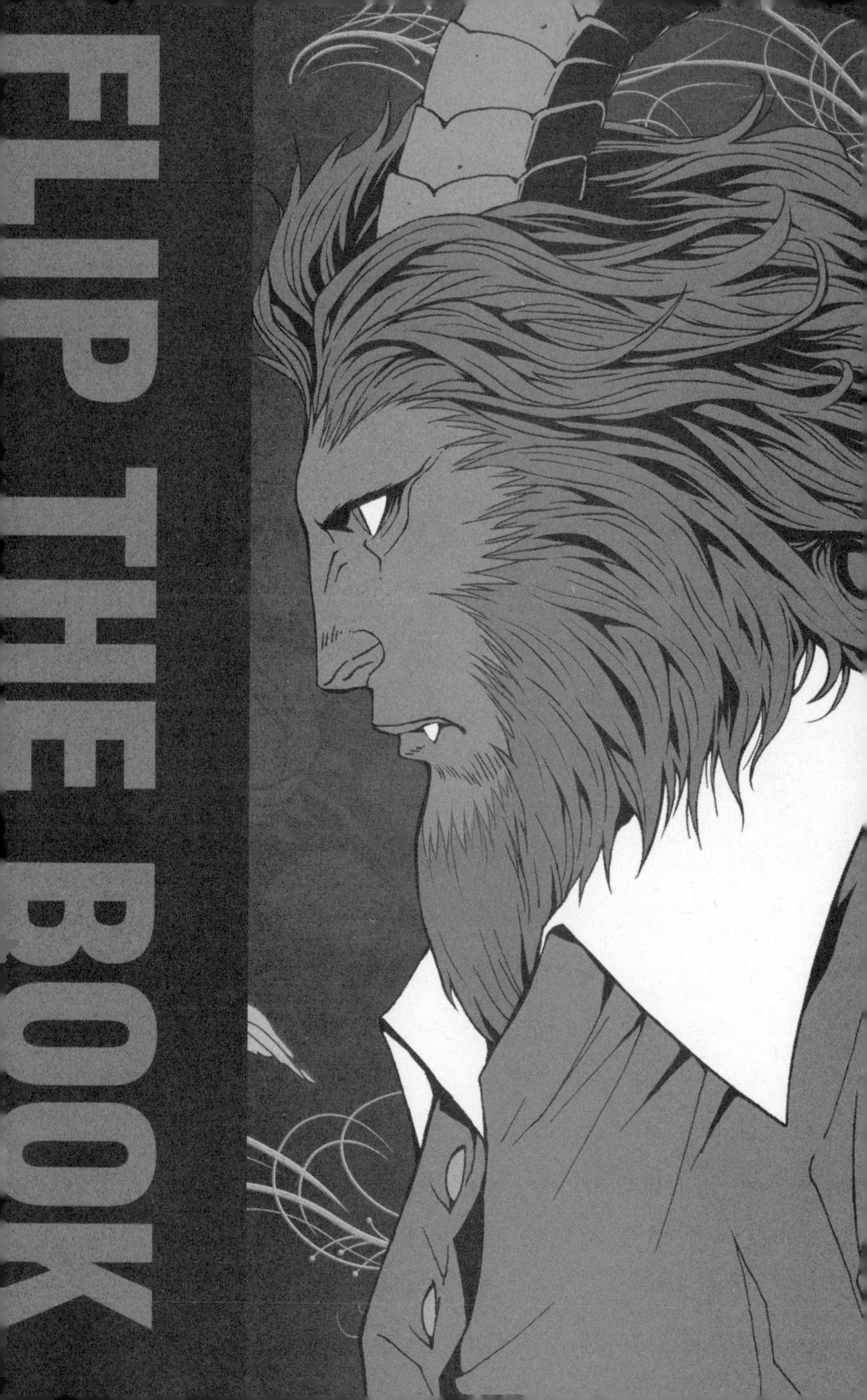
FLIP THE BOOK

Dear Readers:

Welcome to a very special project: the twin companion BEAUTY AND THE BEAST manga set! This particular manga is THE BEAST'S TALE, where we relive the classic story from the Beast's perspective.

Creating a manga image for such a ubiquitous and enigmatic character such as the Beast is a challenge unto itself. Fortunately, we were blessed with an extremely talented team of artists in Japan who ended up with the perfect manga look. To do so, the artists balanced extensive notes and guidance from the Disney team with inherent manga sensibility – and you can experience that process a bit by studying the Concept Art bonus pages near the end of this book.

Further, adapting the gorgeous production design from the film into hand-drawn illustrations in the manga was an exhilarating experience. Our goal was always to satisfy your innate curiosity about this classic world and characters while keeping the manga aesthetic relevant to your reading experience. Hopefully you'll enjoy the visuals as much as we do.

And of course adapting this world-renowned story for the page was critical, especially honing in on the Beast's point of view, which is particularly unique to this book. While BEAUTY AND THE BEAST is famously Belle's story, we wanted to demystify the Beast in a personal and intimate way.

So, in this manga you can dive in and experience this side of the Beast from within – his true emotions, his soul. Join us on a journey into the Beast's mind – and see what Belle saw, and who she fell in love with.

TOKYOPOP is proud to bring you THE BEAST'S TALE!

—Team TOKYOPOP

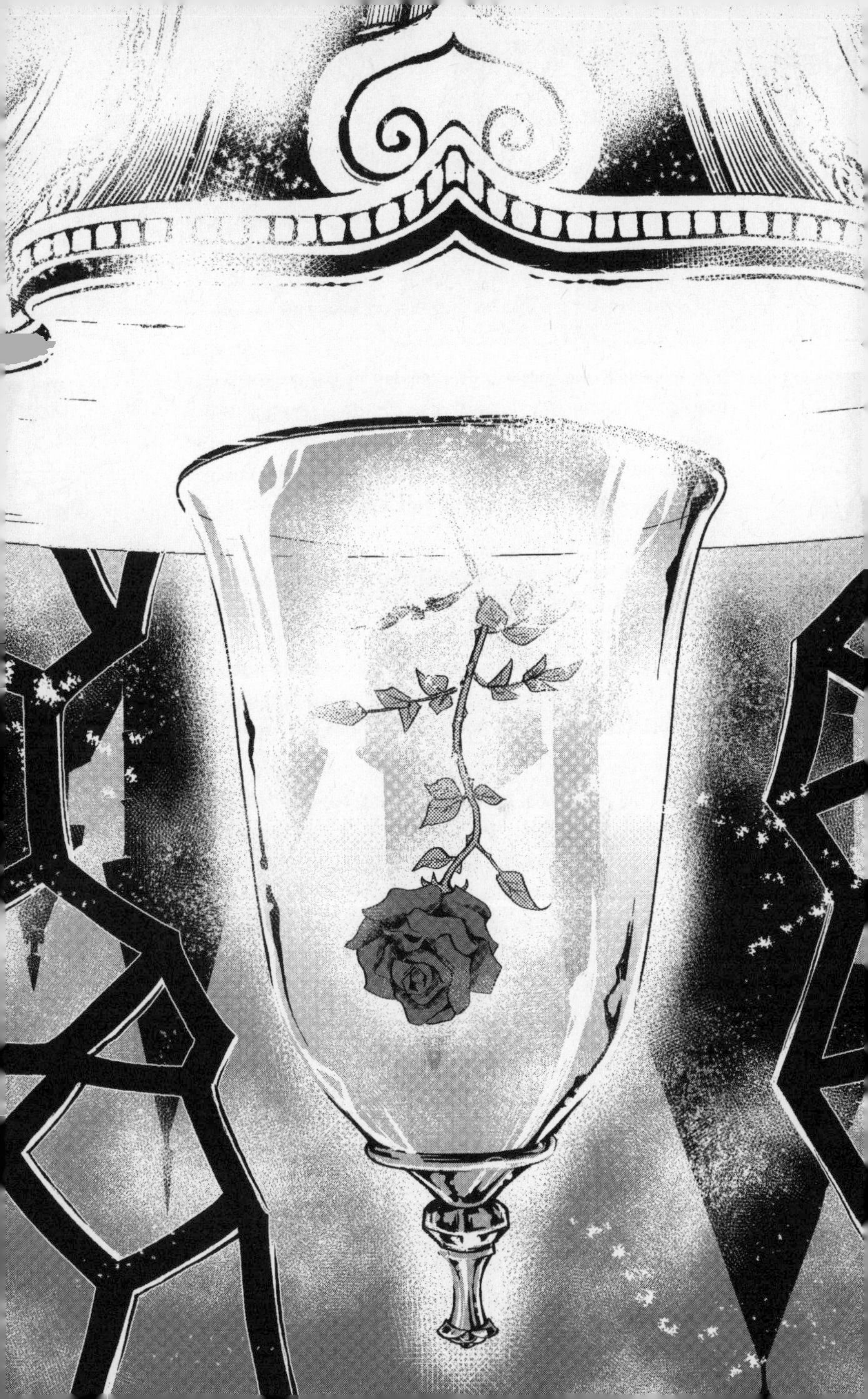

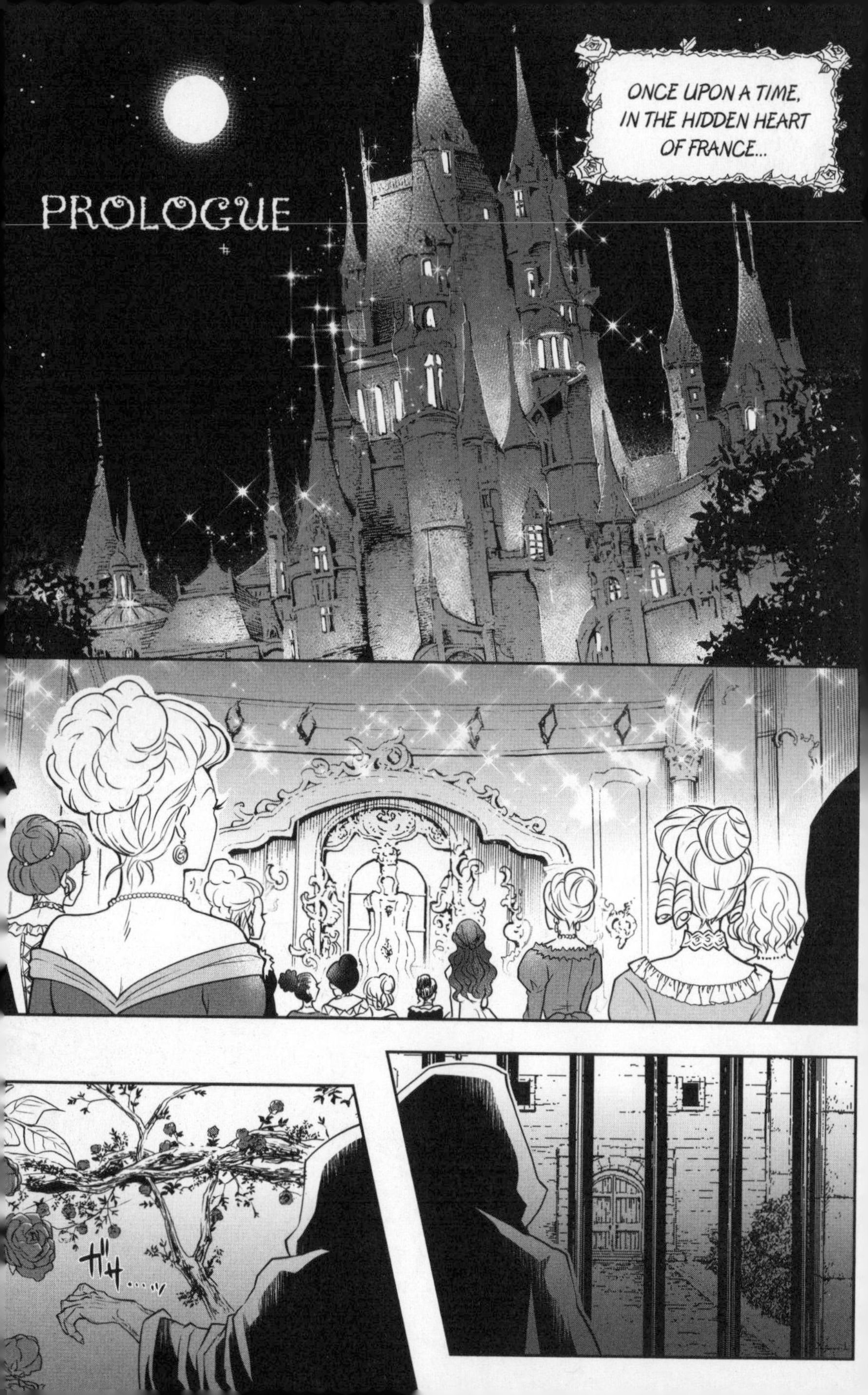
ONCE UPON A TIME, IN THE HIDDEN HEART OF FRANCE...
PROLOGUE
ガサ...ッ

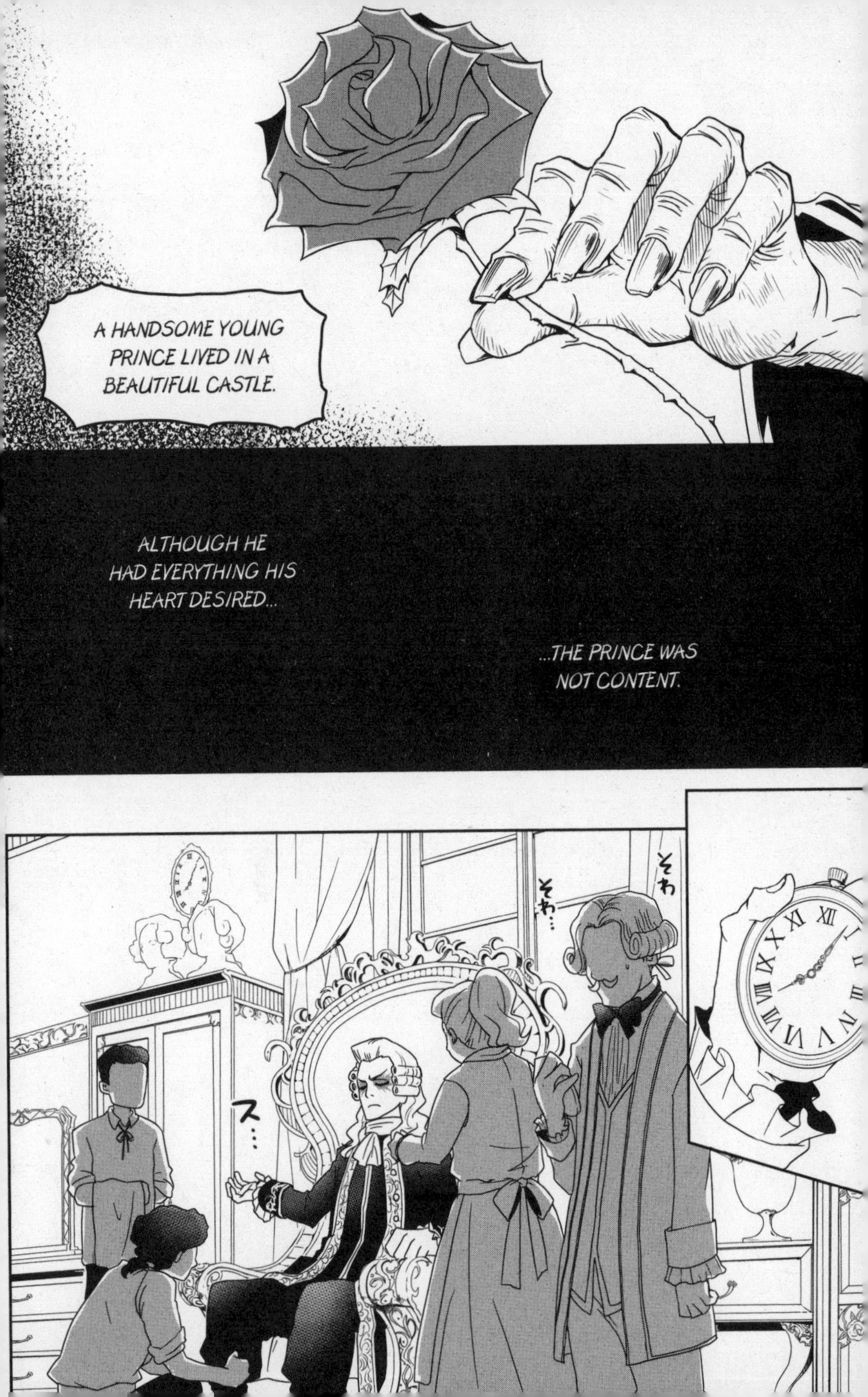
A HANDSOME YOUNG PRINCE LIVED IN A BEAUTIFUL CASTLE.
ALTHOUGH HE HAD EVERYTHING HIS HEART DESIRED...
...THE PRINCE WAS NOT CONTENT.
そわ
そわ…
ス…

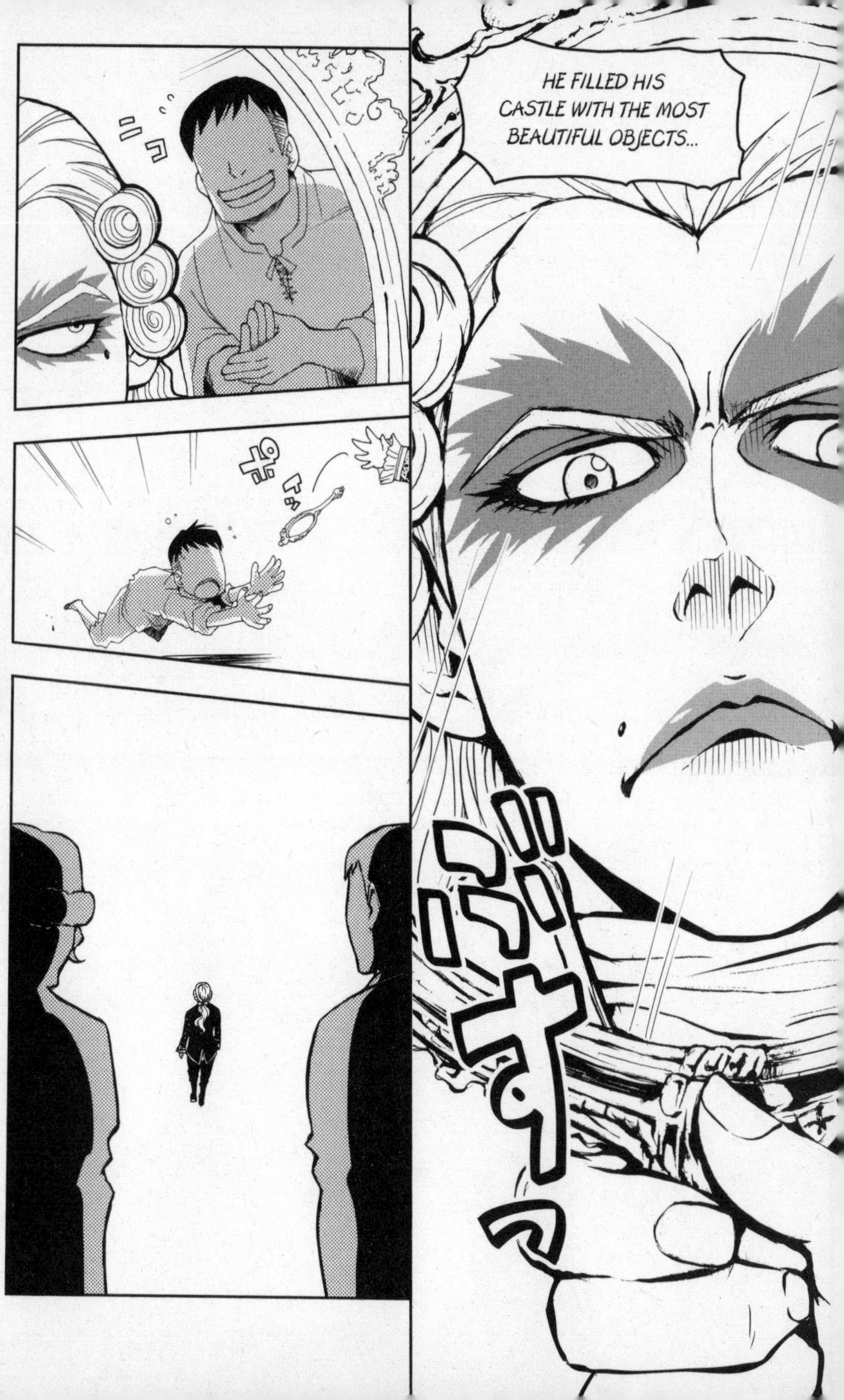
HE FILLED HIS CASTLE WITH THE MOST BEAUTIFUL OBJECTS...

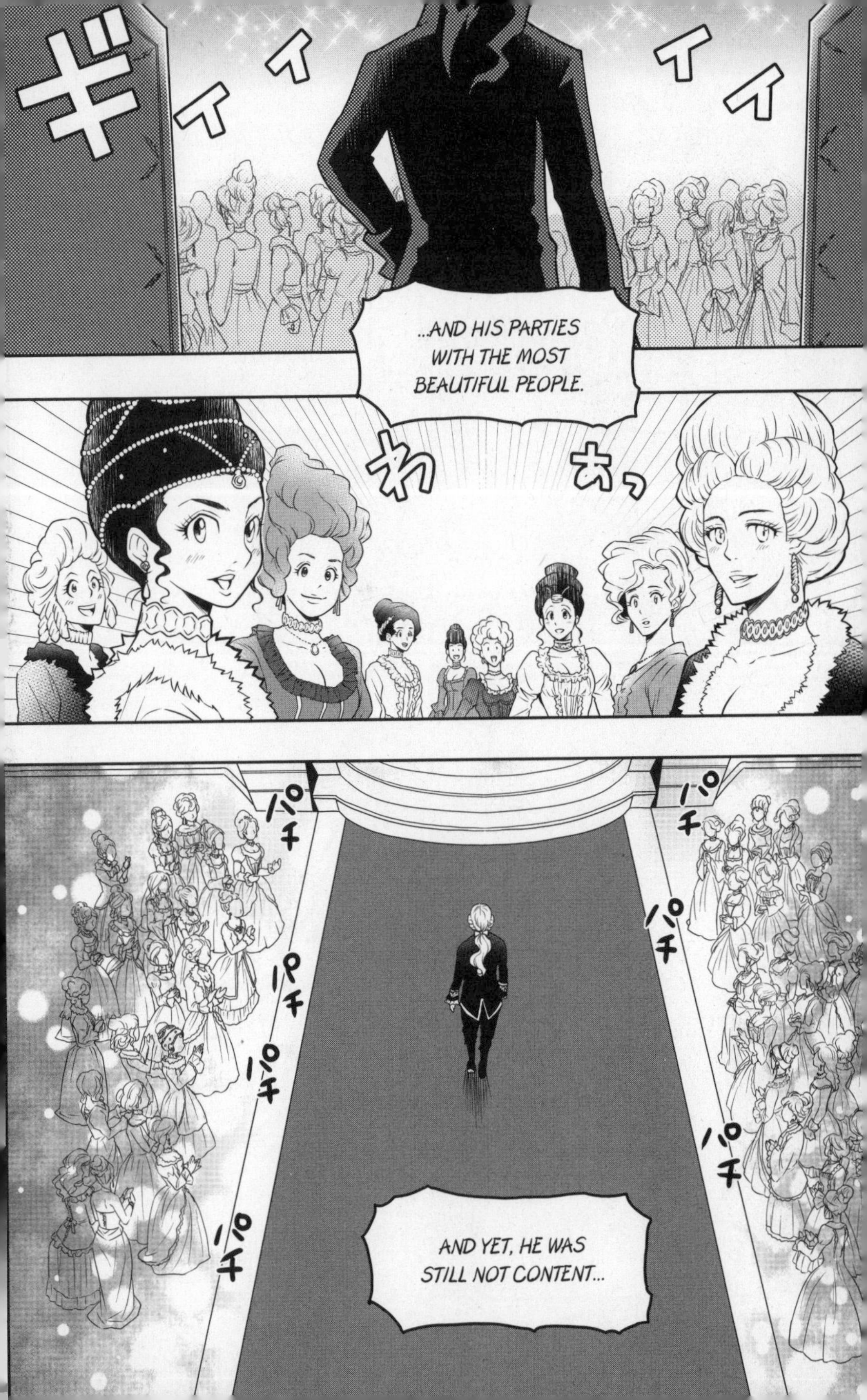
ギィィ
イイ
...AND HIS PARTIES WITH THE MOST BEAUTIFUL PEOPLE.
あっ
わ
パチ
パチ
パチ
パチ
パチ
パチ
パチ
パチ
AND YET, HE WAS STILL NOT CONTENT...

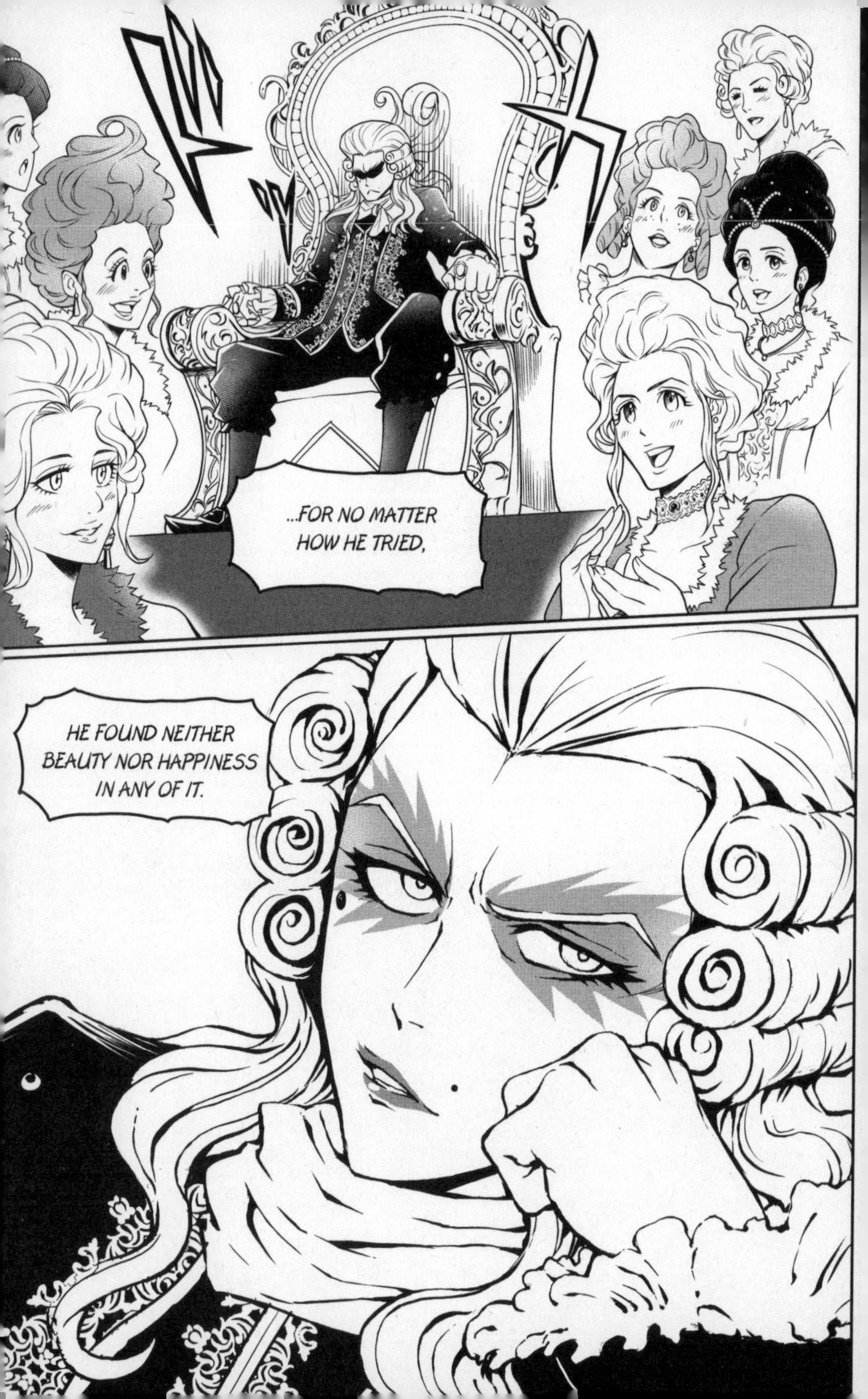
...FOR NO MATTER HOW HE TRIED,
HE FOUND NEITHER BEAUTY NOR HAPPINESS IN ANY OF IT.

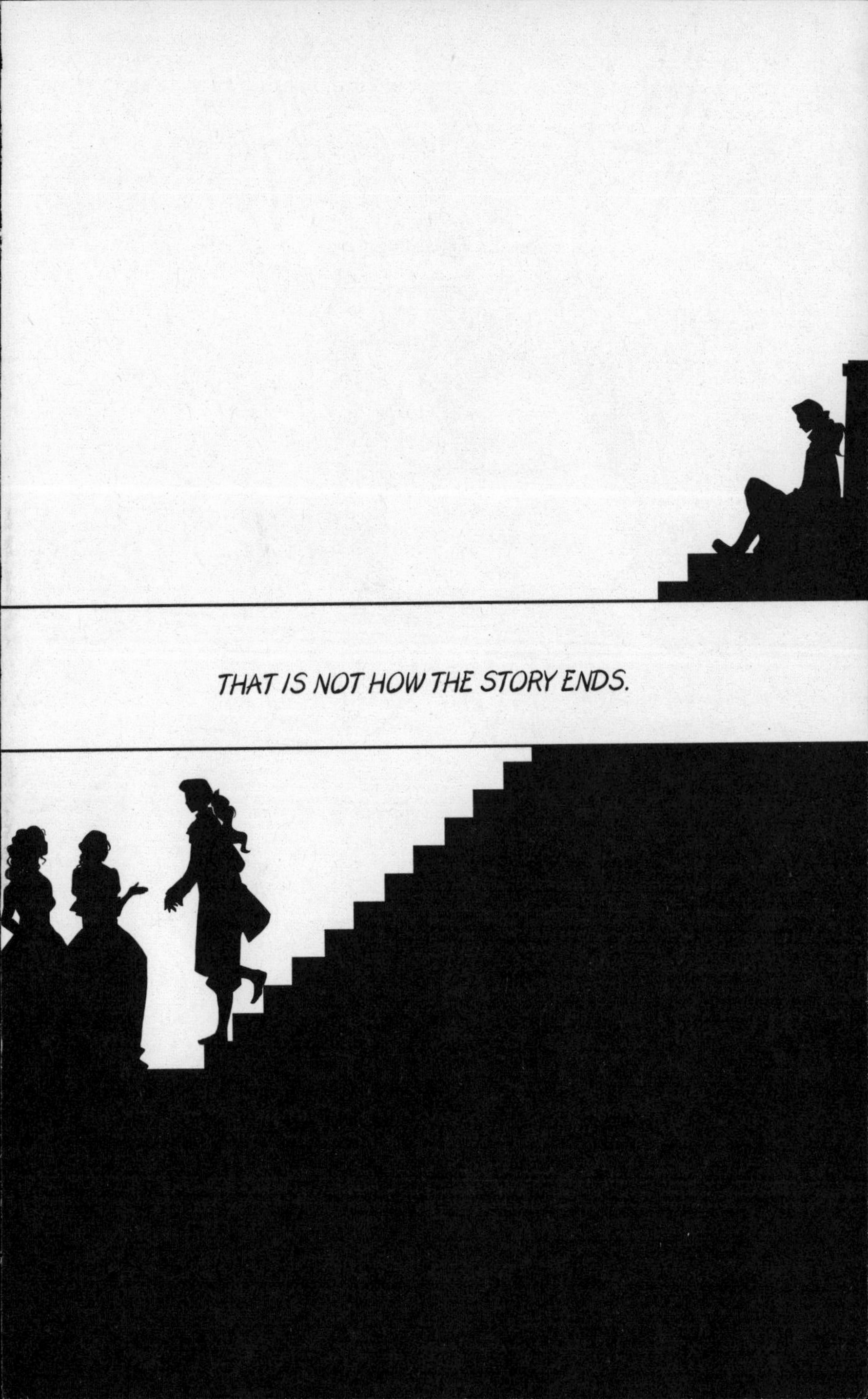
THAT IS NOT HOW THE STORY ENDS.

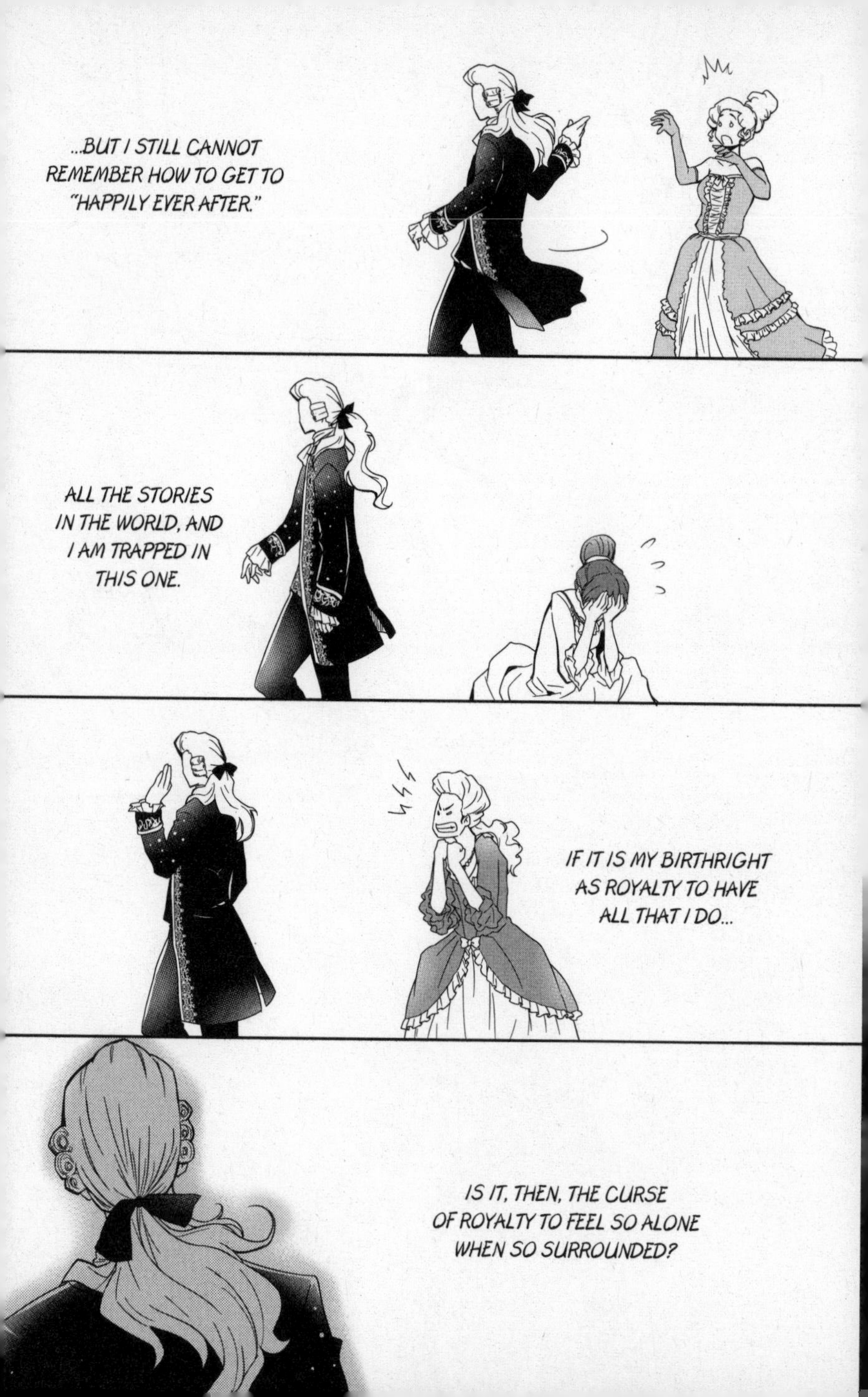

...BUT I STILL CANNOT REMEMBER HOW TO GET TO "HAPPILY EVER AFTER."
ALL THE STORIES IN THE WORLD, AND I AM TRAPPED IN THIS ONE.
IF IT IS MY BIRTHRIGHT AS ROYALTY TO HAVE ALL THAT I DO...
IS IT, THEN, THE CURSE OF ROYALTY TO FEEL SO ALONE WHEN SO SURROUNDED?

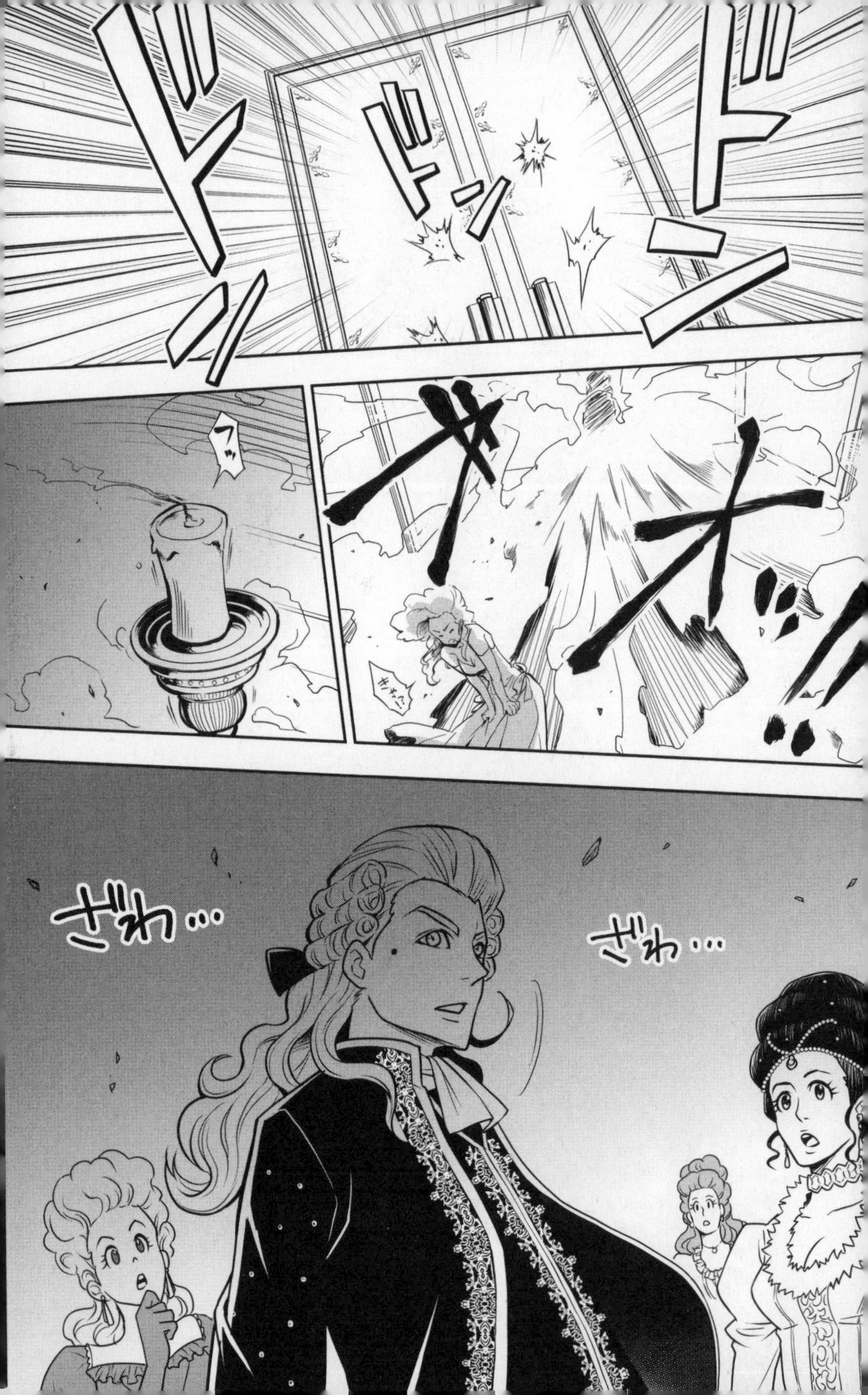
ドン
ドーン
ドン
オオッ!!
きゃっ!?
フッ
ざわ…
ざわ…

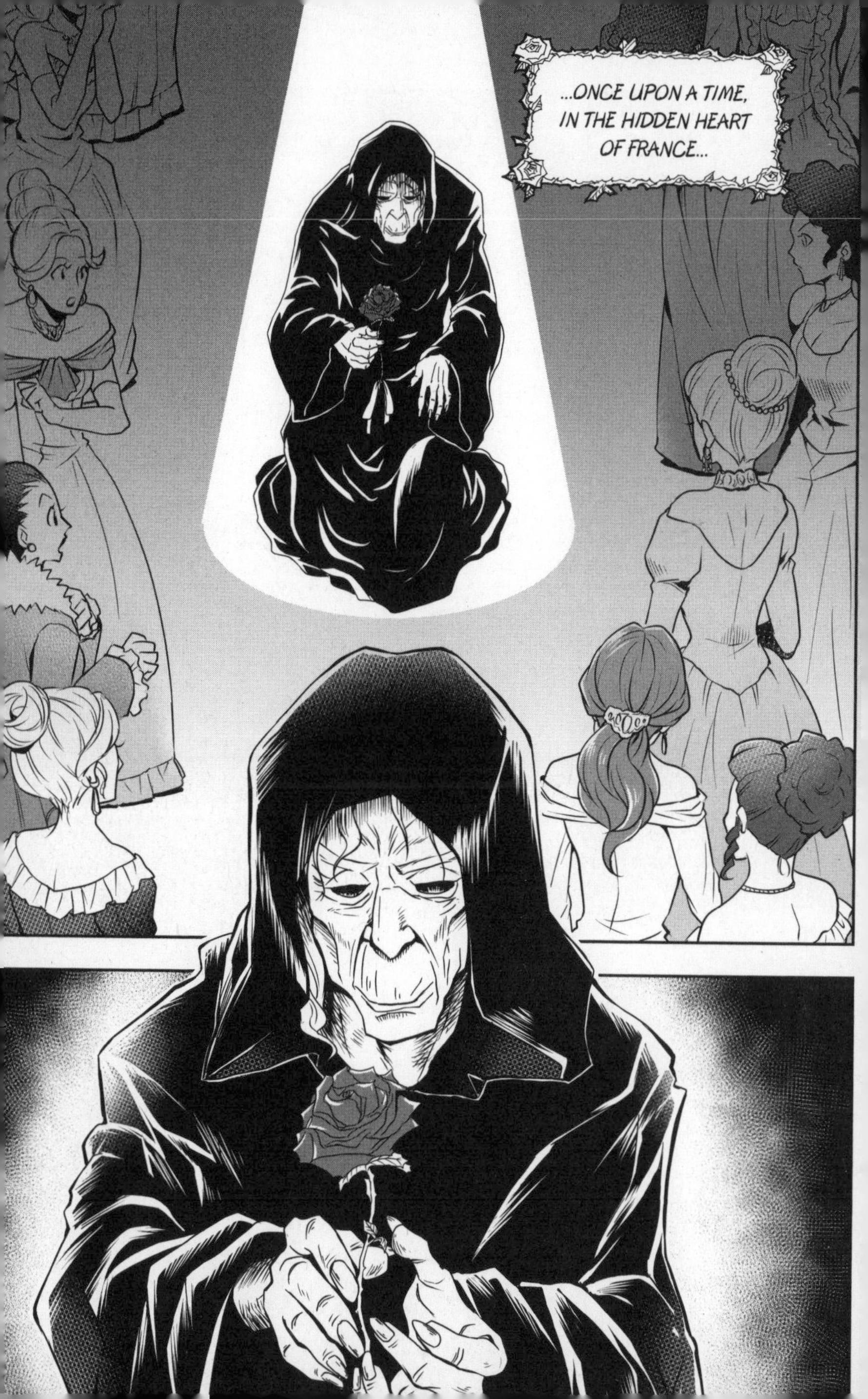
...ONCE UPON A TIME, IN THE HIDDEN HEART OF FRANCE...

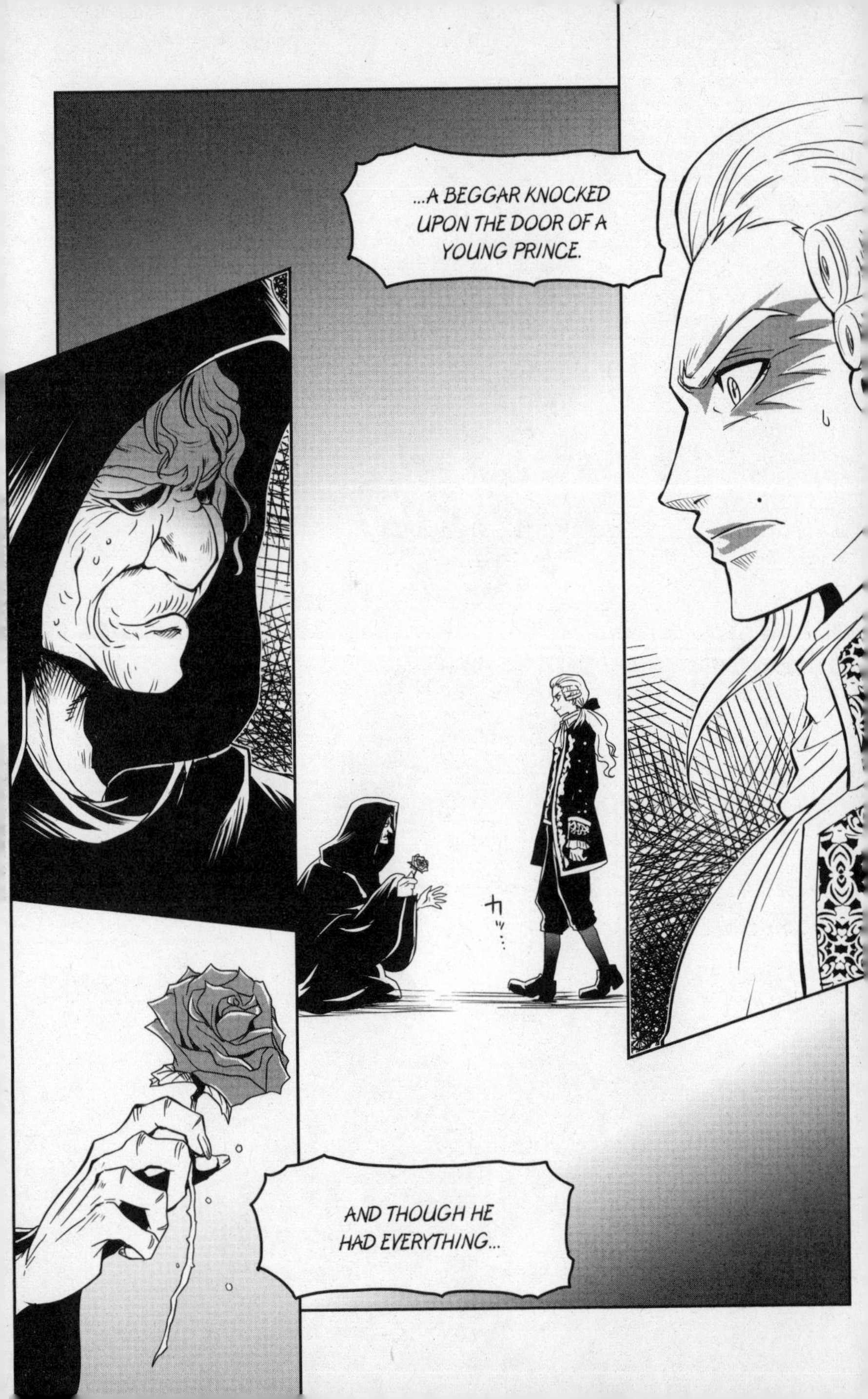
...A BEGGAR KNOCKED UPON THE DOOR OF A YOUNG PRINCE.
カッ...
AND THOUGH HE HAD EVERYTHING...

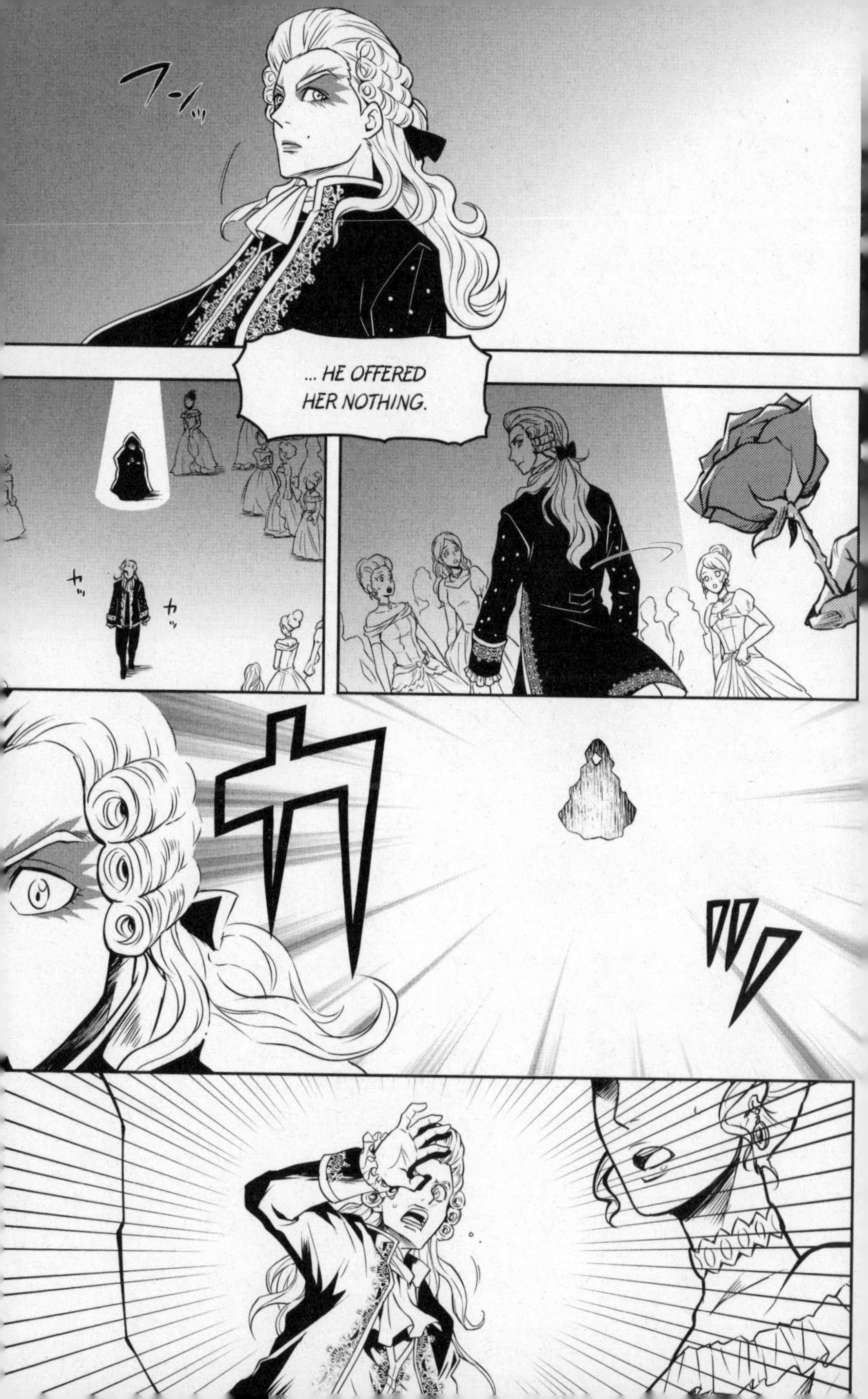
... HE OFFERED HER NOTHING.

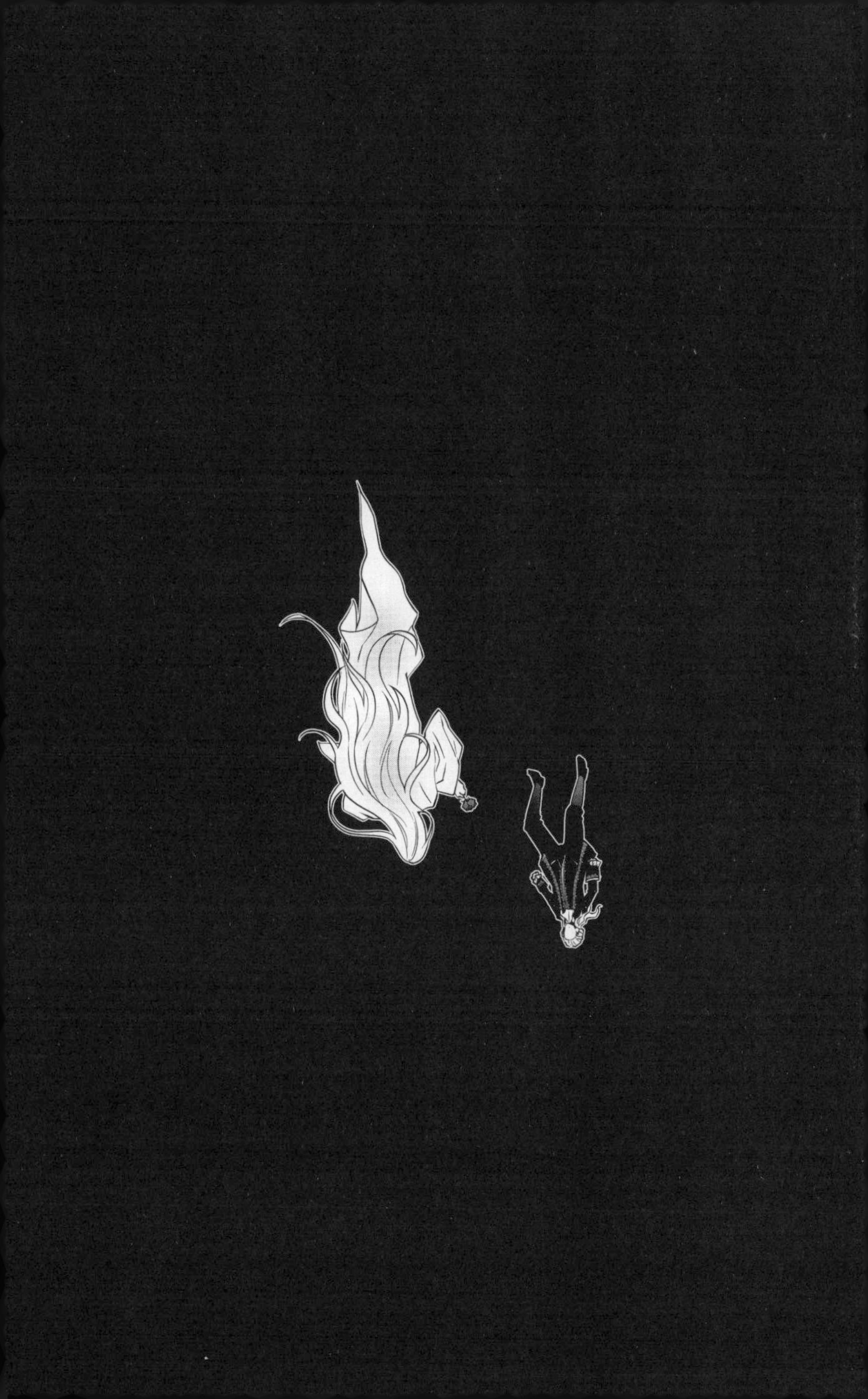

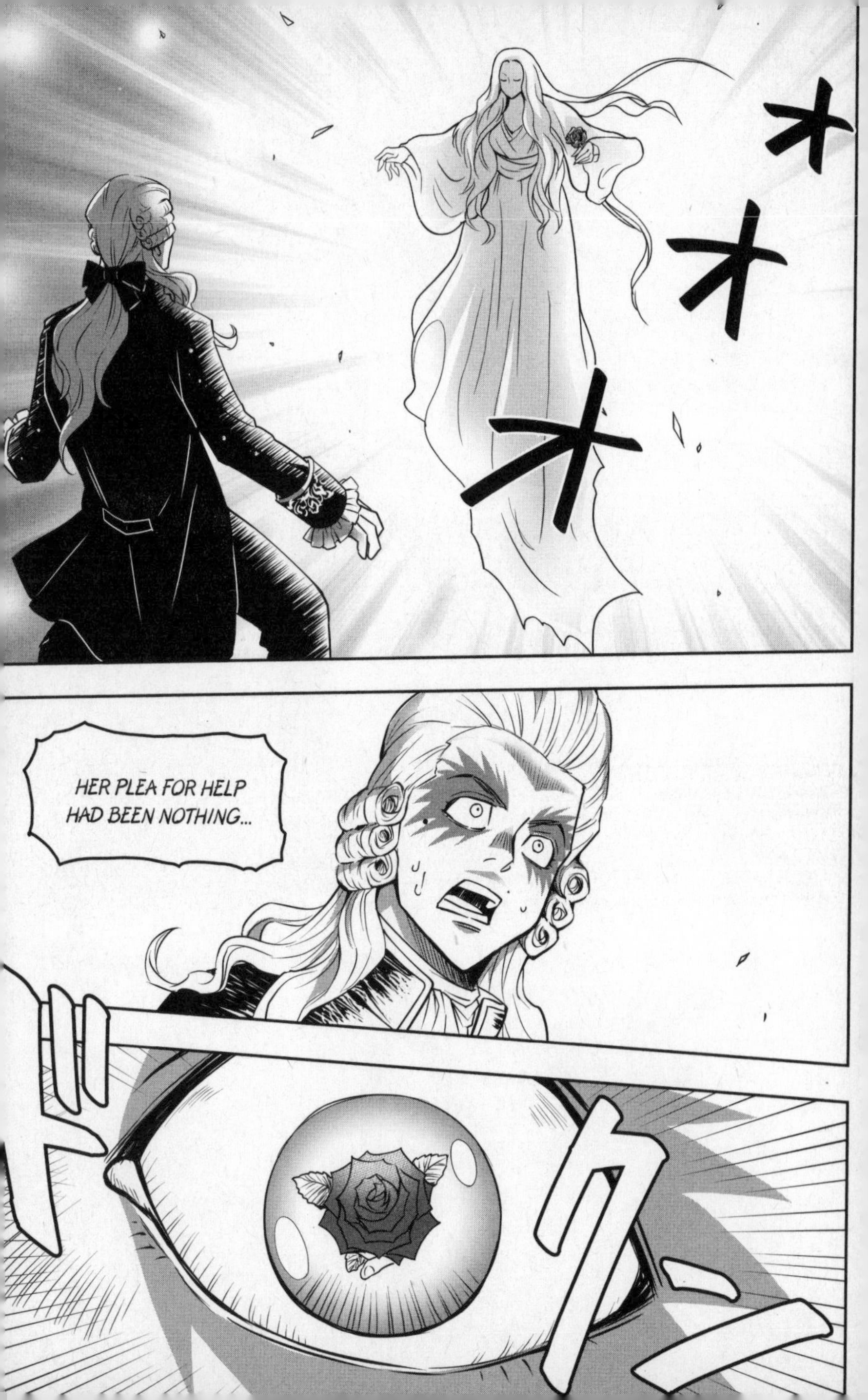
オオオ
HER PLEA FOR HELP HAD BEEN NOTHING...
ドクン

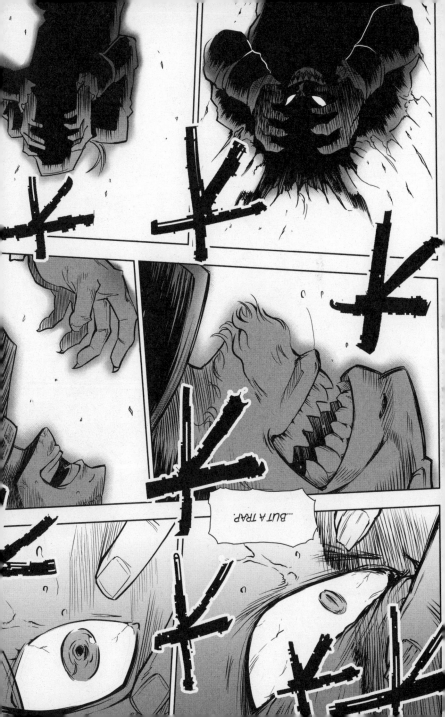

"...BUT A TRAP."

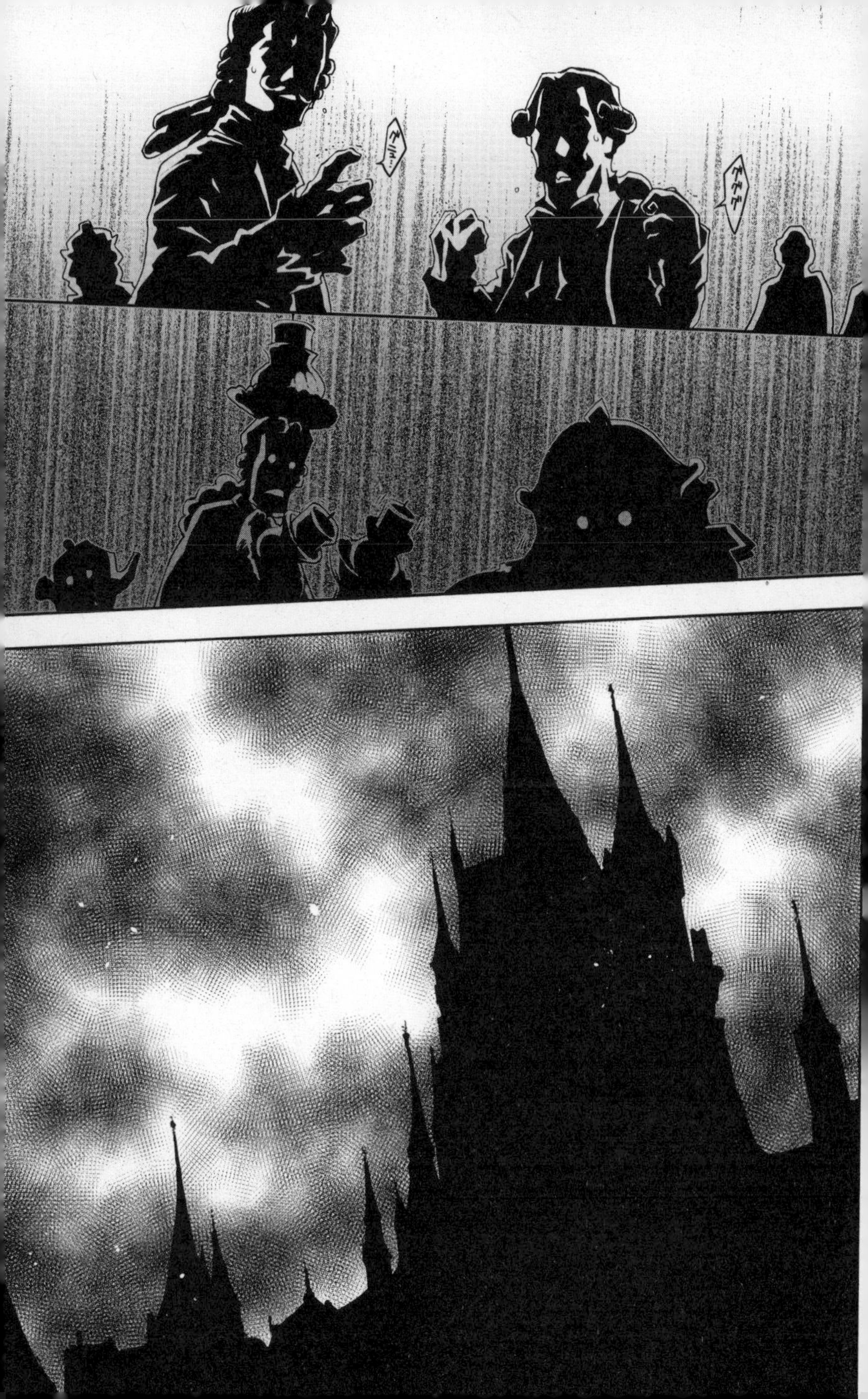
ぞぞぞ

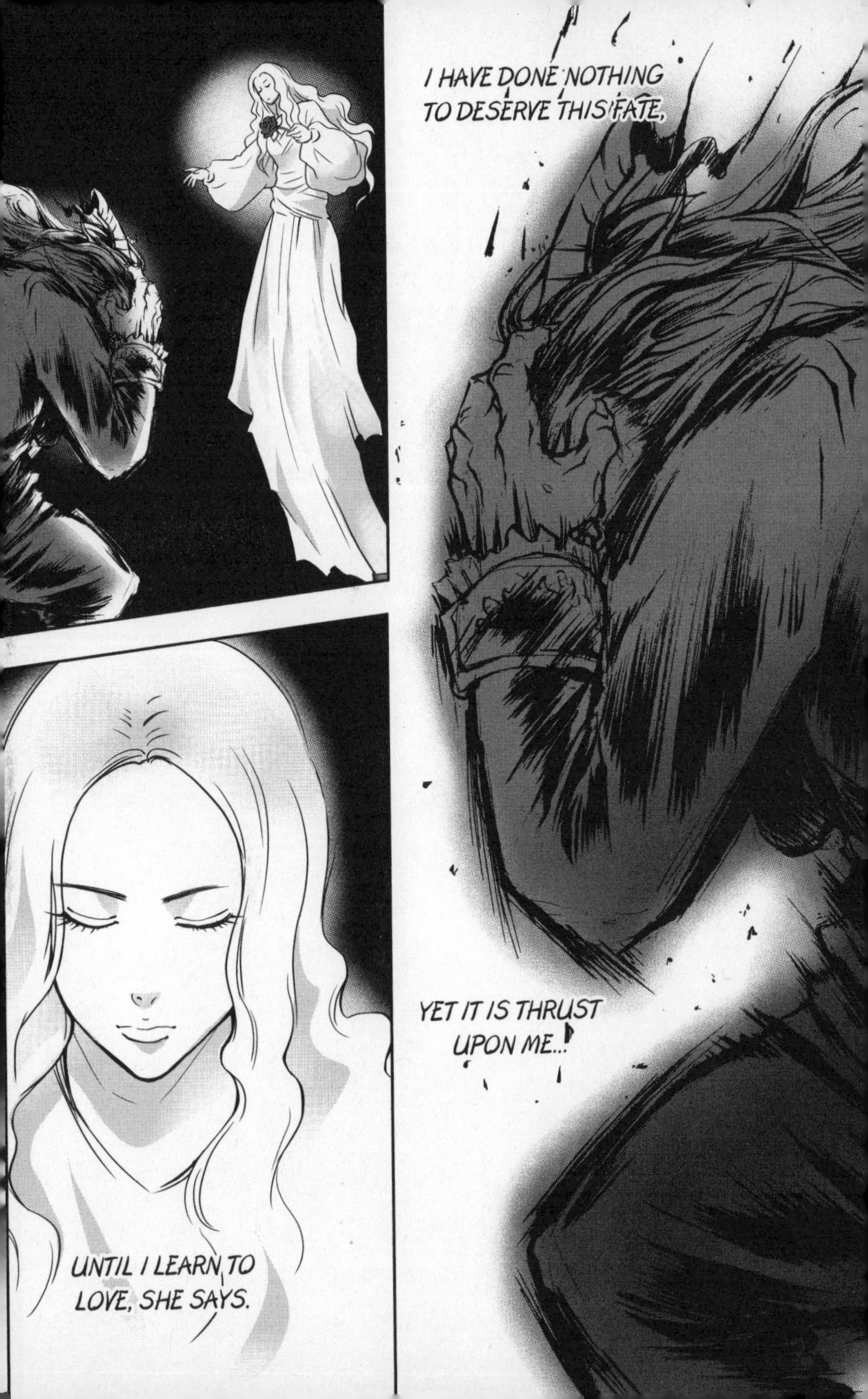
I HAVE DONE NOTHING TO DESERVE THIS FATE,
YET IT IS THRUST UPON ME...!
UNTIL I LEARN TO LOVE, SHE SAYS.

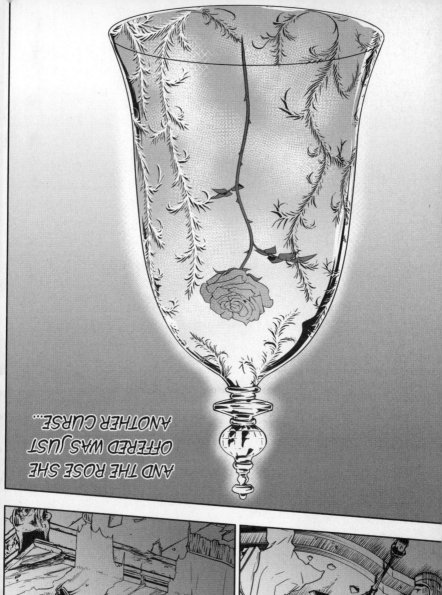

AND THE ROSE SHE OFFERED WAS JUST ANOTHER CURSE....

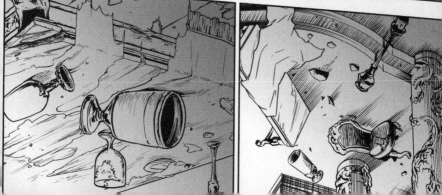

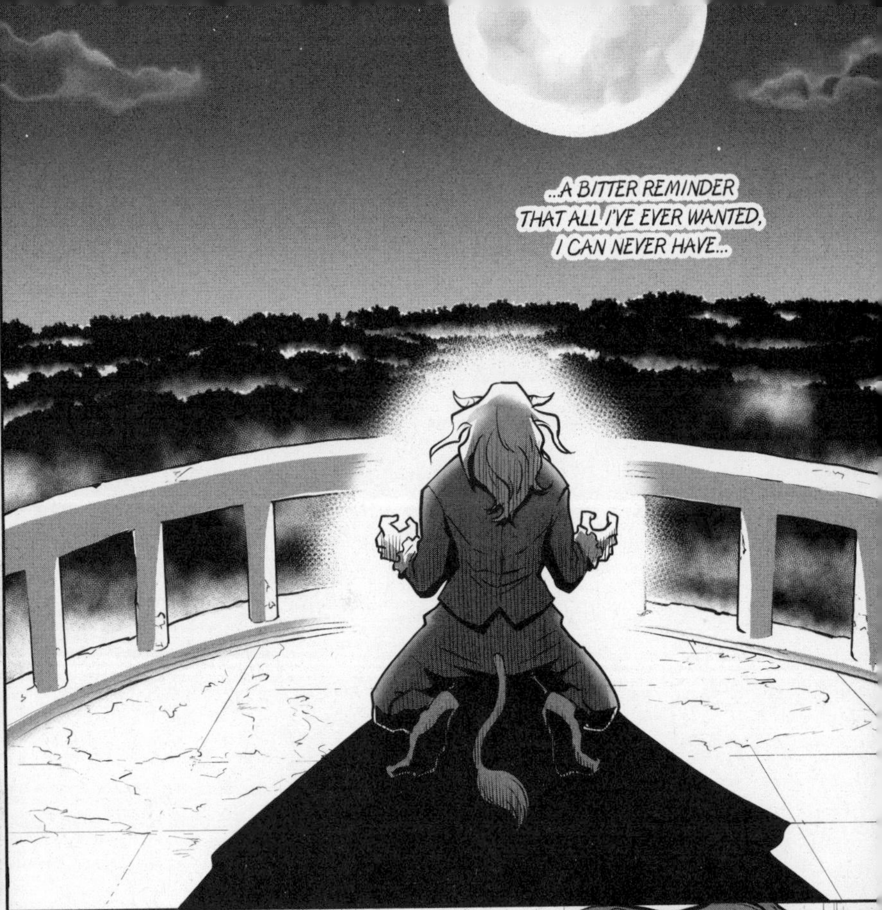
...A BITTER REMINDER THAT ALL I'VE EVER WANTED, I CAN NEVER HAVE...
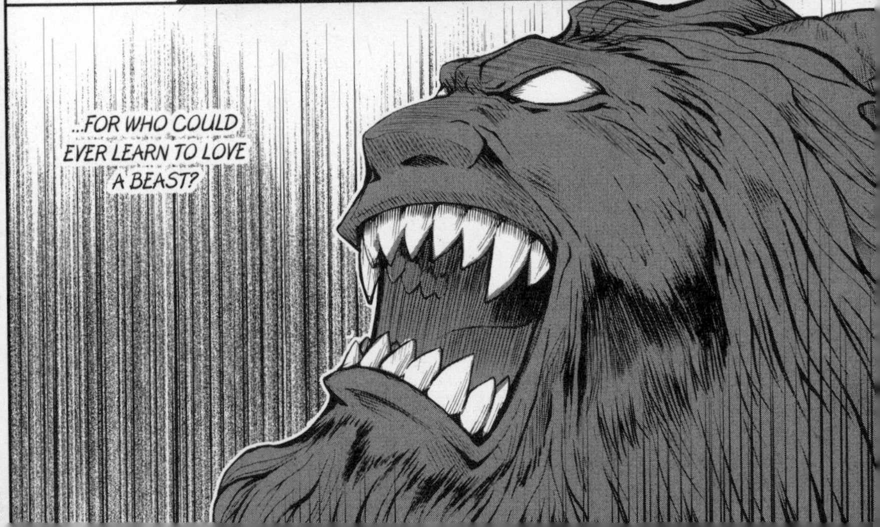
...FOR WHO COULD EVER LEARN TO LOVE A BEAST?

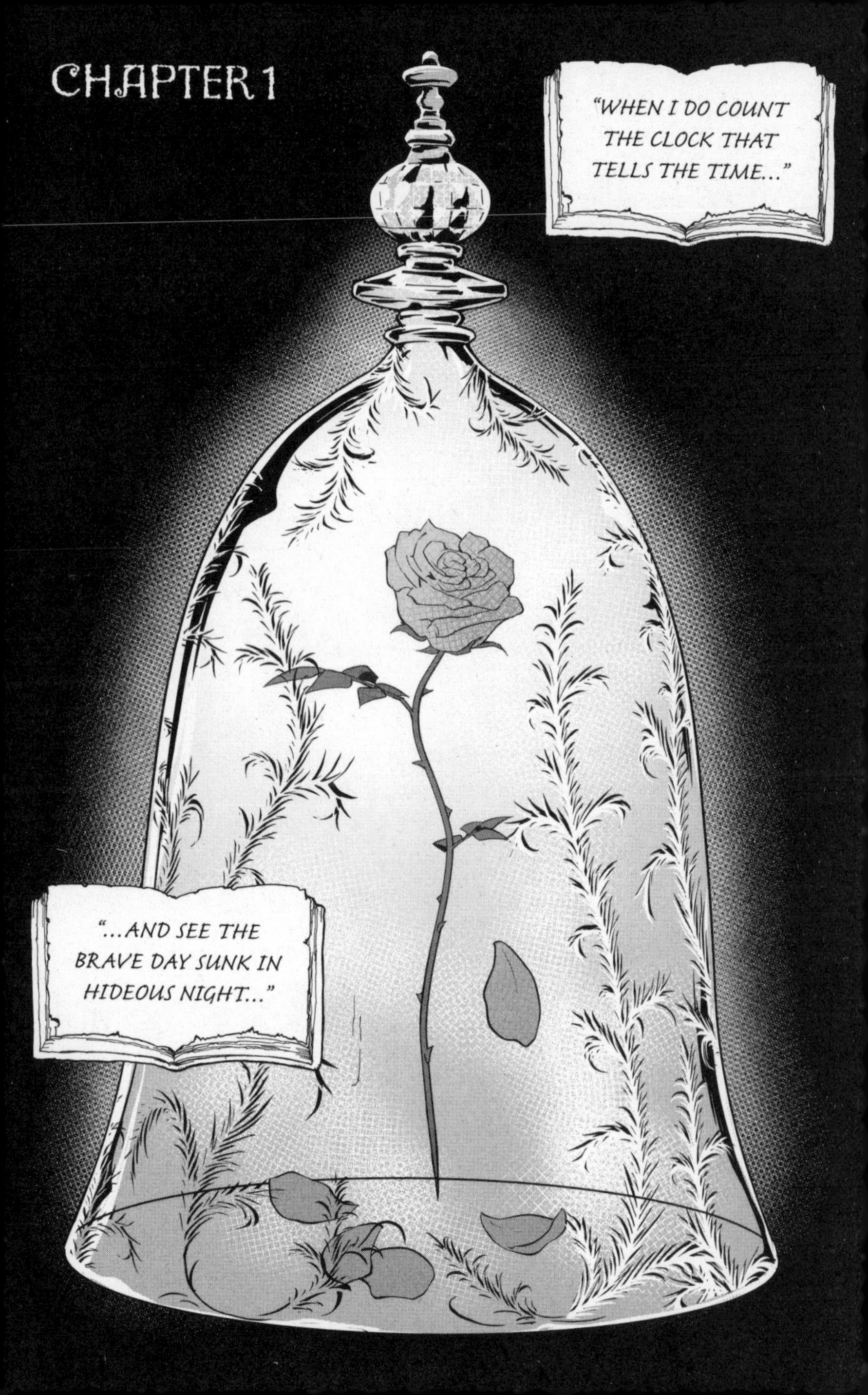
CHAPTER 1
"WHEN I DO COUNT THE CLOCK THAT TELLS THE TIME..."
"...AND SEE THE BRAVE DAY SUNK IN HIDEOUS NIGHT..."

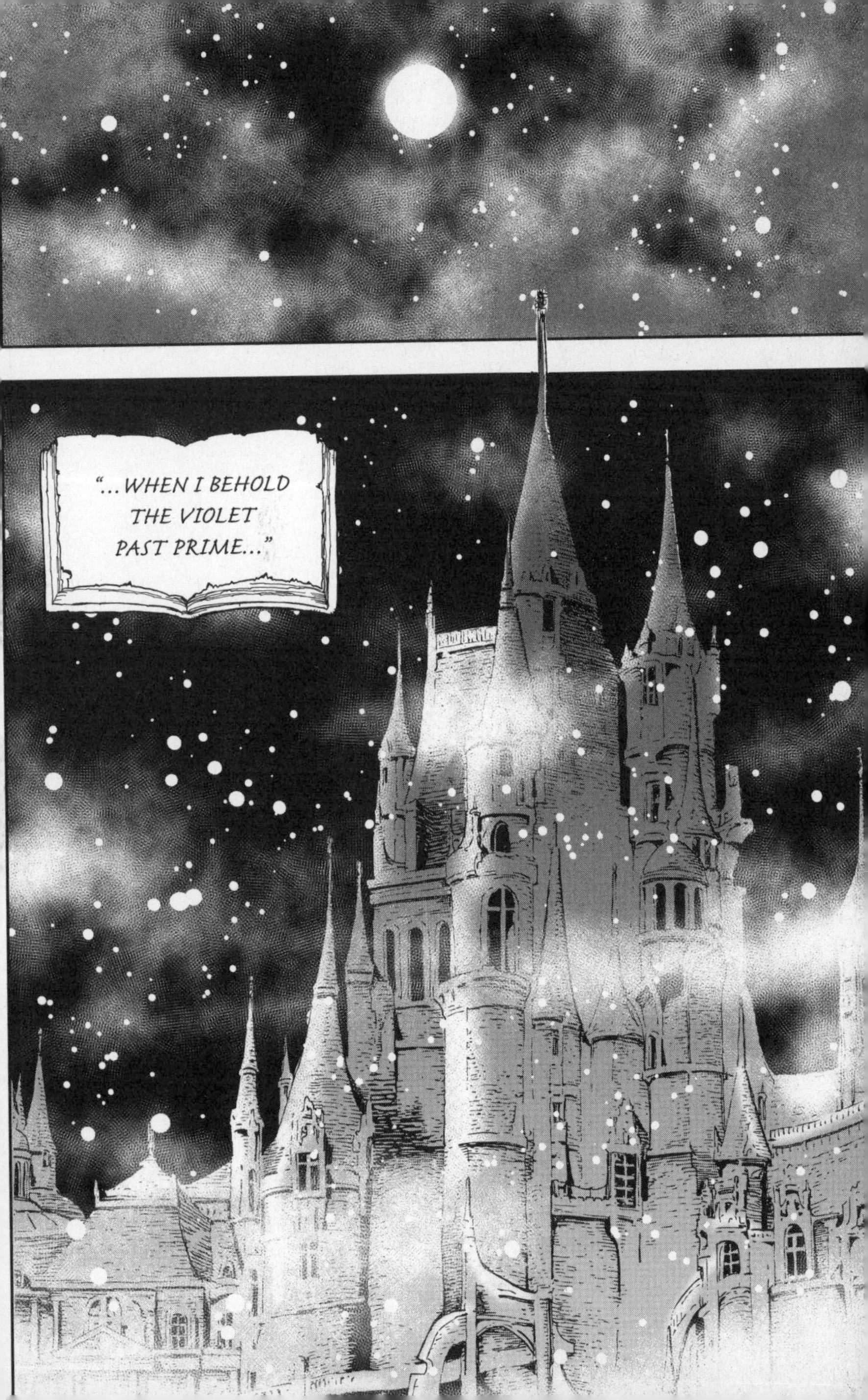
"...WHEN I BEHOLD THE VIOLET PAST PRIME..."

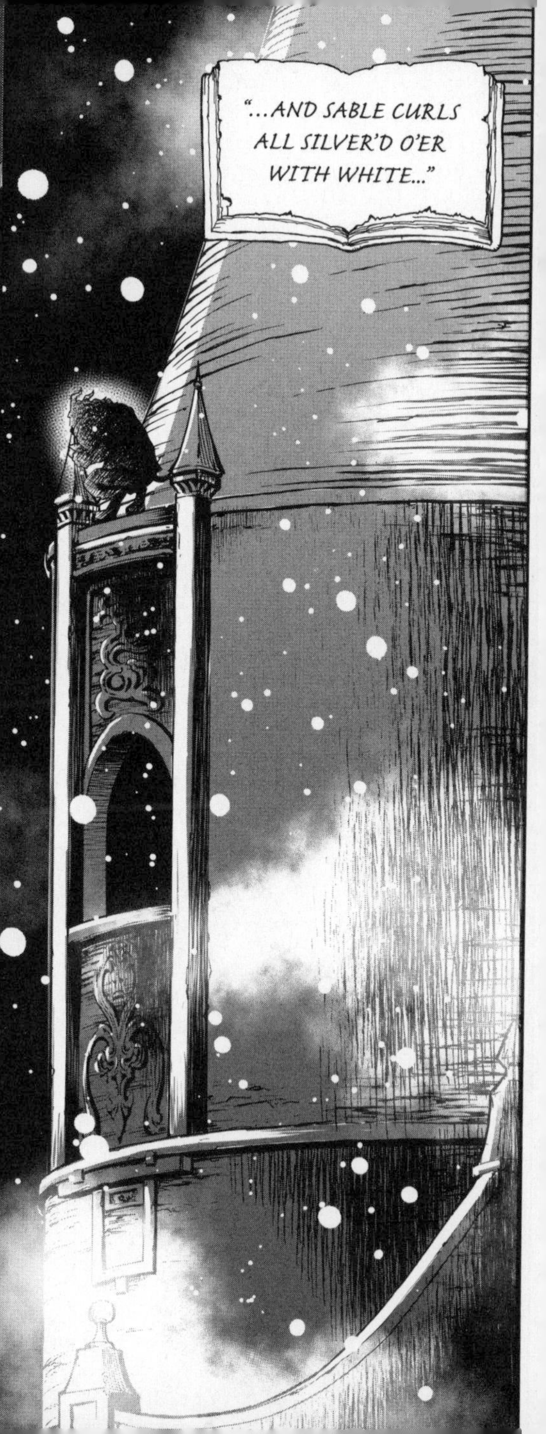
"...AND SABLE CURLS ALL SILVER'D O'ER WITH WHITE..."
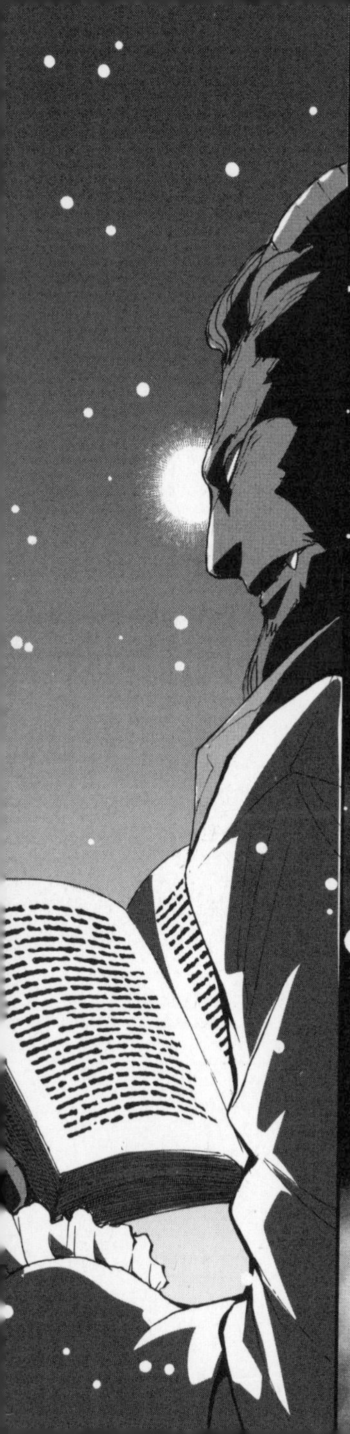

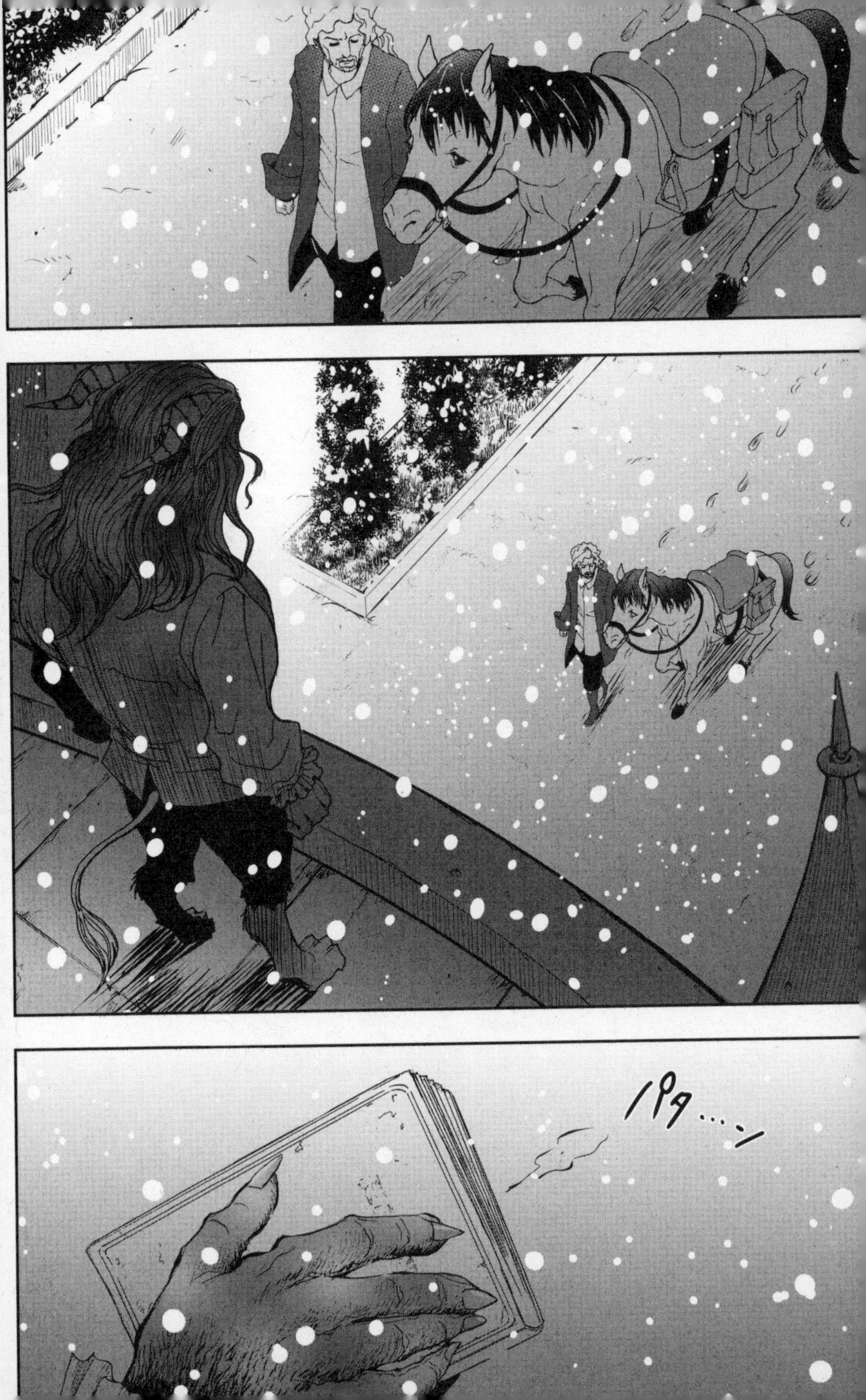
パタ…ン

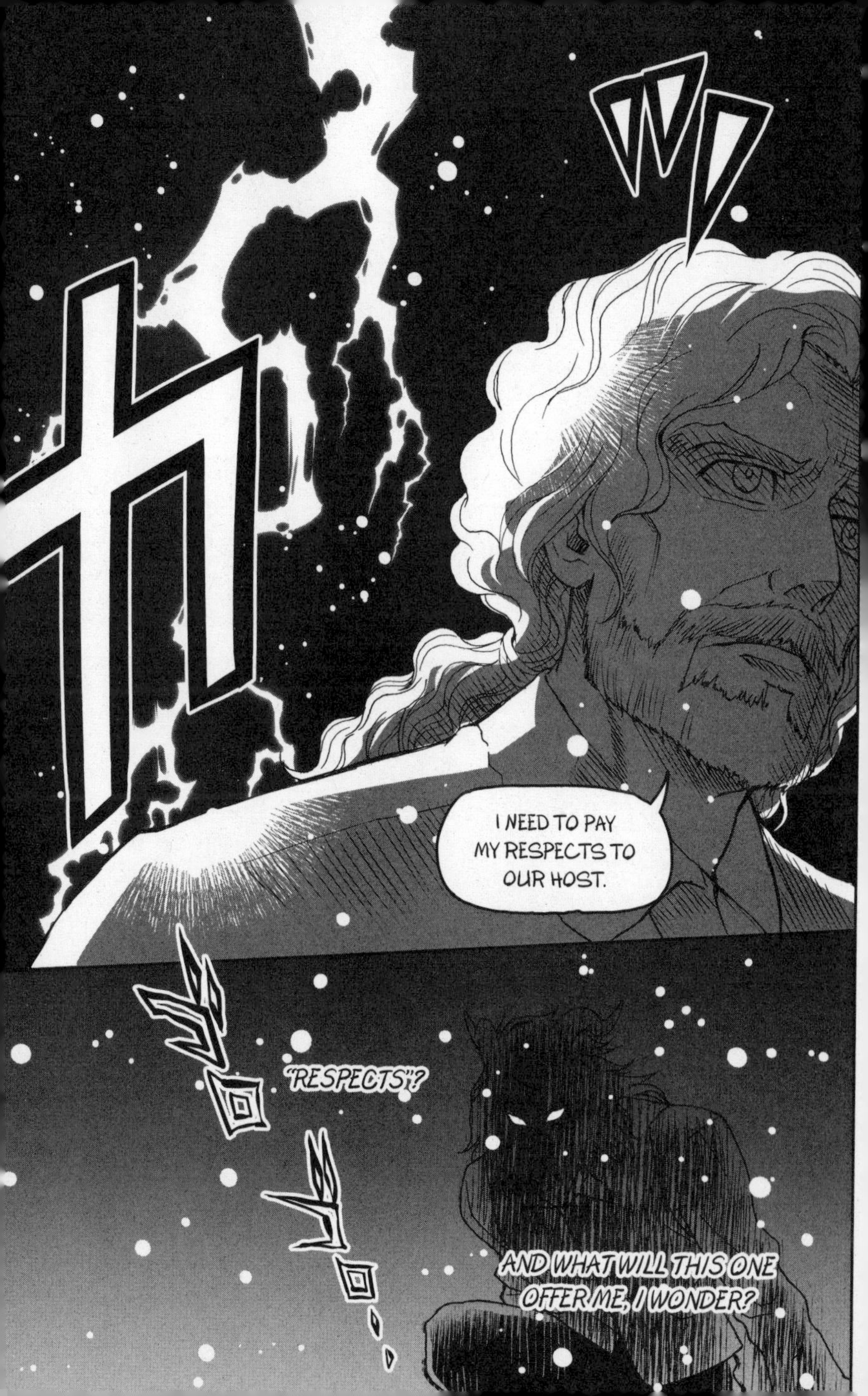
I NEED TO PAY MY RESPECTS TO OUR HOST.
"RESPECTS"?
AND WHAT WILL THIS ONE OFFER ME, I WONDER?

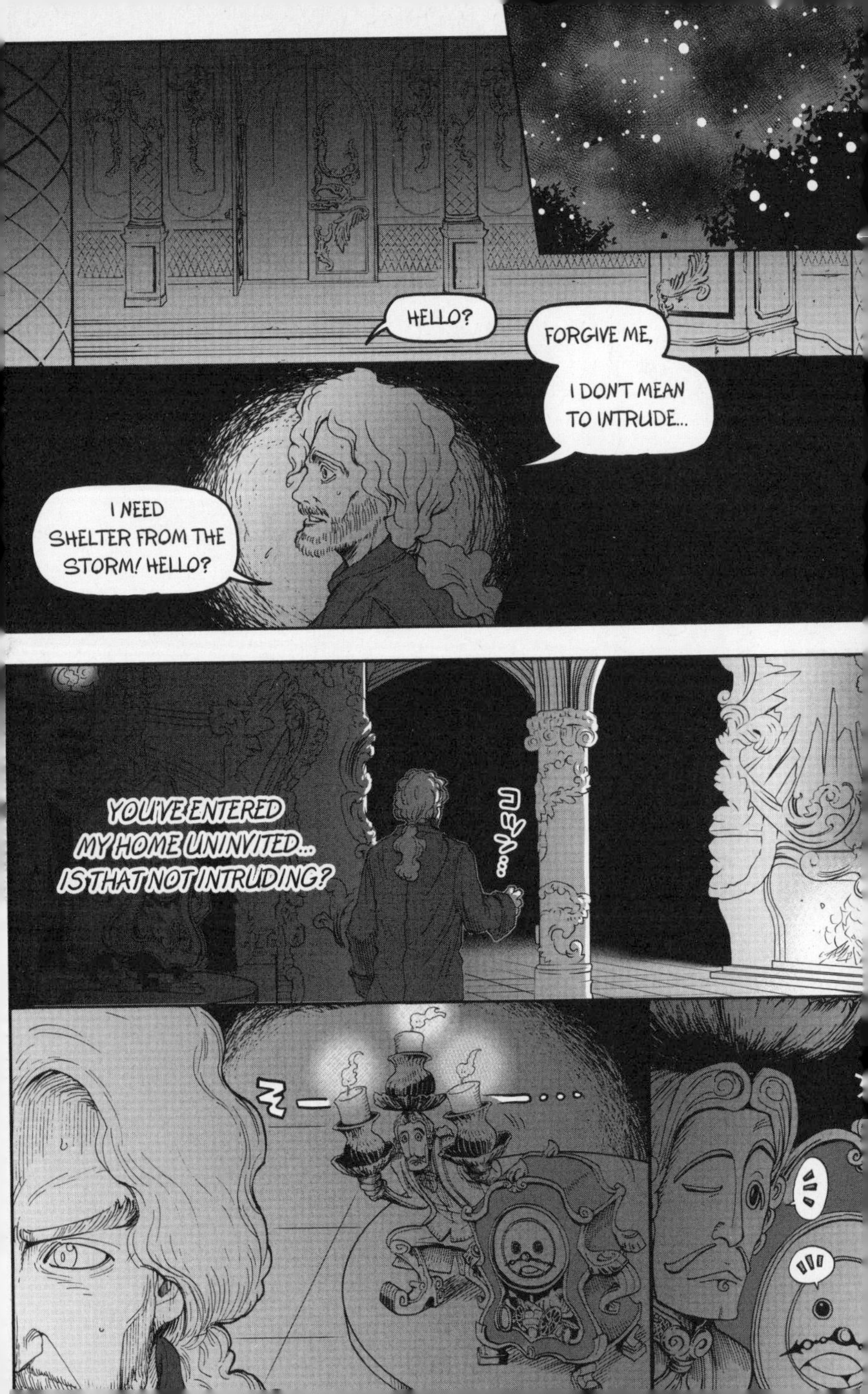
HELLO?
FORGIVE ME,
I DON'T MEAN TO INTRUDE...
I NEED SHELTER FROM THE STORM! HELLO?
コツ...
YOU'VE ENTERED MY HOME UNINVITED... IS THAT NOT INTRUDING?
!!!
!!!

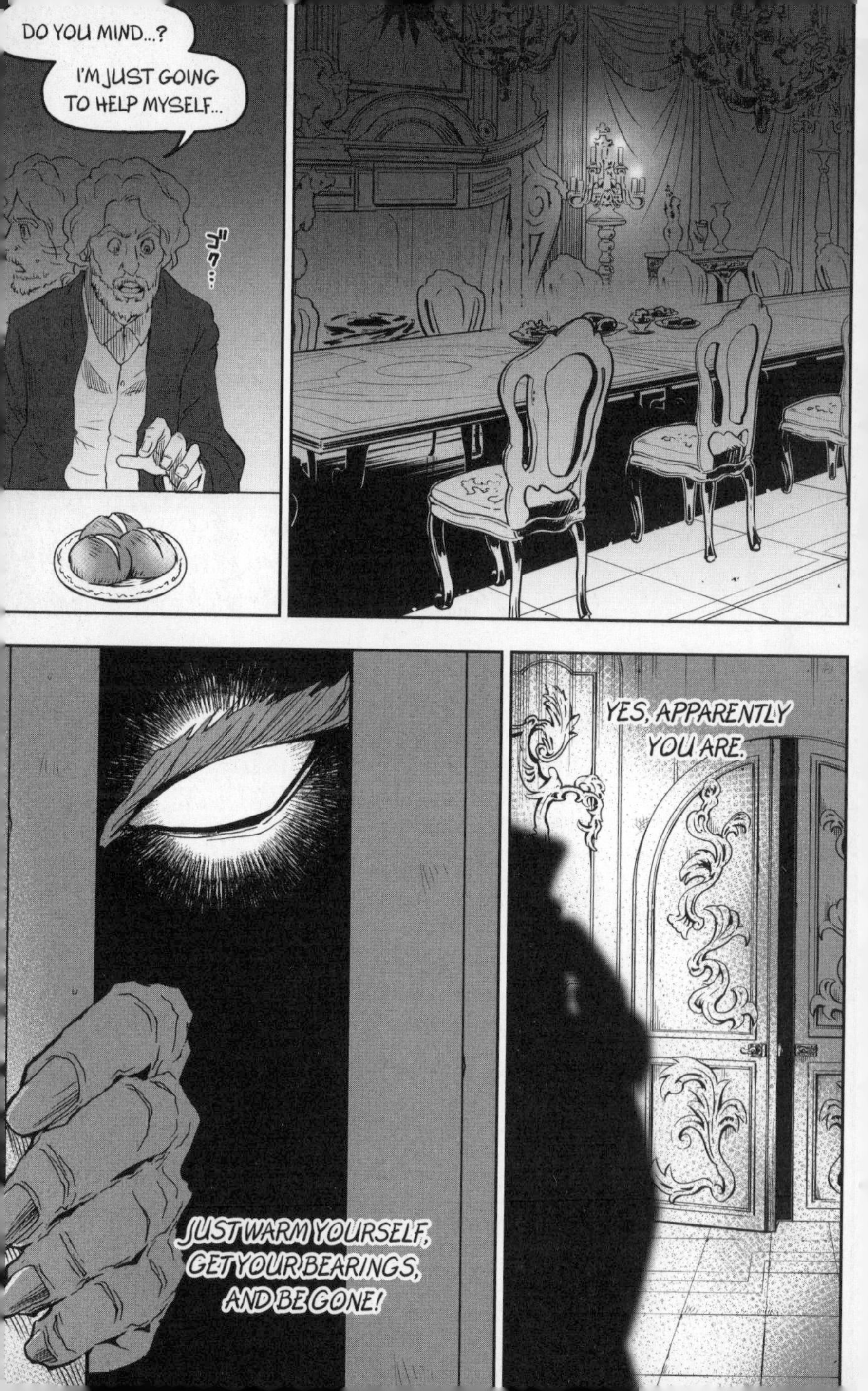
DO YOU MIND...?
I'M JUST GOING TO HELP MYSELF...
ゴク...
YES, APPARENTLY YOU ARE.
JUST WARM YOURSELF, GET YOUR BEARINGS, AND BE GONE!

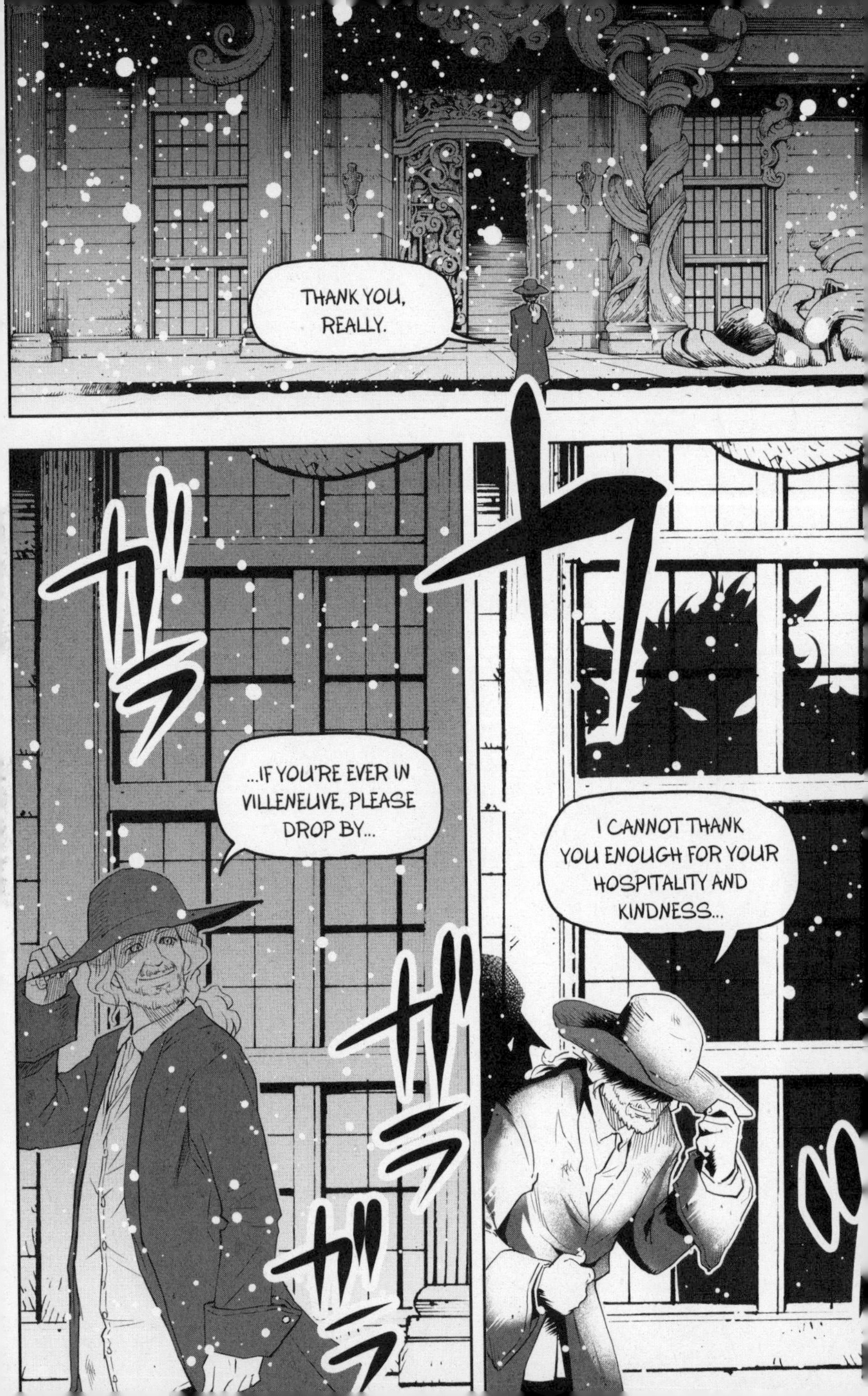
THANK YOU, REALLY.
I CANNOT THANK YOU ENOUGH FOR YOUR HOSPITALITY AND KINDNESS...
...IF YOU'RE EVER IN VILLENEUVE, PLEASE DROP BY...

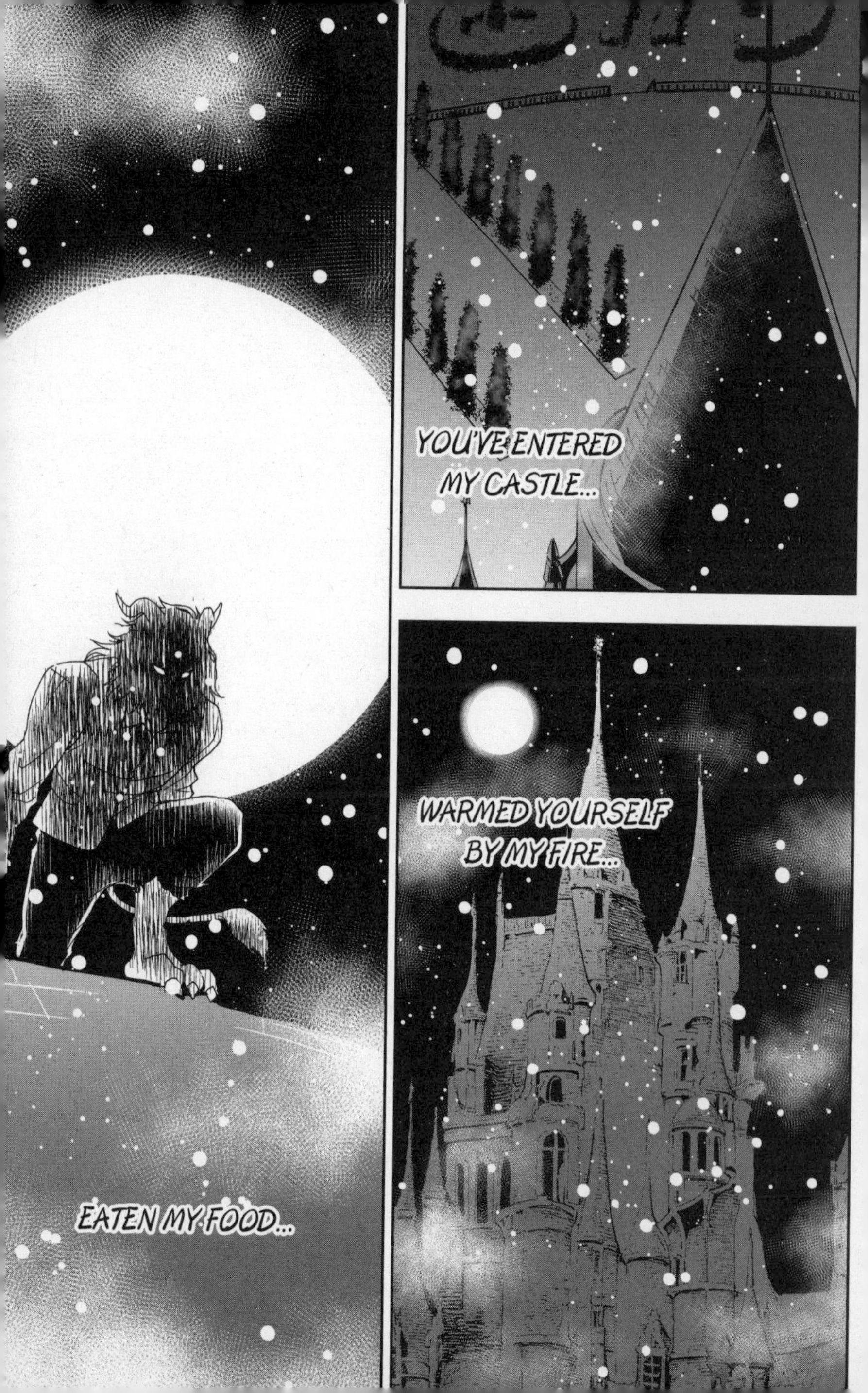
YOU'VE ENTERED MY CASTLE...
WARMED YOURSELF BY MY FIRE...
EATEN MY FOOD...

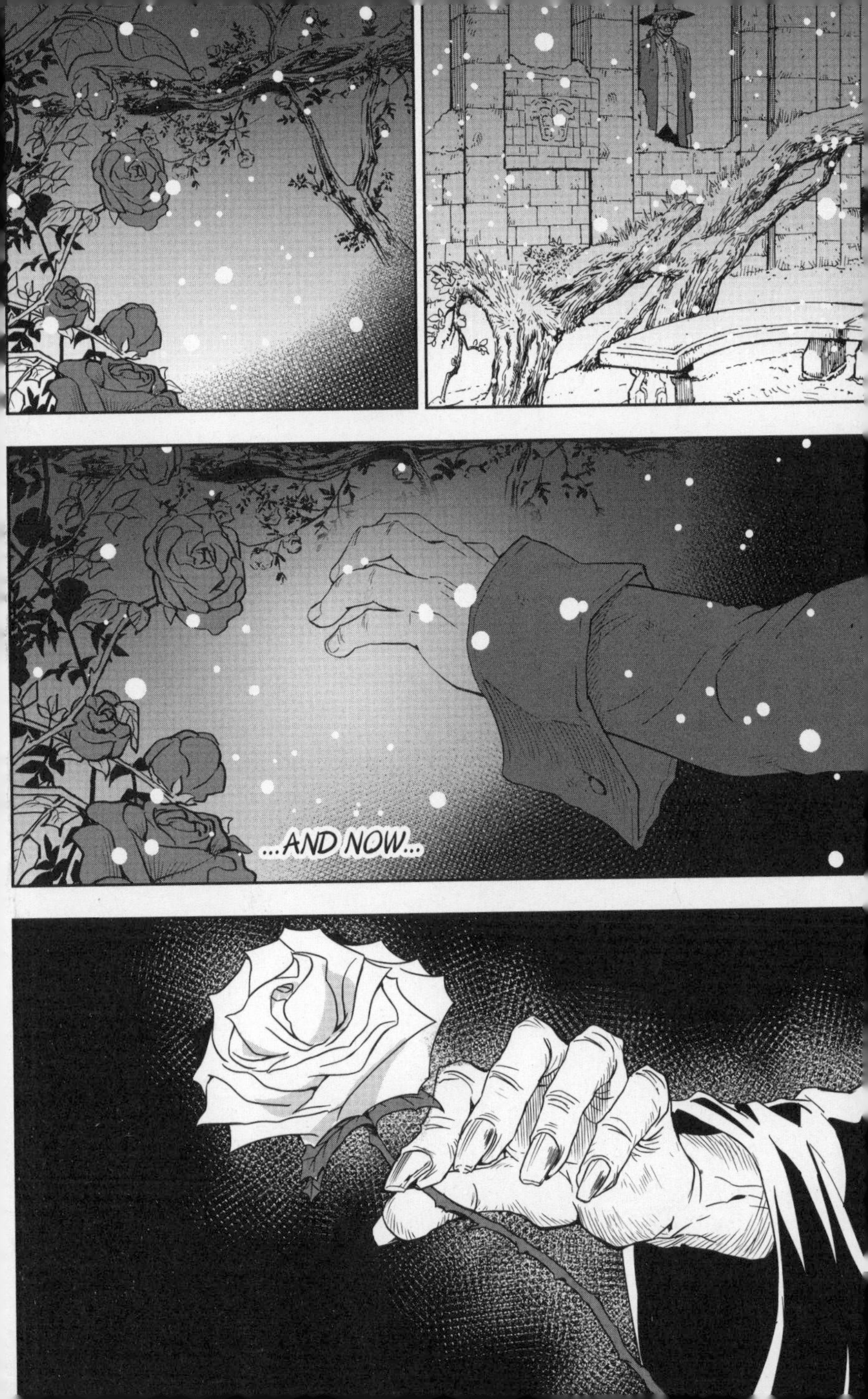
...AND NOW...

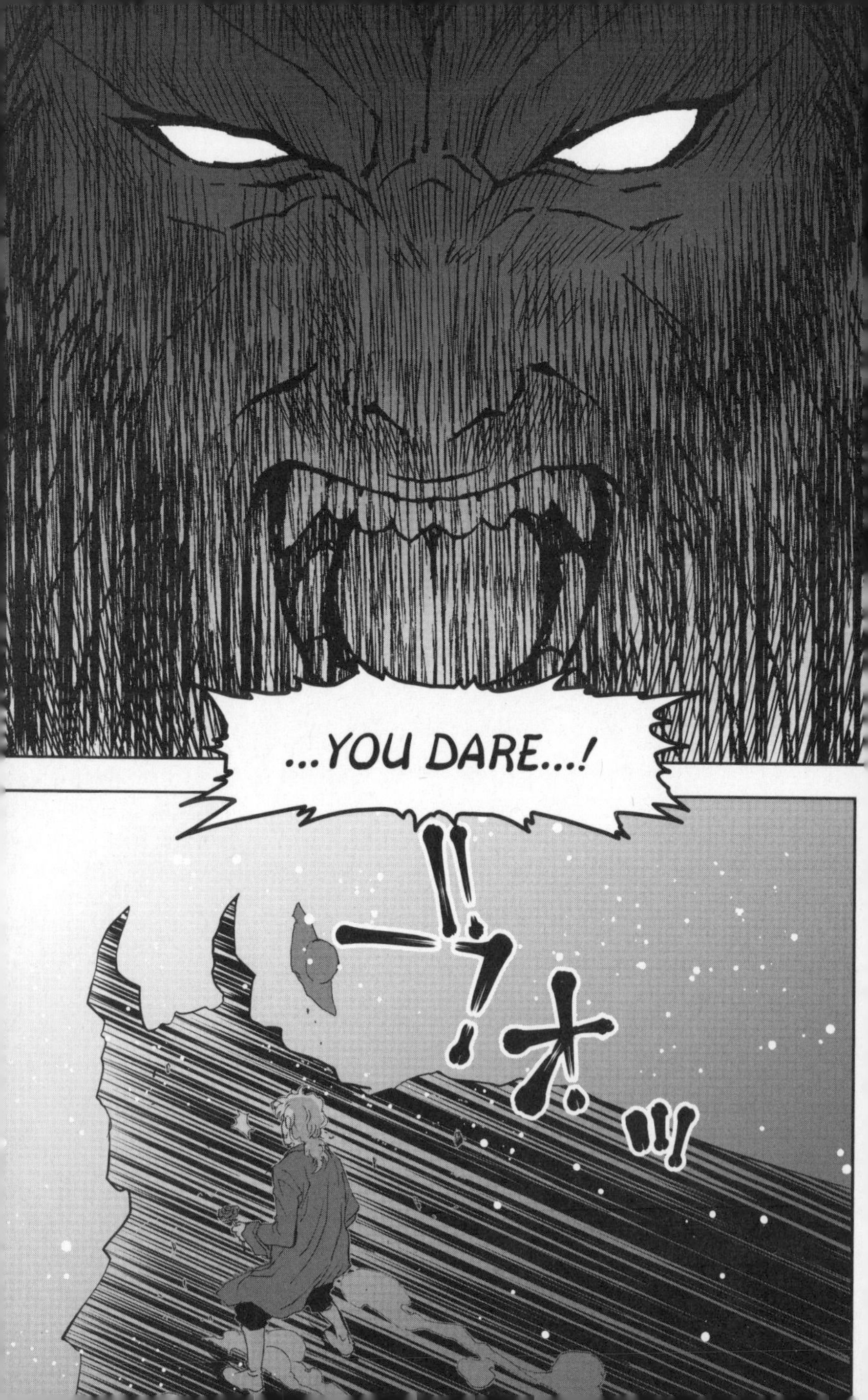
...YOU DARE...!
ゴオ!!

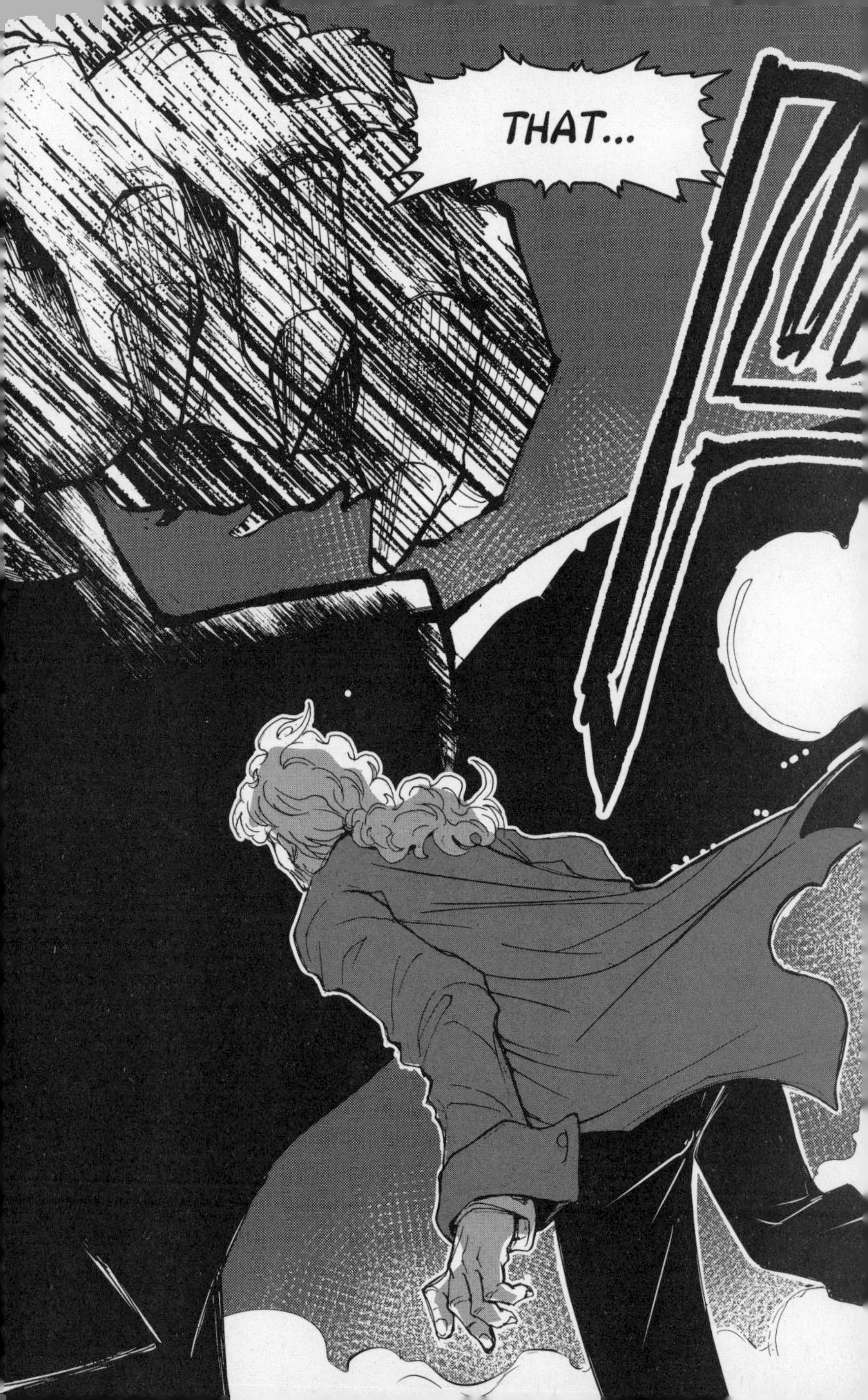
THAT...

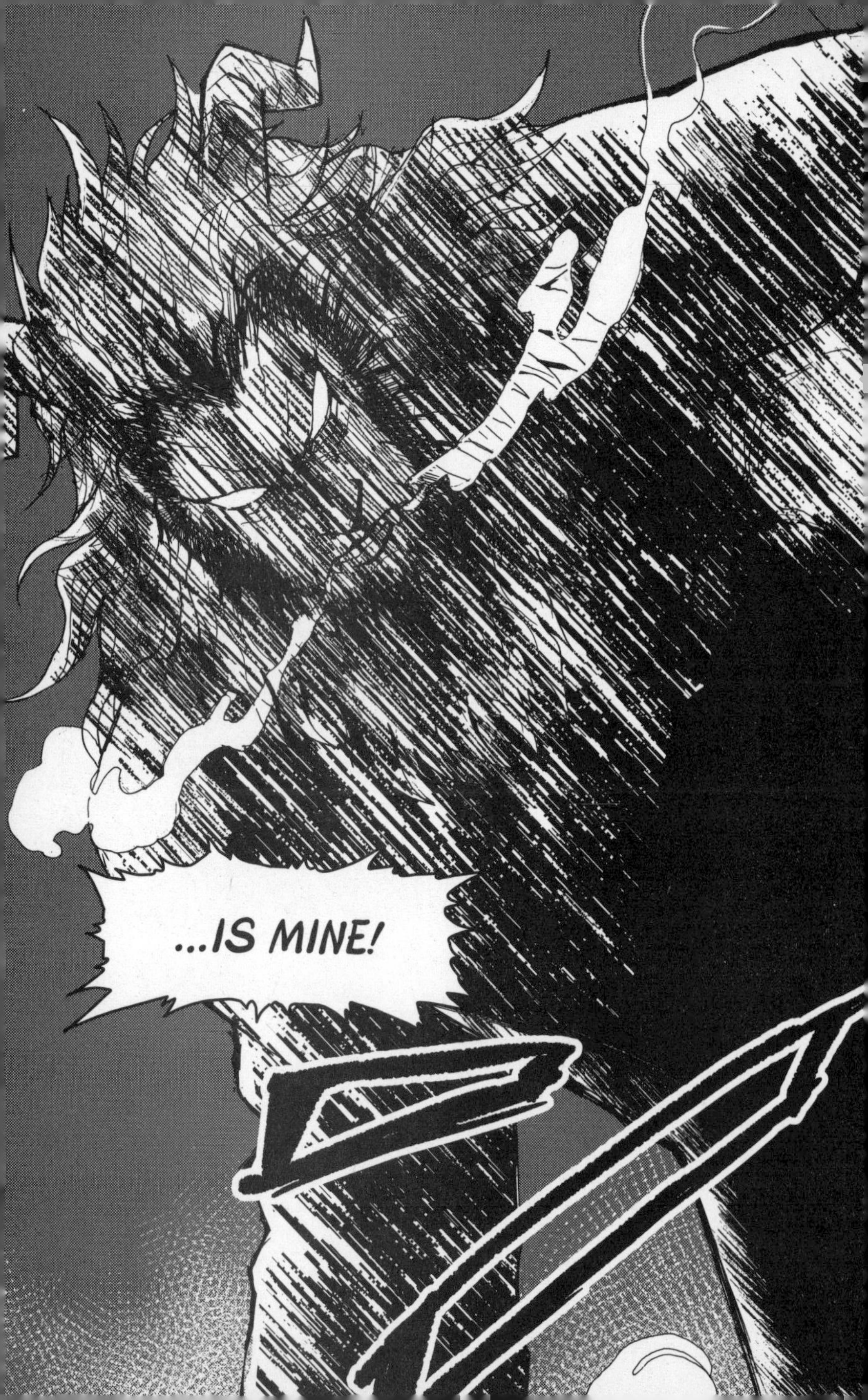
...IS MINE!

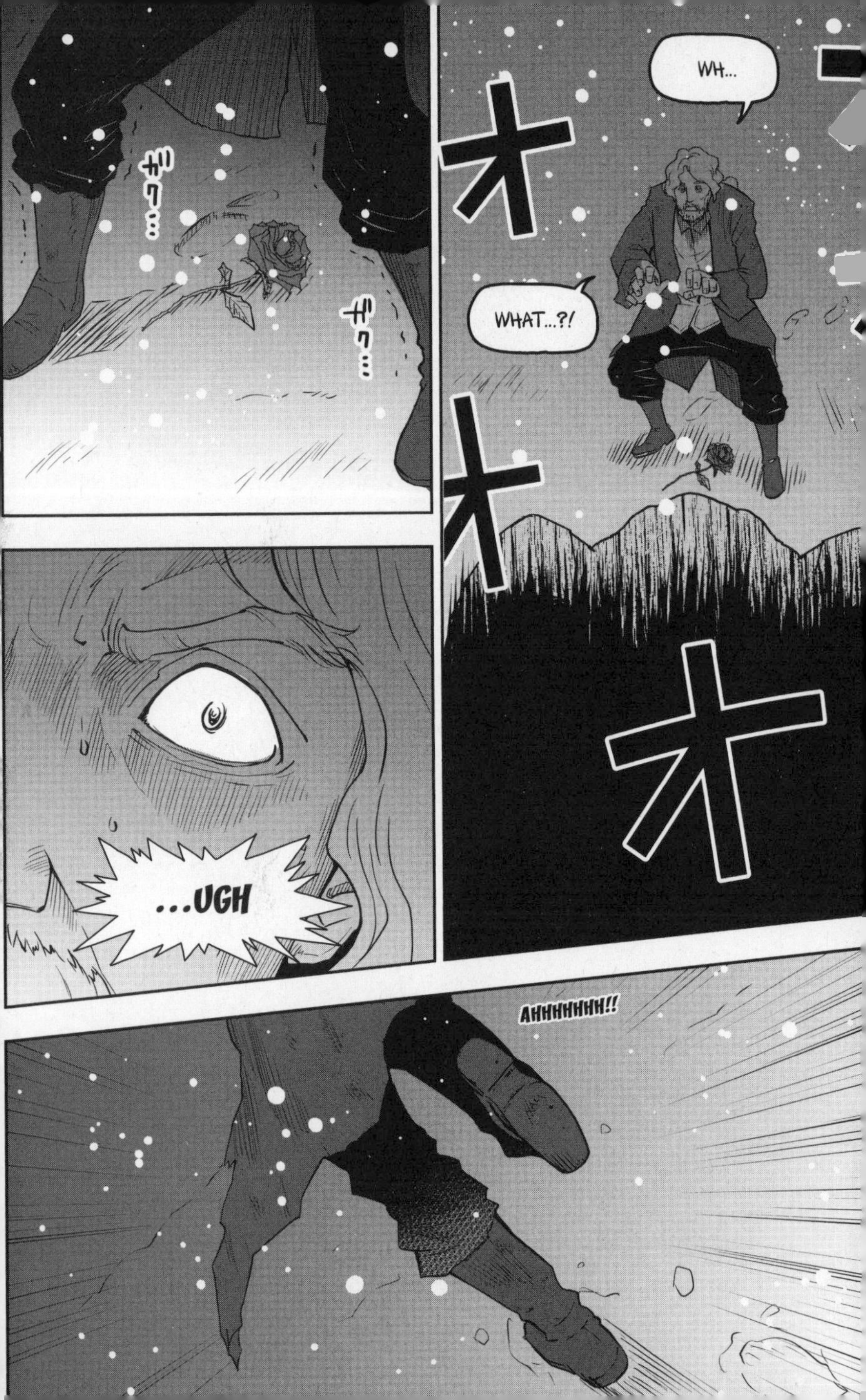
WH...
オ
WHAT...?!
オ
オ
ギク…
ギク…
...UGH
AHHHHHHH!!

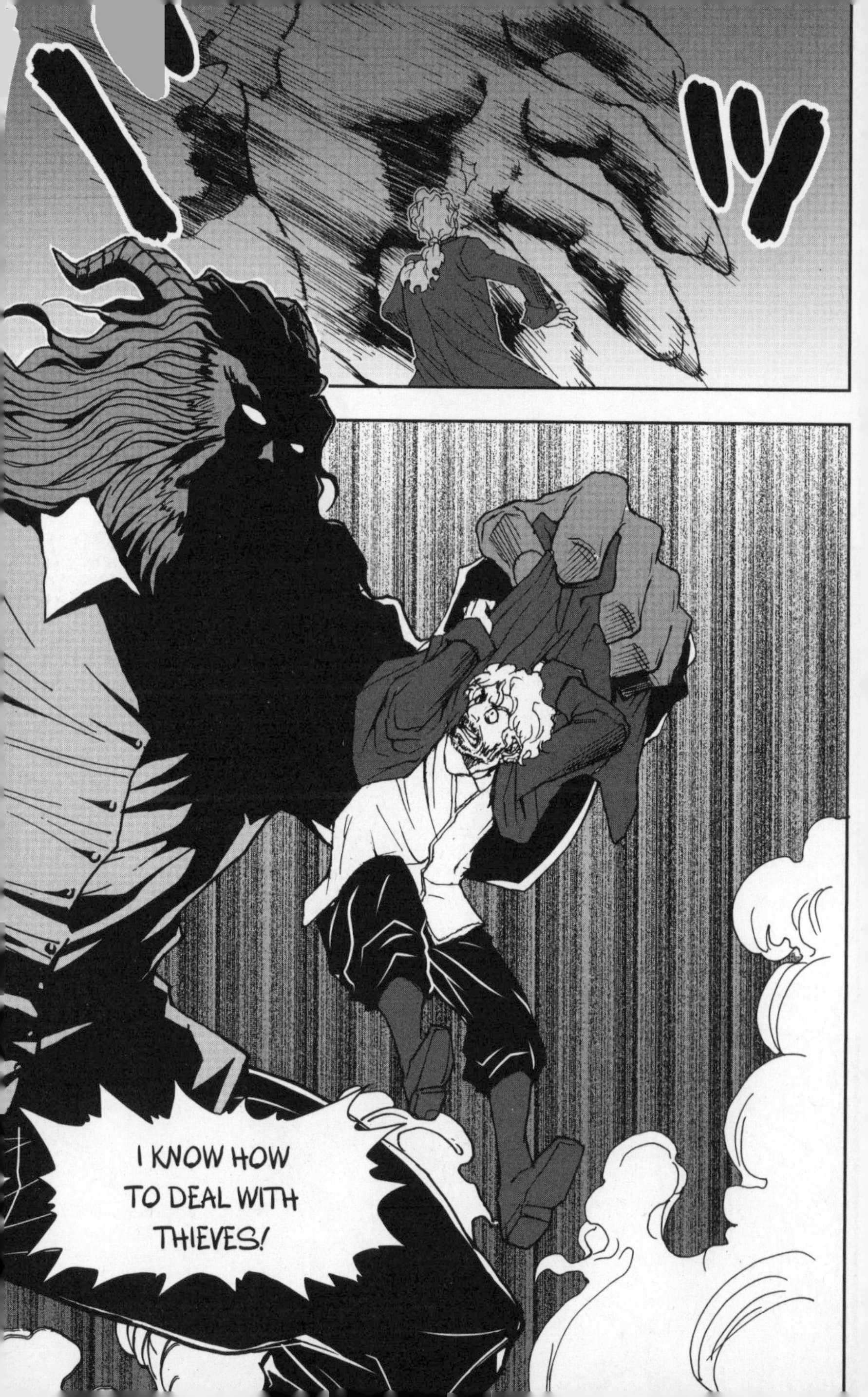
I KNOW HOW TO DEAL WITH THIEVES!

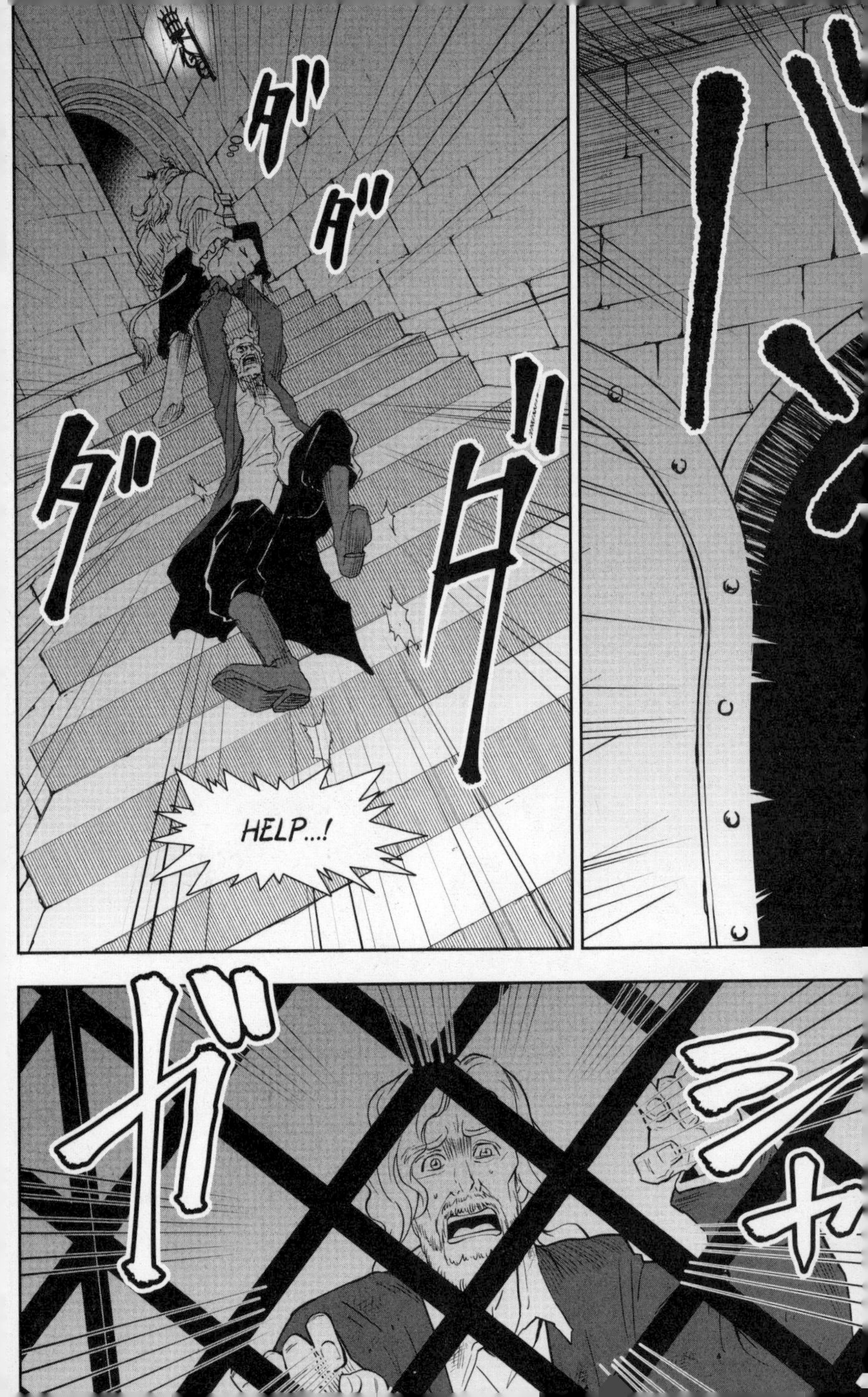

ダ ダ
ダ ダ
HELP...!
ガ

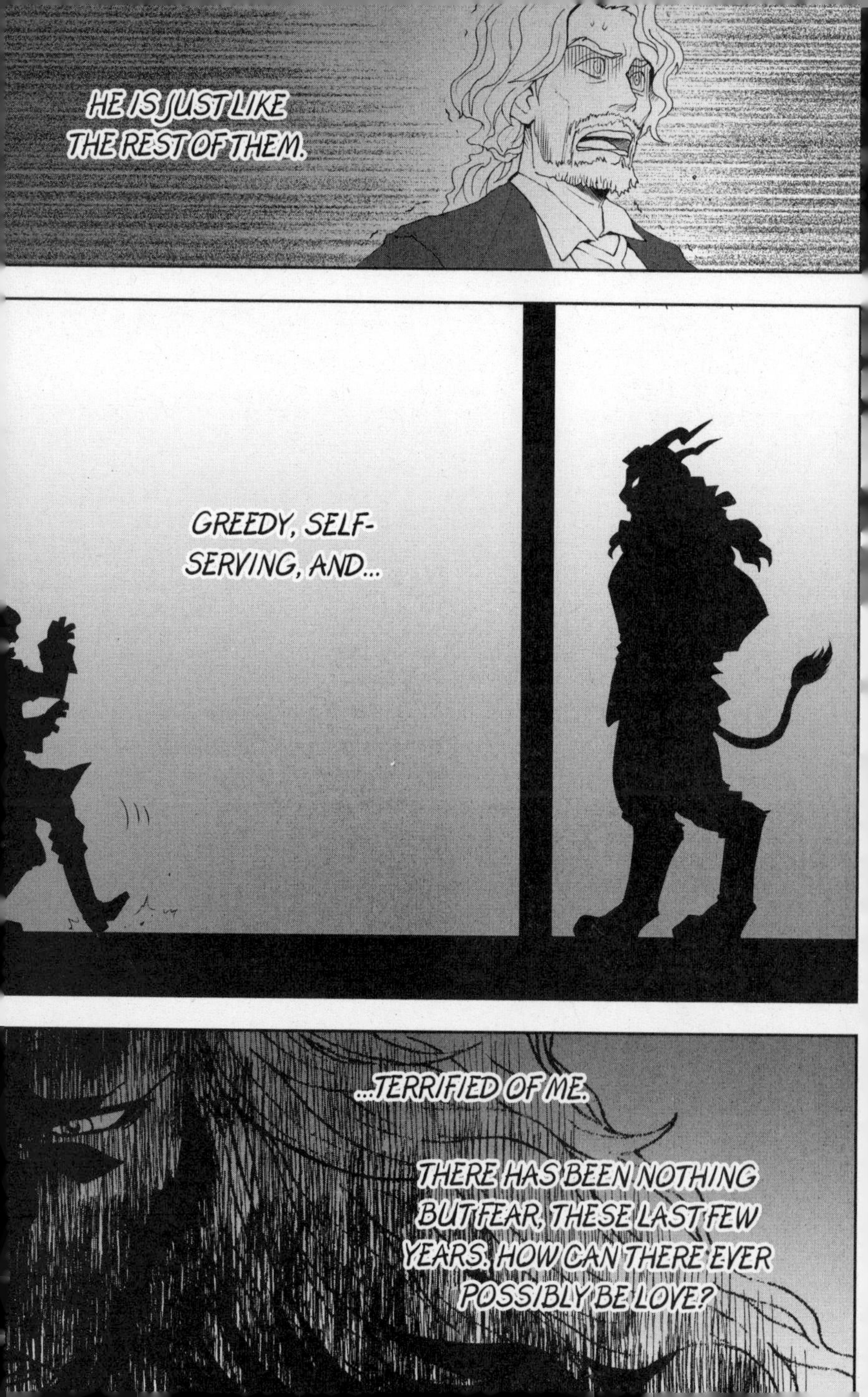
HE IS JUST LIKE THE REST OF THEM.
GREEDY, SELF-SERVING, AND...
...TERRIFIED OF ME.
THERE HAS BEEN NOTHING BUT FEAR, THESE LAST FEW YEARS. HOW CAN THERE EVER POSSIBLY BE LOVE?

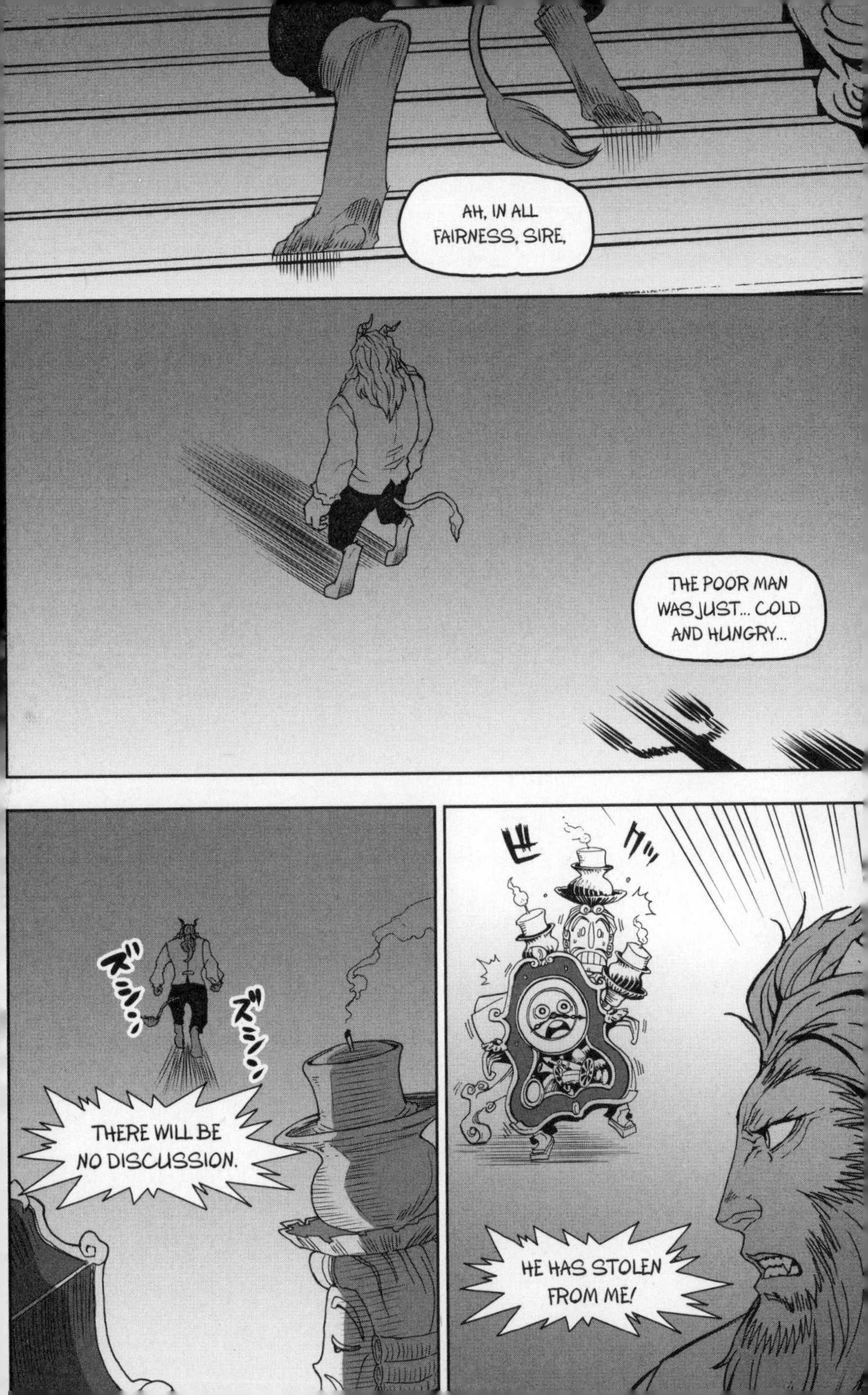
AH, IN ALL FAIRNESS, SIRE,
THE POOR MAN WAS JUST... COLD AND HUNGRY...
ビ
クッ
HE HAS STOLEN FROM ME!
ズシン、
ズシン、
THERE WILL BE NO DISCUSSION.

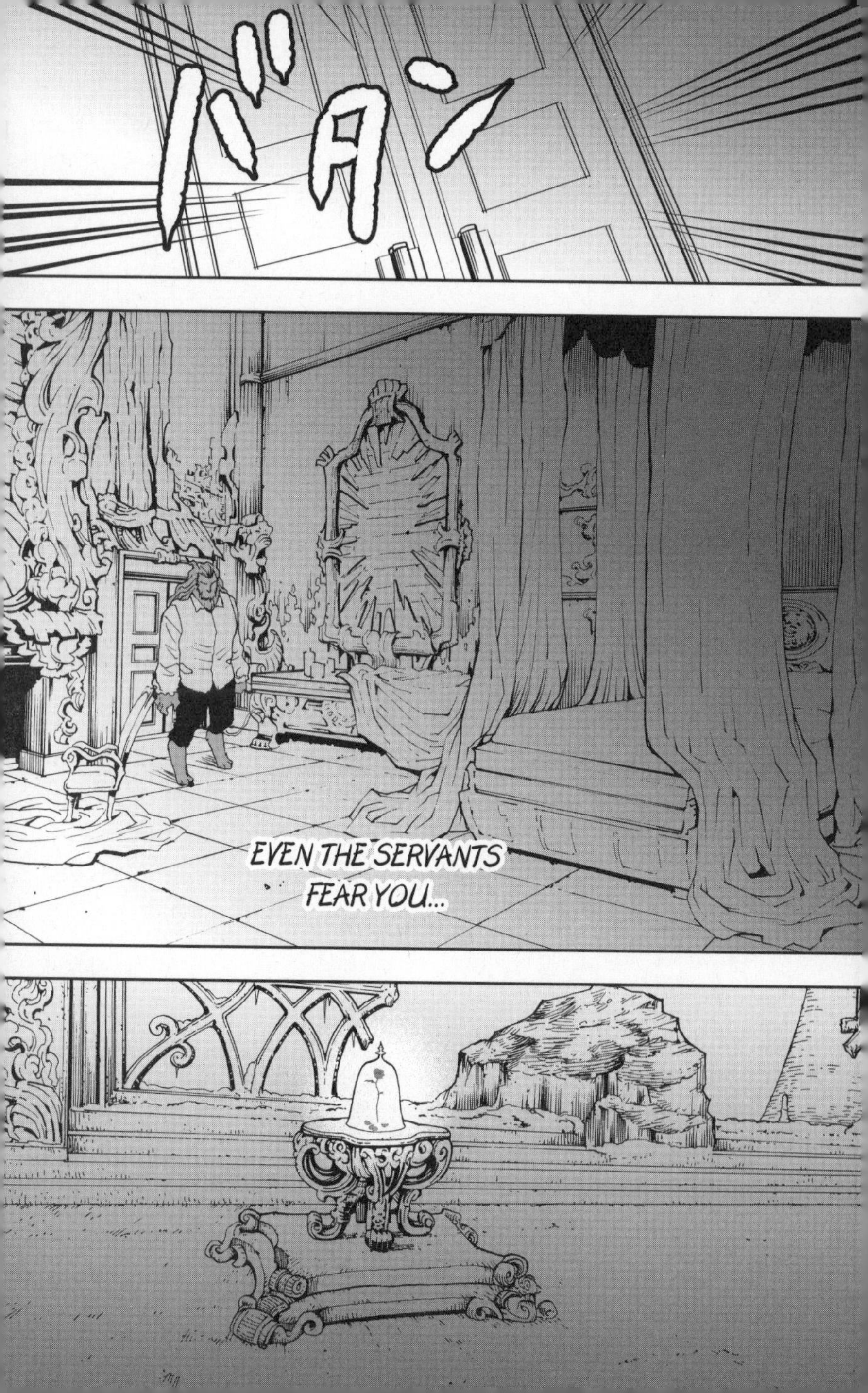
バタン
EVEN THE SERVANTS FEAR YOU...

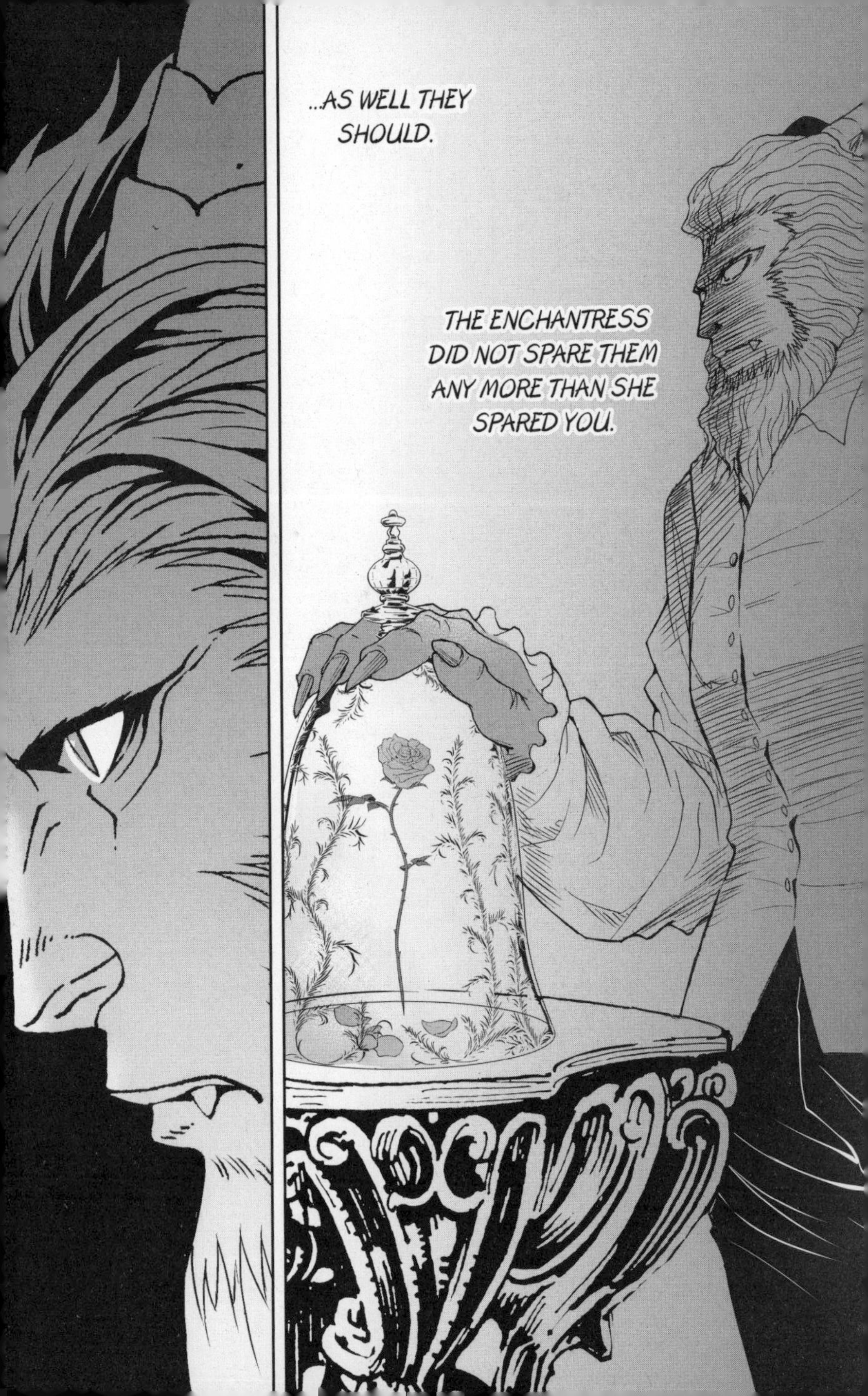
...AS WELL THEY SHOULD.
THE ENCHANTRESS DID NOT SPARE THEM ANY MORE THAN SHE SPARED YOU.

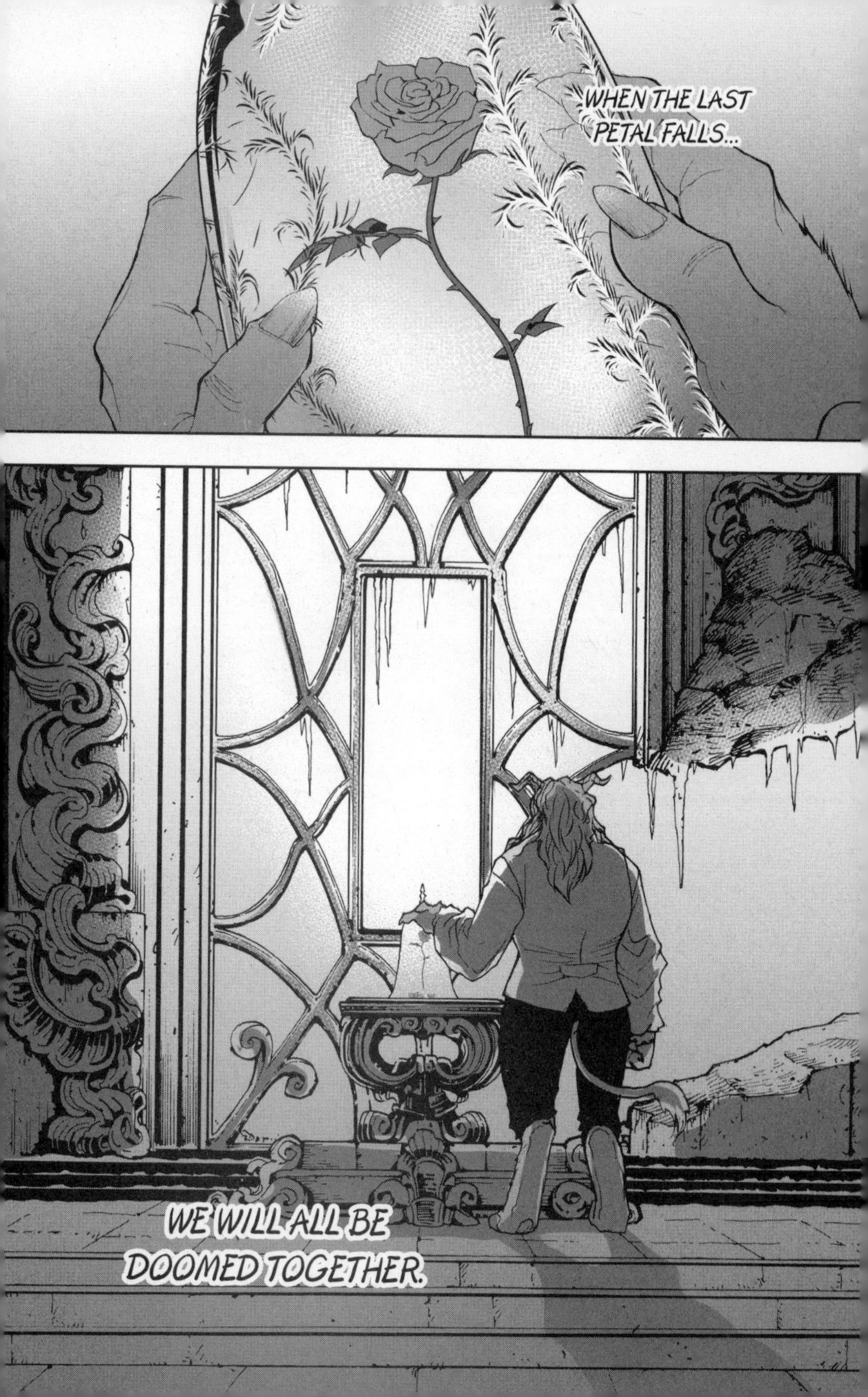
WHEN THE LAST PETAL FALLS...
WE WILL ALL BE DOOMED TOGETHER.

Disney

Beauty and the Beast

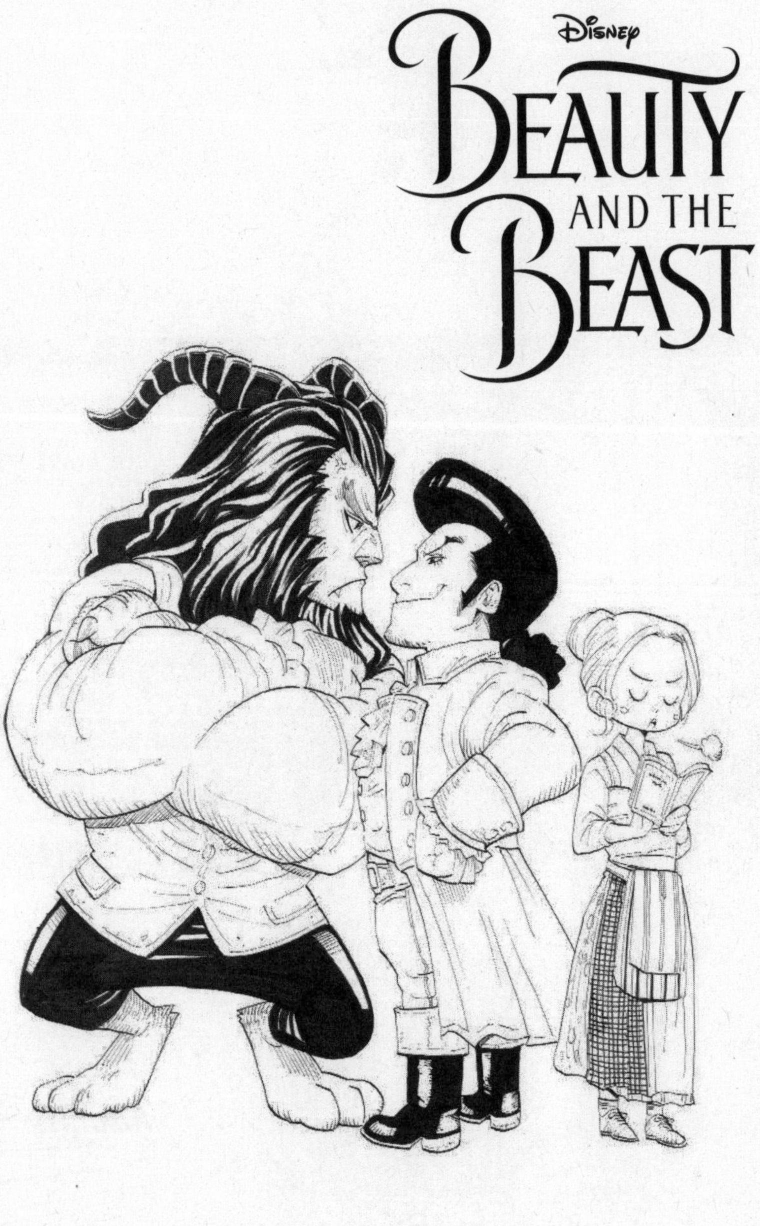

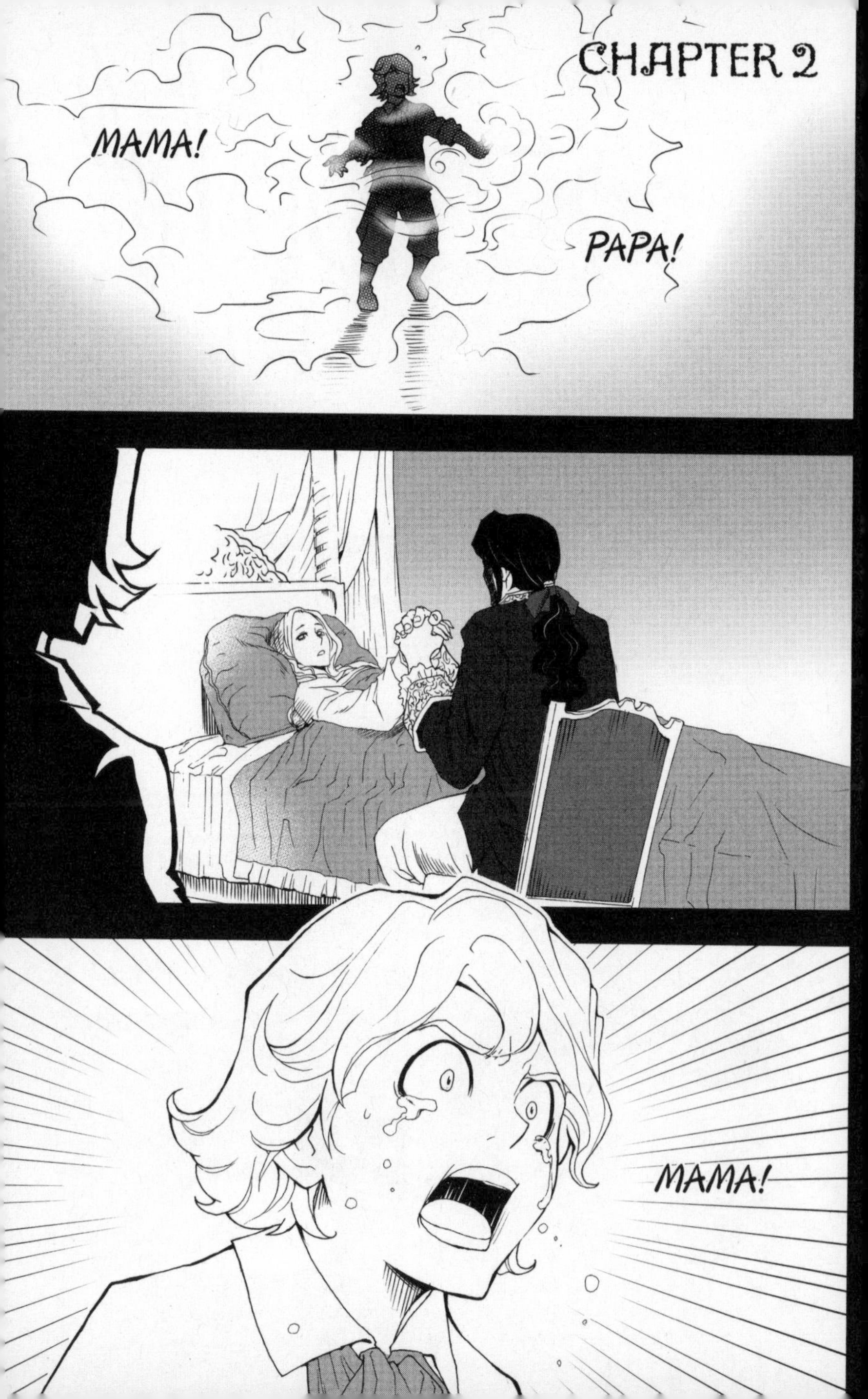
CHAPTER 2
PAPA!
MAMA!
MAMA!

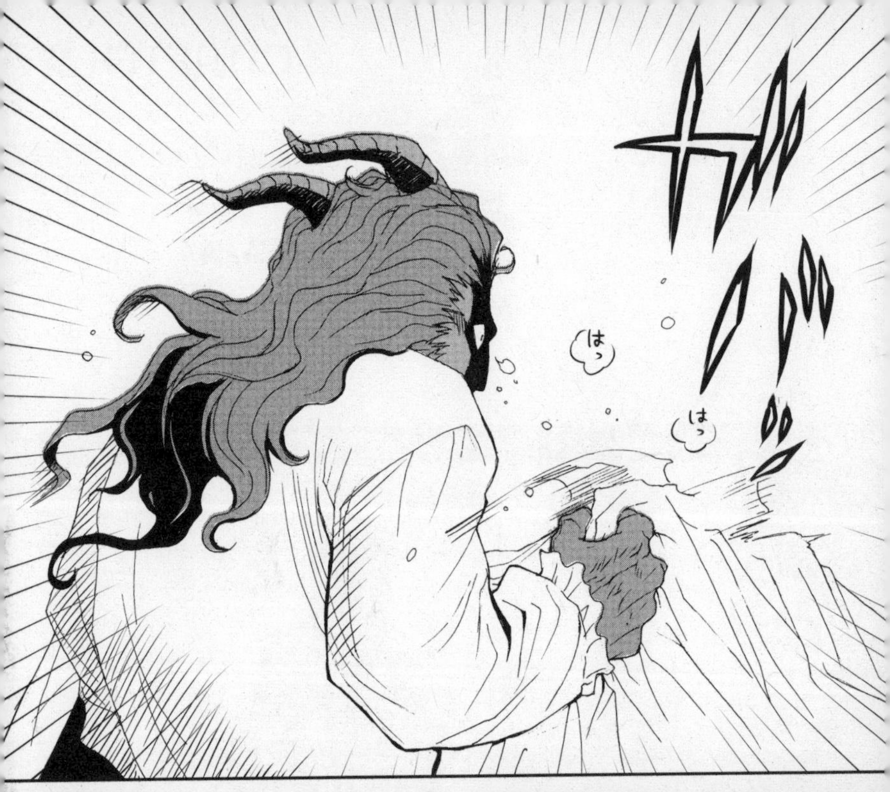
ガバッ
はっ
はっ
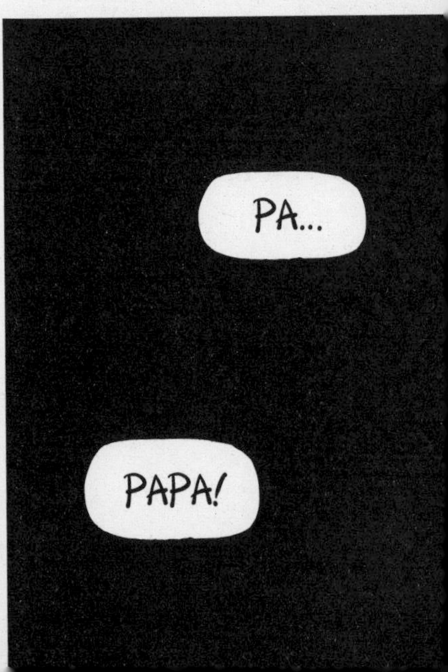
PA...
PAPA!
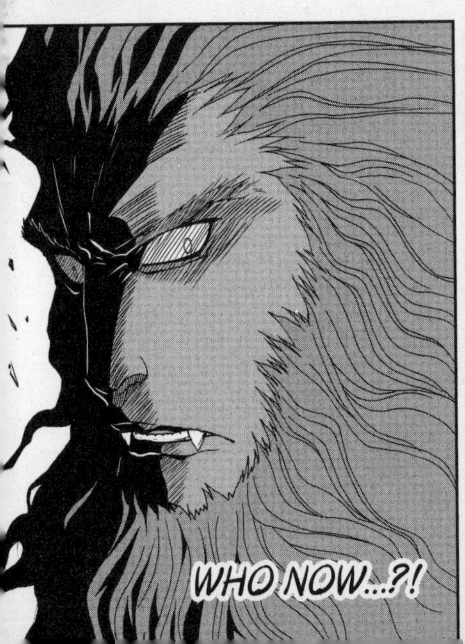
WHO NOW...?!

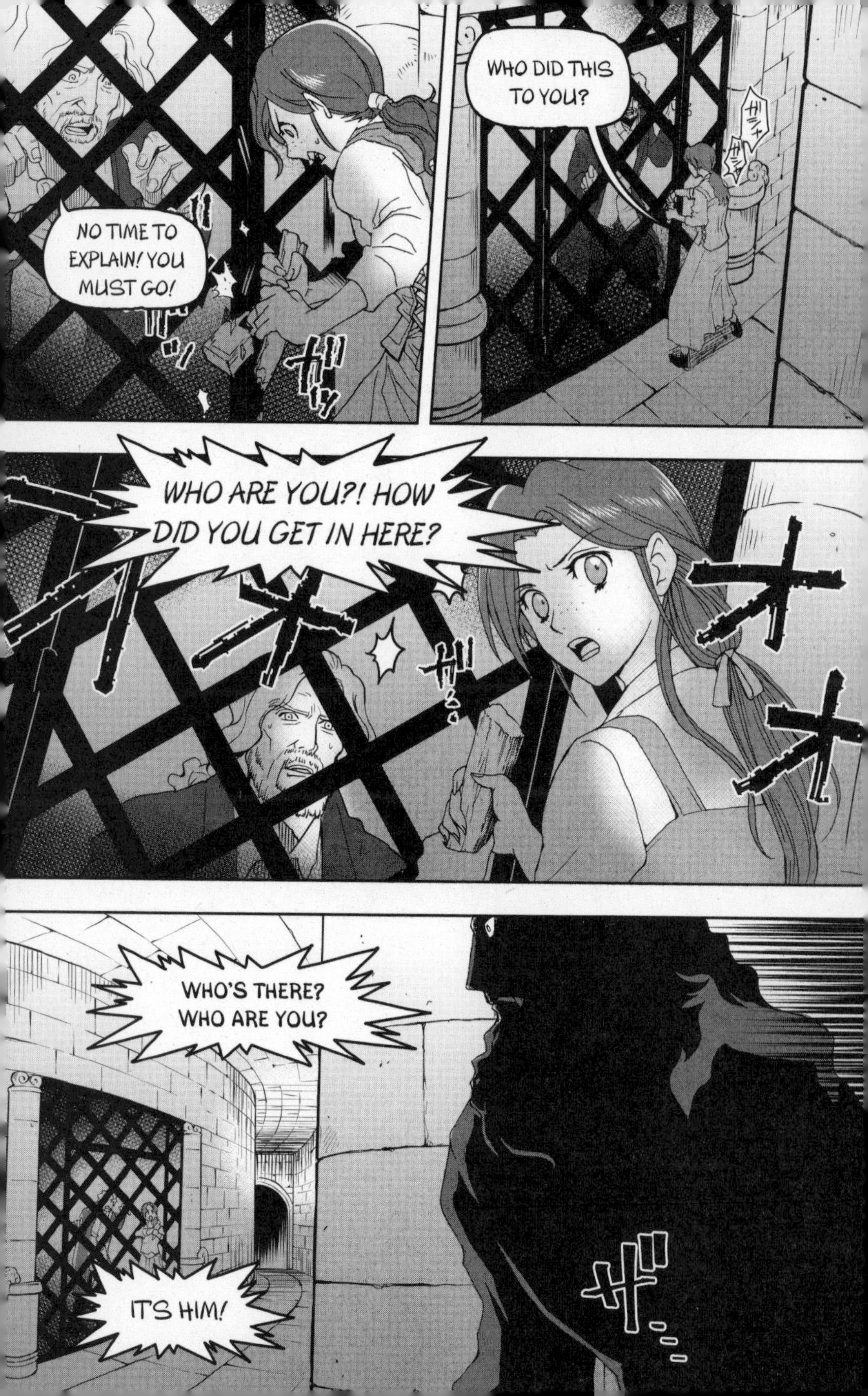
WHO DID THIS TO YOU?
NO TIME TO EXPLAIN! YOU MUST GO!
WHO ARE YOU?! HOW DID YOU GET IN HERE?
WHO'S THERE? WHO ARE YOU?
IT'S HIM!

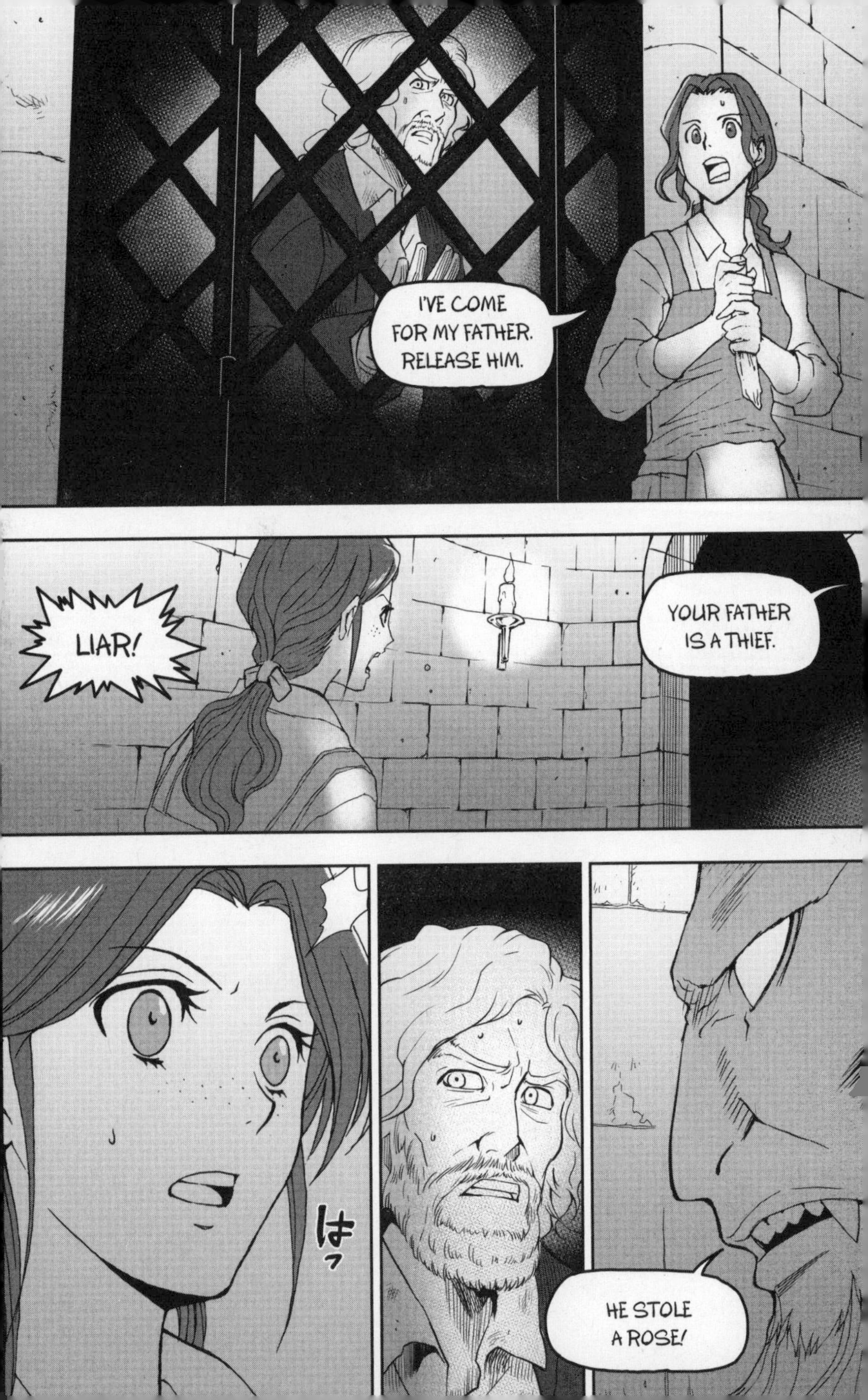
I'VE COME FOR MY FATHER. RELEASE HIM.
YOUR FATHER IS A THIEF.
LIAR!
HE STOLE A ROSE!
はっ

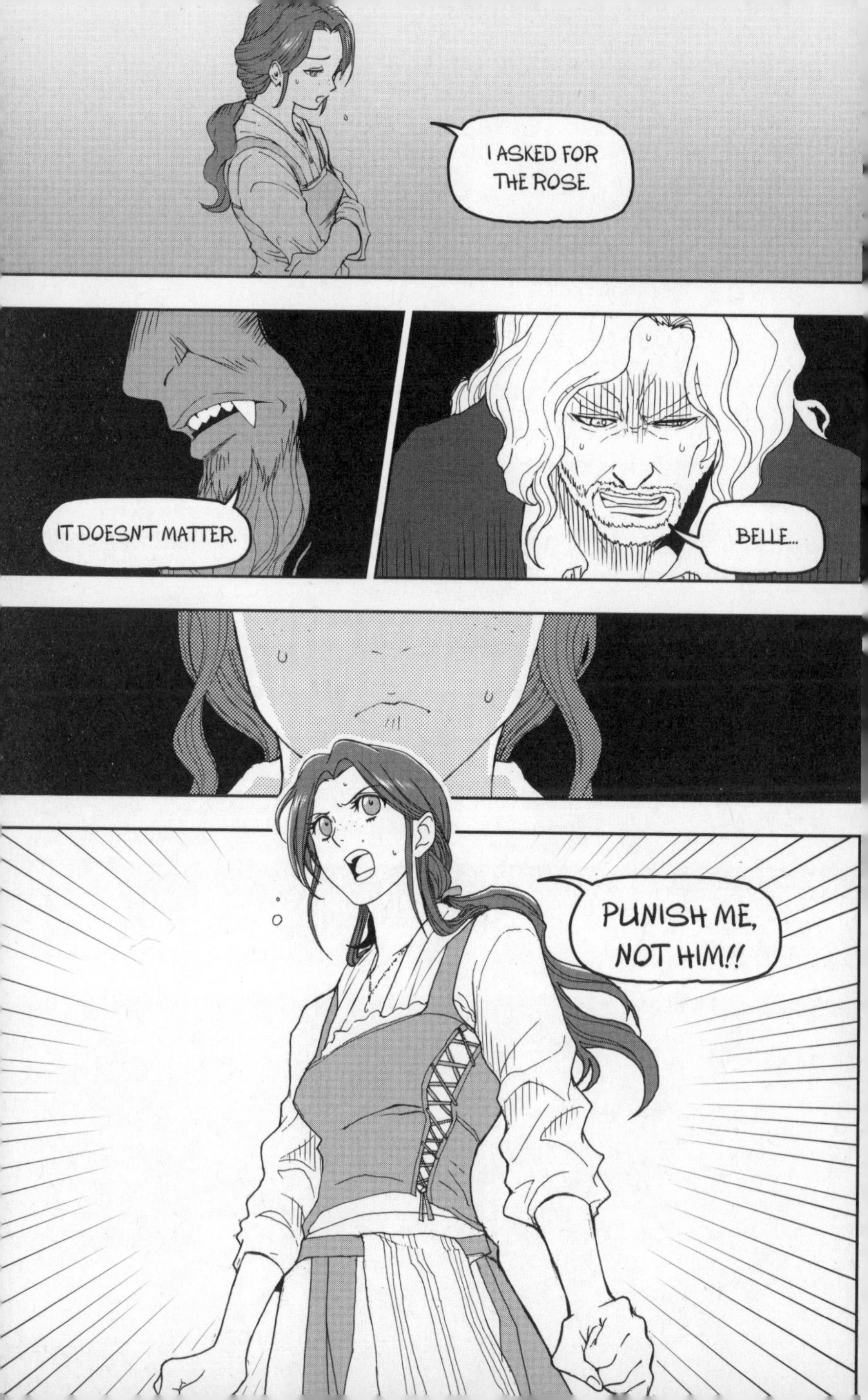
I ASKED FOR THE ROSE.
BELLE...
IT DOESN'T MATTER.
PUNISH ME, NOT HIM!!

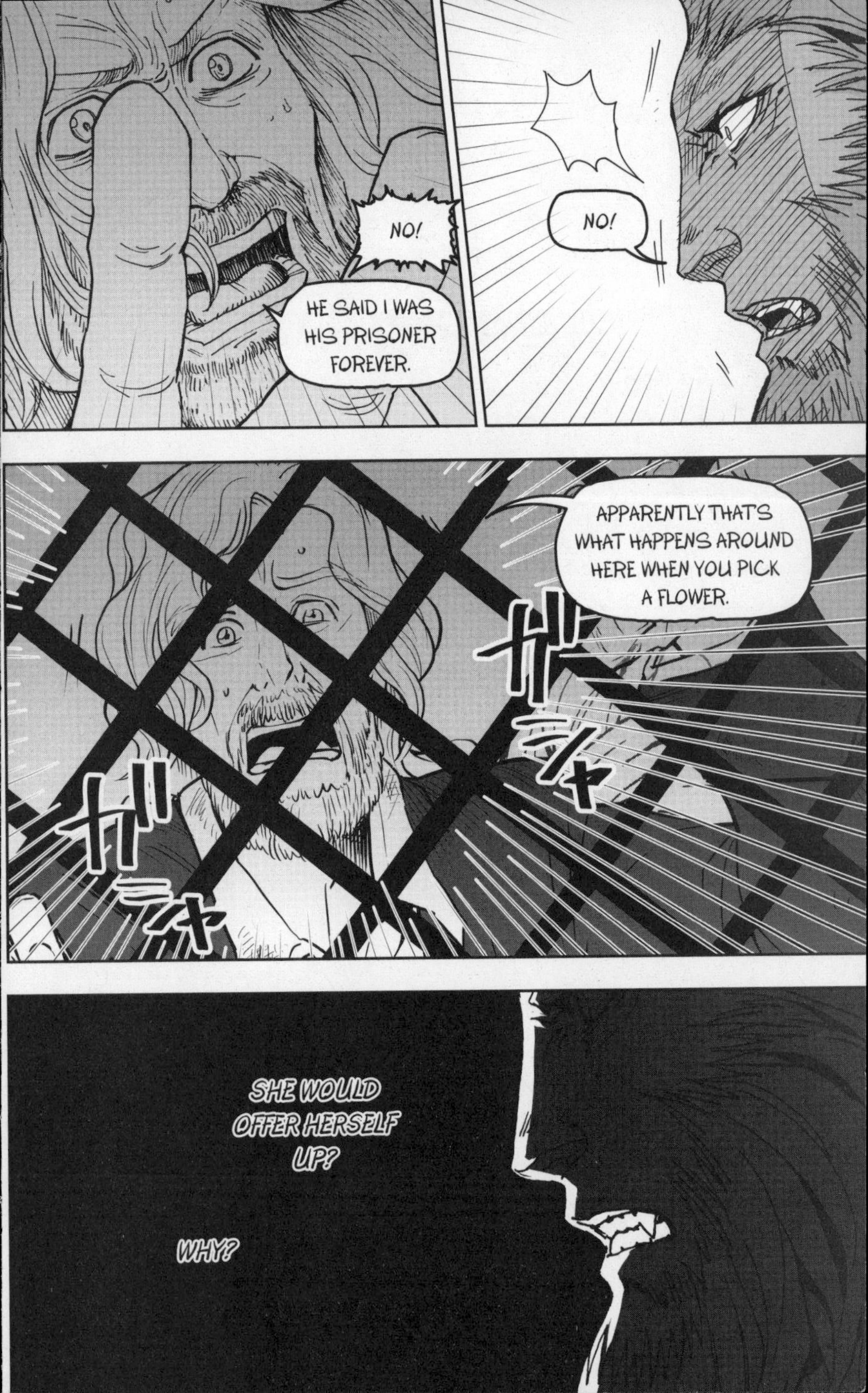
NO!
NO!
HE SAID I WAS HIS PRISONER FOREVER.
APPARENTLY THAT'S WHAT HAPPENS AROUND HERE WHEN YOU PICK A FLOWER.
ガシャ
ガシャ
SHE WOULD OFFER HERSELF UP?
WHY?

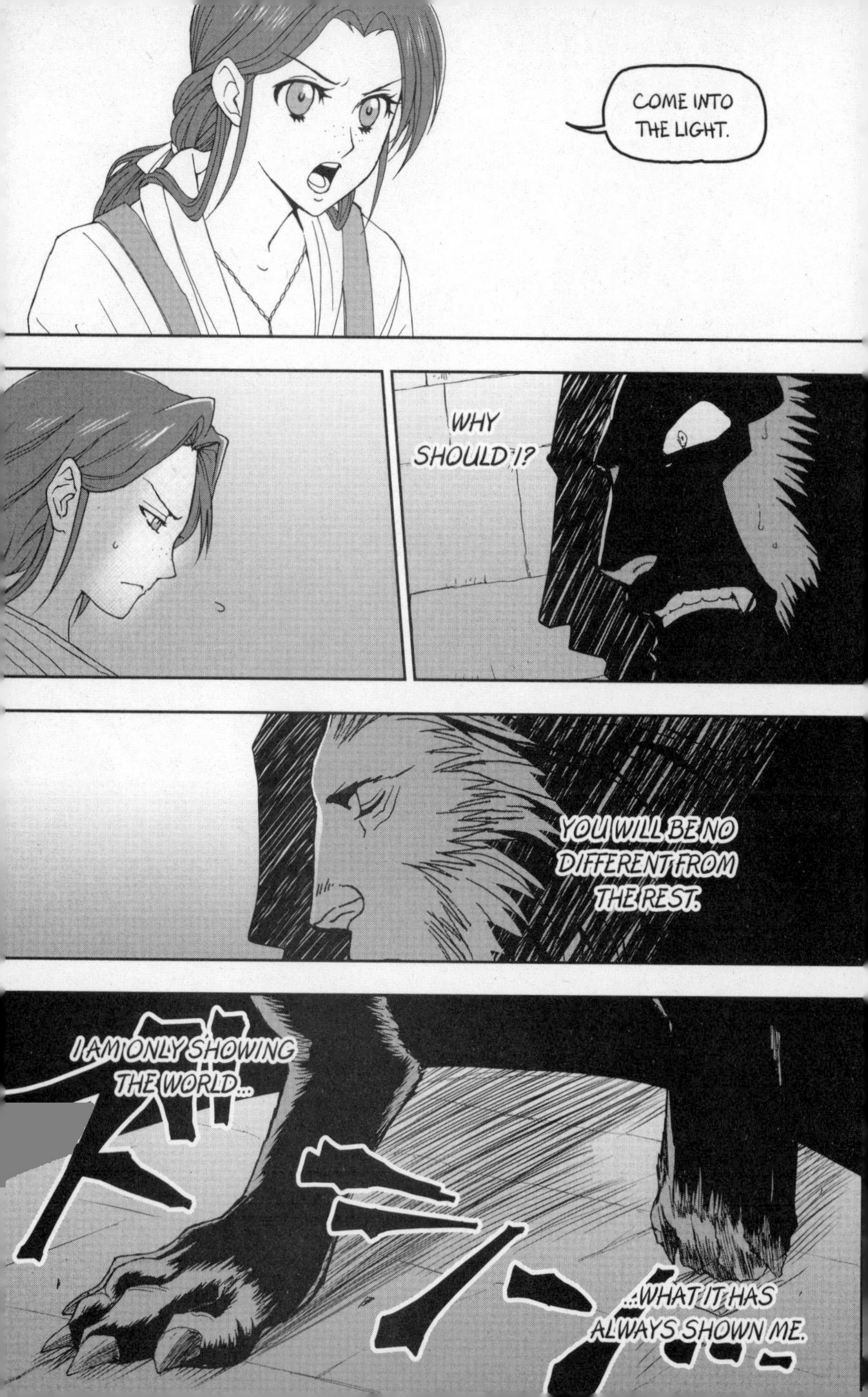
COME INTO THE LIGHT.
WHY SHOULD I?
YOU WILL BE NO DIFFERENT FROM THE REST.
I AM ONLY SHOWING THE WORLD...
...WHAT IT HAS ALWAYS SHOWN ME.

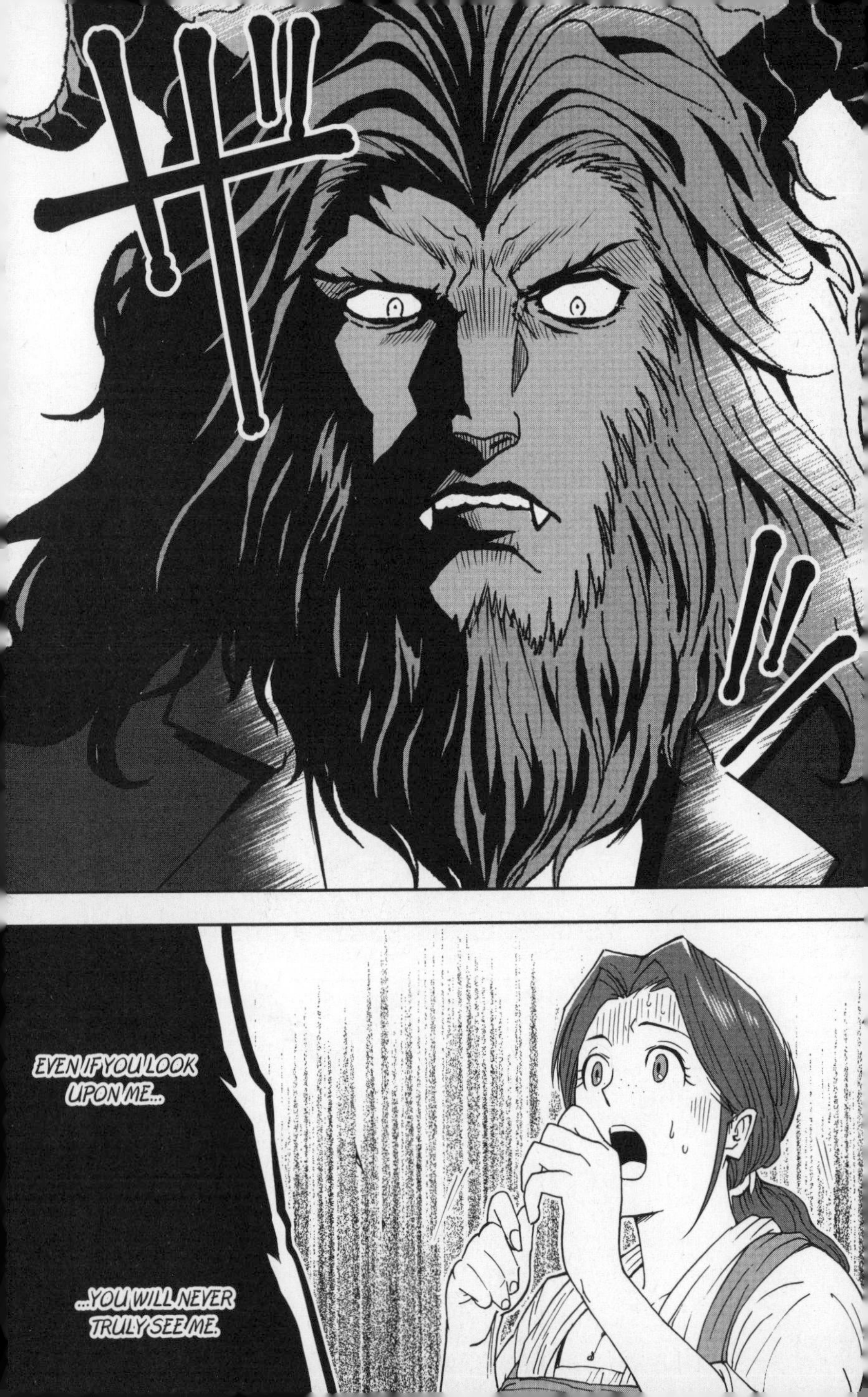
EVEN IF YOU LOOK UPON ME...
...YOU WILL NEVER TRULY SEE ME.

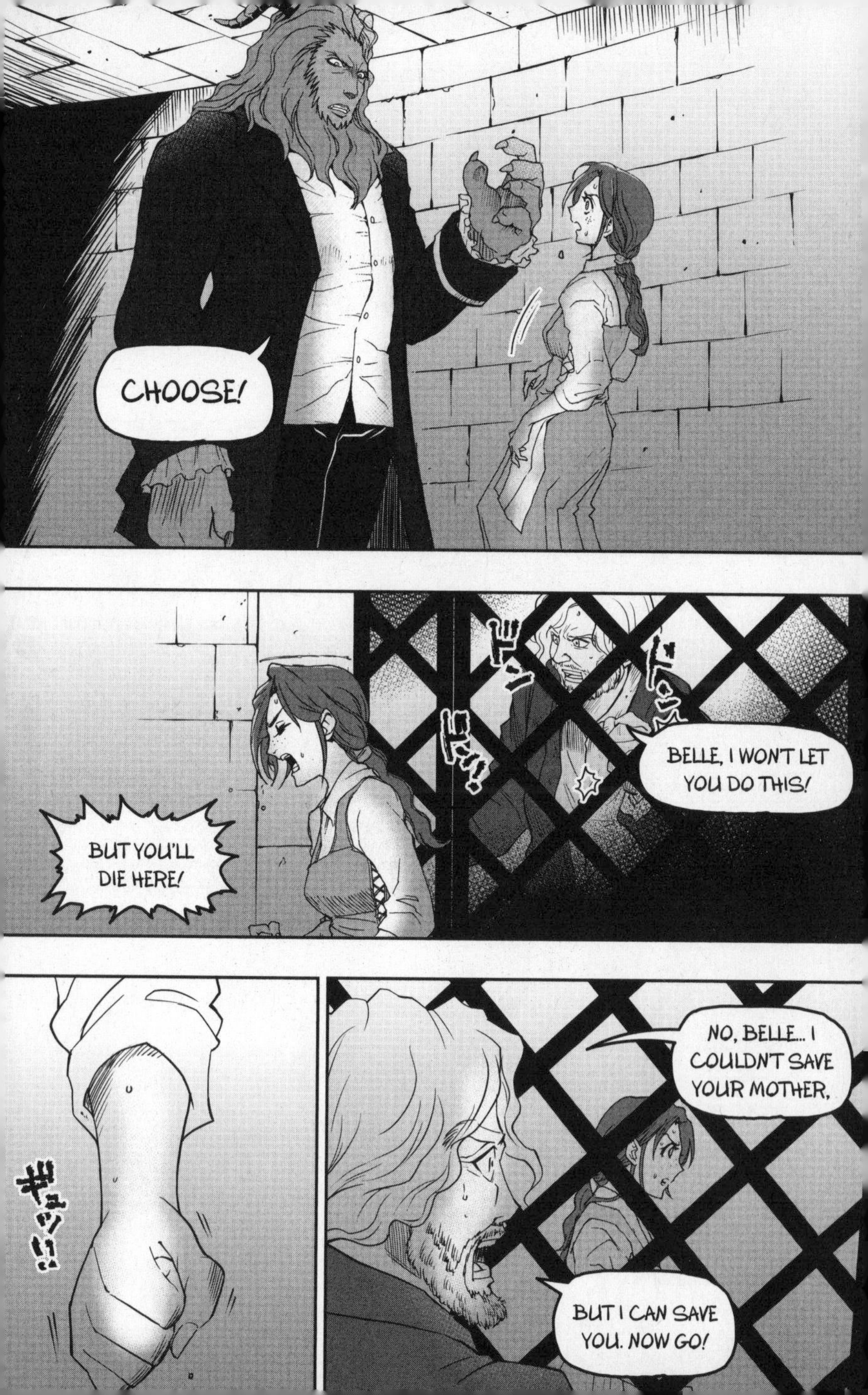
CHOOSE!
BELLE, I WON'T LET YOU DO THIS!
BUT YOU'LL DIE HERE!
NO, BELLE... I COULDN'T SAVE YOUR MOTHER,
BUT I CAN SAVE YOU. NOW GO!
ギュッ!!

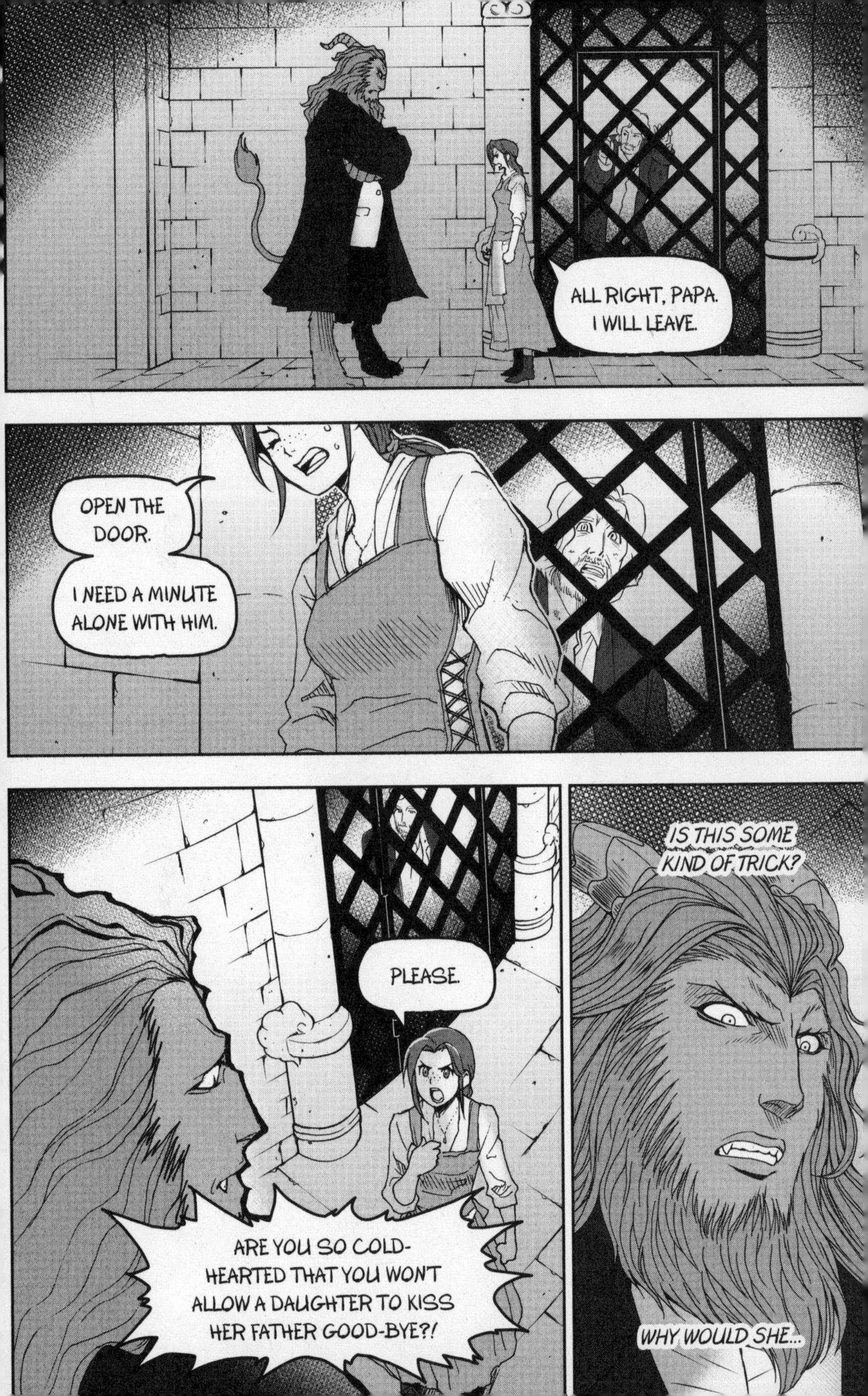
ALL RIGHT, PAPA. I WILL LEAVE.
OPEN THE DOOR.
I NEED A MINUTE ALONE WITH HIM.
IS THIS SOME KIND OF TRICK?
WHY WOULD SHE...
PLEASE.
ARE YOU SO COLD-HEARTED THAT YOU WON'T ALLOW A DAUGHTER TO KISS HER FATHER GOOD-BYE?!

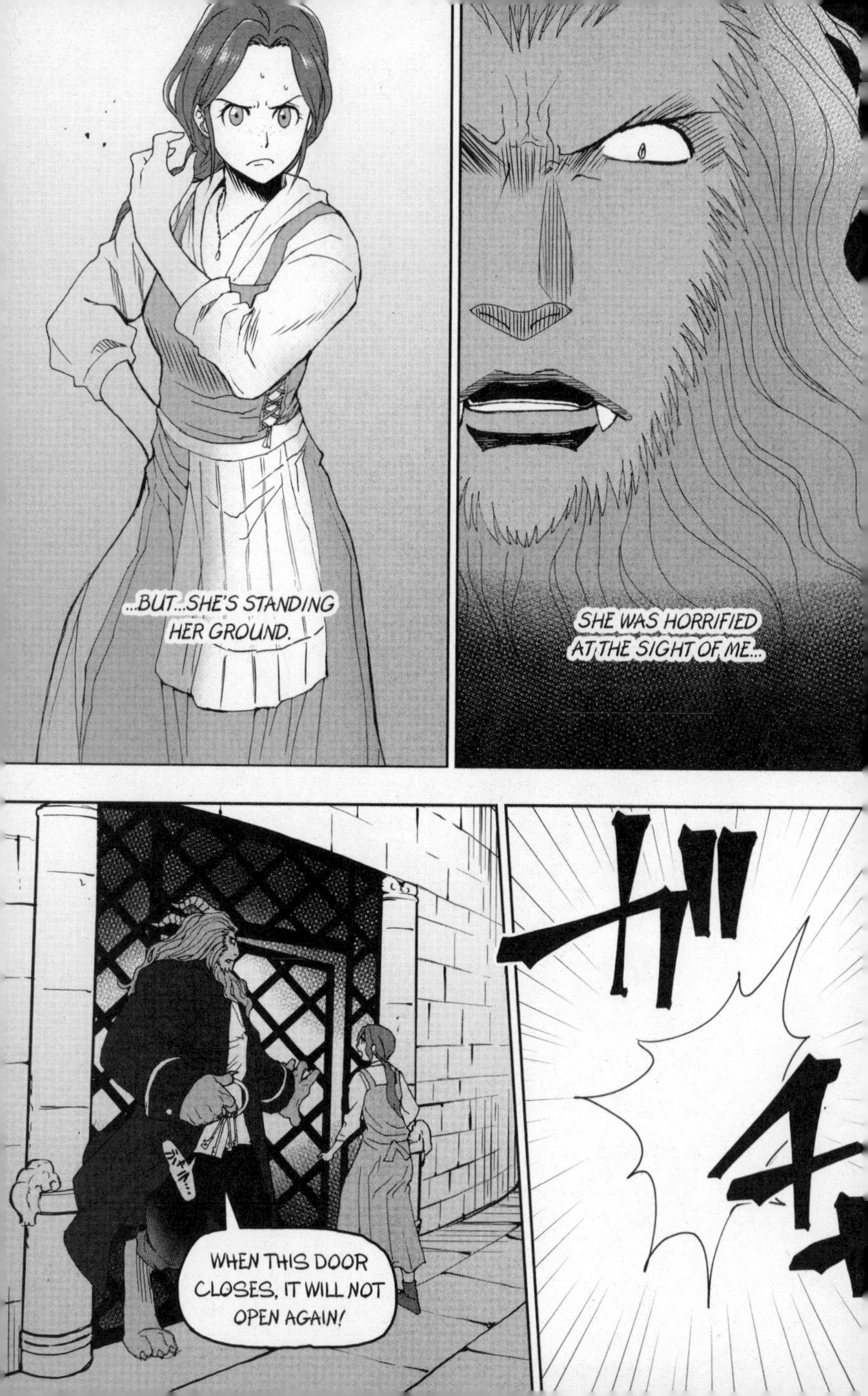
SHE WAS HORRIFIED AT THE SIGHT OF ME...
...BUT...SHE'S STANDING HER GROUND.
WHEN THIS DOOR CLOSES, IT WILL NOT OPEN AGAIN!

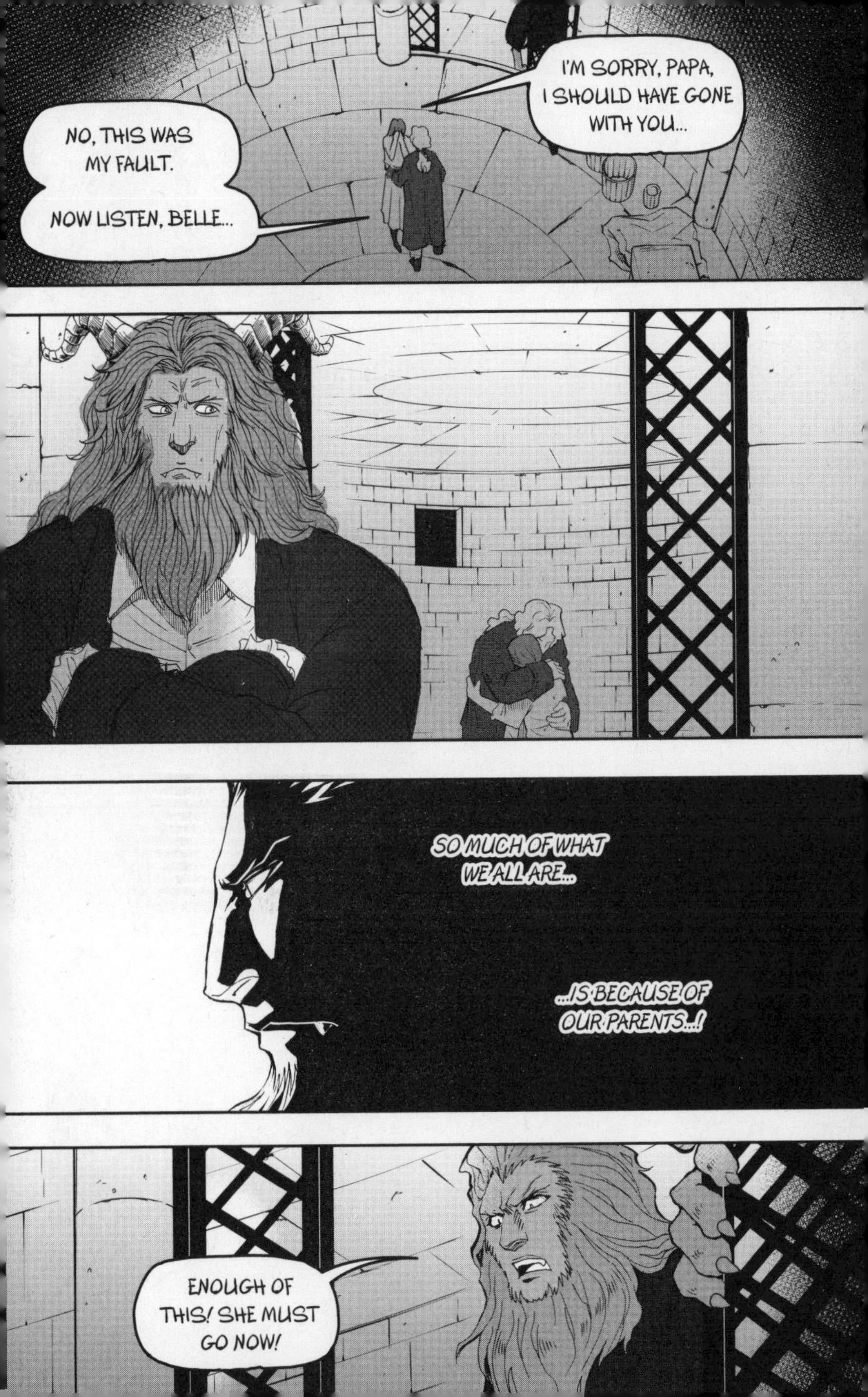
I'M SORRY, PAPA, I SHOULD HAVE GONE WITH YOU...
NO, THIS WAS MY FAULT.
NOW LISTEN, BELLE...
SO MUCH OF WHAT WE ALL ARE...
...IS BECAUSE OF OUR PARENTS...!
ENOUGH OF THIS! SHE MUST GO NOW!

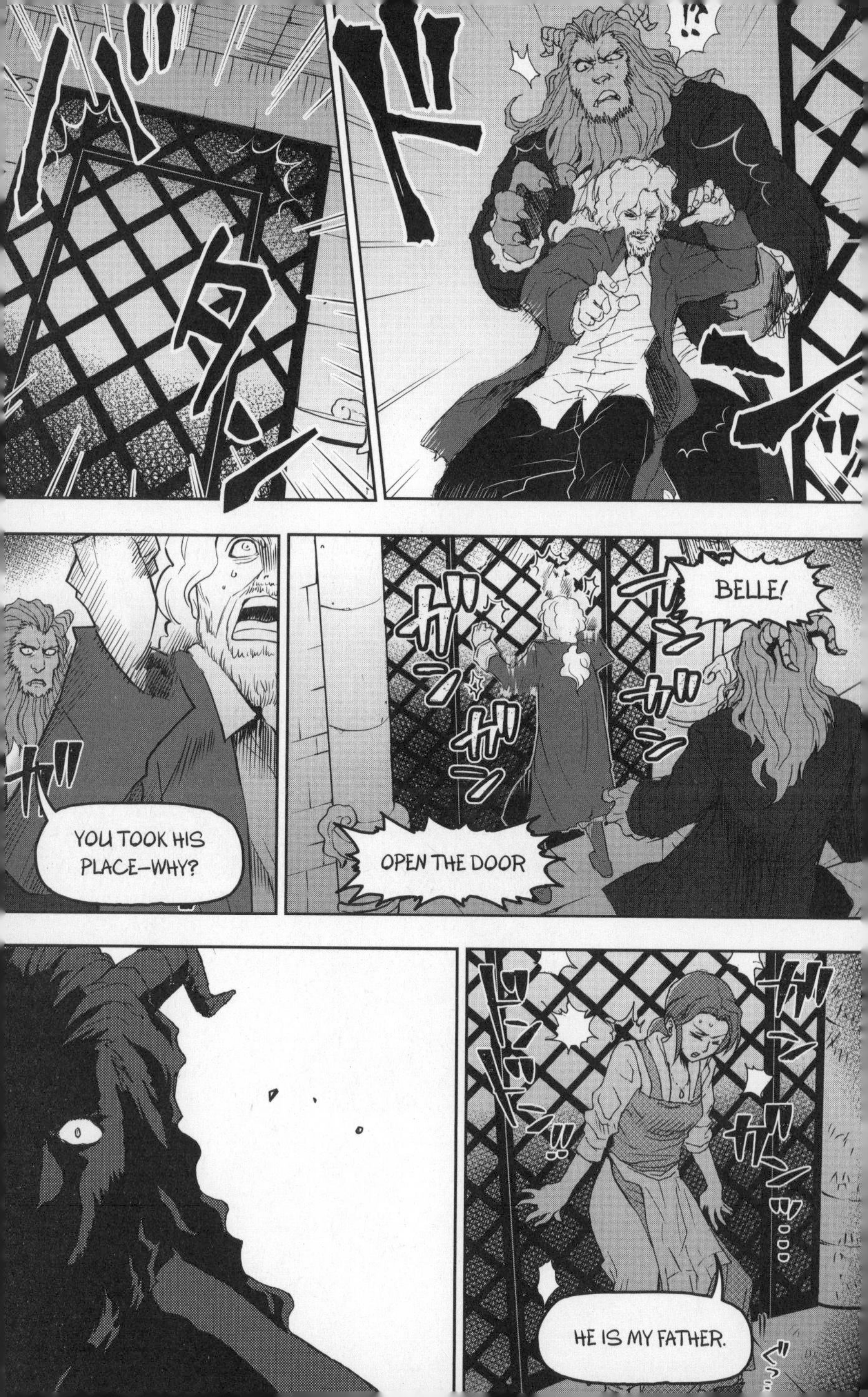
!?
BELLE!
OPEN THE DOOR
YOU TOOK HIS PLACE—WHY?
HE IS MY FATHER.

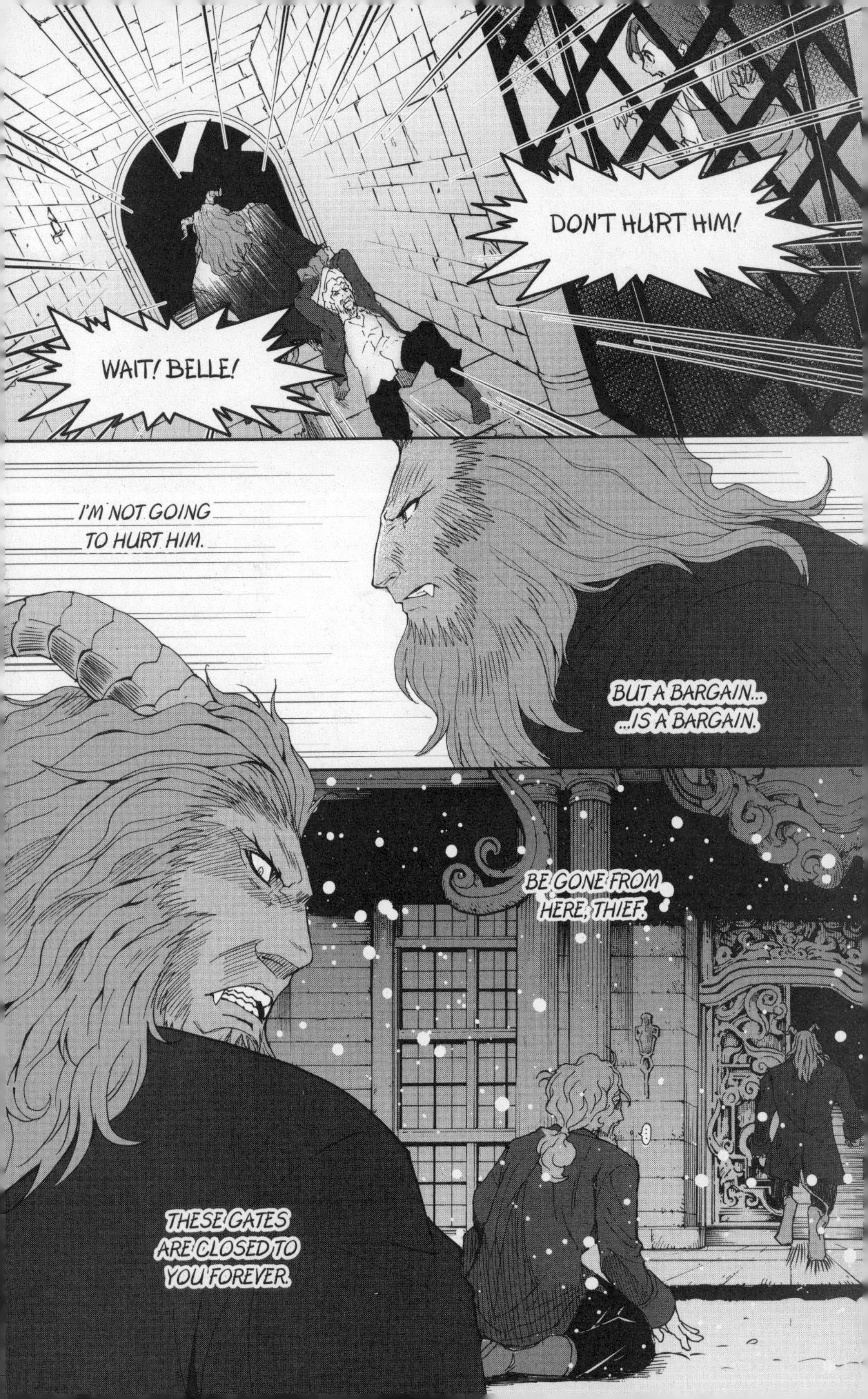
DON'T HURT HIM!
WAIT! BELLE!
I'M NOT GOING TO HURT HIM.
BUT A BARGAIN... ...IS A BARGAIN.
BE GONE FROM HERE, THIEF.
...
THESE GATES ARE CLOSED TO YOU FOREVER.

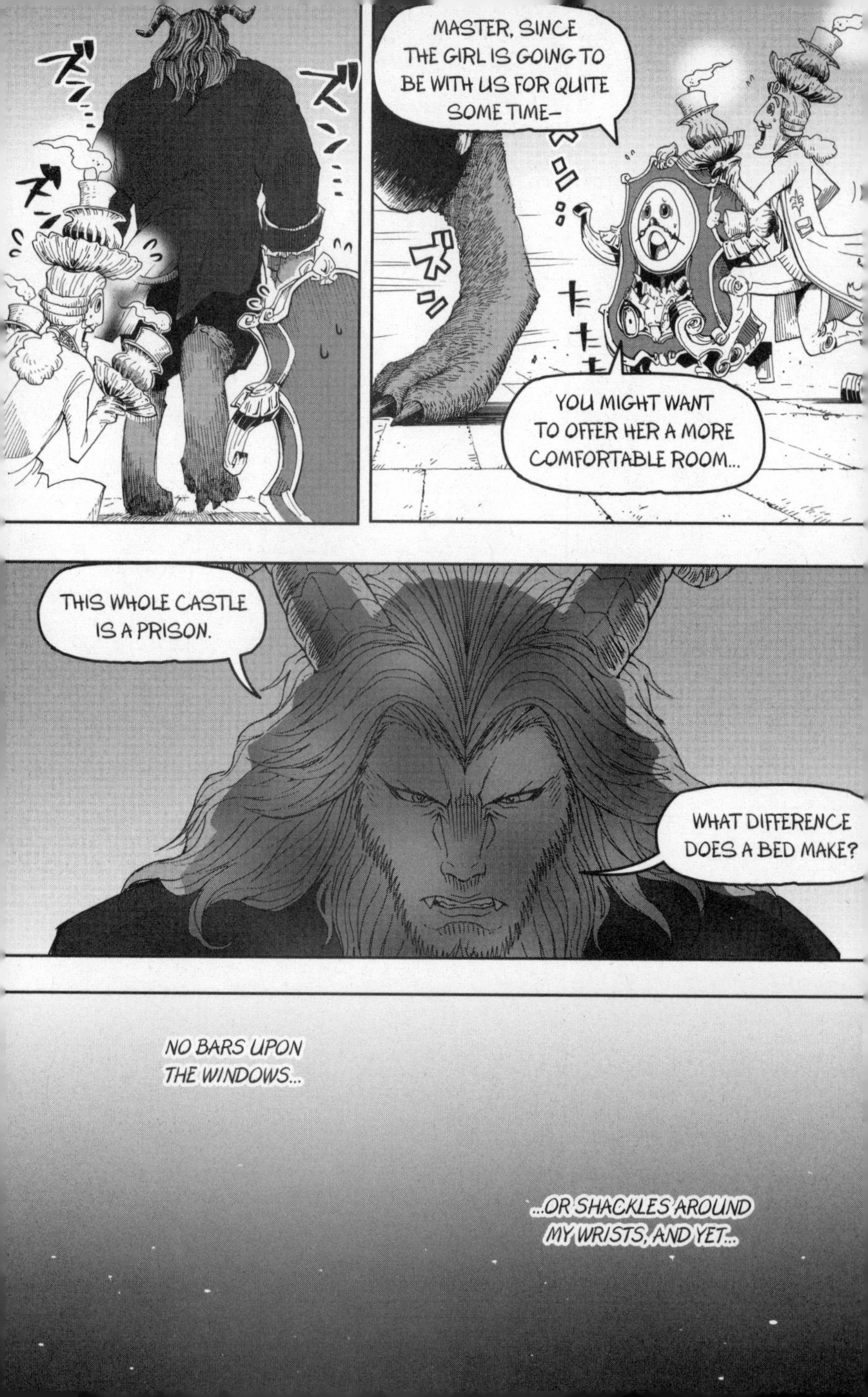
MASTER, SINCE THE GIRL IS GOING TO BE WITH US FOR QUITE SOME TIME—
YOU MIGHT WANT TO OFFER HER A MORE COMFORTABLE ROOM...
THIS WHOLE CASTLE IS A PRISON.
WHAT DIFFERENCE DOES A BED MAKE?
NO BARS UPON THE WINDOWS...
...OR SHACKLES AROUND MY WRISTS, AND YET...

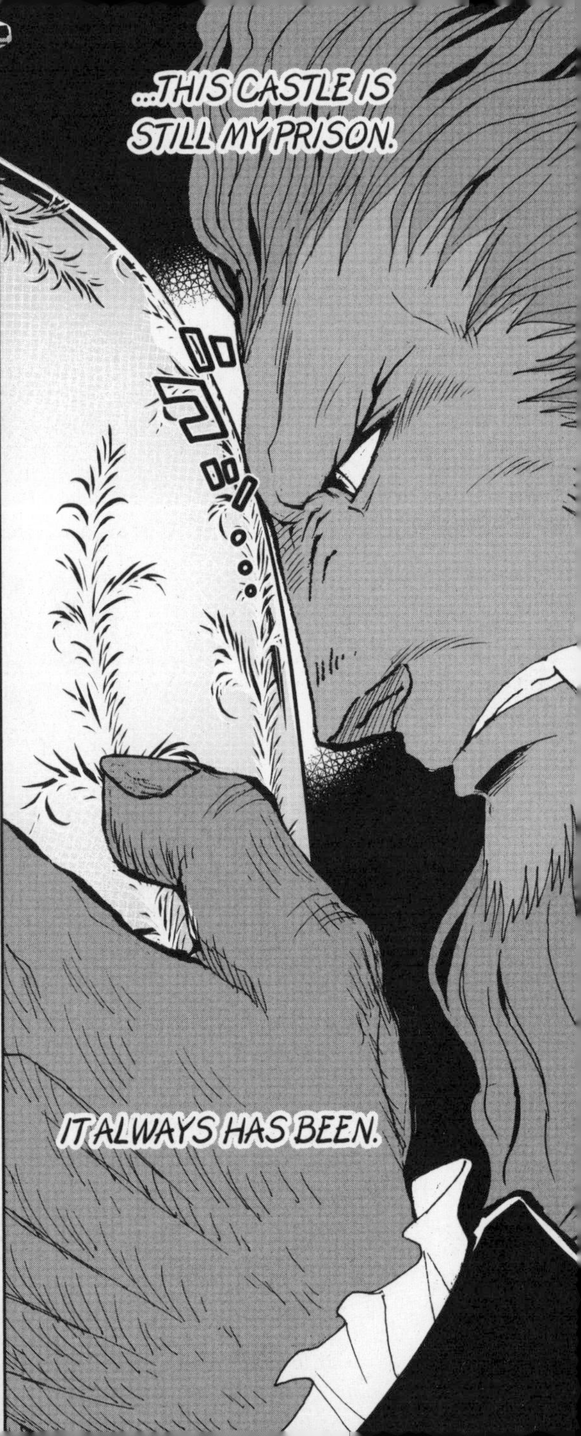
...THIS CASTLE IS
STILL MY PRISON.
IT ALWAYS HAS BEEN.
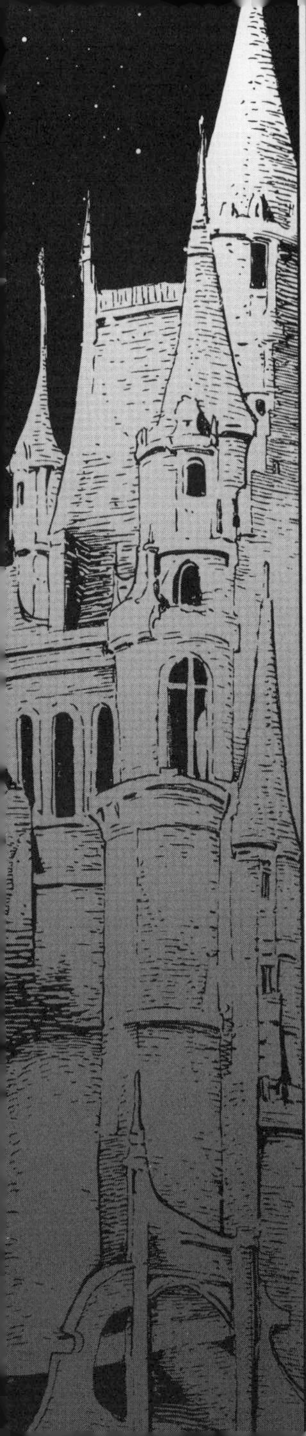

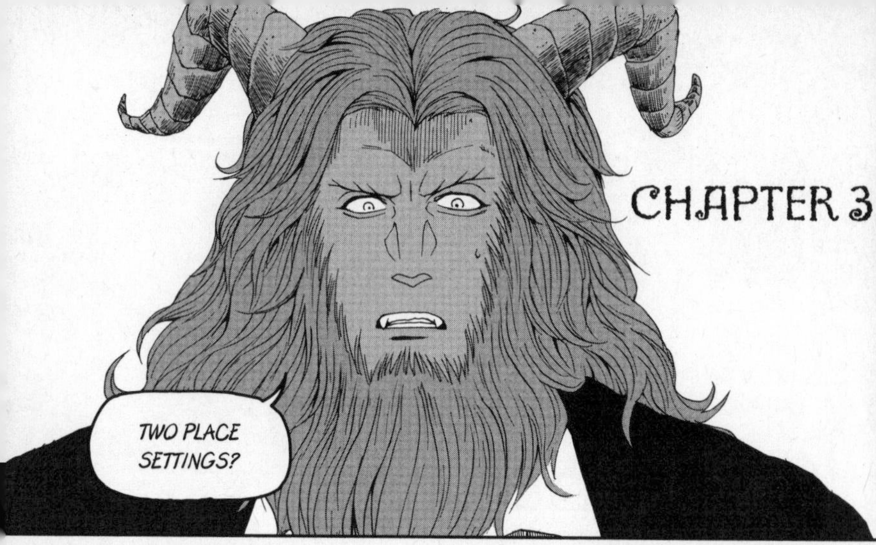
CHAPTER 3
TWO PLACE SETTINGS?
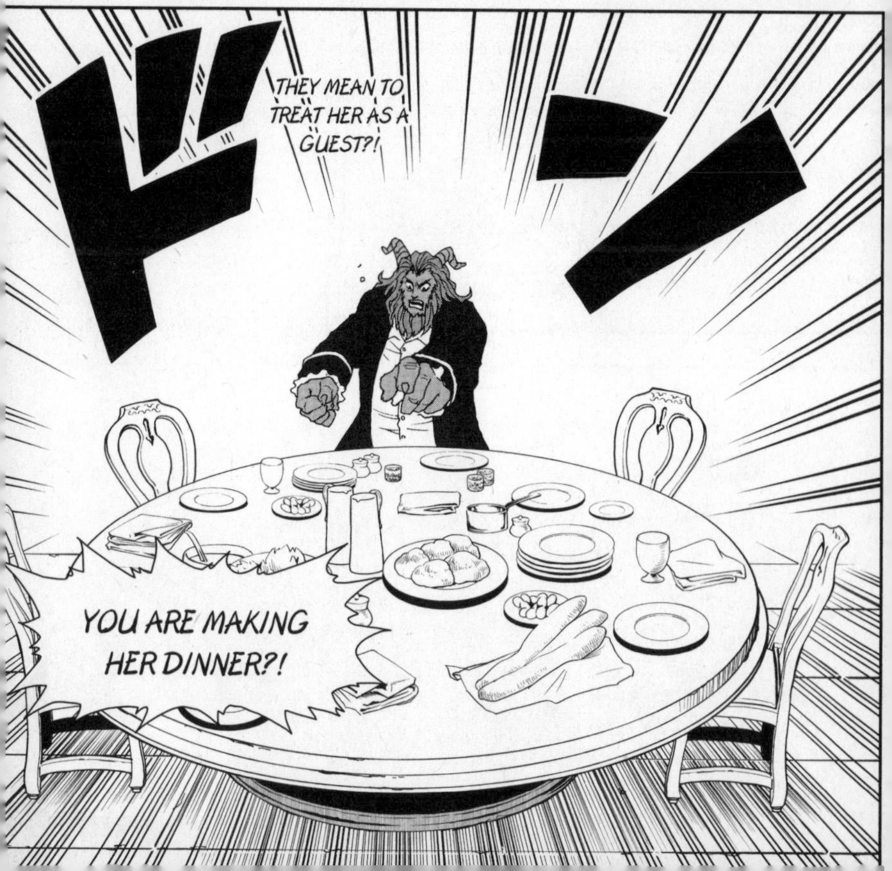
THEY MEAN TO TREAT HER AS A GUEST?!
YOU ARE MAKING HER DINNER?!

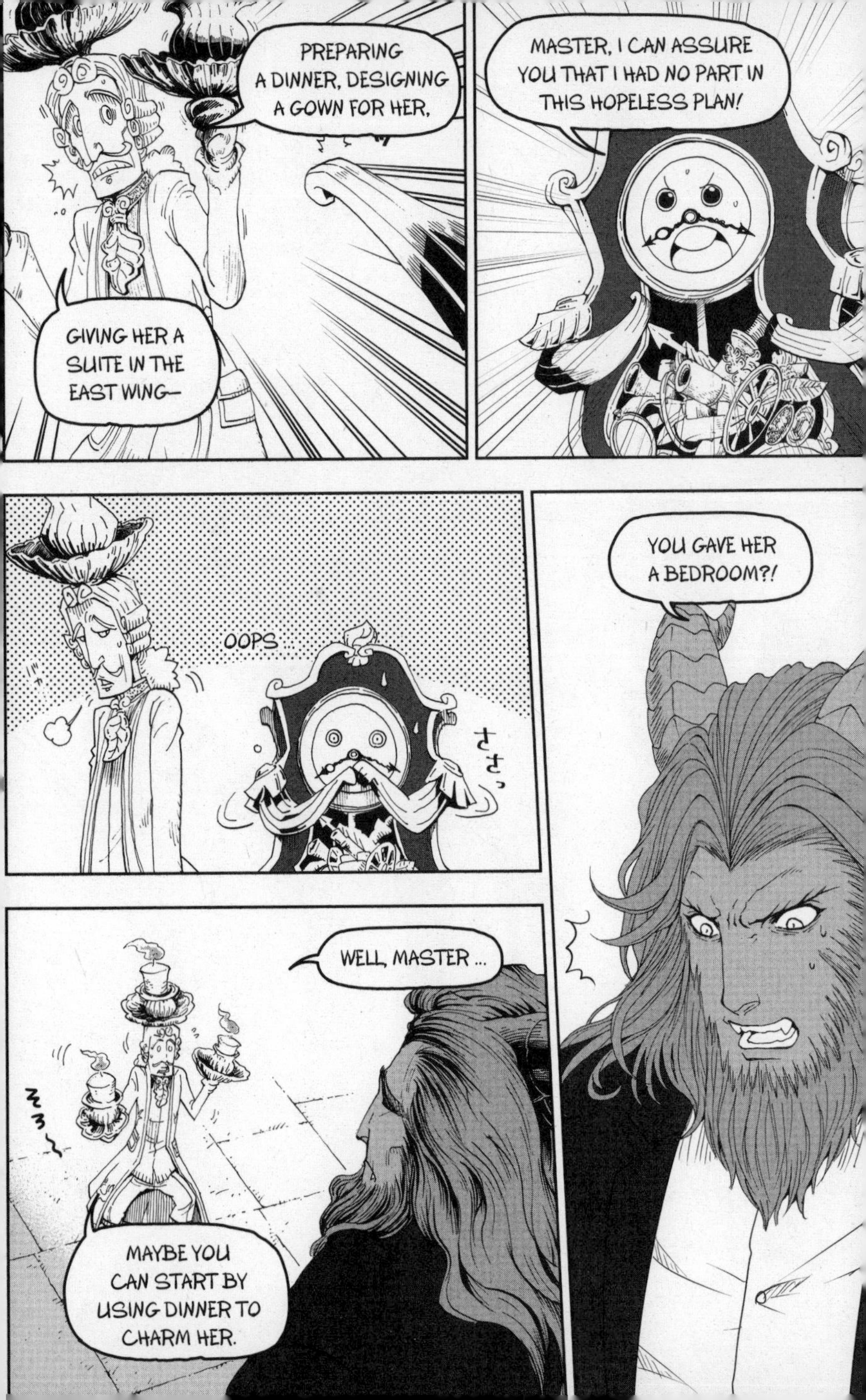
MASTER, I CAN ASSURE YOU THAT I HAD NO PART IN THIS HOPELESS PLAN!
PREPARING A DINNER, DESIGNING A GOWN FOR HER,
GIVING HER A SUITE IN THE EAST WING—
YOU GAVE HER A BEDROOM?!
OOPS
ささっ
WELL, MASTER ...
MAYBE YOU CAN START BY USING DINNER TO CHARM HER.

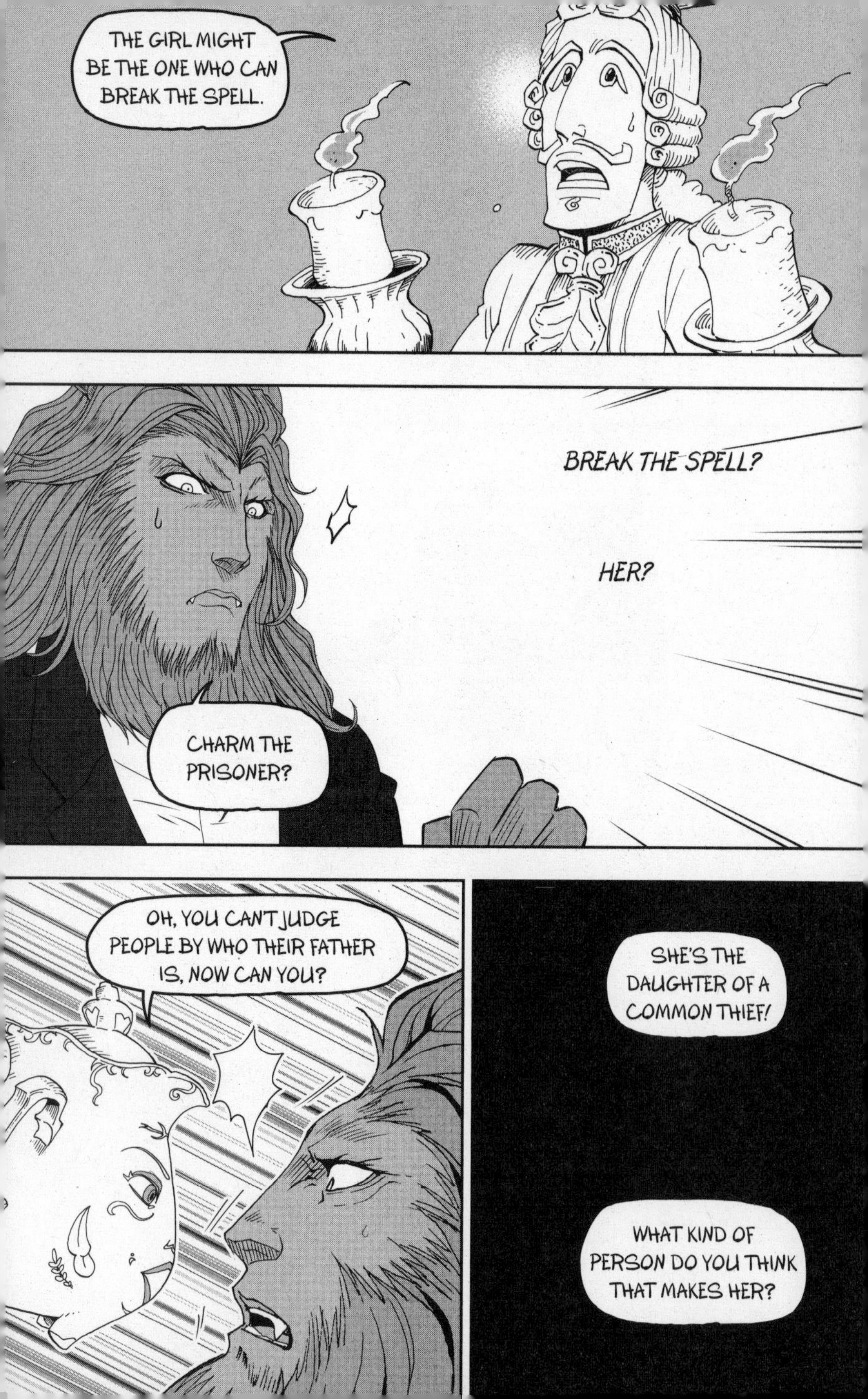
THE GIRL MIGHT BE THE ONE WHO CAN BREAK THE SPELL.
BREAK THE SPELL?
HER?
CHARM THE PRISONER?
SHE'S THE DAUGHTER OF A COMMON THIEF!
WHAT KIND OF PERSON DO YOU THINK THAT MAKES HER?
OH, YOU CAN'T JUDGE PEOPLE BY WHO THEIR FATHER IS, NOW CAN YOU?

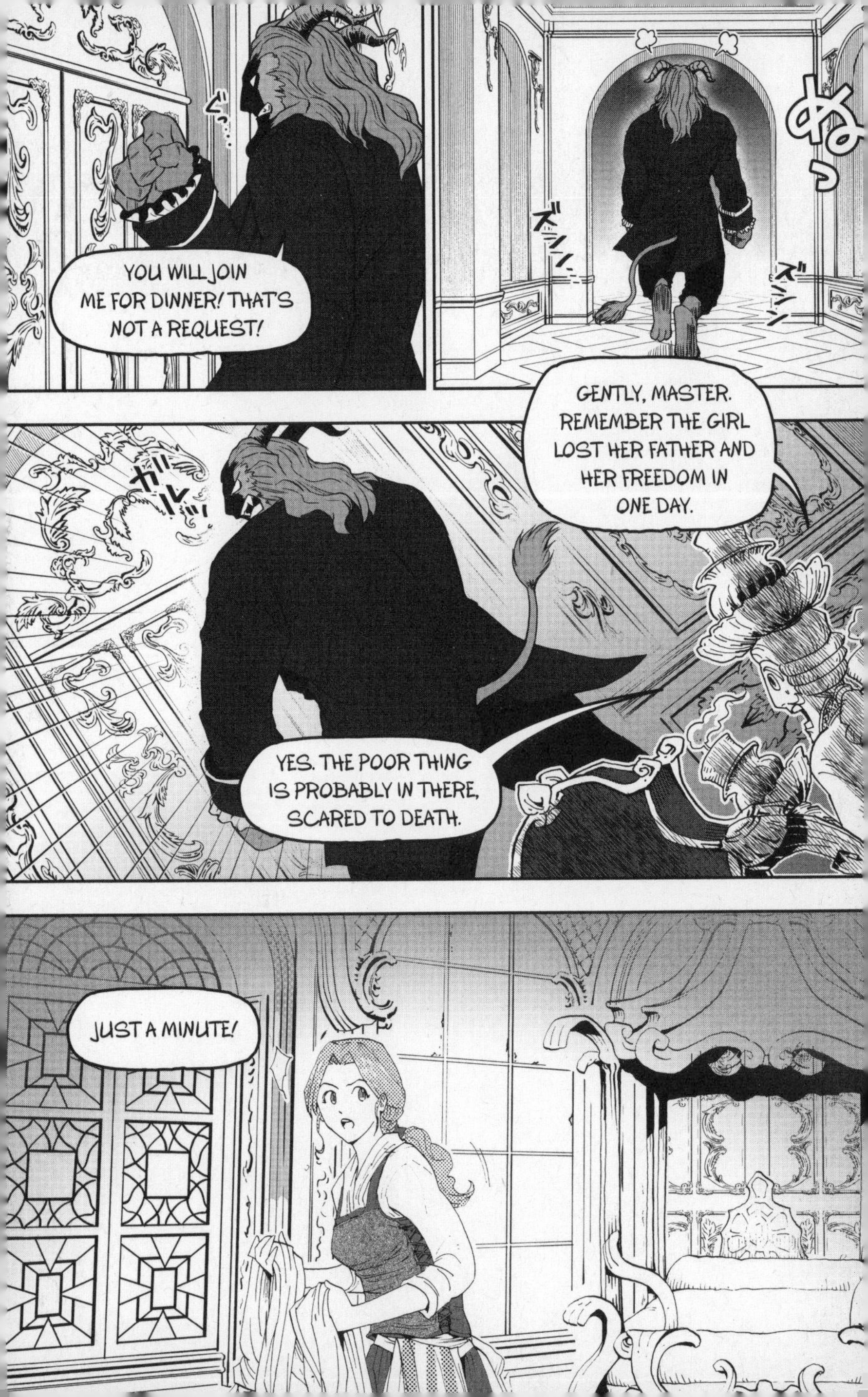
ぬっ
ズシン
ズシン
ぐっ…
YOU WILL JOIN ME FOR DINNER! THAT'S NOT A REQUEST!
GENTLY, MASTER. REMEMBER THE GIRL LOST HER FATHER AND HER FREEDOM IN ONE DAY.
ガルルッ
YES. THE POOR THING IS PROBABLY IN THERE, SCARED TO DEATH.
JUST A MINUTE!

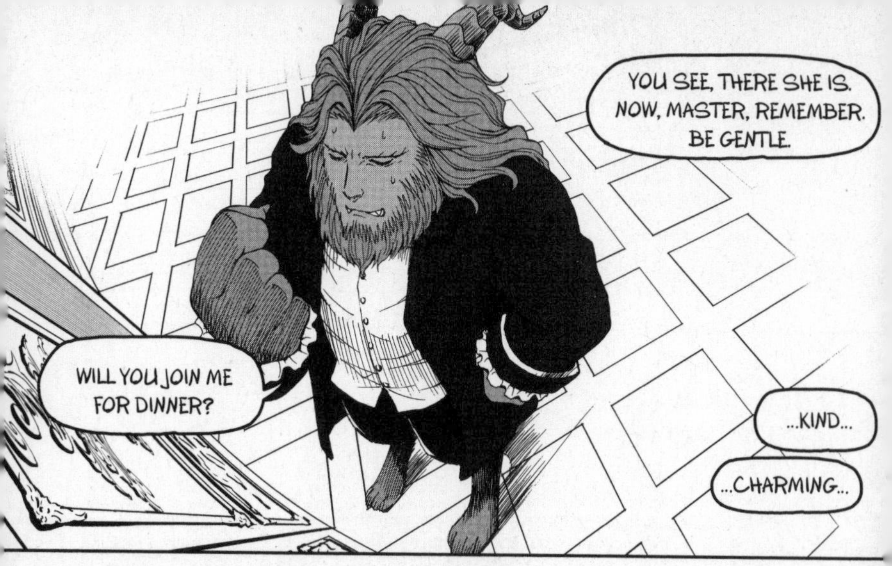
YOU SEE, THERE SHE IS. NOW, MASTER, REMEMBER. BE GENTLE.
...KIND...
...CHARMING...
WILL YOU JOIN ME FOR DINNER?

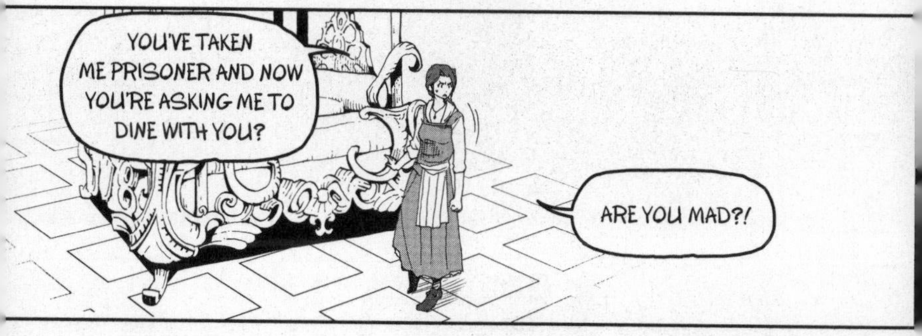
YOU'VE TAKEN ME PRISONER AND NOW YOU'RE ASKING ME TO DINE WITH YOU?
ARE YOU MAD?!

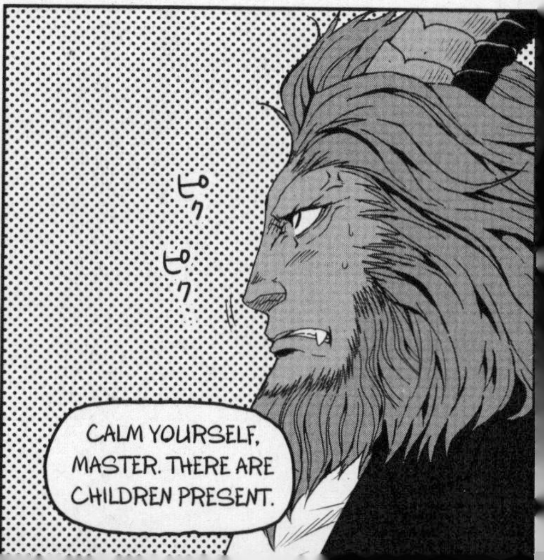
ピク ピク
CALM YOURSELF, MASTER. THERE ARE CHILDREN PRESENT.

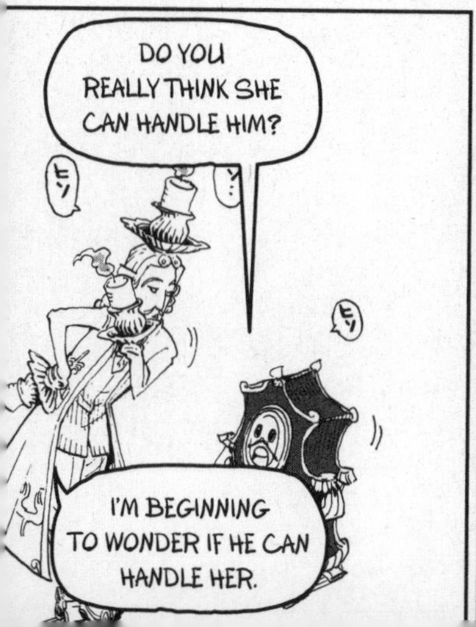
DO YOU REALLY THINK SHE CAN HANDLE HIM?
ヒソ
ヒソ
I'M BEGINNING TO WONDER IF HE CAN HANDLE HER.

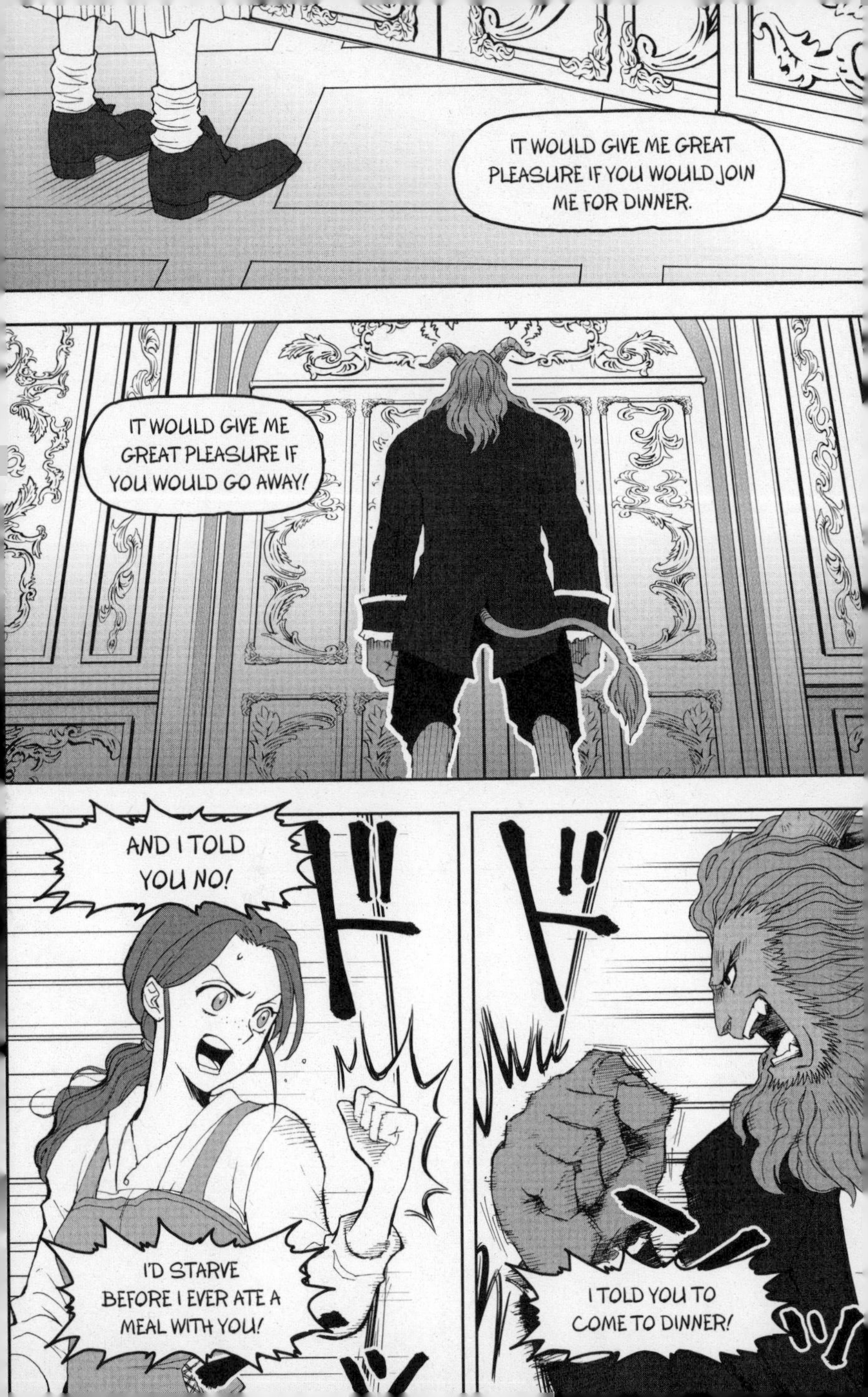
IT WOULD GIVE ME GREAT PLEASURE IF YOU WOULD JOIN ME FOR DINNER.
IT WOULD GIVE ME GREAT PLEASURE IF YOU WOULD GO AWAY!
ド
I TOLD YOU TO COME TO DINNER!
ド
AND I TOLD YOU NO!
I'D STARVE BEFORE I EVER ATE A MEAL WITH YOU!

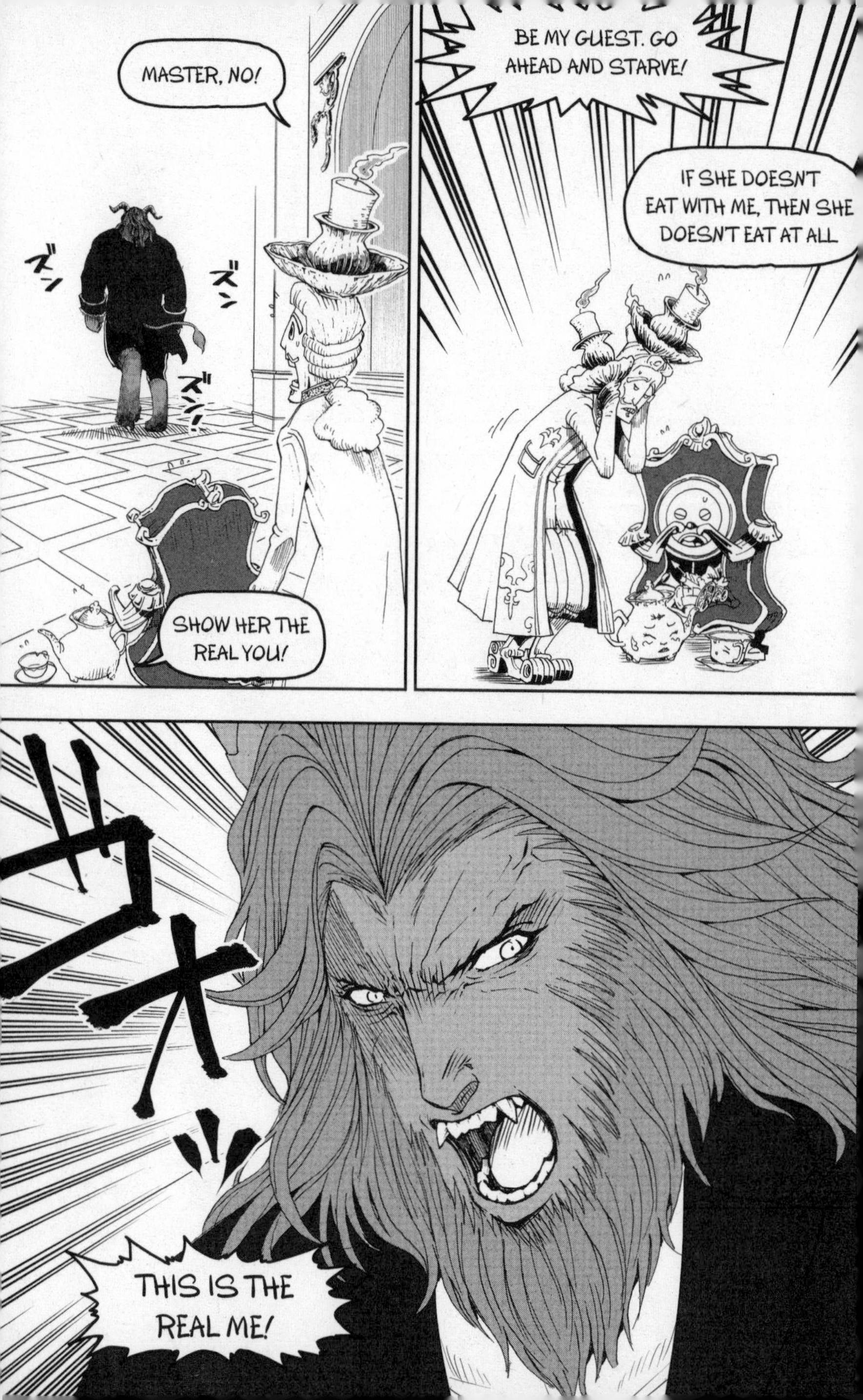
BE MY GUEST. GO AHEAD AND STARVE!
IF SHE DOESN'T EAT WITH ME, THEN SHE DOESN'T EAT AT ALL
MASTER, NO!
ズン
ズン
ズン!
SHOW HER THE REAL YOU!
ガオ!!
THIS IS THE REAL ME!

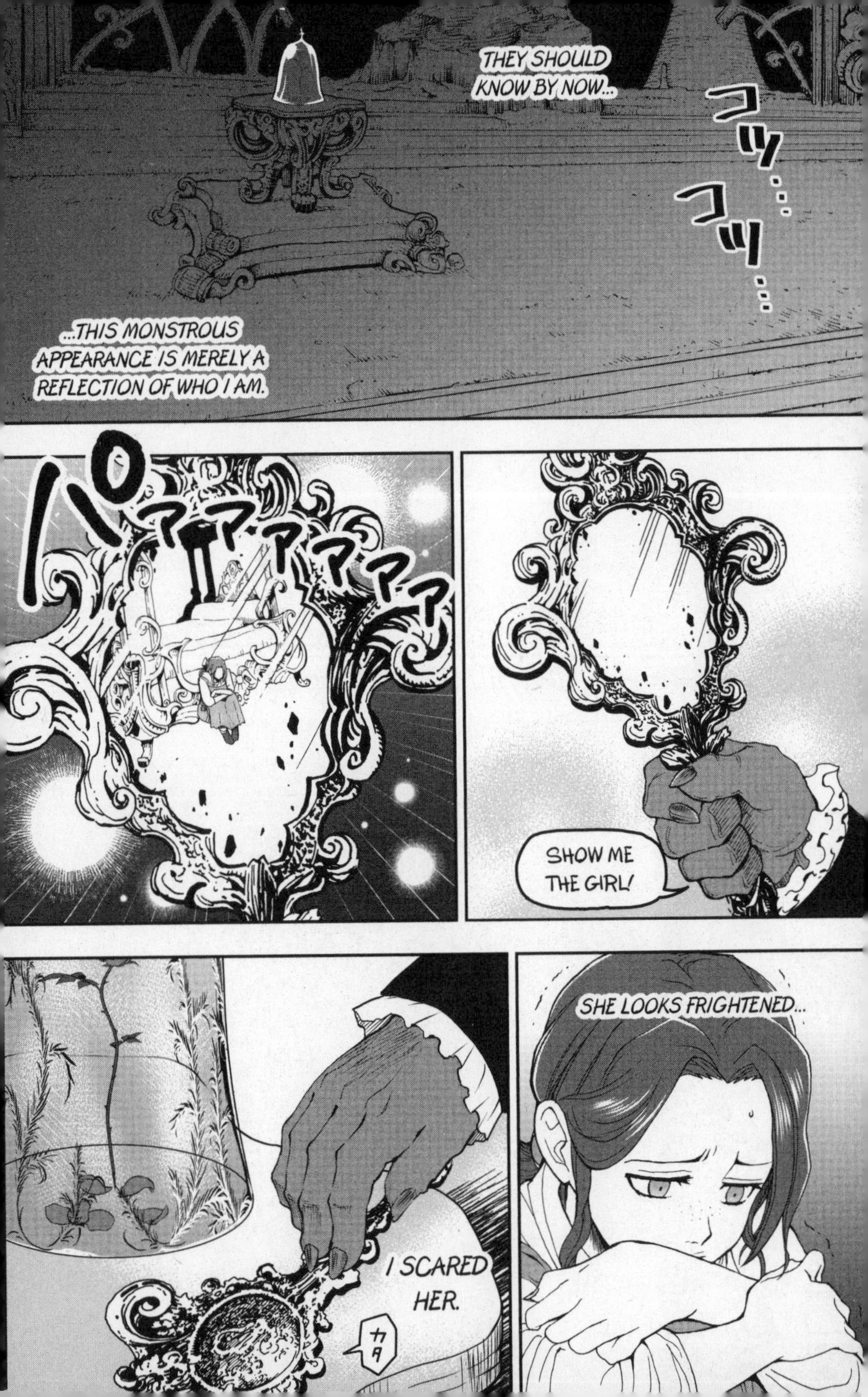
コツ…
コツ…
THEY SHOULD KNOW BY NOW...
...THIS MONSTROUS APPEARANCE IS MERELY A REFLECTION OF WHO I AM.
SHOW ME THE GIRL!
パアアアアアア
SHE LOOKS FRIGHTENED...
I SCARED HER.
カタ

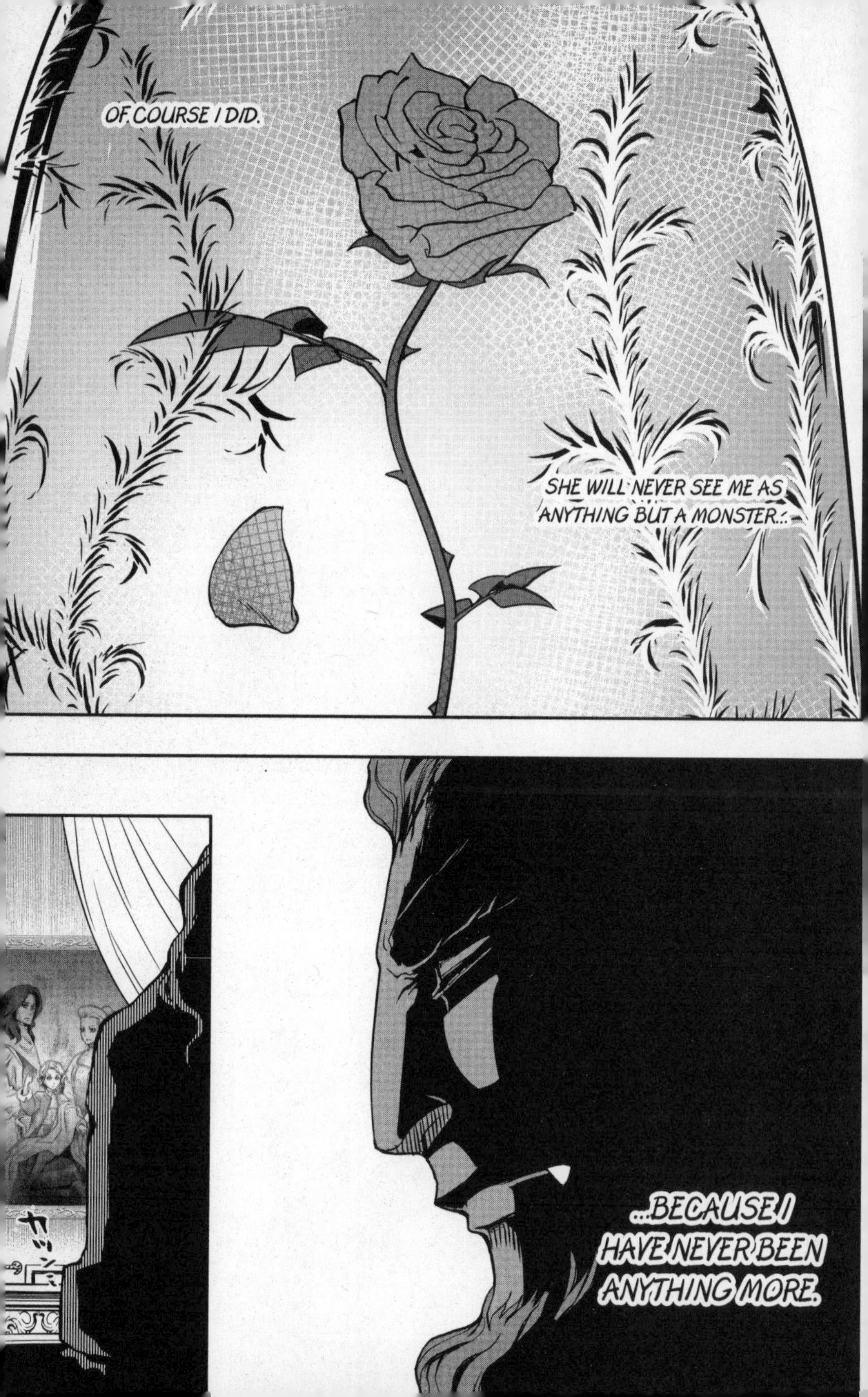
OF COURSE I DID.
SHE WILL NEVER SEE ME AS ANYTHING BUT A MONSTER...
...BECAUSE I HAVE NEVER BEEN ANYTHING MORE.

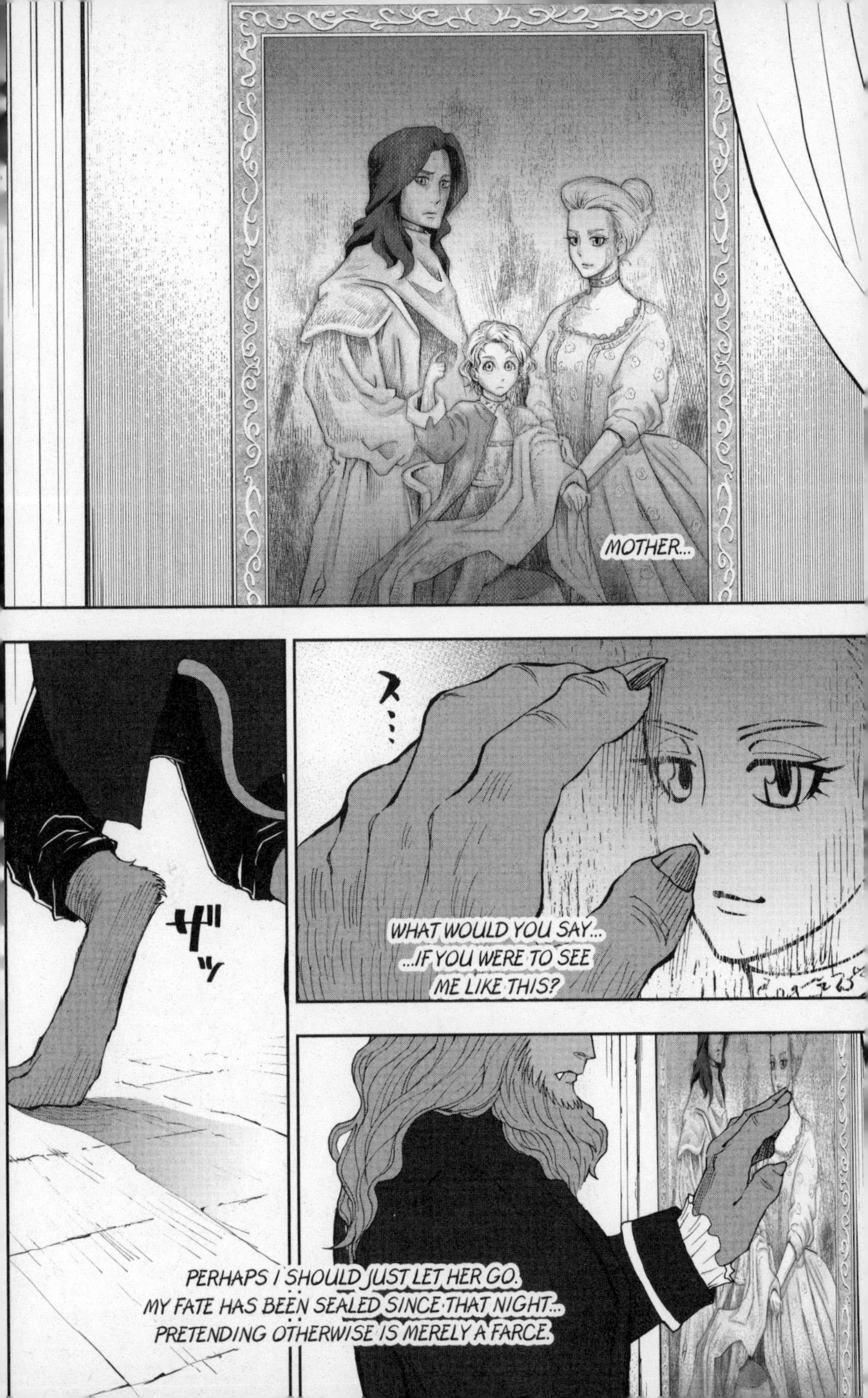
MOTHER...
ス...
WHAT WOULD YOU SAY...
...IF YOU WERE TO SEE ME LIKE THIS?
PERHAPS I SHOULD JUST LET HER GO.
MY FATE HAS BEEN SEALED SINCE THAT NIGHT...
PRETENDING OTHERWISE IS MERELY A FARCE.
ザッ

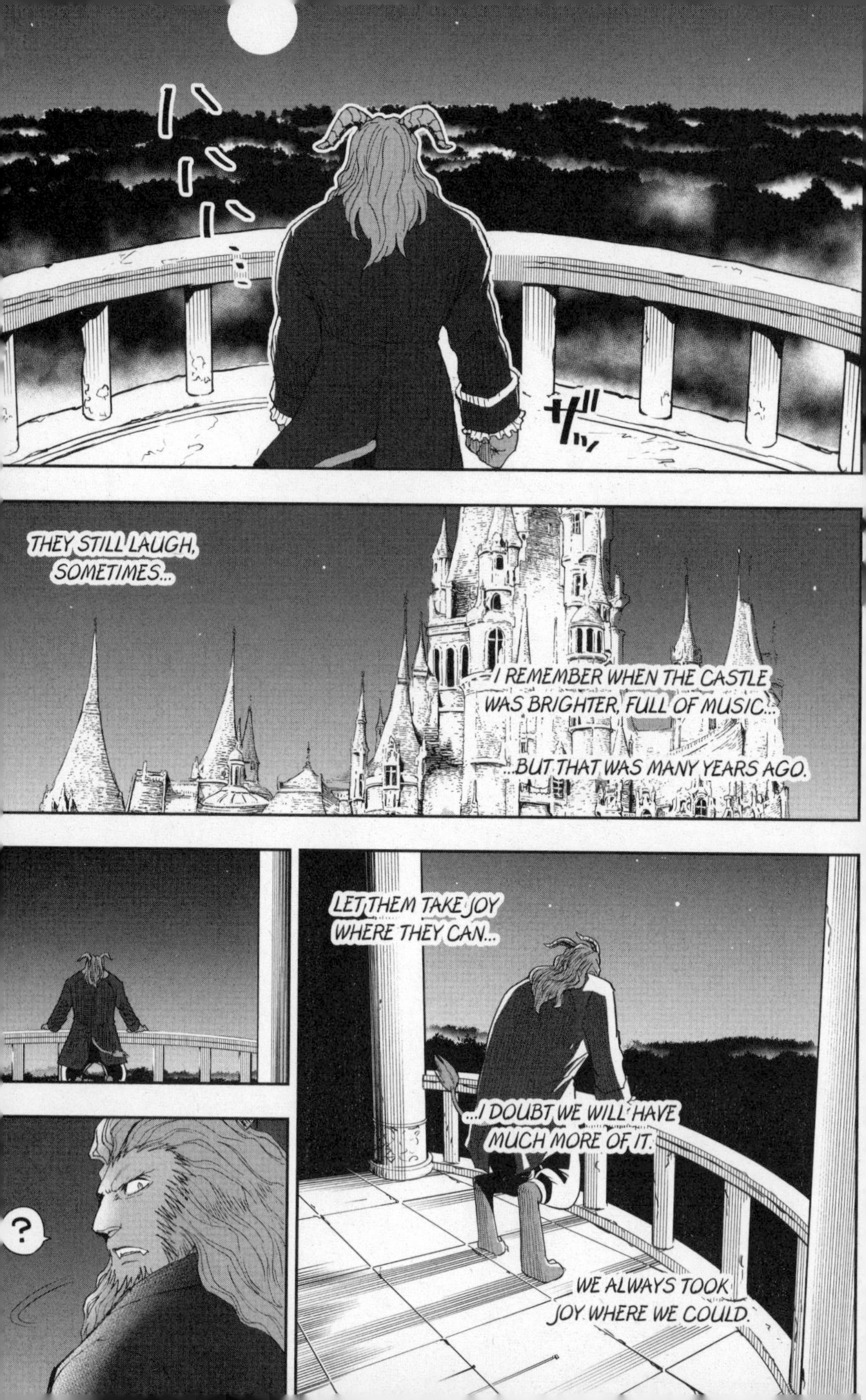
THEY STILL LAUGH, SOMETIMES...
I REMEMBER WHEN THE CASTLE WAS BRIGHTER, FULL OF MUSIC...
...BUT THAT WAS MANY YEARS AGO.
LET THEM TAKE JOY WHERE THEY CAN...
...I DOUBT WE WILL HAVE MUCH MORE OF IT.
WE ALWAYS TOOK JOY WHERE WE COULD.
?

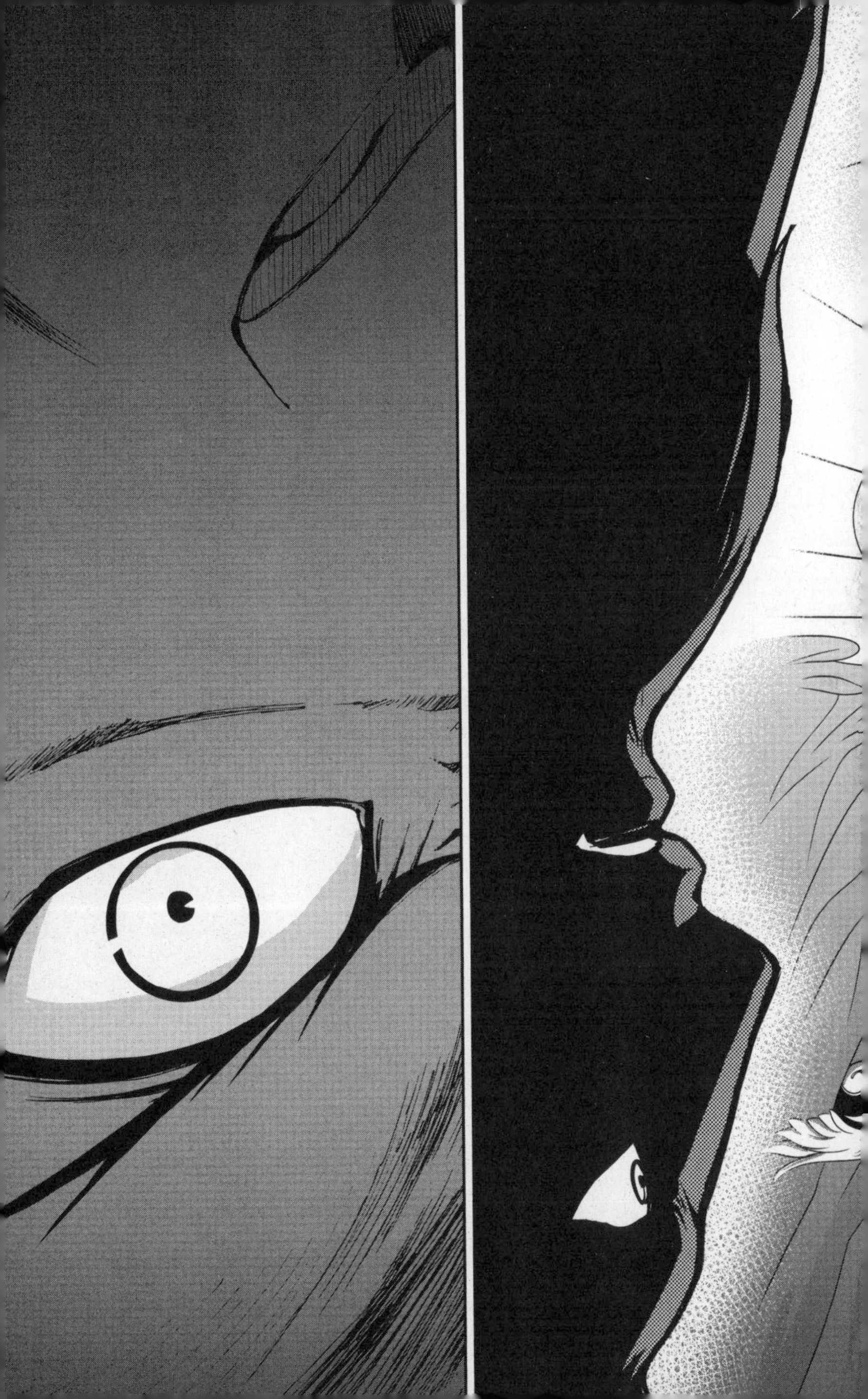

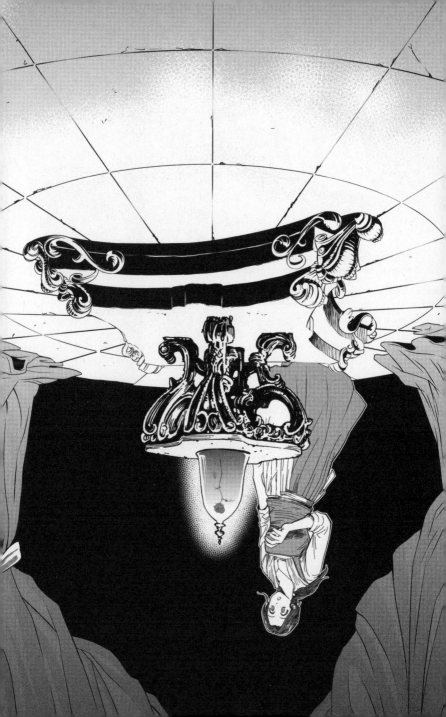

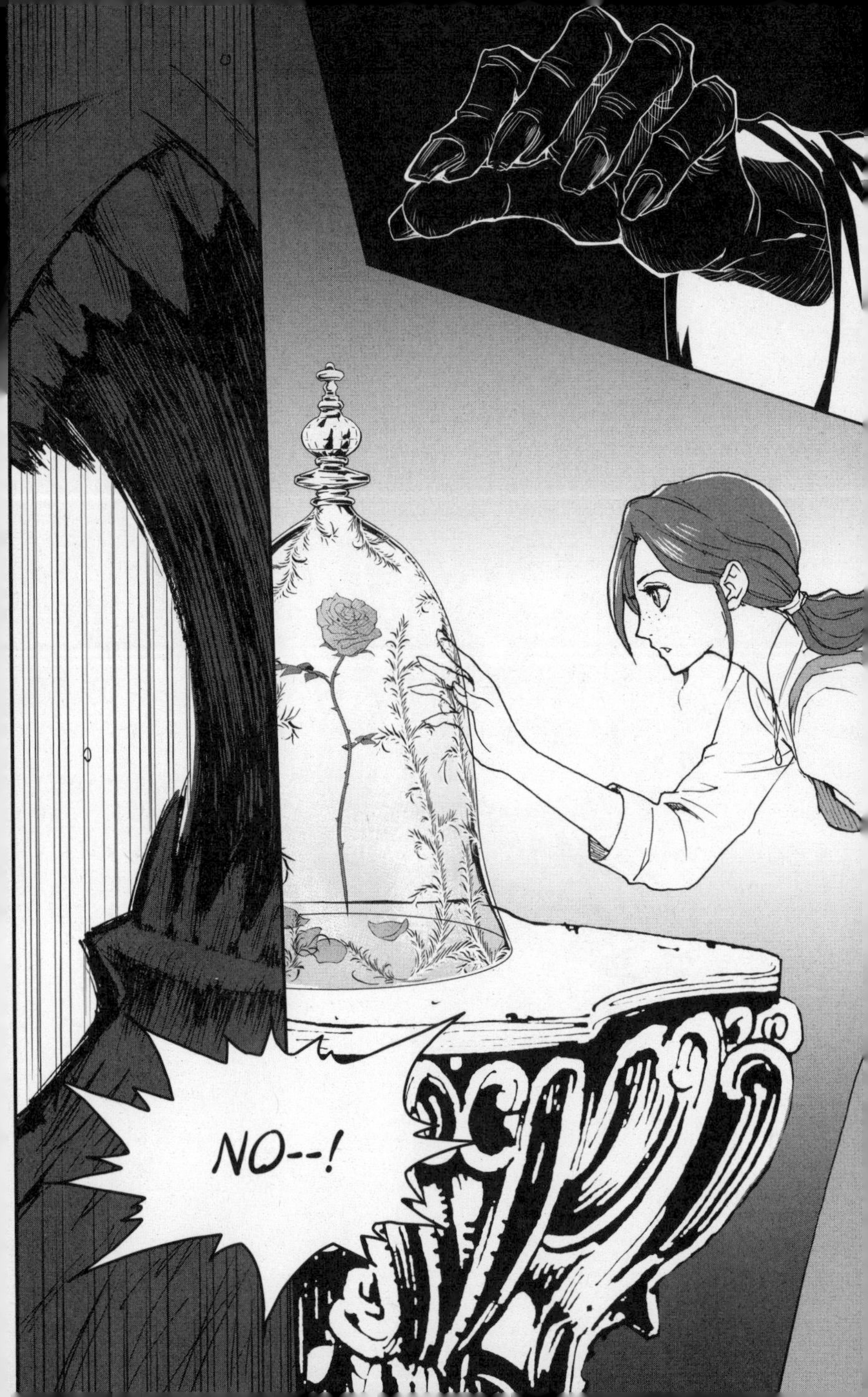
NO--!

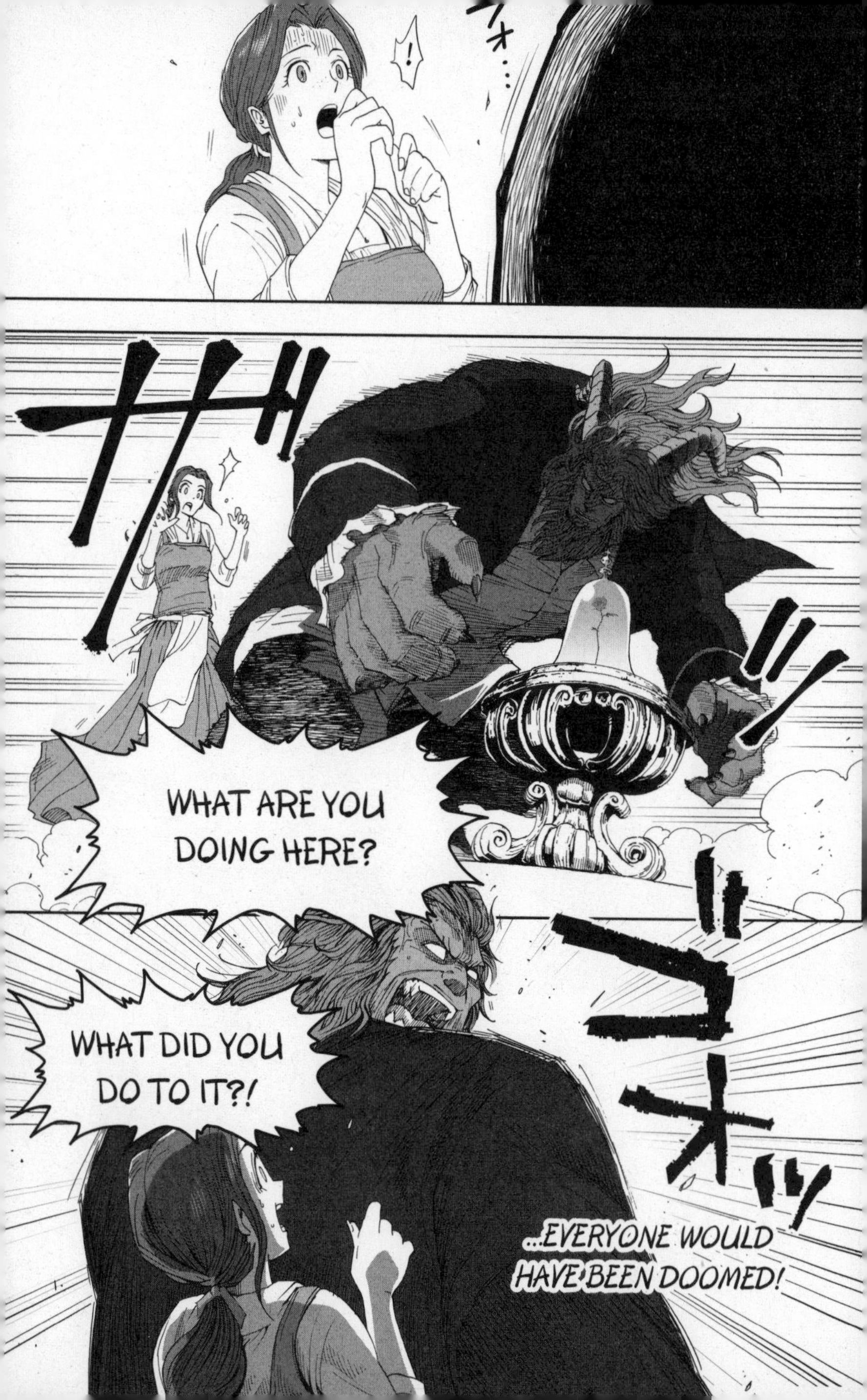
!
WHAT ARE YOU DOING HERE?
WHAT DID YOU DO TO IT?!
...EVERYONE WOULD HAVE BEEN DOOMED!

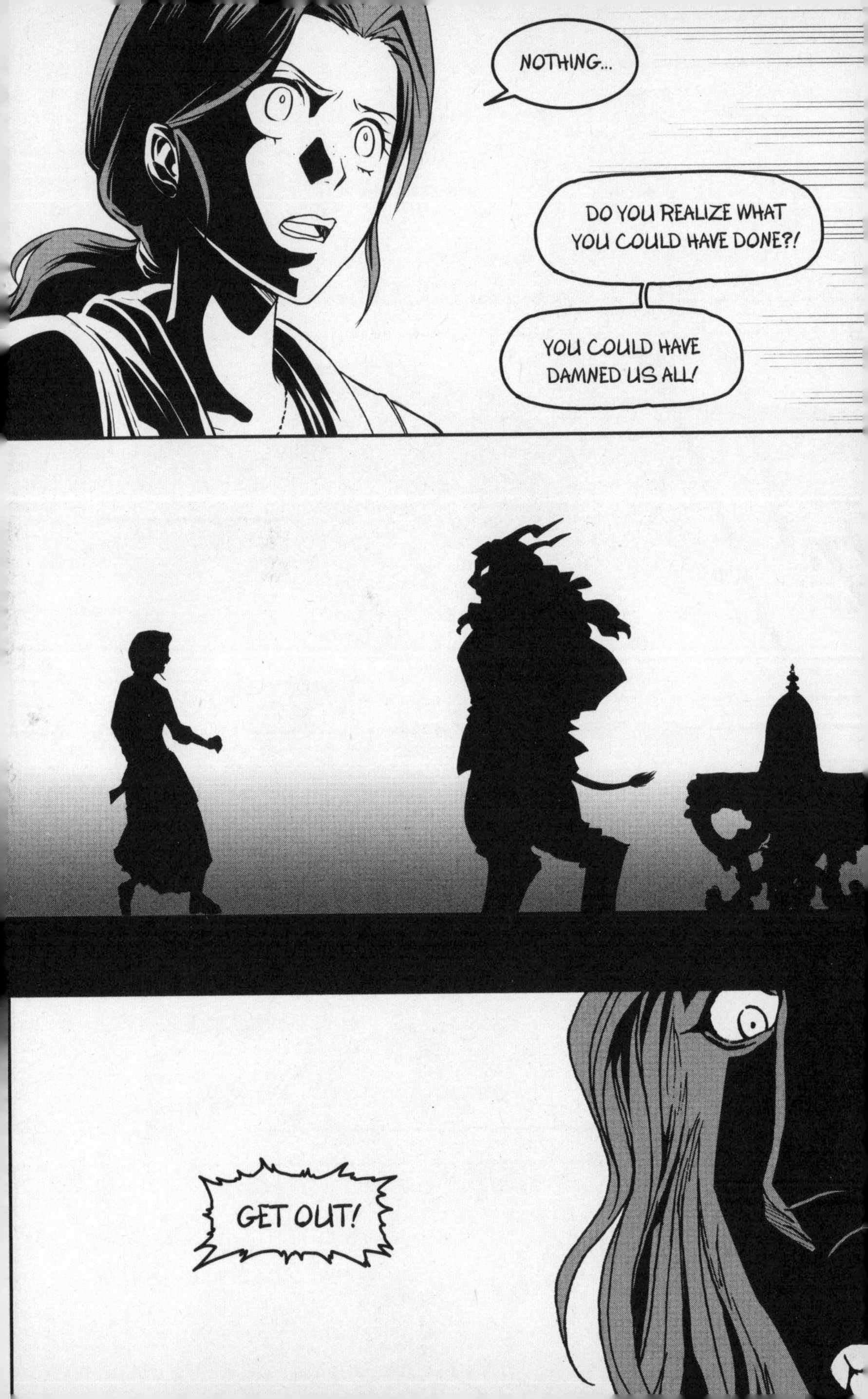
NOTHING...
DO YOU REALIZE WHAT YOU COULD HAVE DONE?!
YOU COULD HAVE DAMNED US ALL!
GET OUT!

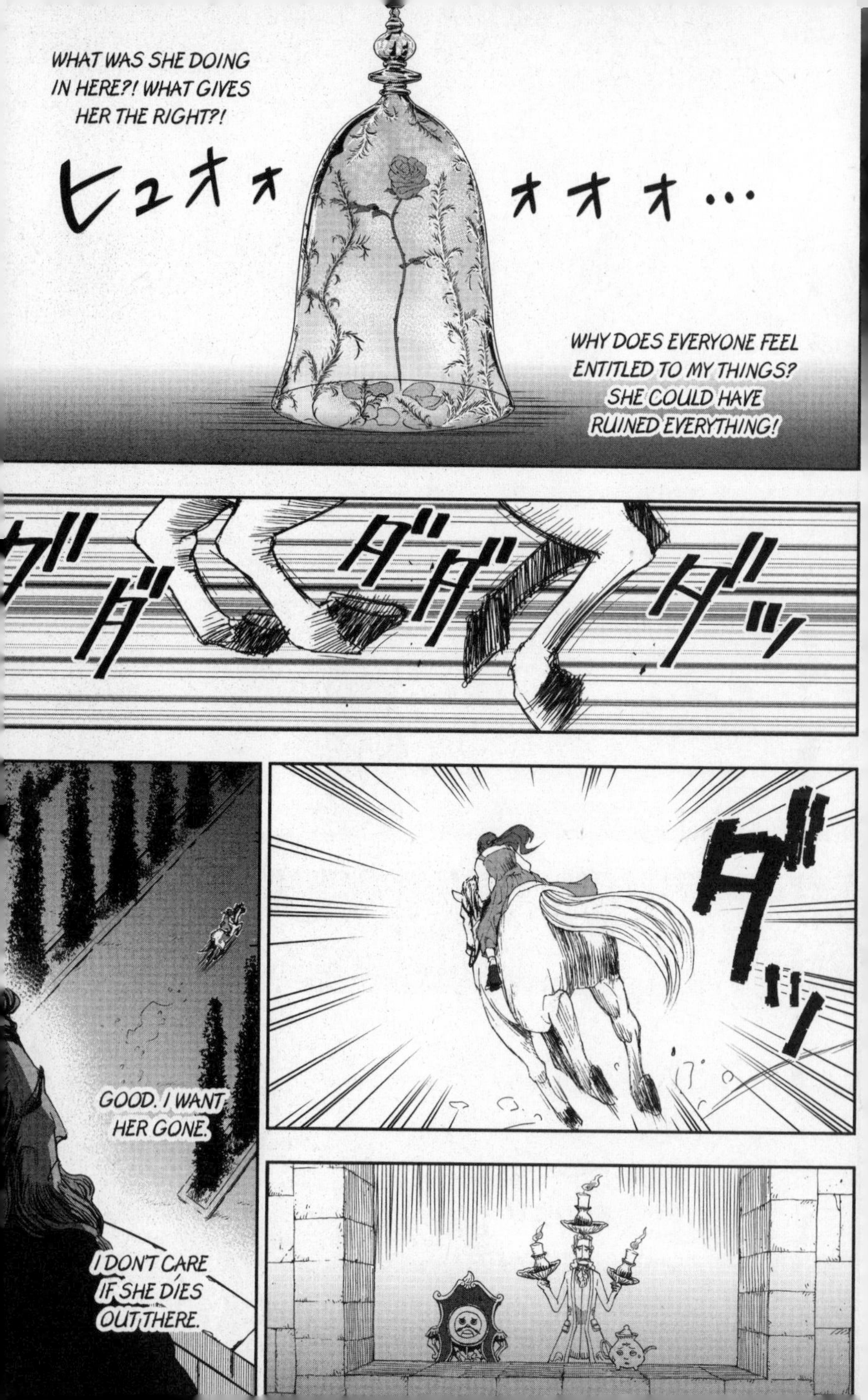
WHAT WAS SHE DOING IN HERE?! WHAT GIVES HER THE RIGHT?!
ヒュオォオオオ…
WHY DOES EVERYONE FEEL ENTITLED TO MY THINGS? SHE COULD HAVE RUINED EVERYTHING!
ダッ
ダダ
ダダ
ダッ
GOOD. I WANT HER GONE.
I DON'T CARE IF SHE DIES OUT THERE.

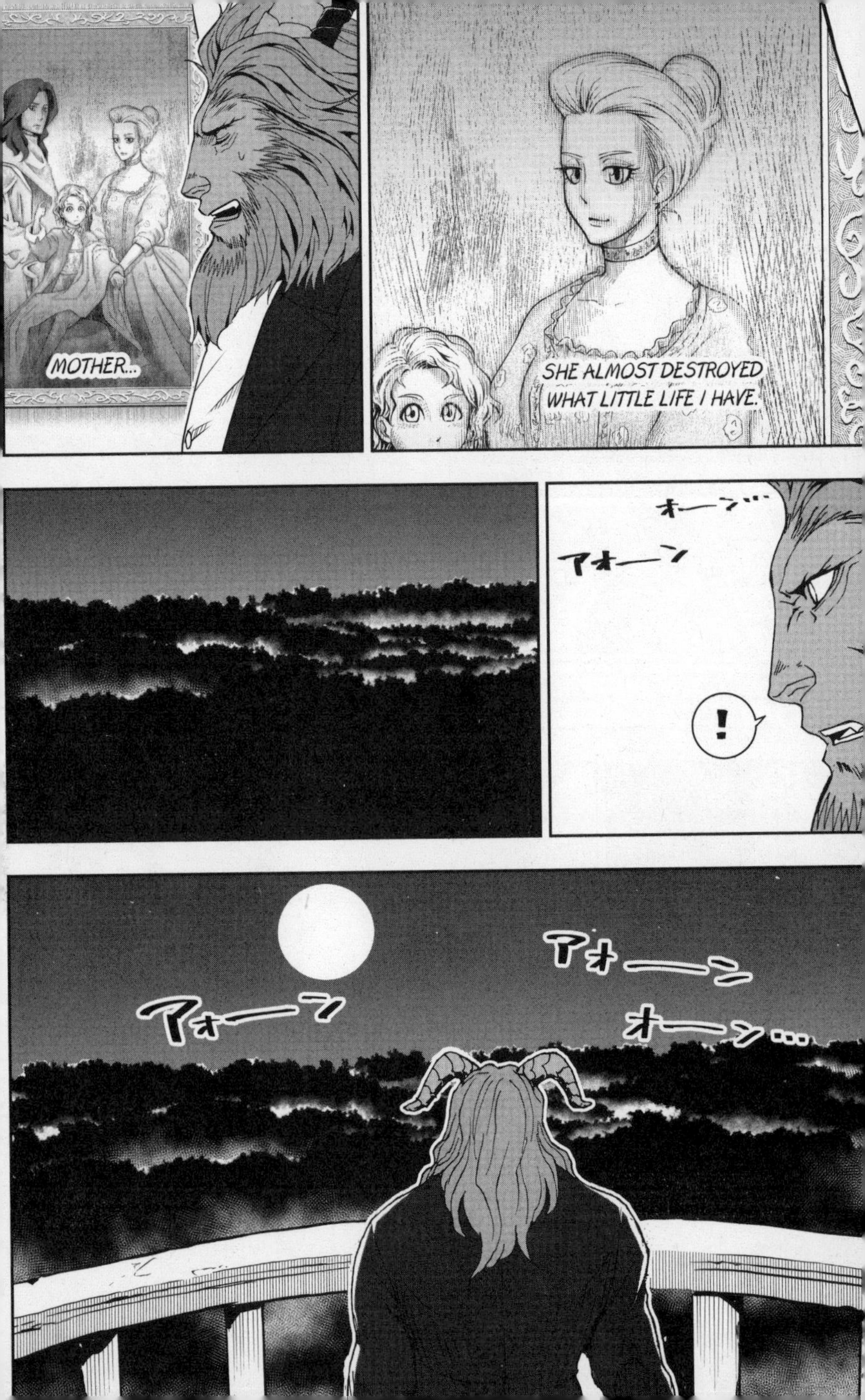
SHE ALMOST DESTROYED WHAT LITTLE LIFE I HAVE.
MOTHER...
オーン…
アオーン
!
アオーン
オーン…
アオーン

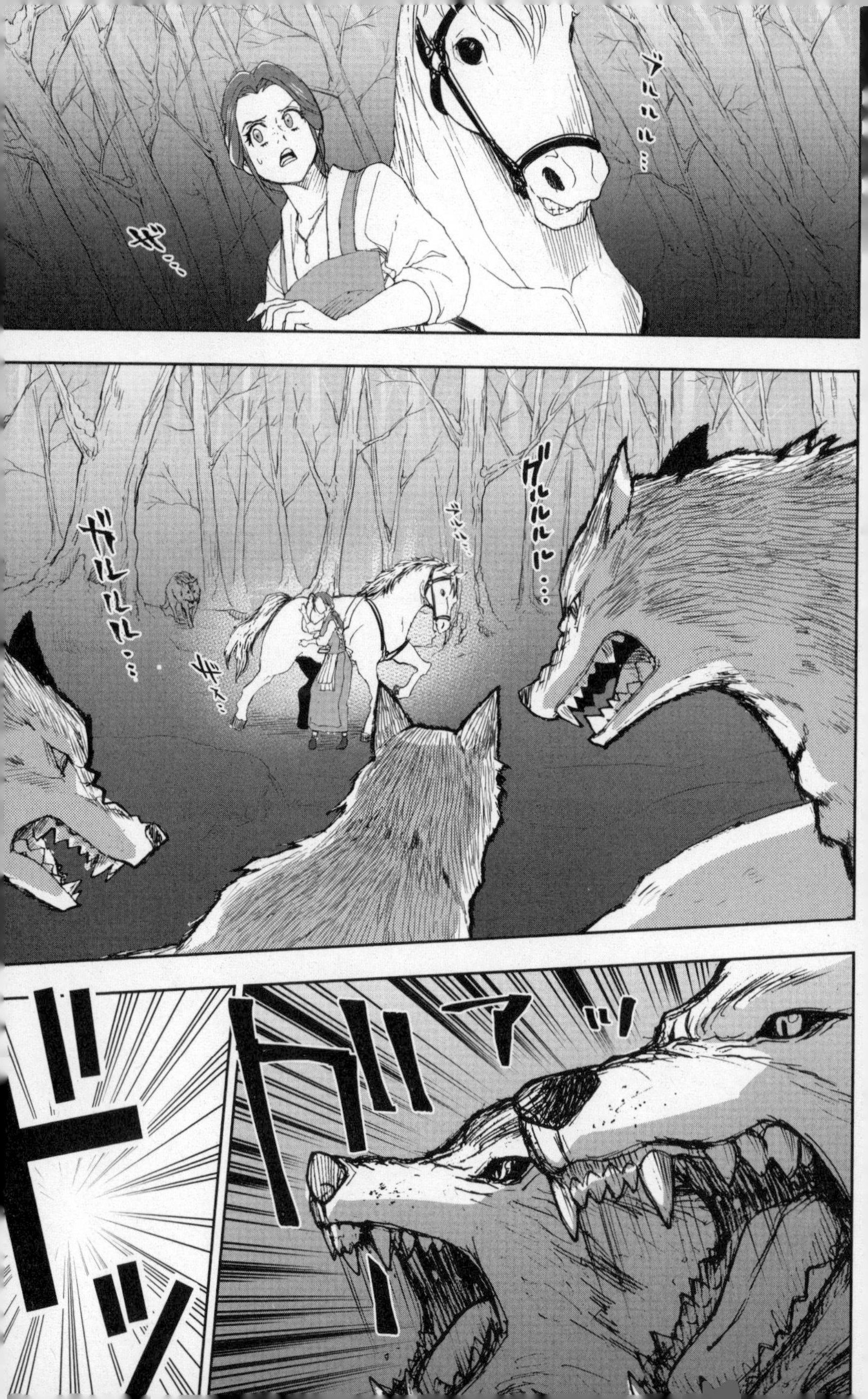
ブルルル…
ザ…
グルルルル…
ギュ…
ガルルルル…
ドガァッ
ドッ

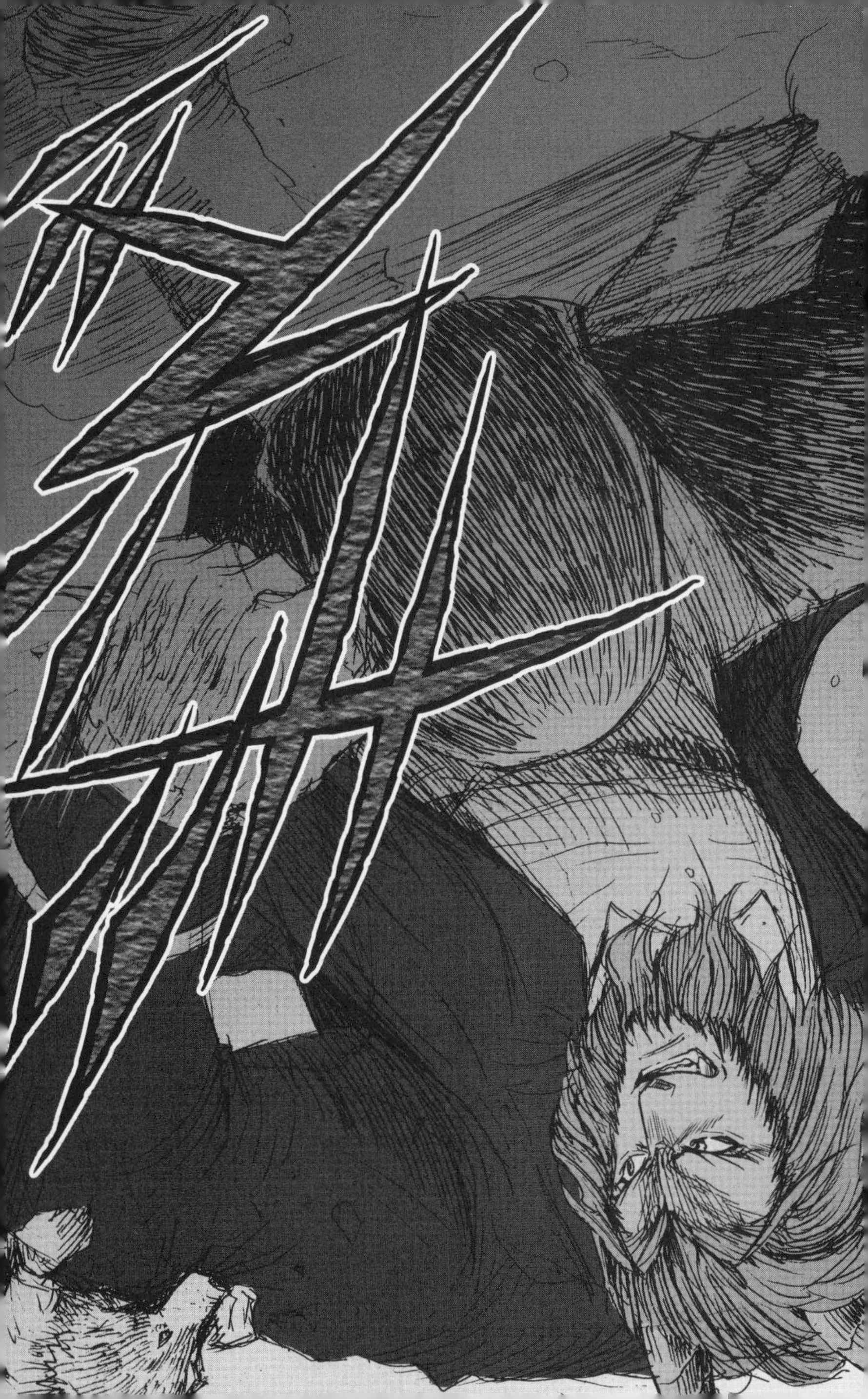

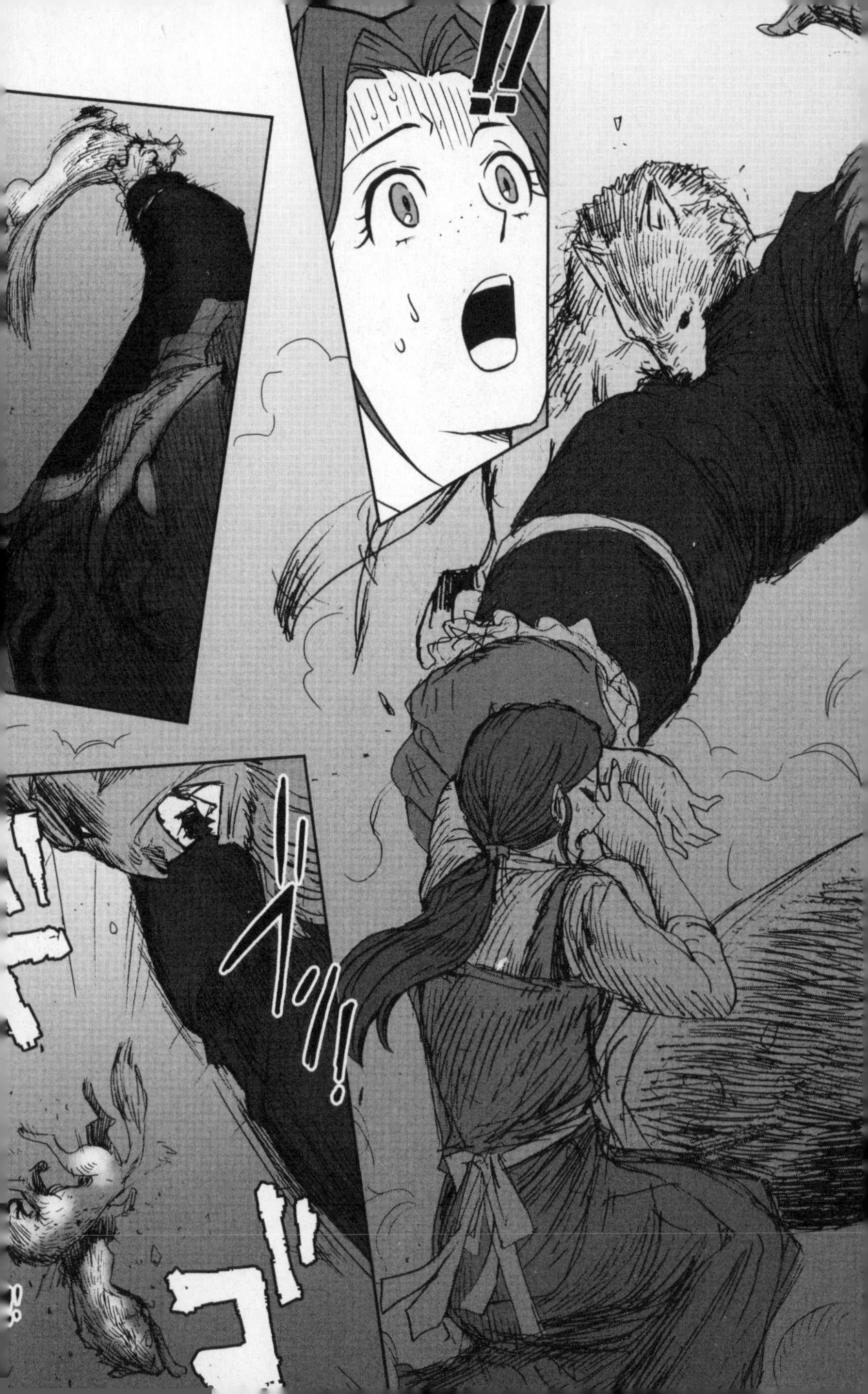
!!

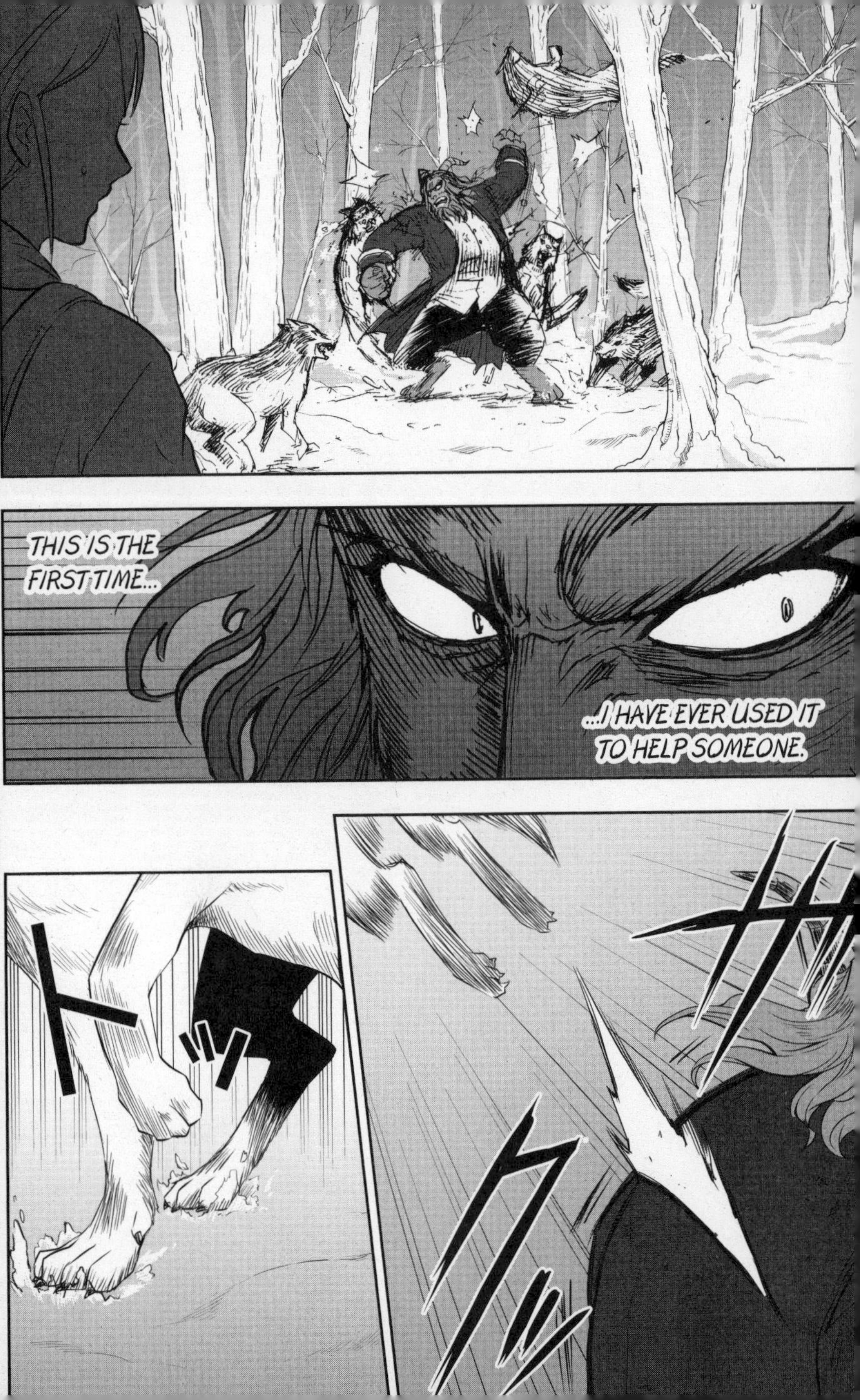
THIS IS THE FIRST TIME...
...I HAVE EVER USED IT TO HELP SOMEONE.

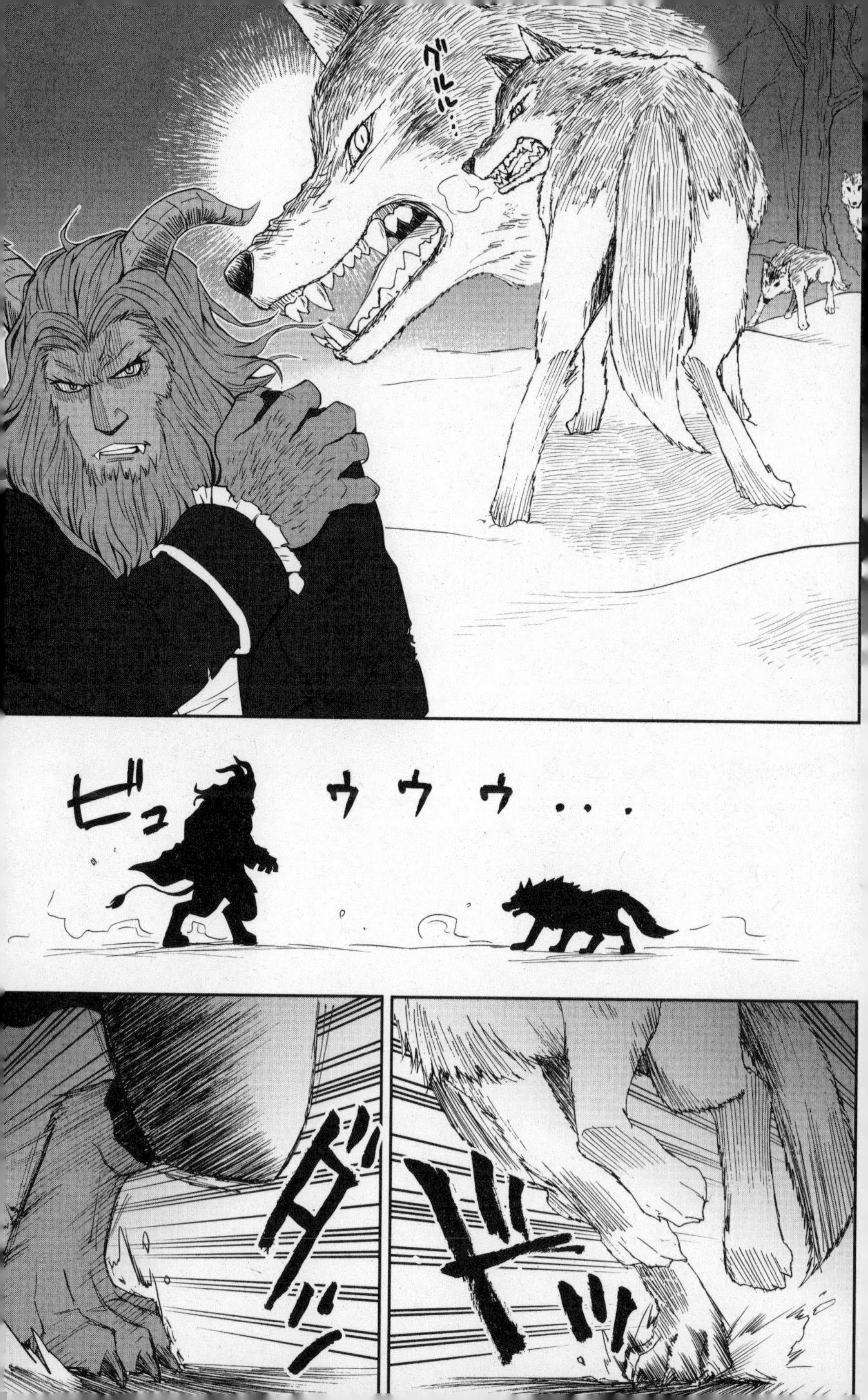
グルル…
ウウウ…
ビュ
ドッ
ダッ

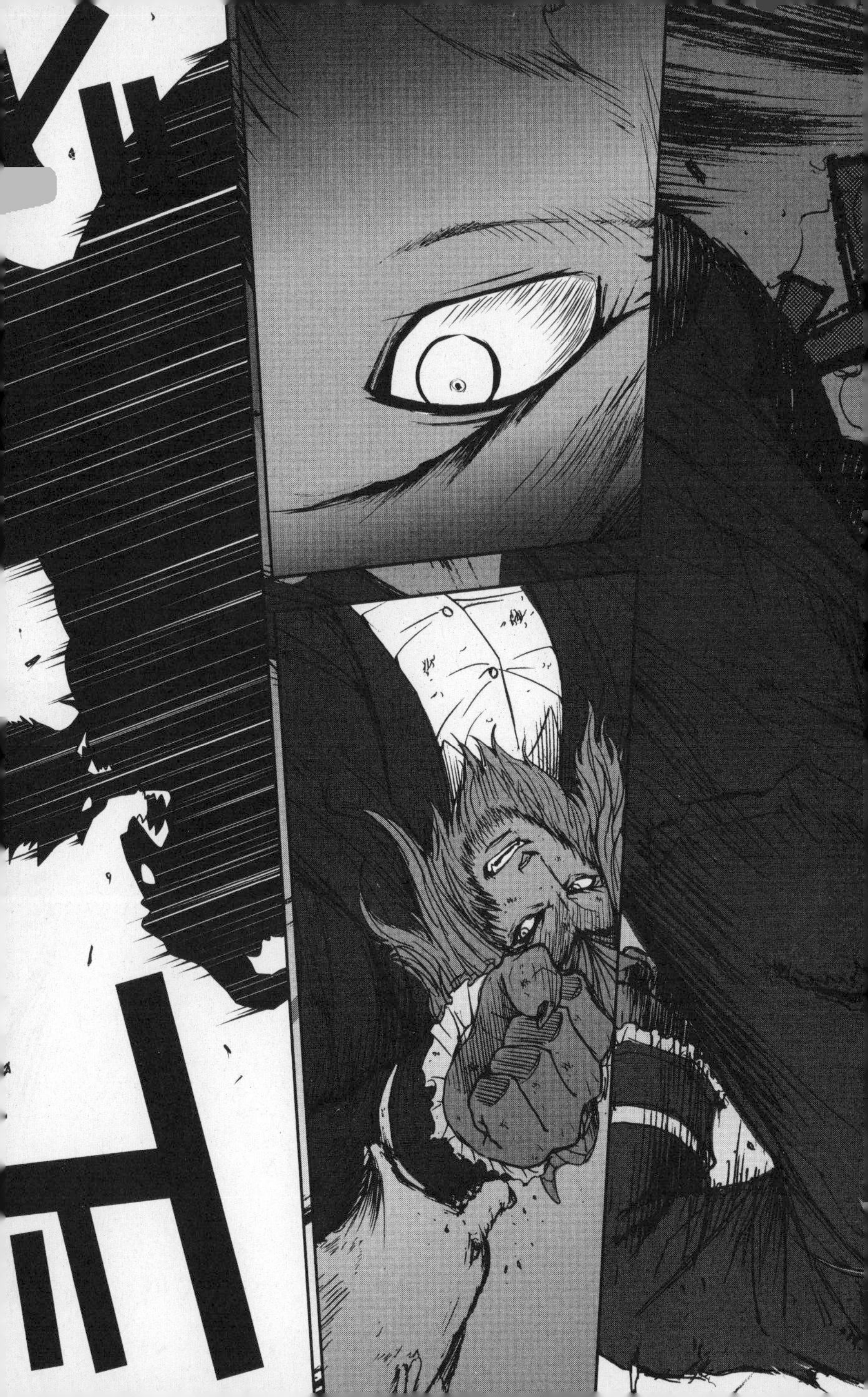

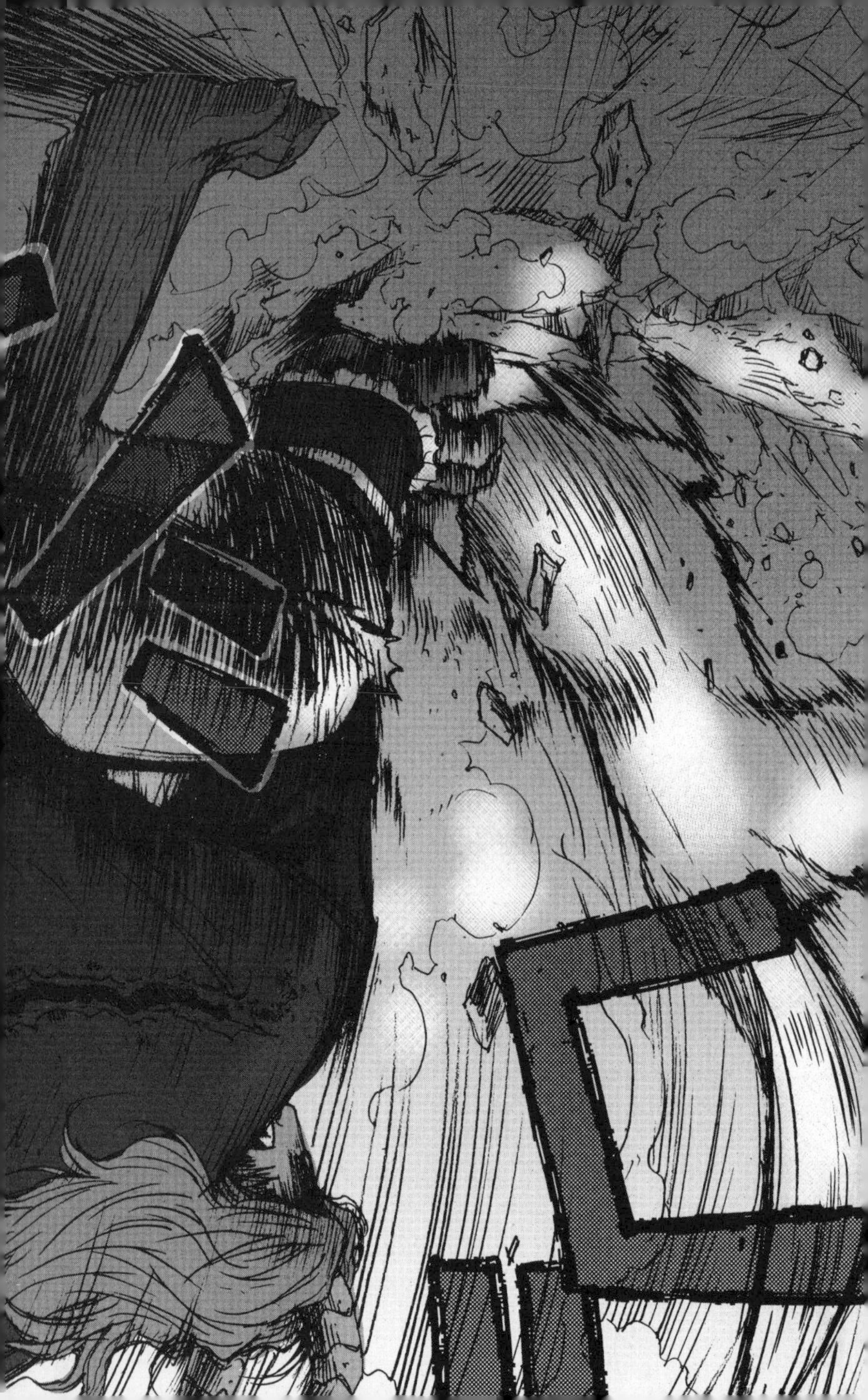

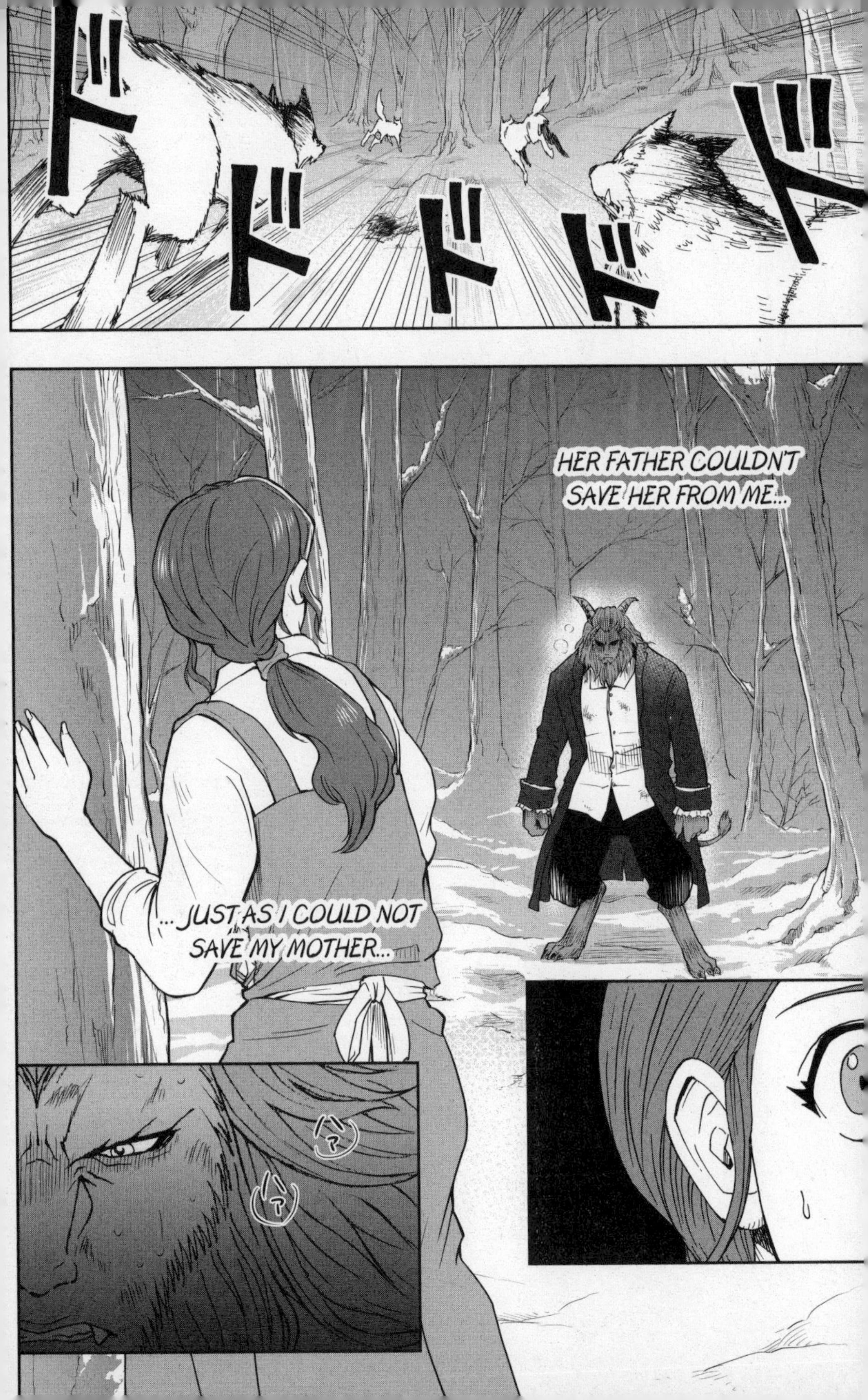
ドドドドド
HER FATHER COULDN'T SAVE HER FROM ME...
...JUST AS I COULD NOT SAVE MY MOTHER...
ハァ
ハァ

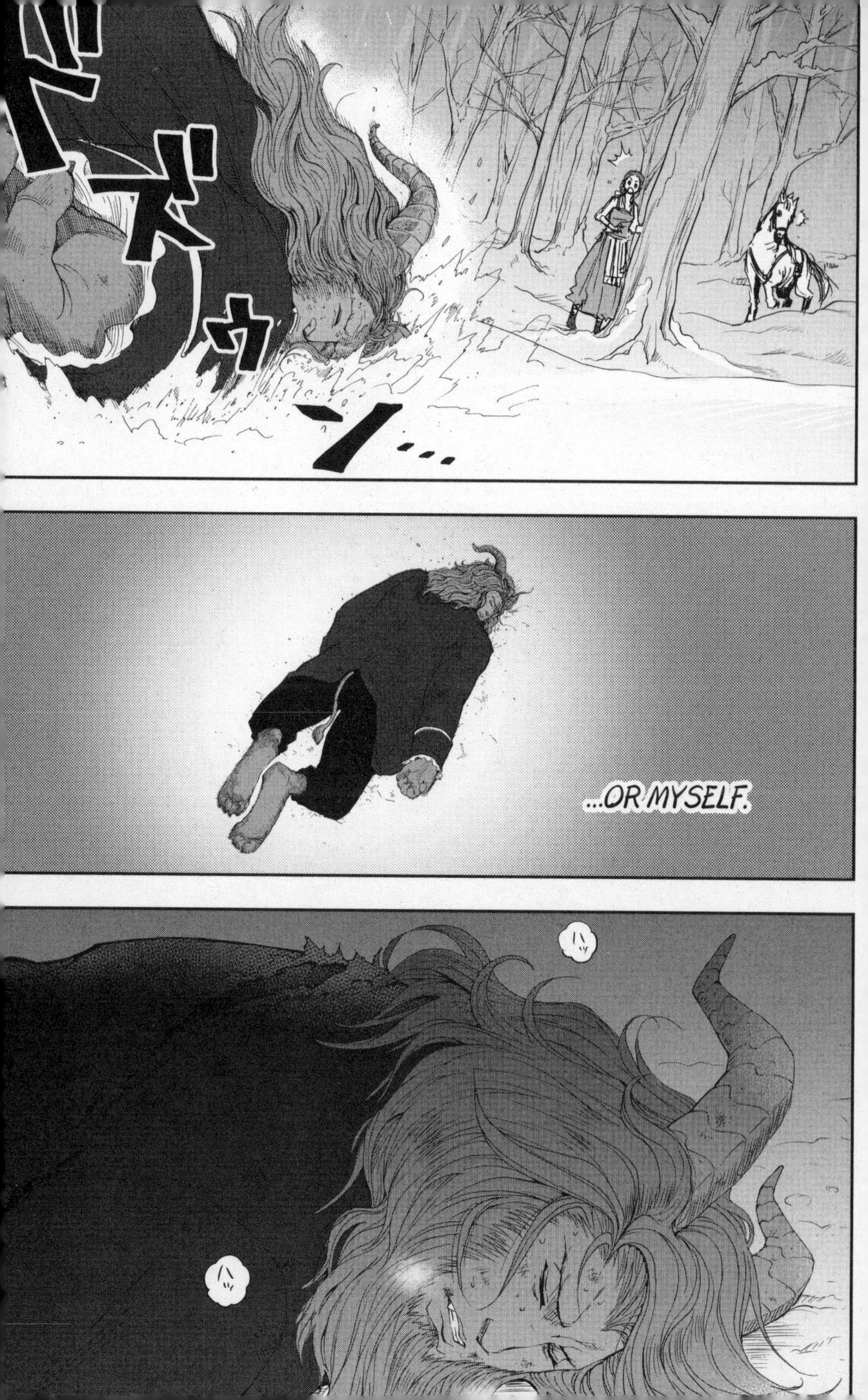
ドズゥ
ン…
…OR MYSELF.
ハッ
ハッ

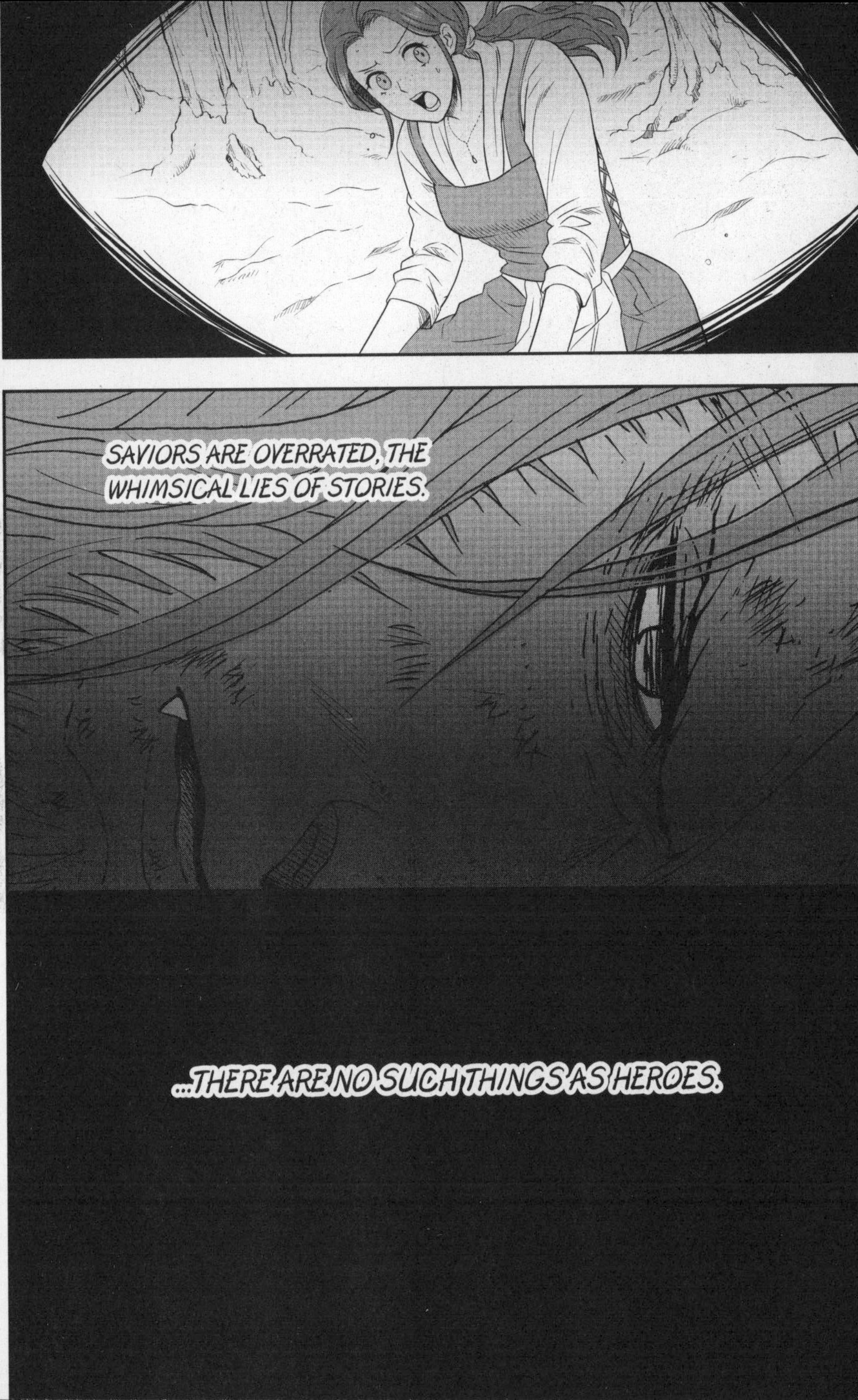
SAVIORS ARE OVERRATED, THE WHIMSICAL LIES OF STORIES.
...THERE ARE NO SUCH THINGS AS HEROES.

"...SHE..."

"...DIDN'T
LEAVE...?"

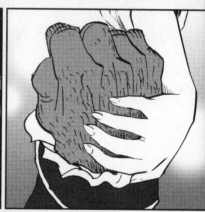

"...I'M..."

"...WARM?"

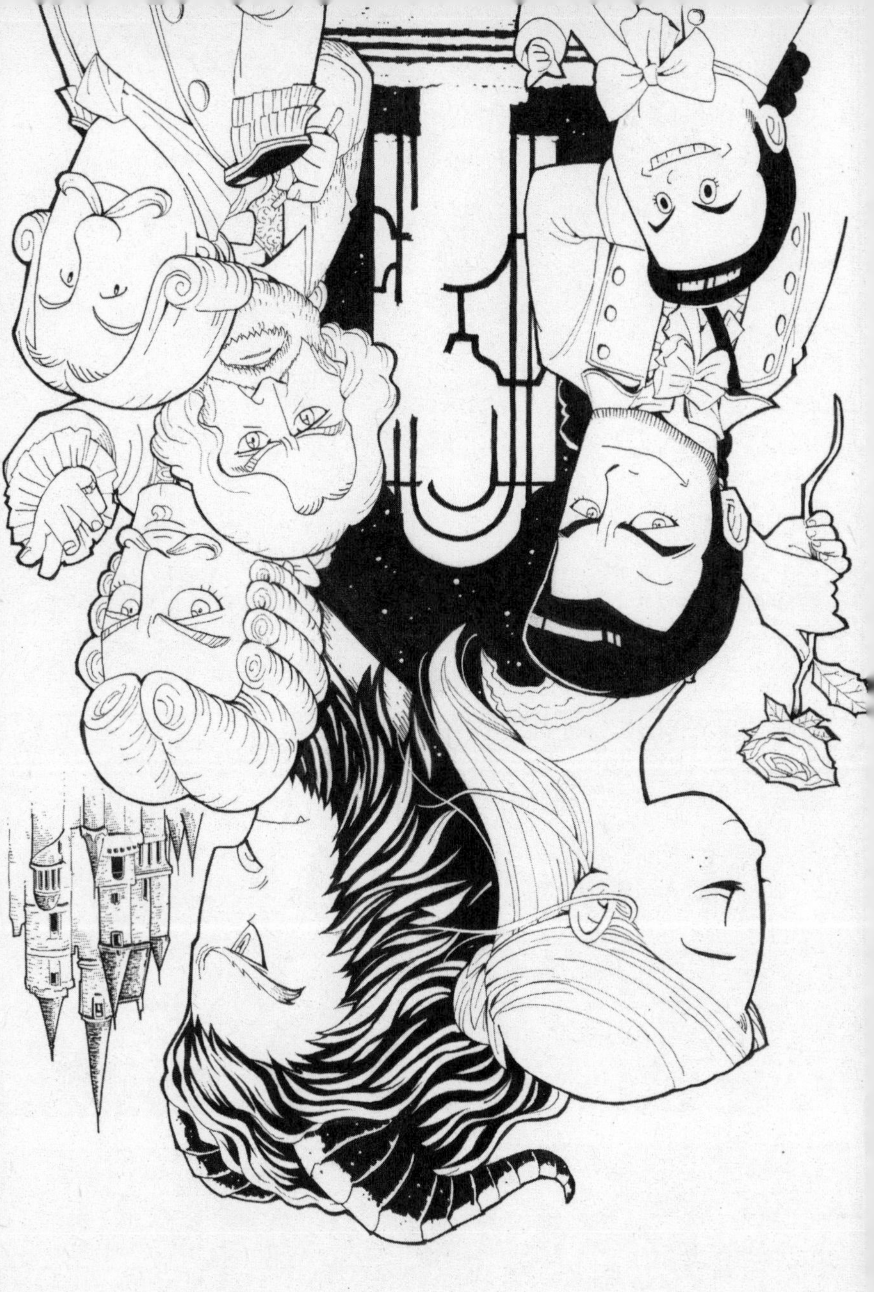

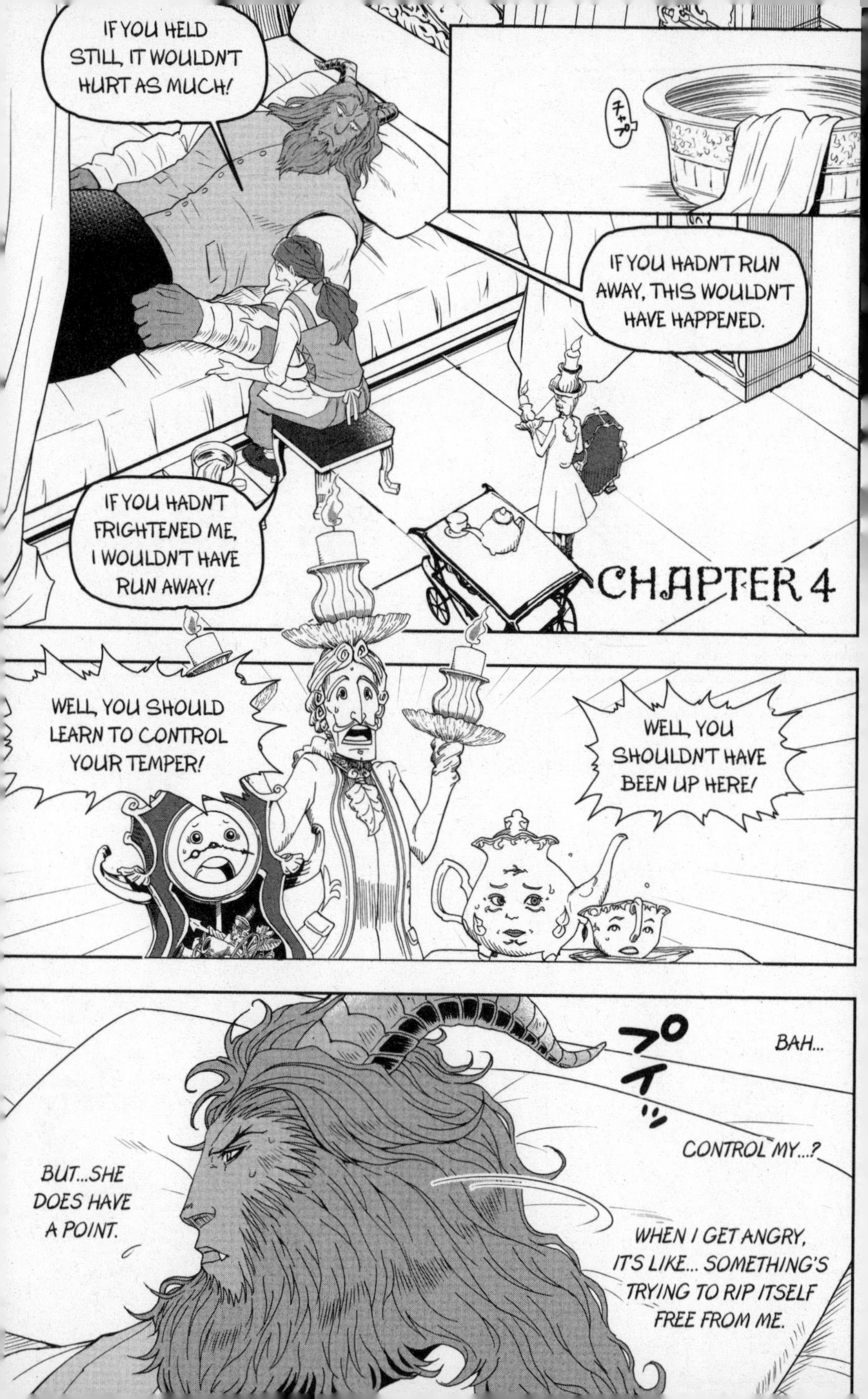
チャプ
IF YOU HELD STILL, IT WOULDN'T HURT AS MUCH!
IF YOU HADN'T RUN AWAY, THIS WOULDN'T HAVE HAPPENED.
IF YOU HADN'T FRIGHTENED ME, I WOULDN'T HAVE RUN AWAY!
CHAPTER 4
WELL, YOU SHOULDN'T HAVE BEEN UP HERE!
WELL, YOU SHOULD LEARN TO CONTROL YOUR TEMPER!
BAH...
プイッ
CONTROL MY...?
WHEN I GET ANGRY, IT'S LIKE... SOMETHING'S TRYING TO RIP ITSELF FREE FROM ME.
BUT...SHE DOES HAVE A POINT.

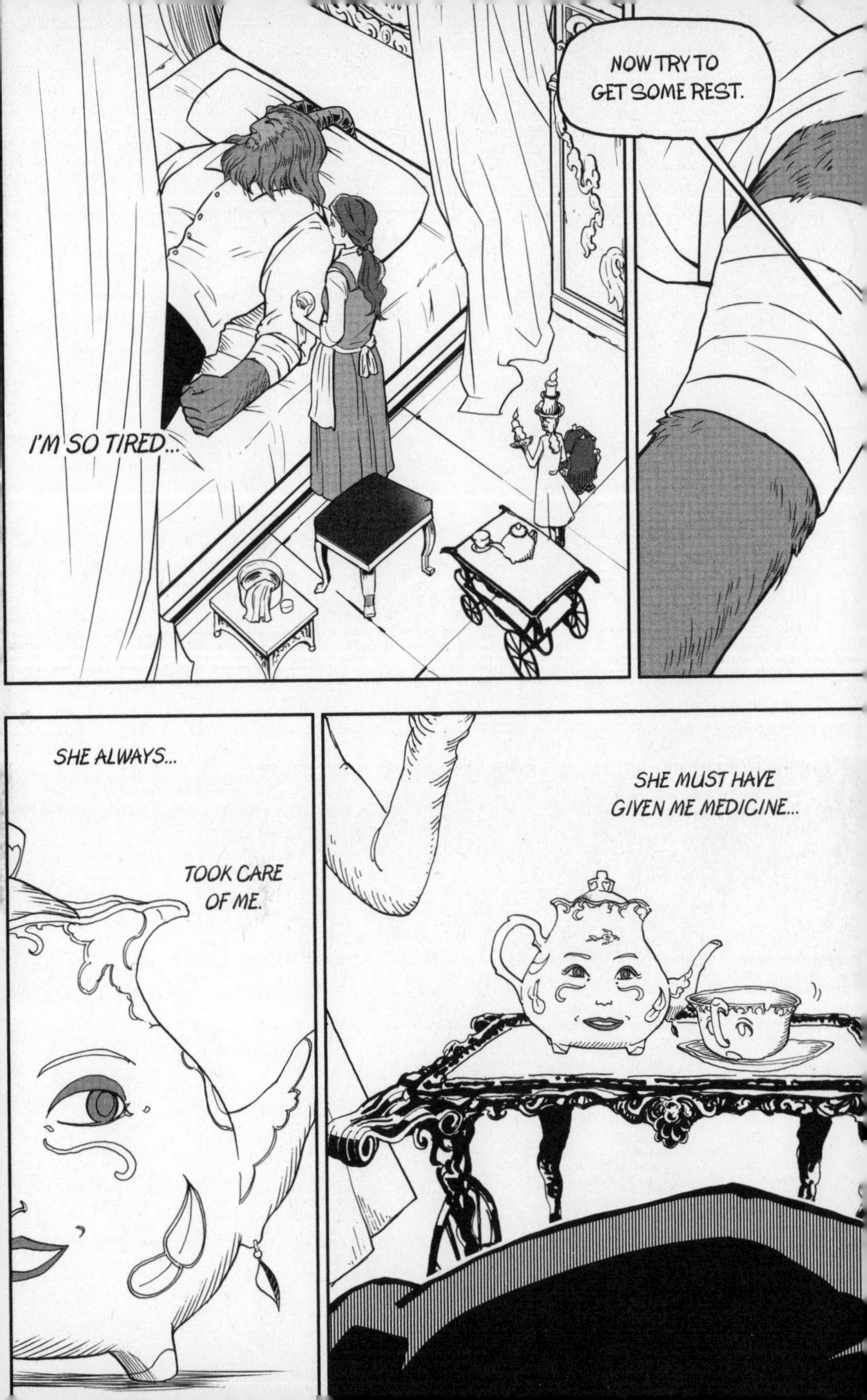
NOW TRY TO GET SOME REST.
I'M SO TIRED...
SHE MUST HAVE GIVEN ME MEDICINE...
SHE ALWAYS...
TOOK CARE OF ME.

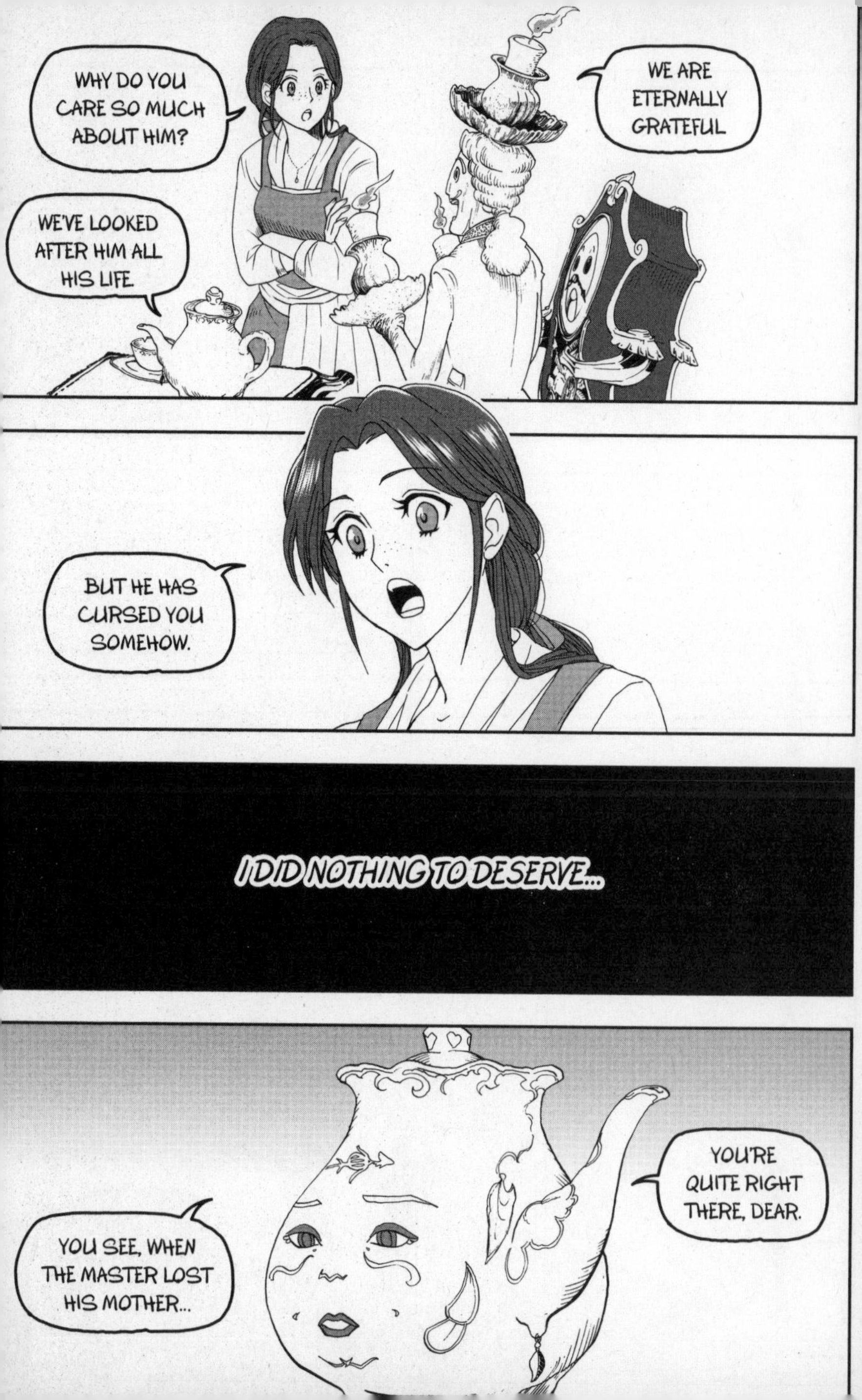
WE ARE ETERNALLY GRATEFUL
WHY DO YOU CARE SO MUCH ABOUT HIM?
WE'VE LOOKED AFTER HIM ALL HIS LIFE.
BUT HE HAS CURSED YOU SOMEHOW.
I DID NOTHING TO DESERVE...
YOU'RE QUITE RIGHT THERE, DEAR.
YOU SEE, WHEN THE MASTER LOST HIS MOTHER...

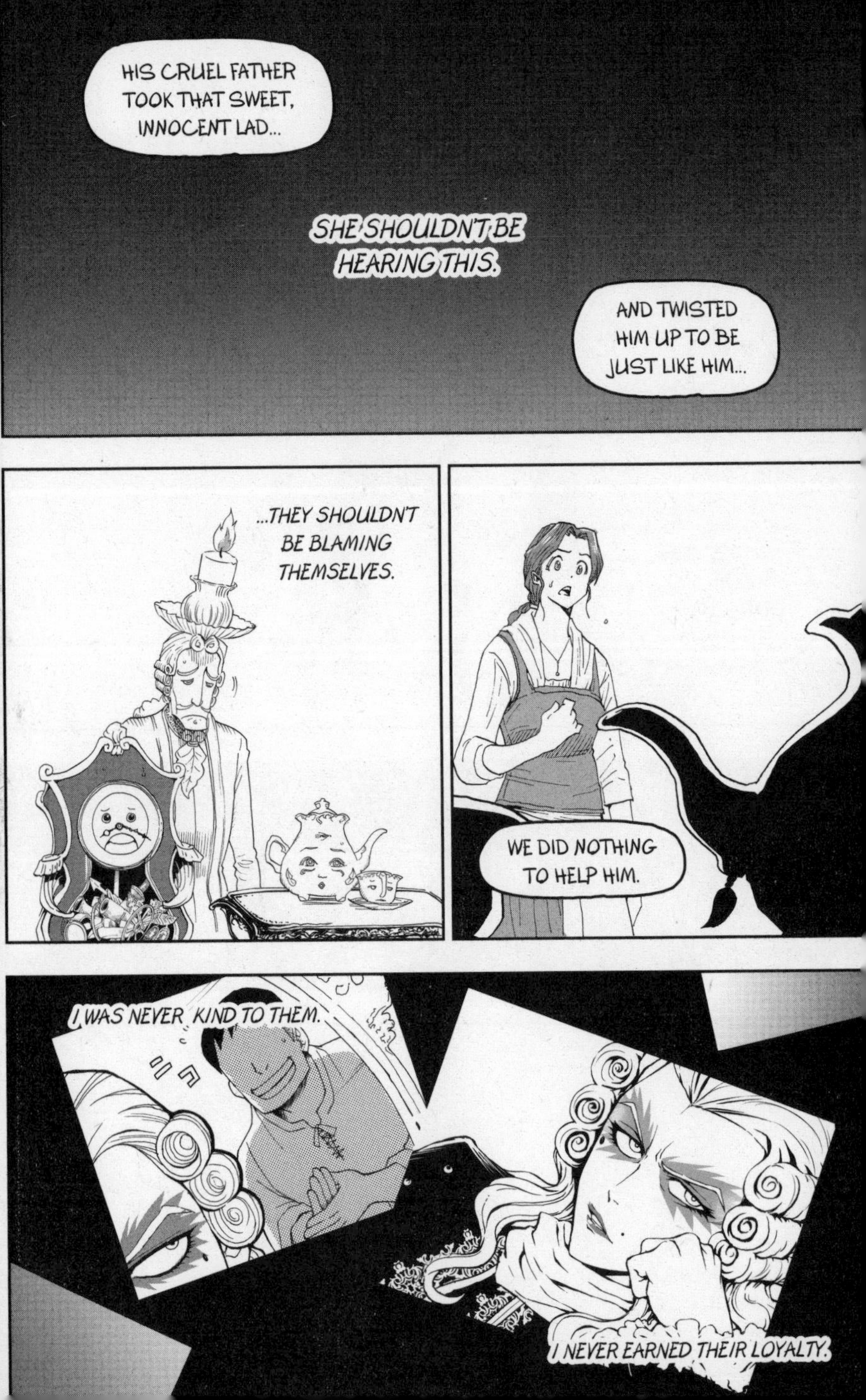
HIS CRUEL FATHER TOOK THAT SWEET, INNOCENT LAD...
SHE SHOULDN'T BE HEARING THIS.
AND TWISTED HIM UP TO BE JUST LIKE HIM...
WE DID NOTHING TO HELP HIM.
...THEY SHOULDN'T BE BLAMING THEMSELVES.
I NEVER EARNED THEIR LOYALTY.
I WAS NEVER KIND TO THEM.

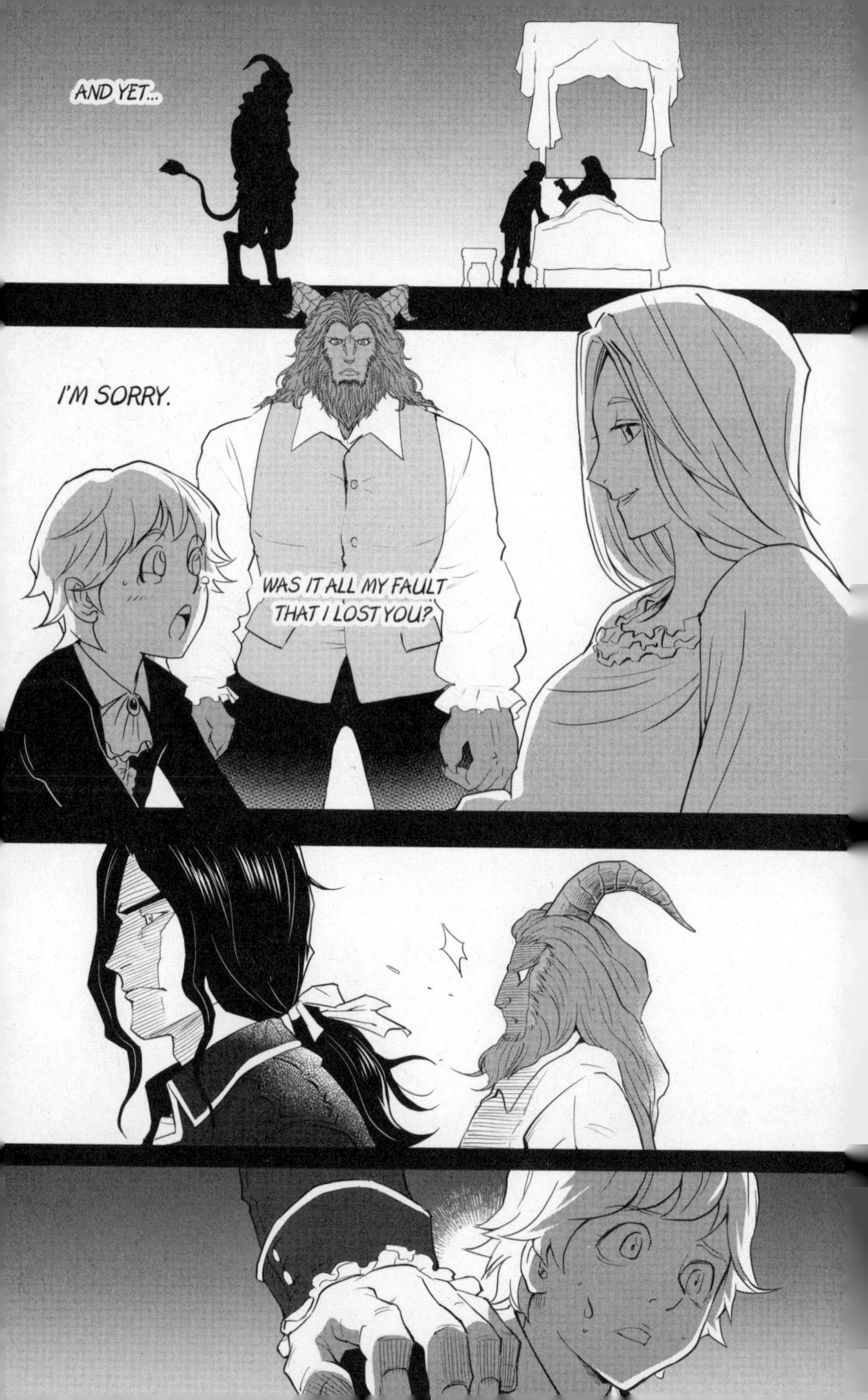
AND YET...
I'M SORRY.
WAS IT ALL MY FAULT THAT I LOST YOU?

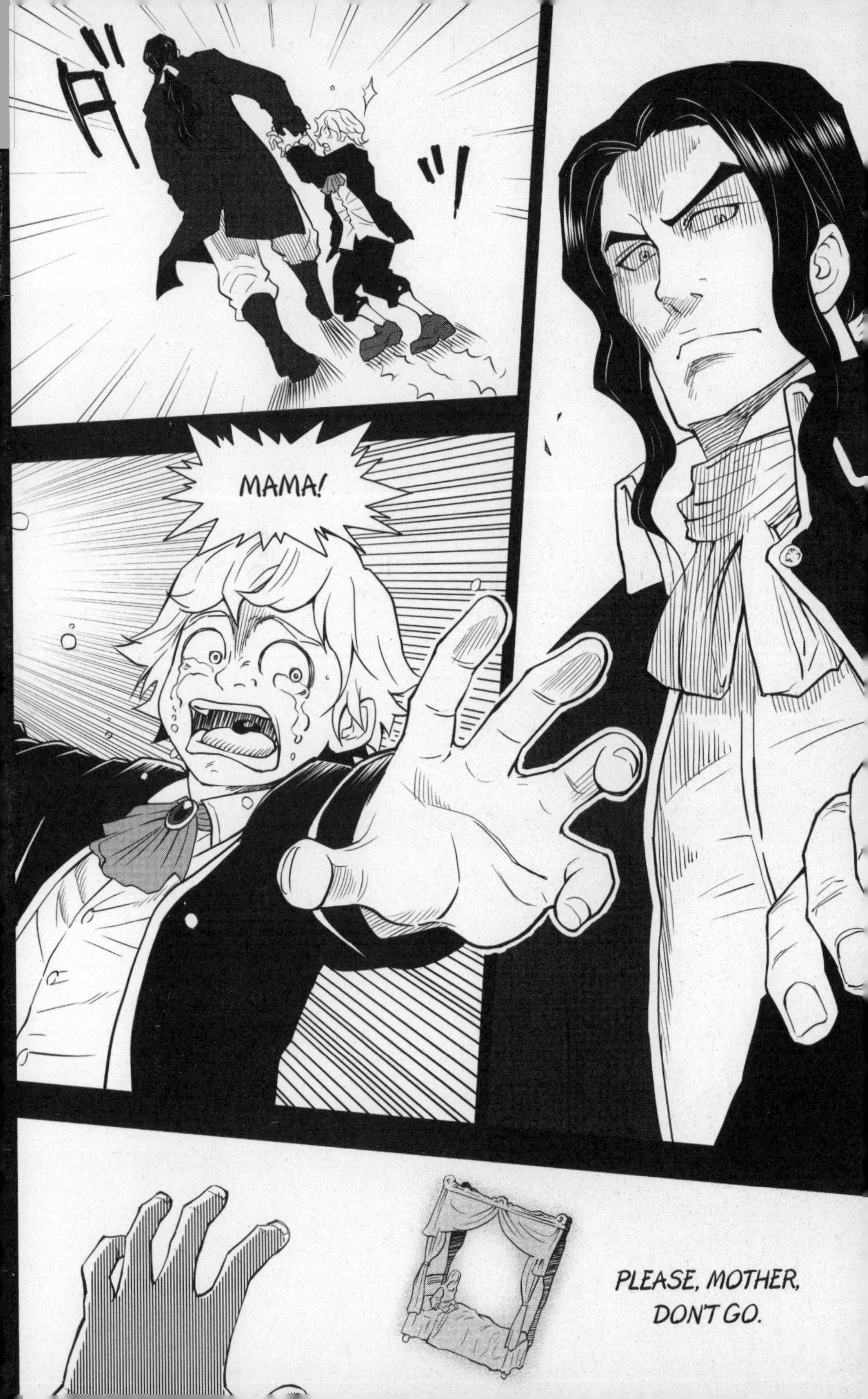
MAMA!
PLEASE, MOTHER, DON'T GO.

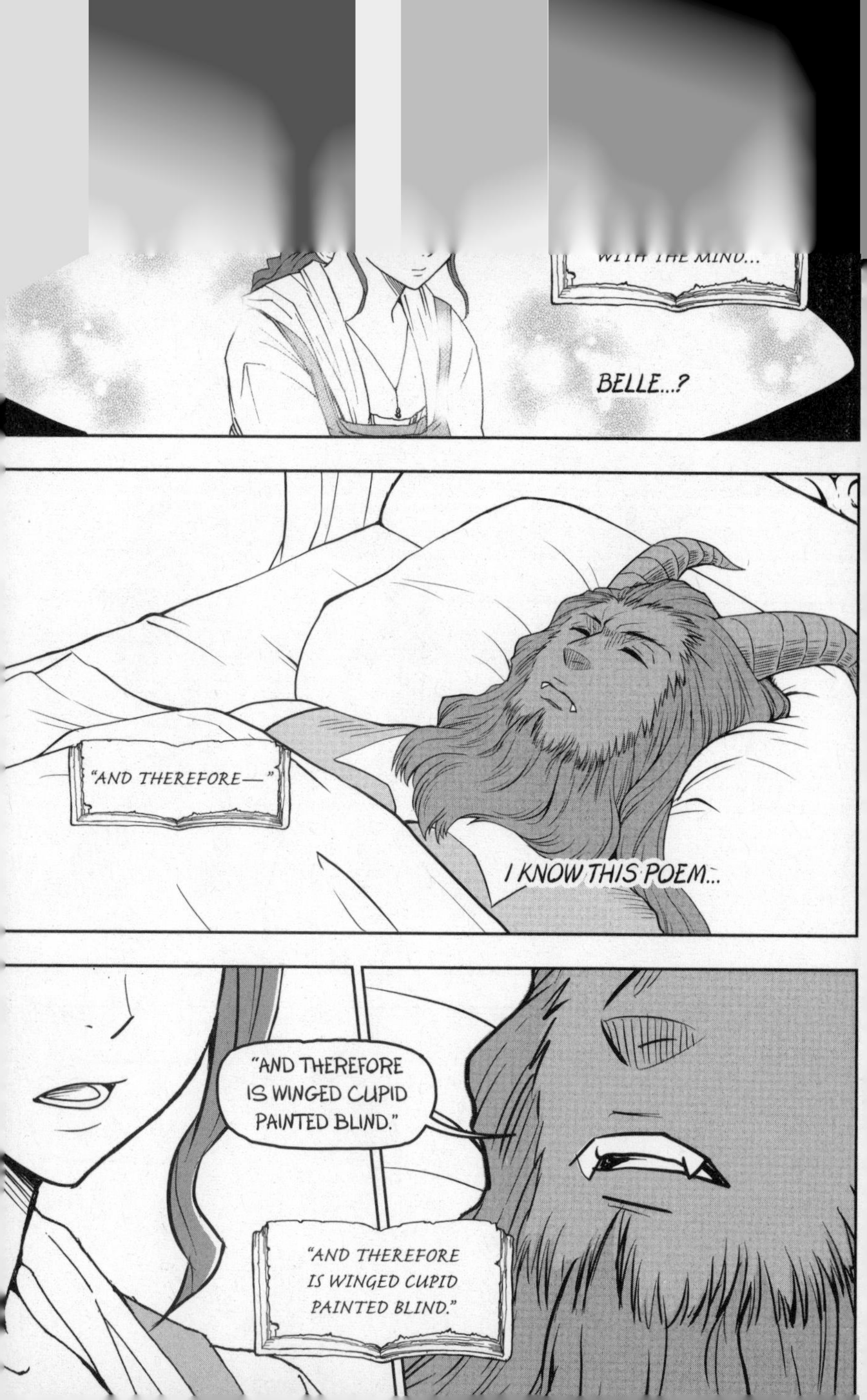
WITH THE MIND...
BELLE...?
"AND THEREFORE—"
I KNOW THIS POEM...
"AND THEREFORE IS WINGED CUPID PAINTED BLIND."
"AND THEREFORE IS WINGED CUPID PAINTED BLIND."

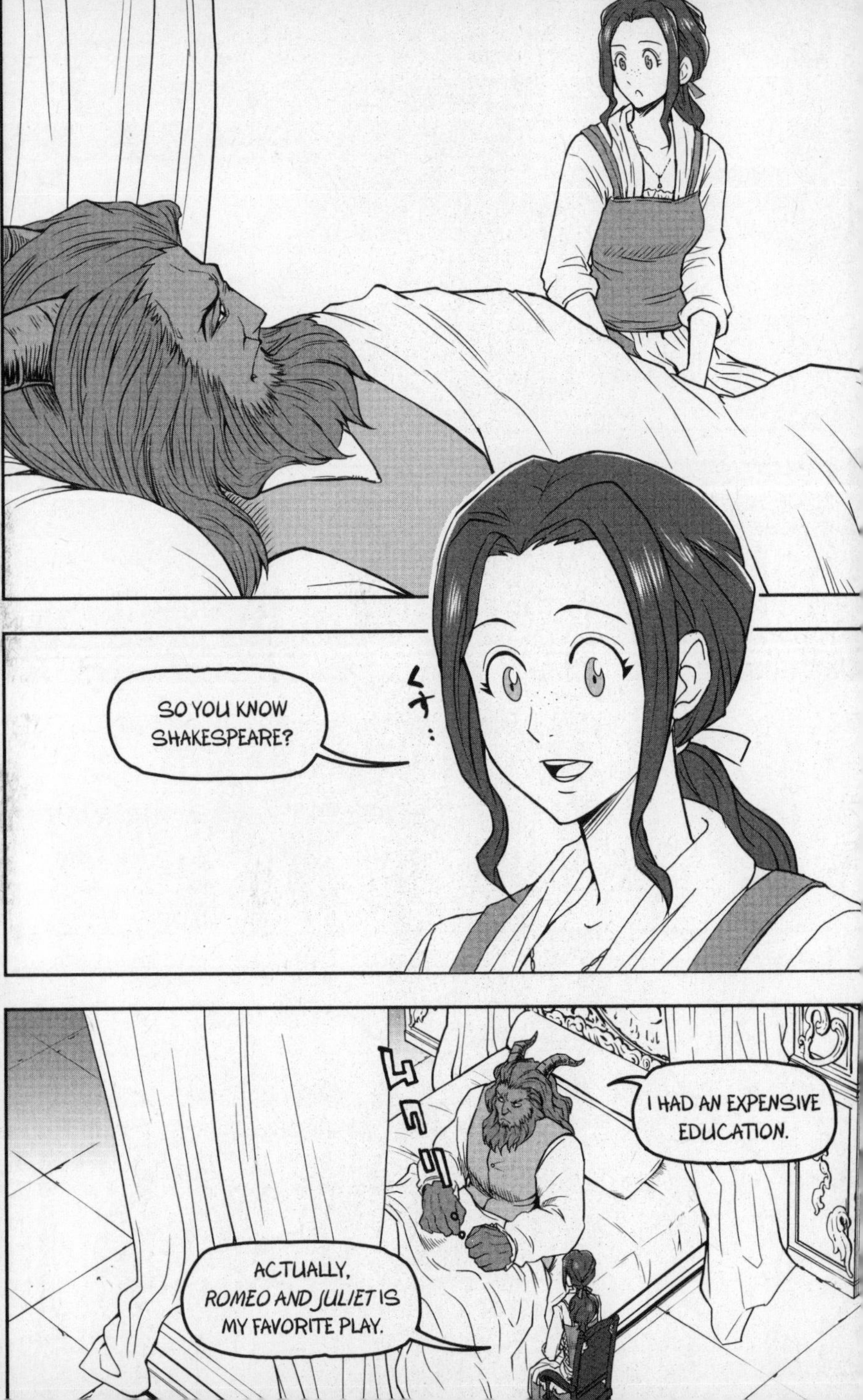

SO YOU KNOW SHAKESPEARE?
I HAD AN EXPENSIVE EDUCATION.
ACTUALLY, *ROMEO AND JULIET* IS MY FAVORITE PLAY.

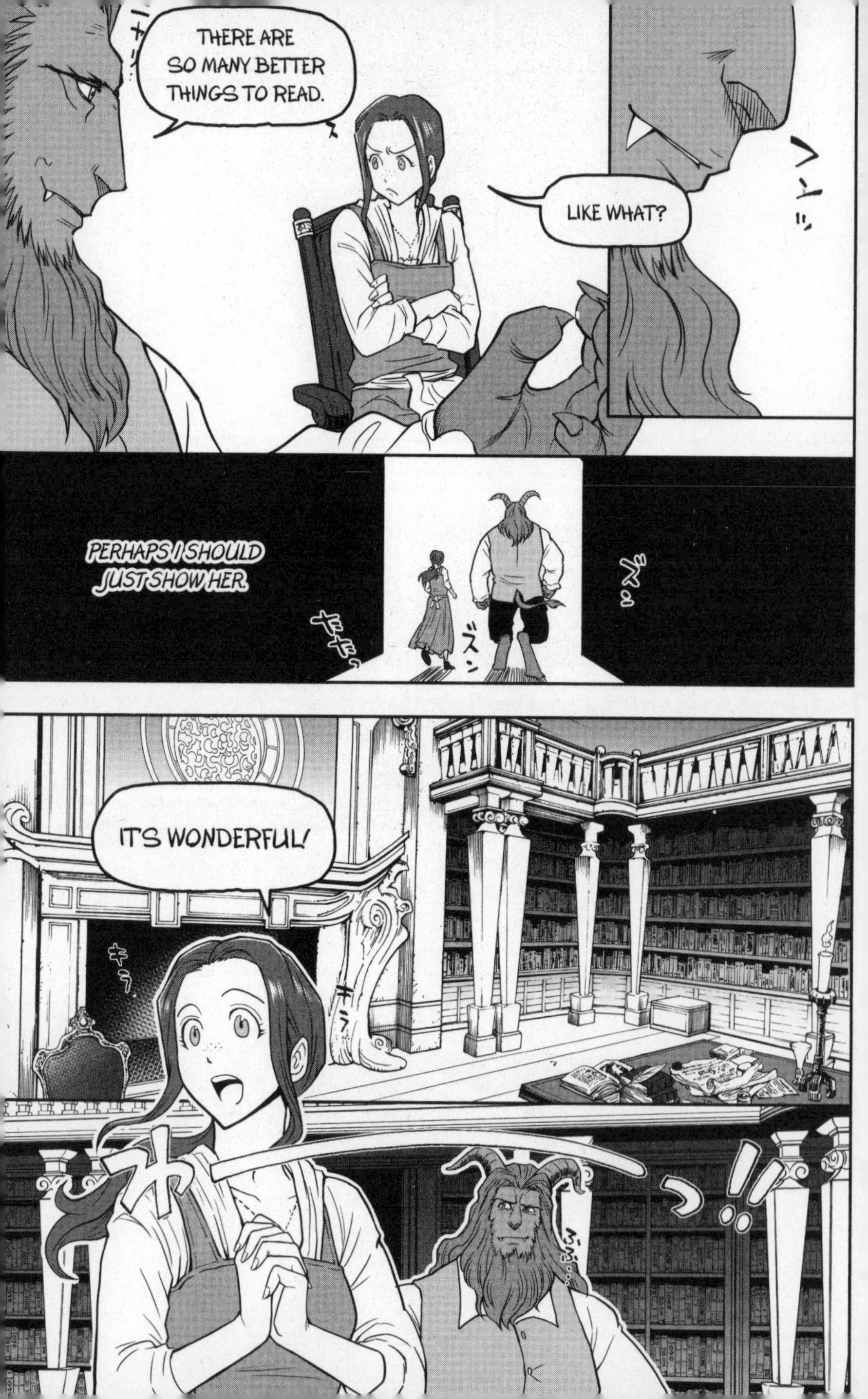

THERE ARE SO MANY BETTER THINGS TO READ.
LIKE WHAT?
PERHAPS I SHOULD JUST SHOW HER.
ズスン
IT'S WONDERFUL!
キラ
わ

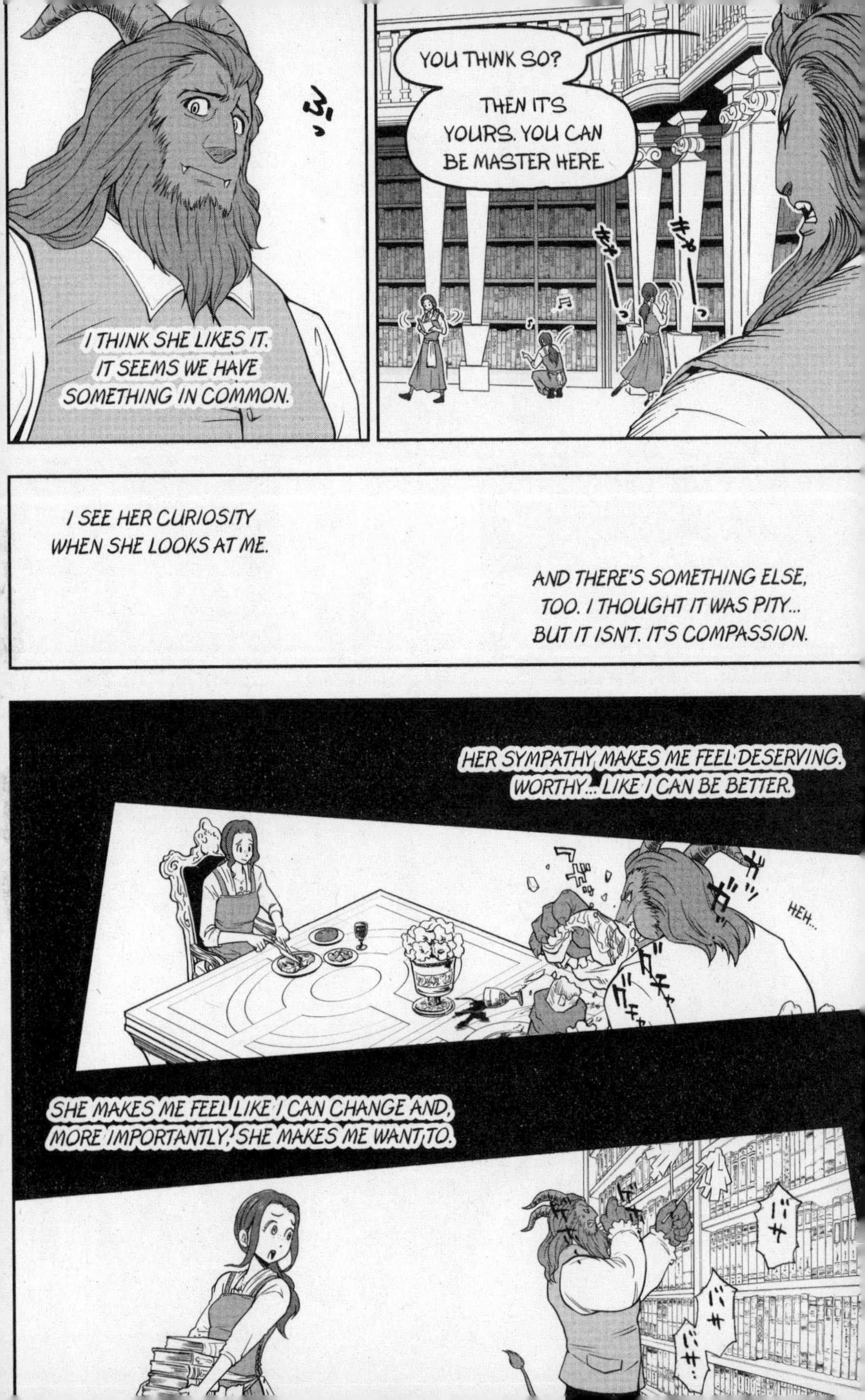
I THINK SHE LIKES IT. IT SEEMS WE HAVE SOMETHING IN COMMON.
YOU THINK SO?
THEN IT'S YOURS. YOU CAN BE MASTER HERE.
I SEE HER CURIOSITY WHEN SHE LOOKS AT ME.
AND THERE'S SOMETHING ELSE, TOO. I THOUGHT IT WAS PITY... BUT IT ISN'T. IT'S COMPASSION.
HER SYMPATHY MAKES ME FEEL DESERVING. WORTHY... LIKE I CAN BE BETTER.
HEH...
SHE MAKES ME FEEL LIKE I CAN CHANGE AND, MORE IMPORTANTLY, SHE MAKES ME WANT TO.

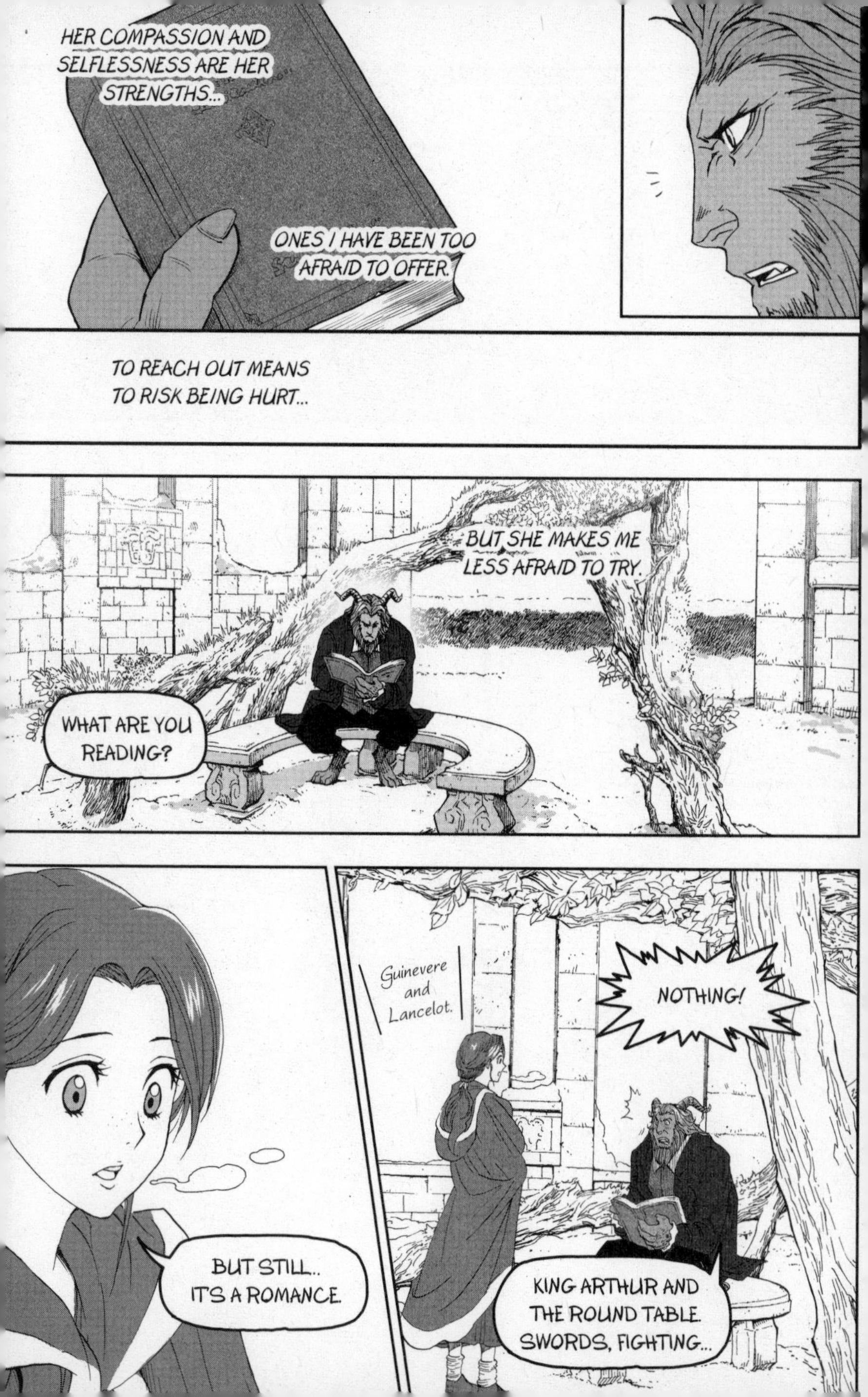
HER COMPASSION AND SELFLESSNESS ARE HER STRENGTHS...
ONES I HAVE BEEN TOO AFRAID TO OFFER.
TO REACH OUT MEANS TO RISK BEING HURT...
BUT SHE MAKES ME LESS AFRAID TO TRY.
WHAT ARE YOU READING?
NOTHING!
Guinevere and Lancelot.
KING ARTHUR AND THE ROUND TABLE. SWORDS, FIGHTING...
BUT STILL... IT'S A ROMANCE.

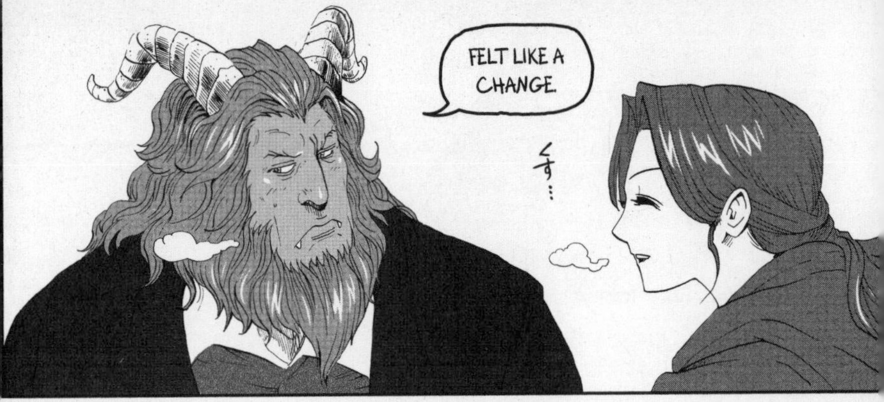
FELT LIKE A CHANGE.
くす…
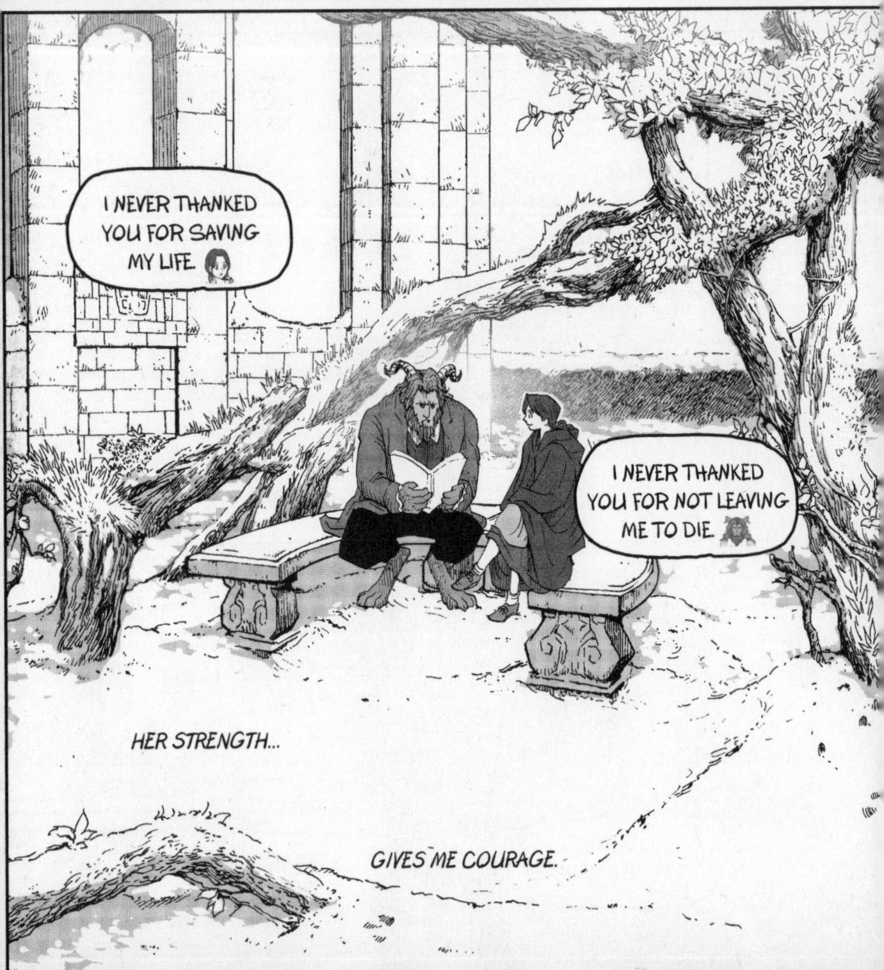
I NEVER THANKED YOU FOR NOT LEAVING ME TO DIE.
I NEVER THANKED YOU FOR SAVING MY LIFE.
HER STRENGTH...
GIVES ME COURAGE.

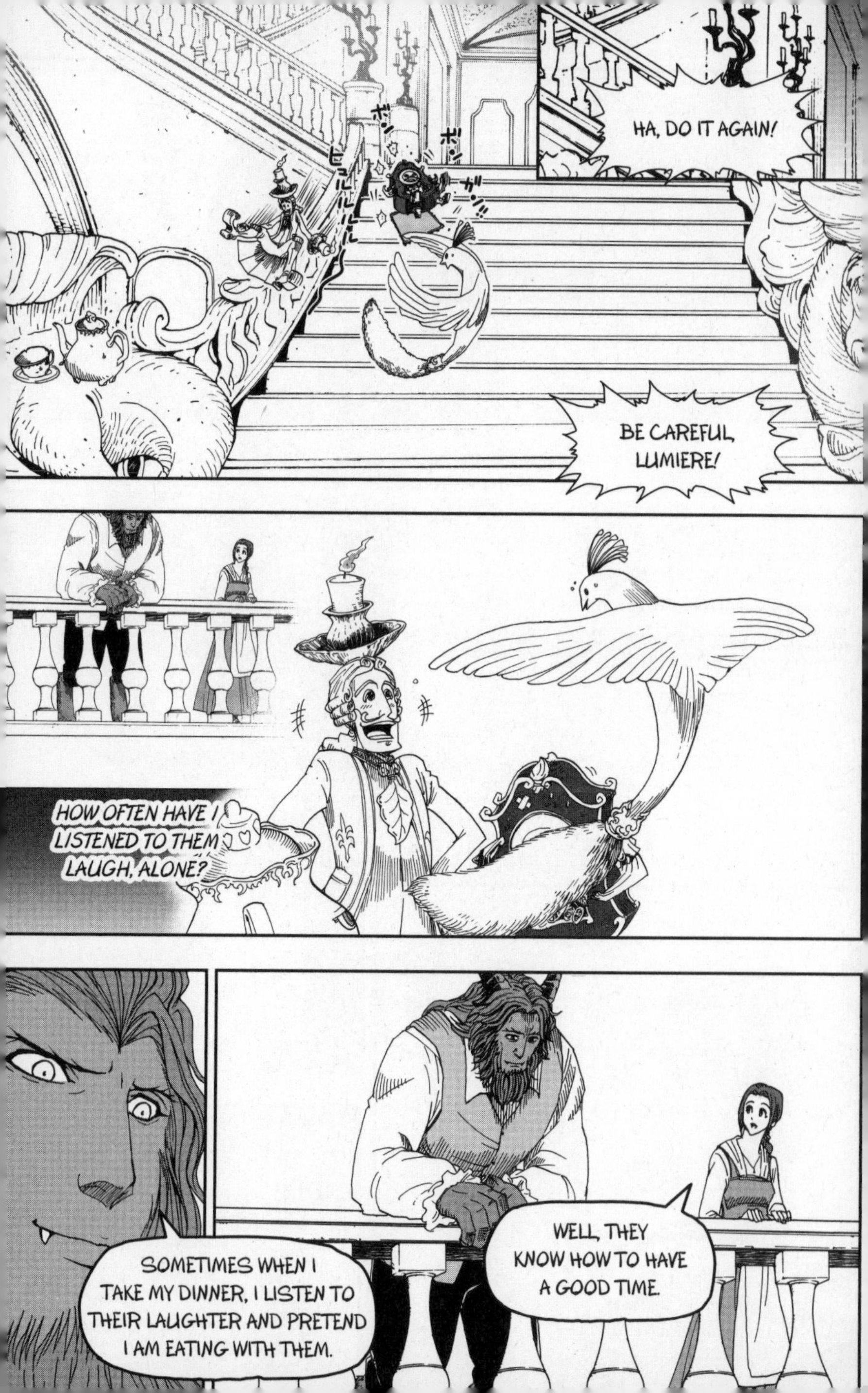
HA, DO IT AGAIN!
BE CAREFUL, LUMIERE!
HOW OFTEN HAVE I LISTENED TO THEM LAUGH, ALONE?
WELL, THEY KNOW HOW TO HAVE A GOOD TIME.
SOMETIMES WHEN I TAKE MY DINNER, I LISTEN TO THEIR LAUGHTER AND PRETEND I AM EATING WITH THEM.

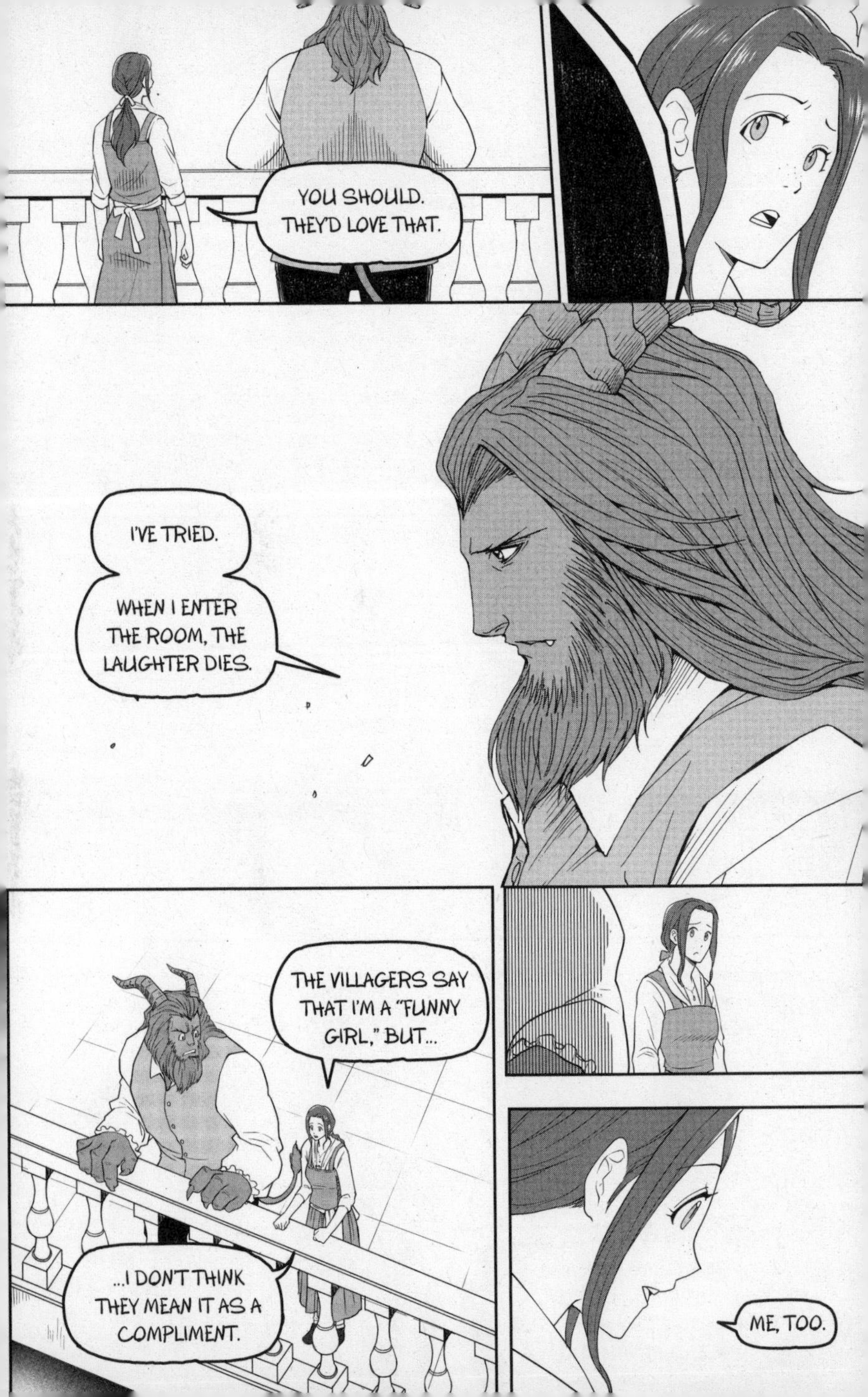
YOU SHOULD. THEY'D LOVE THAT.
I'VE TRIED.
WHEN I ENTER THE ROOM, THE LAUGHTER DIES.
THE VILLAGERS SAY THAT I'M A "FUNNY GIRL," BUT...
...I DON'T THINK THEY MEAN IT AS A COMPLIMENT.
ME, TOO.

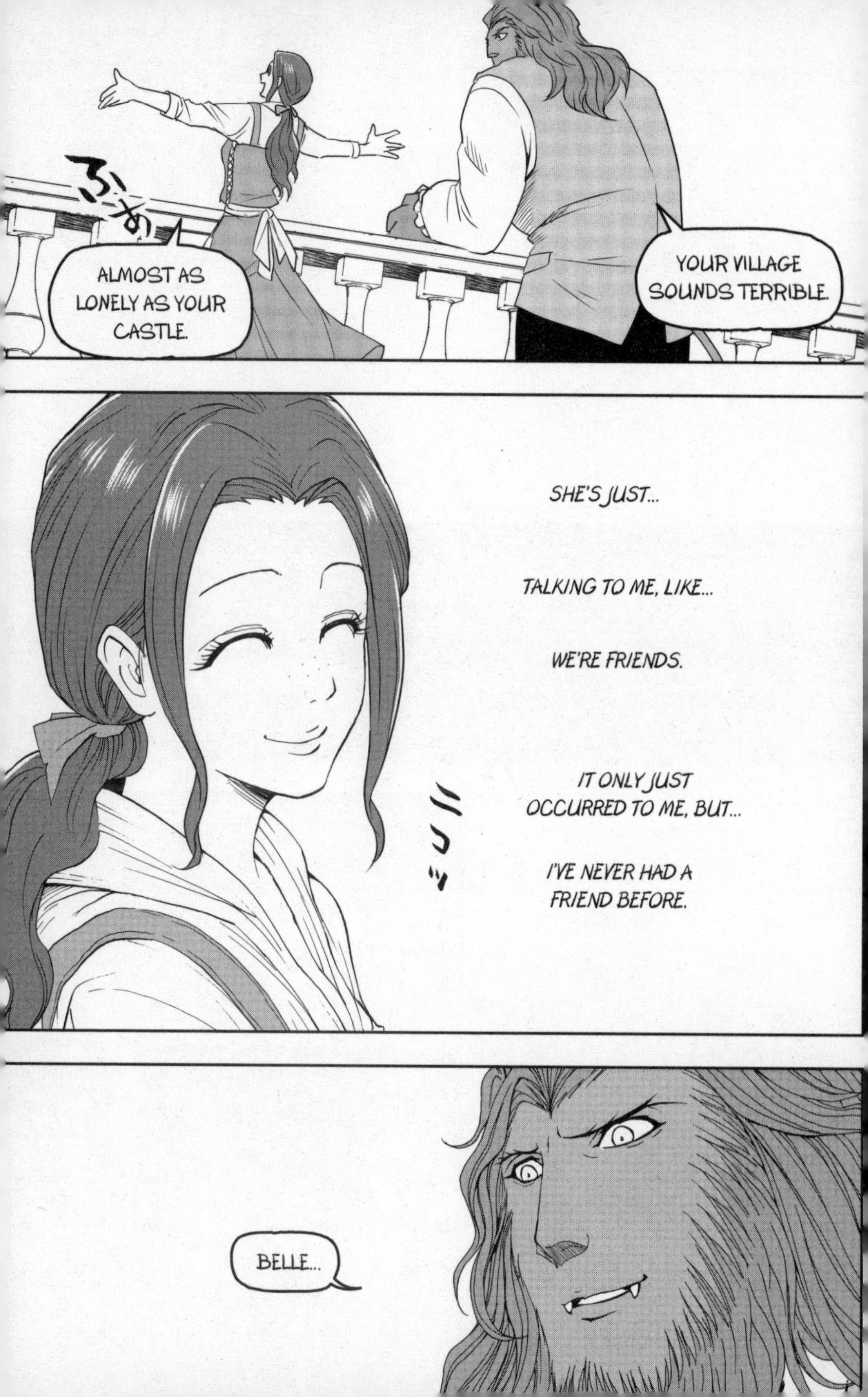
YOUR VILLAGE SOUNDS TERRIBLE.
ALMOST AS LONELY AS YOUR CASTLE.
SHE'S JUST...
TALKING TO ME, LIKE...
WE'RE FRIENDS.
IT ONLY JUST OCCURRED TO ME, BUT...
I'VE NEVER HAD A FRIEND BEFORE.
ニコッ
BELLE...

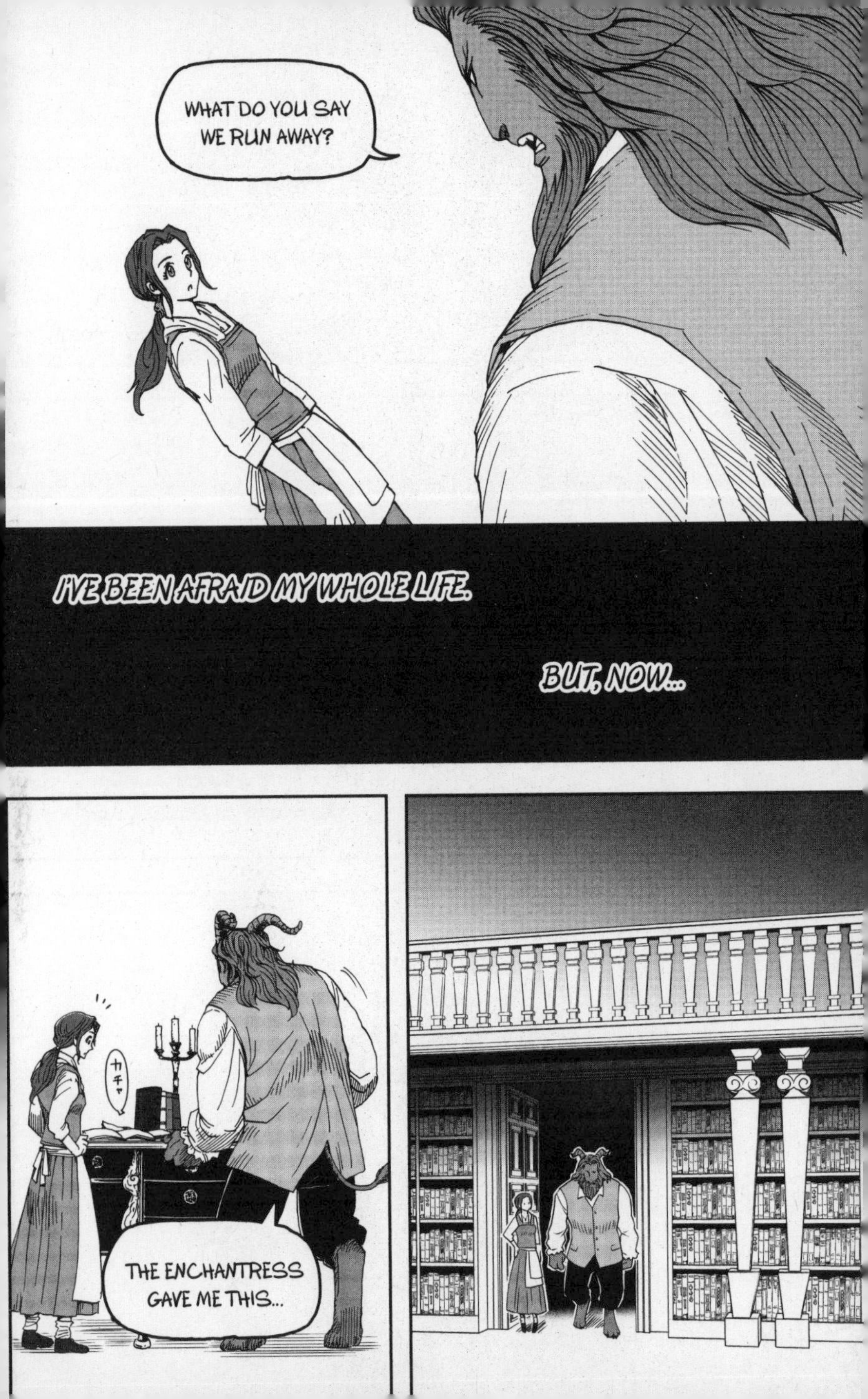
WHAT DO YOU SAY WE RUN AWAY?
I'VE BEEN AFRAID MY WHOLE LIFE.
BUT, NOW...
カチャ
THE ENCHANTRESS GAVE ME THIS...

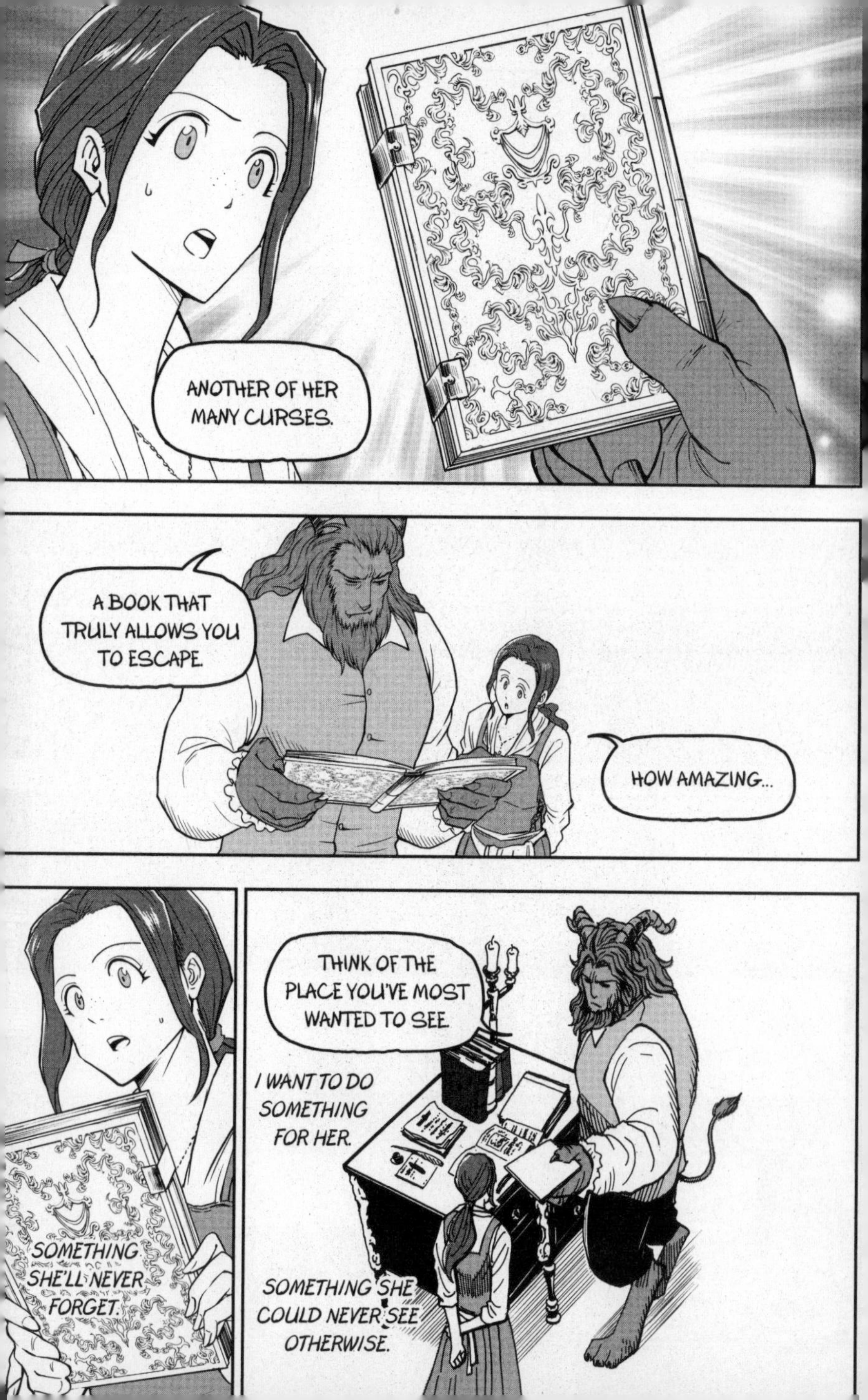
ANOTHER OF HER MANY CURSES.
A BOOK THAT TRULY ALLOWS YOU TO ESCAPE.
HOW AMAZING...
THINK OF THE PLACE YOU'VE MOST WANTED TO SEE.
I WANT TO DO SOMETHING FOR HER.
SOMETHING SHE COULD NEVER SEE OTHERWISE.
SOMETHING SHE'LL NEVER FORGET.

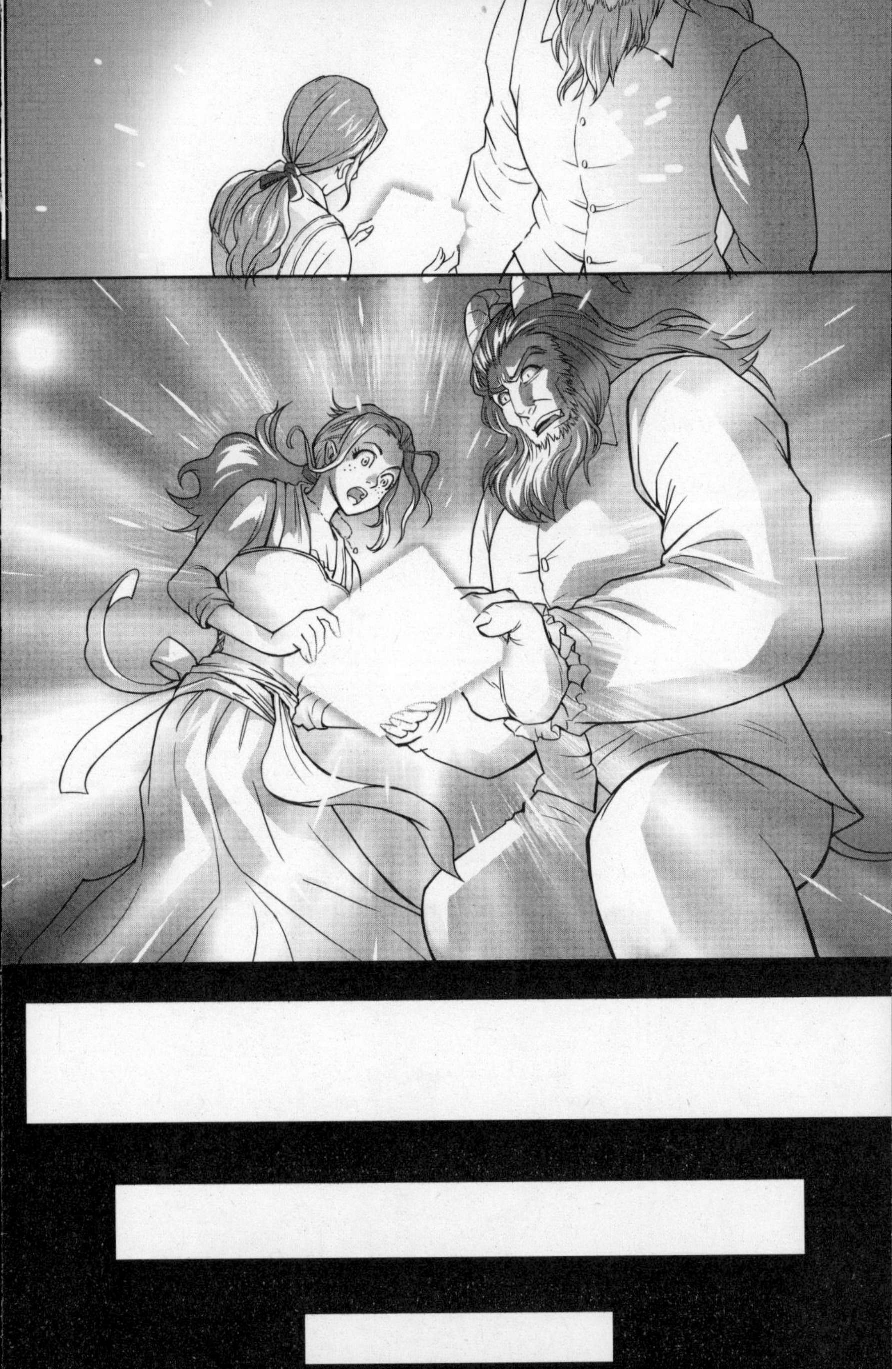

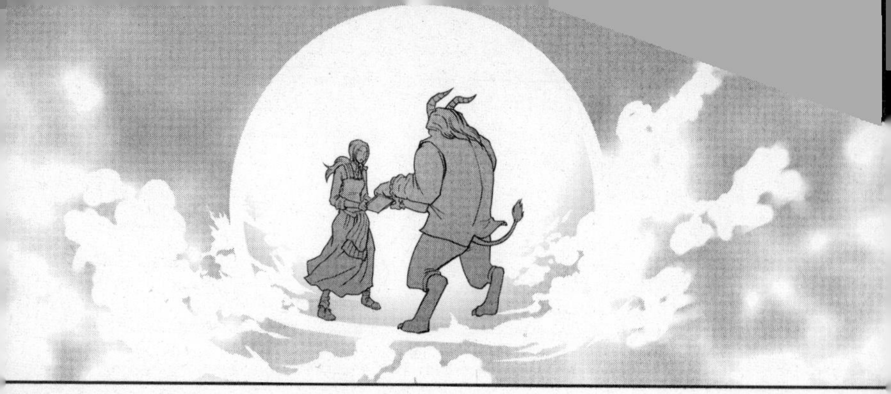

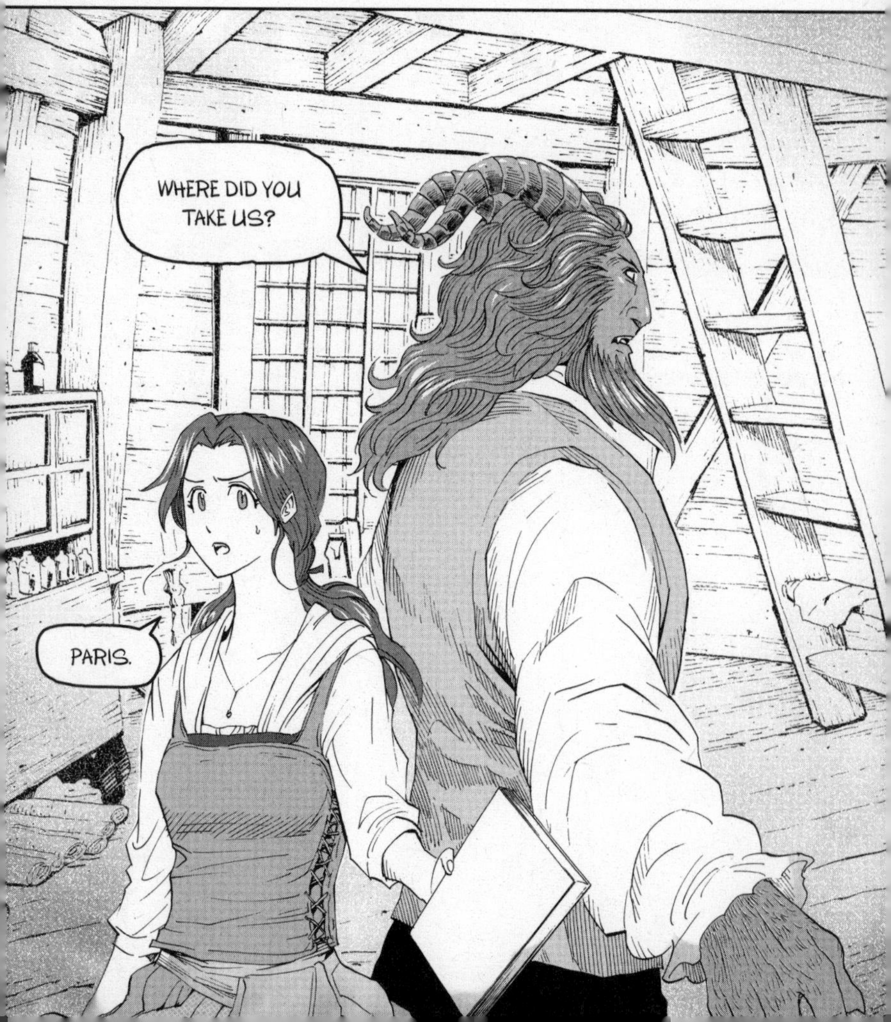
WHERE DID YOU TAKE US?
PARIS.

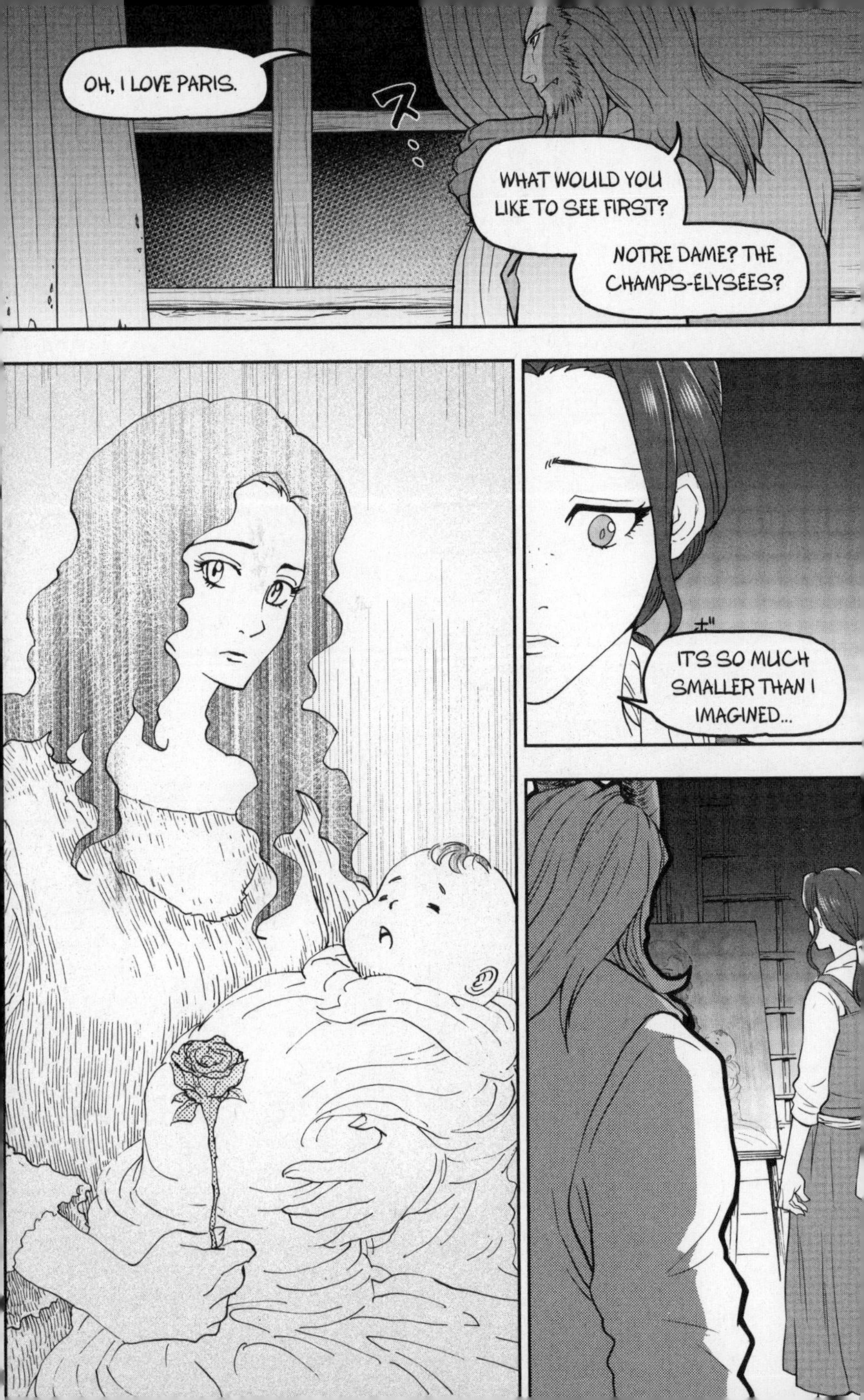
OH, I LOVE PARIS.
WHAT WOULD YOU LIKE TO SEE FIRST?
NOTRE DAME? THE CHAMPS-ELYSEES?
IT'S SO MUCH SMALLER THAN I IMAGINED...

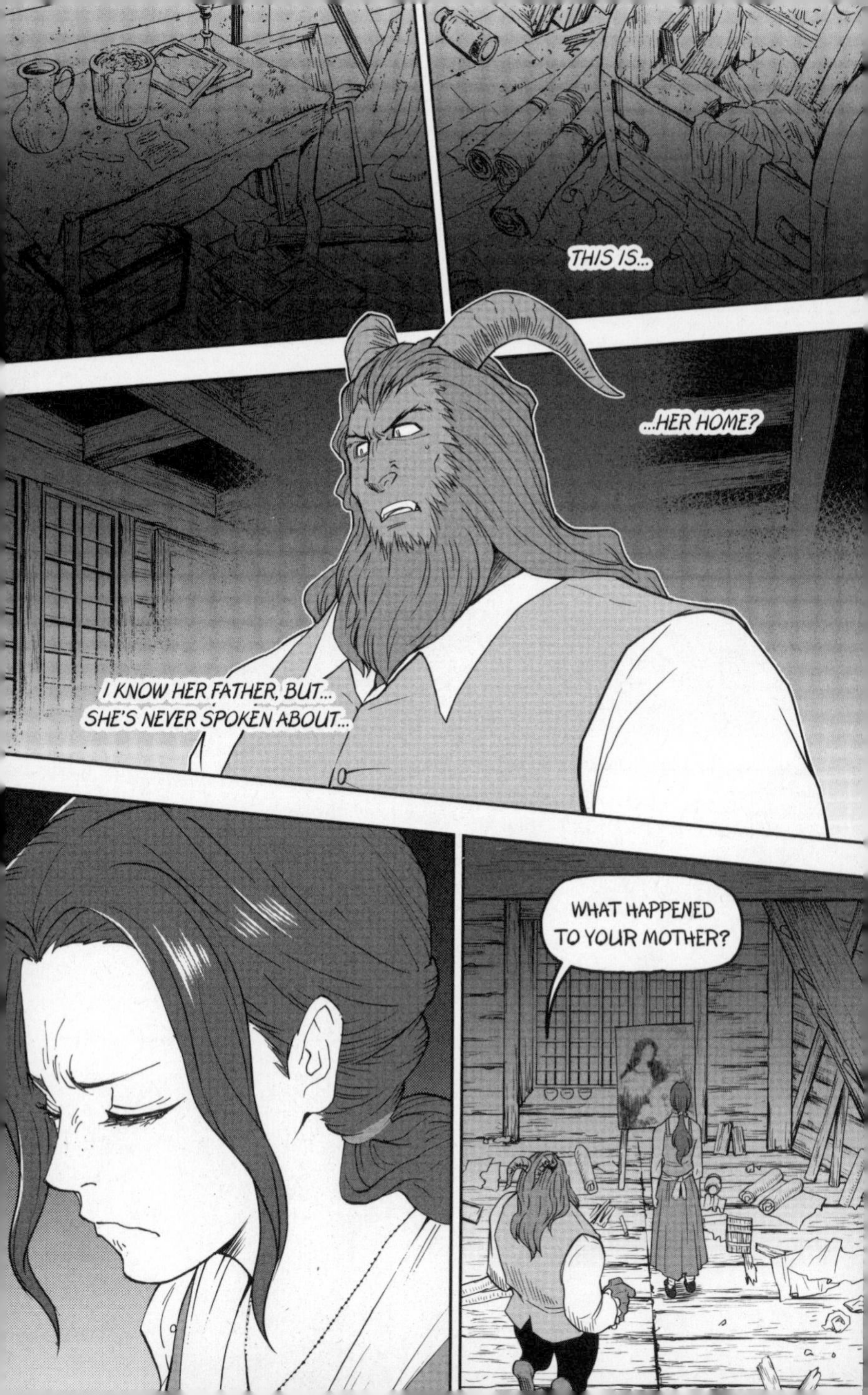
THIS IS...
...HER HOME?
I KNOW HER FATHER, BUT... SHE'S NEVER SPOKEN ABOUT...
WHAT HAPPENED TO YOUR MOTHER?

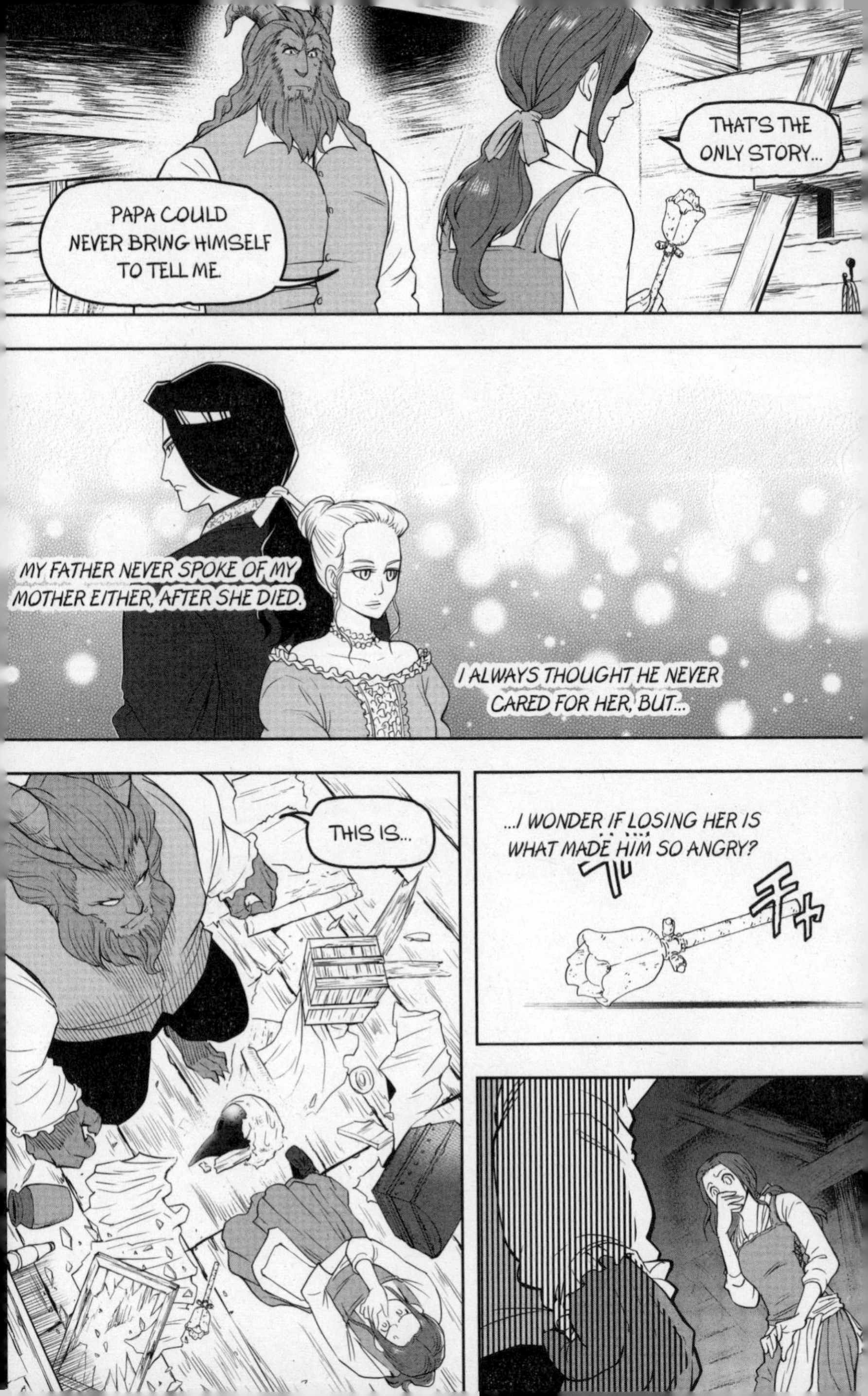
THAT'S THE ONLY STORY...
PAPA COULD NEVER BRING HIMSELF TO TELL ME.
MY FATHER NEVER SPOKE OF MY MOTHER EITHER, AFTER SHE DIED.
I ALWAYS THOUGHT HE NEVER CARED FOR HER, BUT...
...I WONDER IF LOSING HER IS WHAT MADE HIM SO ANGRY?
THIS IS...

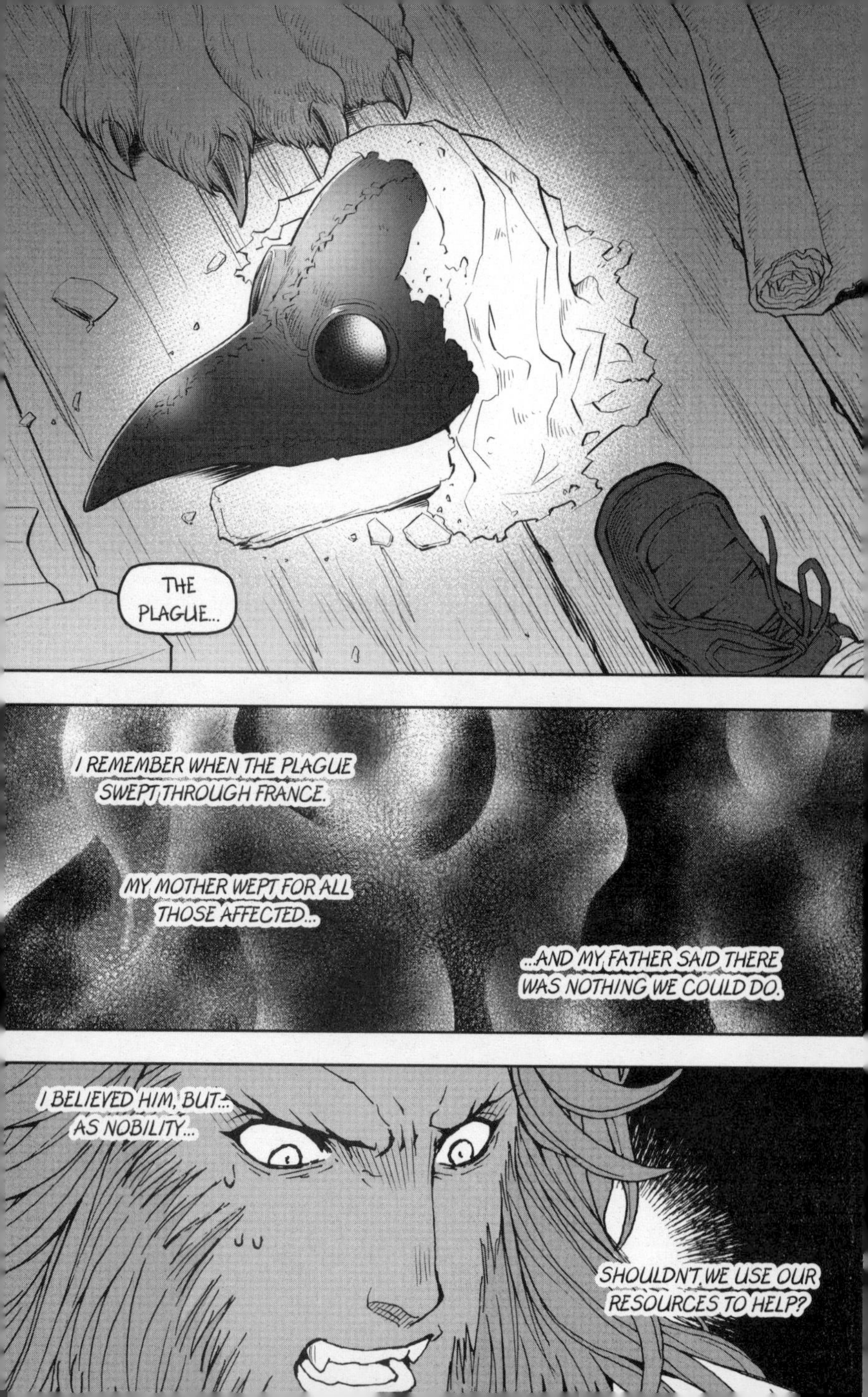
THE PLAGUE...
I REMEMBER WHEN THE PLAGUE SWEPT THROUGH FRANCE.
MY MOTHER WEPT FOR ALL THOSE AFFECTED...
...AND MY FATHER SAID THERE WAS NOTHING WE COULD DO.
I BELIEVED HIM, BUT... AS NOBILITY...
SHOULDN'T WE USE OUR RESOURCES TO HELP?

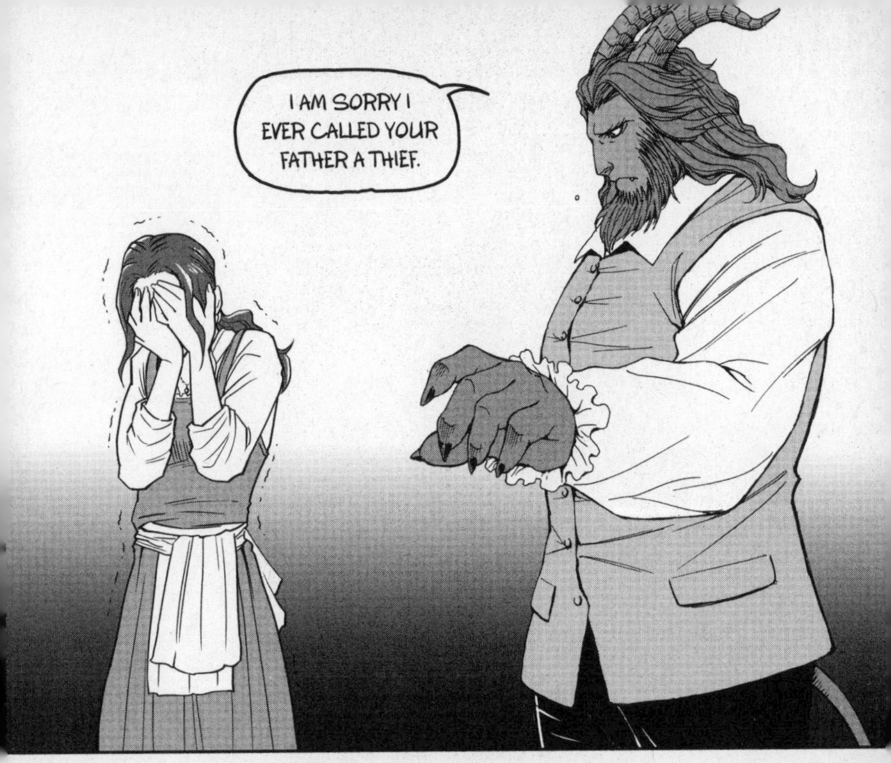
I AM SORRY I EVER CALLED YOUR FATHER A THIEF.
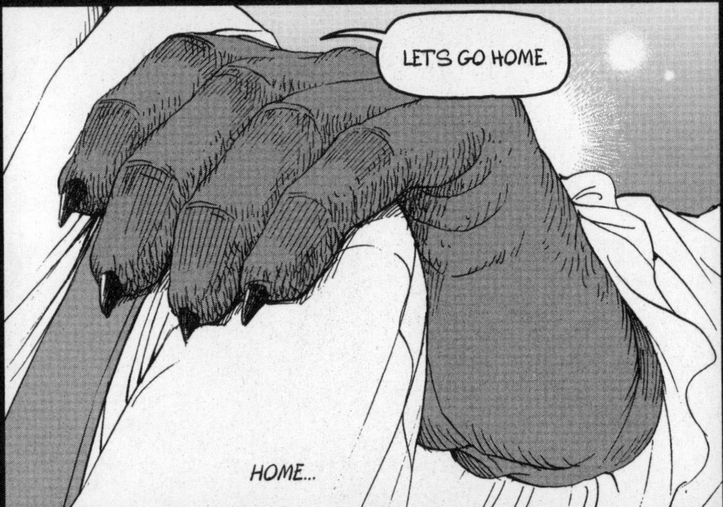
LET'S GO HOME.
HOME...

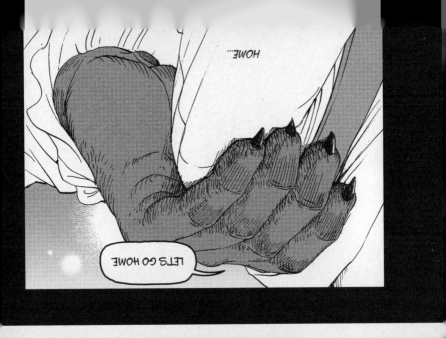

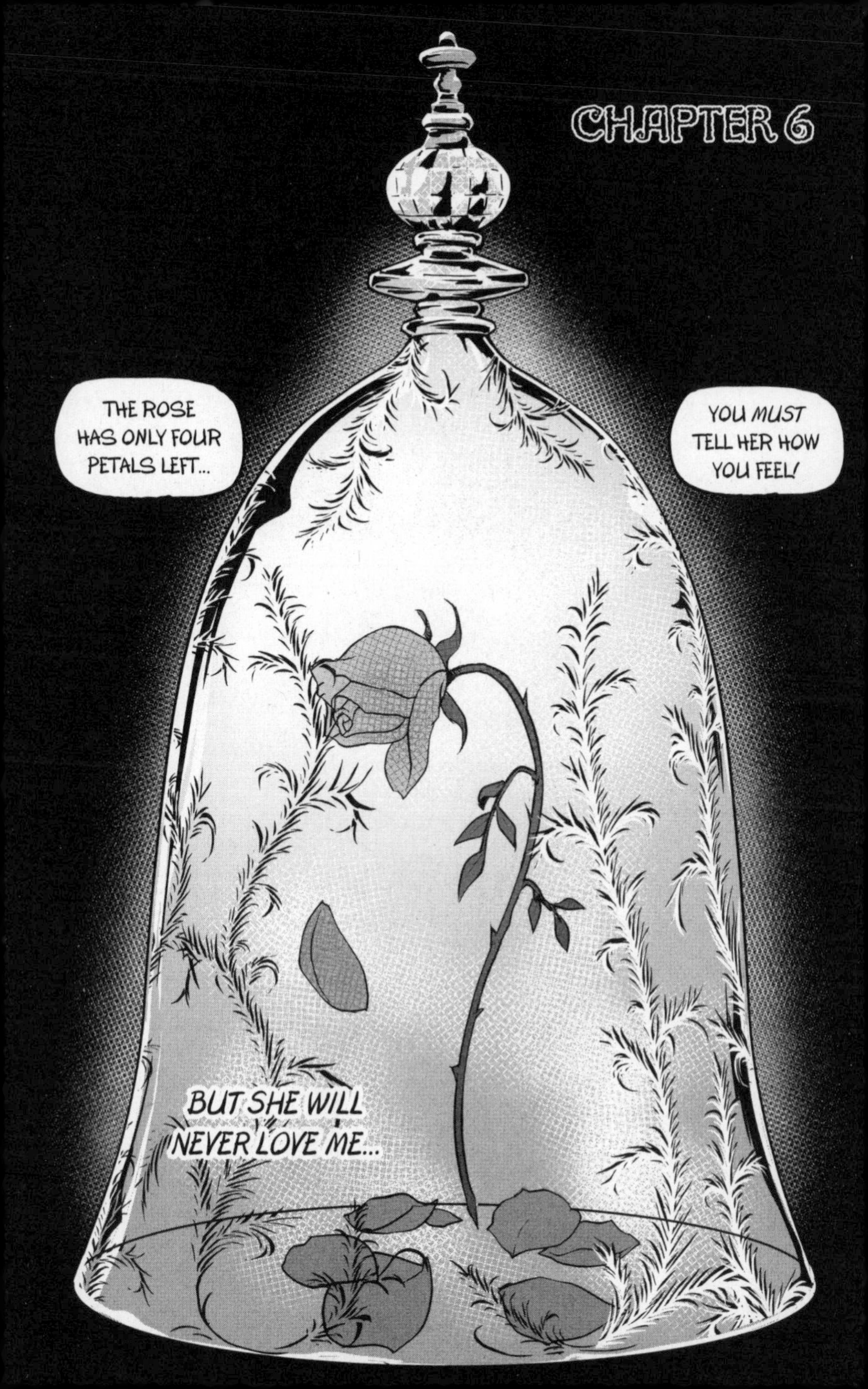
CHAPTER 6
YOU MUST TELL HER HOW YOU FEEL!
THE ROSE HAS ONLY FOUR PETALS LEFT...
BUT SHE WILL NEVER LOVE ME...

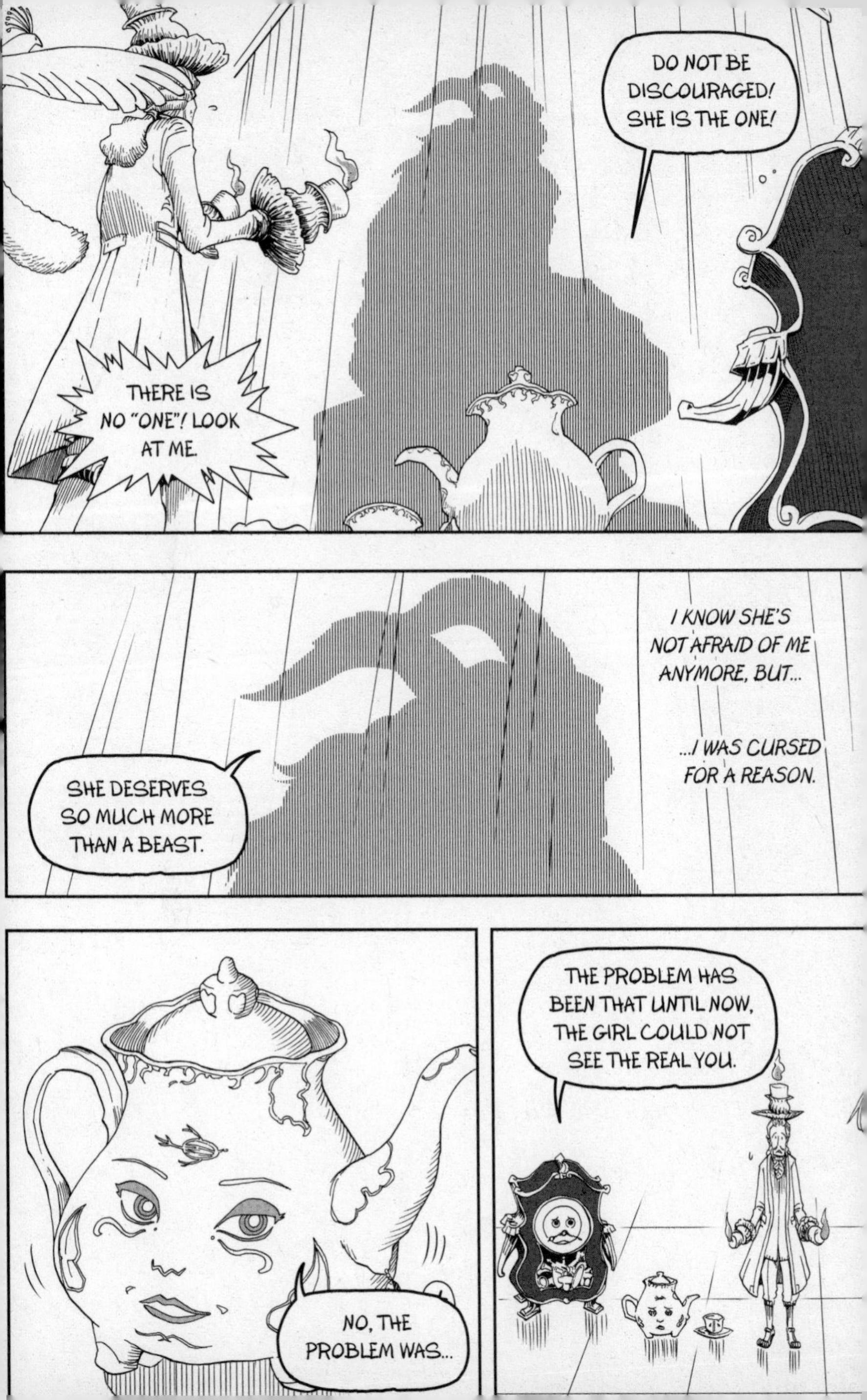
DO NOT BE DISCOURAGED! SHE IS THE ONE!
THERE IS NO "ONE"! LOOK AT ME.
I KNOW SHE'S NOT AFRAID OF ME ANYMORE, BUT...
...I WAS CURSED FOR A REASON.
SHE DESERVES SO MUCH MORE THAN A BEAST.
THE PROBLEM HAS BEEN THAT UNTIL NOW, THE GIRL COULD NOT SEE THE REAL YOU.
NO, THE PROBLEM WAS...

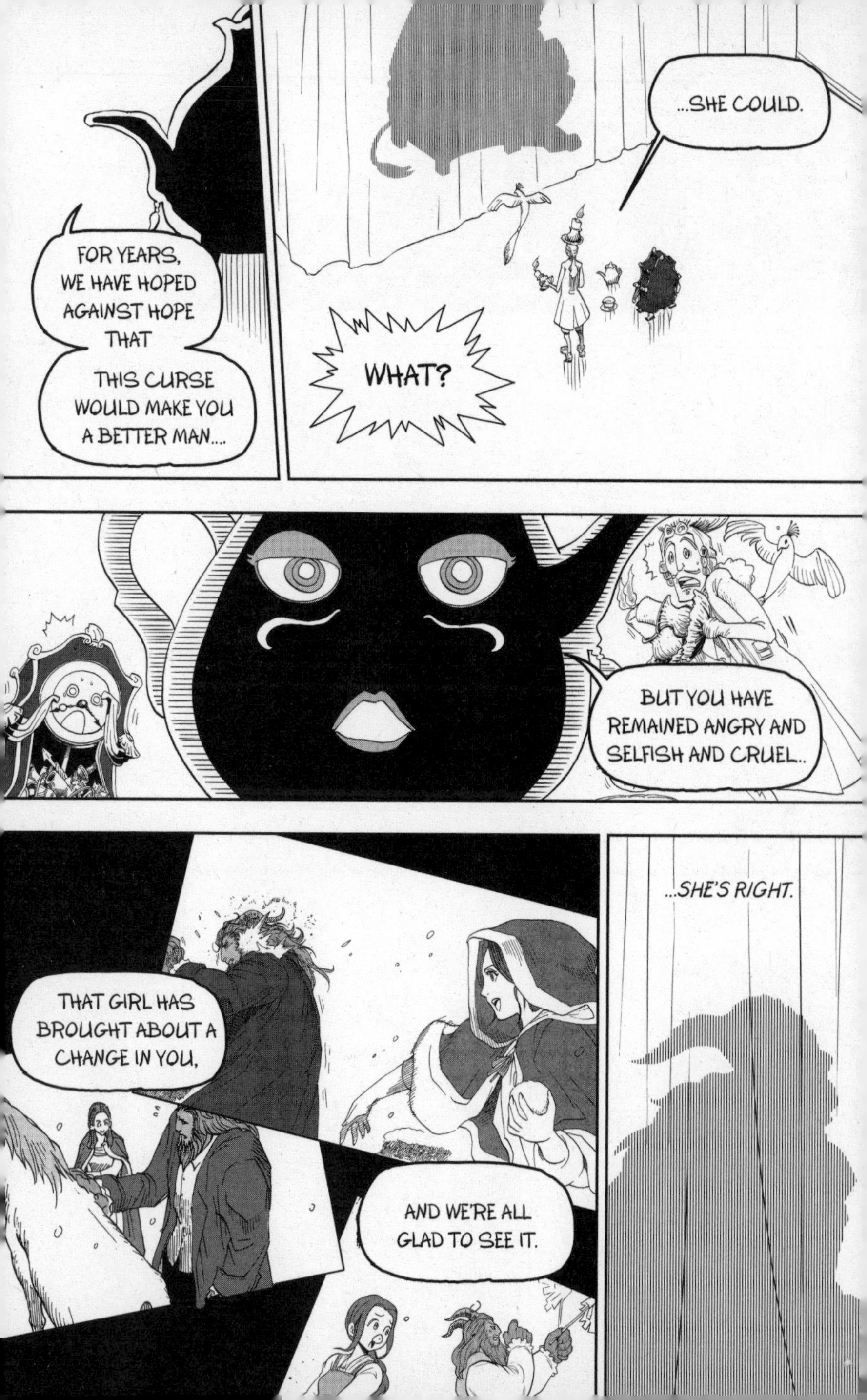
...SHE COULD.
WHAT?
FOR YEARS, WE HAVE HOPED AGAINST HOPE THAT
THIS CURSE WOULD MAKE YOU A BETTER MAN....
BUT YOU HAVE REMAINED ANGRY AND SELFISH AND CRUEL...
...SHE'S RIGHT.
THAT GIRL HAS BROUGHT ABOUT A CHANGE IN YOU,
AND WE'RE ALL GLAD TO SEE IT.

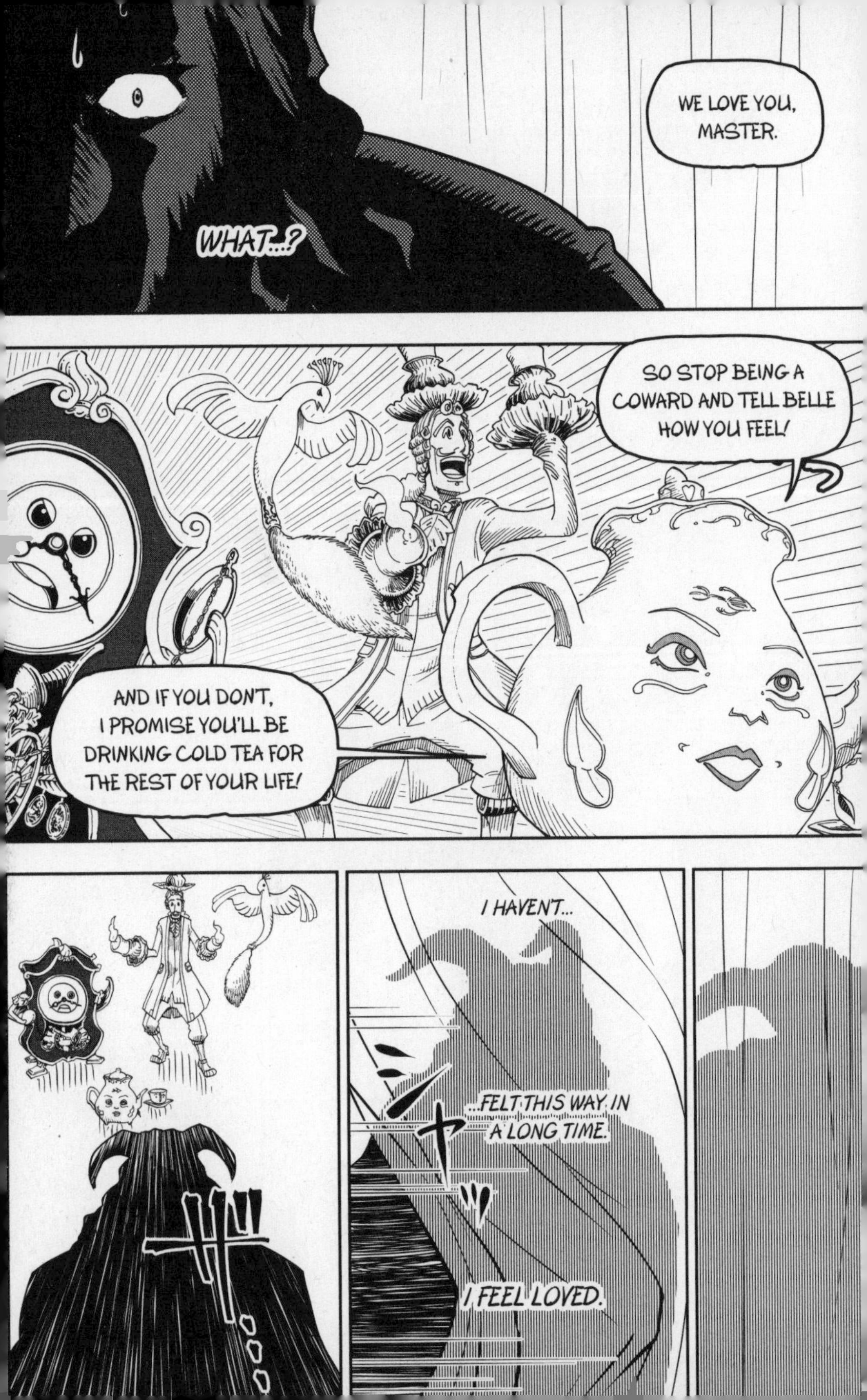
WE LOVE YOU, MASTER.
WHAT...?
SO STOP BEING A COWARD AND TELL BELLE HOW YOU FEEL!
AND IF YOU DON'T, I PROMISE YOU'LL BE DRINKING COLD TEA FOR THE REST OF YOUR LIFE!
I HAVEN'T...
...FELT THIS WAY IN A LONG TIME.
I FEEL LOVED.

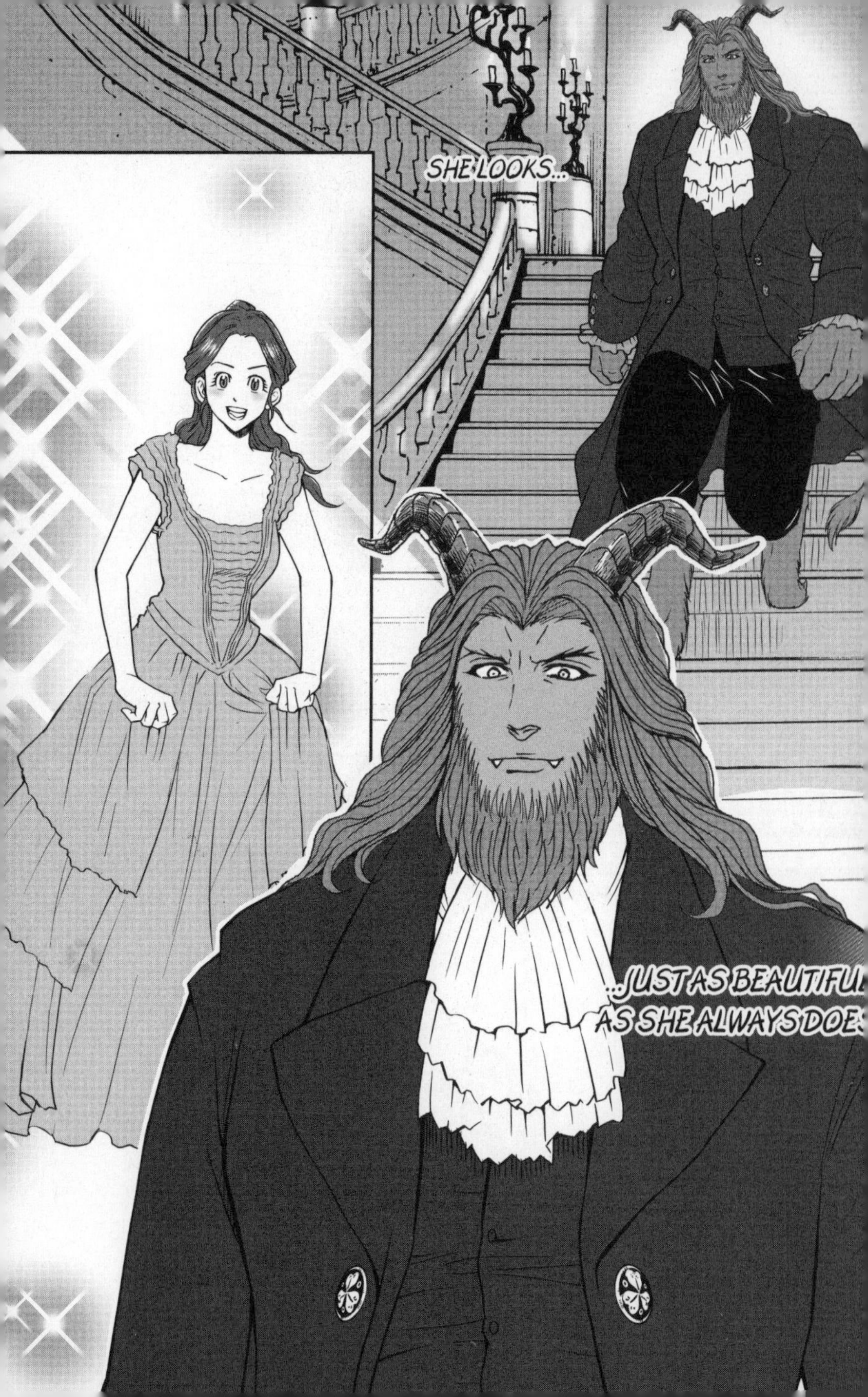
SHE LOOKS...
...JUST AS BEAUTIFU
AS SHE ALWAYS DOE

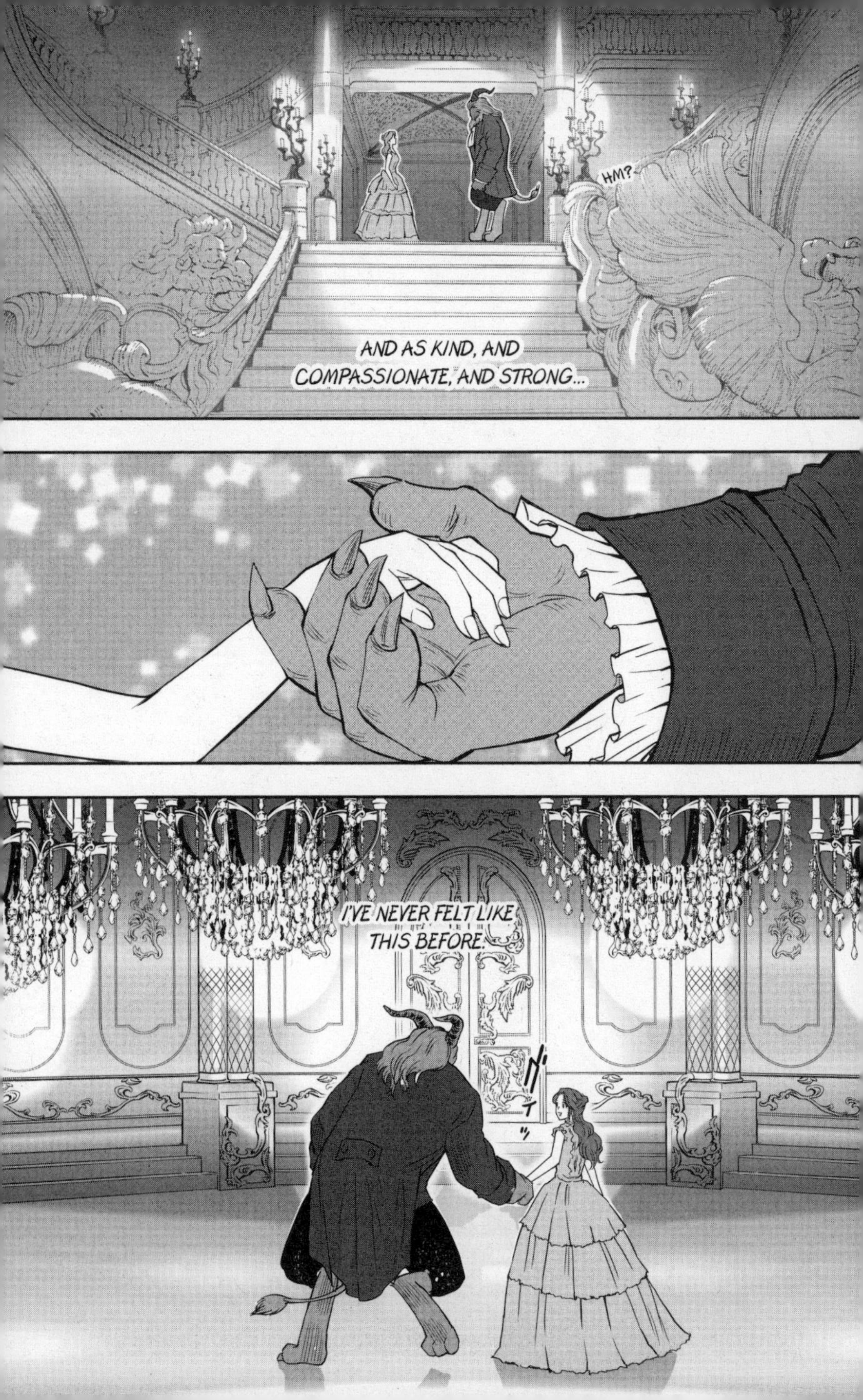
HM?
AND AS KIND, AND COMPASSIONATE, AND STRONG...
I'VE NEVER FELT LIKE THIS BEFORE.

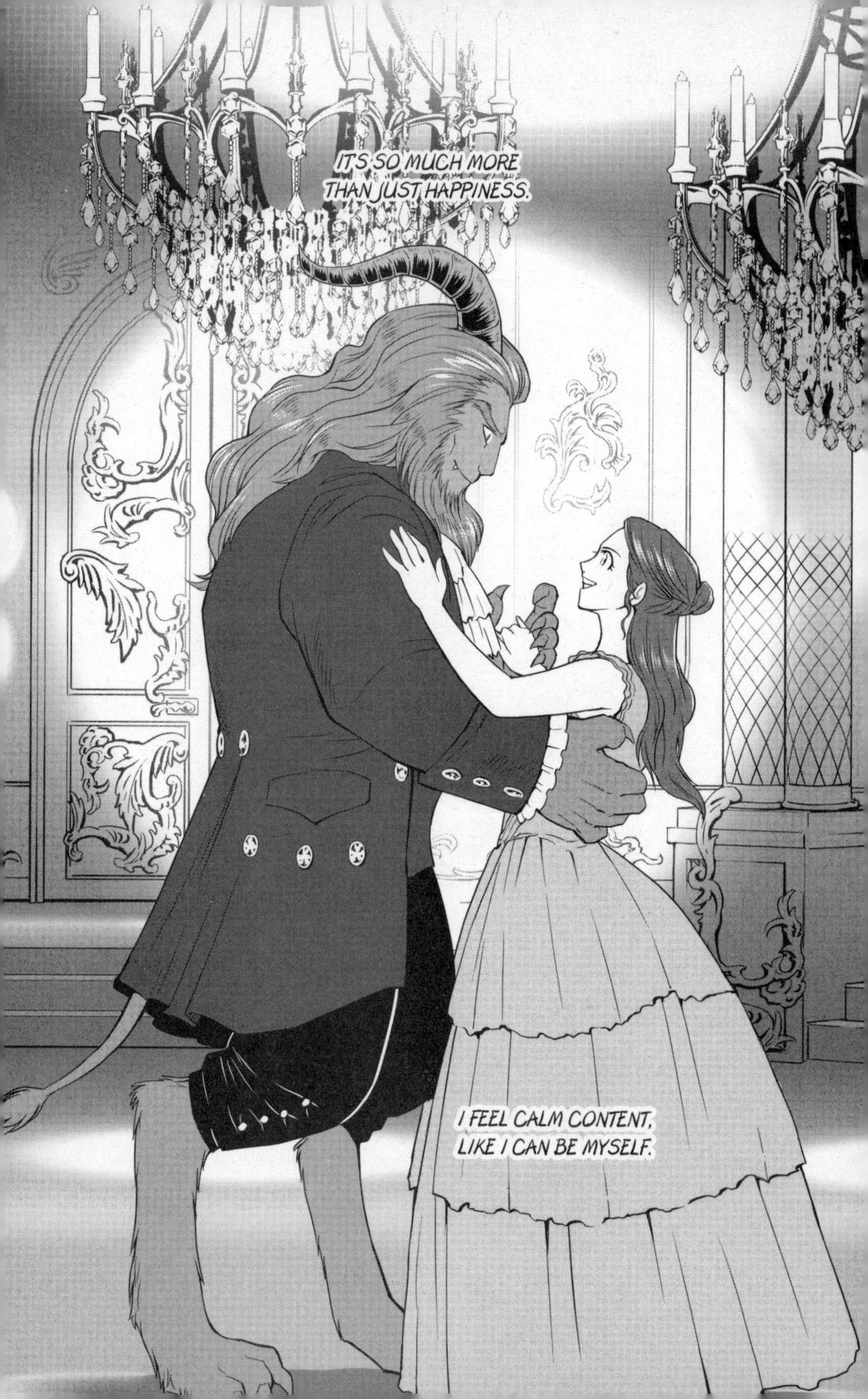
IT'S SO MUCH MORE THAN JUST HAPPINESS.
I FEEL CALM CONTENT, LIKE I CAN BE MYSELF.

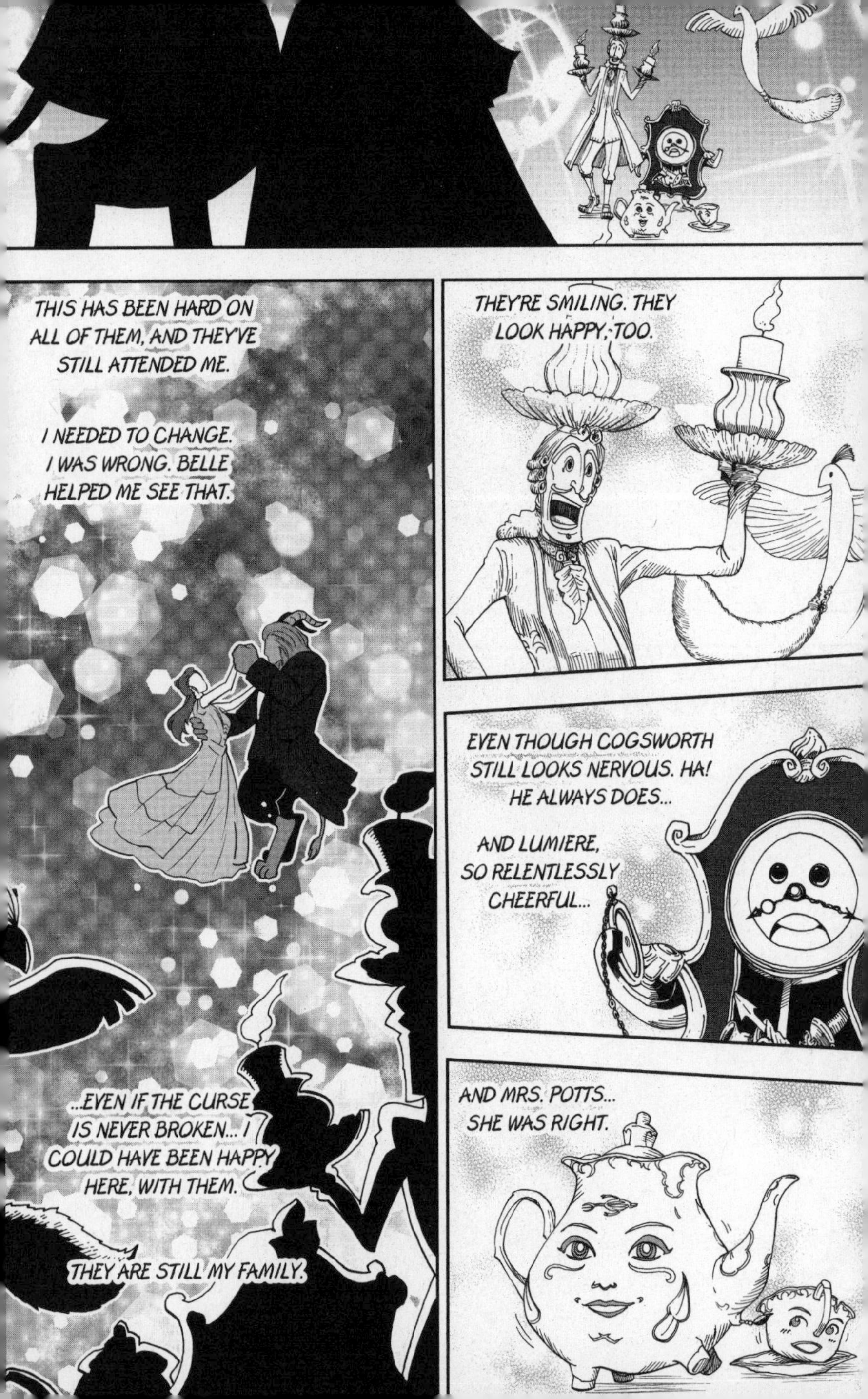
THEY'RE SMILING. THEY LOOK HAPPY, TOO.
EVEN THOUGH COGSWORTH STILL LOOKS NERVOUS. HA! HE ALWAYS DOES...
AND LUMIERE, SO RELENTLESSLY CHEERFUL...
AND MRS. POTTS... SHE WAS RIGHT.
THIS HAS BEEN HARD ON ALL OF THEM, AND THEY'VE STILL ATTENDED ME.
I NEEDED TO CHANGE. I WAS WRONG. BELLE HELPED ME SEE THAT.
...EVEN IF THE CURSE IS NEVER BROKEN... I COULD HAVE BEEN HAPPY HERE, WITH THEM.
THEY ARE STILL MY FAMILY.

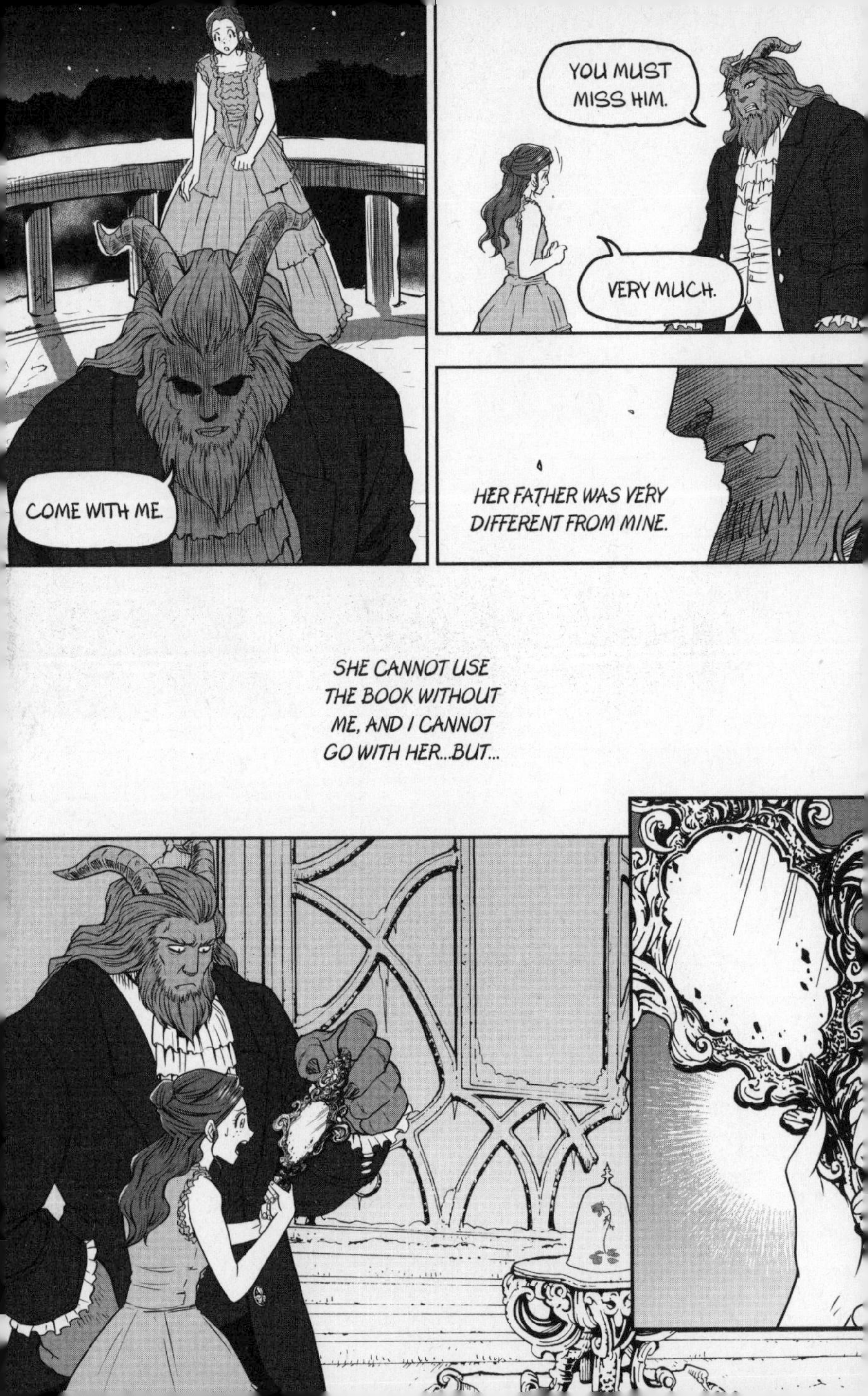
YOU MUST MISS HIM.
VERY MUCH.
HER FATHER WAS VERY DIFFERENT FROM MINE.
COME WITH ME.
SHE CANNOT USE THE BOOK WITHOUT ME, AND I CANNOT GO WITH HER...BUT...

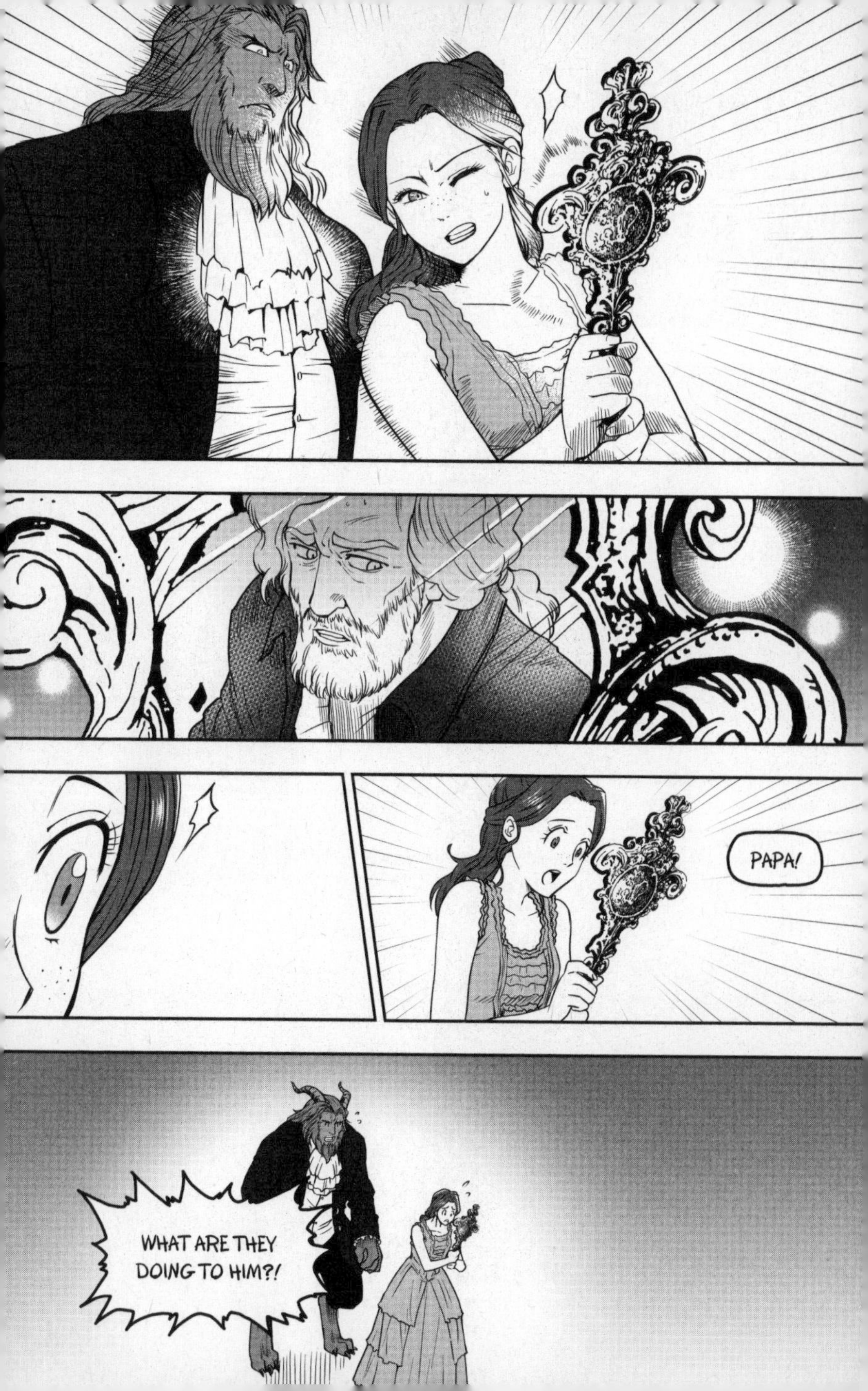
PAPA!
WHAT ARE THEY DOING TO HIM?!

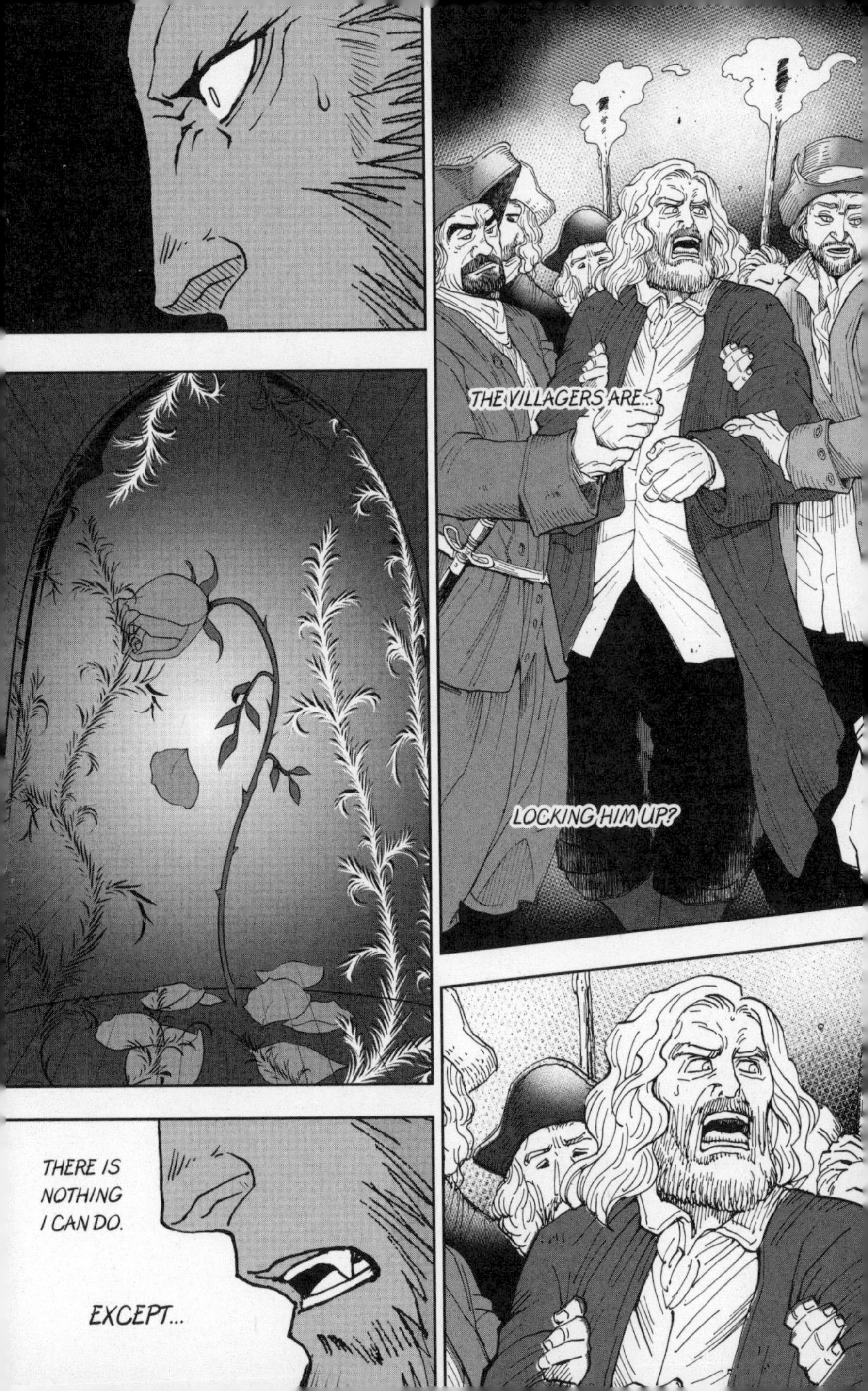
THE VILLAGERS ARE...
LOCKING HIM UP?
THERE IS NOTHING I CAN DO.
EXCEPT...

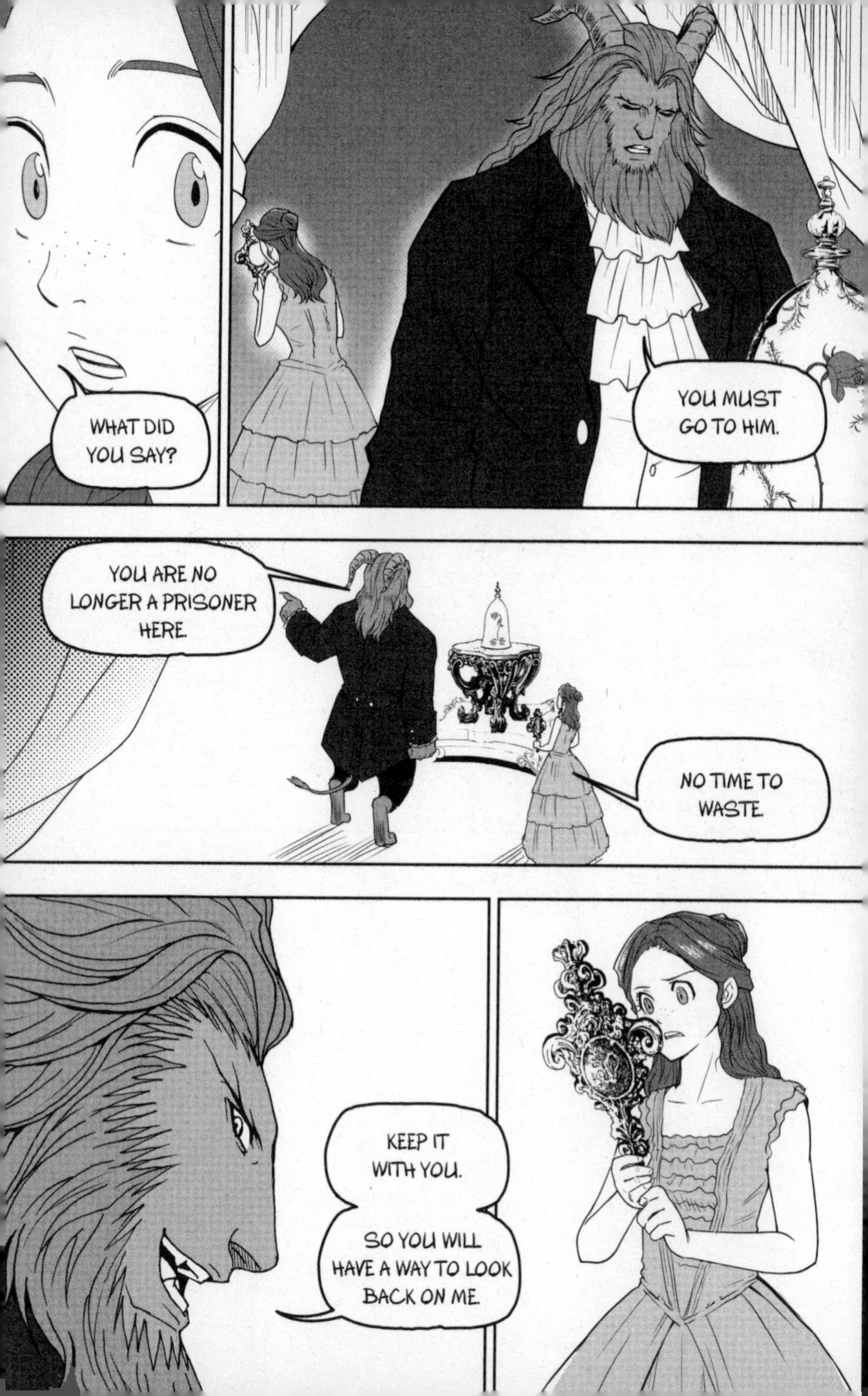
YOU MUST GO TO HIM.
WHAT DID YOU SAY?
YOU ARE NO LONGER A PRISONER HERE.
NO TIME TO WASTE.
KEEP IT WITH YOU.
SO YOU WILL HAVE A WAY TO LOOK BACK ON ME.

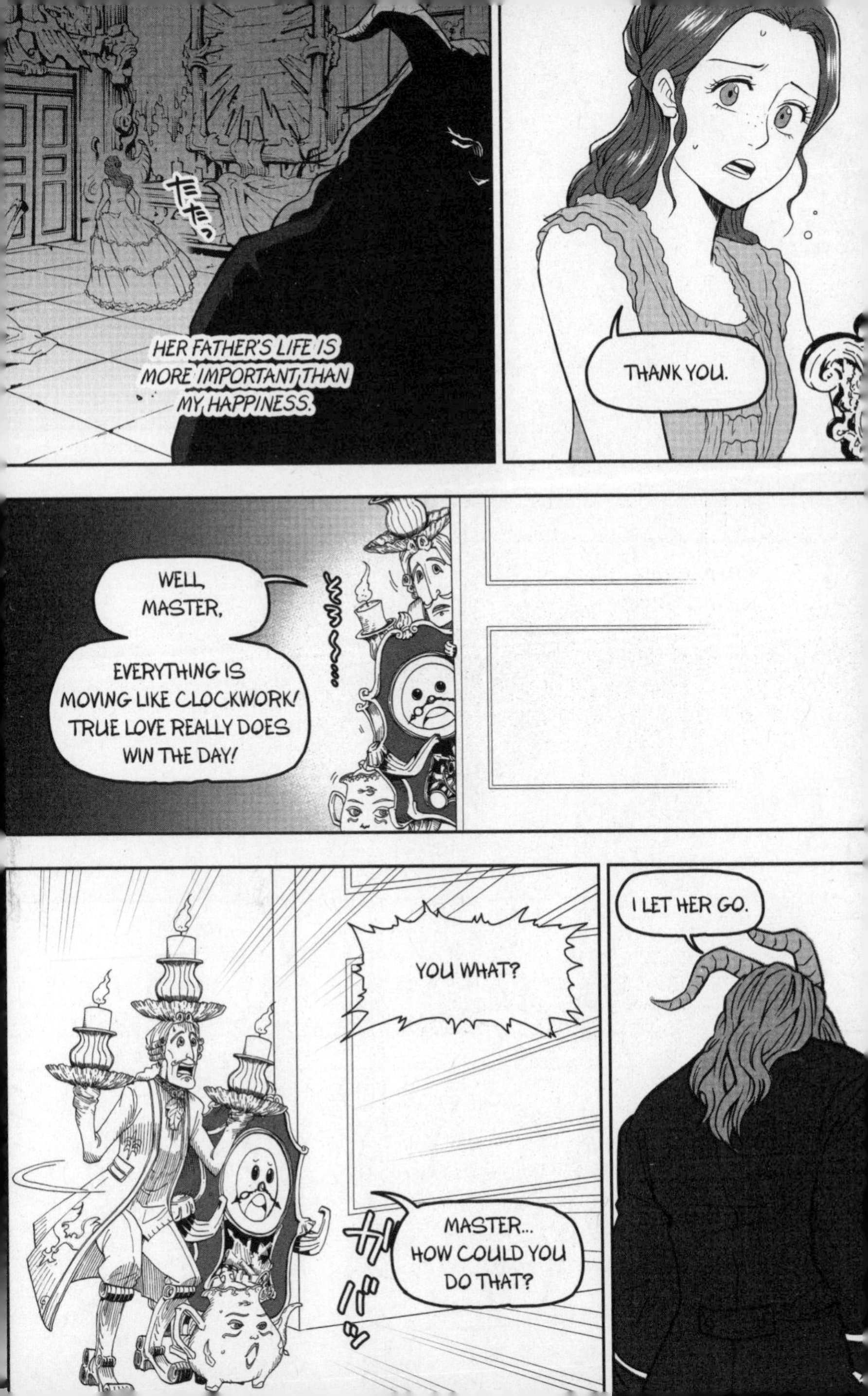
THANK YOU.
HER FATHER'S LIFE IS MORE IMPORTANT THAN MY HAPPINESS.
たたっ
WELL, MASTER,
EVERYTHING IS MOVING LIKE CLOCKWORK! TRUE LOVE REALLY DOES WIN THE DAY!
I LET HER GO.
YOU WHAT?
MASTER... HOW COULD YOU DO THAT?

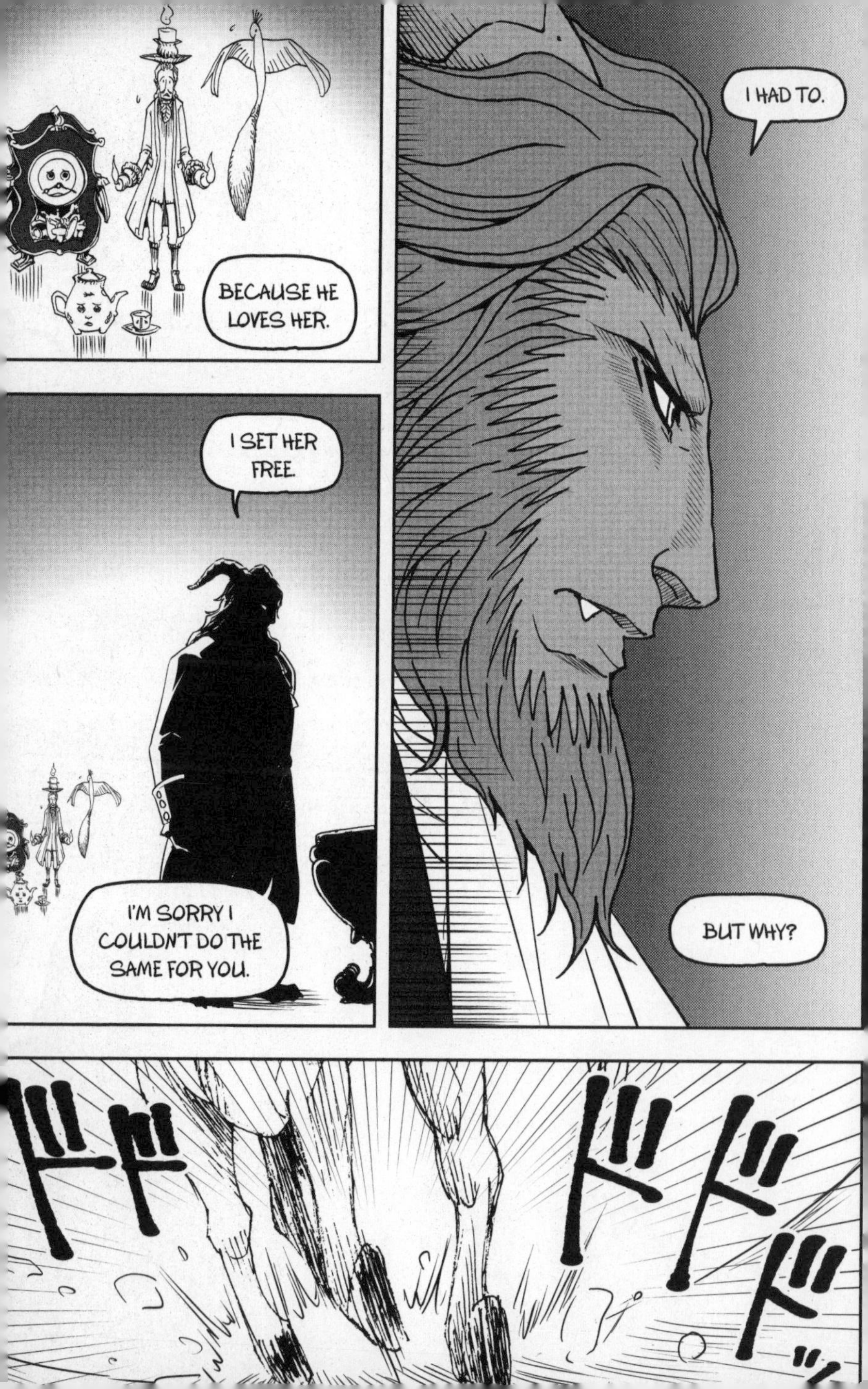
I HAD TO.
BUT WHY?
BECAUSE HE LOVES HER.
I SET HER FREE.
I'M SORRY I COULDN'T DO THE SAME FOR YOU.
ドドドド
ドド

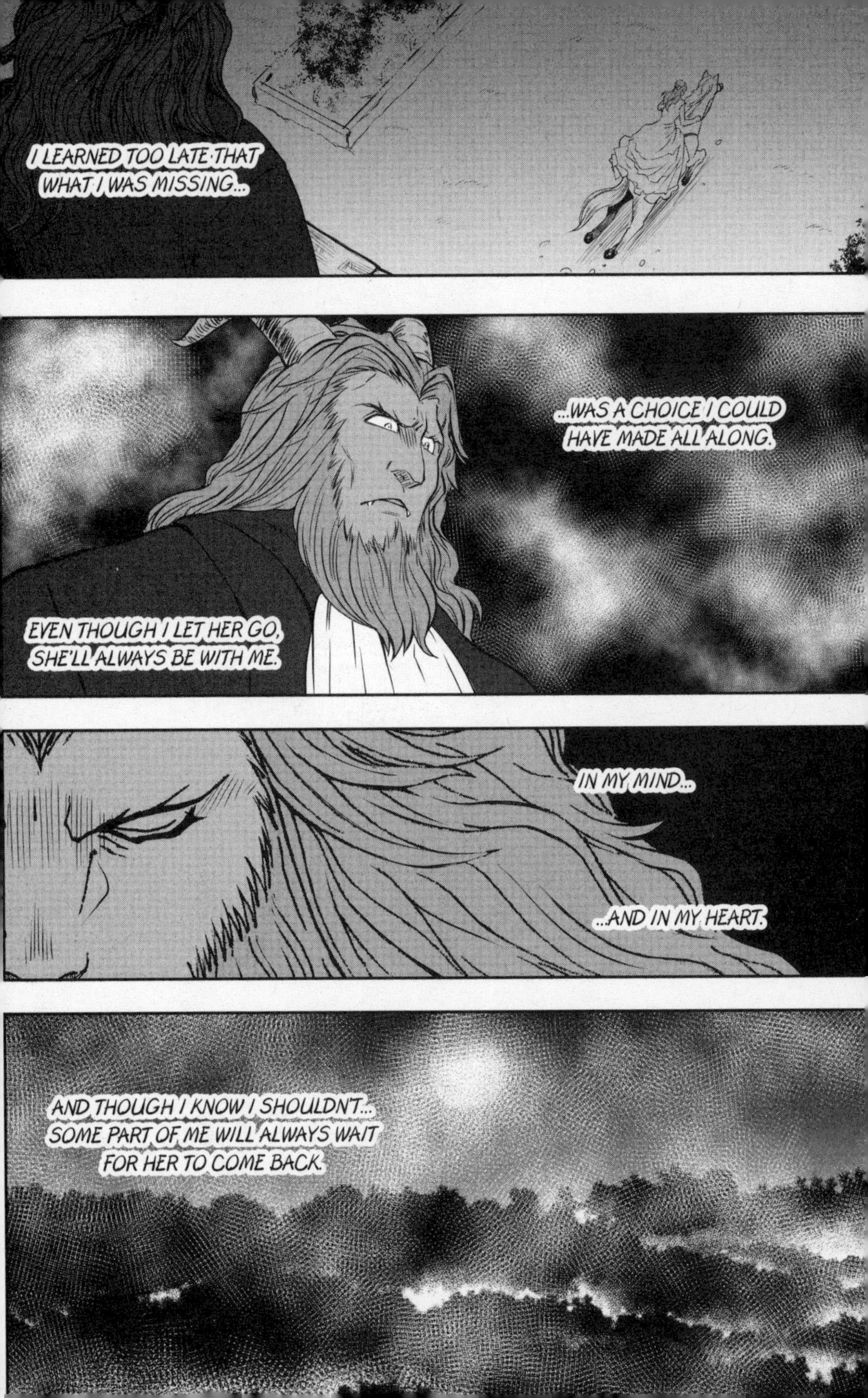
I LEARNED TOO LATE THAT WHAT I WAS MISSING...
...WAS A CHOICE I COULD HAVE MADE ALL ALONG.
EVEN THOUGH I LET HER GO, SHE'LL ALWAYS BE WITH ME.
IN MY MIND...
...AND IN MY HEART.
AND THOUGH I KNOW I SHOULDN'T... SOME PART OF ME WILL ALWAYS WAIT FOR HER TO COME BACK.

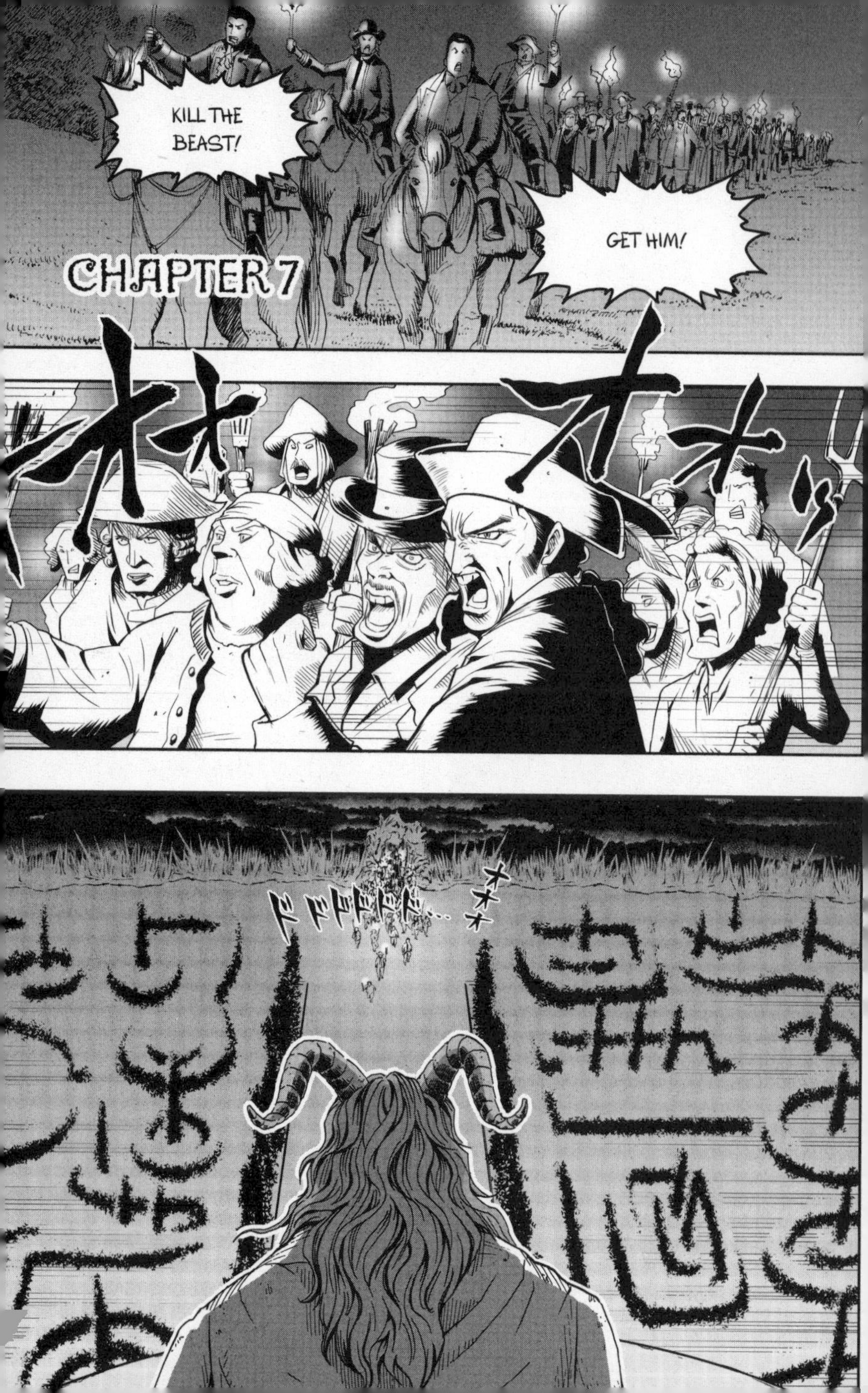
GET HIM!
KILL THE BEAST!
CHAPTER 7
オオッ
オオ
ドドドドドド…
オオオ

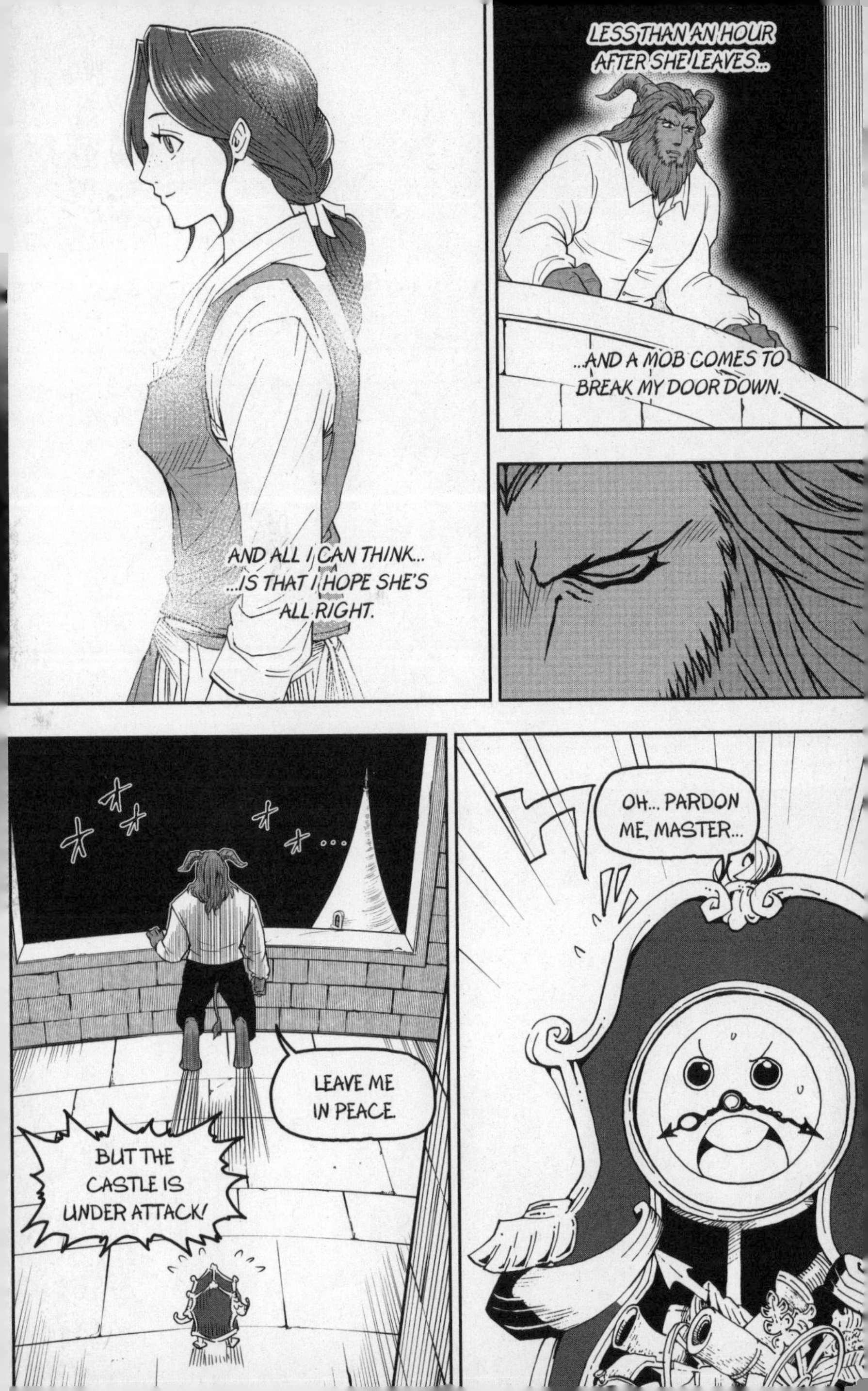
LESS THAN AN HOUR AFTER SHE LEAVES...
...AND A MOB COMES TO BREAK MY DOOR DOWN.
AND ALL I CAN THINK... ...IS THAT I HOPE SHE'S ALL RIGHT.
OH... PARDON ME, MASTER...
LEAVE ME IN PEACE.
BUT THE CASTLE IS UNDER ATTACK!

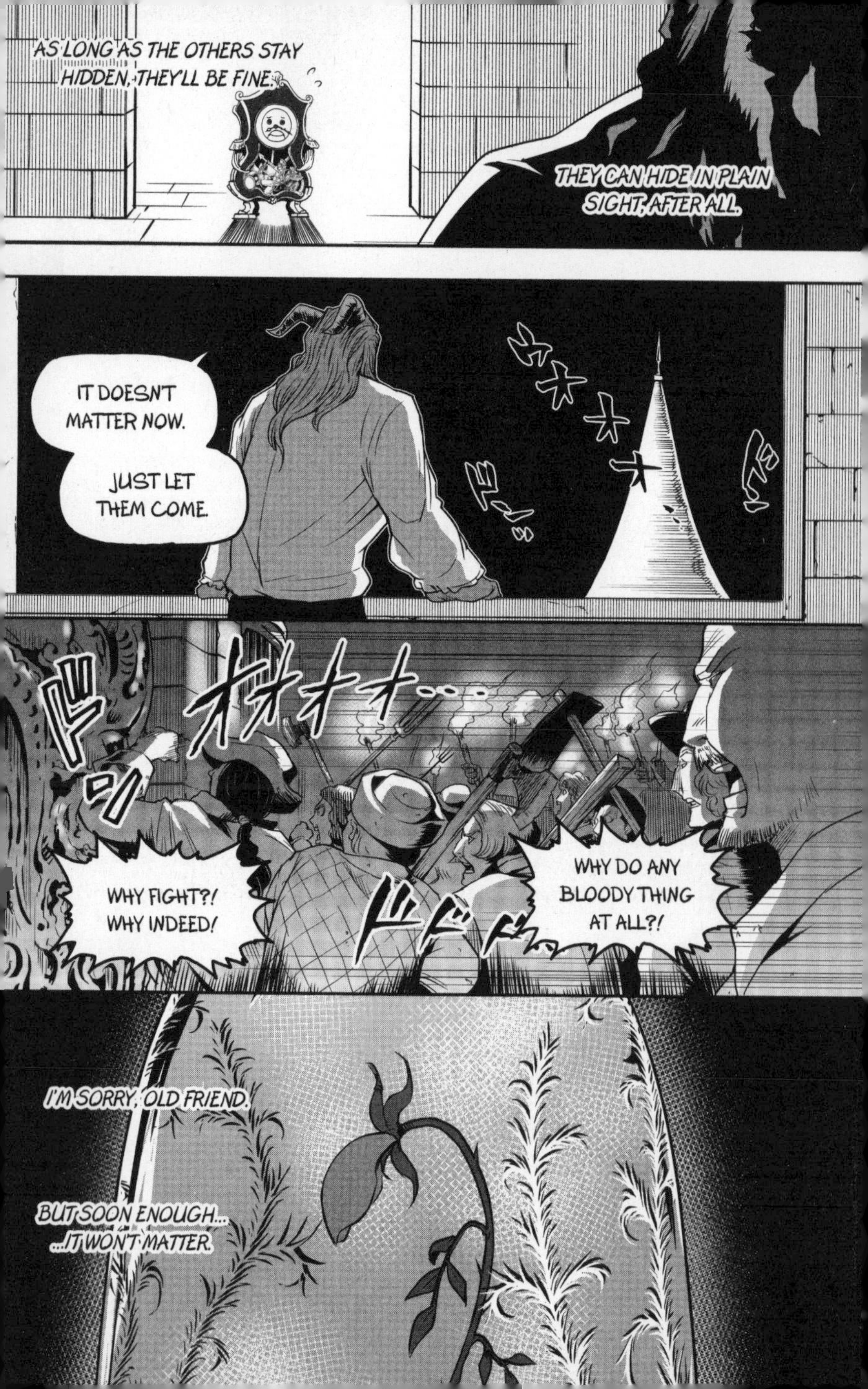
AS LONG AS THE OTHERS STAY HIDDEN, THEY'LL BE FINE.
THEY CAN HIDE IN PLAIN SIGHT, AFTER ALL.
IT DOESN'T MATTER NOW.
JUST LET THEM COME.
WHY DO ANY BLOODY THING AT ALL?!
WHY FIGHT?! WHY INDEED!
I'M SORRY, OLD FRIEND.
BUT SOON ENOUGH...
...IT WON'T MATTER.

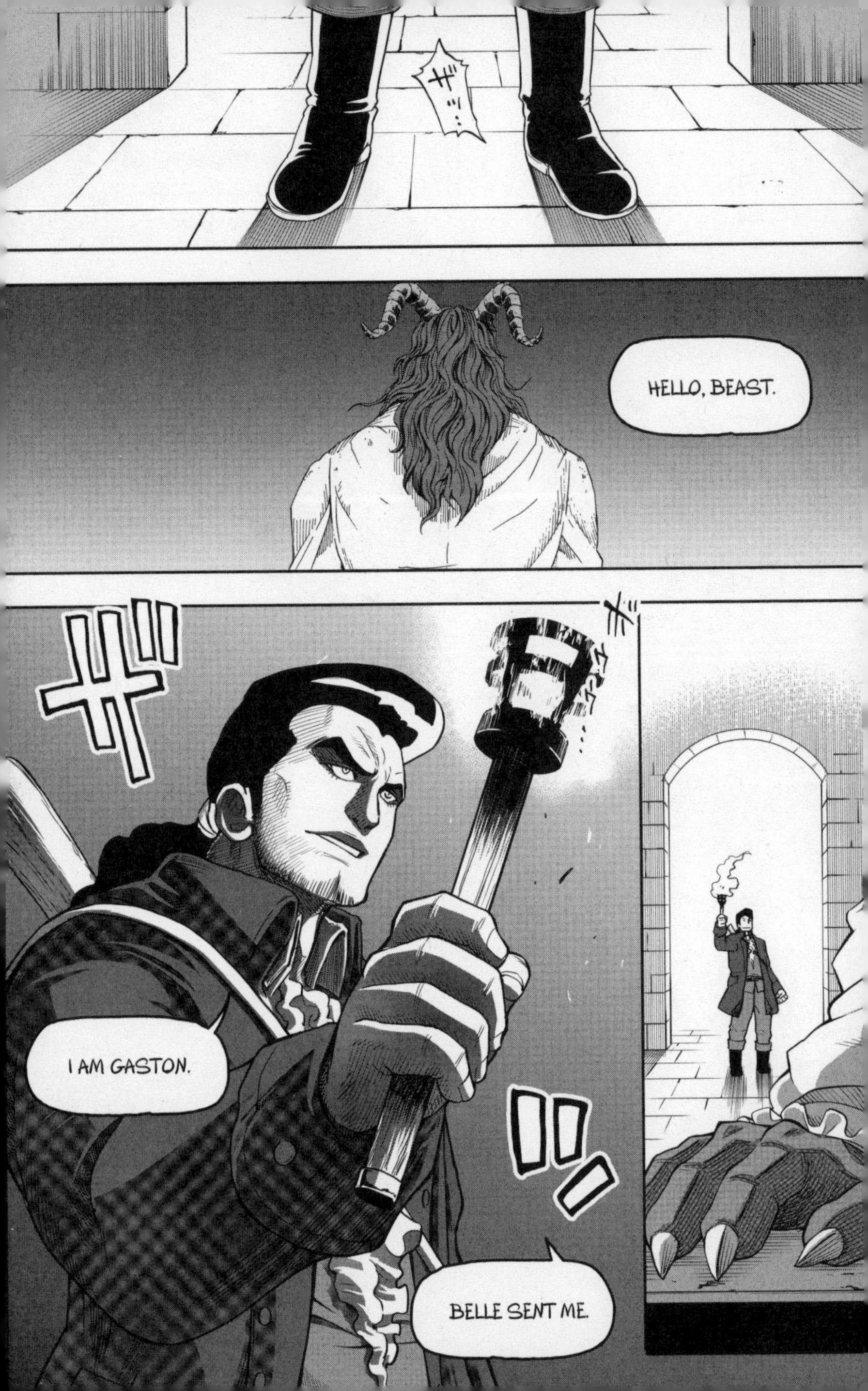
ザッ…
HELLO, BEAST.
ギュッ…
ギリッ
I AM GASTON.
BELLE SENT ME.

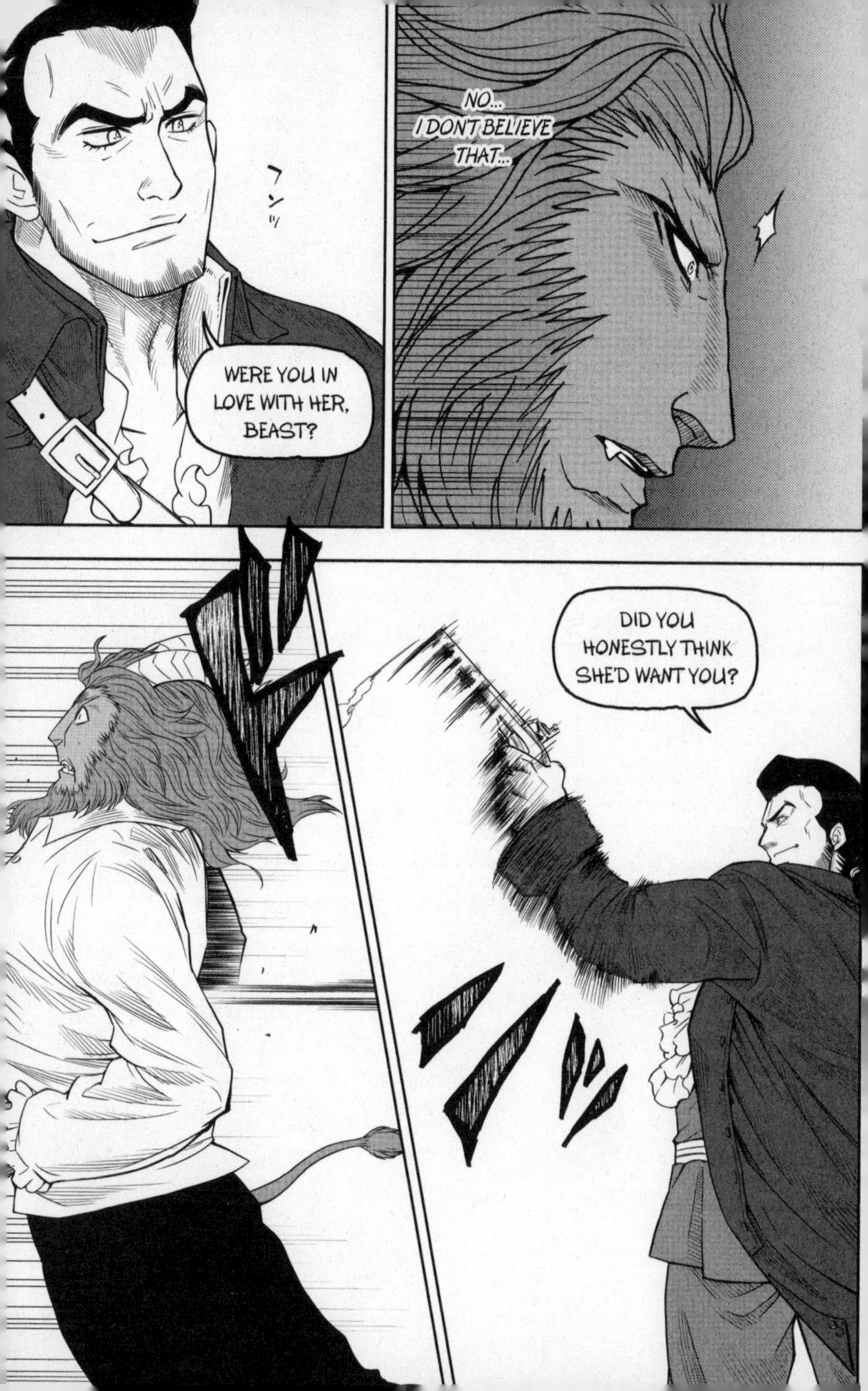
NO...
I DON'T BELIEVE
THAT...
フンッ
WERE YOU IN
LOVE WITH HER,
BEAST?
DID YOU
HONESTLY THINK
SHE'D WANT YOU?

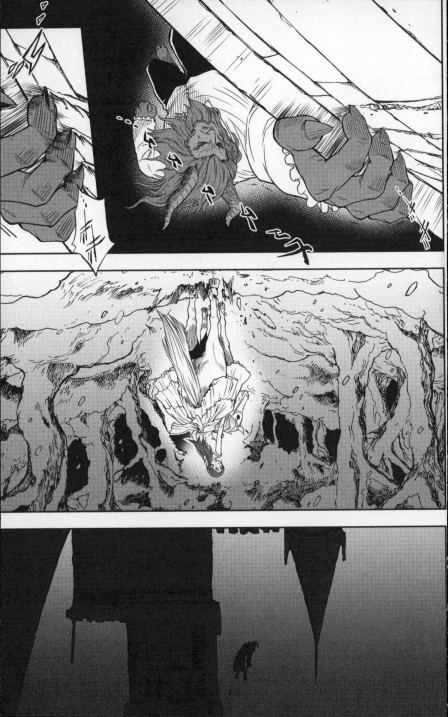

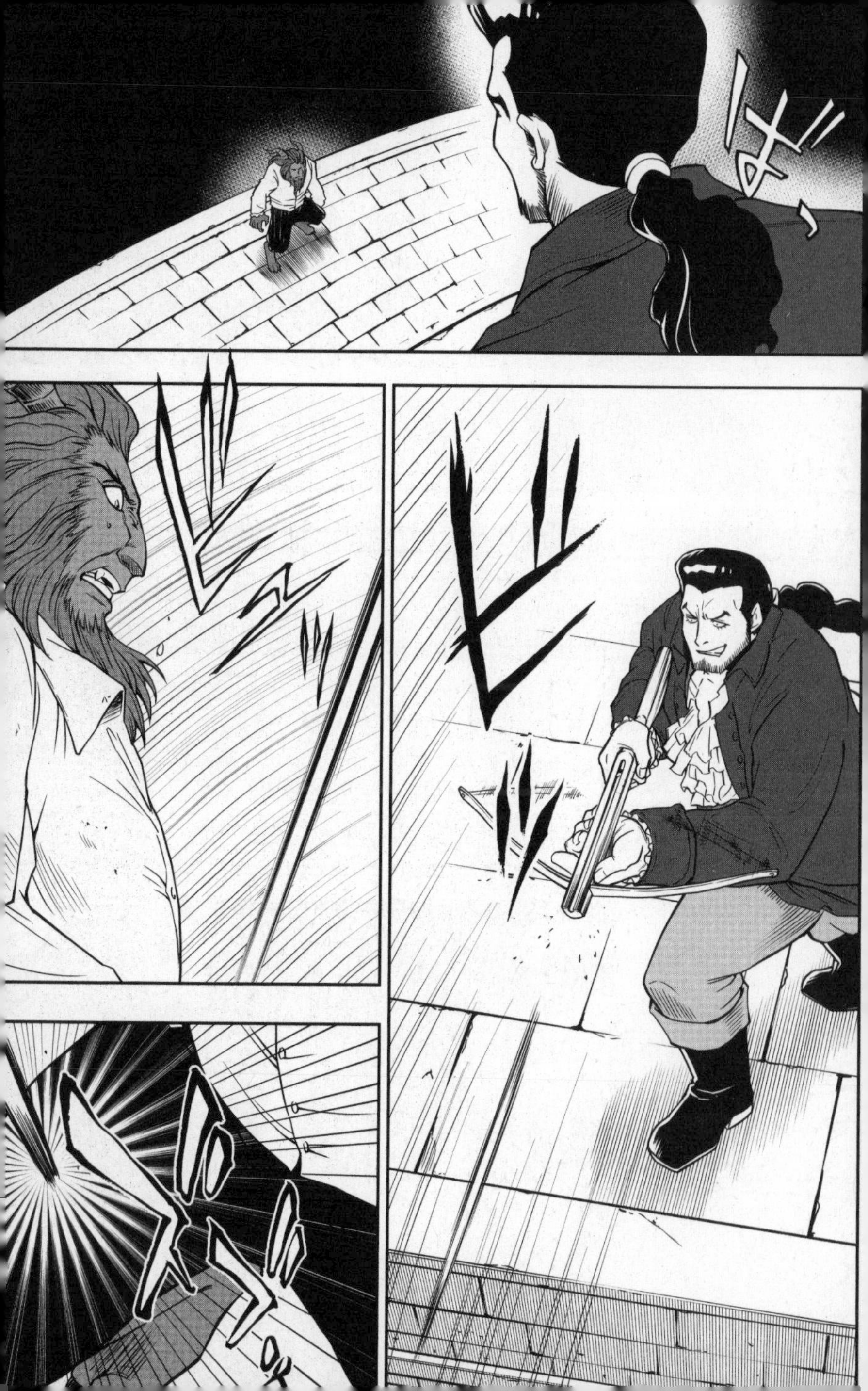
ばっ

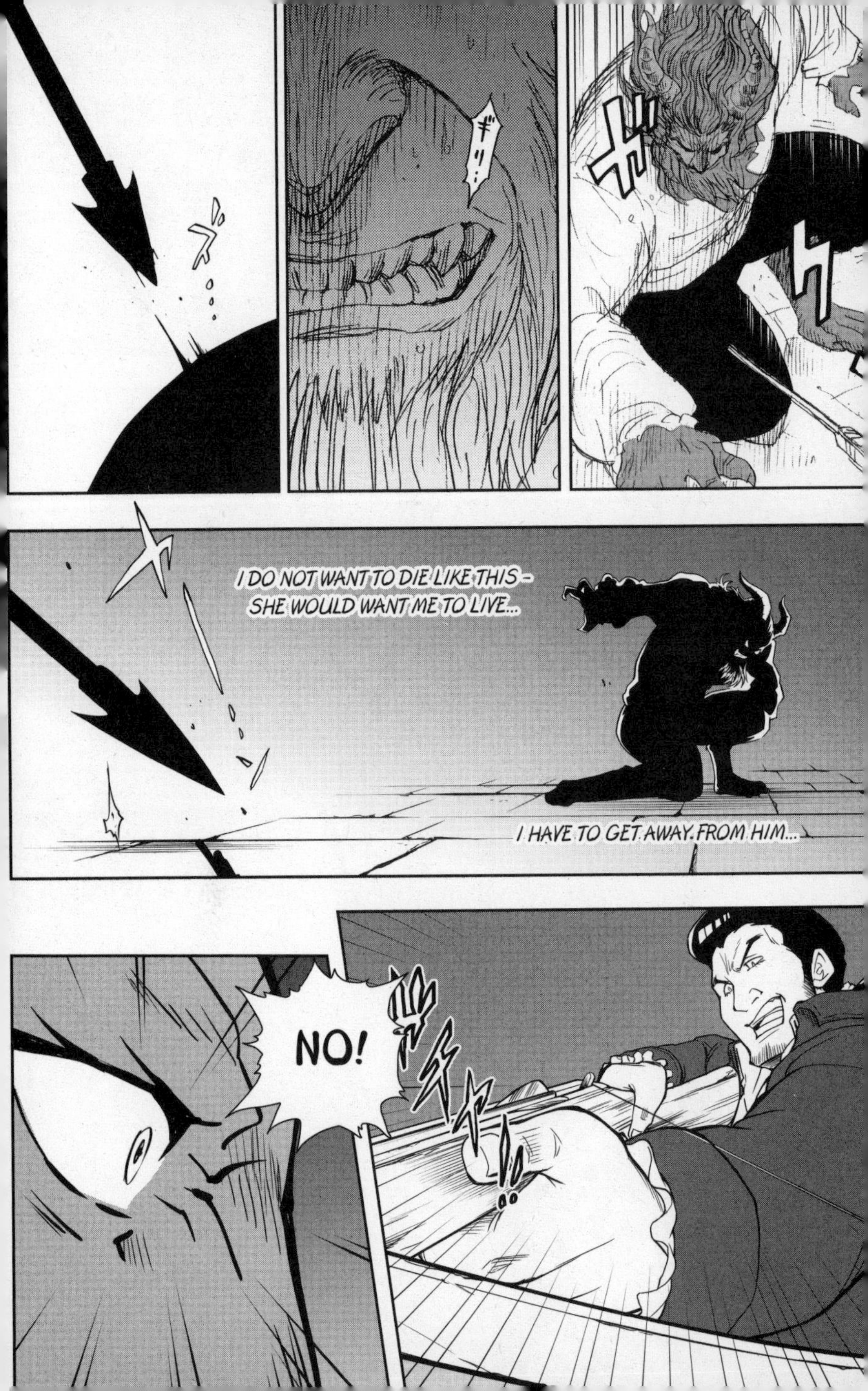
I DO NOT WANT TO DIE LIKE THIS -
SHE WOULD WANT ME TO LIVE...
I HAVE TO GET AWAY FROM HIM...
NO!

BELLE...?
SHE CAME BACK...!
BELLE!

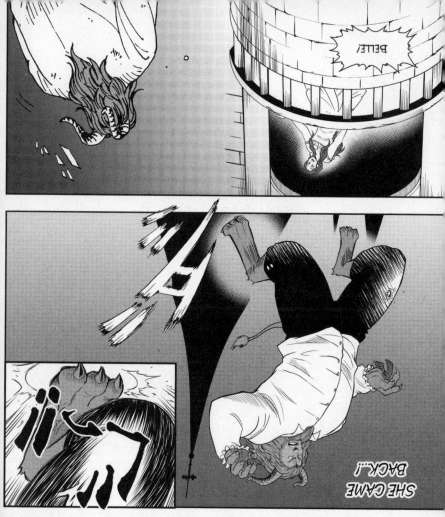

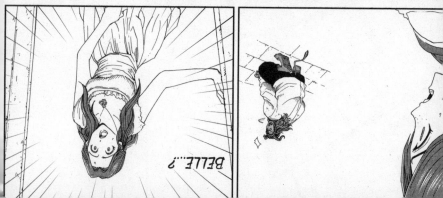

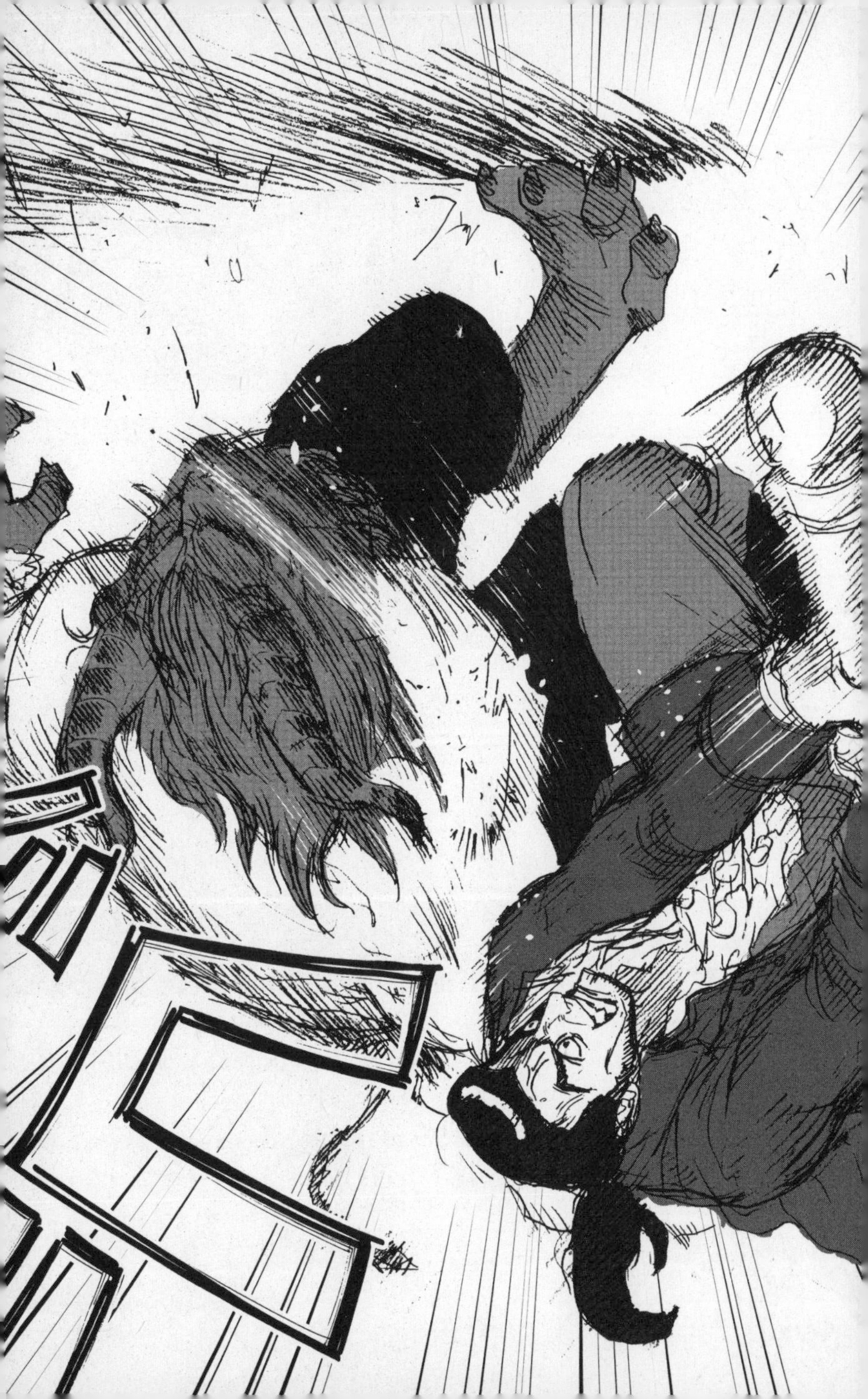

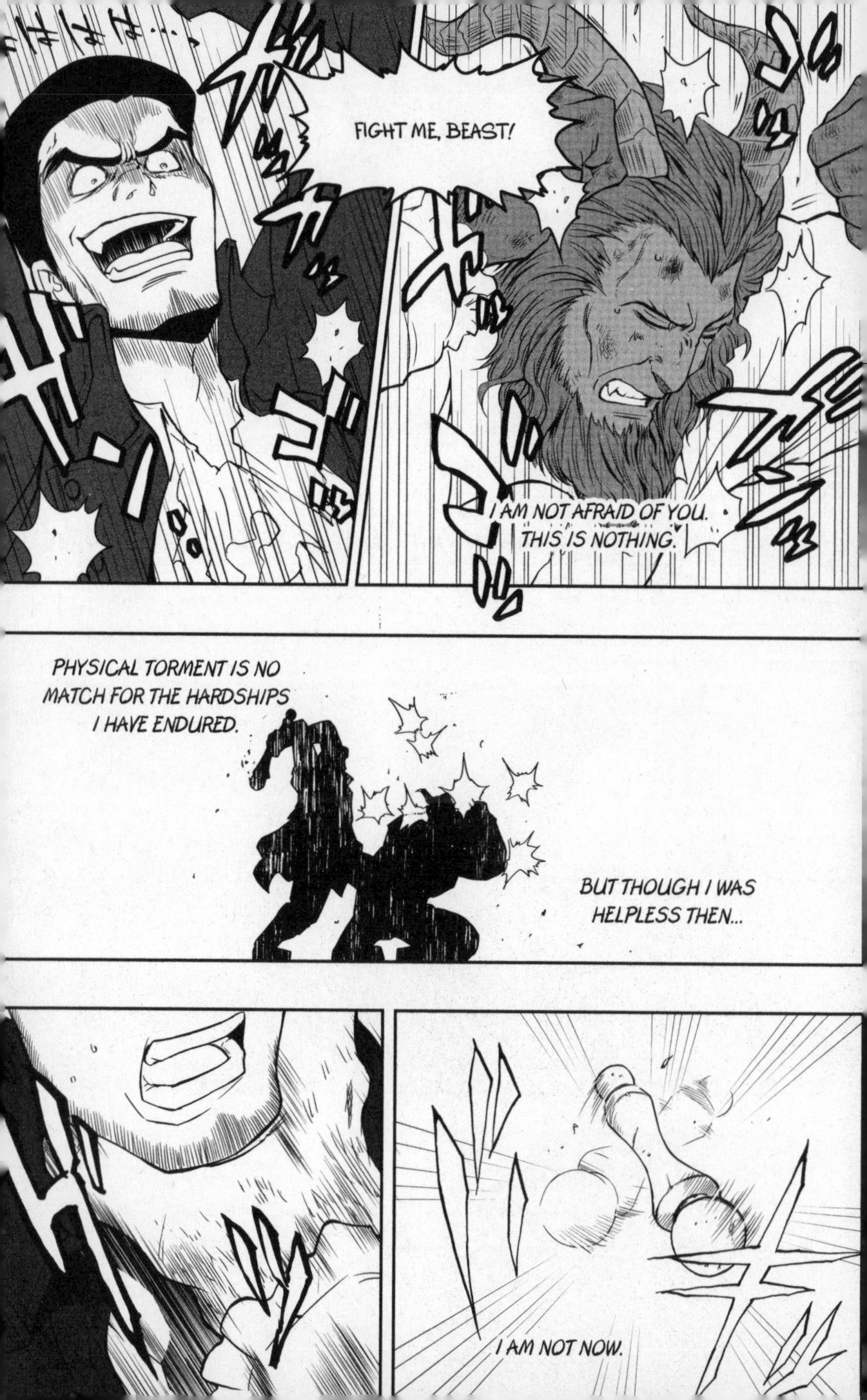
FIGHT ME, BEAST!
I AM NOT AFRAID OF YOU. THIS IS NOTHING.
PHYSICAL TORMENT IS NO MATCH FOR THE HARDSHIPS I HAVE ENDURED.
BUT THOUGH I WAS HELPLESS THEN...
I AM NOT NOW.

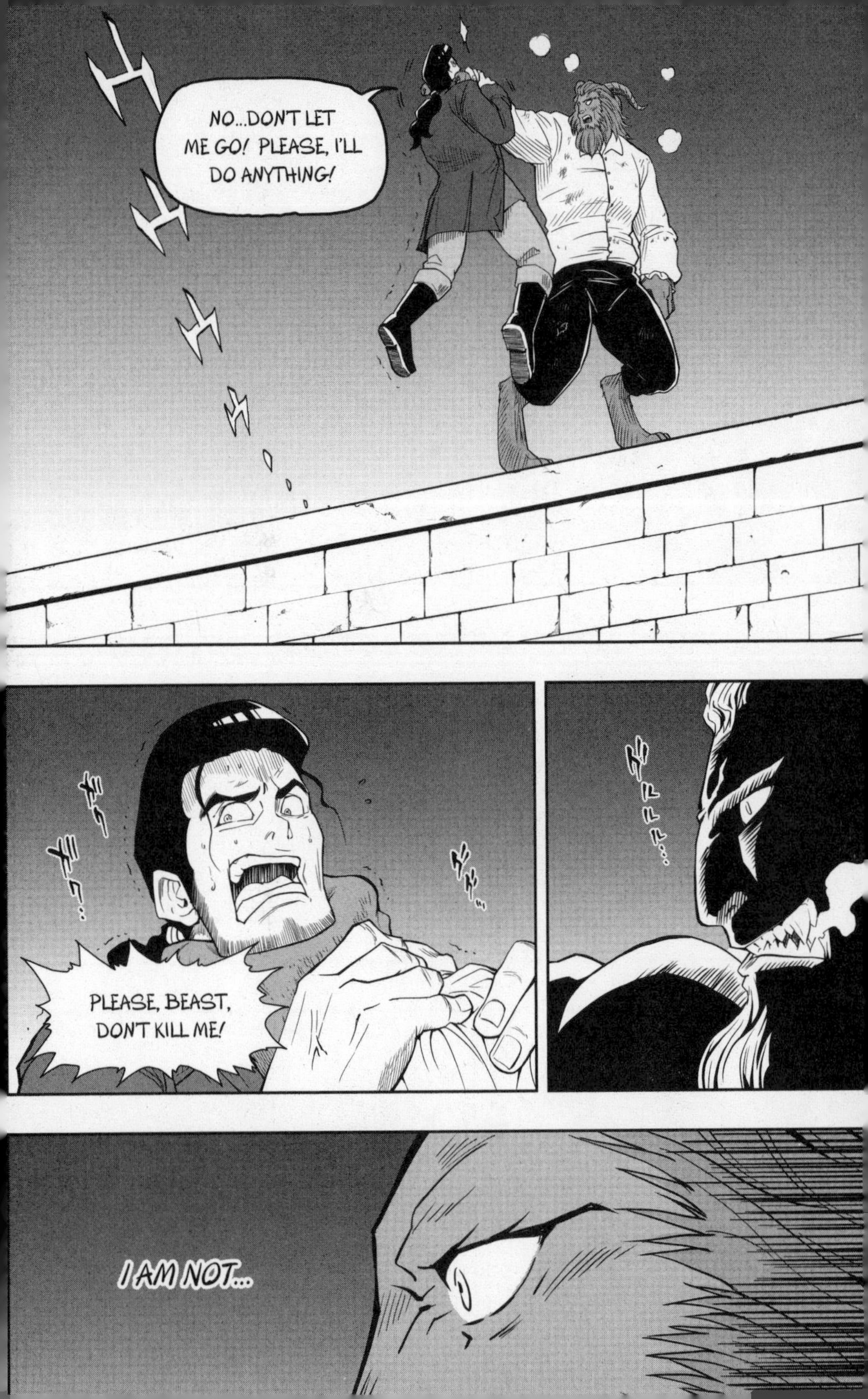
NO...DON'T LET ME GO! PLEASE, I'LL DO ANYTHING!
グルルル…
PLEASE, BEAST, DON'T KILL ME!
I AM NOT...

GO! GET OUT!
I AM NOT A BEAST.
I AM A MAN WHO MADE MISTAKES...
... AND LEARNED.

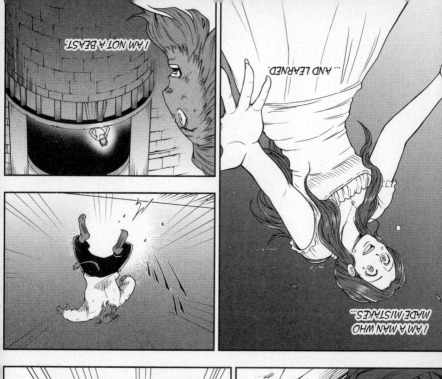

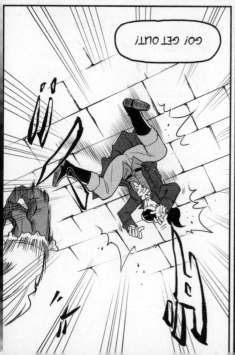

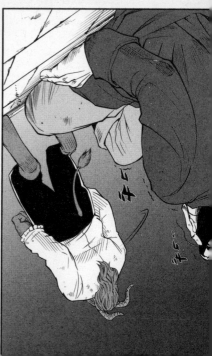

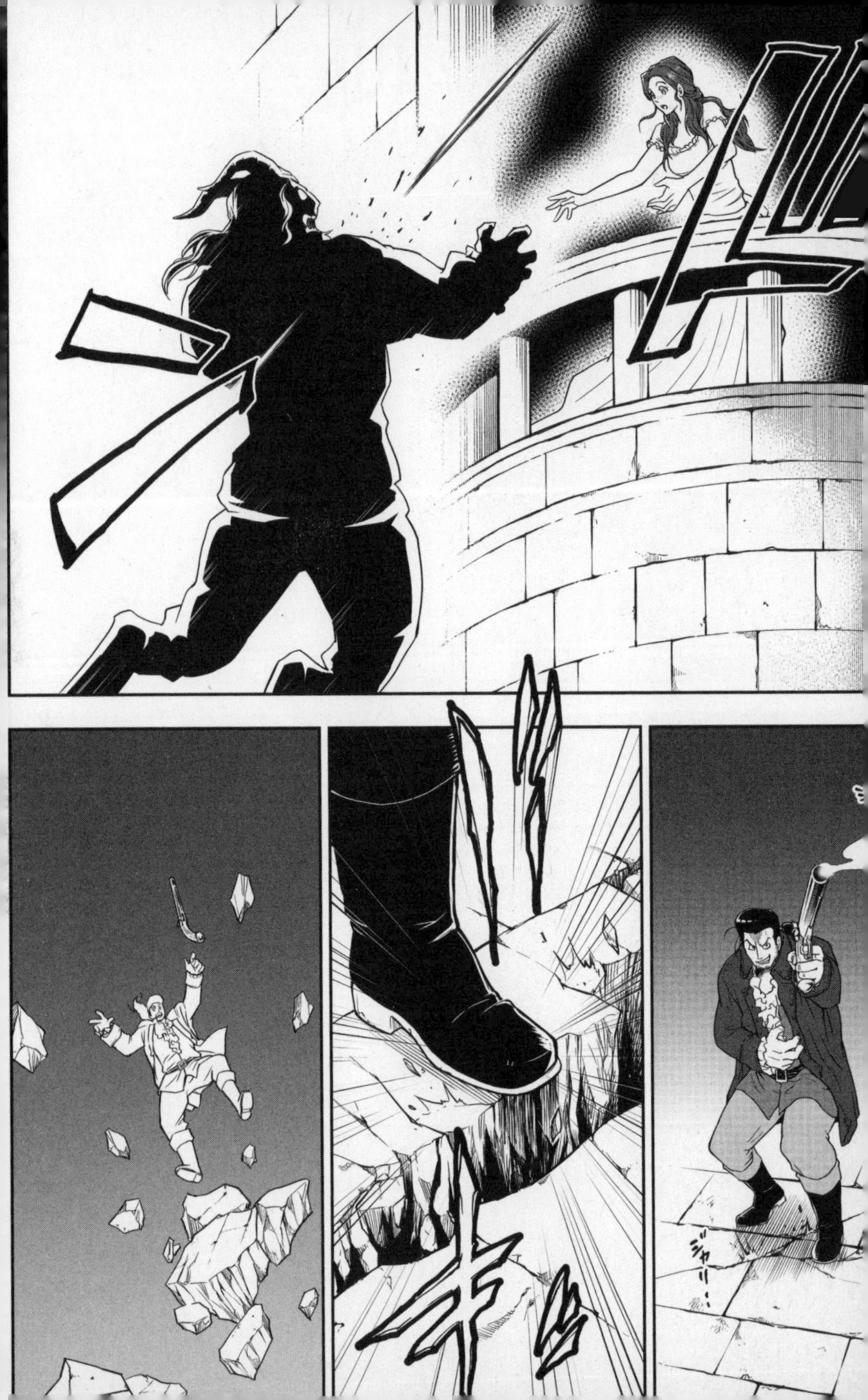
ジャリ…

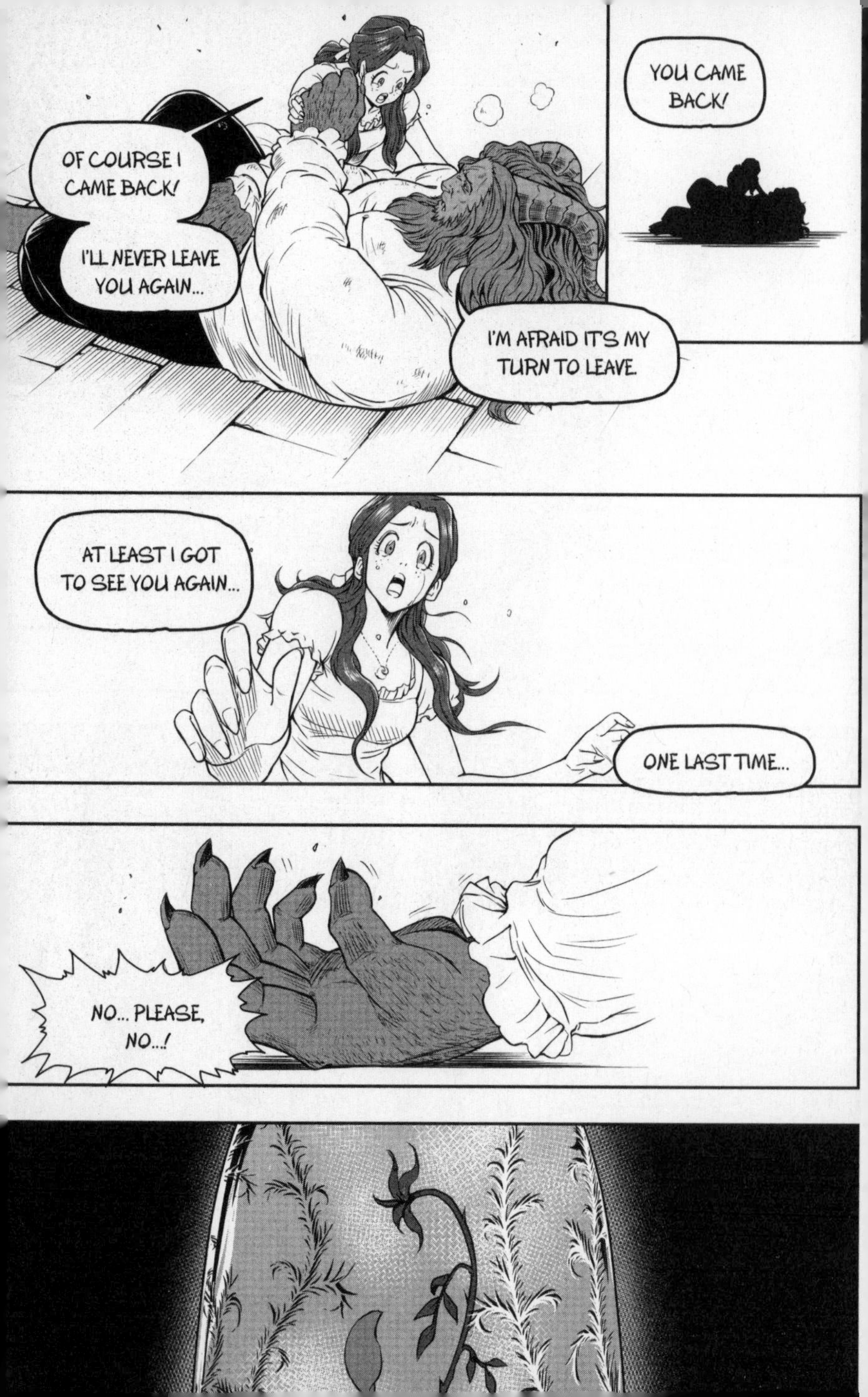
YOU CAME BACK!
OF COURSE I CAME BACK!
I'LL NEVER LEAVE YOU AGAIN...
I'M AFRAID IT'S MY TURN TO LEAVE.
AT LEAST I GOT TO SEE YOU AGAIN...
ONE LAST TIME...
NO... PLEASE, NO...!

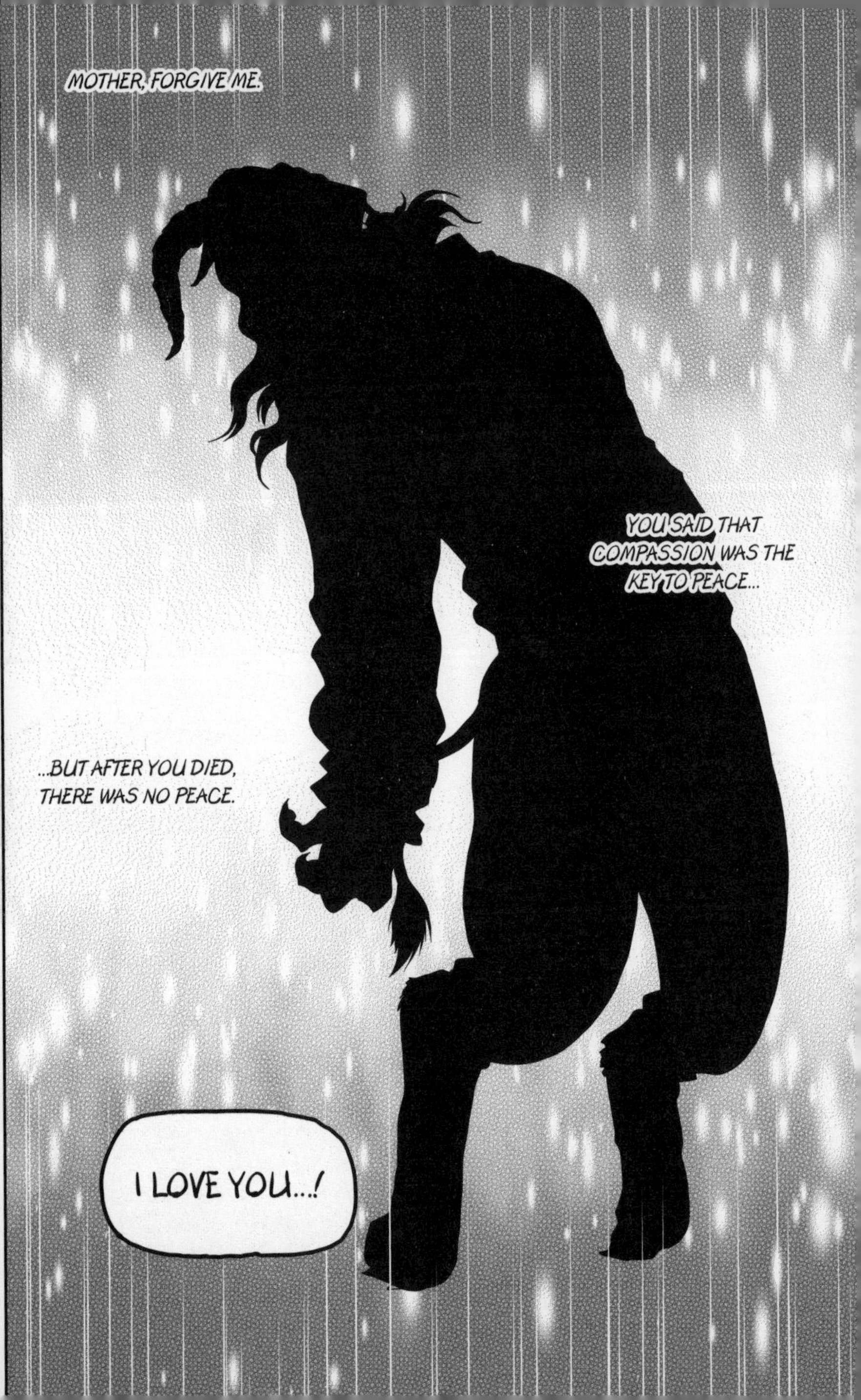
MOTHER, FORGIVE ME.
YOU SAID THAT COMPASSION WAS THE KEY TO PEACE...
...BUT AFTER YOU DIED, THERE WAS NO PEACE.
I LOVE YOU...!

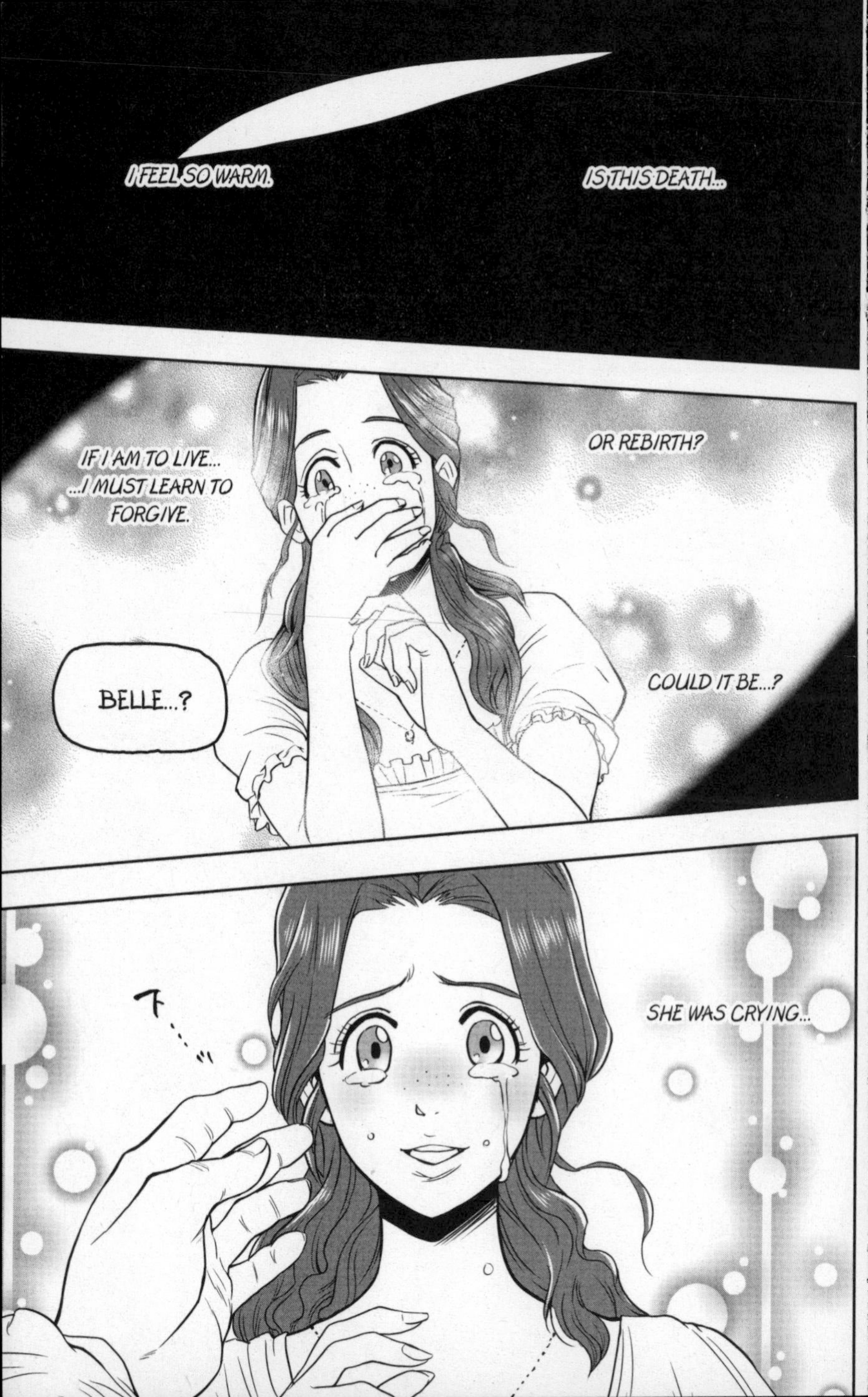
IS THIS DEATH...
I FEEL SO WARM.
OR REBIRTH?
IF I AM TO LIVE...
...I MUST LEARN TO FORGIVE.
COULD IT BE...?
BELLE...?
SHE WAS CRYING...

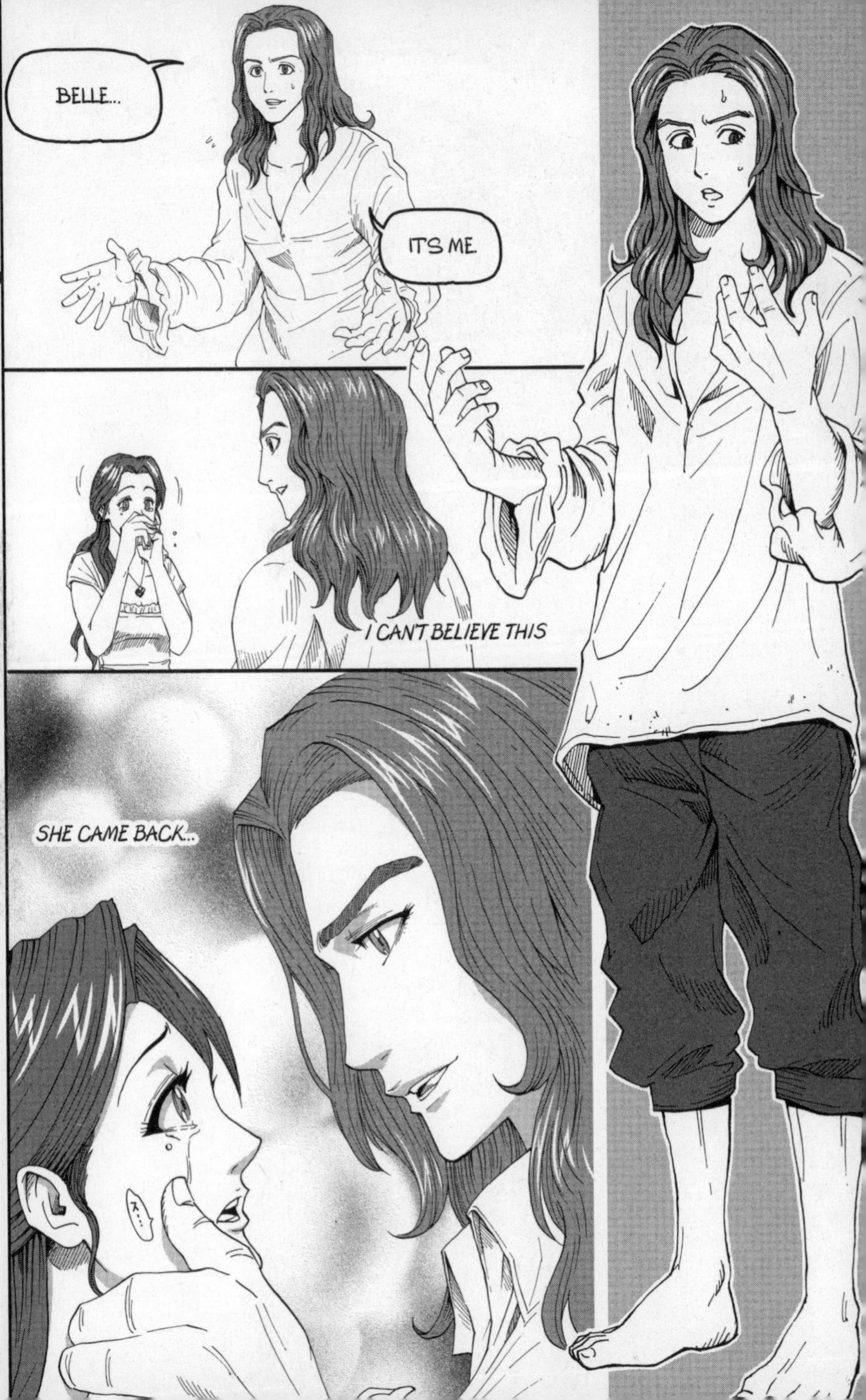
BELLE...
IT'S ME
I CAN'T BELIEVE THIS
SHE CAME BACK...
ス…

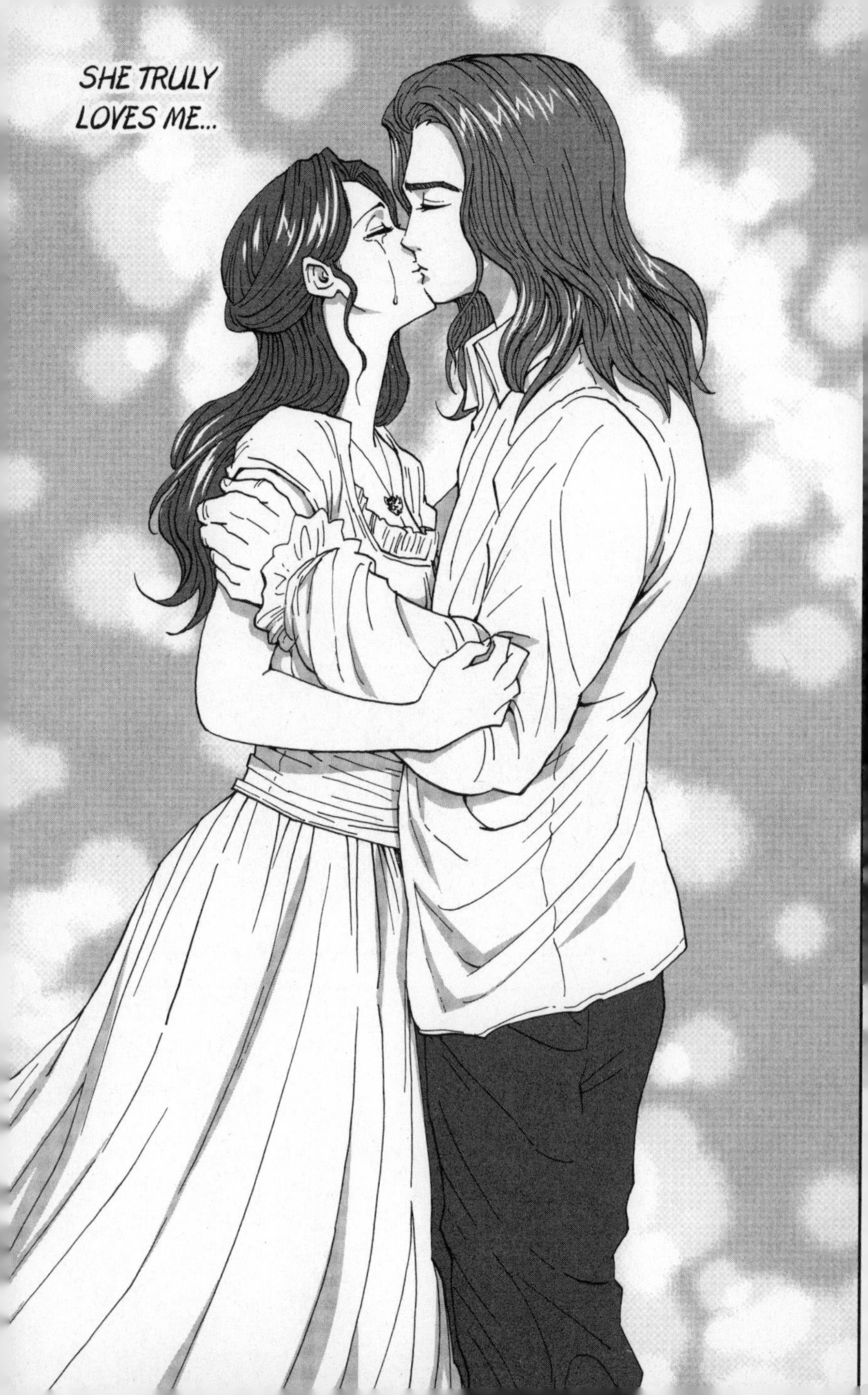
SHE TRULY LOVES ME...

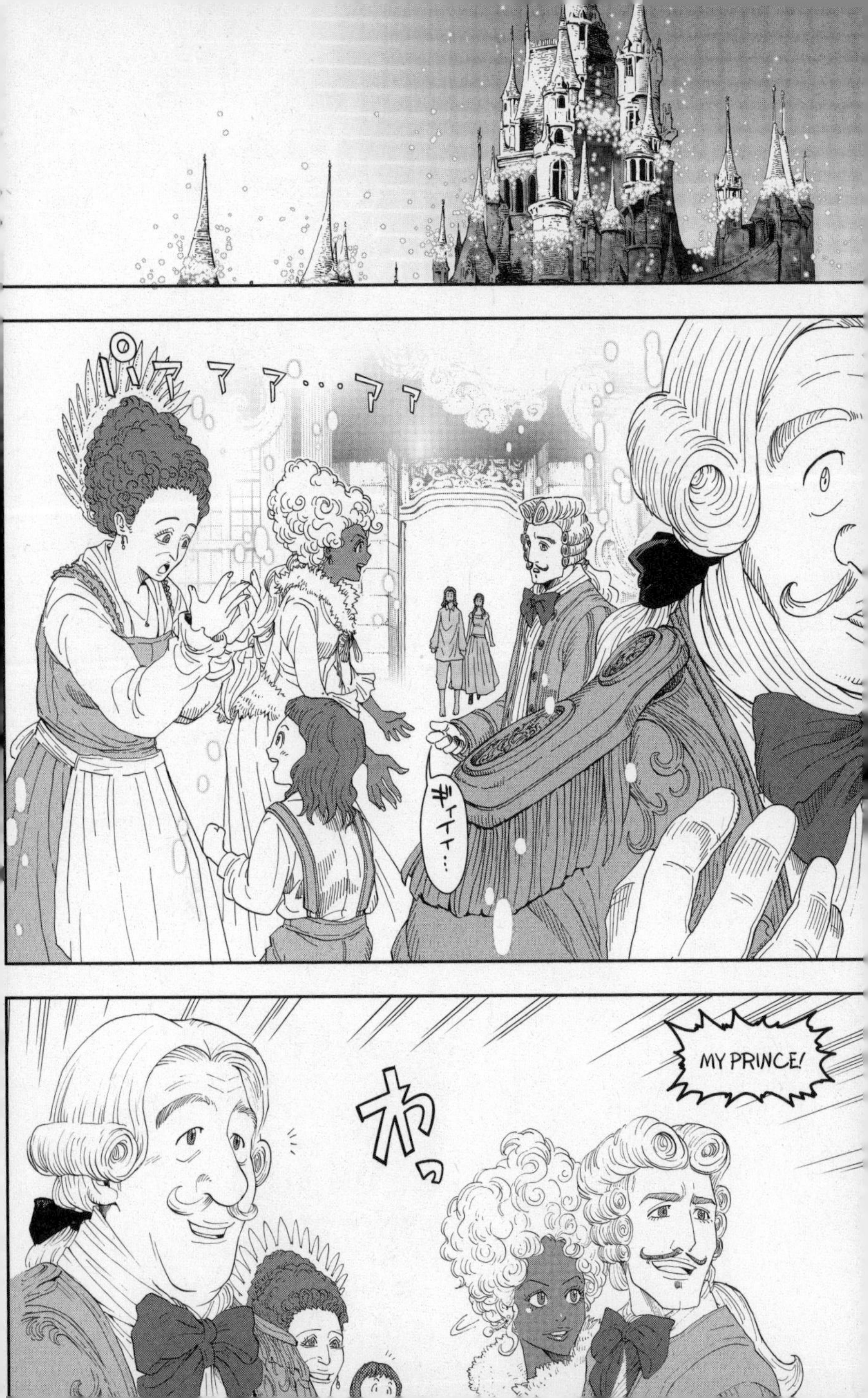
パアアア…アア
ギイイイ…
MY PRINCE!
わっ

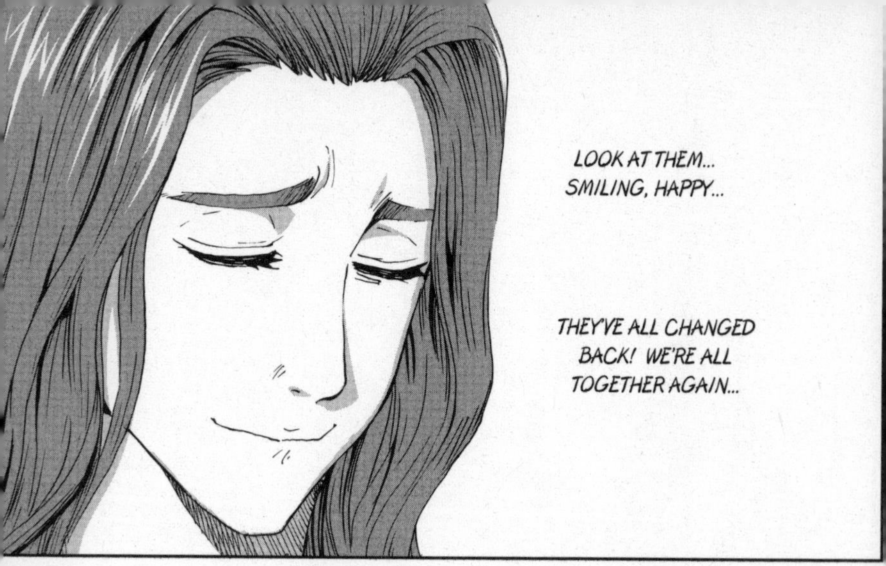
LOOK AT THEM...
SMILING, HAPPY...
THEY'VE ALL CHANGED BACK! WE'RE ALL TOGETHER AGAIN...

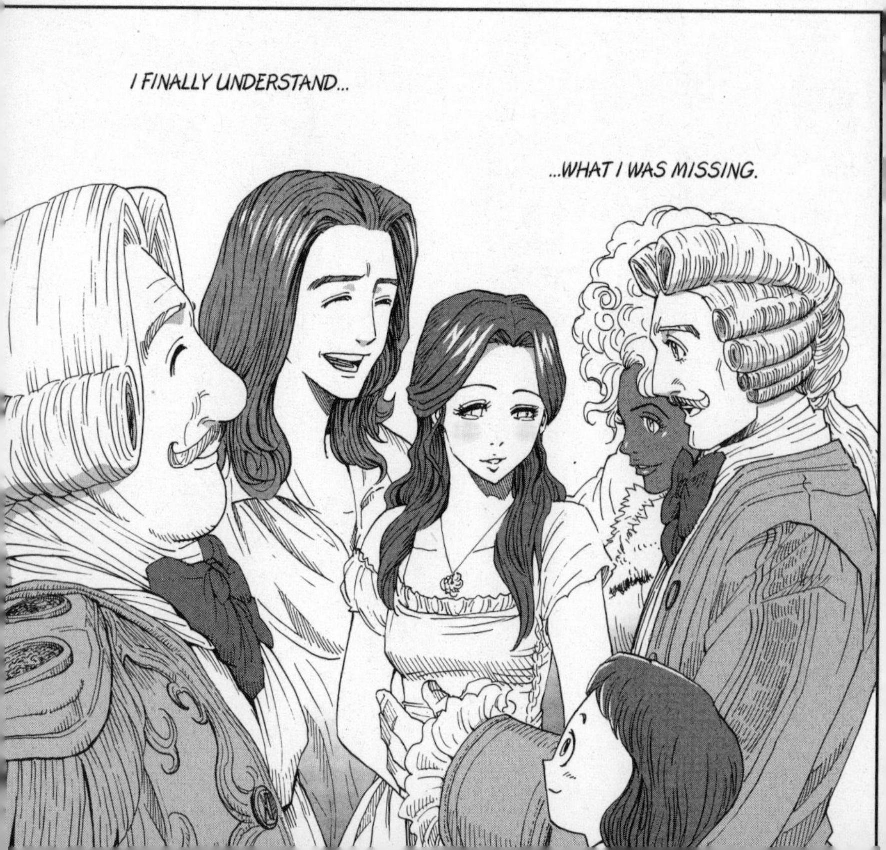
I FINALLY UNDERSTAND...
...WHAT I WAS MISSING.

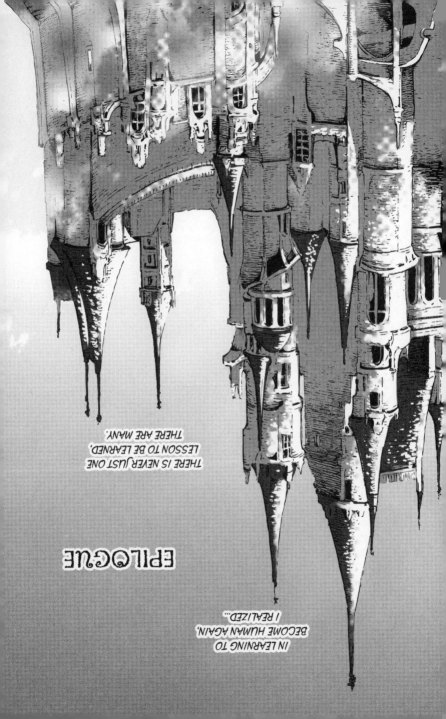

IN LEARNING TO
BECOME HUMAN AGAIN,
I REALIZED...

EPILOGUE

THERE IS NEVER JUST ONE
LESSON TO BE LEARNED,
THERE ARE MANY.

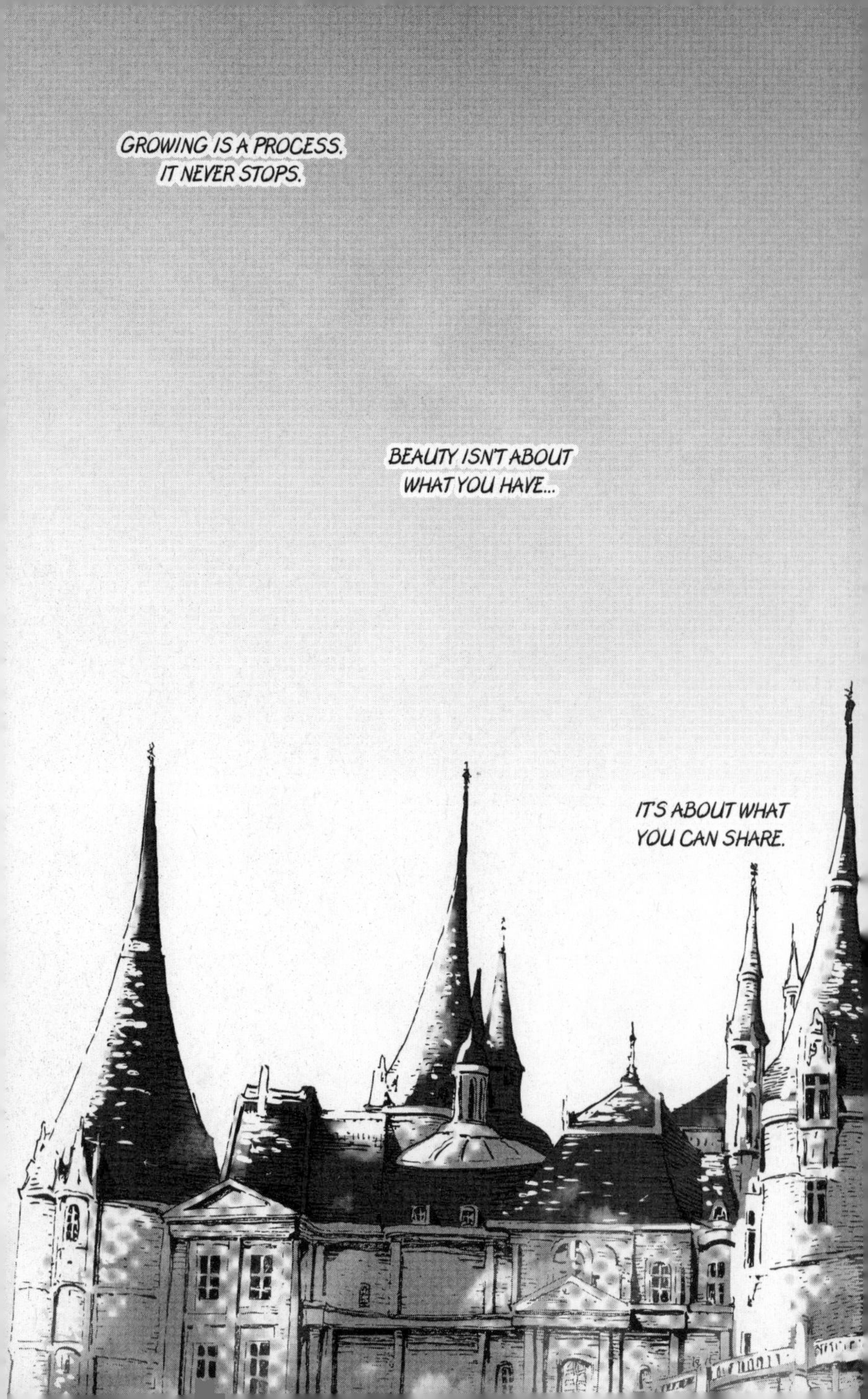
GROWING IS A PROCESS. IT NEVER STOPS.
BEAUTY ISN'T ABOUT WHAT YOU HAVE...
IT'S ABOUT WHAT YOU CAN SHARE.

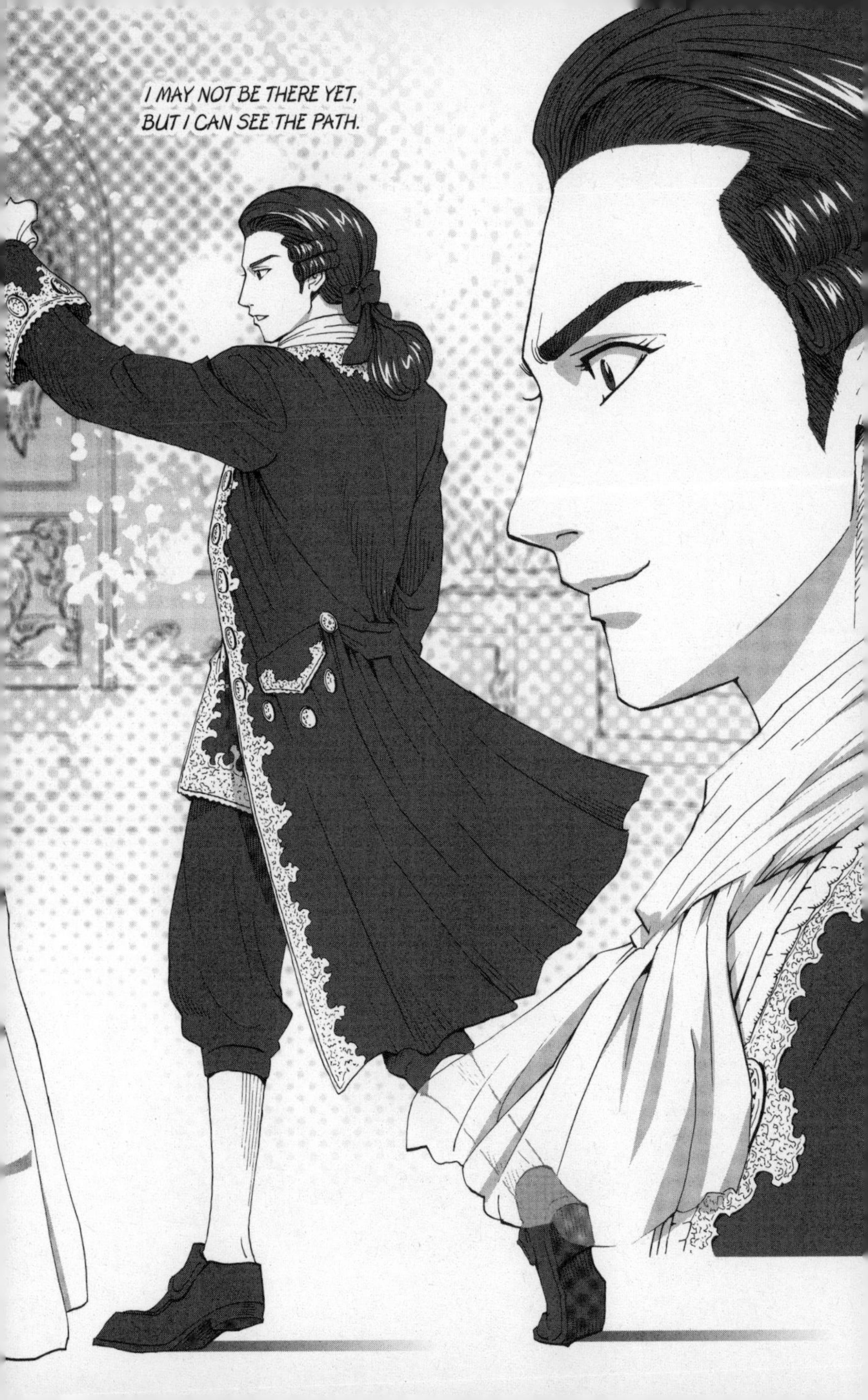
I MAY NOT BE THERE YET, BUT I CAN SEE THE PATH.

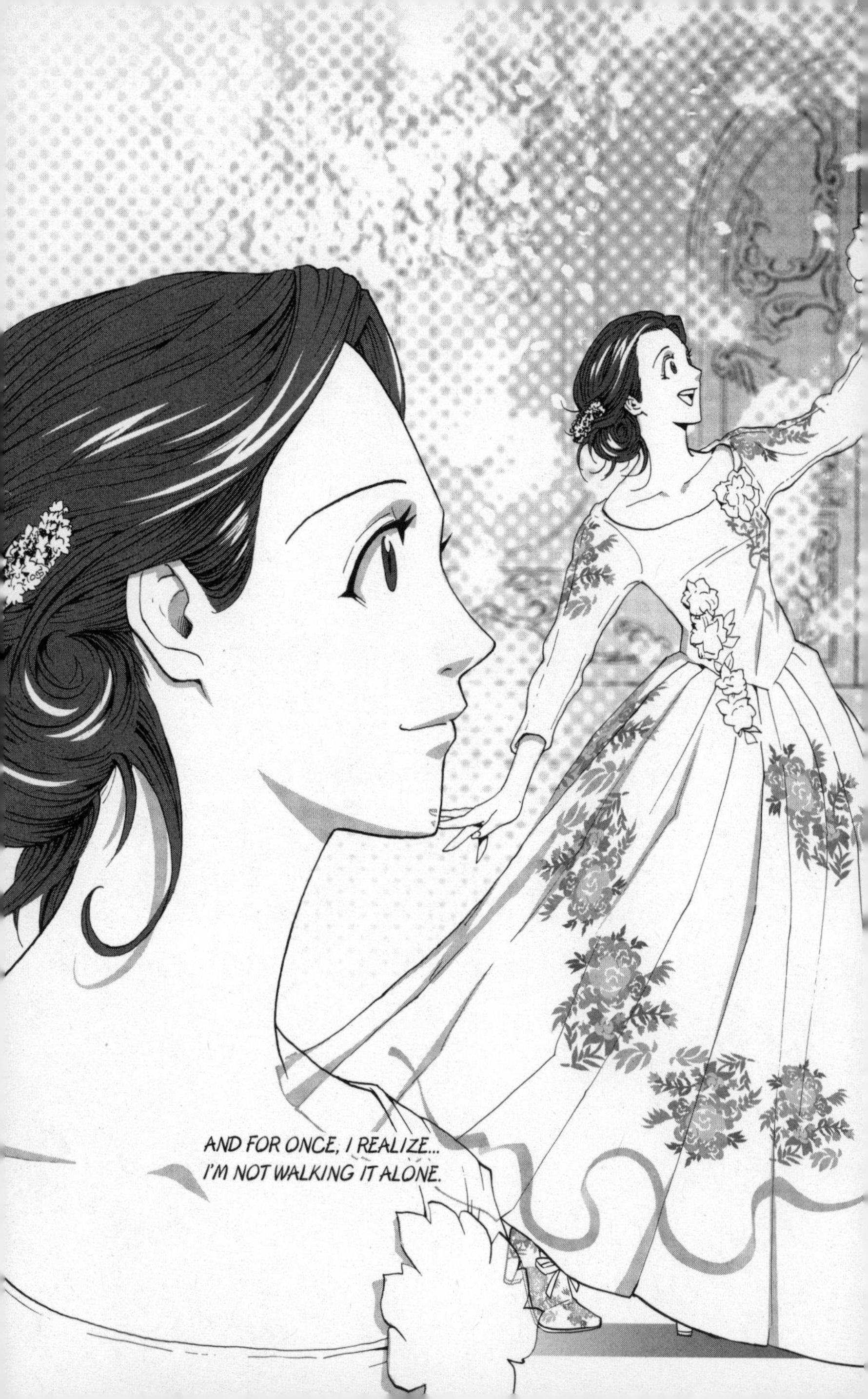
AND FOR ONCE, I REALIZE...
I'M NOT WALKING IT ALONE.

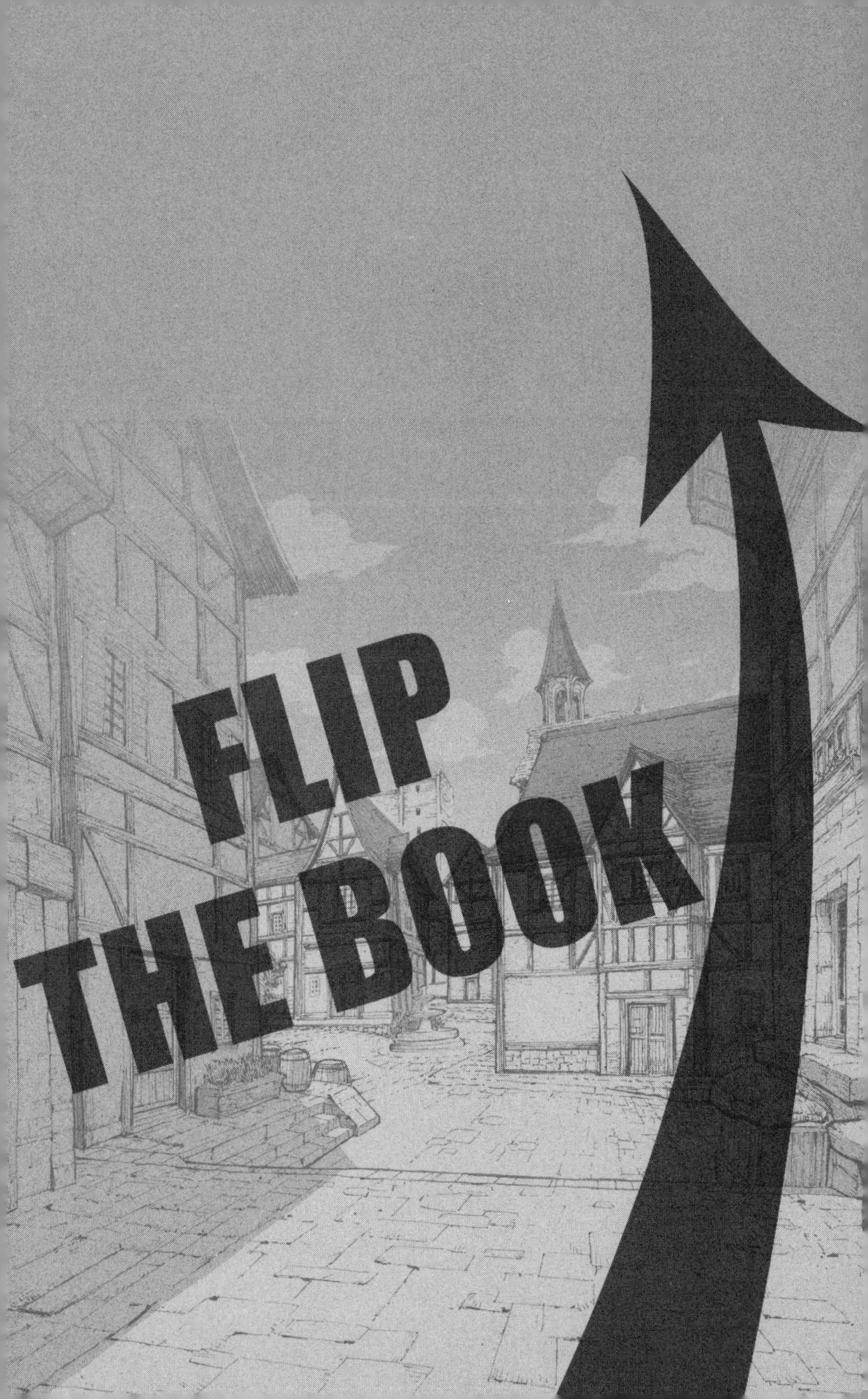
FLIP
THE BOOK

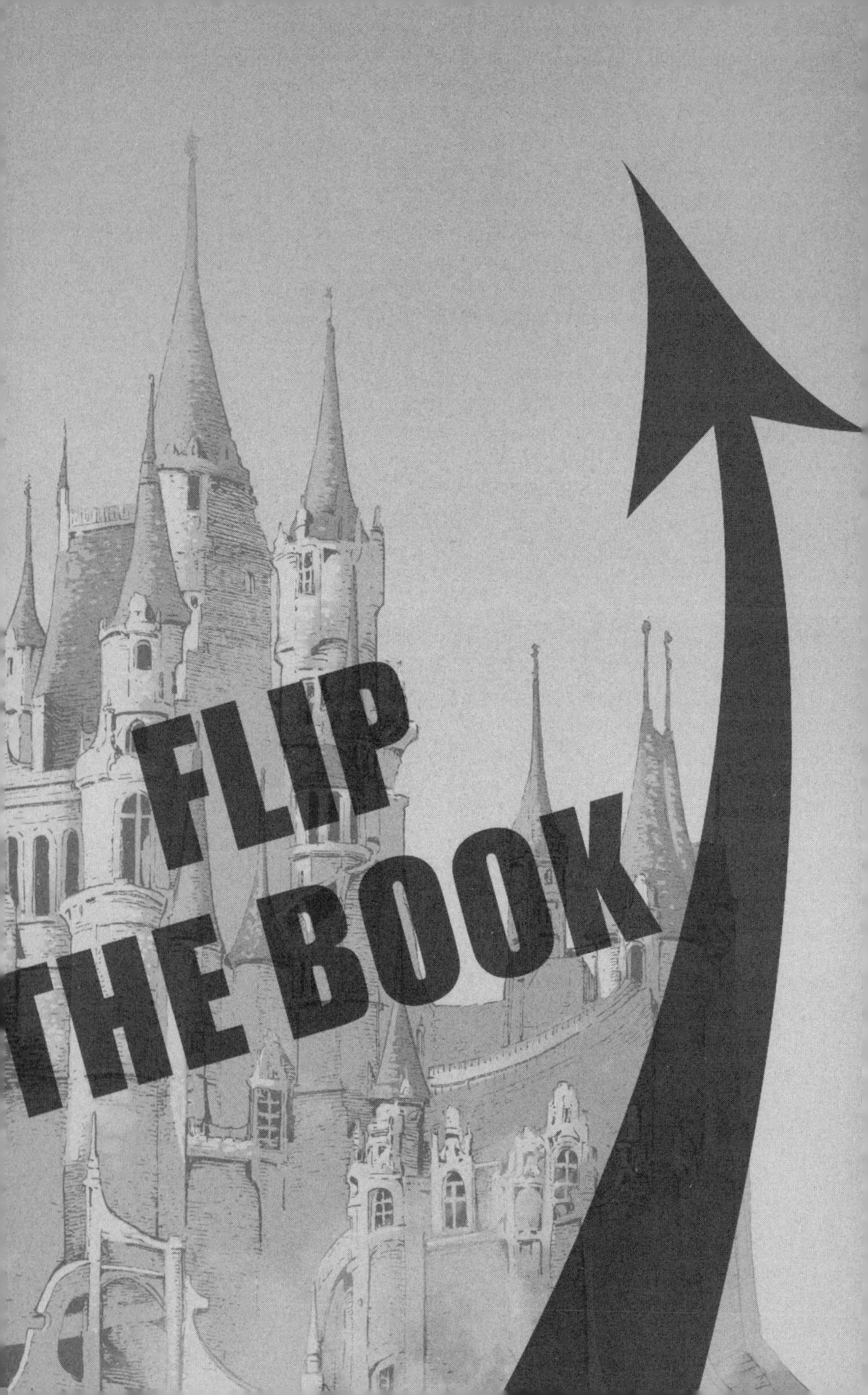
FLIP
THE BOOK

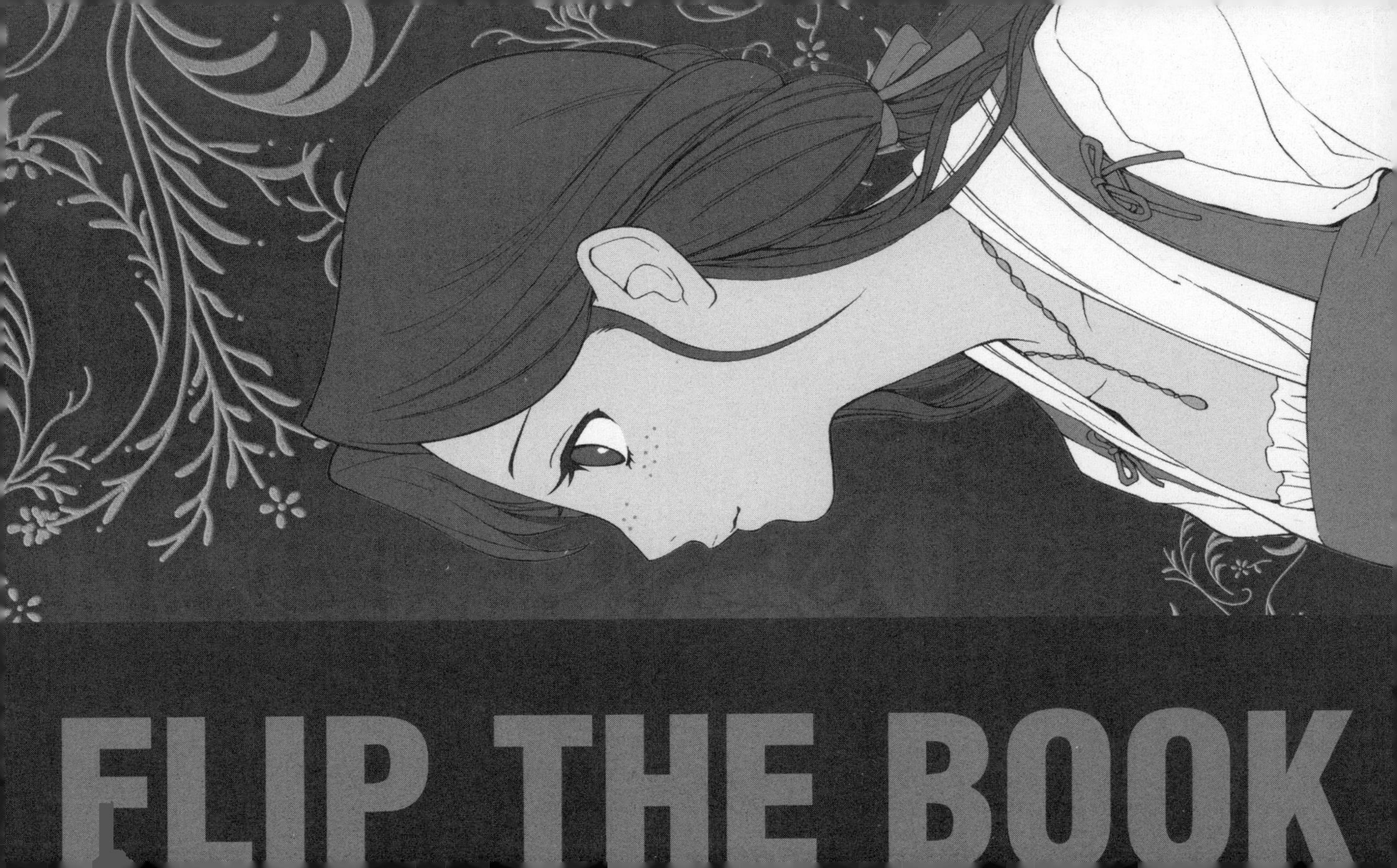
FLIP THE BOOK